CW00970446

Monumental
WORKS GROUP

BOOKS by TY JOHNSTON

THE KOBALOS TRILOGY

City of Rogues

Road to Wrath

Dark King of the North

THE SWORD OF BAYNE TRILOGY

Bayne's Climb

A Thousand Wounds

Under the Mountain

OTHER BOOKS

Mage Hunter Omnibus

The Shieldbreaker Collection

The Castle of Endless Woe

Five Tales from The Rusty Scabbard

The Storm

More Than Kin

100 Years of Blood

Sands of Time

SEVER, SLICE and STAB

THE HORRORS OF BOND TRILOGY OMNIBUS

Collecting all 3 books

Ghosts of the Asylum

Demon Chains

The Company of Seven

The Ursian Chronicles

Ty Johnston

tyjohnston.blogspot.com

a Monumental Works Group author

ISBN-10: 1500527777
ISBN-13: 978-1500527778

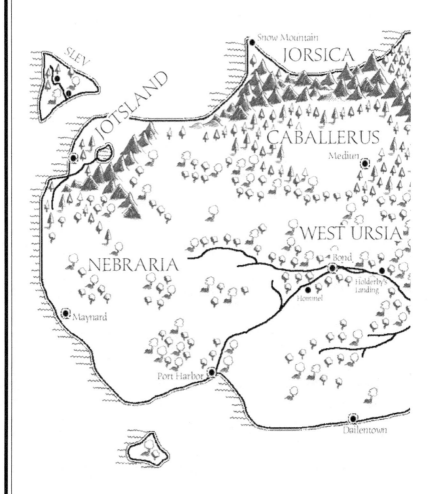

SLEV

JOTSLAND

JORSICA

Snow Mountain

CABALLERUS

Mediun

WEST URSIA

NEBRARIA

Bond

Holderby's
Landing

Hommel

Maynard

Port Harbor

Dailentown

North

Approximately 1,000 miles

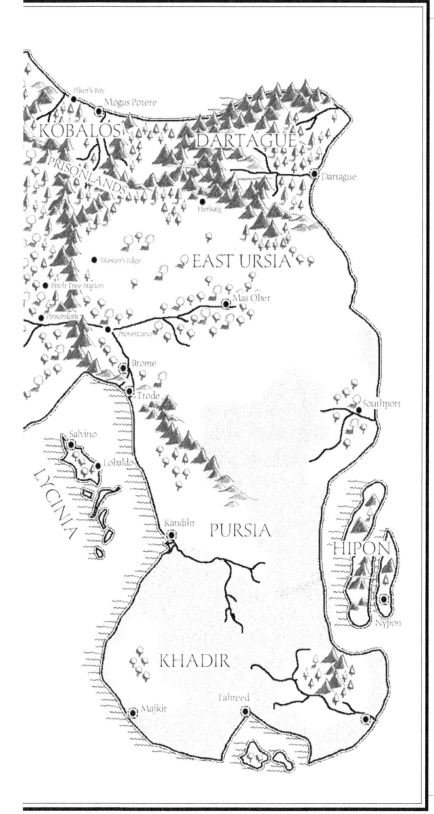

Contents

THE HORRORS OF BOND TRILOGY OMNIBUS

Book I:
GHOSTS OF THE ASYLUM

Part 1:
Burdens

1

1,995 years After Ashal (A.A.)

Taljintus shuffled down a slime-covered step and raised his torch high, staring into the blackness beyond, the bottom of the stairs ending in water as dark as ink.

He couldn't help but grimace as the outline of a body floating face-down glided into view at the edges of the torch's light. The corpse was that of a man, as all of them would be, this one still wearing the river-soaked garb of one of the guards.

Not for the first time, Taljintus asked himself if he truly needed this job. Unfortunately the answer was always 'yes.' He hadn't traveled all the way from Trode after losing his young wife to the pox just to wallow in misery and indebtedness. He had sought a new beginning in the city of Bond far from his homeland, and being an experienced stonemason he had hoped to find steady work here in the West. But he had arrived in the middle of Winter, during the off season for construction. Tough months had followed, the stonemason forced to scrounge as a day laborer just to survive.

Now the Spring had arrived, and Taljintus had put in a bid on the first major job he could find. Fortune had been with him and he had landed the bid.

But standing there in the cold and dark, one hand rubbing at the last dark curls surrounding his balding head, he was beginning to wonder if he should have passed on this project.

The Asylum.

Wincing, he stepped down into the black water, the cold soaking through his thin moccasins and chilling his flesh to the bone. Another step brought the water up to his shins, and the Trodan shivered as the cold ate away at him.

Taljintus cursed at not having the coin to purchase a proper pair of oil-cloth boots, or perhaps even waders layered by the gum of a rubber plant from a southern clime. He promised to add that to his list of needed tools and other items he would purchase as soon as he received his first full payment for this job.

Stepping down further, he came to the floor of the dark tunnel extending before him. The water now rose to his knees.

Taljintus continued to shiver, though he could not be sure if it was the cold water which caused him to do so or the body gently bobbing up and down ahead.

He had known there would be corpses, perhaps lots of corpses. Some kind of magical accident had apparently occurred here last Summer, flooding the Asylum with river water. Other than city workers dragging away the dead on the ground level above, no one had yet to clean the place nor get it into working order. The news Taljintus had managed to overhear on the street was that ownership of the Asylum had changed hands several times during the Winter months, none of the owners seemingly interested in spending the gold it would take to bring the main building and the basement level back to a working condition.

The current owner was of a different mind, and had wanted the Asylum restored to its former state.

The short Trodan grimaced further as he waded nearer the body. He continued to quiver, but now it was at thoughts of the Asylum's current owner. The young man had eyes as dark and foreboding as the water leaking into Taljintus's leggings. At least he had promised to pay well, and his down payment had been enough to secure the stonemason a place of residence in the Swamps for the next few months as well as enough money for daily needs.

But was it worth it? Growing closer to the floating dead man, the Trodan's feelings on the matter were beginning to shift. Yes, he needed the coin, but there had to be other jobs available. Right?

"Stop it," Taljintus whispered to himself. *It's just a job, like any other job.*

Except there were dead bodies, perhaps as many as a hundred or more if the rumors were true.

Why couldn't there have been a nice church that needed a new cathedral? Or a new building for the university on the east side of town?

Taljintus shook his head, driving away all negative thoughts. It was a job. He was being paid well, enough to hire a sizable crew and keep himself in business at least through the Summer. Clearing out the basement level, of water and bodies, was simply part of the job. Then there would be the new roof that had to be constructed for the Asylum, then the main floor had to be rebuilt and --

The Trodan's face turned white.

There was another body. Floating ahead there. Just beyond the dead man he was almost touching.

The new body wore no clothes, its naked skin wrinkled and as pale as a dead fish's gullet. The corpse floated on its back. A pair of dead, white, flat eyes stared up at the bricked ceiling of the basement tunnel.

Taljintus stopped moving. He had come down to the lower level to take in what kind of damage the river water had caused, and to see the extent of the dead, but he had seen enough. His new crew could take care of the bodies. That was part of their job. Taljintus had other things to do, like beginning the drawings for the new roof.

Yes, the new roof. He would get started on that. Let the laborers clean up the mess down here.

He turned to leave.

A wind sprang up from the direction of the steps leading above, a wind so strong tears sprang to the stonemason's eyes and he was forced to blink.

During one of those blinks, his torch died.

Taljintus almost panicked. Almost.

Here he was, stranded in near pitch blackness with the corpses of dead men floating about him. It was not a good place. It was not a place he wanted to be.

At least there was some little light ahead of him there, from the stairwell. A touch of the sun's glow had worked its way through the large hole in the Asylum's roof and had found its way to the top of the stairs. Taljintus could just make out the bottom of the landing above his eye level.

Now all he had to do was work his way over there.

As his feet began to slowly, agonizingly slide along the slick bricks of the tunnel toward the stairwell, the stonemason's mind began to play tricks on him. Had he just heard something move behind him? And how had any wind down here been powerful enough to knock out his torch?

A strong chill grew over the Trodan's skin, raising bumps on his flesh. For a moment he even believed he had seen his breath misting before the light of the steps.

"Stop it," he repeated to himself. *No reason to spook myself. I need this job. What with my own problems and the riots and --*

Slurp.

Taljintus paused. That had definitely been something in the water behind him.

Though not a superstitious man, the Trodan had had enough of snooping around in the dark and the wet with dead bodies. He plunged toward the exit.

And slipped on the floor, falling face-first into the water.

For a moment there was nothing but blackness, even the light from above being denied to the stonemason. He couldn't breath. He tried to suck in air, but murky, muddy water flooded his mouth. Then Taljintus panicked. He could help it no longer.

He thrust up his arms, reaching for the air, and found cold, cold, cold. It was a cold so icy it caused the wet joints of his fingers to ache.

Then his feet found the bottom once more and Taljintus pushed, launching himself with a splash above the water level.

He spit out nasty muck and inhaled, glad to feel the cool breaths rushing down his throat to drive away the burning sensation in his lungs.

That had been close. He had nearly drowned himself, and why? Because of fear and impatience.

Taljintus rubbed at the black little mustache beneath his bulbous nose and leaned against the wall to rest for a moment. He had to get a grip on himself. Whatever noise he had heard, it had probably been a rat, nothing more. In his line of work, he had run across many a rat. Nothing of which to be afraid.

Okay. His breathing normal again despite the chill that had invaded the tunnel, Taljintus pushed off the wall and slowly made his way toward the exit. Yes, let the workers come down here in the dark and clean up the mess.

His right foot touched the bottom step, and he could see daylight flooding into the hallway above, when the skin beneath the Trodan's collar felt as if it were standing up, as if someone had breathed an arctic, bitter mist down his back.

His eyes went wide.

But still, he did not panic again.

Until the cold, wet, clammy flesh of claw-like fingers grasped at the back of his neck.

***

When the scream went up a dozen big, burly workers were outside on the Asylum grounds, busy unloading lead pipes for a manual water pump out of the back of a long, rickety wagon hitched to a team of mules. Beneath morning shadows cast by the fortress-like structure that dominated the walled compound, pipes were dropped with a clanging din and rough men glanced at one another across the back of the wagon. Then their eyes shifted up the hill to the open front entrance of the Asylum. More than a few rough hands reached for hammers or large wrenches hanging from belts or resting in the back of the wagon.

Then there was another scream, this one louder and more shrill. The men jumped, startled. It sounded as if someone was being murdered inside the main building, and the only person who had dared the Asylum in months was their foreman, Taljintus, who had entered but minutes before.

Heavy tools were lifted as if weapons and the group began to make its way up the hill.

To be brought up short by Taljintus himself. The stonemason sprang from shadows into the open doorway, standing frozen for a moment, his arms stretched out to grip the sides of the frame. His chest was heaving. His eyes were large and round. His skin was pale, almost blue, and dripping.

The workers paused to stare at one another. What was wrong with this man?

Then Taljintus screamed again.

And ran down the hill. Never looking back. His short legs kicking up dirt as if the man ran from a demon.

The workers glanced at one another once more. Then they shrugged. So much for this job.

2

A wall of smoke billowed up across Dock Street, blocking the city guards' view of the lane, but the noise of the approaching mob still came to them above the crackling of the flames that had engulfed a half dozen warehouses along the wharfs on the right. The shouts for murder rose on the wind, drowning out not only the sound of the fires themselves, but also the yelled orders within the line of the bucket brigade trying desperately to put out the conflagration.

"This is no good," Sergeant Gris said from the front line of guards, his shield raised into position on his left arm as his right gripped a sturdy cudgel.

He glanced left and right. At least his men were standing their ground and doing so in a straight line. Most of them were local toughs or former construction workers who had recently signed on, but a number of veterans were among the ranks and they seemed to be doing a good job at keeping the morale strong. Thank Ashal for that.

Gris's gaze shifted further to his right across the dusty brick road and along the stone walkway that fronted the burning warehouses. Fifty or so men were lined up there, buckets passing back and forth amongst them, water coming from the shore to be tossed onto the roaring blaze that kept growing and growing. These brave souls were without protection other than the two score city guards stretched across the street next to them.

It wasn't enough, Gris knew. The roaring crowd on the other side of that wall of smoke was numbering into the hundreds, many of them hungry and angry and screaming for blood, more than a few of them also street toughs and sturdy workers.

His men couldn't hold. Not against these numbers.

"Smick!" the sergeant shouted.

"Yes, sergeant!" a voice rang out somewhere behind.

"Front and center," Gris yelled.

The sound of rustling leather and chain armor proceeded a young man in the orange tabard of the guard suddenly forcing himself between a row of his mates and appearing next to his sergeant.

Smick offered a salute. "Yes, sir."

Gris didn't look at the man. His cold eyes remained on the smokey barricade ahead and the growing screams and shouts beyond. "Smick, get a message to Captain Chambers. If we're to hold the Docks, we need reinforcements."

"Yes, sir." The young man gave another salute and a grin his sergeant didn't notice.

"Now!"

"Yes, sir!" The young guard turned to push his way through the line of warriors.

And was hit in the back of the head with a chunk of red brick.

Gris had seen the brick coming. The makeshift weapon had sailed forth from behind the smoke, but it had been flying too fast to cry out a warning.

Smick went down on his knees. Fortunately he had been wearing the round iron helm of the Bond city guard.

"Missiles!" The shout came from down the line.

Another brick, this one whole, shot through the smoke to clash against an upraised shield.

Then the situation became worse. Much worse.

A dozen chunks of rock and broken brick came crashing through the smoke, cracking against shields, then were followed by another barrage, this one much more deadly.

At least a hundred projectiles filled the air. Rocks. Stones. Bricks. Slate roof tiles. Wooden chair legs. Small bags of sand and iron pellets used as ballast aboard ships.

"Shields!"

But it was too late to yell orders.

Most of the sergeant's men had their shields prepared, but some few had not, and the bucket brigade was at the mercy of luck. The solid thunking sounds of missiles connecting with wood and iron filled the air to sound like a hard rain of hail, but just as loud were the cries following crunching flesh and cracking bones.

Then, as swiftly as it had come, the barrage faded.

Gris allowed himself a quick glance from behind his shield and was surprised to find the front line of his guards still held firm. A look to his left revealed the brick warehouses along that side of Dock Street still stood strong, but his view to the right showed a bloody mess. A half dozen of the fire fighters were down, a few not moving, and those still standing now sporting bleeding wounds.

"Sergeant?" The voice was weak, barely above a whisper.

It had come from his feet.

Gris glanced down.

To find a young man stretched out, the fellow's helm nowhere to be seen, his eyes fluttering beneath a mess of short yellow hair now stained with the red of blood.

"Smick." Gris dropped to a knee.

"I'll ... I'll ... get to the captain." The youth's words were weak.

The sergeant dropped his club and gave the young guard a gentle pat on a shoulder. "Don't worry about that right now, Smick. You just take it easy."

"Missiles!"

Gris cursed and raised his shield, stepping forward over his downed comrade.

The sergeant had time to shout, "Healer!" Then flying debris crashed into the wall of guards once more.

Shouts of pain and anger followed more than a few soldiers being knocked to their knees or dropped flat, but to the surprise of all the front line held once more.

Then a light breeze soared into the gulf between the warehouses, those whole and those in flames, and the black smoke was washed away.

Gris looked up along with his remaining men and found the spitting, screaming mob of Bond's lowest citizens less than two dozen yards away. None of the mob showed fear, only madness. Behind the dirty rags of clothing and the muddied faces of Swamps dwellers, there was an intense, irrational hate.

TY JOHNSTON

Within the crowd, weapons were raised, rusting maces and swords that were likely stolen or family heirlooms, though most were clubs with nails driven through them, farming tools and kitchen knives.

This crowd was not going to back down. They did not care they were facing their own townsfolk, their own brothers and neighbors and kin. They did not care they had set aflame the very structures that provided many of them employment as well as sustenance. They did not care they were a ragtag bunch facing armored men. They wanted blood.

Gris realized all this in a matter of moments. "Fall back to the bridge!"

Again, it was too late.

With a shriek, the mob surged.

The sergeant had just enough time to raise his shield over his head and bend to grab Smick by the collar of the young man's tabard.

Then the wave of hate smashed into the wall of city guards. For a moment that wall held. Table legs used as clubs hammered against shields. Woodsman's axes chopped high in search of heads above the line's defenses. Knives slashed and stabbed. Clubs were swung. Makeshift spears were thrust.

And one found a home.

A kitchen knife wrapped with cord around the end of a broom somehow found its way between two shields. The long, rusting blade drove in from below, skewering one of the burlier guards beneath his chin. Iron sank into flesh and buried deep in the man's throat. Warm blood splashed the front of the crowd, and for a moment the mob drew back at the sight of its own ferocity.

There was but a second of relief. Then the madness burst forth once more and scores of young men in rags shoved against the shields and hammered with clubs and stabbed with knives. The noise was nearly deafening, the roar of the crowd like that of a hundred rabid lions tearing at fleeing prey.

The new shock forced Gris to one knee, the sergeant nearly bent back double with his body and uplifted shield the only thing keeping him and the unmoving Smick beneath from death.

The line of guards was breaking. Already a half dozen men were wounded, another half dozen trying to retreat with their shields raised. A few attempted to grab their dead brother, the man with the ripped throat, to pull him back.

The crowd exploded forward, thugs launching themselves off the backs of their compatriots and over the shields, falling with cheap blades flashing and dirty fists flailing. Into the midst of the guards did this new madness plummet.

The men in orange had had enough. If they would not be allowed to flee, they would go down with a fight. A roar went up, this one from the city guards left standing, their throats bellowing a threat and a challenge. Knobby cudgels were raised. They would flee no longer.

The herd of madmen was beyond fearing the clubs of their fellows. And the guards were beyond hoping they would live through the next few minutes.

A general melee ensued, man against man or groups of men tackling single guards.

Gris was knocked to the ground. He managed to roll himself atop the downed Smick, and he lay there unmoving in hope he might be mistaken for the dead. It was the only chance he had of saving his wounded guard. Feet trod across his back, his chain shirt and padded underclothes saving him from broken bones but not a loss of breath. By some miracle the sergeant's helmet remained strapped to his head, keeping him from more than a few brushes with a stomping boot or dropped weapon.

Soon enough Gris found he could not breathe. The crowd was too close, all over him, on top of him. The air was heavy and filled with dust and the reek of sweat and blood and urine. The noise was hurting to the ears, roaring and roaring as if Gris were caught in the throat of a giant beast. He thrust up his gloved hands to close his ears but it was of little use as the jostling and jarring of the crowd constantly knocked aside his arms.

Worse was that Gris could not see, at least not beyond the ever-flowing horde that rolled over him again and again and again. It seemed as if the entire city must be crossing over the sergeant's back, and more than a few were willing to step directly on him.

He tried to look about, to discover what had happened to the remainder of his men and the line of bucketeers near the water. But there was no view the beyond dirty ankles and legs that brushed past with rough blows against his face, leaving bruises and scratches and more than a little blood from a busted lip. There was nothing else to do but duck his head and hope the moment of terror would pass.

Then, just as Gris believed he would suffocate beneath the unending wave or be trampled by uncaring feet, there was a flash of brightness. What followed was the scent of sulfur and something worse, something harsh.

Then another flash. And another.

The crowd was backpedaling. New shouts went up, these filled with anxiety instead of rancor, and the mob was rushing back the way it had come along Dock Street. The retreat was more swift than had been the advance. There was no gradual build-up to an assault, but a rampant revolt filled with fear and panic.

More legs and boots and muddied feet burst past the prostrate sergeant and the youth he protected, all fleeing in the opposite direction they had been headed. Once more there was a general trampling of the downed guards, their armor and padded garb and helmets and shields providing the only protection.

Gris clamped his eyes closed and kept his head down. Soon it would be over. Or he would be dead.

After what felt to be the longest time, there was silence.

The sergeant dared to open his eyes, but he did not yet look up. Instead, he listened. There were moans and grunts close to him, as well as more than a few creaks of leather and jangles of chain armor. The noise of the crackling flames continued unabated, but the loud strength of the mad crowd seemed to have flowed away by a few city blocks. The cries of fear and anger continued, but they were no longer in the immediate vicinity.

A shadow appeared across the sergeant's narrow view of the brick road before his face.

Gris looked up to find a dark-cloaked figure standing over him, the man's hood thrown back to reveal a pale face beneath short, black hair.

"By Ashal, I could've used you three days ago, Kron."

The tall, broad-shouldered man in black offered the sergeant a hand. "My apologies. I have been occupied."

Gris accepted the lift, allowing himself to be pulled to his feet. He glanced down at Smick, saw the young man was still breathing, then scanned the destruction around him. In the mob's wake a dozen of his own men had been left unconscious or dead amidst several pools of blood and garbage strewn across the road. Another score of wounded or dead had been left behind from the mob itself. Those guards still on their feet were carrying or dragging their comrades back along Dock Street toward Frist Bridge and the relative safety of the more sane Southtown. Another dozen guards, fresh recruits, were jogging forward from the bridge, these men ready to lend a hand. The squad that had made up the bucket brigade had dispersed, apparently having fled, leaving behind a dozen of their own unmoving brethren. The fires continued unchecked along the north shore of the Docks, the flames eating away at the wooden structures there, leaving behind blackened, smoking bones.

The sergeant pointed to the nearest guard who was still standing. "Corporal Rogins!"

"Aye, sir," the fellow said, his eyes dazed as he looked about at the results of chaos.

"Snap out of it!"

Rogins blinked. Then, "Yes, sir!"

"Form a retrieval party and get the wounded back to the barracks," Gris ordered, "and send a runner to the captain. We need reinforcements and a new line of bucket men. Now!"

"Yes, sir!" The corporal sprinted off.

"I hope your grenados didn't add to the fire," Gris said without glancing at Kron, referring to his friend's personal weapons which had been used to disperse the crowd.

"No incendiaries," Kron said. "I haven't been able to find an alchemist who can make them for me."

Gris leaned down and gripped Smick under the arms, then lifted the heavy weight of the man over his right shoulder. Glancing to his old friend, he said, "So what was in those things? Thought it was going to make me puke from the stench."

Kron grinned. "Some sulfur. A few other things I've picked up over the years."

The sergeant nodded. Kron practically had been raised as a border warden of the Prisonlands. The younger man had learned much from many different men from many different cultures, including combat, languages, tracking and apparently alchemy.

"Alright, keep your secrets," Gris said, waving an arm around them, "but make yourself useful, won't you?"

Kron gave a two-fingered salute before dropping to a knee to lifting a mewling old man who had been at the front of the mob. The wounded fellow was barely conscious, his face and tunic saturated with blood that continued to leak from a nasty gash across his head.

Soon enough the sergeant and his friend were surrounded by a score of fresh guards, their oranges unstained by dirt and soot and blood. Another group of men, this one larger, jogged up from behind the soldiers, each carrying clubs and buckets and heading toward the still growing flames.

Gris and Kron handed off their wounded, then the two retreated to a post at the north end of Frist Bridge, overlooking the South River behind them and the various brick and stone buildings lining the shore of Southtown across the running brown water. The view was of a much better part of town, full of people coming and going as if they had not a care in the world, traveling between shops and inns and restaurants. The only sign there was anything out of the ordinary was another orange tent, this one much larger than the one Kron and Gris found themselves under, planted just the other side and to the left of the bridge.

Sergeant Gris eased onto an unfolded wooden stool beneath the shade of his small tent and motioned for Kron to do the same next to him.

The man in black did not sit, however, instead staying on his feet, his eyes moving in an unending watch upon the half dozen soldiers surrounding the tent and the constant comings and goings of dozens of other guards from Southtown tramping across the bridge and into the maelstrom that had overwhelmed the part of the city known as the Swamps.

Kron raised a hand toward the buildings burning in the distance. "Why are they rioting?"

Gris did not try again to tempt his friend with a chair. If Kron wanted to stand, Kron would stand. "You really have been busy, haven't you?"

Kron shot him a glance. "The Asylum has been taking up my time. The contractor quit on me, and I've yet to find another."

"What happened? Did you scare him off?"

"Nothing of the sort." Kron turned his gaze back to the line of city guards now carrying the wounded and dead back along the bridge. "The man mumbled. I couldn't understand what he was saying other than he wished to back out of the job. I allowed him to do so, offering to let him keep the down payment. But he would have none of my money. We parted ways."

"And you don't know why?"

"Not a clue."

"You must have spooked him."

"I don't think so," Kron said. "He had been down in the basement of the Asylum just before he resigned the job."

"That could do it." The sergeant had been on the site after river water had flooded the Asylum and killed as many as a hundred men, inmates and guards alike. That had been more than six months ago. There was no telling what condition the bodies would be in after floating around in those dark tunnels all that time.

Kron's stern gaze would not leave the streets. "The riots make no sense."

"Like I said, you've been busy. A lot has happened, and none of it good for the city's granary."

"Food is short?"

"And expensive."

Kron's features grew tight as he continued to watch men run past, some in the direction of the fires, others away and back along the bridge. "I should not have allowed myself to become so distracted."

"Nothing you could do about it," Gris said. "Too much has happened within the last few months. The Eastern pontiff raised the tariffs on all goods heading West. The king up in Caballerus has been dethroned by his brother, who cut off all exports, supposedly only until things settle down there. Then there was that huge rain we had last year which swamped the Swamps and destroyed a year's worth of grain."

"What of last season's harvest?"

"No ships to bring it in. Belgad used to take care of that, but some damn fool went and burned the man's ships."

Kron grimaced. "My apologies."

"You didn't know at the time," Gris said, "besides, it's water under the bridge at this point."

"Are there truly no other ships?"

"None large enough for a major haul. The Ruling Council has been trying for weeks to get some boats up the river from Port Harbor, but all the merchant crafts are at sea this time of year and most of the war galleys are too big for the shallows."

"This is all my fault." Kron appeared dazed as he stared once more at the comings and goings of the soldiers, sounds of the rioters still in the distance.

The sergeant chuckled. "A little full of yourself, aren't you? Thinking you brought a whole city to its knees."

"The whole city? Is it really that bad?"

"Not yet," Gris said. "The folks in the Swamps are feeling it first, of course, because of the rising prices. Southtown is getting by with just a few rumbles from the merchants, and Uptown ... well, the folks in Uptown will hardly notice a little thing like the price of wheat and corn."

"I shouldn't have burnt those ships." Kron turned his back to continue watching the busy street.

"Stop blaming yourself," Gris said. "That was then, this is now. By Ashal, there are enough other factors besides your war with Belgad. It's not like you could have known about Caballerus or the Eastern pope."

Kron half turned, one eye staring at the seated sergeant.

Gris held up his hands. "Okay, okay. Maybe, just maybe, you could have predicted the tariffs." The sergeant chuckled again. "I'd guess the pontiff isn't too happy with the West after everything that went on in Kobalos last year."

Kron turned back to watch the road. "Assuredly not."

The sergeant reached over to a small table and retrieved a clay mug, then began to pour water into it from a pitcher. "What brings you down here, anyway? You said you were busy."

The man in black waved a hand around. "I saw the smoke from the Asylum. Decided to look into it. Good thing, too. I got here just in time."

"My thanks," Gris said, "but I'm surprised you hadn't noticed the riots earlier. Three days they've been going on, though no fires until this morning."

"I'm fairly isolated at the Asylum," Kron explained. "The grounds are large enough and protected by those walls. Plus, you forget the Asylum is at the other end of the Swamps."

"Noise must not have carried," Gris surmised. "Then again, it's no surprise the riots didn't touch there. Not much out your way but Belgad's place and the real swamps beyond. You really spending your nights there?"

"Only on the grounds," Kron said. "The roof won't be repaired for weeks, maybe months, but I've a decent enough shelter in a tent and an old horse stall."

"Thought you had a room at the Rusty Scabbard?" Gris nodded to the far end of the bridge where a hanging sign could be seen out front of the inn and tavern.

"I still do," Kron said, "but I've used it little of late. I was spending so much time at the Asylum, I decided to camp there for a while. Once the re-building begins, I'll likely move back to the Scabbard."

Gris drank deeply from his mug, then clanked the tankard onto the table. "Well, I've got to get back to work. Are you truly here to help? Or do you have to be rushing off?"

"Where do you want me?"

"Just what I wanted to hear," the sergeant said with a gleam in his eyes.

***

Lalo the Finder should have been the happiest of men. He had spent fifteen years of his life helping to create the most powerful underground syndicate the city of Bond had ever known, and he had had much success. Before his time there had been chaos with multiple underworld guilds and cartels vying for position, power and wealth. There had been murders in the middle of the night, street wars, gang violence, honest citizens afraid to walk outside the doors of their homes. Lalo had put an end to all that.

But he had not done so alone. Nor, for that matter, had he been at the head of such ambitions. Lalo the Finder was a kingmaker, not a king. A barbarian chieftain, a famous brigand who had been the only exile to gain freedom from the Prisonlands, had led the charge against the chaos. His street name had been Belgad the Liar.

Lalo could remember the early days, his discovery of Belgad as a champion among the local pit fighters. The huge Dartague warrior had been known for his willingness to commit violence, but he had also been shrewd and had shown much intelligence.

In a matter of years Belgad had managed to clean up the streets, to break the various gangs and underworld guilds, to bring a level of peace and harmony to the city of Bond's less fortunate citizens. All the while Lalo the Finder had been at Belgad's back, performing many of the tasks with which Belgad had had little interest. It had taken a sizable intelligence network and administrative conglomerate to hold together the empire of Belgad the Liar, an empire which had stretched beyond Bond's streets and into the very heart of politics and business within the nation.

After fifteen years Belgad the Liar had arguably become the most powerful man in all of West Ursia, perhaps even within the entire western portion of the Ursian continent. True, there were a handful of politicians or kings who could have claimed to have more wealth or personal power than Belgad, but none had had the freedom of Belgad, and no man west of the mountain range known as The Needles had been as feared or respected.

But Belgad was gone. A series of adventures had taken the Dartague barbarian far to the north to the land of Kobalos, and once there a twist of fate and the will of a retiring prince had landed Belgad on the throne of Kobalos. Now Belgad truly was a king.

Which did Lalo the Finder little good. As had seemed natural months earlier, Lalo had inherited his former master's empire. But it had come at a price. Quite literally. Belgad had sought to divest himself of his financial interests in Bond, which only made sense for the new sovereign of another land as otherwise it could have created ... issues. But Belgad was no fool. He had not simply turned over his underworld kingdom and all financial holdings and concerns. No. He had wanted to be reimbursed. Which made sense considering the size of the investments.

Lalo had paid. It had cost him every single gold, silver and copper coin he himself had saved or invested over the years, but he had paid. Unfortunately, it had still not been enough. He had been forced to borrow in the extreme. He had sold off some few of his new investments in order to pay Belgad, but nearly half of the coin that had gone to the new king of Kobalos had come from various banks and organizations from within Bond.

The tables had been turned. Whereas once the empire had been in complete control, now the empire was feeling the tightening grip of outside influences.

And all of this had happened in less than a year.

Thus were the fortunes, or misfortunes, of Lalo the Finder.

Which was why a frown had appeared on his slender face under the even more slender dark mustache he wore beneath his angular nose.

And it was why he continued to frown while seated in a chair behind the heavy desk in the center of a room that had once been Belgad the Liar's personal library, the walls lined with shelves of scrolls, books and other odds and ends.

It didn't help that seated across from Lalo was one Kerjim, known as Sidewinder on the streets of Bond. Kerjim was fifty years old but still sharp and hardened as if made of ancient steel. His darkened skin bespoke his ancestors' Pursian roots. His simple garb of wool leggings and gray tunic above leather sandals revealed his more recent roots in the Swamps. His hard eyes suggested his past as the head of Bond's thieves guild, back when there had been a thieves guild fifteen years earlier before Belgad the Liar had come along.

Now Kerjim was in charge of something else. Something nearly as crooked as the thieves guild itself.

"As a representative of the Docks Guild workers," the Pursian said, "allow me to say I am here to help you."

I seriously doubt it, Lalo thought, but he kept a smile on his face. "That is much appreciated, Master Kerjim."

The guild spokesman remained still, his eyes unblinking and staring across the desk as if he expected the Finder to have more to say. After several uncomfortable seconds, once it was clear Lalo was to remain silent for the moment, Kerjim opened his mouth.

Then Lalo spoke. "What, however, does the guild believe it can do for me?"

Now Kerjim blinked. He had been interrupted. It was a sign of disrespect. It was also a sign of a minor power struggle. Lalo knew this. Which was why he had done it.

"Not just the Docks Guild," the Pursian finally said with almost a sneer.

Inwardly, Lalo cringed. This was not going to be nice.

"Whom else could you mean, Master Kerjim?"

The former chief of thieves grinned. "*All* of the guilds, of course."

Lalo's eyes narrowed. "Speak plainly, please."

Kerjim sighed and eased back in his chair. "Finder, you and I have been ... acquaintances ... for a long time."

"True."

"We have been comrades and competitors, even back in our younger days."

"Again, true."

"Back in the days before ... Belgad."

The break in Kerjim's words had been intentional, of course. The man had wished to make a point of separating the present from the past. The Finder understood this, and it was another factor which did not make him a happy man. Kerjim was making an obvious point that Belgad was no longer available.

With the bitter flavor of distaste rising in his throat, Lalo forced himself to go on. "As you said, we have known one another for some time. That leads me to believe you realize I am a busy man, as I'm sure are you. Please explain yourself, Master Kerjim, for both our sakes."

The grin on the Pursian's face broadened, so much so crooked teeth were revealed between his dark lips. "Very well. It has become noticeable of late that your enterprises have become a bit ... what is the word? *Stretched.*"

Lalo grumbled, but only to himself. "I asked you to speak plainly."

It seemed impossible, but Kerjim's smile grew even wider. "With the disappearance of Lord Belgad --"

"He did not disappear."

"As you say." Kerjim flung up a hand as if dismissing the Finder's remark. "Since Lord Belgad has gone missing from -- "

"In no way is he missing."

The Pursian's smile vanished.

"I know exactly where Lord Belgad is located," Lalo said, "and I am in communication with him from time to time."

"Where is he?"

"That is a matter he might not wish me to divulge." It was Lalo's turn to grin. "But rest assured, knowledge of his current location and enterprises will become public soon enough. In fact, it would be quite impossible to keep it from becoming public."

"He is the new king in Kobalos, is he not?"

Lalo's smile vanished. "Where did you hear of this?"

Kerjim's grin returned. "I have ears. *We* have ears. Besides, it is no simple task to keep quiet the identity of a titular ruler of a nation, even one as dark and distant as Kobalos."

True enough, but Lalo was not happy to hear the news had traveled so swiftly. He had believed the knowledge about Belgad's new rule was still unknown to the general populace. But then, perhaps it was. Perhaps such knowledge was only known to Kerjim and a handful of others. Still, it was information that would have eventually become common knowledge. That it was becoming known now was unfortunate, as Lalo had still hoped to use the mystery of Belgad's whereabouts to his own financial advantage, but the event wasn't completely unforeseen.

"Your quiet makes me believe I am correct," Kerjim said.

Inwardly, Lalo the Finder cursed. The guild representative had not been sure of Lord Belgad's whereabouts. Now he was. Lalo's silence had confirmed such.

"It must be an interesting story," Kerjim said, "how a former Dartague chieftain and a knight of West Ursia became ruler of a nation, especially considering that nation is Kobalos."

"The details would bore you."

Kerjim chuckled. "Perhaps they would. But we have gotten off onto a side matter."

"Yes, we have."

"We were speaking of the guilds and your current financial difficulties."

Lalo leaned forward, his eyes narrowing again as he stared across the desk's top at the Pursian. "If my finances are in dire straits, and I am in no way suggesting they are, then that would be my concern, not that of the Docks nor any other guild."

"There is where you are wrong. The finances of your ... enterprises ... are of extreme importance to all the guilds of Bond."

Lalo leaned back. His eyes remained slits. "How so?"

Kerjim waved his hands as if to accentuate the obvious. "Whatever Lord Belgad's current situation, you have taken over where he left off. He was a powerful man in Bond. His business interests stretched forth like a thousand chains linking every industry and guild with one another."

"And?"

"You, Lalo the Finder, now occupy the throne upon which Lord Belgad sat."

Lalo feared wrinkles on his face from all the frowning he was doing. "Allow me to explain the situation to you, Master Kerjim. My former employer, the man we know as Belgad Thunderclan, has removed himself from nearly all of his corporate and personal interests not only within Bond, but within all of West Ursia."

"Which makes sense for a king of another land."

"Yes," Lalo went on, nodding, "but with his permission and his blessing I have been allowed to appropriate all of his commercial interests within the West."

"All?"

"Yes, all. That includes all titles to properties and investments. And, through my former association with Lord Belgad and my own experience as his associate, I retain full knowledge and all links to those chains you mentioned. Which means I now stand where Lord Belgad once stood."

"You forget one thing."

"What is that?"

"You also carry the weight of all Lord Belgad's responsibilities."

There was truth to this. The Finder did not know what to reply. Mainly because he had yet any idea exactly why Kerjim Sidewinder was sitting in his office.

The Pursian seemed to read Lalo's mind. "The reason I asked to meet with you is to ease your burden, to help you with your current problem."

"And what problem would that be?"

Kerjim's stare was flat, unemotional but knowing. "You are in over your head."

There. It had been said. And it was true. Lalo was no Belgad, and the Finder knew that, had known it for months now. He had realized years ago that at some point his employer would retire, but he had never thought of Belgad leaving in the manner he had. Lalo had believed he would have time to make plans for his own retirement, which he would have done upon Belgad's own decamping. But events had occurred swiftly, and Belgad's fate had taken him off on other ventures to a land far away. A part of Lalo wished he had gone with his former boss, for bringing a kingdom back from near ruin would have been a proper challenge for someone with the Finder's skills, experience and temperament. But Lalo was a West Ursian. He had been born in Bond and had lived all his life there. He loved the city. It was home. So he had stayed. And now the ravens were circling.

"I mean no insult," Kerjim went on, "but it's a simple fact your finances are not those of Lord Belgad's. It has been difficult not to notice of late you have reached out to secure further finances. Quite a bit of gold has come your way. I and others can only surmise your takeover of Lord Belgad's concerns has come at a hefty price."

Lalo said nothing. The man across the table from him knew too much already, or he suspected too much already, so why speak? Words could only give Kerjim further arrows to sling.

"All of this means you have acquired a rather sizable pile of debt of late," Kerjim continued. "This is a pity. Especially considering the fifty-thousand gold the Docks are expecting from you for --"

Lalo interrupted. "What in the name of Ashal gives you the notion I owe the Docks a single coin, let alone fifty-thousand gold?"

"You forget," Kerjim said. "Last summer Lord Belgad made public his intentions to provide fifty-thousand gold in funding for further development of the Docks."

"And you hold me to that commitment?"

"Obviously. What other way is there to see it? Since you have inherited Lord Belgad's enterprises, you naturally also acquire his obligations."

So, not ravens, but vultures circling.

Lalo grinned, but it was no smile of mirth. "You honestly cannot expect me to accept this debt. It was not I who agreed to such an investment."

"But as a representative of all Docks workers and industries, I *do* hold you accountable," Kerjim said. "There is a desperate need for improvement upon the Docks, especially of late what with the riots and fires."

"Ah." Lalo held up a finger. "Now I understand."

Kerjim blinked as if confused. "What do you mean?"

The Finder's grin showed teeth. "This is an old game, Kerjim, and I would have thought it beneath someone as experienced as yourself. You are trying to shake me down. *Me.* In my own home. Belgad would have had your head separated from your body for such an affront."

Kerjim's own smile returned, and this time it was twisted and full of malice. "But you, Lalo the Finder, are no Belgad Thunderclan."

"No, I am not, and for that you should be grateful. I will merely have you escorted from the premises."

The Finder stood.

"Sit," Kerjim said. It was not a request.

"You are a fool." Lalo raised his head to call for a guard.

"There is a new guild."

Lalo almost called for the guard anyway, but his curiosity got the better of him. He sat. "That's impossible."

"Unlikely, yes, but not impossible," Kerjim said.

"The city council would have to have been petitioned, then there would have been a vote," Lalo said. "I would have been informed if such had occurred."

"As we have pointed out, you are not Belgad the Liar."

It had begun. Lalo had hoped the transition of power from Belgad to himself would have gone smoothly, but that was not to be the case. Already there were those behind the scenes working against the Finder. Those like Kerjim Sidewinder.

"Listen to me very carefully, Finder," Kerjim said. "I will speak plainly and I will tell you the truth. And believe it or not, I am doing you a favor. I know, as do others, that you cannot afford the gold for the Docks refurbishments."

Lalo opened his mouth to speak, but the Pursian cut him off with a brush of a hand.

"But let us forget the Docks for the moment," Kerjim went on. "Even without that debt, you are still up to your neck in liabilities. There is no need to deny this. True, you have all Belgad's properties, personal and otherwise, but *it has cost you.*"

Wait, Lalo thought, gritting his teeth. *Wait and hear all he has to say.*

"It is only a matter of time before you would have to renege on one of these debts," Kerjim said, "because believe me, you do not have the full backing that Belgad carried. There are already those who question your ability to provide consul as did Lord Belgad. Sooner or later, possibly too late, you will realize you cannot bring in the currency that Belgad did. This is why I am here. To offer an alternative."

"Which is?"

"Liquidation."

"Liquidation." The word was clumsy on Lalo's tongue. It was a nasty word to him, one which he had never believed could be used in association with himself.

"Only partial liquidation," Kerjim said. "You would keep the mansion and its grounds, of course, and there are likely some few particular clients who have personal ties with you. Those you would be allowed to keep, upon approval, of course."

"Approval by whom?"

"By the gathering of guild representatives."

"Wait a second." Lalo held up a flat hand. "There is no authoritative body within Bond that acts upon the behalf of *all* the guilds."

"There is now."

Lalo lowered his hand and sank back into the softness of his padded chair. Events were already spiraling out of control and beyond his reach. He had expected such, but there had been no word. He had men on the streets and in the taverns. Why had no news of any of this reached him? He should not have allowed himself to remain indoors so often, caught up in his administrative duties. Belgad had not done so, but then Belgad had had Lalo to take care of many of the managerial duties of his empire. Major changes had occurred within the city's administration, and quite swiftly. Could Lalo pull himself and *his* empire from the brink? He did not know. Perhaps he needed another version of himself, a younger version, a man with the proper skills. Or perhaps --

Kerjim cut off his thoughts. "Again, you are silent. It would seem I have caught you off guard with news of the many alterations of late."

"What else do you have to spring upon me, Kerjim?"

"I mentioned a new guild."

"Yes, you did."

"It is a guild of mages."

Again Lalo went silent in thought. Mages? Why did the wizards suddenly need a guild? True, the mages had not been represented within Bond through a guild, but they had had little need for such. Mages weren't like the members of the guilds, mostly rough men and women who worked with their hands and backs for a living, either through labor or craftsmanship. Mages were scholars. They dominated much of the university with their College of Magic on the eastern side of town. The mages had not been represented because they had not needed representation. They were not working-class people.

"I can see the questions in your eyes," Kerjim said, once more seemingly reading Lalo's mind. "You must be asking yourself why there is a need for a mages guild. The truth has been in front of you all along. Not all of Bond's wizards are the high-brow type who associate at the college. For example, you have such a man in your employ."

"Spider," Lalo said.

"Yes, this Spider. He is a prime example."

"He studied at the university."

"But he did not graduate," Kerjim said. "Instead, he went to work for Lord Belgad. There are others like him, a sizable number of others. Some of them are healers. Others are street magicians who only know a touch of magic, but still they are considered mages. The late, great Trelvigor was such a mage, as was the Jarnac woman who went off with Belgad."

"So, they've formed a guild," Lalo said. "Good for them."

"That is just one example, a strong one, of how matters are changing," Kerjim said. "You have not kept up with the times, Finder, and events are moving past you. My offering is a way for you to find peace with dignity, instead of --"

"Of what?" Lalo asked, his voice slightly raised. "A street war? A return to the old ways? Let us be clear about one thing, Sidewinder, you did not come here to do me a favor. You came here to make a threat, plain and simple."

Kerjim winced. But it was a faked wince, a staged wince. Any street actor could have done as well. "You do me harm to speak in such a manner, Finder."

"Kerjim, enough of these antics. You have promised to speak plainly and to tell the truth. Do so. What is it you want?"

"I have been telling you," the Pursian said. "I am trying to provide you with a means to ease your financial burden, to thwart any future unpleasantry."

"You are trying to blackmail me, Sidewinder," Lalo said. "You have come here with disquieting news in an attempt to rattle my nerves, all the while implying I am inept and unable to perform the task of running my own business interests. You have told me I need to liquidate some of my assets, yet you have not mentioned exactly *which* assets. Tell me, and let us be done with this conversation."

Kerjim's eyes grew bright as if a flame were lit behind them. "Very well. If you wish to be so abrupt."

"I do."

"Then sell me the old contracts for the Thieves Guild."

Lalo blinked. So this was the crux of the matter. Years ago Belgad had managed to shut down the city's thieves guild, as well as the assassins guild, by buying the contracts for each and every individual thief or assassin in town. The price had been exorbitant, but it had been worth it. The streets were safer. The nights were safer. More importantly, it gave Belgad control. By rights of the local underworld, nothing could be stolen nor anyone slain professionally within Bond without Belgad's blessing, which he never gave. Of course over the years there had been the occasional individual operator or a group attempting to form a new guild, but Belgad had always crushed such operations with the swiftest forms of street justice. It also had helped that Belgad's ownership of the contracts had put fear into all other guilds; they feared at some point he might have put those contracts to work for himself against various of their leaders.

Now Kerjim wanted the contracts, at least the ones for the thieves.

"There has not been an operational thieves guild in Bond for more than a decade," Lalo pointed out. "Nor has there been an assassins guild. As Belgad was fond of saying, such was bad for business. I see no reason to change this policy now."

"What if I'm not asking?"

Lalo held back a hiss. "So now you are upfront with the threats."

"I promised to speak plainly, and you are holding me to it."

"What of the assassins guild contracts? Are you not interested in those?"

"No," Kerjim said with a casual wave of a hand. "Fortisquo was the last head of that guild. Let him apply for his own contracts."

"Fortisquo is dead."

The guild representative's eyes went wide. Lalo was glad to see he still had a few surprises of his own.

But the look of shock died away quickly. "Regardless, my only interests are the contracts for the Thieves Guild," Kerjim said.

"There has been relative peace in Bond for years. There is no need for change."

"Do not do this," Kerjim warned. "If you refuse me, the situation could become quite ugly."

"In what manner?" Lalo asked. "Are you threatening a street war? There has not been one in years, and the local government is not going to stand for such. These are not the old days, Kerjim. West Ursia is not quite the new nation it was even a few decades ago, recovering from the war with the East and struggling to find its own way in the world. No, no. Any attempt at such violence would mean the wrath of democracy brought down upon your head. Belgad was no fool, and neither am I. That is why he brought peace to the streets of this city, and that is why I intend to keep that peace."

Kerjim's dark eyes nearly closed, like that of a mad beast about to strike. "You forget the new alliance of guilds, and you forget the power to be found in a guild of mages. That plus your own financial weakness leaves you in a wobbly situation, Finder."

"I believe I can manage."

"Can you?" Kerjim said. "The riots on the Docks have already claimed three of your warehouses, all lost to fire, unfortunately."

"What are you implying?"

"The riots could get worse," the Pursian said, "or they could be prolonged for an indefinite period."

Once more, Lalo the Finder was brought up short, and he was growing sick of that sinking feeling in his stomach. "Are you suggesting these riots are not ... natural?"

"What do you think? It's true enough about the Eastern tariffs and the troubles in Caballerus, but was it an accident the granary was ruined by last year's floods? Do you really think no ships whatsoever could make their way up the South River? Think it through."

Lalo did think it through, in a matter of seconds. He had been set up. The entire city had been set up.

Kerjim went on. "And do you really think a ragtag mob could stand up against our city guard for more than a day or two?"

Realization forced Lalo to sit up straighter. "You're using Docks workers. You're employing bully boys to fan the flames of discontent and to fight in the front lines. It's you who is behind all of this, including the fires at the warehouses."

"I do not work alone," Kerjim corrected. "Let that be a warning to you. Even if something should happen to me, there are plenty of others lending a hand to this operation."

Which was a foolish thing to say. The man had given too much, told too much. Lalo realized that right away. Recognizing one's enemies' weaknesses was a lesson Belgad had passed along to his former protege. Kerjim had overstepped his bounds, had spoken too much.

"Give me what I want, Finder," the Pursian went on, "or things will become very nasty very quickly. Otherwise, I cannot be held responsible for the results, especially considering there are dozens of other guilds lusting for a taste of Belgad's crumbling empire."

The guild chieftain stood. He had said all he meant to say and more. It was time to go.

Lalo leaned forward, placing his elbows on his desk and forming his fingers into an arch. "You have accused me of forgetting much this day, Kerjim, but there is one thing you yourself have forgotten?"

"And what is that?"

"Belgad may no longer be within Bond, but I was his student for many, many years. I learned much from him, and I have no qualms in taking the same measures he himself did."

Kerjim chuckled. "I wish you luck in doing so."

"Whatever the situation with the guilds might be," Lalo said, "I still have a staff of personal guard, and more than a few clients who will side with me."

"Is one of those clients Kron Darkbow?"

The name had seemed to come out of nowhere. How had Kerjim heard the name? What did he know of Darkbow?

"You wear your surprise on your sleeve once more," the Pursian said with a grin. "This is not like you, Lalo. In the old days you would have never been caught off guard so often, nor so easily."

The Docks representative turned to leave.

But Lalo would not let the matter be dropped so swiftly. "Why did you bring up Kron Darkbow?"

Without turning from the door, Kerjim twisted his head to one side and looked at the Finder with a single eye. "It was he who drove Belgad from town. I would think such a man could be an important ally."

Lalo stood, his palms slapping flat on the desktop. "Darkbow did not *drive* Belgad from Bond. You have your information wrong. Belgad *followed* Darkbow out of Bond."

"Yet Belgad did not return, and Darkbow did."

"Which means nothing. Belgad's interests lie elsewhere now. The matter is that simple."

"You might believe such, and possibly so do I," Kerjim said, "but the word on the street is otherwise. Whatever the truth, Kron Darkbow is the cause for Belgad's fleeing Bond. And a man powerful enough to do that is a man to be reckoned with."

Kerjim turned the brass knob on one of the two doors that led from the room, then he opened the door and exited, closing it behind him. His movement was done swiftly, quietly and with calm.

Lalo fumed. Now he understood why he had caught his former master so often hammering a fist against furniture.

After a few minutes, long enough for the representative to have exited the mansion, Lalo crossed the room and opened the door. Outside on the balcony walkway stood two guards, each in chain armor with their backs to Lalo, one to the right and the other to the left.

"Bring me Spider," Lalo ordered.

Both guards looked back at their employer. "My apologies, sir," the one on the right said, "but Spider left with Representative Kerjim. Do you want me to run after him?"

Lalo almost exploded. His face went red and he had to bite his bottom lip to keep from screaming. Fortunately the bite was not so strong as to break skin and draw blood. At least now he knew where Spider stood on the matter of the mages guild.

After a moment, the Finder breathed deeply and steadied himself. "No, no reason to go after him."

He almost closed the door. He needed time to think. But then a name popped into his head.

Lalo stuck his head out the doorway and shouted, "Stilp!"

3

"You are different now." Sergeant Gris watched Kron's cloak fall onto a stool while the man in black pulled an orange tabard over his head. "I mean, since you came back from Kobalos."

"In what way?"

Gris shook his head. "I'm not exactly sure. Maybe you're a bit more reticent than you used to be. A bit more calm?"

Kron frowned and slammed the wooden club he'd been given down upon the table beneath the tent. "Then give me a real weapon. If I'd known there was going to be this much trouble, I would have brought my sword. And why aren't we carrying blades instead of these useless cudgels?"

The sergeant chuckled. "There's the Darkbow I remember."

Kron was having none of his friend's humor. "Seriously, why aren't the guard bringing swords and bows to this fight? I've seen a few with spears, but not many."

It was Gris's turn to frown. This really did sound like the Kron Darkbow of old. "We're not in the Prisonlands any more, and we're not fighting a war against enemy troops. These are West Ursian citizens out there we're dealing with."

"In other words," Kron said, "it would look bad for the politicians if the city guard were spilling blood in the streets of Bond."

The sergeant chuckled again. "That's one way to look at it. And speaking of weapons, how many more grenados do you have?"

"Two, but I don't plan on using them. They are too expensive."

"Good," Gris said. "The last thing we need is for some citizen running to a city council member screaming about us using explosives."

The two men then went about readying themselves for the front lines of what was becoming a regular riot squad. Kron was busy tightening buckles and adjusting his mostly-leather garb while Gris found himself sending off runners with orders for the front line or requests for the captain across the river. The sergeant had held no compunctions about deputizing his old friend, a man he had watched grow to adulthood on the borders of the Prisonlands, and would have made Kron a sergeant himself if such a thing would have been permissible. The man in black had proven himself to Gris over the years in more than one tight situation, though the younger man had an edge that leaned toward the unpredictable.

It was nearly night as the two men made last preparations beneath the tent, the sun dead in the west but still spreading a light blue glow across the sky. Flames controlled the northern shore of the Docks where the wharfs ran out into the river, but the conflagration had been beaten back to some extent due to the seemingly never-ending work of a line of men passing buckets back and forth, the numbers of the group now reaching nearly a hundred. One of the three buildings that had been set aflame earlier was now little more than a black, hulking husk. A line of two-score city guards blocked Dock Street and the near turnoff that led to Beggars Row, with another score of burly men in padded leathers behind them and ready to move in at a moment's notice.

The rioters had quieted since their withdrawal. Occasionally a scream or shout could be heard a block away over rooftops or through alleys, but there had been no new approach of the enraged Swamps dwellers.

Just as the last of the sun's glow faded to a starry sky and torches and lamps were hung about the small, secondary command post, a young man wearing soft hides with an orange cape wrapped over his shoulders came jogging up from the direction of the main base of operations across the South River.

"Sergeant Gris?"

The sergeant stepped forward, "Here," and retrieved a folded paper from the runner.

"What news?" Kron asked.

Gris flipped the paper open and perused its contents. "The water pump I requested won't be coming for some while. It's sprung a leak and the engineers are working on it."

"Anything else?"

"Yes," the sergeant said with a grimace, "we're to reconnoiter the Swamps."

"Not a smart move."

Gris dismissed the runner with a nod. "The captain is leaving the details up to me, but he wants us to do some reconnaissance. Apparently it's been too quiet for a few hours and he wants to know what's going on. I can't say I disagree with him."

"I'll go," Kron volunteered.

"Not by yourself."

The man in black frowned. "You know I work better alone."

"And I know it'll be my ass if something should happen to you. Deputized or not, you're still basically a civilian. If you got yourself hurt or killed, I'd be scrubbing latrines with my tongue until Ashal returns from the dead."

Now it was Kron who had to smile. It was his friend's last words which had brought about the mirth. If Gris only knew the truth about the god he so often mentioned.

"Stop smiling," the sergeant said. "It makes you look crazy, and I don't like it when you look crazy."

"Fair enough." Kron stopped smiling. As simple as that.

"You're still going in," Gris added, "just not alone. I'm not having my best tracker and fighter sitting here on his butt while I send some green recruits into the lion's den."

"Just tell me where to go."

Gris retrieved a vellum scroll from a pack at his feet and unrolled it on the small table, revealing a map of the city. He planted a finger on their position just north of the bridge in a region known as the Point because it was where three rivers converged. Straight ahead ran Dock Street. Veering to the west was Beggars Row. Along both roads were rows of buildings, most two or three stories in height. Between the two roads was the Swamps proper, a maze of structures of all types and sizes, from large warehouses to apartment buildings to mere hovels. The nearest end of the Swamps was also home to a sizable open area that normally operated as a marketplace. A handful of other business establishments dotted the region, including various taverns and whore houses, as well as a few shops. To the east and south were wide snakes of rivers, beyond them shores leading to other, more affluent parts of the city.

One of Kron's gloved hands waved over the eastern portion of the Swamps, the congested area nearest them. "If there is any organization, it is likely working out of the bazaar."

Gris nodded. "That's the most logical spot. They might have a safe house somewhere nearby, but it would be easier to give out orders from the market."

"There's the square." One of Kron's fingers drifted to a blank spot on the northern side of the bazaar. The words "Haven Square" had been written above the unmarked area.

The sergeant slapped his friend on the back. "Good thinking. That's the perfect place. We'll start our search there."

Both men moved away from the map to the edge of the tent, staring out past guards to the darkness that was the Swamps beyond their light. The Swamps was always dark at night other than a few torches or lamps hanging here and there, but tonight it was black and weighted, as if a heaviness were looming over the squalid region.

The occasional cry could still be heard from the direction the mass of citizens had retreated, but outside of magic there was no easy way to determine what exactly was happening. Was another assault in the works? Was the riot dying down for the night? With Ashal's mercy, perhaps the eruption was dying down altogether. Gris needed to know, as did Captain Chambers. The anarchy had so far not burst beyond the eastern portion of the Swamps, and Gris wanted to keep it that way. Better yet, he wanted the riots to just go away. The only way to determine if such was likely or even possible was to send someone in. At any other time, this would not have been a problem. Though seedy, the Swamps was still part of the city, and like any other part of the city people commonly walked its streets, rode horses, drove carriages and so forth. Gris and Kron had both spent plenty of time on those streets.

But now things were different. From their vantage point the two men could spy nothing. No lights were burning on this end of the Swamps tonight, though there was a glow on the clouds hanging low over the buildings to the northwest of the Point. That general area was where the bazaar and Haven Square were located, rows of brick and wooden warehouses blocking any direct view.

"Looks as if you were right about the marketplace," Gris said.

"You sure you won't let me do this alone?" Kron asked. "I'd go in the same way I got to you in the first place, by rooftop. I'd be safer up there than a group will be on the streets."

The sergeant grinned thinking of their days together as border wardens of the Prisonlands. Heights had never been a fear for Kron, if the man had any fears. "You always were a bit of a tree monkey, weren't you?"

"I do what needs done."

Gris turned around slowly and looked down upon the map once more, giving himself a moment for reflection. It was too dangerous to send one man on his own. But then, a single person could possibly slip in and out of the bazaar without being noticed, whereas a small squad would be much more likely to draw attention. If anyone was an expert at sneaking and hiding, it would be Kron Darkbow. The man practically lived the life of a night warrior, able to climb and skirt rooftops as easy as others would walk down a street, all the while keeping himself from being seen. Gris had witnessed it a dozen times in the Prisonlands, but there had been heavy forest and mountains around the Lands. Here there were flat roofs, and the population density was much higher, giving a better probability of someone being seen.

No. Yes. No. Yes. The sergeant couldn't make up his mind, but he realized he had to. It was his duty, his charge, to make such decisions. No man was better suited for this job than Kron, but it was dangerous in so many ways to send the man alone.

The man in black seemed to read his friend's thoughts. "If it makes you feel better, I could take a boat down the river some ways so I would not be approaching directly from here."

Gris glanced to the man. Kron's idea made sense. Anyone watching the city guards from the Swamps wouldn't expect a spy from another direction. Frist Bridge was the only direct path from the Swamps to the main guard barracks. There was a smaller barracks in the western part of the Swamps, but it had been shut down days earlier when the riots began, the soldiers stationed there pulled back across the bridge. Even the flood walls to Uptown had been closed and locked, which could have been done as well for Southtown though Captain Chambers had so far declined the idea on grounds there were citizens needing protection. There was no other road out of the Swamps than the one Gris and his men blocked. Anyone wanting to leave the region would have to take a boat or go by foot through the actual swamps to the far west. The multitudes, the thousands upon thousands, within the Swamps were there to stay.

Unless one were Kron Darkbow.

"All right," Gris finally said, showing little enthusiasm. "You made it here through the rabble during the day, I suppose it would be less dangerous to send you out at night."

Kron pulled the orange tabard over his head and dropped it next to the table.

"But you're to avoid all contact unless absolutely necessary," Gris added.

"Very well."

The sergeant gripped his friend by a shoulder and looked him in the face. "I mean it, Kron. Don't make me regret this. You have a tendency toward the ... "

"Theatrical," the man in black finished.

Gris grinned and nodded. "From time to time, yes."

***

Eel squatted on the roof's edge and stared over the black line that was Beggars Row, across the tops of the warehouses and structures on the other side, then across the river to the lights that made up Southtown. There was a life over there he could only dream of. Which was sad because Southtown was not considered the wealthy part of the city. That would be Uptown, to the north. Southtown was mostly a collection of working-class homes, government buildings, shops, restaurants and inns. It was only a few miles away. But it might as well have been another world.

Eel had been born and raised in the Swamps, the central portion of Bond that lay between the North and South Rivers which came together at the east of the city in the region known as the Point. There the two rivers flowed together into the much larger Ursian River, which continued further east into the mountains and lands beyond. In the western portion of the Swamps there was literally a swamp, but the area within the city had gained its name for its proclivity of flooding whenever a heavier-than-usual rain swept through.

It was home to Eel, and he had rarely stepped foot outside of it. He could have. West Ursia was a free nation, and had been for sixty years, but Eel had hardly ever crossed a bridge into Southtown or into Uptown. He had never taken a ferry or rowed or swam across any of the rivers. He was a "Swamps rat," as the locals said. He wasn't necessarily proud to be a Swamps rat, but he accepted what he was and felt no humility in it.

His mother had died giving birth to him, then his father had been killed a few years later in an accident on the Docks. Apparently a crate had broken loose from a winch while a ship was being loaded and Eel's father had been unfortunate enough to be beneath the crate when it fell. Since that day, more than fifteen years earlier, Eel had lived with his uncle Kerjim.

The early days with his uncle had been almost blessed. They had had plenty to eat and a decent enough place to live in a rented room above The Stone Pony tavern.

Then had come Belgad and things had changed. It had been no secret Kerjim had been the head of the local thieves guild. Though the city officials had seemed to have no qualms with the thieves' organization, Belgad the Liar had made sure the guild was shuttered for good. Tough times had followed. Soon enough Eel himself took to stealing, bringing home crusts of bread and fruits and vegetables snatched from vendors' carts and stalls. His uncle had been proud of him, complimenting Eel handsomely and telling him how delighted he was to have another thief in the family.

Eventually Kerjim had been able to weasel his way into a position with the Docks Guild, and from that time on things had been better, though not as lively nor as affluent as they had been in the early days. When Eel was old enough, he had tried to land a job on the Docks himself, but his uncle would have no part of it.

"No nephew of mine is going to work for a living," the Pursian had said on more than one occasion. "He'll be a thief or he'll starve."

When Eel had first heard those words, he had been confused. What did they mean? Was he to be denied the opportunity to make a living like his father had done, to become a man? But soon enough it became clear Kerjim had plans for young Eel.

Eel was to be a thief. Not only that, he was to bring back the glory days of the Thieves Guild. To that end, Kerjim had spent the years teaching Eel everything he knew. Skulking. Crawling. Climbing. Hiding. How to break a window without making noise. Even some combat skills.

Eel had been a good student. Young and strong, he had also proven to be fast and resourceful. Under his uncle's tutelage, the lad had managed to increase their minor holdings quite well over the last five years. After the end of the Thieves Guild more than a decade earlier, Eel and Kerjim had been forced to live in a shack on the edges of the swamp in the west end, but now they were back in the top floor of The Stone Pony. If they had wanted, they could have afforded to move to another part of town, but that had been out of the question. Eel was a Swamps rat and he would always be a Swamps rat.

Which was why he was perched on a rooftop watching the river beyond and the empty Beggars Row that stretched to the left and right beneath his feet. This was a night for Swamps rats.

On the roof behind the thief squatted a half dozen men in a circle, most of them older, all with their attentions focused upon a dice game going on between them and lighted by lamps made of gourds. Beyond the gamblers, past the other side of the roof, the air opened up into what had once been the central plaza of

Bond hundreds of years earlier before the city had expanded beyond the borders of what would become known as the Swamps. Now that open arena was the marketplace.

Haven Square, north on the other end of the bazaar, was believed by most to be the oldest section of Bond. The youth himself believed such, when he bothered to give it any thought.

The bazaar was usually home to scores of stalls for Swamps merchants to ply their crafts and trades. For as long as anyone could remember, the place had been used as a daily market. But for the last three days the square had been cleared of all merchants' stalls. Instead of the usual wooden lean-to structures sporting decaying fruit and cheap gewgaws, the grounds were littered with ramshackle tents and dirty blankets. Beneath the tents and laid out on the blankets were citizens of the Swamps, a few hundred of them at least. Some were wounded or injured and being attended by others. Some were simply biding their time, roiling in the excitement of the riots because there was nothing else better to do when you had no money or food or drink or home. Still others were big men like those on the roof with Eel, these street warriors sporting makeshift weapons of all sorts.

The only clearing in the bazaar was a circle around a green statue in the middle of the square, a statue of a forgotten Trodan hero with one arm raised as if he were hoisting a sword upon high; if the figure atop a stone dais had ever actually gripped a weapon was beyond the memory of anyone living.

Perched on the podium, one hand wrapped around the waist of the statue, was Eel's uncle. Kerjim was speaking to a circle of burly fellows surrounding the bottom of the dais. At this distance Eel could not hear what was being said over the ebb and flow of the crowd's own tumult, but he paid it little attention. He had heard his uncle's rantings dozens of times before. The people were starving. The promised improvements upon the Docks weren't going to happen. Jobs were needed. The wealthy of Bond were growing fat while those of the Swamps were struggling just to survive. The Ruling Council didn't care. The city council didn't care. The First Councilor and the mayor didn't care. The Western church didn't care. Over and over, it was the same old thing. Some of it was true, Eel had to admit. People were hungry, but he had his doubts about whether any of the targets of Kerjim's yammerings cared. It didn't really matter. Those targets were but a means to an ends. Eel saw that right away. He had been raised by not only the former leader of the Thieves Guild, but by a man who was a shrewd street-level politician. With Belgad's leaving Bond, Kerjim had seen an opportunity.

The worn crowd didn't seem to know any of that, or if any of them did they didn't seem to care. Kerjim and a handful of other guilds leaders spread rumors and gave out orders, and the crowd grew more incensed every day. There had been three days of riots, and Eel expected more to follow. More than likely the riots would not break beyond the borders of the Swamps, but that didn't matter either. What mattered, at least to Eel and his uncle, was that Kerjim would be able to implant himself as something of a replacement for Belgad, or at least bring back the days of the Thieves Guild.

At this point, only a fool would try to interfere.

Which was why the young man's eyes grew wide with surprise when he spotted a half dozen burly figures working their way from the west down the middle of the road beneath the young thief. The moon outlined these sturdy figures, glinting off their chain shirts, helmets and the swords in their hands.

Eel glanced to his left, toward the brightness in the distance that made up the camp of the city guards stationed at Frist Bridge. Nothing from there.

He looked back to the approaching figures, men obviously on a mission. Could these fools be city guards? It didn't seem likely, not coming from deeper in the Swamps. But who else could it be? To Eel's knowledge the only person in the Swamps wealthy enough to afford soldiers on retainer was Lalo the Finder, the heir to Belgad's throne. But why would the Finder send out troops in the middle of the riots? Surely Eel's uncle had made clear the situation to the Finder. And either the men below were idiots or they knew no fear. The street was empty and dark, a rarity except during turbulent times, and the six men stood out like a burning candle atop a mountain.

Eel chuckled, then half-turned to the group of men throwing dice. "Kaf, you're going to want to see this."

The largest of the gamblers, a tall, fat man in a greasy tunic and short pants, rose away from the companions with an audible grunt. "I was losing anyway."

The others laughed as Kaf made his way over to Eel, though the big man kept his distance from the roof's ledge as if he had no great love for heights.

"What is it?" the big man asked.

Eel leaned over the edge and pointed to the six now huddled near a building on the street within an arrow's shot of where he stood.

Looking leery, Kaf leaned forward. Then his eyes went wide. "The fools."

"Absolutely," Eel said with a grin. "Shall we give them a proper Swamps welcome?"

***

Kron slid the skiff behind a thicket of scrub brush, then tromped through mud up the shore, his boots sinking several inches into the muck. Finding the small craft had been no problem, but the fisherman who owned it had put up a bit of a ruckus when Gris had requisitioned it for the city's use. A couple of silver coins from Kron had quieted the man, along with a promise the boat would be returned.

Taking his time in approaching a line of small unkempt houses that backed up against this area of the South River's shore, Kron wrapped his black cloak tighter around his shoulders. The chill of the night was whipping up a mild breeze that played with the edges of his cloak as if it were a dancer.

Skirting fences, he made his way between two low buildings, finding little need for skulking as he approached the bricked Beggars Row. The moon provided the only light. Kron had never seen the Swamps so dark and quiet. Even late at night there were usually a few torches or lamps along the roads, candles beckoning from behind shutters. Tonight, nothing. The usual late-night cavorters also were missing, bringing a quiet to the streets that was like that of a morgue.

As he pulled the hood of his cloak over his head, Kron had to grin. Dark and quiet. It was a perfect night for him.

At the edge of a house he peered out into the street, still finding nothing. Far to his right there was a glow above a scattering of taller buildings. A distant din came to his ears, the subtle, dying roar of a crowd slowly quieting for the night. The riots were over and those who had taken part were healing themselves and resting for the next day's action. That was the direction he needed to go.

He planted a boot forward.

Then pulled it back into shadow.

There had been movement to his left, something heading in his direction.

Kron eased back into complete darkness, flattening himself against a wall. He waited, one hand on a dagger at his belt.

Soon enough he heard the jingling of chain armor and the clomping of booted feet approaching.

Kron slid back along the house another few steps in order to put a little more distance between himself and the approaching men. Just in case.

He did not have to wait much longer. Six beefy-looking fellows came marching along down the middle of the street, their swords out as if they were prepared for trouble.

Kron was nonplussed. Who were these men? They did not look like a city patrol, and surely Gris would have known if such had been working the Swamps. True enough there was a small city barracks in the west end, but Kron's friend had been sure the place was closed down, the soldiers there pulled back across the river to Southtown.

Most likely these men were personal guards, but only Belgad the Liar had kept personal guards of any numbers within the Swamps. A few shopkeepers or tavern owners hired on the occasional goon, but never in these numbers.

Watching the line of hardened men tramp past, Kron found himself flummoxed. Belgad was gone, so who did these men work for? They didn't seem to be part of the rioters. Too well equipped, for one thing. And their demeanor, walking down the road with weapons drawn, told of trouble brewing.

Kron blinked.

He had seen something else, something he had not noticed before.

Struggling to keep up with the six fighters was a smaller figure. The man was no dwarf, not by any means, but his size paled in comparison to that of those marching ahead of him. He also appeared a bit smaller as he was hunkered over, almost as if he was afraid.

Kron had not spotted that seventh man until the group was past him, and now his curiosity was getting the best of him. Who would be foolish enough to head out on a night like this, even with personal guards?

Stepping out of the shadows, Kron eased into the moonlight. There was only one way to find out what was going on, and that was to follow. Moving out nearer the street, he was thankful he had dropped by the Rusty Scabbard to gather his sword, but cursed his luck for having left his bow behind at the Asylum.

***

Eel rolled his shoulders in excitement as he sauntered down the alley, his moccasins kicking up sludge and dead leaves in his wake to shower the booted feet of the dozen fellows following him. His hands were fists on the hilts of the two short swords sticking out of his belt, the blades precious gifts from his uncle who had worn them years earlier during his own thieving days. Tonight was Eel's night. He could feel it. Tonight he was going to prove once and for all he was ready to take the mantle of the new thieves guild Kerjim had in the works.

Whomever those half dozen idiots were ahead in the street, they were going to pay the price for stepping out of doors this night. Kerjim himself, with the backing of other guild leaders, had called for a general curfew. With the city guard having retreated from the Swamps, someone had to keep things in order. The only people who were supposed to be out and about were those on guilds' business, everyone else either behind closed doors or staying the vigil back at the marketplace, waiting for morning and the next round of attacks to begin. Normally the Swamps populace might not have paid attention to a curfew, but when the Docks Guild spoke within the district, people listened. The lower castes had few to speak directly for them within the city, and the Docks Guild was their common champion. A mixture of respect and fear kept most indoors following Kerjim's orders.

The young thief paused at the end of alley, holding up a hand for those behind him to halt and be quiet. He peered around a corner and spied the six chain-clad fools stomping along in the middle of Beggars Row, their swords leading the way.

Eel blinked.

There was a seventh man, someone the thief had not noticed before. The fellow was not as tall as the street fighters ahead of him, nearly invisible in the dark behind the six, hanging back and allowing them to lead the way. If the six swordsmen knew there was another right behind them, they showed no signs of it.

Eel blinked again. For a moment he had thought he had seen a shadow shift further down the street behind the approaching figures, but he must have been mistaken. Staring harder, he noted nothing worth seeing. Perhaps it had been a moth or a bat or something.

Grinning, he pulled himself back into the alley and turned to his companions, all twelve big men with cudgels and knives and other weapons they had been able to grab.

The biggest of the lot, fat Kaf, stepped forward while brandishing a long-handled hatchet, more of a woodsman's tool than a true weapon. "What we got, Eel?"

"I was wrong about their numbers. There's seven of them, but the last one doesn't look like much of a fighter."

Kaf leaned forward to glance around the lad, briefly getting a glimpse of their prey before pulling back. "Little matter. One more won't make a difference."

"Good." Eel's grin widened as he slid his weapons free of his belt.

***

His sword slapping against his back, Kron dropped to the ground behind a water trough next to the road, allowing his cloak to envelope him as he watched the scene ahead. The six swordsmen and their shadowy companion had come to a halt just as a group of a dozen or more tough characters strolled out of an alley on the other side of the road, each of the newcomers flaunting homemade weapons of all varieties and sizes. The swordsmen formed into a defensive position before the man behind them, Kron cursing the moon for not being brighter to reveal the man's face.

The group from the alley stepped into a line across Beggars Row, effectively blocking the street from easy access. A tall, hefty fellow gripping a long-handled axe appeared to be the leader of the pack as he took a step forward and bounced his weapon from one side to the other.

"What business do you have on the streets this night?" the big fellow asked.

One of the swordsmen pointed his long blade at the line of ruffians. "Our business is our own. Step aside!"

A chuckle spread through those from the alley.

The big man switched his axe to his other hand. "Maybe you hadn't heard, but there's a curfew. Nobody's to be out in the Swamps tonight."

Breaching his line of protectors, the smaller man with the guards came forward. "It's still a free country, isn't it?"

Kron recognized that voice, but he couldn't quite remember to whom it belonged. It was a voice he felt he had not heard in some while, at least a few months. Had to be someone here in the city, but who?

The street toughs chuckled once more, and the big man with the long axe rested his weapon over a shoulder.

"Move out of the way," the smaller man said to those blocking the street. "We're on important business this night."

The laughter died.

The leader of the gang took another step forward as if to speak further.

But his words were cut off.

"Enough of this!" One of the swordsmen darted forward, his weapon slashing.

The big man's gut was laid open, intestines spilling onto the street.

A shout, and the fight was on.

Eleven men in grimy and torn leathers charged forward, forgetting their dying comrade as they rounded his dropping form and clashed with the armored guards.

Swords winked in the moonlight, cries and moans went up. Black blood splashed. Kitchen knives and homemade spears lunged. Grunts and roars and the scent of urine filled the air.

Kron remained unmoving. This was not his fight. He had no way of knowing which side he should join.

In a matter of seconds, two of the swordsmen and half of the street thugs were down, their bodies splayed out in a growing pool of wet dark on the brick road. The two groups slid back from one another for a moment in order for everyone to catch their breaths, then launched themselves as one again.

Blades clashed and the thunky sound of metal cutting flesh tortured the ears.

A figure darted off to one side, headed for an alley. It was the smaller fellow who had been protected by the swordsmen.

Kron jumped up to a knee. He should catch that fleeing figure, to find out what he knows about the situation in the Swamps. And perhaps more.

The man in black was just about to dart across the road when another person separated from the melee and ran after the man who had entered an alley.

Now two men were running away, one chasing the other.

Kron had to know what was going on. Not just for Gris and the city guards, but for himself. The curiosity was eating at him.

His boots smacked brick and he pursued.

There was no opposition as he crossed the road behind the remaining combatants, now down to two of the armored guards and three of the thugs, every one of them weaving from exhaustion and probably more than a few bleeding wounds. Kron paid them no mind. The second runner had disappeared into the alley. That man was his immediate goal.

Occupying the far end of the alley was a cul-de-sac, square and littered with refuse and old crates. Eel knew this of course, as any good thief would know his own city, which was one reason he had not hesitated chasing after his prey. Another reason? Eel had yet to wet his sword. The fight had broken out much sooner than the young thief would have believed possible, that first guard charging like a madman and spilling poor Kaf's lifeblood right there in the street. Then the violence had erupted, the chain-clad swordsmen and Eel's companions slamming into one another. Eel had wanted to kill, to prove himself. He had not had the opportunity. As luck had had it, every time he had moved into position to stab or swing one of his two short swords, the foe before him had fallen to another's blow or been blocked by someone moving into Eel's path.

Then that one fellow, the older man, the one who had spoken, he had dashed off down the alley. Eel had seen his chance. There was a dead-end ahead, and the runner had worn a sword on a belt but had not drawn it when conflict presented itself. That told Eel the man ahead of him was no combatant. And while Eel himself was not the most experienced of sword fighters, he had one thing his prey did not. Enthusiasm to kill.

Breaking out of the alley proper and into the dead end, Eel's moccasins skidded through grime as he came to a halt.

His target had disappeared.

Impossible.

Eel glanced about the place. No, not impossible. There were a half dozen sizable wooden crates the fellow could have hidden behind. There was also the possibility the man was as good a climber as Eel himself was, meaning he could have taken to the rooftops already.

But that didn't seem likely. There hadn't been enough time.

A grin slid across the young thief's lips. His quarry was still here in hiding.

"You might as well get this over with," Eel said to the alley's end, the sound of combat now dying on the distant street.

Slammed from behind. Eel went spinning, a shoulder suddenly pained and one sword flying free to crash into a wall. Thank Ashal he remained on his feet.

How did he get behind me? And why didn't I hear him approach?

Gyrating around, Eel caught his footing and came to a stop, his remaining sword flashing out blindly to hit nothing but air. When his vision stopped swirling, he found it was not the man he had been following who now blocked the exit through the alleyway.

"I give you credit for your agility," the stranger said. "Most men would have been knocked from their feet."

The fellow was tall and broad, nearly as big as those sword fighters from the street. He was draped in a black cloak from head to toe, the moon behind him outlining his large figure while hiding his features. Eel felt his hefted weapon's inadequacy as he spotted the large handle of a sword much bigger than his own over the dark man's right shoulder. So far the stranger wasn't reaching for his weapon.

Which meant Eel had only moments to act.

He lunged. His right foot jumped ahead several inches as his right arm extended to its fullest, the short sword launching ahead for a stab.

That never came.

The man in black stepped casually to one side and slapped out with a gloved hand, cracking against a wrist and sending Eel's last sword spinning away into shadows.

The thief cried out and backed away, holding his wounded limb to his chest. The man in black had been so fast, too fast, faster than anyone Eel had ever seen. And with such bulk. How could someone that large move so silently and strike so swiftly?

Eel winced at the pain in his wrist, but he could feel nothing was broken. There would be soreness for a couple of days, but he would be fine soon enough.

The big fellow moved to block the exit once more. "Now, we were about to have a conversation."

Unnerved by not being able to find a face in the dark hole that was the cloak's head, Eel backed away a few more steps. "What are you talking about?"

***

The stained pants, the grubby leather shirt, the greasy cropped hair, it all spoke volumes to Kron, letting him know the young man before him backing deeper into the dead-end alley was a street rat, one of thousands who roamed the Swamps every day and night. This one had shown some little skill, however. Kron had been correct that most men would have been knocked down by the blow the young man had received between his shoulders. Fast footwork had saved the lad from falling. Those two short swords, now having disappeared into the dark, also told a tale. This young man meant serious business, and though he was no expert at the art of the duel, he did have natural ability and had received some little training.

Kron would take him seriously. Especially since this street rat reminded him of another, a younger lad, a boy who had not had the opportunity to grow up because his life had been taken at a tender age. Wyck had been young, much younger than the whelp now before Kron, but he had been smart. The man in black would not make the mistake of underestimating the young man who had wielded two swords.

Allowing his peripheral vision and his ears to take in his surroundings, Kron kept the focus of his attention on the lad edging away. "Looks as if you've lost your mark."

For a moment confusion continued to rein on the young man's features, but then he smiled. "Mark? You mean the fellow I was chasing?"

Kron nodded.

"Don't know where he's gone," the youth said. "I suppose you're one of his protectors."

***

Eel didn't for a moment believe the fellow standing across the alleyway was one of the guards from the street. Eel didn't know who this man before him was. Eel was just trying to buy precious seconds to think, think, think of what to do.

The man in black was too big and too swift for the thief to simply run past him. And evidence so far leaned heavily against Eel being able to fight his way past him, even if he could regain his swords. That left two options, talking or climbing. For now, Eel would try talking. Climbing was a last resort. He could scale the walls here easily enough as they were made of crumbling brick that offered plenty of handholds to one looking for them, but Eel had to consider his current foe might be able to climb as well. He was so damn big, but fast. What other skills did he have beneath all that black demeanor he wore so casually.

The shadowy figure chuckled. "I'm no hired guard."

Eel edged another step away until his back was against one of the taller crates. All he had to do was turn, jump and start climbing. He could do that. In fact, he had done such plenty of times before. But could he do it fast enough to get away from this menacing stranger?

Keep talking. Buy some time.

"Then you're involved in business that's not your own," the young thief said, then decided to add a slight threat. "The guilds won't be happy to hear about this."

"Guilds?"

Right then Eel had almost spun around and prepared himself to mount the wall, but the questioning word caught him off guard. This fool didn't even know he was interfering in guilds' business? Wait until Kerjim and the others heard about this, and the death of Kaf and the others. Someone was going to pay and pay dearly.

He laughed. Standing there at the end of the alley, his back slightly twisted in case he should need to climb, Eel laughed in the face of a man who had so far shown tremendous ease in dealing with him physically.

The black-clad shoulders straightened, the cowled figure standing taller. Until that moment Eel had not realized the fellow had been slightly crouching. Now the figure in black was even more menacing, almost spectral.

The youth's laughter withered.

"You ... uh, you better get out of here, mister." The words were shaky. "Any moment now some of my boys will come along and it'll be end-of-the-road for you."

The dark hood adjusted to one side as if the face behind all that black was scrutinizing the thief. "So the guilds are responsible for the riots." It was not a question.

Perhaps Eel he had said too much. He didn't know who this person or thing was, and he didn't want to know. Enough was enough. Time to go.

***

Kron had expected the move.

The street rat's moccasins skirted to one side and the youth bounced off his feet, twisting in the air and scrambling on top of a wooden crate behind him.

Kron grabbed.

Then from behind felt a tug on his cloak.

Sensing possible danger at his back, the man in black set aside his intentions for the fleeing youth and spun. A shadow was hunched in a corner.

Without thinking, Kron threw a punch.

Which connected with a crack and a cry.

The battered figure dropped to the ground and rolled over in front of the alleyway, the moon suddenly revealing the pale features of a man with thinning brown hair and a broken, bleeding nose.

"Stilp?" It was all Kron could do to keep from laughing.

The pattering sounds of feet scaling brick brought him around before he could deal with the man on the ground.

Kron spotted a leather moccasin disappearing over the edge of the rooftop.

So, the lad was gone.

Of course Kron could catch him. But why bother? He already had someone who could likely tell him what was going on within the Swamps. Stilp must have been the person who had first run into the alley. Stilp would know much being a man of the streets and entwined with Lalo the Finder.

Turning around and kneeling next to the sniveling figure at his feet, the man in black reached out and patted the fellow's shoulder. "My apologies, Stilp, but you shouldn't have come upon me from behind."

The little man on the ground rolled over onto his back and spat a stream of blood off to one side. Then he stared with a touch of pain and malice at the dark-garbed figure leaning over him. "Damn. Darkbow."

4

Finally, peace and relative quiet.

Kerjim nearly collapsed into the folding chair beneath the faded copper statue of the Trodan general reaching for the stars. The Docks Guild chief rubbed his eyes and stretched out his legs, relaxing for the first time all day. Remaking the world that encompassed the streets of Bond, specifically the streets of the Swamps, was no easy task. There had been headaches and heated moments throughout the day. Drumming support among the crowds was a full-time job in and of itself, but there had also been constant messages needing sent off to his lieutenants, meetings with his ground troops, the constant bickering and begging of the rabble, always wanting something, always needing something.

When will we eat? When are we getting food for our children? When will the city guard leave us alone?

It was enough to give Kerjim a headache. Years of experience leading the Thieves Guild and then the Docks had built up his resolve, but dealing with the masses was a different story. These people expected much from him, perhaps too much. But Kerjim would not let them down. He needed them as much as they needed him. He had staked everything on this one ploy, creating chaos in the streets. So far his plan was working.

When Belgad had gone missing from the city months earlier, it was as if a giant whirlpool had sprang up leaving behind a gulf of leadership on the streets.

Kerjim had seen his opportunity, one he had spent a third of his life waiting for. Belgad was gone. Someone had to take control. It was now or never. There was no time to waste, otherwise someone else would pounce upon the opportunity gain power.

In the Pursian's younger days, the underworld of Bond had been controlled by various guilds. Belgad had put a stop to that and consolidated power. For fifteen years the streets had belonged to the barbarian lord, so much so his power had reached into the highest levels of government and beyond the city itself.

That extent of power now sat waiting for the taking. Kerjim was determined to be the man to take it.

Rubbing his tired eyes, he thought of the potential enemies he had, others who might possibly stand between him and his goal. Lalo the Finder was the most obvious, being the last remainder of Belgad's power in the city. But there were a dozen or so others who could present a threat, most of them lower-level politicians or other guild leaders. A handful of the more powerful merchants might try to make a move, but those were people who could not stomach physical confrontation, thus Kerjim put them out of his thoughts. One mage or another might try to impose his will, but there were few powerful wizards within the city and most of those were academics, not a class likely to seek power among the slime and the riffraff.

Then there was Kron Darkbow. Kerjim had spotted him at a distance once, nearly a year earlier at a party Belgad had thrown at his mansion. The notorious man in black had come smashing through a window, embarrassing the lord of the manor and bringing panic to those attending the event. Chaos had ensued. Black smoke had engulfed the room, sending revelers fleeing for their lives, stampeding over one another to escape. Darkbow himself had then fled, apparently after a confrontation of some sort with some of Belgad's guards on the roof.

Kron Darkbow was someone to be reckoned with. Kerjim saw that right away. The man was becoming an enigma of sorts. He had left the city with Belgad chasing after him, then Kron had returned. Belgad had not. Oh, Kerjim knew the truth of the matter, that Belgad was now a king in a faraway land, but the whispers on the street spoke differently. *Belgad was too afraid of Darkbow to return. Darkbow had slain Belgad. Darkbow would be taking Belgad's throne.*

Not if Kerjim could help it. True, the man in black had so far shown little interest in Belgad's world, the underbelly of the city, but that didn't mean Darkbow's curiosity couldn't be aroused. Kerjim did not want that to happen.

Which was why he was busy consolidating his own power base.

He had to admit, the riots had gone better than he had planned. Three, going on four, days of fighting in the streets had shut down the center of the city. So far those outside the Swamps might not care, but they would. It just took time. If nothing else, the Swamps dwellers outnumbered those of the rest of the city by a two-to-one margin. And the Swamps dwellers were voters. The powers-that-be couldn't allow the riots to go on much longer. Food for the masses had to be found. Chaos had to be brought under control. Peace must return.

The Pursian grinned. He had plans for all of that, as well. He just needed a little more time, perhaps not more than a day or two.

Crossing his ankles, he leaned back in his chair, stretching his legs further and surveying his kingdom-in-waiting. Several hundred locals sat or lay in a large circle around him, most of them dozing or trying to find sleep while huddled around dozens of campfires. More than a few were wounded, some badly. Thank Ashal for the local healing tower and its hospitalers and wizards.

Nearby stood a half dozen street toughs, Kerjim's personal guard, men he trusted after working with them for years. A couple were older, hangers-on since the thieves guild days, but most were younger men with broad backs and muscled arms. These men were also the ones to pass along word when Kerjim needed to give out orders to those in the front lines of the riots. These men were integral to the guild leader's success. So far they had proven more than worthy of the charge he had given them. Of course they eventually expected payment, and not necessarily in coin.

Why shouldn't Kerjim be surrounded by such men? All kings had their personal guards. Belgad the Liar had ruled the streets of Bond like some emperor sitting upon high, and that man had been nothing more than a dirty barbarian from the far northern wastes. Kerjim was a Pursian, descended from a people of rajahs and sheiks, a refined people. If anyone deserved to rule here, it was the Docks boss. He had little use for upper-level politics where little men squabbled amongst themselves over petty differences that amounted to nothing. No, real power was down in the grime with the people.

Such people as the one now drawing near, a bedraggled looking fellow covered in a tattered cloak that barely shielded his spare frame. His face was gray and lank, yet showed a willingness to speak with the chief of the Docks Guild.

Kerjim looked up in time to see two of his guards intercept the fellow, questioning him at some distance, slapping open the man's cloak to find whatever might be hidden about his body. No weapons presented themselves.

One of his men glanced back, and the Pursian nodded approval, recognizing the subject of the interrogation.

As the guards allowed the man to approach, Kerjim reeled in his legs and sat up straight. He had to look the part of a leader, grinning at the thought of the long-dead general above him, the statue lending weight to Kerjim's own authority.

The newcomer halted a short distance away, two of the larger fellows at his back. "Master Kerjim."

The Pursian's smile widened. "No need for honorifics. We are all people of the street here."

More than aware of the pair shadowing him, the lanky fellow nodded and cautiously moved closer another step, within distance to speak lower and still be heard by the Docks leader. "The meeting is set. The day after tomorrow."

Kerjim's eyes narrowed, yet his grin remained. "What hour?"

"Seven bells in the morning."

The Pursian scowled. "Why so early?"

The skinny man shrugged. "I am not one to know."

Indeed not. The fellow before him was a street sweeper, the lowliest of municipal positions. Still, Kerjim could guess as to why the meeting was to be so forward in the day. Fewer people on the streets. Fewer eyes to see Kerjim himself coming and going. Less tongues to wag if he were seen. Very well, so be it. The meeting needed to occur, and it was happening within Kerjim's timetable.

"I will be there," he said to the underling. "Inform your ... master."

The sweeper nodded. "Will you be able to cross the rivers?"

"Of course." Kerjim's scowl deepened. How he should cross the South River with all roadways blocked was his business. "Now leave me."

***

Lungs burning as if afire, hands scraped raw from climbing, legs and arms strained and sore, Eel Sidewinder lost his footing and tumbled across a rooftop, rolling until he came to the ledge. He would have gone over, too, if his exhausted mind had not righted itself at the last moment. His left hand shot out and grabbed an iron gutter that ran around the top of the tenement. His body still moving, his legs swung out over the emptiness of a drop down to another alley. Eel strained with a grunt, swinging around his other hand to sink bleeding fingers into the edge of the gutter.

With a jerk, he came to a stop.

Laying on his back, he allowed himself a moment of rest, allowed his chest to fill once more with precious air. After several seconds he back crawled away from the ledge, wincing as he removed his fingers from the black iron of the gutter.

He did not get up. He was too tired. Eel had been running for he knew not how long, but at least he felt assured he was not being followed. He had charged across rooftops, flung himself over open alleys, darted up and down stairwells. There was no way that big bastard in black had kept up with him.

But Eel was paying a price. He tried to curl his fingers back toward his palms but stopped as pain ate through the flesh. He had scrambled too quickly up the side of that wall in the alley, then in a panic had climbed other walls further along his zigzag route. It would be days before his hands could properly heal and he could grip anything with precision.

Grip? *His swords!* He had left behind his uncle's precious short swords, family heirlooms given to Eel in trust. He would have to go back for them, and hopefully the two men in the alley had forgotten the weapons during ... well, during whatever it was they were doing.

The young man forced himself up, wincing once more as he had to use his elbows instead of his hands to sit right. He stared about in the night at his surroundings. Across the black blocks that made up rows upon rows of tenement buildings, he could spy a string of lights along the northern horizon. That would be the lamps marking Mages Way across the North River in Uptown, another place Eel had rarely visited. So, he had crossed the Swamps from east to west. It was quite a distance by rooftop. Any other time he might have been proud of himself, but not tonight.

The first opportunity he had had to prove himself in combat had turned into be a mess. Not only had he been ineffectual during the street fight, but that dark-cloaked figure had snuck up on him and battered him around as if he were nothing. The man hadn't even drawn that large sword of his. And Eel had been practically defenseless. If not for luck, Eel realized he might be dead right now.

Or maybe not. That shadowy man had seemed more intent upon questioning Eel than doing him real harm. The fellow also had been surprised when the thief had mentioned the guilds. What did this man in black have to do with anything? And who had been the other fleeing from the fight?

Eel wished he had had just a few moments more in that alley, then he might have come away with some answers instead of questions.

Speaking of questions, his uncle was likely to have more than a few, and Eel was not looking forward to that meeting. How could he present himself to his uncle in his current condition, especially after that tumultuous street fight and then him losing his swords? But Kerjim needed to know everything that had transpired. There might have been an importance to the events, an importance of which Eel was unaware. His uncle had not placed the young thief in charge of watching the streets without having confidence in the lad, and Eel didn't want to lose that confidence.

He would have to report to his uncle. Everything. The truth.

But first, he was going to rest for another half hour or so. Then he would slink back to the alley. Perhaps he could retrieve his swords.

***

There were only two men remaining standing atop the bloody heap taking up the middle of Beggars Row. Both were Lalo's men, each swaying on their feet and showing a half dozen small wounds beneath the light of an oil lamp one of them was holding high. About them was a circle of death, a dozen chopped and sliced bodies. Four of their comrades were among the dead, as were eight of their attackers. The rest of the thugs from the alley had proven smart enough at the last to flee, realizing their numbers no longer protected them against trained men with swords and chain armor.

One of the two men was moving about the corpses, using his lamp to shed a glow upon the scene, most likely searching for faces of the enemy to see if he recognized anyone. Or perhaps he was seeking to find out if anyone was still alive.

His companion was in worse condition, one arm hanging by only a thread of muscle, blood still filling his boots after saturating his leggings. The bleeding man took a step, his eyes bulging and unblinking as if he were seeing into another world.

Then he fell with a grunt.

The lamp carrier hurried over. "Kilp?"

"I believe Kilp is dead."

The guard spun at the voice, his sword and lamp thrust forward.

Approaching through the darkness was a tall shadowy figure, one sturdy arm holding Stilp by a shoulder. Stilp now sported a twisted nose crusted with blood.

Kron shoved his package toward the remaining guard. "See that he gets home."

Stilp fell at his sole protector's feet, the man unable to catch him because of the weapon and lamp in his hands.

The little man rolled over onto his rear to see the edges of Darkbow's cloak whisking off into the night. "Wait! I've been looking for you."

Easing back into the circle of light, Kron dropped to a knee in front of Stilp as the guard bristled, lifting his sword slightly as if wary. "We no longer have business with one another."

"Lalo sent me to find you," Stilp said, rubbing at the red crust below his nose.

One of Kron's eyebrows rose. "What does he want?"

"Hell if I know."

"I have no time for games, Stilp. Tell your master that."

"Alright, alright." Lalo's lackey sat up straight, flinching when he noticed the corpses laid out around him. He opened his mouth as if to speak further, but the sight of all that death seemed to have frozen him.

Black-gloved finger's snapped in front of the man's face, breaking him out of his shock.

"Focus," Kron said.

Stilp narrowed his attention on Darkbow, which was probably better than looking at all those dead people. "Okay. I don't know much, but it's got to have something to do with the guilds."

"Guilds?"

"At least the Docks Guild."

"What makes you say this?"

"Kerjim paid Lalo a visit right before I was sent out after you," Stilp said.

"I do not know this Kerjim."

"Boss of the Docks Guild."

Kron nodded. "So he showed up at the mansion, and you were sent to find me?"

"That's right," Stilp went on, nodding his head at the guard standing behind him. "We went to the Asylum first, figuring you was there, but it was all dark. Decided to check at the Scabbard, see if you still had your old room there."

Kron grinned as he sat back and glanced up at the big man with the sword. "So the lot of you decided to just waltz your way down the middle of the street in the middle of the riots. Unbelievable."

"It was late, the roads were empty," the guard said. "Thought we had a pretty good chance of no one bothering us."

Chuckling, the man in black got to his feet and turned to leave.

"Wait!" It was Stilp again.

Kron looked back.

"What do I tell the Finder?" Stilp asked.

"Tell him you found me," Kron said, "and tell him I'll see him in the morning."

The guard stepped around Stilp, his sword held with the point toward Kron. "Master Lalo wants to see you *now*."

Kron's gaze lingered on the dead, then returned to the swordsmen. "It would seem you have friends to bury and a client to convey to shelter. I myself have business elsewhere. I will be along in the morning."

Then he spun away. Within seconds he could no longer be seen nor heard.

The guard looked down at Stilp. "Does he always do that?"

5

Rest. A smart soldier knew to take it when he could get it. And that included Gris, reposed on a pile of hay covered with layers of cloaks, though he had never been a regular soldier in any army. First a border warden in the Prisonlands and now a sergeant within the Bond city guard, technically a branch of the West Ursian military, Gris felt he had seen enough action over his thirty-plus years to qualify as a soldier in anyone's mind. By Ashal, he was a veteran.

But he did not let that go to his head. Just because he had seen and shared and dealt out what could probably amount to gallons of blood over the years, did not mean he accounted himself better than other men. He had some small gift for leadership, at least on a squad level, and that was that. Each man had his own skills, his own talents. Some were good at magic, others at weaving or pottery. Some men made good fishermen or hunters or fletchers. Gris, called Griffon in the Lands, was fairly decent at small-level tactics, in part, he knew, because he was willing to listen to his men and realized he did not know everything.

So yes, he considered himself a soldier. And soldiers often did not get rest when they needed it. Which was why the sergeant now took slumber when he could.

His tent was still surrounded by a half dozen men, city guards who would remain on duty until the sun rose in several more hours when they would be replaced by the next shift. Beyond the bright orange tent were a few campfires built in the middle of the intersection where Beggars Row and Dock Street met, around those dancing flames two score men in orange tabards, most sleeping with a few standing watch at the border of the lights. Beyond that border was the quiet and the darkness of the Swamps. The image was not that different than the one in Haven Square except Gris nodded beneath a tent whereas Docks Guild chief Kerjim reclined under the watchful eye of a copper general.

A sharp nudge to a boot brought the sergeant out of his dreams, his left hand grabbing for the dagger at his belt.

"Easy." Kron stood over the reclining figure, the younger man's features outlined by the black of his cloak's hood.

The hand dropped from the dagger as the sergeant sat up and rubbed at his eyes. "What bell?"

"I believe it is about three."

Gris shoved away from his substitute for a bed, yawned and stretched. "By Ashal, man, couldn't you have let me sleep until morning? I think I've had maybe two hours."

"I thought you would want my report," Kron said. "Besides, we need to talk."

Gris had not liked the sound of those words. "If you tell me there's some conspiracy involving assassins and wizards and Ashal-knows-what behind these riots, I'm quitting and heading back to the Prisonlands."

Kron chuckled. "Things were simpler there, weren't they?"

The sergeant yawned again and pointed his friend to a chair as he retrieved his sword belt and wrapped it around his hips. "Simple is correct. There were exiles and there were wardens. They were supposed to stay inside the Lands and it was our job to keep them there. And everybody had fewer headaches."

The man in black tugged his cloak to one side and slipped onto a stool. "We had our fair share of danger."

There was that. The life of a border warden was deadly, often harsh and usually short. Few wardens made it to thirty. Gris had gotten out when he had neared his third decade, figuring his luck was running thin. Kron had left the Prisonlands but a year ago, in his mid-twenties, which was a smart move as far as the city sergeant was concerned. Still, since then Kron had often enough gotten himself into trouble that made the dangers of the Lands pale in comparison.

Gris grabbed a hand cloth from a table and dipped it into a bowl of water, squeezing the small towel nearly dry before patting at his face. "You mentioned we need to talk. What did you see in the Swamps?"

"There was a fight."

The sergeant bristled. Kron was often short on words. Now was not the time for that. "Go on."

"A dozen Docks Guild thugs took on a handful of the Finder's best in the middle of Beggars Row."

Gris dropped the towel. "Hold on. There was an armed conflict in the middle of the streets?"

Kron nodded.

"How do you know it was guild thugs and Lalo's men?"

"Stilp was there," Kron explained. "I saved him from a beating, or possibly worse. Some young pup chased him down an alley and I intervened, though at the time I didn't know it was Stilp being chased."

"Why were you following?"

"I saw no reason to jump into the fight. I didn't know the sides at the time. It was only later, after I'd caught up with Stilp, that I learned some of what is going on."

"Which is?"

"I'm not sure yet."

Gris moaned and spun away to stare between a pair of his guards and out into the dark of night. Sometimes Kron could be infuriating.

He slapped a hand against his leg and turned back to stare at the younger man. "Okay, so exactly how did you find out about the guild and Lalo's involvement?"

Kron sat forward, placing his elbows on his knees. "Apparently some boss of the Docks Guild met with Lalo earlier, then soon after the Finder sent Stilp out to find me."

"You?"

"That's what Stilp said."

"Did he say what for?"

"He said Lalo wanted to meet with me, but he wasn't sure why. He thought it might have something to do with the Docks Guild and the riots."

Nothing was ever easy in this city. Gris rubbed at his eyes again, feeling a headache coming on. "So, are you telling me the guild is responsible for the riots?"

"I'm not sure," Kron said. "Stilp seemed to think so. And then there was the young man who had chased Stilp."

"What of him?"

"He mentioned something about guilds."

"Guilds? As in more than one?"

"He said it at least twice."

Gris shook his head but it did not relieve the growing pressure behind his eyes. "What happened to him, the one chasing Stilp?"

"He climbed a wall and fled. I would have gone after him, but Stilp had been wounded."

"How badly?"

"Just a punch."

The sergeant grinned. "Who did it? You or the other fellow?"

Kron's face remained blank. "It was dark. I did not recognize him at first."

Gris slapped a knee and laughed. Kron and Stilp had some history, and poor Stilp always ended up the worse for it.

"He will be fine," Kron said. "Just a busted nose."

Gris checked himself. He could have a good laugh later. "Okay, so we *think* the Docks Guild might be involved, and possibly other guilds?"

"As I said, 'I'm not sure, yet.'"

The sergeant nodded. "I'll have to report this to Captain Chambers, let him decide what to do next. He might want to send in a squad to make some arrests."

"That would be a foolish tactic."

"Why do you say that?"

"I just left a dozen dead men hacked to pieces on Beggars Row," Kron said. "How many guardsmen could you spare for a mission like the one you're suggesting? Ten? Twenty? You'd need at least a hundred, and even that might not be enough."

"I see your point."

"Besides, I think there must be quite the gathering at the marketplace," Kron said. "Early on I saw lights and heard plenty of people. I didn't take the opportunity to check on it, but there seemed to be a sizable crowd."

Gris picked up a wooden tankard and sat on his bed of hay and clothes. He stared into the cup, finding only dregs rolling around in the bottom. "Well, we can't hold our position here forever, that's for sure." He tossed back the last of some old wine. "I guess I'll leave it up to the captain to decide what to do."

Kron nodded. "That's likely best."

The sergeant planted his mug on the small table between the two men. "But maybe I'll hold off on reporting to him for a few more hours, at least until the sun is rising."

"Why is that?"

"You," Gris said with a glance. "Lalo wants to see you. I'm thinking it won't be just to catch up on old times."

"True enough. I'll find out what I can."

***

At least Eel had retrieved his swords with little problem, the weapons either forgotten or uninteresting to the two men from the alley. That was the only good news he could have brought his uncle, but he had decided against telling that portion of his tale altogether. There was enough hell already raining down upon him.

"By our ancestors!" Kerjim's curse was common enough among Pursians, or at least that's what the uncle had told the thief. Eel had never been to Pursia and had known few natives of his ancestral homeland other than family.

"By the gods!" Kerjim threw a wooden goblet, sending it flying to crash against a wall. This curse was more rare, going back thousands of years.

Standing there in the middle of a warehouse, surrounded by stuffed burlap sacks stacked as high as his shoulders, Eel was wishing right then he could go back those thousands of years. At least he wouldn't be where he was right now, alone with his uncle, a major disappointment to the man who had been a second father to him.

Kerjim turned his back on the nineteen year old, his shoulders flouncing up and down as he seethed. He stared between a row of the piled sacks, his gaze seemingly nailed to the far wall and the windows set high above.

Eel stood motionless, his hands hanging useless at his sides. The lateness of the hour and the noise of water slapping against the nearest wharf outside normally would have lulled him into a near sleep, but not now. Not with his uncle so angry with him.

Turning around slowly, with deliberation, Kerjim's unblinking eyes glared upon his nephew. "You are positive Kaf is dead? And at least nine others?"

Eel nodded. "Yes, sir."

"You checked their bodies yourself?"

"Yes, sir."

"Checked their necks for a heartbeat?"

"Yes, sir."

"Their mouths for air?"

"Yes, sir."

Kerjim growled from the back of his throat. "What in the world made you think a bunch of thugs could take on armored men, boy?"

Eel hated being called a boy. Hated it. His uncle knew this. His uncle also knew that if anyone else had said that one word, there likely would have been a fight. As it was, Eel merely bit his bottom lip until a thin line of scarlet was flowing.

"Answer me!" Kerjim shouted.

"We had them outnumbered two to one." It was the only answer Eel could give.

Kerjim spat in disgust onto the floorboards and turned away once more. "What kind of imbecile have I raised?" He was speaking to himself, to the room at large. The young thief knew better than to answer.

The Docks Guild chief turned around again, once more glaring upon his kin. "You get Kaf killed along with nine others, plus two men seriously wounded. Yet you show not a single injury. How is this?"

Eel held up his hands, the flesh scraped raw.

His uncle snarled. "That's not a wound. You probably did that running away."

The thief lowered his head. It was true. He had been fleeing the man in black with that big sword on his back.

"I suppose it's fortunate for you the other survivors are in no condition to speak at the moment," Kerjim said.

Eel had to say something for himself. He could not allow his uncle to believe he had done nothing while their comrades had been butchered. "One of the others ran into an alley, so I gave chase."

"One of the soldiers?"

"It was a man with them," Eel said. "He wasn't wearing armor, but he had a sword on his belt."

Kerjim sneered. "So you went after easy prey."

"No!" The word was nearly shouted. Eel had to show his uncle he was not worthless, that he could be depended upon. "It looked like he was the one the soldiers were guarding, so I figured he must be important." It wasn't a complete lie, though the youth wasn't about to mention he had not gotten in a single blow during the fight in the street.

"Well, was he important?" Kerjim asked.

"I never got to find out."

The uncle threw up his arms in disgust, allowing them to fall with a slap against his sides. "Eel, Eel, Eel."

The thief waited with a hanging head. He felt a rebuke coming. But he would take it. For the honor of his family and himself, he would take it. What choice did he have?

"I have been working for years to make you a proper thief," Kerjim went on, "and yet I am beginning to have my doubts." He held up a hand to block any possible retorts. "Still, you are young. A few more years of seasoning and ... I suppose it's possible you might be ready to take over the new thieves guild."

Eel's head snapped up. "We're going to do it? There's going to be a new guild?"

Kerjim smiled. "Not everything is set in stone as of yet, but I believe so. There will be a gathering of the guilds tomorrow, and the next day I've a meeting across the rivers. If both meetings go as well as I believe they will, the Finder won't dare hold out on me."

Eel could barely believe it. All his life he had heard tales of adventure about the Thieves Guild, about how his uncle had once been in charge of a hundred or more men, men at his beck and call to slink forth into the night, to take from those who were undeserving and to set things a little right with the world. It was a dream. But now it seemed it might soon be a reality.

"But before I can go further," Kerjim said, "you and I need to finish things here. I pulled you into this warehouse because I didn't want anyone to hear what you might have to say. When the wounded were coming in, I knew something bad had happened. We don't need news of this leaking out."

"Of course," Eel said with a curt nod.

"So tell me," the guild chief continued, "why weren't you able to catch the man who fled the fight?"

"I almost had him," Eel explained. "I'd cornered him in a dead end. Then another man hit me from behind."

"One of the soldiers?"

"No," Eel said. "I don't know who he was. But he surprised me. I don't know how considering his size, but he came up on me without my hearing him. And all that black he wore, I could barely make him out in the alley. If not for some moonlight, I probably wouldn't have seen him at all."

"All in black, you say?"

"Yes, sir."

"What happened when he struck you?"

Eel hesitated. Here was the part he had not wanted to tell his uncle. There had been enough bad news already, so why add to it? A little lie wouldn't hurt. "I swung at him with a sword, but he got out of the way. I kept trying to attack him, but he kept moving around all over the place. I've never seen someone so big move so fast, and without hardly a sound."

"Darkbow," Kerjim said.

"*What*?"

"Kron Darkbow."

Of course Eel had heard the name. What street pup hadn't? Kron Darkbow was a growing legend throughout the city, especially in the Swamps. It was Darkbow, rumor had it, who had rid Bond of Belgad the Liar.

"At least it sounds like Darkbow," Kerjim said upon seeing the glint in his nephew's eyes. "Might not have been. But I'd give a few gold to find out why Kron Darkbow was chasing after you into an alley."

"I tried to take him out, but he was just too fast. Every move I made he countered. And he didn't even draw his sword." There was awe in the youth's voice as he remembered the dark figure from the alley.

"Sounds like the Darkbow I've heard described."

"I'm sorry, uncle," Eel said as way of apology. "When I saw I couldn't get through his defenses, I climbed up to a roof. I didn't know what else to do."

The heat of his anger having burned down to embers, Kerjim harrumphed. "If it was Darkbow, I'm surprised he didn't chase after you."

"Maybe he was only protecting that other man, the one who had run."

"Possibly," Kerjim said, "or perhaps he wanted the man himself for some reason. Regardless, it seems Darkbow is a threat to the guilds, even if simply as an accident of circumstance. I had feared such might happen. A man like that burns hot, and he needs a target. With Belgad gone, who knows what trouble he might get into?"

"You say that almost with regret."

"I do," Kerjim said with a nod of agreement. "I had briefly thought of trying to make the man an ally, but he has been damned difficult to locate. Now it appears he is more likely to be a problem."

"Sad."

"Not completely." Kerjim shot his nephew a grin. "I made plans for this possibility, as well."

***

Rising atop a hillside in the western Swamps like the belly of some slumbering giant, the estate that had once belonged to Belgad the Liar was more like a castle than the typical mansion of the city's wealthier classes. The main house itself was a fortress, and surrounding it were acres of open ground in which a thief or assassin would find few places to hide. Along the edges of the property was a high wall of stone, crenels across its top. To enter the grounds, one had to pass through a tall iron double gate regularly guarded by a pair of well-armed warriors.

The last time Kron Darkbow had paid a visit, he had left the place in flames. He smirked as he strode forward along Beggars Row, interested to see the main structure was still intact and showed signs of recent work. He would have to ask

Lalo the Finder who had been the contractor, as Kron still needed someone to repair the Asylum.

Approaching the gate silently, as was habit with the man in black, he noted the two men on guard were at their posts, one on either side of the gates, and they appeared to be paying attention. Lalo, as had Belgad, hired solid help. Often enough such sentinels would be dozing at this early hour of the morning. Not these two.

Still, they did see Kron until he stepped into the light of the pair of lamps hanging above their heads.

One man reached for his sword.

The other thrust out an arm to stop his comrade. "This one is expected."

Kron nodded at each of the men in silence as the gate was opened for him and he strolled through and onto the yard. A gravel thoroughfare led from the gate, across the acres of grass and up to a circle in front of the house. More than a few lights still burned in the main building. It seemed Kron was expected.

He wasted no time trotting up the path of crushed rocks and bounding up several marble steps to the entrance. The door was already open, Stilp and another guard in chain waiting just inside.

Upon spotting bandages crossing the smaller man's beak, Kron had to chuckle.

"It's not funny," Stilp said, his voice hollow and subdued behind the dressing. "You could have killed me."

"Wouldn't be the first time," Kron said upon entering.

His shoulders sinking, Stilp pointed to his right up a flight of curving steps to a landing above where several doors could be seen behind an iron railing. "He's in the library."

Kron nodded his thanks and turned up the flight of stairs, his eyes taking in the opulence that had been built upon the backs of Bond's lowest citizens. The floor of the lower level as well as the staircase and its twin across the wide room were all made of pale marble. The landings of the second floor were a wood stained dark, the railing along its edges gilded in spots along the top. From the center of the massive chamber's ceiling hung a gigantic chandelier of simple black iron but of exquisite craftsmanship, its arms and cups sporting scrollwork of wood painted gold.

Upon striking the landing, he made his way to the first door on the left, twisted the knob and pushed his way through.

Inside was a room he had never visited, though he had known of its whereabouts. The walls were covered with shelves of dark red wood, upon them resting hundreds upon hundreds of bound books and no few wrapped scrolls. Thick rugs kept the room warm and were helped by a massive hearth far to Kron's right. In the center of the room rested a massive desk of dark wood, a row of windows behind. At this desk sat the lengthy, pale features of Lalo the Finder, looking peaked as he ran a finger along the thin mustache beneath his nose.

The Finder motioned to a pair of heavy oak chairs in front of his desk. "Please have a seat."

A quick glance about the long but narrow chamber revealed the two men were alone. Kron closed the door behind him, noting there was another exit in the same wall further to his right. He did not move deeper into the room. "Forgive me if I prefer to stand."

Lalo allowed a slender grin. "I suppose I cannot blame you. We have had our dealings, haven't we?"

Kron nodded. "I thought we would be clean of one another after you sold me the Asylum."

"I had thought to level the place after what happened there," Lalo said with a shrug. "I've heard you are rebuilding. May I ask why?"

The man in black threw out a casual hand. "Perhaps as a shrine of sorts. Moreover, every man needs a home."

"Yes. The Asylum would seem suited as an abode for *the* Kron Darkbow."

Kron snarled. "Why did you want to see me, Finder? It is late, and I am sure both of us have other things we would rather be doing."

"Actually, it is early. The sun will rise in a few hours or less."

"Don't play word games. I've had no sleep, and my guess would be you haven't either, though you look no worse for it. You must keep some damned strange hours."

Now it was Lalo who nodded. "These days I do. When Stilp had not found you at the Asylum, I resolved to wait until hearing word from him. He informed me you would be arriving in the morning. A man of your habits would not wait until the sun was high. As I was already awake, I saw no reason to risk missing our meeting by napping."

A growl was growing in the back of Darkbow's throat. "As always, you speak much without saying anything."

"You want to know why you are here? Because I wish to present you with an opportunity."

Kron's eyes narrowed. "What could you possibly have that I would want?"

"Not so much want you want as what you will need." Lalo waved a hand to one side as if indicating the future or the outer world or both. "You will need coin, for one. Your purchase of the Asylum must have cost you a hefty amount, and to my knowledge you have not gained steady employment."

"I get by," Kron said. "Sergeant Gris has me working with the guard."

"Yes, the riots." Here the Finder grinned. "But once those break, what then? You do not strike me as the sort of man to be tied down with obligations to a municipality."

"Let me worry about that."

Lalo nodded again. "Very well. Besides money, I can also offer you a certain level of propriety within the life of Bond, on the streets and up to the highest levels. You would find yourself acquainted with --"

Kron cut him off. "Get to the meat of the matter, Lalo. So far you've told me what you can offer, but you've yet to explain what it is you want from *me*? What is it? You wanting to hire me as one of your guards?"

The Finder's face went pale. "Heavens, no. I'd never dream of such a position for someone as talented as yourself."

"What, then?"

"I ... " Lalo hesitated, obviously seeking a way to express himself in a manner most appropriate for his audience. "Since my former master departed, there has been a breach, a chasm left behind in Bond society."

"Belgad left."

"Yes, exactly. His leaving, especially as abruptly as it occurred, has put me in position as his immediate successor. With no humility, and to be blunt about the matter, I am not the man for the job."

Stunned, Kron eased onto the nearest chair. It was obvious where the Finder was going. Kron just wasn't sure he wanted to reach the conclusion.

"You're seeking a replacement," he said, "a replacement for Belgad."

Lalo rested his elbows on the desk and placed his hands together before his face, almost as if he were in prayer. "When you put it that way, it sounds somewhat crude, but yes, that is what I seek."

"And you are thinking I am a candidate?"

"You are the *only* candidate."

Kron sat back in his chair, astonished at the offer, the opportunity. What he could do with the resources of Belgad the Liar. But Belgad had left in part because he was not happy with his own situation in Bond. Being the emperor of the city's underworld was a harrying chore, one that could chain a man down as much as being a prisoner in a walled cell.

"No," Kron said, shaking his head. "No."

Incredulity lit up the Finder's face. "But why in Ashal's name not?"

"I will make my own way, one not involving wearing your fetters."

Lalo reached beneath his desk, using both hands to lift a small silver tray atop which rested a bottle of wine and a pearly mug. Without speaking he poured the red liquid into the mug almost to the rim, then set the bottle to one side and lifted the drinking vessel. For a moment he stared into the depths of dark crimson, then he gulped the drink in one hale swallow.

The mug slammed onto the desk. "This I did not foresee."

"You should have expected as much," Kron said. "You and Belgad spent years stirring anxiety within Bond. Now you can sit and stew in your own mess."

"It is not that simple."

"It is for me."

"How can you say that?" Lalo nearly shouted. "Bond needs someone in charge of the streets. Otherwise there will be chaos!"

"Such as with these riots."

The Finder drooped back in his seat, his gaze off to one side. "Exactly like these riots. Belgad would never have allowed such to happen."

"Not unless it benefited him."

Lalo's head snapped up. "You can think what you want about my former master, and I do not blame you considering your histories, but do not for a second think he did not have the best interests of this city and its citizens at heart."

"Tell that to my parents."

Lalo appeared nonplussed for a moment. Then he poured himself another cup of wine. "That was an accident."

"Accident or not, two people lost their lives."

"We were young," Lalo said as way of explanation. "The times were different."

"Two people died."

Lalo drank, this time only one hardy swallow before returning his mug to the desk. He would not look Darkbow in the eye. "I can offer you no excuses that are meaningful to your loss, but regardless, you know Belgad and myself well enough to realize we had good intentions for this city."

"As long as you were making a profit."

Lalo winced. "The two went hand in hand."

Kron stood, shoving away from his chair.

His eyes full of pleading, the Finder looked up.

"I believe we are finished here," Kron said. "I was hoping to discover information about these riots, but instead I find a weak man grasping at straws."

A hand shot up from, flat against the air. "Wait."

"Do we have anything further to say?" Kron asked.

"Whatever you might think of Belgad and I," Lalo said, "you have to respect what you could do with the power I am offering. You would take Belgad's place, and I would be right behind you as I was with him. The two of us could accomplish much in this city."

A sneer greeted him. "You are a drowning man, Lalo, and you are looking in the wrong direction for a helping hand."

Kron turned to leave.

The Finder shot out of his seat, hands flat on the desk. "The riots!"

The man in black glanced back, a skeptical eye raised. "What of them?"

"We could work together to stop them." Lalo's voice was nearly stuttering in panic. "You mentioned coming here for information. It's the Docks Guild behind the riots."

"One organization is behind these riots?"

"It's all of the guilds. They are working together."

A grin crossed Kron's lips. "If I didn't know better, I'd think *you* were behind the disturbances. You seem to know much of them."

Lalo leaned forward, placing weight upon his hands. "I spoke with Docks Master Kerjim only yesterday. He confirmed my fears. The guilds are trying to take over where Belgad left off."

"Why would the man tell you this?"

"He was trying to frighten me, to threaten me," Lalo said. "He wants the old contracts for the Thieves Guild."

Kron's face screwed up in confusion and disgust. "The Thieves Guild? What does that have to do with anything?"

"It was before your time," Lalo said. "Kerjim was the head thief. He wants to bring the guild back, and to unite it with the other clubs in a coalition of sorts. He even spoke of a new organization for mages."

"Thank you for the information." Kron spun away for the door.

"Wait!"

Kron did not turn around, but he did pause with a hand on the door.

"You and I, we can put a halt this," Lalo said, near begging. "We can end the riots and stop Kerjim from uniting the guilds. If the trade unions should join together -- "

Kron cut him off again. "Things would be just as they were under Belgad, except Kerjim and his gang would be in control instead of you."

The Finder could only sigh at the truth as he sank back into his chair.

"Good luck dealing with the guilds," Kron said. "As for me, I have a boat to return."

And he walked out of the room.

6

The sun had been in the sky less than an hour and it was already blazing heat to the ground, enforcing early the warmest day of the year so far. Throughout the waking city, citizens arose groggy and sticky, sweat clinging their clothes to their skin. The bread bakers, who rose hours before the light of day, likely had it the worst having to bend and lift and press and roll within a few feet of their great brick ovens. The fisherman who were out early fared little better, the heat radiating off the flats and swells of the rivers as if there was a second sun below. But whatever one's particular profession, each figured he or she had it worse than everyone else.

It was that kind of morning.

Sergeant Gris added to the misery by sweeping off his tabard and letting it fall behind him beneath his tent. It was bad enough he had been wearing a studded leather hauberk for nearly a full day, and carrying weighted steel on one's hip helped none. Kicking away from the straw pile that been his bed, he glared at the helmet and shield he had dropped the night before near the small folding table. No, he would not don those iron monstrosities, at least not yet.

Stepping into the brightness, he rubbed at his eyes as the guards around his tent gave him room. "Rogins!"

The guard was suddenly there, snapping to attention in front of his commander.

Bleary eyed and grimacing, Gris did not appear to appreciate his subordinate's diligence. "Anything happen while I was sleeping?"

"No, sir," Rogins' voice clipped.

"Yeah? Well we'll see about that." The sergeant moved past the man before him and surveyed the encampment.

Little in the immediate vicinity had changed since the night before except the handful of campfires were low and had pots brewing above them. Gris yawned. He supposed too there were more guards awake than there had been during the night, but he spied more than a few still curled up beneath blankets.

"Don't know how they can sleep like that in this heat."

Rogins was at his side again. "Did you say something, sir?"

Turning his head slowly to frown upon the corporal, Gris almost cursed. But he held himself back. It wasn't the fault of the likes of Rogins that the sergeant was in such a foul mood. At least Rogins had gotten a full night's rest. Gris had managed a few hours total, but even that had been broken up what with Kron coming and going and other general happenings. The sergeant had had to hand out more than a few orders throughout the night, including dealing with a man trying to sneak across the bridge from the Swamps. Turned out the fellow was a street sweeper who worked in Southtown and was just trying to get through to his job. Gris had seen no reason to accost the fellow and had allowed him to go on through. Funny that during the whole of the night not one other citizen had tried to pass through the line of city guards, in either direction.

Well, night was over. It was time to get to work.

"Rogins, any orders from Captain Chambers?"

"No, sir."

"Any sign of the rioters yet?"

"No, sir."

"Any sign of our scout?" Gris was referring to Kron.

"No, sir."

"Has the next shift arrived yet?"

"No, sir."

The sergeant closed one eye, allowing the other to snarl upon the other fellow. "You are just the bearer of good news this morning, aren't you?"

"Sir?"

Gris chuckled. "Just prodding you, Rogins. Get the rest of the men up and ready for the day. The shift should be changing any time, and I'm sure those who are going home will be more than happy to do so."

"Yes, sir!" Rogins snapped a salute and charged off to do whatever it was he normally did.

Gris heaved a sigh of relief. At least the corporal was dependable. Now the sergeant could find some breakfast while his men prepared for the day's action.

His eyes had just found a plate of biscuits baking away atop a fire when a gloved hand slapped him on the book.

Gris nearly reached for his sword, but the grinning face of Kron Darkbow appeared to one side.

The man in black was all smiles. "Morning, Griffon."

"Says you. What's with the good mood this morning? You're never in a good mood."

Kron stretched his arms wide and yawned as a fresh group of soldiers came trotting over the bridge and mingled with those who had been on duty all night. "I had a most interesting audience with the Finder."

The sergeant nodded to several of the fresh guards and waved on some of the tired ones, sending more than a few home to bed with a pat on the back. It was the least he could do. These men had not only shown their determination the day before, but then they had remained on the scene throughout the night. Fortunately that night had been quiet, but perhaps a little too quiet.

Once a line of withdrawing troops was past, Gris turned back to his friend. "What did Lalo want?"

"The man practically begged me to take Belgad's place."

"*What?*"

Kron shook his head as if he also could not believe it. "He's on a sinking ship and the sharks are circling. Lalo's not the man to fill Belgad's boots, but at least he's smart enough to realize it."

Gris rubbed at his unshaven chin as he watched Rogins form the incoming soldiers into defensive positions around the encampment. In the distance a few of the locals were beginning to stir, bleary-eyed as they stumbled out of their homes onto the streets of the Swamps. So far no one seemed to be looking for trouble, and that fit the pattern of the last three days when the riots hadn't broiled up until noontime.

"It's hard to believe the gall of the man," Gris said. "To ask *you* of all people."

"He seemed to think I would be suited for the position."

Gris turned and one eye winked. "You know, you just might be, at that."

Kron was no longer smiling.

The sergeant chuckled. "By Ashal, there's the Darkbow I know."

"Lalo had plenty more to say."

"Such as?"

"He pretty much confirmed that the Docks Guild is behind the riots," Kron said. "A fellow named Kerjim is apparently leading the charge. I don't know the man."

Gris nodded. "I do. Shrewd. Used to head up the Thieves Guild years ago."

"Yes, Lalo mentioned that. Said this Kerjim wants the contracts for the thieves."

The sergeant chuckled again, but there was no humor in it. "Sounds as if someone is making a play for power in the city."

"I agree," Kron said. "Lalo also mentioned the guilds forming together into some sort of alliance. Sounds as if Kerjim is the leader of a pack, trying to bring back the Thieves Guild and uniting it with the other organizations."

"It's practically Belgad all over again."

"Nearly. But there is one other detail."

"What?"

"Lalo mentioned a guild of mages."

Gris blustered. "Mages? Why would the wizards want their own guild?"

"Makes sense," Kron said. "Not all of them are professors and students. Remember Trelvigor? Spider? Even Randall."

"That's disturbing news. If a group of second-rate wizards are forming a power base in the city, there's no telling where it could lead." The sergeant rubbed his forehead as last night's headache began to return like a needle to the back of his skull. "We'll end up with firefights in the middle of the streets, demon summonings, people being enchanted and robbed, Ashal knows what else."

Kron's grin had returned. "You're getting a little ahead of yourself, aren't you?"

"Perhaps. Perhaps not." That needle suddenly became a spike, jamming in hard right behind the sergeant's eyes. Since coming to Bond he had not had much dealings with wizards other than a handful of healers, but in the Prisonlands there had been squad mages, characters as tough and reliant as any border warden. Gris didn't have anything particular against mages, but magic was dangerous. Such powers shouldn't be unleashed haphazardly upon the populace at large. Most of the magic Gris had witnessed in the Lands had been defensive, as it didn't make much sense throwing around curses and lightning at unarmed men on the run, but there had been a few instances where powerful offensive spells had been used. Such instances had always ended messy, with the fleeing convicts never returning alive.

"I'll have to report all this to the captain," he said as the throbbing in his skull began to fade.

Kron planted a friendly hand on one of the sergeant's shoulders. "You need rest. When is your replacement arriving?"

"He isn't," Gris said. "There is no replacement. This is my engagement and I'm stuck with it unless the captain pulls me off."

"You should request a temporary leave."

Gris glared at his cohort. "Not unless I drop dead. It's my duty. I'll stand it."

"Very well."

Gris felt the last of his headache fade away and was glad Kron was allowing the subject of his removal to drop. "Did you check on the Asylum while on the west end?"

"I did," Kron said. "I had to. My horse is stabled there. Everything was fine. No signs of the riots. No signs of vandalism."

"Funny thing, that," Gris said. "All the action has been here around the bridge and along Dock Street. Everything I've heard says the west side has been quiet."

Kron nodded as he turned to watch soldiers passing back and forth along the bridge while others solidified a front facing the two roads that met at the command post. "I saw very little sign of trouble in those parts. But what can you expect? There's not much out that way but the Asylum and the Finder, the true swamps beyond. There's a couple of taverns nearby and a handful of old warehouses, but those are rarely used."

"I suppose so. Still, it seems odd."

"I also got a good look along the South River," Kron said. "Hell, I should have. I crossed it four times during the night, coming and going."

"Any signs of anything there?"

"Nothing. Not even a barge."

"That's kind of weird, too. There's always some big ship or other going up and down the rivers this time of year."

"Sounds to me this Kerjim might have more going on than we've realized."

Gris grunted. "That wouldn't surprise me. He's always been a crafty one. Let me give out the last orders of the morning and I'll inform Captain Chambers of what -- "

"Sarge! You'll want to see this!" The yell came from the front.

With Kron following, Gris took off at a jog, bustling past several of his men as he came to the front of the standard formation he had come up with days earlier, one man in front with club and shield, a second man behind with a spear. There were two dozen soldiers altogether, only half what Gris wanted. The rest of the men were still stumbling in from sleep or grabbing a morning meal. This was lack security the sergeant knew, but it had been a long night and already a hot morning; so far there had been no signs of yesterday's troubles.

Until now.

Fifty yards away was a growing crowd. Whereas before there had been your typical day folks shuffling out of doors and wandering here and there, now there was a sizable bunch milling about in the middle of Dock Street straight ahead, a smaller but similar group the same distance away on Beggars Row. Most of these newcomers were young people, many in their teens.

This was an obvious change in tactics, proof there was someone behind all this mess. These people out in the street weren't bully boys or wharf workers. These were the youth of the Swamps, the urchins, the back-alley bandits, even the whores. These were little more than children, and they had grown up in a world that offered them little hope for a brighter future. These were people with nothing to lose.

Fortunately, by luck or design, they were not rushing forward. Nor were they spouting curses at the guards. They didn't even carry weapons, at least none that could be seen.

Gris stared at the scene in puzzlement. "This is different."

Kron opened his mouth to speak.

Then the first rock was thrown.

And a hundred followed.

"Incoming!" It was all Gris had time to shout, his head turned to one side to deliver the message to his men further back.

A stone the size of an apple slashed the sergeant's left cheek.

For a moment Gris was stunned. The rock had come at him so fast, sailing over the heads of his men, he had not had time to react.

Grabbing a handful of his friend's black cloak, Gris dropped flat, pulling the man along with him. Fortunately Kron did not struggle, but rolled with the action. The two had just enough time to watch the other guards raise their shields.

Then the deluge came raining in. Like hammers dropped by the gods, the projectiles crashed into the camp, tearing holes in the command tent, knocking cooking pots aside, splashing up flames from the fires. What followed was the thudding sounds of rocks and sticks and a hundred other impromptu missiles slamming into the wood and iron of the guards' shields. More than a few fleshy thunkings sounded, bringing up a handful of screams and shouts.

Kron and Gris ducked their heads, the man in black taking a moment to yank his cloak over both of them, the sergeant wishing he had strapped on his helmet and shield. Stones and chunks of brick peppered the ground around them, but whether from sheer luck or the line of shielding soldiers directly above and behind, the two men received no more than a few scratches and some torn clothing.

As fast as that, the hail of pain ended.

A roar went up from down Beggars Row and several dozen young street toughs came charging, clubs and hatchets and knives suddenly appearing and waving in the air.

Gris shoved off the ground, crawling through the legs of soldiers in formation before standing. His men needed him, especially after he had made the mistake of complacency. *By Ashal, it wouldn't be the first mistake, but just don't let it be the last.* "All arms to the front!"

The order hadn't been needed. Good old Rogins already had the rest of the men in position. A wall of steel-tipped spears, oak shields and hard muscle faced the oncoming wave of ragtag rioters.

Still, the screaming mob came on, showing no fear of their armored foes.

The city guard dug in their boots, ready for the lashing to come.

Gris had just enough time to realize the crowd to their north, along Dock Street, was still hanging back when he noticed Kron was no longer with him.

The sergeant spun around looking for his friend. There was too much going on, too much action, to see everything at once. Where was Kron?

Then one of his men grabbed him by a shoulder and pointed with a spear. "Sarge, there!"

Gris looked.

And didn't know whether to laugh or scream.

Kron was running full tilt at the gang of what had to be fifty desperate, blood-mad maniacs. His arms were out at his sides, his fists gripping the edges of his cloak, making him look almost as if he were gliding along. All that black, all that movement, it had to make the man look bigger than he was, and Kron was pretty big already.

"By Ashal." It was all the sergeant could say. No. No, it wasn't. "Lock spears and shields! Ready for retrieval!"

Wood and steel clanked together as the guards' formation tightened.

"They're going to swamp him," someone said from behind.

But Gris wouldn't look back to curse the man who had spoken.

All eyes were on front.

Twenty yards ahead of the line of soldiers and less than ten yards from the charging mob, the man in black slung an arm ahead of himself and leaped into the air. A blossom of black smoke sprang up in front of the crowd, causing more than a few to scream and fall back, suddenly checking the forward momentum of those behind.

Into this madness, Kron Darkbow fell like a whirlwind. As he landed on top of the front line, his left knee smashed into the chest of one rioter, sending the youth reeling while Kron's right boot kicked out to connect with another's chin. Black-gloved fists lashed out in two directions, spurting blood from a broken nose and cracking against a jaw.

The crowd tried to withdraw from this devil amongst them but they were too many and he was already in their midst, rolling atop them, pummeling and kicking at everything and everyone. It was as if a starving tiger had been dropped atop the masses. The smoke whirled around Kron, restricting the vision of the mob and hiding him from those not near, leaving many with no more than the screams and cries of their compatriots to gauge what was happening in the front.

From their position the city guards could make out the mad figure of Kron Darkbow struggling atop a half dozen, the man in black punching and clouting every which way. But then Kron disappeared amidst the smoke and the hungry masses.

***

The gathering had not even officially begun, yet Kerjim already recognized it would be a success. There were a little more than two score guilds representing workers within Bond, and nearly every one of them had a representative present. What was most amazing was half those present did not live in nor have an official presence within the Swamps, which meant they would have had to sneak across the rivers to attend this meeting. It seemed the absence of a figurehead to take the reins of the streets and alleys of Bond had brought many out for discussion.

With a smile Kerjim leaned back in the tall chair at the end of the long table and stared about the narrow but lengthy back room of The Stone Pony tavern. The delegate from the Beggars Guild was none other than the infamous personage known as The Gnat, the holes of his hawk-shaped nose so large one could count the hairs inside; the man sat forward with his elbows on the far end of the table, facing Kerjim across the distance. To the Pursian's immediate right lounged Captain Tuxra, the leader of the Guild of Bodyguards, the man's huge belly shaking to a joke someone behind him was telling as he stuffed a fried bird wing into his ever-hungry mouth. To Kerjim's left sat rigid the thin, stick-like figure of Kadath Osrm in long black robes, a silvered ring on the woman's right hand revealing her high placement within the city's Guild of Merchants. Extending beyond Osrm and Tuxra all the way to The Gnat were a dozen more chairs on either side of the table, each filled at the moment, most with faces favoring hooded eyes. Behind the chairs loitered another dozen or so figures against the stone walls, most shuffling their feet and mumbling to one another, here and there a joke or a curse spewing forth.

Despite the din of chat and banter spreading about the chamber, it was a tense room. Hearths on either end revealed strained looks and concerned visages while the half dozen candles on the table and the three lamps hanging above showed much the same.

These were business folk ready to get down to business, but Kerjim had all of them waiting. Why were they waiting? None of them had a clue. In the meanwhile they were enjoying or suffering the flow of cheap wine and the placement of cheaper food in their midst.

"How much longer, Kerjim?" Kadath Osrm snapped at one point. "We have been here nearly an hour."

In a fit, Captain Tuxra lost his smile and slapped a chain-clad hand onto the table. "Yes, when will this commence? Some of us have things to do."

Several similar sentiments sprang up throughout the chamber, though none voiced their complaints as loudly as had the first two speakers. Some muttered to one another about wasting their time. Others pointedly spoke with voices raised so Kerjim would notice their displeasure, all in an attempt to prove their own importance, more to themselves than to the rest of the room. Only The Gnat sat quietly, his hands clasped together in front of his face like a rat at feast, his eyes darting about as if to share some secret knowledge.

Kerjim's smile widened. He had all of them in his thrall. Their annoyance showed their lack of leadership, their very dependence upon the man that had been Belgad. But now Belgad was gone and these fools were fumbling around in the dark. Most of them were too young to remember the days before Belgad, when the guilds had individually taken care of their own interests with no interference or control from outside. Oh, yes, they needed a new leader, someone to take charge of the seedier side of the business world, someone to keep their interests safe, and most importantly someone who kept the gold flowing into their coffers. Kerjim was determined to be that someone. His ambition was growing. Upon learning of Belgad's flight from the city, the Docks chief had initially had hopes of bringing back the Thieves Guild, soon after thinking to pass that guild upon to his nephew while retaining control of the powerful Docks Guild. And now? Now he wanted it all.

Taking his time, he sipped at a mug of stale wine, winced at the acrid taste, and only then turned his attention upon Osrm on his left. "Good Kadath, I appreciate your patience. We merely await one more to join us before proceeding."

"Not good enough," spat Tuxra, spraying bits of bread and chunks of fowl. "You promised this would be a meeting of importance, that all of us needed to hear what you had to say. It's bad enough you've turned the Swamps into a war zone under siege, what with the city guard closing all exits. Our pocketbooks are growing thin while you plan and connive, Kerjim, and frankly, most of us see little profit in your actions."

There were more than a few heads nodding agreement.

For a moment it looked as if the group would turn upon the Docks boss, but he held up a hand and the hubbub settled to a low roar with only a few mutterings and whisperings remaining.

Kerjim stood to better be seen, and looked from face to face one at a time to make sure he had the full attention of each and every person in the chamber. "All of you have been patient, and for that I offer my thanks. When the food shortages were made public and the riots began several days ago, chaos threatened the streets of Bond. All of us feared the worst, restrictions from the city council and the mayor, perhaps even from the Ruling Council or First Councilor Menoch."

Captain Tuxra jumped to his feet, his girth smacking the edge of the table. "We already have those restrictions! All ties with the Swamps have been cut off! We can't get to the Docks and our warehouses and ships."

The crowd went ugly once more. Shouts and curses and pointed fingers were directed at Kerjim, but he stood smiling, allowing the disdain to wash over him.

It took nearly a minute, but the group began to simmer instead of burn hot, and the leader of the Docks held up a hand again.

"If we of the Docks had not taken control of the rioting, it could have been much worse," he said, glad to see more than a few nodding heads from one end of the room to the other. Of course he wasn't going to inform those present he and the Docks Guild were responsible for the food shortage and the start of the riots in the first place, but not everyone needed that knowledge. "The closing of access to the Swamps was predictable and to some extent necessary. While it is true we are all suffering from recent events, it is also true the rest of the city suffers as does the countryside beyond. Lest I need remind you, Bond is a major financial center not only for West Ursia, but for all of the Ursian continent, perhaps second only to Mas Ober in the East."

Osrm now stood, more in control than she had been moments earlier. "All you say is true, Master Kerjim, but that does not explain *why* we are suffering. Most of us are here this morning for answers. We want to know when the riots will end and when we can get back to work."

Nods around the chamber again.

"The riots will be finished within two days." The admittance was direct, definite. Kerjim had spoken the words with absolute sturdiness.

The room went silent.

Then Tuxra chuckled. "You must be joking. Something this large cannot come to an end so abruptly."

As if looking upon a simpleton or a child, Kerjim turned his attention upon the captain of the guild of bodyguards. "I have a meeting scheduled with the mayor tomorrow morning. If all goes as I expect, the riots will come to an end by the following day."

"It can't be that simple," Osrm said.

Kerjim turned to face the woman. "Oh, but it is, Kadath. None of you seems to realize what a vise the city finds itself caught within. The very economic problems currently restraining each of us individually is far more damaging to the city and the state at large. They *need* us to get back to work. They need revenue flowing, taxes being paid. How else can the mayor continue to pay the very city guards protecting the decent citizens from the rabble? How else can the First Councilor continue to pay for the university, the wardens sent to the Prisonlands, protection of the trade routes? How can they continue to pay for *anything* without the gold flowing? They can't. And that has them frightened."

The room was silent once more, this time with more than a few eyes wide at the implications being put forth.

"Let me put it this way," Kerjim went on. "If the worst happened and the economy became so depressed all of us went out of business, it would affect each of us personally on a relatively minor scale. We would retire to our homes in the countryside, or perhaps uproot and start again somewhere else. We have those options, and plenty of others. *They* do not."

A door in the wall to the Pursian's left opened, drawing the attention of most in the room. Eel slid through the gap.

Kerjim shot his nephew a glance.

The lad nodded back.

The Pursian gestured in return, Eel exiting the way he had come.

With a smile Kerjim motioned to the other two guild leaders standing. "Captain Tuxra, Mistress Kadath, please find your seats."

No one moved.

Kerjim's smile vanished as he faced the leader of the bodyguards. "Sit down, Tuxra."

With a grunt the captain plopped onto his chair, his belly shaking beneath his tight leather armor.

The Pursian turned his heavy gaze upon Osrm.

Who stared back with rebellion in her eyes.

"Please, Kadath," Kerjim said. "The person we have been waiting for will be here in a matter of moments."

Heat flared in the woman's eyes, but she eased onto her chair.

The only sound was a titter from The Gnat, all eyes in the room finding the crusty beggar now wearing a grin beneath his beak of a nose.

Kerjim's smile returned as he sat, and broadened again as the door opened once more and Eel entered now followed by a short, dark-haired woman wrapped in a gray cloak about tight leather straps encompassing her diminutive figure.

Osrm shot to her feet again. "Frex Nodana."

The newcomer's red lips widened as she nodded to the leader of the Merchants Guild. " Kadath Osrm."

"You two know one another?" Kerjim asked.

Osrm spun to face the Pursian. "We attended the College of Magic at the same time."

"Yes," Nodana said, bypassing Eel and sliding behind those gathered around the table until she was standing next to Kerjim. "We both studied under Professor Markwood."

Kerjim smiled. "Then it will be like a class reunion for the two of you."

Osrm's eyes narrowed. "What are you doing, Kerjim? Nodana is no guild member."

"Oh, but she is," the Pursian said, "or she will be as of tomorrow morning. Not only will she be a member of a guild, but she will be the head of the latest guild."

Grumbles rolled through the room with whispers and traded glances. At the far end of the table, even The Gnat's eyes were large with questions.

The Docks Guild chief held up both arms. "Quiet, please." Once the room had settled, he glanced up to the still standing Osrm. "Kadath?"

The Merchants leader glared at the man for a moment, but then she sighed and eased onto her chair.

Kerjim appeared pleased, lowering his arms and looking about the room. "As some of you are aware, tomorrow I have a meeting across the river."

Several mouths opened as if to speak.

The Pursian's right arm sprang up. "Please hold your questions."

Mouths closed, silence followed.

"Now," Kerjim went on, "my intentions at this meeting are to find a satisfactory agreement to end these riots."

"In other words, you're making demands," Tuxra said.

Kerjim frowned. "Look at it however you wish."

"Thank you, I will," the captain stated.

The look the Pursian gave Tuxra might have killed a lesser man, but the beefy fellow did not seem to notice.

After a tense moment, Kerjim continued. "I will seek to end the riots, but also to put forward our own causes as a gathering of guilds. No longer will the city and its citizens deal with us as individual groups. We will be a collective of collectives, governing ourselves from within and boosting the overall economy of the nation at large."

"If you can get the city council to agree to all this," Osrm said.

Kerjim glared, but went on. "I believe we can come to an agreement with the city. Without us, the rest of them will starve. Remind yourselves of that."

And those gathered did. They were the guild leaders of the city. It was they who controlled the workers and the production and the very produce of Bond and much of West Ursia as a whole. The events of the last few days had already proved devastating to those living within the Swamps, and if matters did not change soon the situation would bleed over into the other sections of the city and would begin to affect the middle and upper classes. The local officials, and perhaps the national ones, would not allow this to happen.

"We have the economic might to do this," Kerjim said, "and we have our fair share of political clout. But where we are lacking is in martial strength, the physical ability to back up our words."

Tuxra raised an eyebrow.

Kerjim waved at the Bodyguards boss. "No doubt the good captain might disagree with me on this matter. And there is no doubt he can put together some of the finest squads to be found within the city. Still, where we are lacking is in the area of magic."

Dumbfounded faces stared back. None of them had an idea where the Pursian was taking them.

"There will be a guild of mages," Kerjim stated plainly.

More eyebrows rose. Concerned glances were traded once more.

But no one spoke.

Until Frex Nodana opened her mouth. "Guild master Kerjim approached me some time ago concerning forming such a guild, of heading up such a guild. I have agreed."

"What makes you believe you can take charge of a guild?" Tuxra asked. "There's more to it, lass, than fancy potions and jiggling your fingers in the air to make some lights dance for a crowd."

Nodana smirked. "Captain, I have spent the last three years as an official liaison to the farming guilds along our borders with Caballerus. Before that, I worked with Master Kerjim in capacity as his personal auxiliary. I believe I have more than enough experience and education to start a new guild."

Kerjim piped up again. "Nodana has proven herself more than capable."

A chain-gloved hand from Tuxra pointed at the Docks Guild chief. "This is unfounded, Kerjim. There has never been a mages guild in Bond. And I do not buy into your assertions we need magic to back us up on the streets or in the city halls. You are walking on very thin ice, my friend, especially considering our alliance of guilds is new."

Nodana's lips parted to speak, but a gentle hand from the Pursian on her arm kept her silent.

Kerjim leaned forward, his elbows on the table, his fingers entwining, gripping one another. "Captain Tuxra, imagine four to six of your men are hired to protect a caravan. This happens often enough, yes?"

With a sour face, the captain nodded.

"Very well," Kerjim continued. "Imagine they are attacked by an equal number of men."

Tuxra chuckled. "The bandits would be fools. My men are --"

"The best trained. Yes, we know." Kerjim's fingers cracked. "But what if these bandits came in larger numbers? Or what if they weren't mere highwaymen? What if they were trained veterans?"

"It happens from time to time," Tuxra admitted. "Men down on their luck and such."

"Yes," Kerjim said. "In such instances, your men would be put to the test, true?"

A nod was the answer.

"And we might also surmise that even should your men be facing mere bandits," Kerjim said, "sometimes even in such circumstances one or more of your men might be wounded, possibly even killed?"

Captain Tuxra nodded again, a scowl reddening his face.

"I thought so." Kerjim loosed his fingers and sat back in his chair. "Now, I want you to imagine one more thing."

"Go on."

"Imagine similar situations, but your men have a mage at their disposal."

The chamber was silent once more. There was no need for the Pursian to say more. A wizard would make a huge difference in such conflicts. Magic itself had only been legal in the nation for a couple of generations, and plenty of people still feared magic and mages. The very presence of a wizard would likely scare off all but the most hardy or foolish of attackers.

"The truth is obvious," Kerjim said after moments of silence. "We can make use of a mage guild. It would empower us politically with the city, the country and on the streets. It gives us power not even Belgad the Liar could have imagined, especially if all of us continue to work together."

There were no arguments otherwise.

The Pursian turned slightly in his chair to look up at Nodana. "As soon as the paperwork is approved by the city, and I feel it shall be, Frex Nodana here will be the first head of our new Mages Guild." He looked back onto the silent chamber. "Then let anyone try to stop us."

***

Sergeant Gris saw his opportunity. With a quick glance along Dock Street to see none of the crowd there was approaching, he grabbed a shield from one of the men in the second line and hefted it high above his head. "First line! Forward!"

The city guard of Bond were not the finest soldiers the army of West Ursia had to offer. In fact, the group as a whole had a reputation for being slovenly, ill trained and unkempt. That day the city guard proved many doubters wrong. The men of the front line marched ahead, one clanking step at a time, their shields up and blocking the occasional thrown detritus, their cudgels gripped close but ready to strike.

Gris just hoped they would get to Kron in time. *No, can't think like that.* "Second line! Right aslant!"

As a group, the spearmen shifted their weapons to face directly along Dock Street. Just in case.

But the sergeant was keeping his attention down Beggars Row where the line of his marching men and the flittering black smoke shielded much of his view. What could be seen was chaos. A few rocks continued to sail from deeper along the road, all clashing against shield before falling useless to the ground. The rioters themselves were retreating in disorder with more than a few screams of pain, but from his position Gris could make out little else.

As the soldiers approached, cudgels were raised and smashed down, cracking against skulls and sending agitators reeling back, some few falling to the ground unconscious. Shields pressed forward, shoving wood and iron tips into the faces, stomachs and backs of those who would not or could not retreat fast enough.

Within seconds the immediate action was over, battered young people running or limping away along Beggars Row.

"Front line! Hold!"

The club-wielding guards came to a halt, standing their ground in the middle of the street. A handful of stones came flying from the direction of the fleeing mob, but none found a mark.

Gris glanced around. "Rogins!"

The corporal appeared next to the sergeant. "Yes, sir!"

Gris grabbed the younger man by a shoulder. "Take command of the second line."

"Yes, sir!"

Then Gris was off, his boots tromping on bricks as fast as his tired legs, body and mind could carry him. As he run up behind the unmoving first line, over the men's shoulders he could make out stragglers fleeing along Beggars Row and more than a few curious citizens sticking their heads out doors and windows or loitering about on stoops or street corners.

But no sign of Kron.

"Where is he?" the sergeant shouted as he pushed his way between the line of soldiers.

Then was brought up short.

A half dozen stunned and unconscious figures were splayed on the street just ahead of the front line, but Kron Darkbow was not one of them. Instead, Kron knelt next to a wounded figure, applying a strip of cloth ripped from his cloak to a bleeding leg.

The man in black had taken a beating. His garb was torn in multiple places, one of his eyes was black and several red lines ran along one side of his jaw. But he was whole and alive.

Gris slowed and sauntered toward his friend. "By Ashal, you'll never stop amazing me."

His friend glanced up with a grin. "Thought I was dead, didn't you?"

"I was assured of it."

"I had to put fear into them," Kron said, returning to wrapping the wounded man's leg. "I knew they would run."

"You *hoped* they would run," Gris said with a chuckle.

Kron let out a laugh as he finished his impromptu bandaging. "That, too."

Not able to stop himself from smiling, the sergeant spun about to face his men. "First line, tend the wounded."

With those words, clubs were stuck into belts and the city guards moved forward to lift and carry off those who needed it.

Kron handed off the man he had been helping, then approached his friend. "If you hadn't given your men the order to come forward, there's no telling what would have happened to me."

The sergeant's face was pained. "None of this should have happened in the first place. I was clumsy and lazy. I should have had the camp ready before the rioters hit the streets."

The two backtracked with the city guards, falling back behind the second line of spearmen, all the while keeping attention focused down both streets. There were no more signs of a riot other than garbage and dropped weapons in the streets; the Swamps was dirty and smelled, but that was nothing new. Those who had run from the fight had dissipated down alleys and into various warehouses or tenements, leaving the streets to the casual citizens who seemed without interest in rushing out into the day and the heat and the danger.

Once the wounded were trotted off and the soldiers formed into position in front of their base of operations, Gris gave orders to Rogins for straightening up the encampment. Only after all that did the sergeant retreat to his tent where he poured himself a mug of water with a shaking hand.

Collapsing onto a chair, Gris looked up at Kron who was standing on the edge of the tent and staring out past the guards. "I should resign as sergeant."

Without turning around, Kron flung a hand in the air to dismiss his friend's suggestion.

"I shouldn't have let the men down like that," Gris said.

This time Kron looked over a shoulder, his eyes narrowed in anger. "You are talking stupidity."

"No, I am not. I am talking sense. I did not --"

"Shut up." Kron's words were filled with venom. "You have had next to no sleep for at least three night and you've been dealing with these riots for days. Gris, you are near exhaustion. If anyone should resign it's this Captain Chambers of yours for not pulling you off the front before now."

There was some truth to what Kron said, but it did not make the sergeant feel better. He should have been prepared, and he should have had his men prepared.

"You need rest," his friend said said.

"What about you?" Gris asked. "Don't you ever get tired? At least I caught a few winks last night. You've not slept at all."

"But I slept well the nights before, whereas you have not."

Kron wasn't going to let up, that was obvious, but his goading was full of truth. At least the privates and corporals only had to work every other shift and could get some rest between. And there was no telling what the captain and his lieutenants were doing across the river, though Gris doubted any of them were missing meals or going without sleep.

He sat up straight in his chair and sipped at his water. "Alright, I'll send a request to the captain as soon as I can catch my wind."

"Good." Kron turned his head to stare at the streets and the backs of the soldiers.

"By the way," Gris went on, "you've got blood on your jaw."

A ripped black glove wiped across Kron's chin and came away with congealing scarlet. "I'll go see Randall once you're settled."

"The healing tower in Southtown is closer, and you won't have to fight your way through rioters."

Kron nodded. "True enough."

"And make sure to stop by the captain's tent for your pay. I'll give you a chit so there won't be any questions asked. Anyway, once they get a look at your current condition, they'll know you've been up front."

Kron chuckled. "I'll do that."

"Then *you* get some rest."

"I'll try." Kron sighed. "I've still got to find a contractor for the Asylum."

More than a few people had questioned Darkbow's sanity over the years, and on occasion Gris had been one of them. Now, after everything that had already happened that morning, the sergeant was a little perturbed and shocked his friend would be concerned with something as banal as construction.

Gris chuckled. "Same old Kron."

***

One by one the guild leaders made their way out the door, more than a few sending timid or dark glances in Kerjim's direction, eventually leaving him alone with his nephew and Frex Nodana in the tavern's back room.

Once they had the chamber to themselves, Nodana poured herself a glass of wine, tugged her cloak to one side and rested on the edge of the table facing the still seated Kerjim, one of her slender legs dangling. "You have them worried."

The Docks Guild leader looked pleased. "They are not used to this much confrontation. When I was a thief, we lived on the edge. These guildsmen today, they are fat accountants, little more."

Nodana smirked over her glass. "Tuxra might be a fool, but do not make the mistake of underestimating Kadath Osrm. The woman is as sharp as a Kobalan dagger."

"And The Gnat makes me nervous," Eel said, plopping onto a stool near the wall, "the way his big eyes always stare, and that big nose of his. Gads! One could go mountain climbing within those nostrils."

Kerjim laughed. "Do not worry about the others. The Gnat is sharp in his own way. The man has had to be to work the Swamps. And once the others get across the rivers and are back in their homes and offices, they will keep to themselves. Each realizes the payoff can be huge, while they leave me to share all the risks."

"Yes," Nodana said with a nod, "you do play a game of high stakes. Do you think any of them realize you are doing all this for yourself, for your precious thieves guild?"

The Pursians eye's narrowed for a moment as he stared at the mage, but then a grin slid across his lips. "That is where you are mistaken. I do this not only for myself, but also for my nephew." Kerjim waved a hand toward Eel. "Once a new guild of thieves is instated, he will be the head thief. I will keep running the Docks."

Nodana laughed and spun away from the table to fall onto a chair, all the while holding out her wine glass without spilling a drop. When she came to a stop, her attention was locked on the Pursian. "I've been wondering how you talked the other guilds into forming this alliance, this guild of guilds. Now I understand. With Belgad no longer on the scene, that leaves the Docks Guild as the most powerful entity within Bond, with the possible exception of one or two banks."

Kerjim remained silent, grinning and sipping at his own drink.

"The Docks control access to all the shipping in and out of the city," Nodana continued, "and with that comes great power. Years ago when I worked for you, Kerjim, I would have never imagined you had such dreams, nor such ruthlessness within you."

"Ha!" The Docks leader returned his drink to the table. "I didn't have such dreams then. It had never occurred to me Belgad would never not be 'on the scene,' as you put it. Oh, in his early days there were more than a few who tried to destroy the man, financially and physically, but he proved strong enough again and again to thwart all dangers. His leaving opened my eyes to an all new situation within the city and on its streets."

"Speaking of the 'situation,'" Nodana said, "do you really believe you can pull this off? A new thieves guild? You remaining in charge of the Docks? A guild of guilds? It seems much, especially so fast."

Kerjim leaned forward and squeezed one of the wizard's knees in a manner most fatherly, then sat back in his chair. "My meeting tomorrow morning will settle everything. Once that is finished, the other guilds will recognize I have led them to a land of golden rivers. Though I will retain my seat as head of the Docks, I fully intend to press others into calling for a vote to elect a chief of the alliance."

"I expect I will be important on that matter," Nodana said.

"Yes, as boss of the new Mages Guild, I would expect no less of you."

"And of me?" Eel asked.

Kerjim turned to look at his nephew. "Of course. As leader of the thieves, I would more than require your support."

Finishing her wine and setting the glass on the table, the wizard bent toward her former employer. "Kerjim, you are forgetting two things?"

"Yes?" He appeared genuinely interested.

"First, there is the Finder," Nodana said.

Kerjim flung up his hands and comically shook them in the air as if warding off a blow. "Lalo is no concern at all, my dear. The guilds are in my pocket, or will be by lunchtime tomorrow. Once they see the riots are coming to an end and business will be returning as usual, none of them will dare cross me. No, Lalo the Finder will be quite washed up."

Nodana smirked again. "Do you think the other guild leaders realize you have a sword over their throats?"

His hands lowering to his sides, Kerjim sat blinking, the very image of innocence. "It had not occurred to me."

The wizard laughed.

Eel sat forward. "What is the other thing we're forgetting?"

The Pursian and the mage shot glances to the young man.

"Nodana mentioned there were two things we are forgetting," Eel said. "The Finder is one. What is the other?"

"Darkbow," the woman said.

The room was silent and tense for a moment, recalling the level of constriction that had surrounded the chamber less than an hour earlier during the larger meeting.

Then it was Kerjim who sat forward, his arms placed on top of the table. "This Darkbow character might be a thorn. Whether relative or not I do not know, but it does seem he placed himself firmly within our sites when he interfered with Eel the other night."

"If it *was* him," Eel pointed out.

"True," Kerjim said with a nod. "It might not have been Kron Darkbow, however much your description sounded like him. Regardless, the fools on the street seem to think Belgad's disappearance had something to do with this Darkbow. Of course we know the truth. But appearances are often more important than the truth. As long as Kron Darkbow lives, many will consider him a potential threat toward anyone who would dare to take Belgad's place, despite the fact Darkbow and Belgad's feud was a personal one and not business related."

"What do you intend to do about him?" Nodana asked.

"Simple enough," Kerjim said. "We will end him."

"We don't even know what he looks like," Nodana said.

The Pursian turned to his nephew once more and snapped his fingers. "Eel, would you be so good as to escort in Spider?"

The young man nodded and jumped off his stool, soon enough exiting the room.

Kerjim faced the wizard. "Nodana, I am going to introduce you to your new lieutenant in the Mages Guild. And rest assured, he is someone who can identify Kron Darkbow."

***

Watching the back of his friend's dark cloak as it receded across Frist Bridge, Gris found himself amazed at just how much Kron had changed over the last year. The sergeant had watched Kron grow from a boy into a young man on the borders of the Prisonlands, then had watched his friend become one of the best border wardens the Lands had ever witnessed. Which was no surprise. There had never been a youth raised in or directly around the Prisonlands. Kron had grown up under the tutelage of his uncle Kuthius and more than a hundred of the toughest, most experienced warriors on the continent, men from all backgrounds, nations, religions and races. There had even been more than a few women who had been wardens, especially among the squad mages, and they too had been willing to share in the education of the dark-headed lad.

Kron could fight. There was ample evidence of that. But he was also one of the best trackers Gris had ever known, and the sergeant had known many among the border wardens. Kron could speak, read and write a dozen languages. He had been trained in various interrogation techniques. He could kill or maim with his hands or with hundreds of different weapons, many of which would be unknown here in the West. Kron also knew a bit of alchemy, having learned the craft from a few of those squad mages.

All in all, his unusual upbringing had made Kron Darkbow one tough opponent for anyone foolish enough to cross his path.

Then there had been the rage, the madness, that had enveloped the young Darkbow. Gris knew the story, had heard much of it from Kuthius and some from Kron himself. The boy had watched his parents murdered before his eyes. The lad had been changed forever.

So much so that until the last few months Gris had never known a Kron Darkbow who was not tense, not always looking over his shoulder with hooded eyes. The boy had grown into a man who trusted few and had the weight of the world resting upon his breast. For more than half his life Kron had sought vengeance for the deaths of his parents, and he had found it in a roundabout manner. However, such tragedies never ended without complexities, and Kron's fate had been no different.

But the man in black was not the same as he had been a year earlier. Had Kron found peace? Gris thought not. A man who lived his life for revenge rarely found true redemption in violence. Kuthius had tried to instill that fact in Kron, but it had not taken. Kron had gone seeking revenge and had found himself embroiled with Bond's underworld, specifically with Belgad, and that had led to a string of misadventures beyond not only the borders of the city, but beyond West Ursia itself.

Gris still didn't know all the details, though Kron and their mutual friend Randall Tendbones had given a few clues. The sergeant knew there had been a long journey to the dark nation of Kobalos, then some confrontation with that country's ruler, Lord Verkain. When the matter was settled, Verkain was vanquished and somehow or other Belgad himself had landed on the throne, making him king of Kobalos.

It seemed farfetched. It seemed weird. It struck Gris as just the thing in which Kron would find himself involved.

But that Kron Darkbow, of mere months earlier, had seemed to have slunk away. True, the sergeant's friend spoke with some bluster and continued to wear his sword and carry his favorite grenados, but those were mere outward appearances. Kron was different. He had changed.

The younger man's wild attack against the mob earlier in the morning reminded Gris of the old Kron. But even that had been different. No sword had been drawn. Even the grenado used had been one of smoke and not of flame. The old Kron would have waded into that riot with blades flashing and explosives going off all around.

Kron had been subdued in his actions. Yes, he had still attacked boldly, one man against scores, a fool's errand, but he had not set out to kill. That alone was a big difference from the Kron Darkbow of last summer, the man who had slain numerous guards who had worked for Belgad the Liar.

Why the change? Gris was not sure, but he had an idea it had something to do with a woman. Adara Corvus had initially been an enemy, but she had traveled with Kron and Randall to Kobalos. She had not returned. Why this was, Gris did not know. Perhaps he would never know. The woman was a subject Kron and Randall had rarely mentioned, and one which Gris was leery to approach.

Now Kron was off to Southtown in search of a healer, a tailor, a building contractor and eventually, hopefully, a night's rest.

Gris wished him well.

A runner approached from the direction Kron had traveled, the young man in simple leathers holding out a folded piece of parchment.

With a nod the sergeant retrieved the paper and opened it.

It was a message from Captain Chambers. Gris had expected such, though not quite this soon. It was barely past mid-morning and he had only sent his own note to the captain less than an hour earlier, outlining to Chambers the information Kron had gathered during the night.

Reading the contents of the captain's message, Gris found himself surprised. They were ordered to pull back across the bridge, giving up the Swamps altogether. The flood gates were to be closed and locked, leaving the rioters to themselves. And to any poor souls trapped with them.

The sergeant grunted, then shoved the parchment into a pocket. He patted the runner on a shoulder. "Find yourself some breakfast, then return to Captain Chambers. Tell him we will be along as soon as we break camp."

The youth grinned and took off at a jog for one of the nearest campfires where a sizzling pan was littered with sausages.

Gris spun around looking for his corporal. "Rogins!"

The man appeared from one side, snapping to attention before the sergeant as if he had been waiting for such an opportunity. Perhaps he had.

"Grab a half dozen men and break camp," Gris ordered. "As soon as they're finished and crossing the bridge, pull back both lines in a two-step sigil formation to be drawn up on the south side. Any questions?"

"No, sir!"

"Get to it, man."

The corporal trotted off, young and anxious, giving out orders to the few guards around the campfires before spurring on to the men in formation facing the streets.

The wooden chair groaning beneath the sergeant's weight, Gris gathered the various maps and other papers that had been laid out atop his folding camp table. As a trio of city guards scrambled beneath the tent to clear away equipment before dismantling of the poles and canvas, Gris reached down at his feet and picked up his helmet, strapping it atop his head; the heat was growing atrocious, but he would rather wear the helm than carry it, especially since he still had his shield and the paperwork tucked under one arm to haul away.

Bending free of the chair to lift his shield, Gris glanced across the bridge once more. No more signs of Kron, but the captain's orange tent still bobbed beneath the breeze. A handful of city guards and runners moved back and forth along the stone connector between the Swamps and Southtown, the men busy carrying off various gear or coming forward to help with the dismantling of the camp.

Gris looked toward the Swamps. The place was quiet now, eerily quiet. A few citizens milled about in the distance, going about whatever daily tasks they normally performed, but the only sight of any rioters was a small flock of young toughs beneath a dead street lamp. Every so often a dark eye or a curse would be tossed in the direction of the guards, but there had been no more signs of an attack. It seemed the rowdiness had settled for the time being. The sergeant wondered what would happen once his men had pulled back and the flood gates closed.

Of course the captain should have ordered the withdrawal yesterday, or perhaps even the day before. Gris and his soldiers had done little more than hold a toe into the Swamps, not really accomplishing anything other than keeping the majority of rioters from crossing into Southtown. The flood gates leading to Uptown had been closed at the first sign of trouble, wealth apparently coming with privileges and fear.

As he moved away from the tent and approached the bridge, Gris continued to wonder what he and his men had achieved over the last four days. There had been reports of more than a few boats and even small ships crossing the river from time to time. A few of them had been stopped, of course, but many had not. Kron himself had even navigated over to the Swamps and back ... what? Was it four times during the night?

Gris had to admit little had been done of any merit the last few days. A lot of people had been wounded, a handful had died, but little more was accomplished.

All because of Kerjim and his plans, whatever they might be. Or so it seemed. Kron had provided some little information, but none of it was definitive. The Docks Guild, and perhaps a few other unions, were working to replace Belgad the Liar as the main power on the streets of Bond. *More power to them*, Gris thought. At least Belgad kept things relatively quiet. Assassinations and thievery within the city had come to a standstill, the lone barbarian underworld leader having accomplished more through fear than the city guard had been able to do with brawn and training. If Kerjim and his gang could accomplish as much, Gris saw little reason to stand in their way.

Yet the situation did not feel right. Gris did not know Kerjim personally, and had only seen the man on a couple of occasions, but he knew the Docks Guild boss by reputation. Kerjim was not known to be bloodthirsty, but he apparently wasn't above stabbing someone in the back if that someone stood in his way. Or at least those were the general rumors. Kerjim's heyday as leader of the thieves had been before the sergeant's time, but the stories still lingered. Belgad had been the one to rein in the violence and the crime, and then had profited from it, of course.

So what was Kerjim up to? Gris shook his head, having no idea. But it had to be big to stir up something as major as the riots. And what kind of man was willing to spend the lives of others for his own power struggles? Such men, and women for that matter, had existed for all of history, Gris well knew. Those types had no qualms about spreading pain and death among their followers, sometimes their worshipers, especially if it meant more power for them in the long run. But how much gold did one man need? How much *power*? Gris could never believe in standing in a man's way when it came to earning for himself or his family, but surely there had to come a point when enough was enough. For the city guard sergeant, that point came when it involved harming others, whether indirectly or directly through violence.

Gris shook his head again. The world never changed. Mankind never changed. There was always someone who wanted more, no matter how much they already had.

As far as he was concerned, Gris had enough for his own life. In his thirties, never married, no children, it was what it was. He was not one for loneliness, nor did he feel any urge to pass along his seed. A handful of women had come and gone in his life, but there had never been an overflowing of emotions on his part and rarely on the part of any of the women. For him, duty was what was important. No, he wasn't some flag-waving fool who only came out on holidays or spent drunken nights in a tavern talking about the days of yore. Gris saw his place in the world as one that could make a difference. He did not want to slur through ale or wine about missed opportunities and long-dead companions. Those existed, as they did for anyone who had done any amount of real soldiering, but that was not enough for the sergeant. His place in the world was one which attempted to bring order to the chaos, and hopefully a little bit of safety to those who could not protect themselves. Gris had spent nearly a decade as a border warden trying to keep the worst of men away from the rest of men, and for the last few years he had spent his time among the Bond guards in an attempt to do the same.

But perhaps that time was at an end.

Watching several of his men folding the field furniture and unrolling the tent, the sergeant realized he had meant his words to Kron. He should resign as a sergeant of the city guard. It was not that he did not find satisfaction in his work, but he was wondering if he was suited for it. Though only a sergeant, he was still a leader of men, and that was the root of his recent thoughts. He had only been a sergeant for a brief period in the Prisonlands, having been a grunt for most of his time there. His experience as a sergeant in the Lands had not been long enough for him to come to any conclusions about his own capabilities. Now he had been a sergeant in Bond for a little more than three years. He now felt he had enough to go on to draw conclusions.

And his conclusion was he did not deserve to be a leader among men, he did not have what it took. That morning had been a strong example, perhaps the strongest. He could have gotten his men killed, *himself* killed. Why had he not jumped up and started handing out orders? Why had he not formed the morning shift into formation as soon as possible? Kron had suggested it was because Gris had been weakened by lack of sleep. Perhaps there was some truth to that, but Gris had been tired before and had always been able to carry out his duties.

No, he had slacked off. His sleepiness could be one culprit, but the truth was he also had been delighted and distracted by Kron's appearance the day before. That should not have happened. Kron had been more than helpful once deputized, but Gris had given too much attention to the man.

Thus, staring back across the bridge to the captain's tent, Sergeant Gris was pondering walking over there and resigning. He was still a good soldier, he knew, and perhaps he could find another line of work. The Bodyguards Guild was always hiring, after all.

7

Finding a healer had been a simple matter. There were two healing towers in Bond, one in the Swamps and the other in Southtown not far from the main barracks for the city guards. Both towers offered free healing to anyone, though donations were accepted. Kron left a hefty donation of two gold coins, a price he believed more than reasonable for the removal of the many bruises and minor cuts he had received in the riot.

A good tailor was not so easy an acquisition as had been a healer. There were plenty of shops and stalls in Southtown, but one look at Kron and all his torn black garb and his big sword caused many a shopkeeper to close up for the day.

Which only brought a chuckle from the man in black.

Eventually, however, he did find a shop with its doors open along South Road not too far from the Rusty Scabbard and Frist Bridge. Kron slid past several customers who were exiting and made his way inside the well-lit establishment before the door could be closed.

"I'm sorry, but we are closed," said the proprietor, a short man with little hair other than a little black mustache beneath his nose.

Kron dropped another two gold onto the front counter.

A little less than an hour later he walked out of the business with a new cloak, shirt and breeches. More importantly, small talk with the shopkeeper had provided a name. Felton Keldaris. Felton was the shopkeeper's brother in law. Felton was also supposedly one of the best building contractors in the region. Funny how life could put things together that way.

But for the time being Kron was putting off going to see this Felton Keldaris, who Kron was told had a small shop further down South Road where a dirt trail lead off toward the guards' barracks.

Kron needed sleep. He had been running hard for more than a day, had gone back and forth all night from the Swamps back to Southtown, and he had engaged in his share of melee. His mind remained sharp, but his body needed the rest.

Which was why he was now walking along South Road heading toward the Rusty Scabbard tavern in the distance. Kron had kept a personal room there for nearly a year, and with work at the Asylum no nearer to being completed he saw little reason to change that arrangement. The only problem was his money was beginning to grow a little short. Oh, he could live quite well on what he had for some time, but purchasing the Asylum had cost the majority of his wealth and had left him with little more than daily funds. Eventually Kron would need steady employment, and he had no idea where to find such. There were logical options, of course, such as the city guard, but that would be a last resort. Kron had not left the Prisonlands simply to become a warrior for hire for a government nor anyone else.

Marching up the wooden steps into the Scabbard, Kron had to ask himself just what it was he sought in life. He paused to give a nod to the proprietor, then made his way up the stairs to his room, pausing outside the door long enough to listen for anyone possibly waiting inside. Old habits died hard. And in this instance were unnecessary. The room was empty, and soon enough he was seated on the edge of his bed, his head in one hand.

What did he want to do for employment? For life itself? He had not a clue. Obviously he was a man of action, and he was experienced with deadly situations and all they entailed. But was violence and the potential for violence all he had to offer? He feared to answer that question. He had lived so long seeking only revenge, he had forgotten there was more to life. Adara had opened his eyes to other possibilities, but that relationship gone sour. All Kron's fault. He could admit that now, months later. She had seen the darkest side of him and had turned away. He couldn't blame the woman for that.

Now he was trying to curtail the darkness within himself. Once he had been vicious. Some might have even labeled him a murderer. Such opinions he could not fault. His personal war against Belgad had claimed a few lives, most of whom had not deserved their fate.

That was the past. Now was the present. Kron no longer wished to be the troubled, angry young man that had ridden all the way from the Prisonlands with murder on his mind. He would likely never be someone filled with love, but that did not mean he couldn't ease his ways. The old Kron would have waded into that riot with sword and grenados flying. So at least he had changed that much. Still, he found himself drawn to a life of violence.

What else was there for him?

***

When he was five years old, Kerjim Sidewinder watched from behind the counter of his father's shop as a knight of the land shoved through customers and proceeded to pick out a dozen items he wanted. The big, burly man with the thick red beard had gone home with a new cloak, two leather belts, a pair of soft moccasins, a fashionable hat for a woman and other sundries. The knight had not paid for any of the items. He had taken what he wanted and left. Afterward, Kerjim's father had retreated behind the curtain to the shop's back room and there he had cried for nearly a half hour. Even at such a young age, Kerjim realized why his father was upset. Everything the knight had taken had cost his father a month's worth of work. Now it was all gone.

Since those days nearly five decades back, things had changed. Knights were less common in West Ursia, as were all nobility in the young republic, and they no longer were allowed to walk into an establishment and take whatever they wanted. Nobles had to pay, just like everyone else.

Kerjim, however, had learned a lesson that day. Those with power got to take what they wanted, and the weak could do nothing about it. Over the years he had expanded upon that lesson, adding other lessons to it. Sometimes even those without power could take what they wanted, and the strong could do little about it. That basic philosophy was why Kerjim had become a thief in the first place, and his early adventures into the trade had earned him his surname of Sidewinder. He was like a snake, slithering into the homes of the wealthy at night and absconding with their prized possessions. Kerjim would admit he had never been the best thief, but he had been good; more importantly he had the intelligence to notice talent in others, such as his young nephew Eel.

Who broke the rooftop silence by speaking. "How do I go about this?"

Kerjim paused for a moment before turning around, staring off across the tops of buildings to the sinking sun beyond. Down the streets and alleys that fell within his view, the Pursian could spy Swamps dwellers by the dozens going about their routines, stumbling in and out of doors, yacking away in the middle of roads, hustling and bustling and nursing and cursing. Out past the rooftops he could spy the hilltop where sat the mansion that had once belonged to Belgad the Liar but was now property of Lalo the Finder. Beyond the walls of that fortress were the greens and grays and browns of the true swamp, all the colors and scents of that damp monstrosity muddled together into a sick mess, one rumored to be inhabited by alligators the size of horses and snakes longer than a man was tall. To Kerjim's ears came the usual babel and clamor from the streets, even the noises from the marketplace behind finding their way to him. All of this would soon be his. Or at least all of it would be under his thumb.

"Uncle?"

Kerjim turned to find his nephew not far from him, kneeling as if a puppy ready to lap from its mother's teat. Past Eel two other figures stood waiting near the entrance to the stairwell that took one downstairs to The Stone Pony. Frex Nodana appeared none the worse for the day's heat despite the cloak enveloping her small figure, but the man of similar stature at her side was sweating beneath his graying hair.

"Are you asking me what to do about Kron Darkbow?" the Pursian asked.

"We need to know who you want involved," Nodana said. "Obviously you and I cannot be implicated, not with your position and mine as a potential guild leader."

The Pursian watched the woman slide nearer with ease as if she was not traversing along a gravel covered rooftop. Her companion's footing was not so light. The little man nearly stumbled as he followed, his thin shoes treading across the small rocks. Kerjim grinned. It was ironic Spider experienced aggravation on a rooftop, the little man having a reputation for being somewhat of a thief himself.

"And what about me?" Eel asked. "I'm supposed to be a guild boss, too."

Kerjim turned to his nephew. "Yours is a different situation. You are to head the Thieves Guild, thus you need to be seen to take part. Frex Nodana and I handle more administrative positions, thus we cannot be involved."

The young thief frowned. "But he's already bested me once, and I don't think he even broke a sweat."

"We are not positive your confrontation was with Darkbow," Kerjim said, "but that is beside the point. The man needs to be taken out of the equation. He is too much of a wild card."

Spider came closer, stopping next to Nodana within speaking distance to the others. "What about me?"

Kerjim grinned. "Yours is quite the important job. You can identify Kron Darkbow."

"I've only seen him a couple of times," Spider said with a frown, "and once was from a distance. Stilp was the one who always had dealings with the man."

"But Stilp is no mage," Kerjim pointed out. "You, dear Spider, have some magical talents, which makes you an important addition to our little group, especially considering Frex Nodana will be compiling contracts for the Mages Guild soon."

The wizard's gaze caught that of the Pursian. "How soon?"

"Possibly by tomorrow afternoon."

The other three shared surprised looks.

Kerjim chuckled and turned back to watch the city. "All depends upon my meeting tomorrow morning, but I have no doubts it will go well."

"You're hiding something," Nodana said to his back. "Actually, I would guess you are hiding several somethings. You've not told the guild masters everything."

The Docks chief laughed once more. "Frex Nodana, you are as intelligent as you are beautiful. Of course I've not revealed everything. That would leave too much open to interference."

The wizard came forward and rounded to Kerjim's left, facing the man's side and standing on the edge of the roof. "I do not like surprises, Master Kerjim. Whatever cards you are hiding in your deck had better be good ones."

The Pursian grinned. "The city needs the riots to end and the gold to begin flowing once more. For that to happen, the Docks need to open and the people need to be fed."

Now it was Nodana who smiled. "You've got grain hidden away."

Kerjim said nothing, keeping his gaze upon the growing dimness of the city streets below.

The mage turned away and chuckled. "I should have known. No wonder all the fighting has been in the east end. You've got warehouses on the west side filled with grain."

Kerjim spun about. "Do not become too intelligent, Nodana."

The woman halted and looked over a shoulder at the Pursian. "And this morning's attack against the city guard. Amazing it was timed with the arrival of our fellow guild masters from across the rivers. I suppose the guards were too busy with the riot to notice a few smaller ships landing at the Docks."

Kerjim's eyes narrowed.

Eel threw up his hands and turned away. "By Ashal, none of this helps me figure out what to do about Darkbow!"

The Docks Guild master stared at the mage for a moment longer, then he watched his nephew's back as the young man strode toward the roof exit. "Eel, don't be a fool. We know the man has a residence at the Asylum. Put together a trustworthy group, then watch the place. He'll show sooner or later. Then you deal with him. It's that simple. Any idiot could do it."

Eel spun about with a pained expression. Apparently the sting of Kerjim's words had wounded the thief's pride.

The Pursian spun around, watching the city once more beneath the drowning sun. "Sometimes I feel like I'm surrounded by imbeciles," he said barely above his breath.

***

Miracle of miracles, Sergeant Gris had been relieved of duty for the day. Once the flood gates across Frist Bridge were closed and locked, he had reported to Captain Chambers. Gris realized he must have looked a ragged mess. The captain had taken one look at him then given him the day off, ordering the sergeant not to report for duty again until the following morning.

Several hours of sleep within his private room at the barracks and a meal of baked beans and sliced pork at the mess hall had done wonders for the sergeant. He almost felt like a new man. His body was still weakened from his lack of rest and he continued to sport a few bruises and stiff muscles, but otherwise he was as bright and strong as he had ever been.

Discarding his rusting, grungy armor, which he had still been wearing upon collapsing into bed, back at his private room Gris climbed into a warm bath drawn by one of the grunts, likely Corporal Rogins. The bath was a surprise. He had not given orders for such. Gris would have to remember this. Someone deserved a pat on the back. Hell, if it were up to Gris someone deserved a big, shiny medal of purest gold with a diamond the size of a walnut embossed in its center.

Once clean and dressed, he felt ready for the world once again, his sword on his belt as it always was. Strolling away along the dirt path that fronted the barracks building, Gris pondered what he should do with his day. If he were smart he would have climbed right back into bed. His body continued to require slumber, but he would have none of that. For days he had been smothered by dust and smoke and sweat. It was time for some peace, even if it should only be temporary.

Nearing where the track connected with the much wider and bricked South Road, the sergeant could spot the angled roof of the Rusty Scabbard in the distance to his right, and beyond that the flapping orange tent of his captain. Just the other side of the tent could be seen the gigantic flood gates of iron, standing upright like massive sentinels on watch. *Well, let them stand watch for a while. I've had enough to last a few days. Besides, things seem to have quieted down in the Swamps.*

Which was true. Since the gates had been locked, halting all road access to and from the Swamps, there had been no signs nor sounds of further troubles across the bridge. What could be seen from the shores was relative quiet, the typical Swamps inhabitants milling about on their side, going about their usual daily doings. There was no evidence of heated mobs, buildings burning, screams, shouts, yells, cries. Nothing.

With the sun making its way lower in the west, Gris just hoped this wasn't the calm before the storm. During the riots the nights had been calm, surprisingly so, but that did not mean the situation could not change.

Watching a city lamplighter move from post to post, his torch held up for ease of his job, Gris realized where his feet were taking him. To the Bodyguards Guild office in the eastern part of Southtown.

Turning right into an alley next to the Scabbard, he kicked away a pile of refuse in his path and continued on his way. *It is time to be truthful with myself.* Yes, the truth often hurt, but there were times when a man had to face it, times when a man had to *force* himself to face it. He had had thoughts of resigning from the guards. Gris told himself he wasn't a leader of men, whether that skill was a natural one or a talent earned through experience. He had questioned his own decisions in the past, but none of those decisions, or lack thereof, had been as foolhardy as the one he had made that morning. *Waking and not getting the men in order. What was I thinking?*

He *hadn't* been thinking, and that was the first harsh truth he forced upon himself as he exited the alley and crossed the dusty Rovers Road, bypassing a stalled wagon loaded with stuffed burlap bags and pulled by oxen. Another alley presented itself, this one more narrow and darker though Gris showed no hesitation upon entering, the walls looming over him mere inches from his shoulders.

He had faced no reprimand from Captain Chambers, the officer apparently unaware of the sergeant's mistake, but it was still time to at least consider other employment. Something simple, like a position as an estate guard. Or perhaps a caravan guard. Something that meant he did not have to think. Something in which his job mainly consisted of having to look tough to keep away any potential trouble, all the while being truly willing to commit violence if it should be called for. Gris had few qualms about spilling blood when absolutely necessary, but he did not enjoy deciding whether other men should have to do so. Nor did he enjoy sending other men into harm's way, facing pain and disfigurement, perhaps even death.

So, he needed to be aware of his options before making a final decision.

Squeezing through the end of the narrow alley, he found himself facing a circular area covered in red brick. At the center was a pool surrounded by black stones, in the water's center a bird bath shaped like a cherub holding up a large clam shell. The birds could wash themselves inside the shell where a small hole in one of the statue's wrists constantly streamed forth water from below. Gris paused to stare at the scene for a moment, giving himself time to clear his mind as a handful of pedestrians crossed his path one way or another.

Then he glanced about to the other side of the fountain, noting the half dozen paved paths that lead away from the waters and up to timber-framed and brick structures of various sizes, all of them obviously guild halls of one sort or another. Directly across the way from the sergeant, next to one path was a wooden sign painted red, burnt into it words naming the building beyond as home to the Bodyguards Guild.

His boots spitting up dust, Gris hitched up his sword belt as he passed the cherub and its waters and walked up the pathway between a verdant yard that fronted the guild's building, a towering edifice of marbled columns, stone slabs for front steps and a wide oak door with a small open window in its center.

Gris pushed his way through the door.

The inside of the guild hall presented a vaulted ceiling that vanished into near darkness but for a black iron candelabrum hanging in the center of the long chamber. To the sides were multiple openings to hallways beyond, ensconced lamps lighting the way. Beneath the sergeant's feet was a floor of black stone that stretched to a desk at a distance. The place was built to be intimidating, but not to the average soldier or mercenary. It was meant to warn off the casual observer. To most grunts the guild hall would be too fashionable, obviously a front for those who actually got their hands dirty doing real work. To the establishment's staff, it was likely a second home.

The sergeant had to grin as he meandered down the center of the room, wondering how the spartan elegance presented here went over with the guild's members. He supposed they must be fine with it, otherwise the place would not be standing.

His boots brought him to a halt in front of the desk. So far the hall had been empty and quiet. He had half expected some clerk to come rushing from one of the side entrances, but none had appeared.

Gris glanced down at the desk of dark wood, his eyes running over a ledger and bottle of ink with a feathered quill. He recognized none of the names on the ledger, but that was not out of the ordinary. Bond was home to hundreds of men who potentially could be members of the Bodyguards Guild, and there was no telling how many transients found their way into the hall.

"Sergeant Gris."

The words came from behind. Gris turned to find the portly figure of Captain Tuxra at the other end of the room, as if he had just entered from outside or had come from along one of the side passages.

"Captain." Gris marched back the way he had come, extending a hand as he did so. He did not know Tuxra on a personal level, but their paths had crossed more than once, which made sense considering the line of work both were in.

The captain stood his ground as the sergeant approached, extending an arm only upon Gris's nearing.

Their hands met and Gris immediately felt the tenseness in Tuxra's touch. Looking up he noticed how the guild chief would not meet his eyes, the man glancing down at the chain gloves he gripped in his free hand.

Their palms parted.

"I must have missed the rain," the sergeant said.

"What?" Captain Tuxra now looked at him, his eyes shaking as if nervous.

Gris pointed down. "Your boots. I notice mud on them."

Tuxra leaned forward to peer over his monumental stomach. "Ah." He offered no explanation.

"I am glad we ran into one another," Gris went on, "instead of my having to deal with some clerk or office accountant."

The captain looked up. "Really? Why is it you are here?"

Gris almost took a step back in surprise. Tuxra was generally more affable and less clumsy, at least when dealing with a city official. Still, the sergeant was now here, so he might as well press ahead. "Actually, I've been considering changing professions."

"So you're looking to join the guild?" Tuxra showed no signs of moving, no signs of offering a seat in a near office. Again, unusual.

Gris nodded. "Possibly. I wanted to explore my options."

"Ah." It was the second time the captain had said such. It was as if he were dazed. "Well, we have no available contracts at the moment, but you might consider an independent source."

The sergeant's breath caught in his throat. *Did I hear correctly? Is a guild leader actually sending me off to his competition.*

"I hear Lalo the Finder is in need of several men," Captain Tuxra continued. "Seems there was some fracas having to do with the riots and he lost several guards."

This also brought Gris to a pause. How would the guild chief know of this already? The events had taken place but the night before. Word often spread fast in the city, but the sergeant hadn't gotten the impression there was much talk of the fight on the streets, at least not yet. Of course Gris had been busy with other matters, but still.

"I heard about the street fight," he said to the captain. "It's been reported and Chambers will likely have blank warrants issued before nightfall. Not sure what good it will do, though, since we don't know the names of those involved."

"See?" Tuxra said with a fake smile as he turned to open the path to the exit. "All the more reason to address the Finder. While there you can ask his men if they know who they fought, and then you can ask the Finder if he is hiring."

Yes, something was most definitely wrong. Kron's word had lead Gris and Captain Chambers to believe there was more than one guild involved with the riots. Could the Bodyguards Guild be one of them?

Now was not the time to push. Gris was caught off guard. He needed time to think, and perhaps a plan for approaching the captain. He would sleep on his suspicions for a while, at least until morning.

The sergeant offered his own smile. "Thank you, captain. As soon as these riots wind down, I'll make sure to do that." He nodded and walked past the man. It was time to leave.

"Sorry we did not have anything available, Sergeant Gris." The words came floating to the Gris's back as he pushed open the door. He didn't believe them for a second.

But if Tuxra was involved somehow with the riots, he truly would be sorry. Eventually.

8

Morning came as it had for millions of years across the rolling plains and blots of forest that marked the land of West Ursia, the sun leaning forth and stretching its golden rays as if ever reaching for something unattainable, grasping at the night's cold that still lingered upon the ground and tugging it away, sometimes in mist, sometimes without notice. Here and there across this expanse were towns of variable sizes and the occasional city, each a relatively new blemish upon the land in the larger scheme and from above looking like giant teeth strewn about individually as if broken and fallen from the jaw of some long-dead monster or god.

The largest of the region's cities was spread out over low hills and swamps and flatlands, centering upon the convergence of three rivers. On the muddy shores of one such river, Kerjim Sidewinder climbed out of a rowboat, his shoes sinking into the muck and bringing a grimace to his face.

The man cursed but then followed it up with a grin. Why should he be angered by something as unimportant as muddying his footwear? It was *his* day. His recent plans would be coming to fruition within mere hours. He knew this. There were no doubts nor second guesses. He had been squeezing this city in a vice, and he would continue to do so unless his demands were met. Which they would be.

Glancing over a shoulder, he waved a hand toward the burly fellow who had rowed him across from the Swamps, then proceeded on his way, climbing the shallow bank, each step sinking a little less deep than the one before. Upon reaching dry ground layered with high weeds and grass, Kerjim looked back one last time to see his recent companion using an oar to shove back into the waters. No need to hang around in case any city guards came wandering along.

The Docks Guild chief grinned once more and turned away from the scene, the sun sprouting diamonds of light off the river waters. Ahead lay a narrow strip of grass, past that a walkway of graying lumber. Beyond was the easternmost section of Bond, a portion of a long northerly strip known as Uptown.

This was where the wealthy lived. This were where the grounds of the University of Ursia were located. More importantly, this was where the city's mayor's office could be found.

Taking his time between two smaller warehouses as he approached a bricked road, Kerjim could not help but continue his smile. Yes, it was his day.

***

During the night, the flood gates facing Frist Bridge had been turned into a makeshift defensive wall. On the Southtown side of the gates a scaffold of lumber and piping had been erected, now manned by a dozen city guards, each man with hooded eyes beneath a helm of steel, spears and shields at the ready, cudgels looped on their belts.

As he approached the command tent, Sergeant Gris was actually surprised the captain had taken the initiative in having the temporary rampart built. It seemed overly excessive. The night had remained quiet, or at least that's what Gris had been told by sentries.

Beneath the orange tent he found better accommodations than he himself had had on the far side of the bridge. Here there were the familiar folding tables and chairs, but an iron stove had been placed on one side, piping running up to spread smoke into the sky. Also, on one of the tables rested a silvered tray topped with several soft-paste porcelain goblets. Within the cups stirred a dark red wine. Upon the tray were small white plates, also porcelain, layered with slices of fruit and bread and some obscure soft, white cheese the sergeant did not recognize.

But of the captain and his retinue there was no sign. Instead, Gris found his corporal standing near the table, the man stuffing his face with one of the slices of dark brown bread.

"Rogins!"

The corporal nearly chocked as he dropped the bread and spewed crumbs. He spun about, clicking to attention and raising a hand for a salute.

The sergeant chuckled. "At ease, corporal."

The younger man's eyes blinked as his shoulders sagged.

Gris neared and lifted a slice of the cheese, biting into it and noting a hint of smooth sweetness followed by a bitter aftertaste as he swallowed. *Decent stuff. Probably cost a fortune.* He looked to his corporal. "Where is the captain?"

"Retired for the morning, sir."

"He didn't even wait for me to show?"

"He left when I arrived, sir. Said he had a meeting to attend to. And if I might add, it seemed he was not feeling well."

Gris chuckled. "One night and he's already fatigued. I guess he didn't think to put another sergeant on this front."

"Sir, apparently all other sergeants are on watch at the other bridges,or on leave."

"Well." Which it was not, actually. It wasn't like Captain Chambers to leave a corporal in charge. It wasn't like *any* captain of the guards to leave a corporal in charge. Chambers must have been truly ill. First Gris himself had fallen down on the job, now the captain appeared to be doing much the same. Gris decided to drop in on the old bastard later in the day, if he had the opportunity. He still hadn't made up his mind about resigning, and Tuxra's reaction to his appearance had the sergeant curious.

He motioned toward the rampart. "Have you checked things yet this morning?"

"No, sir," Rogins said. "I thought my first duty should be to see to the change of shifts and to hand out placement orders for the morning."

"Good thinking." Rogins would probably make a good sergeant himself some day, perhaps soon if Gris decided to leave the guard. The sergeant made his way over to the flood gates. "Shall we take a look?"

Within seconds the two armored men had scrambled to the top of the temporary platform behind the gates, a line of guards spaced out every dozen feet moving down to make room.

Gris found himself surprised as he stared out over the bridge, the brightness from the sun revealing an open expanse across the moving waters of the river. There was nothing else there. No rioters. Not even debris. Across the distance he could spot a few people milling around at the other end of the bridge almost in the exact spot where his command post had been the day before. But there were no signs of fires, nor shouts or screams. Once again it was quiet. Had the tide finally turned? Were the riots finished? It didn't feel right. Something was brewing.

The sergeant had to admit despite the damage done, the chaos had been relatively contained, and not because of the work of the city guard. When the riots had initially begun four days earlier, the first major attack had been upon the guards' station in the west end of the Swamps. The men there had found themselves overwhelmed and were forced to pull out, scrambling for the nearest bridge. Soon after Gris and the other sergeants had been ordered to block off the exits from the Swamps. Everyone was pulled in, even those on temporary leave, and more than a few local militia members had been deputized, much as Kron had been. Barricades were initially put up between the soldiers and the mobs, but they had proved more of a hindrance than a help, protecting the rioters while holding back the guards. To limit the violence, the flood gates were closed on all fronts other than Frist Bridge, Captain Chambers wanting to leave one opening in case he should have to bring in aid from the army. The city guard alone might not be able to quell the riots, but the army could if unleashed.

Then the real violence had begun. Flames had been set to warehouses along Dock Street, and Gris had been forced to send his men and the fire fighters in to battle the blazes. The angry mob had wanted none of that. They had wanted the buildings to burn.

The situation had remained static, following similar burnings and violence for the last couple of days before the captain had called for Gris to pull back across the bridge and to lock down the last of the gates. Since the minor engagement the morning before, all had been as if the riots had never happened, as if there had been some agreement to a truce.

Now that was a thought. Perhaps Chambers and city officials were in talks with someone from the opposite side of the river, someone who was behind the attacks. Being a lowly sergeant, it wasn't as if Gris would be aware of anything going on behind the scenes.

One thing he was aware of, however, was that the riots had been purposeful. Despite the lack of food in the city, these attacks had been controlled. The west end had suffered little other than the initial assault on the barracks. At the rivers there had been fires, but they had not seemed random. Gris didn't know who owned what buildings, but it had been odd at the time that some buildings had been spared while others were left smoking.

And then there had been the looting. Or the lack of. That had seemed most odd of all. Riots always had looting. *Always*. But not this time. To Gris's knowledge, not one business establishment had been broken into. Not one item had been stolen. There had just been the burnings.

Weird.

All of it.

And it made his head hurt thinking about it.

*****

Three little bronze statues, mere inches high, told everything there was to know about Melanda Karn, mayor of the city of Bond. The statue in the middle, facing away from the desk as were its companions, was of a cloaked figure with a noose around its neck; this was a representation of the Almighty Ashal, the God Who Walked Among Men. Another statue was of a little girl seated behind a desk while she reads a book; this miniature represented the mayor's educational background at the university. The final figurine was of a knightly figure, sword held high, shield at his side; that last one showed Karn's ties to the nation's nobles.

The mayor came from nobility, after all. Her grandfather had been a duke, back in the days when there had still been dukes in West Ursia. The war sixty years earlier had changed all that. Now the only nobility left in the West were a handful of knights, figures descended from nobility or appointed to their knighthood by the church. Melanda Karn's father had shunned his family's claims to nobility, which meant at birth she had no longer been qualified to become a knight by right. Her only hopes of returning to the folds of nobility had been through the church, and though she had been a good Ashalite all her life, the Western pontiff had never noticed the woman.

Which was why she had turned to politics. The wealth she had inherited had to be put to good use, after all, and the sheep still needed a shepherd. Years of struggle, years as a city council member and years of hard work had finally landed her the mayor's role in Bond. Twelve years and three elections later, she still held the position. And being mayor was a lofty position, similar to that which should have been hers by birth.

All of this meant she was not pleased to be slumped behind her desk while a cretin from the Swamps, this particular cretin being the boss of the Docks Guild, explained to her his demands.

Demands. Of all things. By what rights did this ... this *scum*, have to tell her what he wanted or the riots would continue, the food shortage would continue and the slowed economy would continue? It was out and out extortion.

And that fool Captain Chambers was little help, the old chain-clad idiot slumped into the chair on the left facing her desk.

She sat up straight, staring with flaring eyes at Kerjim Sidewinder. "Allow me to make clear to you that this city will not tolerate ... exaction ... of any kind. I will not stand for this, not while I am in office."

Kerjim grinned from the seat on the woman's right. "Mayor Karn, you seem to be under the impression I am here to blackmail you. And the city."

Chambers grunted, his long gray mustache fluffing beneath his round nose. "Isn't that what you're doing? You can fancy it up with all kinds of words, but it comes down to the same thing."

The Pursian glanced to the captain. "But I am not making demands. I asked for this meeting merely to present ideas which I believe would bring to an end this nasty business in the Swamps district."

Chambers grunted again and stared at the mayor as if to ask, "Do you believe any of this?"

"Master Kerjim," Karn said, leaning forward, "I have yet to see how your *ideas* will end the riots. You have asked for three new guild licenses, all blank, which I daresay I do not have the authority to authorize. These things are decided upon by the city council. Once approved, then and only then does my office have the power to sign off on such things. You have come to the wrong place. Not only can I not help you, but even if I were to do so, I do not see how three new guilds would rectify the current situation in the Swamps."

Any other man Karn had ever known would have at least blanched after her words. She had spoken straight-forward truths. Her hands were tied, and the guild chief's proposal seemed to lack competence. But Kerjim, this lowlife, simply eased back in the padded chair and grinned.

She wished she could slap him.

But she wouldn't. No. The Docks Guild was the most powerful in the city, at least since Belgad's departure. Perhaps Kerjim would eventually get around to saying something useful.

"Do I need to explain?" the Pursian asked, looking from the mayor to the captain then back again.

Silence greeted his question.

"Very well." Kerjim now sat forward, crossing his hands in his lap. "One of the licenses I seek will be for a coalition of guilds. Call it a guild of guilds, if you like. It will consist of a chamber of guild leaders, who will meet from time to time as does any guild, to decide upon --"

"Out of the question," Karn said, jabbing a finger into her desk's top. "Such a guild has no precedent within Bond, and the council would roar if I tried to push through a motion to declare such an organization legal."

"You have emergency executive powers during times of strife, yes?" Kerjim asked.

Karn nodded. "I do."

"Then use them here," the Pursian said. "Allow me the licenses and --"

"*Blank* licenses," Chambers pointed out.

Kerjim glanced to the captain, frowning at yet another interruption.

"That's an additional thing," Karn said, leaning forward on her desk again as if to push her points. "Blank guild licenses? That's quite unusual. Why blank?"

Kerjim kept on smiling. "Because of the emergency situation. We do not have time for the council to quibble about this and that. The Swamps district is being torn apart. Warehouses are burning. Food is nearly non-existent. Something has to be done."

"And you think this guild of guilds can end all that?" Chambers asked.

"It would give the various guild leaders authority to work together to handle the situation, yes."

Karn saw where the Docks boss was going. "You want a way to bypass the collusion laws."

Kerjim shook his head but continued to grin, as if he were a salesman. "From the outside it might appear such, but that would not be the reason for the collective of guild leaders. Such an organization would simply cut through some of the bureaucracy that hinders a resurgence of the local economy."

The captain's mustache drooped. "Ending these riots would bring a resurgence to the economy."

"That is one way of looking at it," Kerjim said, "but the other side of the coin is that improving the economy would end the riots."

A sneer crossed Karn's lips as she leaned back. "Alright, so you want this guild of guilds. What about the other two licenses?"

"One would be for a new thieves guild, the other a mages guild."

Silence.

The mayor and the captain looked at one another. Then both looked to the Pursian.

"You're out of your mind," Chambers said.

Kerjim brought up a hand, one finger uplifted. "We have had a thieves guild before."

The captain growled. "And an end was put to it. Good riddance, too. Damned thieves sneaking about at night, taking goods from honest, hard-working people."

The two men bickered back and forth while Karn's mind turned away from them. She knew Kerjim's history. He had once been head of the Thieves Guild in the days before Belgad. It seemed this was a matter of pride for the Pursian. Belgad was gone, and Kerjim wanted his guild back. He couldn't very well just start up the old guild as the contracts were long gone, bought out by Belgad himself. But a new guild? A license for such a guild would give Kerjim what he wanted.

"What a second!" She thrust up an arm, halting the argument. "How exactly would a new thieves guild help end the riots?"

Beneath the glare of the city guard captain, Kerjim eased out to the edge of his seat. "I'm glad you asked, Mayor Karn. The guild would be a provincial one, with no authority outside the Swamps. It would operate under the old rules. No city property would be touched, nor that of members of other guilds. Its purpose would not be to take goods from the honest, the voters, as the captain has suggested, but would include an additional charter to retrieve goods conscripted by the dishonest."

"A policing force of sorts?" the mayor asked.

"Not exactly. More like protectors of the Docks, and the Swamps. We have enough problems with pirates and bandits that we could use the protection. This would also provide employment for a good number of our younger citizens in the Swamps."

Karn glanced to the captain again. Neither was believing.

"Why not just hire guards?" Chambers asked.

"Another good question," Kerjim said. "Why *not* hire guards? Because guards simply guard. This new guild would have authority beyond that."

Karn waved a hand. "The retrievals you mentioned?"

"Exactly."

"Okay, fine." The mayor shifted in her seat. All of this was foolishness. Kerjim was playing some personal game on a larger scale, impressing the other guilds and the Swamps and now the rest of the city into his pettiness. But Karn was interested in hearing his nonsense, to see how far he would push. "What was this about a mages guild, then?"

It seemed impossible, but the Pursian's grin grew wider. "Yes. As you might know, there are a number of citizens who engage in magical exertions within the city, yet they are not formally trained at the university. Many of them learned their skills from --"

"We know what a street mage is, Kerjim," Chambers pointed out.

"Yes, well." For a moment the Docks leader seemed phased, but then he snapped out of it. "To put it bluntly, then, there are a number of street mages within the city who have no representation. A guild would give them such, within the rankings of the business community and within city politics."

Karn threw up her hands. "Master Kerjim, my apologies, but it seems we have wasted one another's time this day. Even if I were to provide the papers you seek, I am yet to understand how these three new guilds would immediately improve the city's finances so much these riots would come to an end."

The Pursian started to speak, but the mayor thrust a hand toward him. "Let me finish! While your mages guild might help the economy in some small sense, this notion of a thieves guild is beyond considering. Our city is looking to the future, not the past. We have moved beyond such ancient vagaries as a thieves or assassins guild, and while licenses from the city would allow such guilds to operate beside current law, I am not inclined to approve such on moral grounds.

"Then there is this guild of guilds. While I admit there are possibilities here which might benefit the city in the long run, you have presented no evidence that such a collective would end the riots. And you show a certain naivete when it comes to politics. The council would not be likely to approve a license for this guild, and for me to utilize my emergency powers to force through such a license would be political suicide."

She stopped talking.

Captain Chambers sat quiet, like a lump, with a disgruntled face.

And Kerjim, damn him, continued to smile.

"May I speak now?" the Pursian asked.

Mayor Karn nodded.

"Very well." Kerjim looked down at the ground for a moment as if putting together his words. Then he looked up, and he was no longer the same person. The smile was gone. His eyes were heated. "Madam mayor, captain, I have tried to approach the city with the usual niceties, but I see that will not suffice here. So I must push ahead with a more direct approach."

All eyes were on the Docks leader.

"The Swamps is starving," Kerjim went on, "and unless a sizable harvest is supplied within a matter of days, people will begin to die from starvation. While the rest of the city might frown down their noses at those of us in the Swamps, we Swamps dwellers are still voters. Remember that."

Karn and Chambers said nothing to this. They had been told nothing they did not already know.

Kerjim continued. "On top of that, all are aware of the economic and political might of the Docks Guild. We control the majority of goods moving in and out of the city. With the Swamps shut down, the docks are shut down, and that means the Docks Guild is shut down. Which means the gold flowing into the city's coffers has not been quite strangled, but it has been cut short."

Karn's lips opened as if to speak, but now it was the Docks chief who threw up a hand.

"Allow me to go on," he said. "As your time is important, I will no longer take up much of it. Instead, I will be blunt. I control the docks, and I can obtain a harvest large enough to feed the Swamps and, for that matter, the rest of the city."

There. It had been said. Perhaps not quite plainly, but the implications were obvious. Kerjim wanted his three guilds, and unless he got them, the Swamps would starve and the city's finances would continue to sputter.

The mayor leaned forward once more. "How soon can you provide this harvest?"

"Within two days, perhaps sooner."

Chambers slammed a fist onto the desk. "Karn, arrest this fool! Don't play his petty games. He's got a ship or a warehouse somewhere stuffed with grain, and all we have to do is find it. Throw him in a dungeon and me and my men will get to work searching."

"No." The single word was barely above a whisper as the mayor motioned off her city guard captain. Karn needed time to think. Was the Docks boss truly vain enough to have brought about all this mess simply for his ego? To bring back the Thieves Guild? No, there was more to it than that.

"I am not asking for much," Kerjim pointed out. "Three licenses for three guilds. Then the city can get back to its normal self."

Karn turned her stalling hand toward the Pursian. *All right*, she told herself, *what is he* really *trying to do?* As head of the Docks Guild, Kerjim would be in a tenable position with his proposed association of guilds. If he were somehow to manage to become head of this guild of guilds, he would be one of the most powerful men in Bond, expanding his already consequential strengths. What would this gain him that he already didn't have?

She stared at the backs of the three tiny statues on the other side of the desk, her gaze falling upon that of the knight lifting up his sword. She blinked.

Of course.

"You're setting yourself up to be the new Belgad," she said to the Pursian.

Kerjim was grinning again. "Perhaps I am, but that is beside the point. Give me what I want, and your immediate troubles will go away. As a sign of good faith, I have kept the riots under control the last day or so. But that can end as soon as I leave here."

"*Karn*." Captain Chambers growled the word as a warning.

She glanced to the older man and saw the fury in his face. If he had his way, he would likely jump up, draw his sword and cut down the man sitting next to him. But Bond was a civilized city. The mayor would have none of that. Even Belgad, as frightening as he could be, had eventually seen that violence was not the answer. The Dartague had done more than anyone, even more than the city guard, to bring peace to the streets. He had even brought a level of prosperity. Could Kerjim do the same? Did he *want* to?

Politics was often a gamble, Karn realized not for the first time, and sometimes you had to show your cards. If she did not give into the Docks boss, people would starve, the riots would continue and her political career would be finished. However, if she *did* give the man what he wanted, only her career would be ended. There would be no more attacks, no more deaths, no more starvation.

"Very well," she said, her voice soft. "Kerjim, if you can give me a few minutes, I will have one of my staff find the proper paperwork for you."

Chambers smacked the side of his chair.

"You'll sign the licenses?" Kerjim asked. "Blank ones, which I can fill in later?"

The mayor nodded. "Yes. I'll need to know how many contracts you want for each license."

The Pursian's smile was so wide it looked as if his face would crack. "A couple of dozen for two of them. Fifty for the other."

The captain's face was red. He forced himself out of his chair and turned to leave the room, coughing as he did.

"You should see someone about that," Kerjim suggested.

Chambers raised a fist as if to strike, but then the coughing hit him again and he rushed past the seated man, pushing his way out the door.

Karn simply sat there, staring at the center of her desk. So this was how her political career would end? With three signatures. Ah, well. At least she had her family fortunes to fall back upon.

Kerjim prodded the front of the desk.

The mayor looked up.

"Shouldn't you be calling for a member of your staff?" the Pursian asked.

9

The unnerving quiet remained on the other side of Frist Bridge. Gris and Rogins and a line of sentries stood watching for some little while, expecting anything, but there was little to see other than the river flowing by beneath and the occasional pedestrian moving about on the far side.

"Enough of this." Gris climbed down the scaffolding, his boots landing hard on the brick road, the corporal following right behind. "This is the worst part of soldiering, the waiting."

"Yes, sir." What else was Rogins going to say?

"Sergeant Gris!"

The call came from down the busy South Road where the morning traffic was already picking up, almost to the Rusty Scabbard.

Gris raised a hand to shield his eyes and stared through the crowd of those walking or milling about in front of the tavern. A young man dressed in the simple but pricey finery of a city clerk was approaching, his white satin shirt flapping as he strode forward with a hand outstretched, an envelope extended.

Snagging the paper from the fop's hand, the sergeant tore it open, flipping back the pages for reading. His eyes followed the written words for several seconds before he folded the papers and stuffed them into a pocket.

"Inform the mayor her orders have been received," Gris said to the clerk. He then turned to Rogins. "Corporal, get a work crew together. It's time to take down this wall and open the gates."

"Yes, sir!" The young man's boots clicked together and he trotted off to do his duty.

"Does this mean you're going into the Swamps again?"

The sergeant turned at the question, expecting the dandy to be standing over his shoulder like some preening vulture. Instead, he was pleasantly surprised to find Kron Darkbow standing there.

"It looks that way," he said to his friend. "The mayor gave orders to cross the bridge and reestablish the barracks in the west end."

"The mayor?"

Gris shook his head. "Chambers is rumored to be ill. He must be doing poorly for Karn to be handing out orders directly."

"Or he has refused to give the order."

Now the sergeant nodded. "That's not an impossibility. The old bastard can be stubborn at times."

The grunts of working men and clangings of metal piping caused the two men to face the flood gate where the temporary rampart was being dismantled. Corporal Rogins was giving directions to a group of soldiers off to one side while a city crew, each man without shirts beneath the growing warmth of the day, was banging away at the scaffolding.

"Looks like you'll be moving out within the hour," Kron commented. "I'll be going with you."

Gris shot a glance to his friend. "Thought you'd be busy finding your new contractor."

"I found one earlier this morning," Kron said. "Told me he would be there as soon as the riots break up."

"Well, they might be broken up already."

Kron gave a quizzical look. "How so?"

"It's been quiet since your little stunt yesterday morning," the sergeant explained. "There's been no further contact. Of course it helps that we pulled back across the bridge, but still, you'd expect something. An angry mob throwing garbage at the gates, if nothing else."

"Seems as if this was all planned."

Gris nodded. "That's what I've been thinking. Your talk about some guilds being involved might be spot on, especially after an interesting meeting I had yesterday."

"With whom?"

"Captain of the Bodyguards Guild."

"What did he have to say?"

"It wasn't so much what he said as his reaction at my appearance," Gris said. "Chambers gave me the afternoon off, so I thought I'd drop by the guild to see if they have any openings. The captain was a bit anxious. He wasn't rude or anything, but he did give me the brush off. Suggested I seek employment with the Finder."

Kron guffawed. "Why in the world would you want a job with the Finder?"

The sergeant shrugged. "I'm still considering resigning."

The man in black moved around so he was facing his friend directly, then reached out a hand to grip a shoulder. "Gris, you're a fine sergeant. Yesterday morning was a fluke. There is no need for you to quit. Besides, I've not been in town quite a year. What would it say about me if you left off after I showed up?"

The sergeant chuckled. "I don't know what it would say about *you*, but it might show *I've* got some sense."

The two laughed together.

"I do get myself into situations, don't I?" Kron said.

***

Rage. It was not an emotion common to Eel Sidewinder. He had never felt it. He had rarely witnessed it. Anger was the strongest of the dark emotions he had personally ever felt. Even with the loss of his parents there had not been rage, but a sadness, an inner sickness that had left him feeling hollow for the longest time. But true rage? Never. He had done his share of street fighting during his nineteen years, but not once had rage entered the scene. At least not until the combat he had witnessed on Beggars Row two nights earlier. But even that had not been true rage. Eel himself had dealt nary a blow, and the men who had fought and bled and died had shown animosity, possibly even hatred, but not true rage. Not the deep rage that made a person into a living monstrosity, that pushed aside all other factors and people and emotions. Not the rage that could lead to annihilation of one's self.

Now Eel faced such rage, and it frightened him to the depths of his very soul. He himself was not full of animosity, but the hefty woman before him looked as if she would kill him simply because he had informed her of her son's death.

Mama Kaf huffed, spun about and slammed a fist the size of a large ham onto a table. The wood cracked beneath the force, leaving two halves of a piece of furniture that would likely end up kindling by nightfall. Mugs and cups flew through the air, drenching more than a few of the clientele of The Stone Pony.

No one said a word as the big woman tromped through the main room of the tavern, her head sunk between her broad shoulders, her eyes red with hate beneath the stringy, greasy hair that hung from atop her head. All paths were cleared for her, this hulking woman who reminded others of some great bear on the hunt.

She kicked open the exit and squeezed her shoulders through the opening, not bothering to close the door as she exited the establishment and entered daylight.

More than a few sighs of relief went up throughout the room.

Then Kerjim appeared in the doorway, glancing behind as if watching the woman treading down the road. After a moment he shrugged and turned about to face the interior, a broad smile stretching across his features.

Two dozen mute faces stared back at him, including that of his nephew.

"What?" the Pursian asked.

Those gathered looked into their drinks, not wanting to provide any answers.

Seeing he was alone in this, Eel came forward. "Uncle, I ... I ..."

"Spit it out, boy."

"I told Mama Kaf about her son's death the other night."

The smile flickered for a moment, but it remained. Kerjim slapped a hand onto his kin's shoulder and spun the lad about, leading him toward the tavern's long bar to their right. "She had to find out sooner or later."

"She wants to know who did it," Eel said with a visible gulp. "I think -- "

"You think she wants to pound some fool's head into the ground." Kerjim released his nephew and waved for the bartender to bring a mug. "Easy enough. Tell her Kron Darkbow was responsible."

Eel nearly choked despite his lack of a drink. "She'll pulverize the man."

"That's the point," the Pursian said as he was handed a goblet. "Hold off a night or two, let the city calm itself just a little, then strike at the man."

Mug in hand, Kerjim spun about and leaned on the bar, facing the nervous denizens of The Stone Pony. There was no talk among the crowd, and all eyes were upon the Docks boss. A few of these men were local thugs, tough characters who worked for the Docks and thus worked for Kerjim. But the majority were everyday folk, which here in the Swamps meant they were likely without regular employ. All wanted to know what Kerjim had to say. Everyone knew the man had been across the river in Uptown, or was it Southtown? They didn't know for sure, and the details weren't important. The results were what mattered. Most of their faces appeared desperate.

"Gentlemen," Kerjim said, holding up his mug with a widening smile, "drinks are on me."

And with those words, the riots officially ended.

***

Miracle of miracles, within an hour of the city guard marching in a six-by-six square formation across Frist Bridge and into the Swamps, an anonymous Docks

Guild inspector discovered two ancient warehouses on the southwest shore of the South River were heavy with bags of grain. How long they had been there, no one could say. Why they had not been accounted for or discovered before, no one could say. And never mind the burlap sacks were tattooed with city tax stamps less than a month old. None of that mattered. What mattered was food had been found, and it was plentiful, even if only wheat.

Who owned this grain? No one could tell. The two warehouses were older than anyone living, from back in the days when Ursia had been one united nation. Perhaps the buildings had belonged to the eastern pope, perhaps to some long-dead noble. Regardless, the Docks Guild would claim the warehouses and their contents under its charter from the city.

Within minutes of the discovery a line had formed in front of the warehouses. Some of these citizens had been living on shoe leather or neighbors' pets for days, and they were eager for real sustenance. In a show of benevolence, the grain was doled out for free, several groups of clerks from the Docks Guild weighing and measuring the grain and placing it into cups or sacks or hands that were outreaching. A band of tough characters were on site to make sure no one took more than their allotment, and that no one tried anything foolish like attempting to force their way into the warehouses.

By the time Sergeant Gris and his men had made their way along Beggars Row to the west end, meeting up with the troops of Sergeant Thag coming from the north side and the bridge to Uptown, word had spread about the free grain. Swamps dwellers came from everywhere, from doorways, from refuse-laden alleys, from holes in the ground that rumor said were entrances to tunnels and sewers and worse. The line of those seeking food stretched back nearly a mile. Others remained on their stoops, watching the line form, waiting for things to thin out a little before fetching their own free meals.

"This won't last," Gris said to Kron as the guards formed into a defensive position in front of the log structure that made up the smaller Swamps barracks. "They can't give out free food forever."

"The bridges are open now," the man in black said in return. "People can get back to work. By tomorrow morning the Docks will be charging for the grain."

A quick conference among the sergeants decided Thag and his four squads would remain at the barracks, double the normal retinue for the Swamps, while Gris and his men would proceed to what had been considered the heart of the riots, Haven Square and the marketplace. What was to be found there was anyone's guess, but the sergeants agreed they wanted a full reconnoitering of the Swamps before informing Captain Chambers of their findings.

Gris and his squads, with Kron following, backtracked along Beggars Row, then with shields raised and cudgels at the ready, made their way along various refuse-ridden side roads to the edges of the marketplace.

What they discovered was a quick return to normality. Stalls had already been resurrected. Hawkers were shouting about their wares. Customers were few, but there were some, old women milling about to spend hoarded coppers on kitchen staples they had been denied during the troubles, street urchins scampering here and there in search of a crust or a dropped coin, working-class folk waiting to go back to work but meanwhile spending their hard-earned funds on vegetables and breads and meats for their lunch.

Upon sight of all this, Gris removed his helmet and scratched his head.

A call went up and the city guards were drawn to the other side of the marketplace, brushing their way through the shoppers and pedestrians with no trouble. Not even a harsh glance nor cursing words were thrown their way. It was as if the riots had never occurred.

The scene at Haven Square proper told a different story. Here were stretched two dozen citizens, each laid out upon the ground with coverings pulled up to their chins, another half dozen with their faces covered. These were the sick and wounded, the dead and dying. Some coughed, some shivered, some winced from pain. Here and there blood could be seen, as well as a few limbs bent in unnatural directions.

Around this group was formed a circle of onlookers, women clucking their tongues, men shaking their heads, children with wide eyes. These were the friends and family, huddling beneath the green copper statue that loomed above all. Attending to those on the ground were a handful of healers identified by the white robes that were their professional garb.

Kron stepped to the fore of the city guards and pointed. "There's Randall."

A young man in white looked up from kneeling over an unconscious woman. His face was long and narrow, still boyish other than the anguish currently gripping his features.

As Gris and his men began to take control of the environment, Kron moved through the crowd toward the healer.

Randall Tendbones knelt again and muttered ancient words while pressing a hand against the side of the stricken woman's forehead. She did not waken, but the pained look on her face eased. Only when the man in black was near did Randall stand again and turn away from those in need.

"I suppose you were involved in all this." He spoke with calm outrage, waving a hand toward the ill and wounded.

Kron was taken back by the accusatory words. Randall had rarely been one to show anger. "I acted to protect my friend and the city itself, nothing more."

The healer's eyes narrowed. "How many of these people did you put here?"

The man in black glanced toward those on the ground, then returned to his friend. "To my knowledge, none of them. Randall, what is this? What is bothering you?"

"What do you expect?" The healer turned his back and raised his arms over the square, his voice shaking. "People starving and the best this city can do is beat them down? Why shouldn't I be outraged? Every man and woman in this city should be outraged! The riots ended too soon, as far as I'm concerned, if this is the treatment we can expect from our representatives."

Kron moved around to the front of the healer and placed a gentle gloved hand on one of Randall's arms. "You seem to forget the city guard did not seek this fight, my friend. If not for the attacks in the streets and the burning of buildings, none of this would have happened."

The healer dropped his arms and stared at the blood-slick bricks beneath his shoes. "If the people had been fed, none of this would have happened."

"Randall," Kron said, his voice soft.

The young man showed no sign of hearing his name.

"Randall, look at me."

The healer looked up, tears in his eyes.

Kron nodded, keeping his voice low. "Good. Now that I've got your attention, there are some things you should know. I cannot go into detail here and now, but ... there is evidence these people did not need to go hungry, that the riots were ... *arranged*."

Randall's wet eyes widened.

"Yes," Kron said. "I can tell you more about it later. But for now, we need to get these people to the healing tower."

With a sleeve, Randall wiped away his tears. "The tower is already at capacity. That's why we had to leave these people here. There was no room for them."

Kron nodded again. "We'll have them carted to the tower in Southtown. I seriously doubt the city will let these people go untended."

The man in black's words were soon proven true. Gris sent a pair of runners back to Frist Bridge with orders to have Corporal Rogins take command of as many hospital wagons as he could find at the healing tower in Southtown.

"Satisfied?" Kron asked his friend.

It was Randall's turn to nod. "As much as I can be at the moment."

"Come." Kron motioned toward a side street. "Let's leave Gris to deal with this. It's his job, after all. Return to the healing tower with me and I'll tell you what I know."

The healer grinned but shook his head. "I'm needed here, but stop by tomorrow. You can meet my new assistant. She's going to love you."

10

The night brought a change in the weather. The sun had ruled the skies for a week, adding to the tension of the riots through a heat that would not relent. Now that a level of peace had returned to the Swamps, another storm had brewed on the horizon. This storm, however, was quite literal.

Waves of rain washed across the central region of Bond, bringing with it the expected mud and creeks. Within a half hour of the storm's arrival, not a person would step out into the muck that had become the streets of the Swamps. Memories still lingered of the flooding from the year before, and longer memories could recall other floods going back decades. The Swamps had earned its name honestly.

The following morning was another bright one, however. The rains had poured in, done their business, then gone about their way to other parts of the land, like some god sprinkling baptisms upon the faithful before departing to another parish. The Swamps had been washed clean of much of its usual grime, though that would return in time, probably before many had eaten their lunch.

Drops of wet remained about the city, bringing extra brightness to the morning as the sun returned and caught upon each globule. Though no longer falling, the rain water lingered, clinging here and there where it could find a purchase.

The ground remained muddy in many places where there was not grass or road, and one such place included the grounds within the estate walls of the Asylum.

With a scowl ruling his features, Felton Keldaris stood in mud that covered the toes of his weathered boots. He scratched at the patch of white fuzz still atop his head as he stared up at the main building, the Asylum proper. He was not happy.

The Asylum job was a big one. The place needed a new roof, and it needed a new floor on the main level. The basement had to be pumped free of all that river water that had been sitting for nearly a year, and Ashal only knew how many corpses were floating around down there. But none of this was what bothered the old man. Coming so soon, within a day of the end of the riots, he was glad to get back to work. Of course he had heard all the rumors about the place, about how it was haunted and there had been big magic here and all that. But it was nonsense. Besides, a man had to make a living, after all.

No, what he did not like was the person who had contracted him for the job.

This Kron Darkbow fellow. Felton had heard stories. He knew when someone was no good. And this Kron Darkbow looked no good. Waltzing around in all those black clothes, that black cloak floating around behind him like he was some giant bat or something ready to float away. And Felton believed a man who didn't smile was a man out to do in his neighbors. Kron Darkbow didn't smile.

The contractor turned his gaze from the towering building to the towering figure in black standing next to him. He grunted. Neither one looked like much.

"Do you think you can handle the job?" Kron asked, his own eyes turned up to the roof, squinting beneath the sun.

Felton spat into the mud at his feet. Of course he could handle it. He'd been a professional stone mason and building contractor for half a century, and all that time spent right here in Bond. He had the tools, he had the men, he even had all the right paperwork for the guilds and the city. What he didn't have, as of yet, was a down payment on his fee.

Apparently noting the silence, Kron glanced down at the sour face next to him. "My apologies." He reached within the folds of his cloak and removed a small bag that jingled in his hand, tossing it to the older man.

Felton caught it, immediately untying the top and peering inside. His mind worked with speed, and in no time he had it all counted.

"It'll do for a start," he said, still with a sour face.

Kron was no longer paying attention. With a dozen of Felton's workers behind them unloading tools from a cart at the bottom of the path leading to the building, the man in black had once more turned his gaze upon the Asylum.

A frame of steel pipes and lumbered boards had been built up one side of the structure, reaching to the edges of the roof. The scaffolding had been there for months, likely constructed by the city or workmen of a former owner. Why? Likely for the work Kron was now paying to be completed.

With a discerning look, Felton grabbed a rung of a metal ladder built into the outside of the framework. He ran a hand along the piping, tugged a little, then pulled away a wet palm. "Still wet from last night. A little shaky, too. Thing's been standing too long. We'll have to put up a new one."

"I climbed it just last week," Kron said without looking to the contractor. His words were flat, not boastful nor reproaching.

"Is that so?" Felton asked. He glanced back at his men to make sure they were doing their jobs, which they were, then returned to facing the scaffolding. Despite being paid, he still didn't like the looks of this Kron Darkbow. Yet the man didn't seem to be a liar nor a braggart. Maybe he was telling the truth about the climb. "What condition was the roof in?"

Kron shrugged. "I'm no expert. There's a big hole in the center, lots of wood and stonework sticking out here and there. Most of the roof tiles are gone."

Felton harrumphed. "Well, I guess I'll just have to climb up there and take a look." He grabbed the ladder.

"Don't you want to wait for the water to dry?" Kron asked. "Or for your men to build a new frame?"

The old man didn't answer. Hand over hand, boot over boot, he scaled the outside of the structure of pipes and planks. It would take a day to build a new scaffold tower, and he didn't have that much patience. He wanted to see that roof, to find out just what kind of job was ahead of him. As for the rain slicking his fingers, he knew to be careful. As far as he was concerned, his callouses could act as gloves. And he wasn't going to let this young fellow in black think he could do something which Felton could not.

Halfway up the ladder the contractor heard the scuff of leather on metal and paused in his climb long enough to glance down between his legs. The fool in black was beneath, ascending several rungs beneath Felton.

The old man sighed and kept climbing.

Once he had gone as high as he could go, he slung a leg over an iron bar and pulled himself onto the topmost plank. Kron did the same next to him, the two standing there for a moment to catch their breath as they stared down at the men working at the wagon, beyond them a tent Kron had erected and near the wall a small stables where could be seen Kron's tied horse. Across the road in front of the Asylum walls and the blackened rooftops that made up the Swamps, a hundred chimneys belched into the bright morning sky, leaving slow trails of black smoke like climbing snails.

"It's beautiful in its own way," Kron remarked.

Felton grunted. "It's crap. It's the Swamps."

Then the old man grabbed hold of the railing and slowly turned around to get a better view of the roof. He found a simple gabled covering of tiles made from dark gray slate. Of course many of the tiles were missing, flat boards and wooden and iron beams exposed beneath, as well as some stonework along the edges of the structure. In the center was a great big hole. There was no other way to describe it. Just a hole. It was big enough for a twelve-horse carriage to ride through without touching the sides.

Felton frowned.

"Is it hopeless?" Kron asked.

The old man snapped out of his thoughts. "Not at all. But we're going to have to replace nearly everything. You're going to need new rafters, joists, beams ... all of it. New roofing tiles, too."

Felton leaned forward, almost over the railing. "That looks like iron beams there in the shadows. Hard to tell from here."

"Is that a problem?"

The contractor shook his head as he leaned just a little more. "Just unusual. I'd have thought this building too old for iron. I'll be able to tell more once we get a scaffold erected inside."

The old man was about to pull back then. He had seen enough. He was ready to climb back down and get to work, away from the prying eyes of this swarthy character next to him. But one thing stopped him from retreating behind the rails.

It was a hand. Pale, small, almost glittering in the sunlight, attached to nothing. It floated in the air mere inches from him, and Felton was confounded not because the hand existed, but because he could see through it to the black hole in the roof beyond.

It grabbed his collar.

The man jerked, trying to fight his way back, to plant his feet fully on the plank boards, but that grip was like cold steel. It would not let go. Not only would it not let go, but it was pulling him, tugging him, as if it wanted him to explore that hole in the roof a little more closely.

Felton cried out. He felt another hand, this one gloved, grab him by the back of a leg.

But it was too late.

That spectral appendage dragged the contractor forward, his legs kicking up above the railing, one boot connecting with Kron's jaw and sending the younger man reeling back.

Felton landed with a thumping noise and a sudden pain to his chest. He had not fallen far, near the ledge of the remaining roof, but his vision was clouded and he could hardly breath.

Then he was sliding. Toward the outer edge.

Ignoring the ache to his lungs, the old man flung out his arms and kicked with his legs. The scaffolding was right behind him, but there was a gap between it and the building. Unless the contractor could grab hold of something, there was a good chance he was going to fall to his death. And he hadn't worked this long and this hard to die on some damn work site. He was supposed to die at home in bed like a decent person.

His boots flailed out over the ledge of the roof. In a panic, Felton flung himself over onto his back. With a quick brush of a hand he wiped away the tears of pain that had blurred his eyes. If he were to die here, he would face it like a man. Better yet, now that he could see, he had a better chance of grabbing onto something to save his life.

There! A hanging rope. With a glance Felton could tell it was old and frail and raveled, just like himself. That rope had probably been hanging there throughout the winter, left behind by some worker who had been on the crew erecting the scaffold. After months out in the cold and rain and beneath the sun and the elements, that rope had probably about had it. But it was all he had.

He pushed himself off his rear and lunged for the line.

And was swatted away by a glowing blur of white.

It was a chilled, hard slap to the face that threw the contractor onto his back again. He cried out and slid a few more inches down the side of the tattered roof.

Then there was no more roof. He was beyond it, plummeting upside down, the ground rolling up toward him.

Something snagged at his left leg. There was a snapping sound and a crack as if of a whip, then the old man was jolted so hard he nearly lost his breakfast.

He was hanging there in the air, the platform of bars and boards next to him, blood rushing to his face, his eyes wet once more.

What was holding him? Why wasn't he falling? The old man glanced up. A black cord ending in a small grapnel was wrapped around his left ankle, that cord trailing up in a straight line to the black gloves of Kron Darkbow on top of the scaffold.

The man in black's face was strained as his arms bulged from the weight of the old man.

Felton chuckled and looked at his former employer. "Changed my mind. I don't want the job this bad."

11

The scene was a familiar one. The same long room in the back of The Stone Pony. The same fifty or so representatives of the various guilds around the city. Even the food and wine were the same, as were the seating arrangements. Those standing, men and women from guilds of lesser importance to the overall economy and strength of Bond, were lined against the wall in nearly the same places and poses they had been but days earlier.

There were subtle differences, however. The room was a little more crowded, with Eel and Spider and the mage Frex Nodana standing against the wall behind the Docks Guild chief.

Still, that small change could not alleviate the sullen faces throughout the chamber, another similarity to the earlier meeting. No one was happy.

Captain Tuxra slammed a fist onto the extended table, toppling his empty mug and scattering the few pewter plates before his huge belly. "The riots have ended, Kerjim, but I see little different than before! Where is our new-found power? Where is all the gold you said would flow into our coffers?"

There were nods of agreement throughout the room.

Seated in his familiar spot at one end, the Docks boss grinned as he lifted a hand from beneath the table. In that hand were three folded sheets of paper. "Here are the licenses for three new guilds, signed by the mayor herself. Captain Tuxra, I made no promises of immediate riches, if you will remember. These things take time. The riots themselves ended but in the last day."

Kadath Osrm leaned forward on the table to make her presence felt. "What you say is true, Master Kerjim, but we have yet to see how these new guilds will benefit us. Each of us, and those we represent, have given up much this last month. We expect a return for our patience."

The Pursian fluttered the papers before slapping them on the table. His smile was gone. "I have explained and explained and explained. The Thieves Guild, I admit, is a personal matter, one of pride for myself. But the Mages Guild will provide us with strength, and the coalition of guilds will ensure that strength, all the while allowing us to fill our coffers. This is a simple matter. All we need do is sign these forms, have them filed with the city, and then we are masters of Bond, each of us. No more Belgad. No more of others telling us what to do, lifting the silvers from our purses."

"Belgad is already gone," Tuxra reminded, "and his man Lalo is weakened. It seems to me we have what we want without your recent interference. Or perhaps we need to be talking to the man who rid us of Belgad?"

Osrm nodded. "You have pushed your powers as Docks representative to their limits, Kerjim. These riots were unnecessary. Time would have handed us what we seek, without the mess."

"The riots would have gotten out of control without the Docks," the Pursian said. "Without us there would have been mass looting, likely killings."

"Without you, there would have been no food shortage in the first place," Tuxra said.

The room went silent, tense. A weighty charge had been laid down. A shift had occurred.

With a slow hand, Kerjim slid the papers from the table and handed them back to his nephew, who took them in silence.

Then the Docks boss looked up at those gathered, his heavy gaze moving from man to woman, woman to man. "Let me make something clear to all of you. Believe want you want, but the Docks Guild just saved this city. Without us, the Swamps would still be shut off from you. Without us, your warehouses and wharfs and boats would likely be in flames, all of your stored goods up in smoke. The Docks Guild brought food back to this city, and we opened the gates once more. Us. The Docks. *Me*!"

He smacked the table, sending his wine glass spiraling off to one side, spraying red across the light yellow blouse of the Flower Sellers Guild representative. The woman shrieked and dabbed at her shirt with a rag before fleeing the room.

A few chuckles went up around the chamber, breaking the tension. The Gnat tittered on his end of the table.

"My apologies," Kerjim said, rubbing at the side of his brow as if recovering from a headache. "We are all in this together, and the new guild of guilds will mean we must work together even more. We must trust one another, combining our efforts for the benefit of all."

"That is all well and good," Osrm spoke up, "and there is little denial a coalition of our efforts could profit everyone, but where do we go from here? The thieves and mages guilds can take care of themselves, and those we leave to your guidance, Master Kerjim. But for this guild of guilds, we are walking uncharted lands. Traditionally a new guild would have a vote among its members to elect a master of the guild, but who could we vote into such a position?"

Tuxra smacked the table once more, but more gently this time. "Yes! My very feelings. Who would we trust to take the reins of this guild of guilds?"

Kerjim nodded. "That is a natural concern, especially considering any number of us here would be qualified to lead the guild. I suggest we compile the list of members, each of us signing contracts for the license, then we do this the old fashioned way. We allow for a period of campaigning, say ... two weeks? Then we hold a vote."

"Why two weeks?" Osrm asked.

"It could be longer, or shorter," Kerjim said with a shrug. "It was merely a suggestion on my part. My thinking was anything less would not give each of us enough time to weigh our options, and anything more could lead to excessive lobbying, a burden none of us wants to face."

Captain Tuxra nodded. "Sounds well thought out to me."

Kerjim glanced about the room. "Any objections?"

He was greeted with a lull, a few nods, nothing more.

"Very well." The Pursian reached beneath the table once more and retrieved an iron stylus and several more sheets of paper. "We can sign our names and finally create this guild of guilds."

He looked up with the smile of an assassin. "And then the contest begins."

Unlike his long friendship with Sergeant Gris, Kron had known Randall Tendbones not quite a year. During that time the two had shared many misadventures and secrets, which built a wall of trust around the two. Kron knew Randall was more than a simple wizard and healer. Much, much more, in fact. In turn, Randall had learned of Kron's dark past, and had come to realize this character who thrived in shadows was basically a good man at heart, and was working on tempering his harsher ways. Somehow the two meshed, one wearing white, the other black, mirroring their souls and demeanors. Friends they were, but it had not always been an easy friendship.

The thought of such gave Kron a chuckle as he rode over the winding side streets of the Swamps, reaching down to pet his horse as he steered around another corner on his way to the healing tower. The walk was not a long one from the Asylum to the tower, but the steed had been tied and penned too long in Kron's estimation. The animal needed an opportunity to stretch its legs, thus the ride. Perhaps he would take the beast outside the city gates for a while later in the day, letting it run over the verdant fields and rolling hills surrounding Bond. It would do the horse good, and perhaps Kron, as well.

Trotting past a cart loaded with browning fruits and vegetables, the man in black came out upon a wider expanse and slowed his animal nearly to a standstill. Across the way, through the bustle of the afternoon amblers, rose the Swamps healing tower.

In truth, calling such a building a tower was a misnomer. It was indeed round like many a tower, and its three stories were higher than the surrounding structures. But there the similarities ended, other than perhaps the walls of gray stone. The building known as the healing tower was the largest construction in all of the Swamps, a handful of warehouses notwithstanding. It was bigger than the Asylum, bigger than Lalo's mansion. Within its walls were halls that wrapped the outer edges of the structure, the inner workings being taken up by offices, surgical chambers and rooms where physicians or magical healers could tend the ill or injured. The upper levels provided apartments for a few healers in residence, and sometimes served as temporary or final homes for the ill who were bedridden.

For the first time, Kron noted the age of the building. It was old, going back hundreds of years. Some benevolent pope likely had it built, though other than a small chapel on the bottom floor there were no signs of priestly influence. Which was no surprise. West Ursia had become a secular nation since breaking the chains held by the True Church in the East some sixty years earlier.

Spurring his ride ahead, the man in black wound around the side of the building until coming upon a leaning stall to one side. He rode forth and reined in, handing the leathers off to a young man in the white garb of the healers.

"Take care of her," Kron said with a smile. "I should only be a half hour."

The youth nodded back, grinning himself, and led the horse off to the stable where it would be brushed and readied for Kron's return.

It was a familiar routine for the man in black, though he had not visited the tower in some while, and he had full trust in those the healer's trusted. The boy taking care of the horses, Kron's and the other three inside the stall, probably earned a pittance.

117

At least the healers did not charge, which was a small mercy to those of the Swamps. Donations were welcome, of course, and Kron had on more than one occasion left behind a sizable grant.

He reached within the folds of his cloak and withdrew two copper coins. "Lad!"

The youth tied off Kron's horse and looked over his shoulder.

Kron tossed the coins.

Which were caught with another smile.

The man in black gave a brief, two-fingered salute, then spun about and headed for the nearest entrance to the tower.

The inner hall was a bustling place, more busy than Kron had before witnessed. Cots lined the outer wall, upon each an invalid or suppliant seeking ease of their misery. Most appeared sickly, undernourished, though more than a few showed signs of violence, bruises, broken limbs, even some blood. Here and there hastened the volunteers, the backbone of the tower's workforce, men and women who might or might not have some little healing skills, but who at the least were willing to lend a hand, many of them former patients themselves showing gratitude through their labors.

Kron came to a standstill and watched all this with a stiffened back and steady eyes. People should not have to suffer such. They should not be put in a position to suffer in this manner, piled into corridors nearly one on top of the other. Those attending did the best they could, as did the professional staff, but this situation went far beyond the inadequacies of the healing tower or even of the Swamps itself. Economic differences between here and the rest of the city could only account for so much. These people, the sick and the injured, were used almost daily by those with the power to do so. The riots had been just one more tool in that, making others rich while stomping on the necks of those in need.

He spun away from the scene, his mind's eye blurred for the moment, then tromped along the hall, rounding the outer corridor until he came to a familiar door.

A knock and the door opened, a young woman standing inside. Kron did not recognize her. She appeared plain, though not unattractive, long dark brown hair hanging straight down both sides of her face to make her unblinking eyes appear larger than they really were. A simple gray tunic hung too large for her, covering nearly half of her light brown dress.

"I'm sorry," Kron said, glancing up and down the corridor, "I must have found the wrong room."

In silence the woman shook her head, then she stepped back into the chamber to provide entry.

Kron glanced inside and recognized Randall's outer office, a simple wooden desk with a chair behind it up against the right wall, two more chairs in front of the desk, another doorway on the far wall. The room was lit well by several candelabras placed throughout and a series of lamps hanging on the entrance wall.

With a sweep of her arm, the woman beckoned him to enter.

Kron did so, stepping inside as she closed the door behind him.

Just then the opposite door opened, Randall Tendbones coming out with a stern look on his face, one that was flushed away upon seeing his friend. "Kron!"

"It seems I've met your new assistant," the swordsman said, nodding to the quiet woman.

"Yes." Coming forward, the healer motioned from the woman to the man in black. "Althurna, this is Kron Darkbow."

At the sound of the name a frown formed on the woman's lips. Still, she managed a short curtsy.

Kron chuckled. "It seems you have already told her about me."

Randall wore a thin smile. "Yes. Perhaps too much."

The healer turned toward his assistant. "Althurna, young Wesley needs a changing of his bandages, if you would be so kind."

The woman nodded and approached the other door, her narrowed eyes never leaving the tall figure in the black cloak until she shut the door behind her.

"She does not say much," Kron noted.

"That is true," Randall said, easing around behind his desk where the wooden chair groaned beneath his weight. "There's nothing physically wrong with her, and I have heard her speak when necessary, but it seems some trauma from a young age keeps her quiet."

The healer motioned toward the two chairs facing him. "Won't you sit?"

Kron pulled back one of the chairs and settled onto it. "Seems she doesn't care for me, either."

Randall chuckled. "You must forgive her. The last few months she has become quite fond of me, and I made the mistake of telling her about our trip to Kobalos."

Kron's eyes flared. "Did you tell her ... everything?"

"No, of course not," Randall said with a wave of his hand, as if to knock aside his secrets. "What happened in Mogus Potere remains between you and I, and Belgad and a handful of others, of course. They have remained silent, at least to my knowledge, and I have no wish to make public certain ... intricacies ... of the events that occurred there."

Kron gestured toward the outer hall. "It seems the riots have kept you busy."

A scowl grew upon the healer's face. "Yes, too much so."

"My apologies for my role in that."

"None needed," Randall said. "We discussed that yesterday. Which is why I am glad you are here. You mentioned the riots were ... I believe 'arranged' was the word you used."

Kron hesitated for a moment, then speared ahead. "During the riots I did some spying work for Gris. I had an encounter with a young man who hinted there were guilds ... not singular ... somehow behind the riots."

"An encounter?"

Kron grinned. "Do not fret. The fellow was unharmed, at least by me. In fact, he escaped my attentions while I was busy retracting Stilp from a situation."

"Stilp? Lalo's man?"

"The very same," Kron said. "I spoke with him as well, and later the Finder himself. Both confirmed the guilds were involved, with the Docks Guild leading the pack."

The healer nodded while rubbing his chin, looking off to one side as if remembering something. "That fits in with what I saw during the riots. It didn't occur to me the Docks was behind all this, nor any of the other guilds, but Kerjim and his bullies were always at the forefront of stirring up the trouble. I just figured they were part of the crowd, but now it seems their presence was more ominous."

"I've yet to meet this Kerjim character, but when I do, I'll have some questions for him."

Randall looked up. "Even if he was behind the riots, what can be done about it now? The fighting is over."

Kron shrugged. "Perhaps nothing. Gris has put in for a handful of arrest warrants, but I doubt there'll be one with Kerjim's name on it. There's not exactly direct evidence a guild leader was behind the troubles."

Looking much like his assistant from minutes earlier, the young healer frowned. "You're not going to handle this situation personally, are you?"

The man in black grinned as he waved off the question. "I learned my lessons about rage in Kobalos, my friend. If Kerjim and his ilk should cross my path, that is one thing, but I'm not about to blaze another trail of vengeance across the city. Once was enough, I would say."

Randall nodded agreement. "As would I."

"However," Kron went on, "since you are still dealing with the consequences of the riots, I'm sure Gris would appreciate if you kept your ears open for anything suspicious."

"I'll do that," the healer said. "Are you working with the city guard now?"

"It was only on a provisional basis. My talents came in useful during the riots, but I am a free agent once again."

"I suppose that frees you up to finish your work at the Asylum. How are things going there, by the way?"

Kron chuckled. "I've hired two contractors and both quit on me."

"Because of the riots?"

"No, more of a ... spectral ... situation."

"Spectral?"

"The first man fled screaming about ghosts. The other nearly lost his life in a fall, then recounted a tale of a mysterious hand appearing in the air and pulling him off a scaffold."

"Do you believe any of this?"

Kron shrugged again. "I suppose it's possible. The Asylum was a scene of tragedy, after all, and before that it had its share of murder and madness."

The healer's eyes reddened upon hearing those words.

"Do not blame yourself," Kron said. "If anyone, I'm to blame for what happened. If I hadn't opened that door to the river, the place would not have flooded."

Randall nodded. "Very well. It is the past. There is nothing we can do for all those lost souls."

"Perhaps, perhaps not," Kron continued. "If there truly are spirits at the Asylum, I suppose I should do something about it."

"You've not seen any signs yourself?"

"No. I rarely go inside the actual building. I spend my nights either at the Scabbard or camping on the Asylum grounds."

"If it's a haunting, perhaps it is limited to the building."

"Possible. That's where everyone died."

Randall's face grew serious. "Kron, listen to me, don't try to tackle this on your own. I can check with my contacts at the university. Perhaps we can find a necromancer or exorcist who can cleanse the place for you."

Darkbow offered a friendly smile. "All I want to do is finish the reconstruction. If that means I have to hire a wizard, then so be it. I don't suppose *you* would have the time to deal with it?"

120

The healer threw back his head and sighed. "I wish I did. As you can tell by the full hallways, the tower is keeping me more than engaged."

Kron's grin broadened. "I suppose it doesn't hurt you've gained a reputation as the best healer in town."

Randall gave a brief laugh. "Unfortunately that reputation comes with heavy responsibilities. It's one of the reasons I hired on an assistant."

"Yes." Kron glanced toward the door to the other room. "It seems she does not like me very much."

"I don't believe she likes the idea of me traipsing across the continent on grand adventures."

"Or maybe she fears you will do so again, leaving her behind."

The healer's gaze narrowed. "Perhaps you are right."

Silence rolled over the two for steady moments.

"Well." Kron slapped his hands together and briskly stood. "I could sit here all day chatting, but you've got tending to do and I need to find another contractor."

Randall came to his feet behind his desk. "Before you go, one last thing."

"Yes?"

"I meant what I said about not dealing with these ghosts on your own," Randall said. "A man unarmed against them could find himself in dire straits. Ghosts can feed on emotions, growing stronger by them, especially ghosts of tragedy, and their abilities can be numerous and unpredictable.."

Turning to the exit, Kron winked to his friend. "When have I ever gotten myself into dire straits?"

***

"As provisional guild leaders, I expect full support from both of you in my bid for master of the Guild of Guilds."

Frex Nodana and Eel trailed just behind Kerjim as he paraded between pews across a plank floor, kicking up dust in his wake. Spider watched from the far end of the chamber near the exit of double doors. The view of the room was gloomy, hampered by scattered dirt and the dull light from rectangular windows near the ceiling.

In past generations the building had been a temple to Ashal, one of the smaller neighborhood churches that had once dotted the landscape of the Swamps. In recent memory the structure had sat abandoned, home only to rats and the occasional vagrant. The place smelled of urine and worse, with dark streaks smeared upon its inner walls over layers of graffiti older than Eel himself. The stench was nearly enough to make one vomit, but Kerjim had insisted upon inspecting the building as a possible birthplace for the new Thieves Guild. According to the older man, this place had once been a minor gathering spot under the old guild, which had taken over years after the Ashalite priests had moved on.

The Pursian paused as he neared the front of the chamber, a dark spot on the floor revealing where a small rug or altar had once stood. He turned around to face the others. "I will have your support, will I not?"

Eel blanched as if unsure of himself. "Of course, but I don't know if it will be worth much."

The Docks boss frowned. "What is *that* supposed to mean?"

With a look of chagrin, Eel's hooded eyes remained focused on a spot on the floor in front of his soft leather moccasins. "Just what I said. We're not even guild bosses yet, so I don't see how we can be of much help."

"The two of you will head your guilds within the next two days," Kerjim explained, "and the vote for master of the Guild of Guilds doesn't come for two weeks. I will need all the influence I can muster with Osrm and that fat fool Tuxra likely running for the spot, perhaps others as well."

"That's just it," Eel said, "I don't even know how we become guild bosses. There has to be a vote or something, right?"

Kerjim glanced to the woman, then back to his nephew. "Eel, sometimes I wonder that we are related."

The lad looked up, a touch of anger stirring behind his eyes.

"Calm down," the Pursian said with an upthrust hand to ward off his kin's ire. "It's a simple matter. All you and Nodana have to do is get a dozen signatures for each of your licenses, then we file the papers with the mayor's office."

"Any signatures will do?" the mage asked.

Kerjim nodded. "As long as the names aren't repeated and the signatures don't match too closely. You can even have some of the same names on each of your licenses, as citizens can have a contract with more than one guild."

The woman playfully nudged Eel in the side with a slender elbow. "I told you not to worry."

Spider came rambling up behind the group, his voice hushed. "Should we really be talking about this in a temple?"

Kerjim chuckled. "Far worse has been contemplated on this spot, my friend, and Ashal never struck anyone dead."

Eel snickered. "Perhaps we could ask Ashal to deal with Kron Darkbow."

Kerjim placed a hand on his nephew's right shoulder and squeezed slightly, in an almost fatherly fashion. "But that is your job, my young nephew. Darkbow's fall will be a sign to the other guilds we are a force to be taken seriously. Have you made arrangements?"

Eel nodded. "I'm meeting up with Mama Kaf and a bunch later tonight at the Pony."

Spider's boots shifted nervously on the planks. "So it's tonight, then? Good. I want to get this over with. There's something wrong with that Kaf woman."

"It's called rage," Kerjim said.

12

Night is a time that brings fear to many. Perhaps this is because of residual memories from the ancestors, hidden histories that recall huddling in caves while beasts of darkness roamed the lands. Or perhaps it is simply the lack of being able to see that unnerves. Threats looming in the bright of day at least can be faced, challenged. No one sees the dagger sliding toward their throat from the shadows, nor the jungle cat ready to pounce from the shelter of high trees.

Yes, the night can leave many with nerves tingling.

Kron Darkbow was not such a person. He had been born in the night, one particular night, watching his parents laid low by arrows on a backstreet in Southtown. Such tragedy would have reinforced abhorrence of the darkness for most, bringing trembles and heightened trepidation. For Kron, the tragedy had been a beginning, a creation. He had been another person, a boy, before the murders. Nearly sixteen years later he was a different man, one who had even chosen a different name for himself than the one his parents had known.

Would they be proud of their son if they could see him? Kron did not know. He rarely believed it worth considering. He had had experiences that proved to him there was some kind of existence beyond the physical life with which he was familiar, but he had no evidence his parents continued to watch him or that they knew of his habits. If they did, he was not so sure they would disagree with the paths he had taken. Marcus and Aurelia Tallerus had been but merchants, but they had not been the kind to idly sit behind a counter while hawking goods. She had been a specialist in gems and jewelry, he an authority on rare woods and opulent furnishings. They had made a good living, dealing mostly with a higher-end clientele. They had also been exceptionally well traveled and educated, and had included their son on more than a few trips to other lands before they were taken from him when he was but ten years of age. At a time when most children were barely learning to read and write, the boy who would become Kron Darkbow could already speak, read and write several languages fluently and a half dozen other tongues with some little skill. His parents had gifted him with that, and with a sense of adventure.

Which was why he had few worries about them passing judgment upon him from beyond. They might not approve of everything he had done over the years, but they knew in his heart he was a man who sought justice for others. And the harsh things of which he had been a part ... well, amends could not be made, but he could work to make himself a better man.

So Kron Darkbow did not fear the night, nor the judgment of the dead. With rare thoughts for those passed, he embraced the night, allowing it to wrap him in its arms like the parents who were no longer with him.

His lack of fear was what allowed him to ride the city's streets during the dark hours, a practice that had become common for him the last few months before the riots, a reminder of his days on patrol in the Prisonlands. There was no need for these tours other than Kron felt they kept him alert, kept his senses in tune with the dark. Surviving on what few funds were left of his venture to Kobalos, his parents' savings gone long ago, he could have found a steady position that took advantage of his various skills, a position that would also have kept his talents well oiled. But he also could have done much worse, spending his nights drinking away past sorrows.

As it was, he spent most of his nights in solitude, riding through the city. It gave him time to think, to ponder, to plan. His immediate goal was to get the Asylum finished. Why he needed the building reconstructed was beyond the few who knew him, and even beyond himself. Men had died there, and Kron had been partly responsible. Was the Asylum to be a shrine to them? Or to companions who had fallen at Kron's side? He could not fathom his own depths. Perhaps rebuilding the Asylum was a step along his path of self amelioration.

There were to be no major changes in the Asylum's layout. From the beginning he had wanted the building to reflect exactly what it had been a year earlier when he had been but one of scores of guards working there. With the wealth he had received in Kobalos, he could have flattened the Asylum's main building and constructed a small estate, but that had not felt proper, had not felt clean. Perhaps asepsis was what was important here. Perhaps Kron was attempting to wipe from his soul the stain caused at the Asylum, or perhaps he was attempting to cleanse the souls of those who had died there.

He gave a low chuckle as he steered his animal through an alley, heading in the direction of the Asylum, the place which was allegedly haunted. He supposed if any site within the city could contain ghosts, it would be the Asylum what with the madness that had run through the place when it was alive, and then the tragedy of the many in the place's death.

Kron was not yet convinced of the hauntings, but he had seen enough in his days to know it was not impossible. Perhaps Randall was right and he should seek out a necromancer or some priestly exorcist.

The alley came to an end, revealing the black strip of Beggars Row stretching from left to right before him. On his side of the road were row upon row of two- and three-story tenements, across the way the entrance to the Asylum, its dark walls reaching out to the sides.

He almost spurred his riding beast forward, but paused before doing so. Something felt not right. He sat in the saddle and considered for long seconds, allowing his senses to work to their full extent.

After some while he noticed what was wrong. The street was empty, for one, and there were no sounds and no light coming from behind the windows of the buildings around him. True, it was late at night, but he was near the center of one of the largest cities on the continent. There should have been some activity. A few drunks walking the street. A handful of toughs hanging around doorways. Prostitutes walking their familiar paths. Something. Someone.

He edged his horse forward slightly, right to the end of the alley, and craned forward in the saddle, glancing left and right and back again. Then he looked straight across at the Asylum.

Except for his complete solitude, everything seemed in place. Everything seemed normal.

Kron had experienced too many similar situations in the Prisonlands to know he could be riding into a trap. Or perhaps not. Maybe the night was just quiet.

Maybe everyone was tired after the riots. Besides, his few living enemies posed little or no threat. Belgad, the most logical option, was thousands of miles away, and would not use assassins to conclude his own dirty work.

Kron grinned thinking about his hated foe. The two men had set aside their differences, but if the Dartague barbarian wanted Kron dead, at least he would ride right up to the man in black, two-handed sword swinging. Kron could appreciate that, though it wasn't necessarily his way.

So, if this were a trap, who would want Kron dead?

Perhaps the Finder, but violence did not seem that man's mode. Anyone else? There had been that youth in the alley a few nights earlier. Kron would recognize him if he saw him, but they had not traded names. If the boy wanted revenge for a mere fright, which was truly all he had faced, then first he would have to find out Kron's name. And that name might scare the lad off. Kron had to admit, his tangle with Belgad had brought him to the attention of many within the city, and on more than one occasion Gris and Randal had pointed this out. People were beginning to know who he was.

And his odd habit of rebuilding the Asylum only drew more attention.

He stared across at the walls of the place and its locked iron gate.

Then he shrugged. *If there's danger here, so be it. There is no way to discover it except ride right into it.*

He kneed his animal and the two trucked ahead one clopping step at a time.

It was slow going, and Kron kept it that way, his grip like a vice on the reins. Without turning his head, he allowed his eyes to scan his surroundings. He spotted no one, no movement. No sounds, no lights. Nothing.

Perhaps he was being foolish.

Nearing the gate, he turned his horse sideways and fished a long iron key from a pocket. Instead of dismounting, he leaned down and forward in the saddle, reaching for the lock hanging from the gate.

Click. Kron slid the lock free, returned the key to its hiding hole and shoved on the gate of iron bars, sending it to sway back.

Another swift glance revealed nothing untoward. *So far so good.* He twisted the reins once more and rode the horse through the opening and onto the Asylum grounds.

Inside the walls, Kron kept his steed at an angle, allowing him to swing the gate closed once more. Again he leaned forward, wrapping the lock around the gate's bars before retrieving the key to secure the lock in place.

The lock closed once more. He sat up straight, ready to turn toward the stable.

Thunk! Thunk!

The pain was excruciating, like a red hot poker had been jammed into him. Kron cried out, the key falling from his fingers into the dirt as his steed reared, the animal screaming. He fought to stay in the saddle, the horse beneath him bucking and thrashing, and leaned into the beast to keep from falling.

Only then did he notice the feathered end of an arrow extending from the side of the animal's head. The animal would not live. Kron realized that right away. He had seen too many similar wounds in riding beasts to think otherwise. More important to his own survival, he knew he had but seconds to act.

With the beast dropping back to the ground, Kron tried to shove away, to slide off the back of the saddle.

He did not budge.

More pain pounded into his left leg, jabbing like spikes dipped in acid. A quick glance betrayed the fact the horse had not been the only one hit. An arrow protruded from Kron's thigh and held him tight to his seat. The head of the dart had broken through the other side of his leg, pinning him to the front cinch below the saddle.

With a death cry from his steed, the arrow through Kron's leg became the least of his concerns.

Like a ship crashing into the heavy rocks of a shoreline, his horse slammed into the ground once more, its legs sliding out from under it as the beast rolled toward one side.

A black glove snapped down, cracking off the feathered end of the arrow in Kron's leg. With a pitched bellow he flung himself away from the dead animal, the shaft of the arrow sliding clean through his thigh.

He landed in the shadows of the Asylum's walls, sending up a cloud of dirt as he kept in motion, rolling away from the collapsing horse. Each cycle of his body sent fresh anguish through his leg as it hit and hit and hit against the ground.

Coming to a halt several yards from his slain beast, Kron lay unmoving, the hood of his cloak enfolding his head. Let anyone watching think for the moment he was dead or unconscious.

Through the lines of hair hanging in his face, he surveyed the scene as well as he could.

The horse was no longer moving. Poor beast. He would have to see it properly taken care of.

But for now there was a threat near, more than one. Those had been crossbow bolts, he was sure. Probably from behind the wagon Felton's workers had yet to retrieve. At least two archers, probably more.

And here he was in the middle of an open, flat area, wounded and with a wall at his back.

Figures appeared from behind the wagon, as expected, but others slid from inside the tent Kron had erected, shambling their way out of deeper pockets of shadow.

Without turning his head, Kron could not count their numbers. But it mattered little. He was still bleeding, and in little condition to travel. If he were going to make a move, it would have to be soon.

No time like the present.

With gritted teeth he shoved himself off the ground, hopping onto his good leg.

A couple of surprised gasps greeted him, but none too near.

The black hood twisted, glaring across the dark yard. Six approached, two carrying the expected crossbows. The others gripped knives and swords, the blades glinting beneath the moonlight.

Kron's movement had surprised them. To a person they became still, their eyes hidden by shadows in the sockets of their skulls but unmistakably locked on the man in black.

The wind grew chill. Cloaks flapped on the night. Hard gazes were shared.

"Rush him!" It was a youthful voice.

Kron jumped back nearer the wall and stretched up a hand to grab the pommel of his sword.

Which was gone.

126

He slapped at his back, but the weapon was no longer there. Must have fallen off during the tumble from the horse. No time to look for it.

The assassins drew nearer, their leather-clad feet slapping the ground.

Kron sank down, keeping his pained leg outstretched while putting all his weight on his good, bent leg.

Let them come closer. Let them draw near. *I shall spread Hell among them.*

Seeing their target apparently fallen, the killers surged, one of them with a shout of almost joy.

They were nearly upon their victim, within knife-throwing distance, when he sprang up off one leg, an arm flashing out from the shadows.

The night erupted. Light. Fire and the scent of sulfur.

The two nearest Kron were ablaze, and stupid enough not to drop to the ground. Instead they screamed, letting go their weapons and turning back toward their comrades as if seeking sanctuary from the pain that ate away at their flesh.

The other assassins fled to the sides, giving their companions ample room to run through.

Kron watched briefly while hanging from the side of the wall, one hand extended, the fingers gripping the top and barely holding. He slung around his other hand for a better hold and tugged, a scream escaping his lungs as he pulled himself to the top of the wall. He rolled over without thinking of the fall beyond.

Kron dropped, the cold wind pressing upon him, then landed with a thudding noise, the breath knocked from between his lips as his face dug into dirt.

He lay still for a moment, making sure nothing had been broken. *Lucky fool.* Then he pushed off the ground once more. He needed to move. It would not take long for his attackers to scale the wall. Even without his sword, he still had two daggers on him and a handful of throwing darts. That had been the last of his grenados, and his bow was at the tent fifty yards away on the other side of the wall. In the open, wounded and with no major weapons, he was in no condition to face off with four men, perhaps more. It was time to leave, his best hope to hobble his way to the nearest dark alley and disappear.

Kron spun toward the street.

And cursed.

Another half dozen figures jogged toward him, outlined by the moon's glow. The two nearest came at him from directly across the street, from the alley he had ridden through but minutes earlier. The others moved in at angles from his sides, from alleyways further down. They had been waiting for him. Hiding.

The man in black sighed.

There was nowhere to go. He was without benefit of shelter of any kind. He could already hear those behind him scrambling up the wall. Any second now he would be bombarded with nearly a dozen attackers intent upon slaying him.

He could not win this. There were too many of them, especially considering his condition, and it was obvious someone wanted him dead. His only chance at survival would be to force his way through the two coming directly for him, then to charge into the alley, hoping he could lose them in the dark winding paths of the city's belly.

He grinned. Yes, he had tried to turn from violence as much as possible, but this lot was forcing it upon him. If they wished to unleash the beast that lay curled within Kron Darkbow's heart, then so be it.

The fingers of his right hand slid into the back of his left's glove, removing three small throwing darts the color of the sky beyond the stars. His other hand retrieved a large dagger from the belt around his waist.

The scrambling sounds continued from behind, with more than a few huffs and puffs.

And then the nearest attackers were there, right in front of Kron, one sliding around a curved sword from the right, the other bringing up some kind of club on the left.

A black glove snapped out, launching the throwing darts.

A scream as the one with the sword dropped his blade and grabbed at his throat.

Kron dipped down on his good leg, gritting away the pain that once more detonated in his thigh, the club sailing high over his head. He came up with two quick slashes, one cutting across the wrist holding the cudgel, the other deep into an arm pit, laying open cloth and skin and splashing blood.

The two wounded men howled.

Kron had no more time for these two.

He launched himself between them, dragging his bleeding, aching leg as fast as he could. The alley was not far ahead. The other attackers on the street were closing but still some distance away.

A sonorous, clanging din filled the air from behind, followed by a metallic crunching noise that shook the ground and continued with a banging, banging, banging. Nearly to the shadows, Kron dared a glance over his shoulder to see what fate was now throwing at him.

He nearly tripped at the sight. A humongous figure stood like a mountain on the other side of the Asylum gate, battering the iron bars down with a hammer the size of a small tree. Kron had a moment to wonder how he had not spotted such a beast when he had been within the walls, but then he stumbled into the black of the alley.

Pausing for a moment to catch his breath and give his wounded leg some relief, he slid his dagger back home as his fingers went to work unfurling the silk rope that always hung from the back of his weapons belt.

Shouts from the street. They had seen where he had gone, which was no surprise. Across the road that banging, banging, banging continued, and Kron was thankful for the heavy bars of the gate.

He twirled the rope, sending the grappling hook at its end spinning over and under his right arm. He had but seconds, then the killers would be on him, charging into the alley. He could hear their footfalls now, just to the left and right of the entrance. Across the way there were no signs of climbers, the group there apparently waiting for the gate to come down.

Which it did, with a jangle of broken metal.

Kron flung out a hand, sending the grapnel spiraling toward the roof. For the first time in a long while, he muttered a prayer in hopes the hook would find a home.

It did, though he had no way to be sure as he was unable to see where the grapnel had fallen in the shadows of the roof's ledge.

There was no time for hesitation.

Kron pulled on the cord and felt the line go straight.

Stompings of boots almost to him. A bellow, a shout from across the road.

There's only one way to find out if the rope will hold. He jumped, breathing a sigh of relief as the weight was taken off his bad leg, but then grunting as he slammed against the side of a tenement building, the rope holding.

Kron gave his legs a moment of rest and strained and pulled with his arms, the muscles standing out beneath the thin layer of his black cloak. A few feet up and he brought his good leg around to press against the wall, hopping up the side of the building one small step at a time.

Then voices and hurried footfalls below. They were running right beneath him, mere inches away. Kron became still, motionless, thanking Ashal for the blackness of the alley and the blackness of his garb. He held his breath, waiting, hoping his dangling rope would not draw attention and that those below did not have the intelligence to look up.

***

Everything had happened so fast, but of one thing Eel was sure. Whether Kron Darkbow or not, the man on the horse was the same whom he had fled from during the riots. No one else so large moved so swiftly, especially after having been hit with a crossbow bolt. And despite being struck, the man still had set two of Eel's comrades aflame and carved his way through two more. Was there no stopping him?

Thinking mainly of not looking a fool in front of the gang he had put together, the youth barreled into the blackness of the alley across from the Asylum, right on the heels of Spider and several others as they all charged ahead. Mama Kaf and a handful of others remained at the gate the woman had destroyed with her sledgehammer, creating a noise likely to draw the attention of the city guard now they were again stationed in the Swamps. But the guard didn't matter. Mere minutes had passed, and Eel was positive within a short while he and his gang would have their prey. He had no hate for this Darkbow, but he had to prove himself, had to show his uncle and the others he could take care of business. He was chief of the Thieves Guild, after all, and expected to gain all the signatures he needed tonight.

His moccasins smacking against the bricks of the alley floor, Eel heard his comrades cursing ahead of him.

He bumped into the back of one man and bounced away, uttered curses following him and revealing it was Spider he had nearly skewered with his two swords. Thankfully the weapons had been lowered.

Eel halted, noticing the others had come to a standstill at the end of the alley in front of him, another road stretching across before them, more tenements beyond. "Why did we stop?"

A head shifted in the darkness, facing him. A low, rough voice whispered. "We've lost him."

"What?" Eel elbowed his way through the others and came to the alley's end.

There was no one there. He glanced up and down the street and across to narrower lanes on the other side of the road, but there was no sign of the man they had attacked.

Impossible.

Eel turned to where he believed Spider was standing. "It was Darkbow, wasn't it?"

"Looked like him to me," Spider's voice answered.

"Okay, okay." Eel muttered the words more to himself than the others, giving himself precious seconds to think. They had watched the man in black hop into the alley. A minute had not passed before they had waded in behind him. There was no way anyone with such a serious leg wound could have traversed the alley so quickly and gone beyond the street at the other end.

Think! Eel gently prodded the side of his head with the hilt of a sword. He tried to imagine what he would have done in Darkbow's position.

Then Eel grinned in the dark. "The rooftops. He's taken to the rooftops."

***

Kron rolled over the roof's ledge onto his back and lay there, allowing fresh air to fill his lungs and giving his wound a moment of rest. One gloved hand dangled over the side, working to draw the silk cord back to its master. His gambit had worked, the fools running directly below him without stopping, but he doubted his luck was strong enough they would give up the search that easily. They might even take to the rooftops to look for him.

He planned on not being around long enough to find out. He had to get somewhere where there were people, and that was not going to be an easy task in the middle of the night. The closest guard barracks was too far away. The healing tower was relatively close, but Kron did not want to take the chance on bringing a fight to the halls of the healers. A handful of taverns would still have open doors, but it was not likely he would find solace within.

Where to go? If not someplace with a crowd, then a place where he could not be found.

At any rate, he had to keep moving. Remaining in the same vicinity as his attackers was not an option.

Warm blood pooling in his left boot, Kron shoved himself up from the roof. He swayed as he stood, thrusting out an arm to steady himself, thankful he had not gone into shock or that his wounded limb was cramping. *Lucky.* Twice lucky because the arrow had not broken bone. But how much longer could he continue without attention to his wound, especially considering the strain forced upon his body? It was a question he could not readily answer, but staying in the same spot increased his chances of being killed.

He scanned his surroundings and after several seconds of squinting through darkness discovered a hatch that provided access to and from the roof. He limped forward, more blood draining down his leg.

***

The group clustered together near where they had originally entered the alley, a lantern having been lit and forming a circle of light around them.

Eel turned to his street mage. "Spider? Can you find him?"

The small, gray-haired man closed his eyes as if in deep thought.

"Spider?"

The mage held up a hand. "Give me a moment. I'm not exactly some big university wizard."

The group waited, the others from across the road slowly approaching, the gigantic figure of Mama Kaf leading the way.

Spider's eyes opened. "He's above us, but I'm not sure exactly where."

Eel glanced from side to side. Two buildings, both three stories, either of which would have made decent climbing material what with various handholds in the bricks and window ledges. He was amazed Darkbow had made the ascent so fast, especially considering his bad leg. Even if the man had had a rope of some sort, it wouldn't have been an easy climb.

"Okay." The young leader of the pack looked around at his crew, for a moment nearly giddy at the idea he was actually in charge of something. He pointed to the building on his right. "Spider, take one guy with you and head up to that roof."

"What about the rest of us?" someone asked from behind.

Eel glanced about at the others as Spider slapped a man on a shoulder and they took off for the front of their assigned structure. He nodded toward the other building. "I'll take someone with me. The rest of you hang around down here in case Darkbow slips past us. Don't forget to watch the alleys."

A muted grunt from Mama Kaf was the only response, the big woman hefting her giant hammer from one hand to the other.

Eel nodded and tagged a comrade on the shoulder, both taking off at a trot for the front door of the nearest building.

***

Kron nearly stumbled as he neared the closed hatch. Only thrusting out both arms to level his balance kept him from falling on his face. He paused for a moment, breathing slowly, grinding his teeth to get past the pain eating up his thigh. He took several moments to use a dagger to slice a long strip from the end of his cloak, then tied the makeshift cord high and tight around his thigh to cut off the flow of blood.

A door or window slammed open somewhere behind him, followed by the sounds of footfalls upon the roof next door. So, they were still looking for him, and smart enough to check the roofs.

Going through the hatch no longer felt like the right idea.

He glanced to the back of the roof upon which he stood, away from Beggars Row and the Asylum. It was difficult to make out in the dark, but it seemed there was another building, another roof at a lower level. He tried to remember if there was a two-story tenement back there, but his thoughts were absorbed by the burning in his leg.

The hatch? Or another rooftop? Both ideas had possibilities. Both had potential dangers. He had to decide. He wouldn't be able to walk much longer, expecting the growing numbness to turn into cramps or worse at any moment.

Kron cursed as he lumbered toward the back of the building. The hatch would be too dangerous. There was no telling what he would run into once inside the tenement, and it was likely another party of killers was climbing the steps at that very moment.

The end of the roof. The alley behind was narrow, less than five feet across, the building there one story shorter than where Kron stood. An easy jump for a man with working legs. Also an easy fall.

What to do?

Another slamming, this time much closer.

Kron looked over his shoulder. Yes, the hatch had been thrown open. He could already make out a shadowy figure climbing up from below.

Cursing was becoming a regular habit for the man in black.

He eased away from the edge of the roof to give himself running room while untying the rope and grapnel from his belt. He was hoping not to need the silk cord but wanted to have it in hand just in case.

131

"There he is!"

No time like the present.

As fast as he could force himself, Kron lurched, blundering forward more than running.

Charging boot steps right behind.

Then Kron was airborn.

Falling.

Plummeting.

Landing on his good foot, balancing for just a moment as if a dancer pausing in mid-twirl, then cascading forward.

His chin hit the hard gravel of the rooftop, driving his bottom teeth into his top lip and cutting flesh. Blood spurted. Then the wind was driven from him as his chest hit, hammering him as if struck by a giant.

Kron rolled to one side and tried to groan, but his mouth was filled with a wet mess. He spat, sending a black line spiraling as he attempted to sit up, almost falling again in the process.

An explosion of motion next to him as a shadowy figure landed, another jumper, this one also loosing his footing and dropping flat to the rooftop.

Kron could not give this newcomer time to recover. The man in block rolled toward his barely seen foe, the downed figure silhouetted by moonlight alone. Kron did not take the time to reach for a dagger, instead coming up on his good knee and hammering away with a fist, then again, and again.

There was silence as Kron felt his target go limp, flattening out unmoving on the gravel.

Would there be another jumper? Kron had vaguely seen only the one man at the hatchway, but that didn't mean anything. The fellow could have had an army waiting below him. Kron wasn't going to wait to find out.

He crawled away from the unconscious figure, for a moment considering searching the person for weapons before deciding time was of importance. Time and space. He needed to put both between him and his pursuers.

After several feet he used his hands to push up onto his right leg, wobbling for a moment before finding his balance and hopping ahead toward the far edge of the roof where there was light from tall lamps along Cabbage Street. What help could he find on that road? None. He needed to hide, to stop running.

A smashing sound, another person falling and landing, cut through any notions of staying put.

Kron dared a look back. He could barely make out the latest arrival, but the outline seemed male, not too large but not too small. And this one had been elegant enough to land on his feet. Probably young. Probably in great physical condition. Great.

A dagger slid free of Kron's belt as he heard shouts from the alley and other rooftops.

**

The young boss of the Thieves Guild couldn't believe his luck. It was true a couple of his companions were likely dead, at least as many seriously wounded, but now here he was alone with Kron Darkbow, the man battered, tired, breathing heavy and seriously wounded. More over, the enemy was standing hunkered over on the far side of the roof in the middle of the glow from the street lamps, making himself a perfect target despite being wrapped in his cloak of black.

This would be an easy kill, Eel's first. After tonight, everyone would know he had slain Kron Darkbow, the very man who had driven Belgad the Liar from the city.

The youth slowed in his approach, taking his time to enjoy the moment as he twirled his two swords out at his sides. The man in black did not move, a dark eye over his shoulder revealing he recognized his doom approaching. What did he think he was doing moving to the ledge like that? There would be no help for him in Cabbage Street beyond, especially not this time of night. Was he thinking of climbing down, of trying one last desperate bid at escape?

Too bad.

Eel closed, the sword in his right hand coming in low, the sword in his left coming in high. So long Kron Darkbow.

***

The attacker had natural talent, Kron would give him that, but there was little training there.

Just as the youth reached the border of light and dark, Kron snapped up the end of his cloak, popping the young man in the face. It was not a move meant to wound, but a mere distraction.

It worked.

The boy flinched.

With one hand Kron grabbed him by his leather jerkin, twisted and slammed the lad down on the rooftop, all but falling on top of him.

***

Eel didn't know what had happened. He had just been about to skewer his target when something had hit him in the face, blinding him for only a second, maybe less, but it had been enough. He had been pulled forward, the youth expecting a knife to the gut at any moment, but instead was thrown to one side, his back hammered down upon the roof, the wind knocked from his lungs.

Eel felt the extra weight of one of his foe's knees on his chest, and he thought it possible he might not ever breathe again.

In the streetlight, a dagger was raised, the man in black's hood falling back.

Eel stared up into those dark, harsh eyes, the last he believed he would ever see. Then Darkbow blinked, and his eyes went soft.

The dagger edged to the boy's throat, coming short of slicing his neck open.

"You're the one from the alley," Darkbow's heavy voice said, "the one chasing Stilp."

Stilp? That idiot who worked for Lalo the Finder? That was who he had been chasing that night? Eel couldn't help himself. He laughed, laughed at death staring him in the face.

The dagger poked, drawing a dot of red.

Eel stopped laughing.

Darkbow leaned closer, and the youth could now see blood staining the man's lips. "I see nothing humorous about your situation."

"You will once my crew catches up to you," Eel cracked back. Why not? If he was going to die, at least throw out one last little threat.

The dagger slid away, but not far, and Darkbow's face came nearer, their noses almost touching as the man in black's eyes once more turned to iron. "You don't understand. I don't want this. I don't want to kill you. Just go away and leave me be."

Then the cloaked figure shoved away, towering over the downed youth for a moment before hobbling back into the shadows.

***

Kron knew he should have killed the lad. There was one simple reason why he had not. The boy was young, far too young. As bad as the boy might be, he deserved life, at least enough of it to decide what kind of man he would become. Was he even twenty? Kron thought not. And though the man in black did not dwell upon it, the lad also reminded him of another young person he had once known, a boy slain with far too few years in his life, a boy who would have been but five or six years younger than this one on the roof.

Kron clumped across the rooftop, angling toward a back corner away from the youth with the two swords. He kept a watch on that downed figure, but for whatever reason, the young man just lay there, his arms out at his sides, his hands still gripping his weapons.

***

Eel could barely breathe. He was so amazed to be alive, he didn't know what to think. By all rights, he should have been dead. Darkbow should have cut his throat from ear to ear, but the man had not. Why? He had said he did not want to kill Eel. Would a killer say such? True, the man in black had shown little reluctance against Eel's comrades, but that had been open combat. When Darkbow had risen above the lad with that dagger flashing, something had brought a pause to the man. There had been a change in his features, a loosening of the eyes. Darkbow had taken one look at Eel's face and everything had changed.

Kron Darkbow had spared Eel's life, for what reason the young man did not know. What he *did* know was the man he had claimed as an enemy was not a heartless monster, not some nameless face that posed a threat. Despite his demeanor, Kron Darkbow was a man with a certain sense of honor.

Eel could not kill such a man.

When he had not known Kron's face, before he had interacted with the fellow, it was an easy matter to think of his foe as blank, without a face, without a soul. But Eel had seen just a bit of Darkbow's soul, and it had left him reeling.

He could not get up. Though the man in black no longer pressed upon his chest with a knee, it was as if he was still there, pressing with his spirit, with his conscious.

No, Kron Darkbow was not a man who needed killing, who *deserved* killing.

A banging noise snapped the youth's head around to one side. A door on the rooftop had been opened. There, against a light from inside the small building that housed the top of the stairwell, multiples figures could be seen pouring forth.

Eel rolled over on his side and stretched out a hand to his companions. "Wait." He had tried to shout the word, but it had come out as a weak croak.

There were three of them, that much Kron could tell in the shadows. The two on the wings were average size, average build, shaking out weapons in their hands. But the one in the middle, that one was a wall of dark blocking out the stars beyond. That one was the size of a warhorse, and snorted like one. It was the beast that had battered down the Asylum gate, now returned to spread more violence.

Would this night never end? Kron's shoulders sagged as he edged toward the side of the building, slumping as if it would help to hide him in the dark. His right boot felt the ledge, another alley just under him, and he winced at the growing numbness spreading through his other leg. He would not be able to move much longer. His left thigh was already stiffened, the knee locking up.

He glanced behind into the back street, a river of darkness nearly beneath his boots. A two-story drop. Could he make it? He thought he could hang-drop from the ledge, but he did not have time in his condition to kneel down and climb over the side, nor did he have time to work out his rope and grapnel.

The three assassins moved in, weapons hefted, their bodies outlined by the night's sky beyond.

"You killed my Kaf," the biggest one said with a voice of gravel.

Kron's eyes narrowed from confusion. Kaf? He did not know a Kaf. He had killed a number of people over the years, so this monstrosity could somehow be related to any of them.

As the largest figure hefted its enormous hammer above a bulky shoulder like that of hillside, Kron pondered that he had never experienced another human so large other than the mountain folks of The Needles range, and that was a place far from civilization. To witness such a mass here in the city was unnerving, a giant striding the streets of Bond. He readied his dagger, and on second thought slid his left hand down to retrieve the other, smaller blade from his boot. He did not want to kill, but he was not going down without a fight.

The youth laying in the streetlight was suddenly sitting up, rolling onto his knees, one hand extended towards his companions in the shadows.

It was enough to draw Kron's attention for a moment.

In a blur the giant bucked forward, the sledgehammer whizzing in from Kron's left at the height of his head. The man in black ducked and hopped one step forward within the swinging distance of the brute, slicing up with both blades.

One dagger raked across an arm as wide as a mule's neck, opening flesh. The other blade glanced across a rib, sprouting a few drops of blood unnoticed in the darkness.

Neither attack seemed to effect the giant. The hammer spiraled around and slid back, now gripped in two monstrous hands, the weapon's head low and to one side.

Kron took a step back, as much from surprise at the failing of his assault as from an attempt at putting distance between him and his would-be killer.

His left leg went out from under him, having had enough. He tilted back, one dagger twirling from his hand as he stuck out an arm in an attempt to regain balance.

Two massive arms worked like pistons and shot the giant hammer forward, the flat of its head springing toward the man in black's jaw.

Sensing more than seeing the intended blow, Kron tried to roll his head back, throwing himself further off his equilibrium.

The hammer caught him across the chin, just barely. But it was enough to crack his head back and send him flying toward the alleyway beyond.

Kron saw stars for a moment as he realized he had never been hit so hard in his life. He felt cold wind rushing past him.

Then darkness.

***

There were snappings and crackings after the man in black went over the edge, the sounds like that of wood breaking. Or bone. Lots of bone.

Silence followed.

The bulk of Mama Kaf moved to the side of the building facing the alley and stared down into that inky blackness. What she was hoping to see, Eel had not a clue considering how dark it was.

The big woman spun around and marched toward the roof exit. "I want to see the body. I want to *know* he's dead."

None of the other three on the rooftop had any argument with that, and none of them stood in her way.

Once she was gone, Eel glanced into the shadows at the other two. There in the last he had not wanted Kron Darkbow dead, and had hoped to spare the man, but there was little to be done about it now. Mama Kaf had sought revenge and she had found it.

What else was there to do? The young thief slid his swords into their scabbards and took off at a jog after the big woman.

Soon enough the remaining thugs were gathered in front of the two-story building, shouts soon bringing Spider and the rest. Another lantern was sparked and the pack headed toward the alley where Darkbow was expected to be found dead.

A whistle. Shrill, not too distant.

Then a shout. "Halt there, you lot!"

Eel's head snapped around to the west. City guards! A half dozen of them jogging up the street.

"Run!" someone yawped.

Then they were fleeing, the whole group, thoughts of Kron Darkbow temporarily out of their minds. Even Mama Kaf only gave the approaching guards a snarl, and as huge as she was managed to keep up with those who were much younger and lighter.

The whistle sounded again, a little more distant this time but followed by the noises of boots smacking against the brick road.

The race was on.

So much for retrieving Darkbow's body.

13

The world swam in blackness, blacker than the night, blacker than the heart of a cave, blacker than the soul of a killer. Kron found himself afloat in that world, gently tossed about on waves of nothingness, his mind reeling as if he were drunk. For the longest time he supposed he must be dead and this was the afterlife afforded him by whatever resided beyond the veil of the living. There was no pain here other than a meek rolling of his stomach, nor was their warmth or cold. He floated upon a breaker of foaming air, being pushed along as if by the guiding hand of some ancient, benevolent god.

He tried to blink, but found he had no lids for such. For that matter, he discovered he had no eyes nor limbs nor body of any sort. He simply was. All that was left of him was an expression of will, perhaps the deepest part of him, the soul or spirit or whatsoever the philosophers and priests would call it. There were no emotions, no flickerings of past hates and loves, no feelings of regret.

Just a gliding and hovering sensation.

Where were his parents? His uncle? What of Wyck and the wizard Maslin Markwood, former companions recently dead? Were not those who had gone before supposed to greet him in the afterworld? There was no light to long for, no blaze of glory to reach out to. Had all the tales of the churches been wrong? Or had he found himself doomed so some layer of a hell? If Hell, he doubted the awfulness of the place. So far the sensations had been not unpleasant. Also, if Hell, where were the demons? Kron had met such beasts before, had experienced them personally threatening and in combat, thus he knew them to exist.

Once before he had believed himself dead, but that experience had been far different from this one. There had been fields of green, mountains along the horizon. He had not been dead, of course, Randall having pulled him back from the brink. But there was no Randall here and now.

Or was each death different? Did a man or woman expect too much, only to find varying worlds beyond life?

A sharp pain stabbed Kron in the side, followed by a similar one in his left leg. Then anguish encircled him, not as hard as those first pains but low and steady and throbbing. How? He had had no body but moments before, now here he was, feeling as if raked with a slow fire.

Since he once more had a body, that meant he also had eyes. He tried to open them, fighting against a heaviness upon his orbs. His body did not want to cooperate. It did not want to open his eyes. Perhaps it knew best, but he forced himself to look anyway, the simple process of lifting his lids like shredding a piece of his soul.

Blackness. More blackness. But different than what he had been experiencing. Here there was no dipping and swelling, no sensation of sailing upon invisible waves. This blackness was flat, cold, unrelenting. As for floating, here there was nothing to float upon. His back was pressed against something hard, here and there a sensation as of sharp pins poking into his flesh. A familiar numbness crept through his lower extremities, heavier on his left side, making him feel weighted down. For a moment he was dizzy, disoriented, almost as if returning to that invisible ocean of but moments earlier.

A harsh shrillness blasted his ears, tugging him fully into consciousness and new levels of pain. He nearly cried out as agony wracked his body. There was nowhere upon him which did not hurt. Some areas were pained less than others, holding only a vague bruising pressure that was tolerable. His left leg and his back were not so lucky, experiencing torment like that of torture. Kron rolled to one side, felt himself lightheaded once more, and nearly gagged as vomit filled his throat. For a second his lips held back, then he could help it no more and expelled his dinner from earlier.

Once he was reduced to dry heaves he lay panting, something hard pressing into the side he laid upon. The sound of shouts and people running came to his ears, followed once more by that shrill dissonance. It was a whistle, a whistle of the city guard.

More shouts. Growing faint. Boots tromping. The jangle of chain armor. Faint. Fainter.

Gone.

Kron chuckled, flecks of regurgitated food flying from his lips in the darkness. It mattered little the city guards had not found him. It was not likely they could do anything for him. Even if he had been able to manage it, calling for assistance would have been futile. He believed he was dying.

He had lost too much blood. He could feel it. Though the wound in his leg had dried, there had been too much loss, too much stress put upon his heart. Then, there had been ... a fall? No, first a knock to the chin. A mountain had slammed into him, knocking him back into blackness. Then ... what?

He had fallen, of course. Into the alley which he had been standing above. But what had he landed upon? Surely that was not dirt or brick pressing into his back.

He twisted his head in order to search for a source of light and discovered new levels of pain. His neck. His jaw. He felt as if his head had been dipped into a pool filled with lightning. His mouth locked up, sending jarring shivers throughout his frame.

Kron rolled further to the side, hoping to break himself from this torture.

And he was falling once more.

It was not far. Something tore at his side and he heard cloth tearing. Then he slammed into a dusty hardness that splashed his face with grit. For a moment he could not take in air, the taste of dirt on his tongue and filling his nostrils, the sudden jolt of landing pushing against his ribs. His head sunk and air seeped back into him, slowly keeping him alive. He closed his eyes for a moment, just a moment, needing the rest from the physical abuse, the pain, the tiredness.

Kron lifted his head, his neck cracking and his jaw shaking once more. He opened his eyes. His line of sight was from a low position, and he realized he was laying on packed earth. Ahead of him was the end of an alley facing a well-lit street. Cabbage Street. He had been trying to reach that road but minutes earlier. Or had it been hours? Or days? It mattered little. From there had come the sounds of running and whistles. If he could manage to move, he would not go that direction. He might run into the city guard which eventually would lead to aid, but he just as likely could come up against those who wanted him dead. He had no idea of what he would find out there.

With a gasp he twisted his head around to look up at the sky bordered by two tall, black walls. There was no sign of the moon, but stars continued their slow travels across the universe. Still night, then, so no more than a few hours at most had likely passed, if that.

His wavering eyes traveled the ledges of the rooftops, seeking any sign of his pursuers. He found nothing, which didn't necessarily mean he was safe. They might still be up there, or they might be making their way down to him. He doubted both. The sounds from the street made him think the guards had shown up, chasing away his would-be killers. Which still did not give him motivation to want to reach the street. Too many lights. There was no telling who might see him, who might inform others about the dying man in the road.

At least Beggars Row was dark on this end of town, the strip in front of the Asylum nearly black at night. One of Kron's pet projects had been to add a pair of lamps outside the gate, but now he was glad he had yet to do so. That way there would be darkness. That way would also be a direction his assassins would not expect him to travel, not as injured as he was. Considering his options, to Kron, returning to the Asylum made perfect sense. He was little closer to the healing tower, and no closer to the guard barracks. There was no chance he would allow himself to appear in the open on the lit streets, which meant his opportunities for travel were limited. The path to the Asylum, back along alleys and then across a dark road, offered his best opportunity for survival. If he could reach his tent, there were bandages and some few herbs and salves, nothing that would heal him completely but would at least strengthen his body to some little extent and give him a better chance of fighting off infection.

The Asylum it was to be. If he could make it there and wrap his wounds, then when the morning came he could call for help. More than likely the city guard would notice or be called to his front gate. It would be difficult for the waking citizens to not notice the battered gate and the dead horse just beyond. Such an image would stand out even in the Swamps.

The problem was in reaching the Asylum. Even with his pounding head, Kron could guess about where he was within the labyrinth of alleys, and the Asylum was not far. The gate was probably within one hundred yards, the tent no more than half that from the grounds entrance. Not so long a distance to travel, unless one had had an arrow through their leg, a nearly broken jaw and dozens of other minor wounds.

Well, he would never get there unless he tried.

He used both hands to push himself up, then shifted his weight to his right knee. For a moment he swayed, sticking out a hand to steady himself. Instead of touching a wall, his gloved fingers came up against something heavy made of wood. He ran his hand along the length and edges of the object and came to realize there were wooden crates stacked between him and the building on his right. Those must have been what he had first landed upon during his plummet from the roof. Those crates had likely saved his life, or at least saved him from a broken neck. Then he had rolled off the side of the top crate, and that had been the second, shorter fall.

Kron promised himself he would have to find out what merchant or warehouse worker had placed those wooden boxes. They deserved a few gold coins, or a tankard of ale.

First he would have to live through the night to keep that promise.

Leaning against the crates, he forced himself up on his good leg, wincing all the while. Slowly he turned about to face the depths of the alley. His eyes had adjusted somewhat to the dark, but he could still barely make out the path ahead. If memory served, this alley ended in a three-way junction with new arteries running right and left. Kron wanted to go left.

***

"You *think* Kron Darkbow is dead?"

The words did not sound promising, and Eel realized his uncle meant them to be full of skepticism. Laying there in bed, barely awake with the covers pulled up to his chest, Kerjim did not look happy. And when Kerjim was not happy, Eel usually was not happy.

"We barely got out of there without being caught," the young thief tried to explain, his own look a mixture of amazement and bewilderment. "He set two of my men on fire. *Fire*. Whoever heard of such a thing? I'd almost think he was a mage."

Kerjim scowled as he sat up in the bed. "A simple trick. Rare in this part of the world, but back in the homeland it was common enough."

Eel wasn't finished, his voice shaking, almost panicked. "Then he nearly cut a man open, and impaled another with these little darts. He pounded poor Kurif, and all with a hole in his leg. I've never seen someone take so much abuse then keep dishing it out."

Kerjim stretched forth a hand and snapped his fingers to draw his nephew's focus. "He's just a man, Eel. Don't let it distract you. Many a soldier has kept on fighting while his guts are spilling out all around them. It happens."

The youth's wide eyes stared back at his uncle. "But he spared me. He was right on top of me, his dagger ready to plunge. Then he backed off. I don't know why."

The Pursian frowned. Then he smacked the side of the bed, causing it to shake. "Forget that nonsense! I wanted you to make sure Darkbow was dead, and it sounds as if you failed to accomplish this. What happened?"

Eel shook his head to clear his mind, the memories rushing back upon him as he stood there in the small chamber above The Stone Pony. "We were on a roof. There were shadows everywhere. He was barely able to stand, and I thought he'd fall down before any of us got to him. But Mama Kaf, she went right to him. He got in a couple of wounds on her, but then she tagged him with that big hammer of hers. He went falling over the side of the roof into an alley. We heard all kinds of crashing noises. Sounded like he landed in a pile of lumber."

Kerjim nodded. "Did you go down to see the corpse?"

"We were going to, but then a squad of city guards showed up. They must have heard the fighting, or maybe somebody from one of the apartments sent word to them."

The Docks boss closed his eyes and rubbed at them. "So you didn't see the body?"

"We couldn't," Eel said. "The guard were on our tails. Like I said, we were lucky to get away. If I hadn't already ordered the wounded to be carried off, we would have been arrested."

Kerjim opened his eyes and sighed. "Nephew, I am disappointed, but I suppose you did the best you could manage."

Eel nodded.

"However," the Pursian went on, "we need to make sure this man is dead."

Eel kept nodding. "I'll send someone to --"

"No. Do this yourself. Find that body. Or make sure he's dead."

***

Sliiide. Lurch. *Sliiide.* Lurch. His movement was like that of a drunken ship, drifting to one side before righting himself and forging ahead. It was nearly enough to make Kron want to vomit again, but there was nothing left in his stomach. He was forced to keep his head down to lessen the vertigo as the growing sensation of numbness spread throughout his body, slowly beating back the pains, small and large, that layered him.

At least he was within the grounds of the Asylum once more, having worked his way through the rubbish that remained of his gate and then around his dead horse, the poor beast. He glanced about for his sword, still believing it must have fallen during his tumult near the gate, but had no luck spotting the weapon in the dark.

Fortunate to have made it so far, he realized he would not be able to walk much longer. The path across Beggars Row had been slow going, and the occasional sound of voices in the distance had brought concerns of his enemies returning. Still, the alleys had been far worse, stumbling along in the dark with only brick walls as a guide, refuse consistently in his path to be avoided or trodden upon. The twists and turns in the veins of the city had brought new levels of pain, bringing Kron's left leg back from numbness temporarily to share with him what felt to be the flames of Hell rushing throughout his body. He might have fainted, perhaps more than once. He could not remember. His mind, like his eyesight, was blurry.

Now, here at the bottom of the hill leading up to the Asylum's main building, he lifted his head just enough, the cloak's hood hanging almost into his eyes. Up ahead lay his tent. If he could find any hope of survival, it would start there.

Sliiide. Lurch. *Sliiide.* Stumble, almost falling. He stuck a hand out for balance, managing to keep on his feet. He stood there for a moment, hoping to retain his equilibrium. Finding he was not going to plant himself on the ground again, Kron continued forward, knowing if he had fallen he might never have gotten up again.

Hours passed. Or so it seemed. The sky moved little, the moon now hiding but the stars continuing to keep their sentry positions.

The next time Kron looked up, he had to force a grin. The tent was right in front of him, mere inches away.

He brushed aside a flap and pitched through the entrance, collapsing on a pallet layered in blankets. Instant relief came to his limbs and bruises, and he could breathe easier.

Laying there in the dark he allowed the sounds of the city to come to him once more. This corner of the Swamps was relatively quiet compared to other areas, especially here around the Asylum and a near cemetery to the east, but there were still a few abstracted voices and other noises able to reach him. He had heard similar sounds on the street, but none directly around him. Beggars

Row had been quiet and empty. Someone had paid off the closest inhabitants of the apartments across from Kron's property, or threats had been made. Either way, money or power were involved. To send a dozen or more assassins after one man meant planning, which meant a planner. Someone had wanted him dead. The youth from the rooftop, the very one he had encountered days earlier during the riots, seemed unlikely to be behind the night's attack. There was someone else. During their first meeting, the boy had mentioned involvement of the guilds. Then Gris had brought up the name Kerjim, apparently the head of the Docks Guild, the most powerful union in the city since Belgad's exit. Could this Kerjim be the one behind the attack? Kron had to wonder what the man would have against him. Perhaps there was someone else, someone whom Kron had overlooked or forgotten. The monster with the giant hammer had mentioned a name, informing Kron he had slain someone named Kaf. It was a name unfamiliar to him. But even that large figure wielding the hammer had not struck Kron as the leader of the pack, more like a spearhead thrust ahead of a charge.

More importantly, Kron had to decide what he was going to do about the attempted assassination.

He had lived so much of his early life concentrating upon vengeance, he had known no other path than one of rage, of extreme violence. Then he had learned of another path, another way. A dark-haired beauty with midnight eyes had opened possibilities for the young man that was Kron Darkbow. They had never kissed. They had rarely touched. But still, her influence had arrested his soul, had given him sentiments of a life beyond revenge and caprice and acrimony. In the end, their end, his dark side had been too much for her. Such was life. But he had promised himself he would improve, he would no longer be a man of wild abandon who allowed his lust for carnage to get the better of him.

He had known no other ways than ones of violence, but that did not mean he had to kill. He did not have to bring agony, to torture, to rampage. There was little gentleness in him, but he could lay aside his harshest of weapons, his heavy burden of guilt that came with the tempest of his actions.

Only now did Kron realize his mistake.

He had gone too far to the other edge. No, he was not the pacifist, not the peace monger. He was no Randall Tendbones. But he tried to keep reined the dark beast that lurked within his heart, a beast that had lain in hiding for some time.

In life there were lessons, and this night Kron Darkbow had been taught another one. Some men you could not ignore. Some men you could not approach with an olive branch. They came for you, with all arms. These men, they were not ones to be pitied or overlooked. They would not allow themselves to be. When one's very existence was a threat to them, no matter Kron had not known he was a threat, there was no avoidance.

Kron could flee or he could hide.

Or he could fight back.

It would not be the first time he had exploded a personal vendetta upon the city of Bond. This time, however, he would do it differently. He had always been silent in his vengeance, but it had been an emphatic silence, one that could not be ignored by those outside his ring of destruction. Now he would bind himself to the shadows more than he ever had, waiting and watching, prodding his foe.

Yes, Kron Darkbow had hoped to turn from violence. Instead he had found new excuses for it and a new direction.

His eyes closed, and he could feel himself drifting off to sleep. He forced himself up on one elbow. Now was not the time to enter a coma.

A gloved hand searched his surroundings, fumbling over tools and papers and other equipment in the black of the tent. Eventually Kron found what he was looking for and several seconds later there was a flaring as a lamp caught fire.

He held the light up and glanced about his temporary home. Despite the small ruckus he had just brought about within the tent, everything appeared where it had been when he had last seen it. His would-be assassins who had hidden here had not touched anything, at least not that he could tell.

The lamp placed on the ground next to his bed, he pulled a small leather bag to him and fumbled through its contents before withdrawing a roll of pale cloth that could be used as bandages and several small metal vials.

He popped a cork from one of the containers and downed its liquid contents, resting back on an elbow once more to allow the elixir to do its work. It wouldn't be much, but it would help.

After several minutes of repose he got to work with the bandages, cutting strips and layering them with a powder of herbs from one of the other bottles. It took some time for him to strip down his clothes, but eventually he managed with more than a few winces and pain-filled bellows. Wrapping his leg was an easy enough task, the numbness there having deadened most of the pain. Here and there on his arms and chest were lesser wounds which he bandaged as best he could. When he was finished, he pulled on his tattered garb and opened another vial, taking another swig.

Sitting on the edge of his bed, he already felt stronger. Not much, but enough for now.

A flickering from outside drew his attention.

He glanced about, found and retrieved his longbow along with a handful of arrows, then doused the lamp.

Stringing the bow was a difficult task, taking more muscle than he would have liked to use, but he gritted past the pain and prepared the weapon. Placing an arrow against the string, he elbowed through the opening and glanced outside.

There was no sign of his attackers returning, only a slight glow from the Asylum itself.

Kron stepped out into the night and stared up at the entrance to the building. The main door hung open, dancing lights beyond the portal.

Who could be there? To his knowledge there were only two keys to that door, one in his possession in a small bag on his belt, the other locked away in a box in an Uptown depository. Of course it was not impossible the lock had been picked, but who would want to go into the Asylum?

The only thing that made sense was one or more of his antagonists had forced their way into the place earlier. Kron did not remember noticing a light when he had approached, but he had been in little mind of anything. Or perhaps his attackers had returned and were in waiting for him.

He paused to think. He was stronger than he had been but an hour earlier, but was he in any condition to enter another fight? Feeling the stiffness of his left leg, the taste of copper still on his tongue, he knew he was in no state for a confrontation. Which, in his mind, made it a challenge.

Stubborn as always, he pulled back slightly on the bow's drawstring and limped his way up the rest of the hill to the Asylum door. All the while he kept his eyes open for any signs of an ambush or movement within shadows. Being the dark of night, he saw nothing. It did not help his eyes were still weak and somewhat blurred.

Staring down the arrow against his bow, his weapon hand also gripping the other arrows, he approached the entrance to the building, staring as if mesmerized by the faint orange light dancing upon the inner walls. Someone had lit the torches within. As far as Kron knew, those wrapped bundles of straw had not been alive within the Asylum since the disaster there last summer.

He paused outside the door, pulling the bowstring back just a little further, staring in at the dust on the floor. Clean marks showed the former location of a giant cage that had once surrounded the entrance, the iron bars having been taken down at some point, likely by workers or possibly locals stealing the metal before Kron had become owner. There were no other signs anyone had passed through the entrance. Still, someone clever or making use of magic could have accomplished as much. Kron knew he could have so with a little planning.

Enough. The burning lights were adequate evidence someone was inside.

He crouched to make himself a smaller target, once more grimacing at the tightness of his left leg, then vaulted through the opening.

The bow swung from left to right, sweeping the room for any immediate dangers.

There were none.

The only movement other than himself came from the frolicking flames atop the many ensconced torches.

Kron stared up and down the long room, then across its width to the high, three-storied wall of walkways and prison cells. The only sounds were of the crackling fires and dripping noises coming from the ragged edges of a large hole in the center of the room, chunks of stone and lumber and iron sticking up from it and appearing much like its twin in the roof far above.

Kron's shoulders sagged. What was this? Some kind of trick?

He glanced about and found a long, heavy desk shoved up against one wall. He remembered this had once been the desk of Chief Guard Shaltros, the poor man having been killed during the tumult at the Asylum. How the desk had wound up here Kron had not a clue, as it originally had been in a room far down one of the pair of halls that ran off from the main chamber. But since it was available, he would make use of it. He edged his way over and leaned against the heavy piece of furniture, giving his tired body a momentary respite.

A metallic din not unlike that of a an iron bar being struck sounded from the blackness of the massive pit in the middle of the chamber. Kron shifted so as to have a better line of sight with his bow should someone or something pop out of the hole.

The floor gently shook beneath his boots, just enough to send shivers up his legs and spine, minor pains springing to life once more throughout his body. As swiftly as it had come, the shaking drifted away.

A hollow moan built up from the direction of the hall far to Kron's left. The rolling intonation grew gradually, building louder and deeper before simpering away to a hissing noise that became nothing.

Kron shifted again, his arrow facing the hallway. "Is someone there?"

The response was faded, much like a languid wind as it whistled through an open window.

"Show yourself," Kron said.

The entrance door slammed shut, jarring the room.

The fires died.

A cold wind blew across the man in black's face.

Wrapped in complete darkness, not even the stars shining through the hole in the ceiling, Kron eased back on the desk, lowering his bow and resting his arms. There was nothing to see, thus nothing at which to aim. Whatever was coming for him would come, whether he could catch sight of it or not.

A crackling noise as of bones crunching filled the air.

Kron sat motionless, unblinking, his nerves tight and ready to respond.

From the jagged edges of the hole in the floor an eerie bloom grew in luminescence, shedding its glow across the floor to the bottom edges of the walls. A faint smoke distended from the pit, climbing the air, thin arms of the fog stretching upward, clawing at nothingness.

"If you mean to frighten me," Kron spoke aloud, "your actions are wasted. I have fought cannibals and demons. I have faced down immortals. Do you think a handful of ghosts will scare me?"

As if in response, the smoke exploded in a silent blossom of pale colors, a thousand slender limbs reaching outward, forward. A face grew in the center of the misty globule, snarling and filled with hate.

Kron sneered. "So you come for me, the man who killed all of you. I was beginning to have doubts you existed."

The features of the mystical visage elongated into that of a scream. A roar pealed. A heated blast shot forth from the maw with the force of a hurricane and pressed upon Kron, flapping his cloak behind him and furrowing into his flesh, warming him. He was nearly thrown back flat upon the desk, his weakened but muscled legs still holding him up as he dropped his weapon and arrows and braced his hands against the table beneath him.

A shadow darted from one side, slashing into the smoky face, cutting it in half. Another roar bellowed throughout the chamber, rocking the floor yet again, then the glowing mist was sucked back into the pit.

The torches sprang to life once more. The door creaked open.

Kron shook his head to clear his senses. What had just happened?

Images leaped into his mind, memories of his past. It was the Asylum he saw, still complete, the cells filled with screaming lunatics, guards and healers scurrying to and fro in desperate bids to quiet the madness. He watched prison doors pulled open, dirty and grimy maniacs rushing forth, clawing and tearing at those who were their keepers. Cudgels flashed. The insane were beaten down, some few of the strongest standing firm and retaliating, taking their opponents' weapons and using them. Skulls were crushed. Ragged teeth tore away throats. Blood and madness ruled.

That had been the Asylum but a year earlier, Kron well remembered. The place had not always been like that, often quiet and sad, but there had been moments of mania, when it seemed every patient was seething. He had been one of the handful of guards there to protect the inmates from themselves, and also to protect the outside world from having to deal with the madmen.

It seemed even in death the lunacy lived on, at least here in the Asylum.

A gloved hand rose to rub at his brow, to ease the headache left behind by the failing images in his mind.

Another set of impressions rushed into him, their force knocking him back against the desk nearly as hard as had the heated scream. He saw the rugged figure of Chief Guard Shaltros before him, behind him a line of others garbed in the fashion of the late Asylum guards, each wearing the gray tunics and black, floppy hats. The old man Vitman was there, as well as Triple, a man Kron had watched die, stabbed to death by an inmate. There was a pleading in their looks, a wanting, a yearning.

Kron tossed back his head and yelled, "What is it you want of me?"

Peace. The word was not spoken. It brushed across his thoughts, sending shivers along his shoulders. Another image formed behind his eyes, this one also of the guards, the dead men working together to place the mad patients back inside their cells. There was little violence to these motions, the figures of the inmates shackled at wrists and ankles, the guards gentle with them as doors of iron bars were opened then closed.

Kron slid from the edge of the desk, falling to his knees, for the moment dulled beyond the anguish that tore at his leg. Emotions swamped him as he grasped what was being asked of him, and he clasped his hands together before his closed eyes. The spirits of the dead wanted him to fulfill the duties he had performed so many times before, that of a gaoler. From the Prisonlands to the Asylum, his tasks had been those of imprisoning others, of harboring from the world the worst of the wicked and the aberrant. The dead, the ghosts of the Asylum guards, were seeking help in constraining the inmates, the patients, the insane, the dangerous.

His body wracked by waves of grief mixed with fury, he wrapped his arms around himself and rocked back and forth on the cold floor. In the distance moans grew and grew, like a living storm howling out its anguish. The torches flickered, some few sparking. Colors of all shades danced upon the walls, rays of light springing forth from the pit to blaze across the high wall of prison cells. Lightning clapped from the outside, followed by thunder that rolled across the building, shaking the walls. There was a battle going on within all that Kron witnessed, the souls of the protectors entwining and combating with those of the unhinged. The battle was for the Asylum itself, for the soul of the single man alive within the structure, for the freedom of good men to move on to the next world, and for the freedom of the depraved to continue to bring grief amongst the living.

Kron threw back his head once more, and with red, heated eyes glared at the dancing lights before him, the moans and lightning mixing into a tumultuous explosion of light and sound that made it impossible to hear anything else, even one's own words.

"There are men, living men, who deserve the same fate," the man in black spoke.

The storm within the building's walls calmed for a moment, coalescing into a silent, gigantic ball of crackling white flame, hovering above the pit into the Asylum's nether regions.

Kron stared blinking into that white glow. "Let us deal together, then"

There was no explanation from the spirits of the dead. They understood or they did not.

"It is said you feed upon emotion." The man in black bared his teeth and reached up to his throat, grasping the cloth of his shirt, tearing and ripping to reveal his chest thrust forward. "Then have your fill of mine!"

***

TY JOHNSTON

Climbing over the dead horse one of his comrade's had managed to kill, Eel nearly fell when the light show erupted at the main structure. Upon approaching the Asylum he had noticed a luminescence coming from the open entrance to the building, figuring Darkbow must be within. What the man would be doing Eel could only guess, probably tending to his wounds or perhaps seeking aid from a servant or someone. The thief had traveled back to the alley where he was sure Kron had fallen, but upon finding no body he decided the nearest place to look would be the Asylum itself.

Now he was here, in front of the place, and he was not sure he wanted to go closer. The glow from the doorway had exploded into rays of light reaching out, followed by crackles of thunder and lightning from a clear sky above. Most unsettling were the sounds, the moans and groans like those of men in their death throes. The experience was disturbing, enough to make the youth reconsider going forward.

But Eel had to know if Kron Darkbow were alive or dead. His uncle wanted to know for certain the man in black was vanquished, relieving any possibilities of Darkbow being a threat while, more importantly, giving Kerjim something to hold over the heads of the other guilds. Darkbow's slaying at the hands of Kerjim's associates, Eel specifically, would prove without a doubt the Pursian was the person who should run the Guild of Guilds, who should potentially replace Belgad the Liar.

Eel himself hoped Kron was still alive. The man could have killed him, but had not. To Eel, that meant something. Exactly what it meant, he was not yet sure. His emotions were unsettled on the matter. Darkbow was to be his target, his enemy, yet he had shown a sense of compassion, though only momentary. It made sense for the man in black to have defended himself during combat with the others, but he had shown restraint when confronting a downed Eel, the thief having been at Darkbow's mercy.

There was only one way to determine the dark man's fate. Eel had to climb that hill and look through that door, even though his senses were being assaulted by what he guessed to be magic most spectral, possibly by some entity beyond his reckoning.

One shaky foot moved him ahead, but he was brought up short again as a glint of steel caught his attention to one side. He turned in that direction and knelt, discovering a lengthy sword laid out upon the ground. The weapon was plain but in excellent condition, it's brass hilt wrapped in black leather. None of his own men would have carried such a fine blade.

He lifted the weapon and tucked it beneath his left arm. What he would do with it was beyond him at the moment, but there was no reason to leave such quality steel unsheltered beneath the elements and available for anyone to take.

Back on track, step by step he made his way up the mild bluff, the flashing of colors from inside the Asylum continuing to enliven the darkness of the night just outside the doorway.

As he grew nearer, the glow from within seemed to lessen though not completely fade. Eel thought he heard a voice, a rugged man's voice. Was this Darkbow? And to whom was he speaking? Eel had heard no one else other than those ghastly cries that had died away.

Drawing his short swords gradually so as to keep them from making noise, the young man edged toward the door.

147

The lights flared once more, brighter than ever, stabbing so hard Eel's eyes sprang tears.

But he would not be denied. He had to know.

The youth charged the last few steps, planting himself in the doorway.

What he saw he swore he would never tell to another living soul.

Part 2:
Deliverance

14

A considerable magical occurrence had happened within the city during the night. Of this Randall was aware as soon as he woke that morning. Such events were not common within Bond and would be noted by the handful of more experienced mages within the city. It was no exaggeration upon Randall's part that he was the most powerful of all, being the most powerful magical entity on the planet. Noticing a burgeoning of such energy came natural to him, as it would for anyone most would consider a god if they were only aware of his true identity.

The event came from the corner of the city where the Asylum was located, which brought additional concerns to the healer. Not only did his friend sometimes live there, but the last time there had been powerful magics within Bond, the Asylum had been involved. That time Randall himself had been partly to blame, but it did his nerves no good wondering what had happened this time. *Has Lord Verkain returned?*

He yanked a white tunic over his head, slipped on a pair of simple street clogs and scarfed down a quick breakfast of porridge with milk before heading out into the already bustling streets beneath the morning sun. As he made his way through the crowded intersections, he couldn't help but notice there were more people out and about than usual, walking this way and that about their daily business. It seemed ending the riots had brought the Swamps back to life. Randall was pleased to see this, though he was concerned about Kron.

Advancing along Beggars Row, he was passing the fenced cemetery on his right when he spotted two city guards standing at the Asylum walls. The two soldiers faced outward, shooing aside anyone seemingly curious.

Randall hustled ahead, slowing only when he saw the battered gate to the Asylum grounds, the gate busted from the inside, as if someone or something had wanted out. The corpse of Kron's horse just inside the gate did nothing to lessen the mage's concerns, nor did the sight of two more orange-clad figures standing over the poor beast.

As the healer approached, one of the guards in front of the gate's remains waved him on.

"Sergeant Gris!" Randall shouted past the sentries.

The larger of the two men studying the dead animal glanced toward the gate. "Let him through, Rogins."

The nearest soldier motioned for the healer to enter.

Randall wasted no time climbing over the twisted iron bars and rushing up to the sergeant. "Have you found him?"

Gris wore a look of concern. "No sight of him, but we've yet to investigate the main building."

Randall looked up the slight hill to the dark, massive structure, its front door hanging open.

The sergeant turned to follow the healer's gaze, then looked back to him. "What brought you here? Do you know something?"

Randall shook his head. "I sensed powerful magics. That's all I know."

Gris knelt and pointed to various disturbances in the grass and dirt around the horse. "There was obviously combat. Whatever happened, Kron didn't give them an easy target."

"How many were there?" the healer asked.

Gris stood and shrugged. "At least half a dozen. Likely more. A few locals said they heard screams and fighting in the middle of the night."

The healer turned away and began a march up the incline.

Leaving the other guards behind, the sergeant hustled after the mage, catching up as they passed Kron's tent. "Randall, we need to be prepared for the worst."

"He's not dead," the healer said with a nervous grin. "Believe me, I'd know."

Gris didn't question. Wizards had their secrets, after all, Randall more than most.

As the two approached the Asylum entrance, a shadow appeared in the doorway.

Gris put a hand on his sword.

A familiar black glove lifted in a weak salute and Kron appeared from the darkness beyond, his face as pale as that of a dead man.

Randall gasped at the sight of his friend. Dried blood caked Kron's left leg from the thigh down, and the man walked with a slight limp. His cloak had been shredded along the bottom, various other minor tears sprouting ragged threads throughout the black garb. Worst of all were Kron's white, flat features and wide, unblinking eyes. It was almost as if he were in a daze.

"Kron?" Gris asked with caution.

"Hello." Kron's voice sounded as if it came from deep within a well. "What do I have the pleasure of your visits?"

The healer and the city guardsman looked at one another as if the answer should be obvious.

Gris pointed down the hill where more of his men were appearing along with a few city workers, long knives in hands and a mule-driven wagon outside the gate. "There was obviously a disturbance last night. I'm here to investigate."

"Oh, that." The man in black shook his head. "A simple matter really. A group of assassins tried to kill me."

Randall and Gris traded looks once more.

"Are you alright?" the healer asked.

"I am fine."

Randall started. "Let me see to your wounds."

Kron held up a hand to halt his friend's approach. "I have been attended to already."

"You still look as if you need healing." Randall did not appear accept the man in black's disregard of aid.

His movements stiff, Kron glanced down at his body. "I do look the worse for wear, don't I?" His head came back up. "Regardless, I am fine. At worst, my muscles continue to be a little sore. I will walk it off."

He took off past his friends, his strides wide with purpose down the hill.

The two turned and rushed after him, Gris running around in front and bringing all of them to a halt.

"I can't just let you leave, Kron," the sergeant said. "I'll need answers about what happened here last night."

"There is little I can tell you," Kron said.

Gris planted his fists on his hips. "You could start by telling me who attacked you."

"I know none of their names."

For the third time, the healer and sergeant traded glances. This was not the Kron Darkbow they knew. He was often standoffish, sometimes even morose, but the man before them was almost mechanical.

"Perhaps you should come back to the tower with me," Randall suggested.

"I have someplace to be." Kron motioned toward his two friends standing in front of him. "If you would be so kind as to move, I can be on my way."

"Where are you going?" Gris asked.

"To speak with the Finder."

Gris sighed and shook his head. "So it was Lalo's men who attacked you?"

"I do not believe so," Kron said. His features grew perturbed. "I have told you what little I know of last night's events, and I am well. May I be on my way?"

"I still need to talk to you about what happened here," the sergeant said.

"There is nothing further to tell."

Gris raised a brow, his other eye narrowing. "I can have you arrested, by Ashal. Then I could ask my questions back at the barracks."

Kron's eyes compressed to mere slits and locked onto his friend's features. "That ... would not be suggested."

The healer and the sergeant took a step back. Both had witnessed Kron's darkest side before, but rarely if ever had it been turned upon them.

Gris cursed, then shrugged. "Alright. Be on your way, then. Just make sure to stop by the barracks later today for questioning. I'll need answers when I have to explain to someone why city guards and a street crew were needed to clean up a mess at the Asylum."

Kron gave a curt nod, then sidestepped the two and stalked down the hillside.

"That wasn't Kron," Gris said to the other man.

"Oh, I think it was," Randall responded, "but I'm not sure he's alone."

***

The boy was asleep. Kerjim should have known. A wild night of gallivanting about town with his crew, without Darkbow's body to show for it. The Docks boss was beginning to wonder if his nephew truly had what it took to be a leader of a pack of thieves.

He kicked the edge of the bed, jarring the youth awake. Eel sat up straight, still dressed in his clothes from the night before, his hands reaching for daggers at his belt.

Perhaps the boy has some talents, after all. But Kerjim wouldn't let Eel know that. "Wake up."

The thief bunched a pillow behind him before leaning back against it. His eyes slowly glazed over again from lack of sleep. "Do you need something, uncle?"

"Do I *need* something?" Kerjim's voice was high. "You imbecile! Do you remember what you were supposed to be doing?"

"Taken care of."

Kerjim halted. His tongue had been ready for a lashing, but the youth's words had brought him up short. The Pursian sank into a chair near the bedroom's door. "He is dead, then?"

Eel nodded, rubbing at his eyes.

"You saw the body?" the Pursian asked.

Eel rolled over and thrust a hand beneath his bed, that hand rummaging around and making clunking sounds of metal upon wood. When the hand withdrew, it gripped the handle of a lengthy sword.

The youth held the weapon between himself and his uncle. "Proof enough for you?"

Kerjim glanced at the blade. He could not be positive it had belonged to the man known as Kron Darkbow, but it obviously was not a street weapon, not something Eel or any of his friends or Kerjim's Docks thugs could afford. Either Eel had found Darkbow's body and then retrieved the weapon, or he had stolen it from someone else. It made no sense for the lad to have gone to the trouble of taking the weapon from elsewhere, so logic dictated the sword had belonged to the late, great Kron Darkbow.

Kerjim smiled, reaching out for the long blade.

"I want it back," Eel said.

The Pursian darted his nephew a dark look while hefting the weapon in his hands. "Why should you have it?"

"I earned it," Eel said. "Not only did I lead the attack, but I'm the one who went back to discover the body."

Kerjim squinted. "Where did you find him?"

"In the alley where we left him."

"Dead?"

"Dead."

Kerjim gave a nod of approval, then returned the weapon to his kin. "Very well, but take good care of this sword."

"I will." Eel returned the weapon to its hiding spot beneath his bed, then glanced back to his uncle. "Anything else?"

His nephew was becoming a little flippant. Kerjim might have to do something about that, but not now, not when he had so much to do. The Pursian stood. "I'll need those signatures for the Thieves Guild."

"You'll have them by tomorrow morning," Eel said.

"I'd better." Kerjim snapped a nod and exited the room.

<u>15</u>

Staring into his third glass of red wine for the day, Lalo the Finder was already deciding it would not be his last, and it was not even lunchtime yet. Reclining on a wooden folding chair, he took a hefty sip from his drink, lifted his head and stared out from the second-story veranda on the back of his mansion. At the edge of the estate's grounds was the tall stone wall he had watched constructed more than ten years earlier. Beyond that wall lay the depths of a marshland that had given the Swamps its name who knew how many hundreds of years earlier.

Watching the frogs and lizards and other beasts swirling through the muck, Lalo recognized the swamp was not that different from what his life had become of late. Layered, filled with reptiles and worse. Scavenger birds darted here and there for a brief meal, plucking away at anything small and living before scaling off to lands unknown. Lalo knew the feeling.

He did not react when the door behind him opened, but merely brought his glass to his lips once more.

"It is early to be drinking, isn't it?" The words were cold, stilted, but the voice was recognizable as that of Kron Darkbow.

Without looking around, the Finder waved his glass toward the quagmire. "I am busy reading my future."

"I did not realize you were a fortuneteller."

Lalo chuckled, then glanced over a shoulder. What he saw killed his laughter. Darkbow looked worse for wear than usual, what with his tattered clothing and the blood caking one leg, but that was not what brought the Finder up short. It was that face, white as the moon, and those eyes with a hint of lightning behind them. Something had happened to Darkbow since they had last met.

"Am I disturbing you?" Kron asked.

The wine glass was placed upon a small table to one side. "By all means, have a seat."

The man in black moved onto the veranda, stationing himself behind a chair opposite the Finder, but he did not sit. "My apologies for coming upon you like this. The front door was open. I was surprised to find no guards."

Lalo tore his eyes away with difficulty, finding the view beyond the grounds little better. Still, looking away he found it somewhat easier to be himself. He flitted a hand in the air as if he had no concerns. "There were those killed during the riots, the rest ... well, they could no longer resist the urgings of the Guild of Bodyguards. They left, quit. The remaining servants fled, fearing some old enemy of Belgad's would return seeking vengeance. I believe Stilp is still around here somewhere, if you can find him. Probably filling his gullet in the kitchen."

"I have no need of him at the moment," Kron said, his tone level, his voice flat.

Lalo almost glanced to the man again but decided against it. Darkbow was obviously not an immediate threat. Otherwise, the Finder believed he would already be dead. But there was something changed, something *wrong*, about this Kron Darkbow. It was almost as if he was not the same man, but a puppet, a shadow, of the figure known as Kron Darkbow. Whatever was going on, Lalo doubted he wanted any part of it.

Still, the man had come here for a reason. "What can I do for you, Master Darkbow?"

Kron moved around to the front of the other chair and sat, grimacing as his left leg stretched out. "I may have a proposal for you."

The Finder could no longer help himself. He looked to the other man, finding himself unnerved by those unblinking eyes. He was barely able to talk, his words little more than a whisper. "I made you a proposal but days ago. You refused me."

"The situation in the city has changed."

Lalo nodded. He had to agree.

"First," Kron said, "tell me about the guilds."

"What is it you want to know?"

"Everything."

Lalo nearly choked. "There is much to tell."

"Start with the leadership," Kron prodded, "especially concerning the Docks."

Lalo forced his gaze away once more. It was the only way he could converse with this pale fellow. "You mean Master Kerjim."

"Yes, *Kerjim*. Tell me about him."

Lalo reached for his wine once more and took a drink. This was going to be a long conversation. "He has a nephew ..."

***

A haze preceded the smoke from the hearth, laying a thin layer of smog across the ceiling of The Stone Pony's main room. The patrons seemed not to notice, sharing their drinks and slurred speech at the bar or quaffing a mug or slurping gruel at a table.

Spider was one of them, sitting alone in the back next to the stairs that went to rooms on the level above. He sat with his back to the corner while munching a hunk of dark stale bread, a wooden plate before him showing the remains of some kind of small foul, a leather jack off to one side still reeking of the cheap liquid the establishment called ale.

Eating his lunch, he glanced around the room at the others present. A few he recognized from the streets, but most were unknown to him. He had spent too many years as one of Belgad's own, dealing mostly with lower-level local officials and the like, and knew he was out of touch with the common man. It didn't help that he had some few talents in the magical arena, marking him as a street mage and someone to be avoided until needed. None of this bothered Spider much. His personal goals had little to do with infamy or even dignity. Wealth was not even a major concern, though he was not one to shun coin. No, what Spider sought more than anything in the world was to be accepted, and to some extent protected, by the powers that be.

He had no major political aspirations, but simply wanted to be useful, to be noted. Which was why he had gone to work for Belgad the Liar in the first place. Belgad had been the biggest of the big shots in town. Now Belgad was gone, and though the Finder was a decent enough fellow and smart, he was not much of a leader. Kerjim, on the other hand, had had the audacity to step in and take control of things in Belgad's wake. Spider wanted to be with the winners, always, and lately it seemed Kerjim and his boys at the Docks were the winners. Though not stupid, Spider was a bit shallow in regard to others and what they could do for him and what he could do for them, but at least he could admit that to himself.

Which was all the more reason he put on a smile when he noticed Eel trouncing down the stairs from his room above. The smile vanished soon enough, however, when the street mage caught a glance of Eel's new possession, a big sword strapped to his back.

The young thief brushed past the table without paying the slightest attention to Spider, making a straight line for the exit.

"Hey, Eel," Spider called out, dropping the remains of his bread.

The thief stopped and turned around. "Spider." He shook his head as if he wasn't quite awake yet, which was possible. "Sorry, I didn't see you there."

"Care for some lunch?"

"Lunch?"

Spider laughed. "For you it's probably breakfast. Heard you were up even later than the rest of us."

Eel frowned and moved closer to the mage's table. "What are you talking about?"

"Kerjim is already spreading the word," Spider said. "Darkbow is gone, and you're the man who did it. I take it that's the dead man's sword on your back?"

Eel's face went white. "I didn't ... It was Mama Kaf who did it. I just found the body."

"Maybe so," the mage went on, "but you were in charge when the great man went down. To the leader goes the spoils."

The thief stood their in stunned muteness. It was obvious he didn't know what to say.

Spider patted a chair next to him. "Have a seat and get some food in you. You'll need it after last night's work."

His mind obviously elsewhere, Eel slid onto the offered seat. His eyes darted up to those of his companion. "So my uncle is telling everyone?"

"Of course. And why not? You'll be a big shot in this town soon, just like him. Hell, in a few years you might even be bigger."

Eel gave a slow nod.

Spider pointed over the youth's shoulder. "And that big sword you're carrying around is advertising enough. Soon everyone will know who you are. They'll know you're the man who killed Kron Darkbow."

"I'll be known as the man who killed the man who killed Belgad."

Spider chuckled again. "That's right. I hadn't thought of it that way."

Eel's eyes locked on the mage's again. "But how soon until someone wants to kill *me*?"

An uncomfortable feeling settled in Spider's stomach. He didn't like this sort of talk. Eel had too many worries, when he should have been glorifying in his success. It was time to change the subject. "You still accepting signatures for the Thieves Guild?"

Eel nodded, reaching inside his belt to withdraw the folded contract papers.

"You think I can sign up?" Spider asked.

Eel held up the papers. "I thought you were joining the Mages Guild."

"I am," the street mage said. "Your uncle says we can sign with more than one. Figured I'd melt into both guilds. Makes sense, don't you think, considering my background?"

The young thief nodded, then dropped the papers on the table as he pushed back his chair and stood. "Tell you what, Spider. Not only can you join, but you can be in charge." He turned and walked away.

Spider glanced to the papers, then looked up to the receding back of the youth. "Eel!"

The young man paused at the door to the outside, but he did not turn around.

"You sure about this?" Spider asked.

Eel nodded. "It's all yours."

Then he stepped out into the sunlight, bypassing a fellow in a city guard uniform coming in the door, the soldier pausing only long enough to admire the sword on the youth's back.

16

Some women were born beautiful. Some with luck. Some, talent. Others, intelligence. Kadath Osrm was born with three out of the four, and she figured that was a fair balance for a lack of beauty. It was not that she was an ugly woman, nor that she was plain. Staring into a hand mirror, she had to admit there were certain charms to her looks, most crafted by expensive cosmetics and a hint of magic. But she would never be classified as beautiful.

Which was fine with her. Who wanted to be one of a million honey-haired tramps who spread their knees for any horse-faced fool with a peanut swinging between his legs? Not Kadath Osrm, and she prided herself on that.

Returning the mirror to its home atop her vanity of white wood, she swiveled atop a stool and faced the open doors of the armoire on the other side of the room. Within were rows upon rows of silken finery in all colors imaginable. Jorsican blues, Hyponese reds, even Kobalan blacks. All crafted by regional hands with regional dyes. Being the head of the Merchants Guild had its perks after all, such as knowing when new shipments of expensive bolts of cloth were arriving, and how to get one's hands upon them for lower-than-market values.

She stood and crossed the room, the bottom of her lavender robes swashing across the smooth, lacquered floor. In front of the wardrobe she stopped and reached inside, brushing aside several cloaks and robes before her hands fell upon a cobalt-colored garment layered with darker frills around the short sleeves and the bottom of the floor-length skirt. Her eyes roamed over the piece, trying to remember if she had ever worn it. The outfit was a few years out of style, but she prided herself on being one who set trends, not followed them. Yes, this would be her garb for the upcoming meeting of guild masters.

A knock came at her door.

Osrm's brows knitted as she turned toward the room's only exit. "Toyler, I said I wanted no guests."

The door creaked open, revealing the stern features of the Bodyguards Guild master.

Osrm sighed as she tossed her hands down at her side. "What is it you want, Tuxra?"

"My apologies, Lady Osrm," the big man said. "Your servant was most insistent you were not to be interrupted, but there is a matter I felt should be brought to your attention immediately."

She glared at the man for a moment, then crossed the room and sat before her vanity once more. She threw up her arms from exasperation. "Very well, get on with it so I can return to my solitude."

Captain Tuxra grinned, showing teeth inside his beard. "Kron Darkbow is dead."

"What?" Osrm got to her feet once more.

"Kerjim's whelp, this Eel, he killed him."

"Are you positive?"

"The lad is showing off the bastard's sword everywhere he goes. Wears it on his back like some kind of war trophy, as if he'll ever see a front line."

Osrm sank onto her stool once more, her hands in her lap fidgeting. "This is unexpected."

"By you, perhaps," the captain said. "I'm not surprised, not completely. Whether he wanted to or not, Darkbow was gaining a name for himself. I think it's a bunch of hogwash, but there are plenty of simpletons who think he was responsible for Belgad's leaving."

The woman looked up, her unblinking eyes locking on those of the guard captain. "You realize what this means, don't you?"

Tuxra chuckled, his large belly bouncing. "Of course. It means Kerjim is going to be the head of the Guild of Guilds. None of the lesser guilds will vote against him now, and you and I alone aren't enough to thwart his being elected."

"What of The Gnat?" There was a glint of hope in the woman's eyes.

"You can't trust that crazy fool. I doubt he will want to support Kerjim, but one never knows what the beady-eyed little freak will do."

"We have to do *something*." Frantic, Osrm shot out of her chair. "We can have Eel arrested. He's young. He'll likely talk. Then Kerjim will face the gaol, too."

Tuxra shook his head. "What evidence is there? The boy carries a sword, so what? At best, that's proof of thievery because we know he couldn't afford such a weapon."

"There has to be a body," Osrm pointed out. "Has anyone seen it?"

The captain kept shaking his head. "Not to my knowledge, but I don't believe Kerjim would lie about such. If he is, sooner or later Darkbow will show up. No, I doubt the man is lying."

The mage brought her hands up to her chin as if she were about to chew her nails. "What do we do?"

"We wait," the captain said. "That's all we can do. If Kerjim wins this vote, then so be it. We'll be under his thumb, but we'll survive. Besides, if he weren't pulling his stunts, it would mean you and I would be at one another's throats." Here Tuxra grinned.

*   *   *

The pressure swirled behind his eyes, building and building and building. A lesser man could not have held it in, would have gone insane. But Kron Darkbow had already faced insanity more than once in his twenty-six years, and he had come out the other side stronger for it. Each time he had fallen, there had been mayhem of a drastic sort, of last resorts. Men had died, more than a few. A line of the dead swept from Bond more than a thousand miles north to Kobalos, the Prisonlands holding a handful of souls who had fallen to the sword of Darkbow.

That was no longer him, however. He had changed, had become a different man, a *better* man. He had tried to put aside violence, or at least the highest levels of violence. Trained and bred to be a hunter of men, Kron knew little else, but he had learned control.

Now that control threatened to evaporate, to explode upon the city once more. So far he had managed to keep in check, to push down the hundred spirits that now haunted him, encircled him, were *within* him. More than half of those ghosts were beyond the insanity of even Kron Darkbow, were truly insane, filled with nothing but lusts, often lusts to kill. The rest of the spirits floating around inside his skull were men he had known, some well and others only by acquaintance or on sight. For the most part these were fairly honorable men, men with families, men with levels of honor, those who kept the mad at bay.

Conflict raged behind Kron's dark eyes, the prisoners versus those who would imprison. He knew which side he came down upon, and there was no emotional conflict for him. But the madmen had numbers on their side, and their tarnished ghosts were not afraid to push the boundaries of their madness to new extremes.

It was a convergence Kron had brought upon himself in order to quell the hauntings of the Asylum, and also to give him a powerful tool in his latest war. He was yet fully aware of who the target would be, though he had strong suspicions. Lalo had confirmed much. Until Kron could be assured of his target, he would manage to keep the madness within. Once he found his target, well ... he promised himself there would be no more violence on his part. He would not take lives except in defense of himself or others. Whether the mad souls hiding behind his eyes would go along with this was yet to be seen.

To reach his goals, however, to discover for certainty who was behind the attack upon him, he might have to disappear for some little while. Those who sought his death might believe he was indeed dead, but he doubted it. Enough people had seen him leave the Asylum grounds through what was left of the front gate, and tongues would definitely wag. No, what he hoped to instill in his enemies was a sense of the unknown. Let them wonder where he was, what he was doing. His reputation would proceed him. They would not have a moment's rest, a night's sleep, without concerning themselves whether Kron Darkbow was about to blaze into their lives with sword swinging and arrows flying.

Let them ponder.

Let them worry.

Let them *fear.*

To vanish he would have to cut ties with certain individuals, mainly the two who he considered friends, Randall and Gris. If he were to simply go away without informing them, then they would become the worried ones, and there was no telling what extent they would go to to find him. Gris through his ties with the city guard, Randall with his magic. Kron did not want to be found, and he wanted no danger to come to his friends, thus he would go his own way after speaking with each of them.

Randall was first, as the healing tower in the Swamps was not far from the Finder's estate.

A gloved fist cracked against the door to the healer's quarters.

Kron did not have to wait long. The portal was opened, a dour-faced Althurna standing there.

"Is he in?" Kron asked.

She nodded then stepped back, allowing the man in black entrance.

Randall was seated at his desk, his hands busy utilizing a stone pestle to crush some kind of yellow flowers in a thick, wooden bowl. He looked up, smiling for a moment before his features wrinkled with concern.

"Kron?"

The man in black nodded to the woman, then approached the table, standing at one end. "Randall."

The healer slid his tools to one side. "Please, have a seat."

"I won't be staying long."

Randall's shoulders slumped. "I wish you would allow me to look you over."

"There is no need," Kron said. "I understand your apprehension, but I am fine."

Randall leaned forward, his voice low. "Kron, you are playing with powers beyond your control. As soon as I saw you this morning I knew -- "

The man in black looked away as if uninterested in continuing this line of the conversation. "I came here to tell you I will be ... missing for some little while."

Randall's face scrunched up. "What does that mean? Are you going away?"

"I will merely be going ... underground."

"I don't like the sound of that."

A guffaw from Althurna brought both men to look around, but she stood there by the still open door, her emotions unreadable.

Kron turned back to the desk. "I wanted to tell you so you would not be alarmed."

Randall stood, one hand held out as if to hold onto his friend. "You know you can turn to me no matter your troubles. If you need -- "

"I must do this on my own," Kron said. "I will be fine."

"Where will you be staying? On the streets? And for how long?"

Kron shook his head. "Do not concern yourself with such. The less you know, the safer you will be."

The healer squinted, a hint of audacity in his eyes. "It's me you're talking to, Kron. Remember? I doubt there is anything you are facing which I need fear."

"All the more reason I need to deal with this on my own."

Randall lowered his hand and sat back in his chair, seemingly resigned to whatever fate awaited his friend. "It appears I can not talk you out of this."

A slim grin slid across Kron's face. "Randall, you are a good friend, but you forget you cannot save the world."

The healer looked up. "What if I could?"

Kron snorted. "You would be wasting your time. The world doesn't want to be saved. It wants to be coddled." He turned away.

And walked out of the room.

Only then did Althurna close the door. She turned to face the healer.

"Don't give me that look," he said.

***

His soft leather boots kicking up dust behind him, Spider scurried across the bridge into Uptown, a part of the city mostly unfamiliar to him other than the university district. He paused upon reaching the shore, glancing to the side of the road where a board listed several main roads with small painted arrows showing the directions to each. He had visited the place he sought several times before, but that had been years earlier, during his student days, and he had forgotten much. Upon spotting directions to the establishment, he turned left and trotted west along Mages Way.

News. News. News. He had important news, and Kerjim wasn't going to like it. Damn the luck the guild leaders had decided upon the Twelve Chairs tavern for their next gathering. Spider had had to travel to Southtown to confirm his fears with a client, then run back across a bridge and through the Swamps and now across another bridge. It was enough to give the little man a heart attack. He wasn't exactly old, but he wasn't young anymore, either. If he weren't so cheap, he would have hired a buggy.

He came to a stop a block from the tavern. Ahead of him there were a dozen or so younger guild bosses standing outside the building, each man or woman chatting away as if they had not a care in the world. Perhaps they didn't, since the riots had ended. But their presence meant the gathering was close to starting.

Spider rushed forward, hoping he still had time.

A few grunts and curses followed him elbowing his way through the crowd and into the Twelve Chairs. He paused at the entrance and stared about the small front chamber for Kerjim. Long bar on the left, twelve padded stools in front of it. A dozen or so tall tables spread throughout the room, none with chairs of their own. Small but likely the nicest tavern in all of Bond, and packed at the moment. It was a standing-room-only affair. Spider spotted Captain Tuxra's weight crushing one of the stools at the bar, the ugly face of Nelgrave the bartender offering up a jack of ale. The Gnat huddled at the other end of the room, listening intently to whatever Osrm was going on about. Everywhere there were people in finery gossiping and whispering and yacking and ... whatever it was the rich and powerful did when talking to one another. But there was no sign of the Docks boss.

Spider bolted up to the bar. "Nelgrave!"

The big, ogre-faced bartender nodded to Tuxra and moved toward the end of the counter where Spider stood with the exit at his back. "Long time since I've seen you in here, Spelcher."

The little man hissed. "I don't use that name anymore!"

Nelgrave shrugged. "Alright, mister whoever-you-is, what can I do for you?"

"I'm looking for Docks Master Kerjim."

The bartender glanced around at the packed establishment, shrugged once more, then looked back to Spider. "He was just here a minute ago. Might be in the back room preparing for whatever he's up to tonight. Rented the place out, so I guess he's got something going on."

Spider nodded. "Thanks!" Then he rushed through the crowd, shoving his way between the less prestigious lot but careful enough to walk tenderly around those who were more powerful. Soon enough he came to the only other door in the place besides the front one, the door he supposed lead to whatever back room there was.

He pushed through.

It was a storage cupboard, but a big one, almost as large as the serving room itself. Wooden shelves lined the walls, loaded down with barrels and bottles and boxes of all sizes and makes. Most importantly, Master Kerjim sat on a stool in the other side of the room, ruffling through a handful of papers and scrolls. Standing next to him and looking over his shoulder was the new master of the mages guild.

Kerjim and Frex Nodana looked up at the intrusion, neither apparently happy to see Spider.

"What is it?" the Pursian asked.

Spider slid into the room and closed the door behind him, cutting off the loud chatter of the cliques. "We've got trouble."

Kerjim's frown deepened. "What kind of trouble?"

"Darkbow is alive."

The Pursian shot to his feet, pages and scrolls forgotten and falling from his fingers to scatter upon the floor. "What are you talking about?"

"I might not work for Lalo anymore, but I've still got contacts," Spider said. "I heard it from one of them not a few hours ago."

"What kind of contact?" Nodana asked.

"City guardsman," Spider said. "If anybody would know, it'd be him. I made sure to confirm with another guard I know at the barracks. They said they saw Darkbow walk out of the Asylum this morning."

Kerjim cursed, then kicked at the papers at his feet, sending them fluttering away. "That damn nephew of mine!"

The mage remained calm. "Perhaps there has been a mistake."

The Docks boss glared at the woman. "Oh, there's been a mistake, alright. My nephew made a mistake in lying to me! I knew something was not right with him."

Nodana held up her hands. "Hold on a moment. We need to ascertain the facts before --"

"Before *nothing*!" Kerjim spat on the floor and spun around to face Spider. "Tell the others the meeting has been canceled."

"Me?" the little, gray-haired man asked, fear in his eyes.

Kerjim brought himself up short, standing straight, calming himself. "No, you're right." He looked to the mage. "Nodana, please inform the other guild leaders the meeting will have to be postponed."

"They're not going to like it," the woman said.

"I don't give a damn. Tell them I had to rush off to get a few more signatures for the Thieves Guild charter. That will keep them from too much conjecture."

"Oh, about that ..." Spider reached inside a pocket of his dark pants and lifted out a folded sheet of paper. "Eel ... he, uh ... he gave me the license for the Thieves Guild."

Kerjim's eyes grew to the size of gold coins. Big gold coins. "He did *what*?"

Spider shrugged. "Before he walked out of The Stone Pony, he said I could be boss of the guild."

The Pursian fumed. It was in his eyes, his twitching eyes. It looked as if his head were about to pop off his body, leaving a stiffened trunk behind. Nodana calmed him with the mutter of a few magical words and a hand on one arm.

Kerjim slumped, but the back of his eyes continued to boil. "Okay. Alright. I'm going to find my nephew and clear up all this nonsense. Then I'll meet the two of you at the Pony by nightfall." He glanced from Spider to the mage. "And no word of any of this to anyone, understood?"

Two heads nodded.

"Good." Kerjim pushed past Spider, slammed the door open and stormed out the storage room.

***

Holding down the ends of the unrolled scroll with both hands, Sergeant Gris could only stare at the written words and the mayor's seal in dried red wax at the bottom. The paper had been brought directly from Karn's office mere minutes earlier. Gris had expected something pertaining to Captain Chambers as the old fellow had been feeling under the weather the last few days. The sergeant had believed there would be a temporary replacement named to take the captain's place. As it turned out, that was exactly to what the scroll pertained. The shocker was that *he* was the one named interim captain.

Gris sat back in his office chair, allowing the scroll to roll up on its own. He closed his eyes, listening to the comings and goings of booted feet outside his door. It was late afternoon, time for the changing of shifts. He himself was scheduled to go home for the day at this time, but that was not likely to happen soon.

Captain. It was not a position he had sought. Not even one he had wanted. He was not worthy. It was almost like a bad joke. Here he had been considering resigning from the guard, and what happens? They promote him. Oh, it was only temporary, the letter spelling out that Gris would be relieved of his captain's duties once Chambers was back up to snuff or, in case of the old man's retirement or continued illness, another was permanently appointed.

Still, provisional or not, Gris did not deserve this honor nor the corresponding responsibilities. There had to be another sergeant who could fill in until Chambers was back on his feet. If it were not so late in the day already, Gris would have marched over to Karn's office and refused the position. If pushed and prodded, he might very well have gone ahead and resigned. Now all that would have to wait until morning.

It was not that he did not want to be a city guard, but he doubted his abilities to command. If he could not be a guard, *simply* a guard, without rank, then he might have to move on elsewhere. Once the morning came and he had everything squared away with the mayor's office, and once Chambers returned as captain, Gris would have to pay another visit to Tuxra. Something could be worked out.

The door to his office chamber opened, bringing his head up.

Rogins poked his head through the opening. "Sergeant, there's a ... er, uh, um ... I mean *captain*, your acquaintance in the black cloak is here to see you."

"Show him in, corporal."

The door closed briefly, then swung open once more, revealing Kron Darkbow, who promptly shifted his way into the room and gently closed the door behind him.

Gris stared up at his friend. Kron looked a little better than he had that morning, but not much. His limp was gone, but he still wore the same tattered clothes that looked as if they came from a battlefield, which perhaps they had in their own way. And his face was as pale as a sheet. Whatever had happened last night at the Asylum, it had changed the man. Of that, if nothing else, Gris was positive.

"Have a seat," the new captain said, motioning to one of two chairs in front of his desk.

"I won't be long."

Gris shrugged. "Thank you for stopping by. I still want to ask you about last night."

Kron ignored the statement. "Congratulations on your promotion."

"Now, what -- " Gris caught himself. "You've already heard?"

"Your men were talking outside."

"Can't keep their mouths shut, by Ashal." His chair creaked as the captain leaned back, the top rail resting against the wall. "It's only temporary, by the way. Chambers is ill."

"I can think of no one more deserving."

Gris could tell he meant those words. Even with whatever was going on behind those eyes of cold iron, or maybe because of it, there had been no sarcasm or irony in what Kron said.

The captain chuckled. "I just remembered. Rumor on the street is you're dead."

"I am sorry to disappoint." A slight grin appeared on one corner of Kron's lips.

Gris leaned forward. "Word is you were killed at the Asylum last night. You care to explain what went on there?"

The grin disappeared. "I have told you, I was attacked by a group of assassins. Their names I do not know."

"But you have some suspicions?"

Kron gave a brief nod. "I am working on it."

Gris cursed. "Do you remember the last time something like this happened?"

"Of course," Kron said. "It was only last summer."

The captain's eyes narrowed. "Am I going to have another mess to clean up after you're through spreading vengeance all over Ashal's good earth?"

The man in black gave a brief shake of his head. "I promise you, there will be no slayings upon my part. Not unless I am forced to act in self defense."

Gris locked gazes with the other for long moments, trying to gauge what was going on behind that steely look, but gave up after several moments. He slumped some little bit. "Kron, I just don't want a repeat of last year. The city has had enough. *I've* had enough. It's only been days since the riots, and we've still got a ton of warrants to serve over that little fracas. The last thing I need is you on the road to wrath again."

"I understand, but you are going to have to trust me on this, Griffon. I am also sick of the killing."

The captain looked up at Kron. "Do you mean that? Or is this just what you're telling me to get me off your back?"

"Actually, I came by to tell you I would not be available for some little while."

Gris blew out a breath of exasperated air. "Oh, that makes me feel *so* much better. You disappearing on me. The last time you pulled that stunt there was nearly a war between the East and West, and there's no telling what all happened up in Kobalos."

Kron's slanted smile reappeared. "Nothing like that this time. I merely need to find some information."

"About what?"

"About who tried to kill me last night."

Wood cracked on stone as Gris's chair came down, the man placing his elbows on his desk. "And then I suppose you'll make them pay?"

"Gris, I have said I will kill no one, except in defense. And I mean that."

The captain still wasn't pushed to believe. True, Kron wasn't quite the man he had been even a year earlier, and whatever events occurred last night seemed to have changed him further, but he did have a history of a wild streak. But then, what could he do? He had no reason to hold the man, and he would not do that to a friend, one who had been wronged. Perhaps there was another way to put a stop to all this.

"What if I could tell you who attacked you last night?" the captain asked.

"My guess is it was Eel Sidewinder and friends."

Gris's eyes grew large. "So you've heard?"

"I've heard nothing," Kron said, "but I have been given a description, and it matches that of a young man who confronted me last night. It also happens to be the same person who I ran into during the riots the night I found Stilp."

"It also seems he has your sword," Gris said.

"Eel?"

"Eel. He's been seen on the streets with a big sword on his back. I figured it had to be yours."

Kron nodded. "I am not surprised."

"I suspect you will try to retrieve your property."

"Let him keep it. I can replace the blade, but I cannot replace his life if we should meet again."

Gris nodded approval. "Sound words. I'm glad to hear you talking this way. And since you're pretty sure Eel was involved, you won't need to vanish on me."

"Eel was working for someone," Kron said. "I mean to find out who."

Gris sighed as his face sank into one of his hands. "You just don't give up, do you?"

"Last night men tried to kill me, and I have no explanation as to why," Kron said.

"You know who it was, Kron. If Eel was involved, it had to be his uncle that put him up to it."

Kron nodded. "Quite possible. It seems the Docks Guild has been making a lot of power plays of late, and for some reason they find me a threat."

The captain grumbled. "I can't fault you for thinking that way, what with all you found out during the riots."

Kron's crooked smile showed once more, "Of course, you could simply arrest Master Kerjim and bring him in for questioning. Then we could find out what we want."

"Ha ha. Very funny. Just what I need, the mayor's office screaming down at me for arresting one of our guild bosses while I have no more evidence than your word."

Kron leaned over the desk, stretched out a hand and placed it on his friend's shoulder.

The two men locked eyes.

"Listen," the man in black said, "if I can find evidence Kerjim was behind not only my attack but the riots as well, I will bring it to you. Then you can arrest him."

Gris didn't know what to say.

Before he could think of something, Kron removed his hand and stood away from the desk.

"I will not be gone long," the man in black said. "Probably no more than a few days."

Gris nodded. "You be careful."

"I will."

"And if you run into any trouble, do not hesitate to look me up."

"I will."

Then Kron turned and exited the room without another sound.

Gris groaned and slid down in his chair, his head clunking back against the top rail.

***

There often comes a point in a person's life when they must decide what direction they are to take. Such choices are sometimes easy ones, though frequently they are difficult. None can read the future, cannot tell which is the better road for them. Here is a choice, there is a choice. Sometimes there are even multiple choices, just to make things fun. When such decisions are ones to be taken serious, it can churn a person's stomach, hammer away at their mind, even break their heart.

Eel Sidewinder found himself facing such a decision.

One moment had changed his life. When Kron Darkbow had spared him on that rooftop. Eel almost wished the man in black had plunged that knife into the youth's chest. At least then there would be no decision needing made.

Eel felt like a traitor. Not yet twenty, he had spent nearly all his life at the foot of his uncle Kerjim. He had listened to the tales of adventure and wealth about the old thieves guild. He had believed most of them. He had spent years as a street urchin, an education more rough and tumble than that delivered upon most youths, but in its own ways just as rewarding. Eel was a product of the Swamps, a street rat. He had few aspirations for anything more.

Except he *did* have aspirations, to some extent. Kerjim had had high hopes for the lad, and Eel had played right along with it, thinking it would be a challenge and even fun to head up a new guild. Such a title as master or boss would give him a name within the Swamps, a name that proved he was someone to be reckoned with.

In a blink of an eye, all of that had vanished.

He was not uncertain about his prospects for a thieves guild. He wanted no part of it. Morality had not so much come to play a role in the boy's life as had fear of the future. When Darkbow's blade had glinted beneath the street lights, it was not thoughts of the past that darted through Eel's head. Instead, there had been thoughts of the future, a future that would not have come if that dagger had descended. For the first time, Eel truly had to face his own future, what kind of man he wanted to be.

What he found surprised him. He did not want to be a thief. Oh, he didn't mind lurking about at night and climbing along rafters. He also didn't mind the possibility of violence, though recent events had shown him he was no expert fighter. All of that was excitement, a little bit of spice to his often humdrum world. But was that *all* there was? Kerjim had often enough talked about power and money, but Eel had rarely held either in the palm of his hand. What could he do with power? Control others? To what end? To gain more power? Again, for what? The money might be nice, but what could Eel do with it if he had it? The Swamps was his home, so it was not as if he would ever move away. And there was only so much a man needed. A roof, food, a bed, what else? Women?

Eel wasn't the most handsome fellow around, but he had never had a problem finding a woman if he wanted one. Love was a different matter, one he rarely thought about because it was foreign to him. He had never fallen for a woman, and more often than not chuckled at any of his young friends who had become enchanted by feminine charms. Someday Eel might find love, but he had to figure out who he was before he would try to figure out a woman's heart.

He squatted in the dust of the old shack, watching the day's dying light through an open window, its shutters hanging crooked. From outside rang the bells of passing ships, the soft lapping of water splashing against a shoreline. He only came to this place when he needed time alone to think, which was rare enough. Kerjim had been doing all the thinking for him for years.

But no more. Eel did not know what he was going to do, where he was going to go, but he was finished with his uncle. He wished the man no ill will, but the boy could no longer follow him. Following Kerjim had nearly gotten him killed. Only his enemy had showed any signs of compassion.

Eel stood, the weight of Darkbow's sword shifting over his shoulders and reminding him there was a man out there who might be hunting for him, a man in league with spirits of the dead. There was little to be done about Darkbow. Eel couldn't confront him, and wasn't sure he wanted to. The best thing for Eel to leave town for a while, to lay low until everything had been worked out with the guilds. Perhaps after a few months Darkbow might forget about his sword and the attack. Eel doubted that for some reason, perhaps the hard glint in the dark man's eyes, but leaving was better than staying here and waking up with a slit throat.

He chuckled. And here he had been just telling himself he could never leave the Swamps.

"I'm glad you find humor in your situation."

Eel spun.

Kerjim stood in the doorway, which the lad had not even heard creak open. Beyond the Docks boss was a dirt path, past that a row of shacks just like this one, abandoned for years, empty, dying.

The young man glared at his uncle. "What situation would that be?"

"You lied to me."

Eel shrugged. "It happens."

"Why?" Kerjim asked. "After everything I've done for you over the years, why would you suddenly turn on me?"

The youth chortled. "What exactly *have* you done for me over the years, except use me, try to mold me to fit into your plans?"

The Pursian lunged, his right hand lashing out, smacking Eel hard enough to send the boy reeling to the floor.

Eel rolled onto his back, facing his uncle, heat alive in both their features.

But Kerjim no longer moved. He stood motionless, menacing over his nephew. Only his lips moved, quivering from anger. "Kron Darkbow is alive because you are a coward. We will look like fools."

Eel turned his head to one side and spat blood. "Maybe he deserves to live. Maybe he's a better man than you and me put together."

An evil grin slipped into the Pursian's features. "You think so? What has he done that's so noble?"

The boy remained silent, simply glaring at his uncle.

A boot jolted Eel across the chin, dropping him back on the floor where his head smacked against the boards, sending up whisps of dust.

"I knew I would find you here," the Pursian said. "This is where you always come when you want to cry like a little boy. Too bad your father can't see you now, sniveling in his own house. He would be so proud."

Eel scooted away across the floor, putting space between himself and his uncle. "Don't talk to me about my father. He was a working man, not like you."

Kerjim chuckled. "Your father was an idiot, and it seems he's passed it along to his brat."

The youth pushed himself off the floor, a dribble of blood trailing down from one corner of his mouth. "You can say what you want, uncle, but I'm through. I'll have nothing to do with your guilds."

Kerjim stared in silence, thoughts obviously working behind his eyes. Then he pointed at the lad. "I'll have those swords on your belt. They belong with a *real* thief, not to some caitiff."

Keeping his eyes on his kin, Eel raised one hand and unbuckled his weapons belt. He tossed the leather straps and steel blades at his uncle's feet where they landed with a clunk. "Satisfied?"

The Pursian's gaze went to the lad's right shoulder, then back to the youth's eyes. "You might as well give me Darkbow's sword. I do not how you came by it, but it's obvious you were not man enough to take it from him."

Eel took another step back. "I'll not part with the long sword."

Kerjim grinned, then forced a chuckle. He bent at the knees, keeping his gaze on his nephew, and lifted the weapons belt, throwing it over a shoulder. Reaching up, he grasped the pommel of one of the short swords and drew it part of the way. The Docks boss shifted his eyes to stare at the steel.

Then he slammed the weapon home and spun away, pausing only when the reached the open doorway. He glanced over a shoulder. "You have made a grave mistake, nephew. I suggest we not cross paths again. Next time ... "

Without finishing his sentence, he walked out into the streets.

Eel stood with his legs quivering, staring as the last of the day's glow faded to night.

17

Give us our freedoms and we will lets you lives! Now!

The voices would not let up. Kron had been hearing them since the afternoon, soon after leaving the city guards barracks in Southtown. At first there had been but a few mumbles, only a word or two making sense, but the clarity and the strength of the voices had grown and grown.

It was the spirits of the dead trying to break out of their most recent cell, the flesh that was Kron Darkbow.

Frees us!

He had not known at the Asylum what would happen when he had presented himself, his full self, to the spirits. Frustration and his formidable ire had gotten the best of him. In a brief fit of rage, an emotion he had promised he would no longer allow to control him, he had opened himself to the dead, the spirits who had wandered the Asylum, the guards and the mad inmates alike. For a moment at the Asylum he had believed himself lost, the ghosts of the dangerous vying for his body, his soul, but by sheer force of will he had fought back. The souls of the Asylum guards and staff had been instrumental in that victory, even allowing for some physical healing of the man in black, their unfortunate penance locking them inside Kron along with the others. At least they were used to it, being entwined with the tormenters.

But Kron was beginning to wonder how long he could hold out. The sun had dipped though it had yet to be a full day since his ... *entwinement*, and he was already having trouble dealing with the dead trying to claim his body or force their freedom from it.

The worst had not come until he had finished at the Rusty Scabbard, returning to his apartment there and retrieving fresh clothes and a handful of secondary weapons. A bath had followed, a long, warm cleansing needed to wipe away the grit and grime and blood that had layered him throughout the day. Upon descending the stairs inside the Scabbard, the voices in his mind had gained in strength, had pressed and pushed and pulled.

They were tugging at his very soul, trying to entrap it, or worse, destroy it utterly.

Gives up! You is buts skins and bones and bloods, mortal mans!

Of course Kron Darkbow could not allow such. A plan had been formulating in his mind since leaving the Asylum, and it involved the very ghosts chambered within. He must hold the dead at bay until his scheme came to fruition, though he hoped that would be no longer than a matter of days. Could he hold that long? He did not know, and was beginning to doubt. Regardless, he still had work to do. He had enemies out there who must be dealt with.

Unusual for him, there were no thoughts of vengeance upon his mind. He wondered if it was because none he loved had been the target of his attackers, but he himself had been the target. Still, someone wanted him dead and he did not know why. As he was not willing to spend the rest of his life hunkering in some hole or fleeing along open roads, he had to find his enemy.

Of course he could have simply discovered Kerjim's home and beat upon the man until he admitted everything. But that was too simplistic, and Kron had promised Gris there would be no violence. He hoped to keep his word. Besides, there were worse things than pain or even death for men like Kerjim Sidewinder, and Kron planned to introduce the man to such.

Now parading along Beggars Row, the sight of Lalo the Finder's estate growing in his vision, Kron pondered the young man who had somehow ended up with his sword. The boy had nearly been scared to death when Kron had loomed over him, dagger raised. Eel Sidewinder might wear two short swords, and more than likely he had lived a rough life on the streets of the Swamps, but he was not an experienced fighter. He had probably been in a scuffle or two over the years, the usual street urchin nonsense, but he wasn't someone with a past of spilling blood. That much was obvious. It was also obvious he should not have been on that rooftop last night. No commander with sense would have put one of his youngest and inexperienced troops into the middle of that fracas. Eel should have stayed on the ground with others and allowed more experienced combatants to step in, though Kron was somewhat thankful for Eel's involvement, otherwise he might have faced that monster with the big hammer much sooner. His chin still stung, and there was a stiffness to his jaw he expected to last for weeks; if not for his spectral healing at the Asylum, there was no telling what shape his face might be in.

He pushed his way through the lonely gate at the estate's wall, then closed it behind him. Turning to march up the incline to the main house, he wondered if he should have hidden his entrance. There were few people on the street even though it was not yet late, but perhaps he should have --

Lets us go nows or we will drives a spike through your heads! And tears the flesh from your skins with our nasty little teeths!

Kron stopped halfway up the grade. "Quiet," he whispered, rubbing at the side of his head. He had nearly forgotten about the ghosts since they had given him a few moments of peace. What to do about them? "If you continue to give me trouble, I'll throw myself into a river and drown. What would that do for you, hmm?"

Silence was the answer.

"I thought as much. Now remain quiet." He continued his walk, surprised there were lights burning within the mansion. Lalo and Stilp must have decided they could survive without servants, after all.

***

"Where is this nephew of yours?"

A shadow fell across his table as Kerjim looked up from his dinner into a set of round, dark eyes surrounded by stringy gray hairs atop a mammoth head. The Docks Guild chief lifted a red napkin with frayed ends, the best The Stone Pony had to offer, dabbed at the corners of his mouth, then slid away his nearly finished bowl of pigeon stew. "He is no longer any family of mine," he said as he lifted a cup of ale and sipped from it.

The big woman huffed and those present in the tavern's main room went quiet. All conversation stopped, as did any slurping of drinks or scraping of plates. All eyes were on the monstrosity that was Mama Kaf as she leaned forward, towering over the seated Pursian.

"*Where is he?*" she asked.

Kerjim set down his drink and looked up at her. "I have no idea. Perhaps he is upstairs in his room packing to leave. That would be the smartest thing he has done of late."

The big woman grumbled and tromped off to one side, heading toward the stairs to the Pony's upper level.

Kerjim grinned as he reached for his cup once more. *Nephew, you are a fool, and you are about to be taught one of life's hardest lessons. I wish I could feel pity for you.*

***

Slipping past his uncle and the tavern's regulars who would recognize him had been an easy task. Eel had climbed up the alley walls on the outside of the building, stuck a dagger through the crack of the shutters, lifted the inner latch, then withdrawn and sheathed the dagger. Pulling the shutters back and crawling inside his darkened room had been simple enough, but the youth threw up a brief thanks to Ashal for the moonlight that had eased his tasks.

He had not wanted to come back to the room, but it had been necessary. Where he was going, he did not know, but he would need clothes and food, if nothing else.

After closing and latching the shutters once more, Eel dared to light a lamp on a table next to his bed. He glanced around, not bothering to say goodbye to the room that had been his home for several years. Instead he got to work, pulling a burlap sack from a corner and stuffing it with the few shirts and pants he owned. He briefly paused over a pair of low buckskin shoes, then decided against them. It wasn't likely he would need another pair of foot gear in the near future, and it would be one less thing to carry. He did, however, retrieve a pair of daggers hidden beneath his mattress. One never knew when extra weapons would be needed.

Food was harder to come by. The only source of sustenance readily available was a dried hunk of black bread resting next to the lamp. He took it, stuffing it into the sack on top of his clothes.

Kneeling next to the bed, he took out the same small blade he had used to open the window's shutters, then went to work sawing into the stuffed pillow where he had rested his head for many a year. Within seconds there was a hole big enough and he reached inside. A frown grew upon his face, quickly dismissed as his fingers felt the surface of the small leather package he had been seeking.

Withdrawing the sack, he pulled on its top strings and looked inside. A handful of coppers and silvers, a couple of gold pieces. It was literally his life savings, and it wasn't a bad amount for a young man only a few years beyond being a street urchin. It wasn't enough to last forever, but it could last some little while if he was careful.

Eel jammed the weighty sack into his belt, returned his knife to its sheath and hefted the bag holding his clothes over a shoulder. It was time to leave, and there was no reason to look back.

That was when he noticed the thudding of heavy boot steps. Someone was in the hall, right outside his door.

A cracking, snapping, the door bursting open to slam against the wall.

Mama Kaf stood in the opening, a bandage wrapped around one arm, her giant hammer in both hands. The sheer mass of the woman filled the doorway. She did not look happy.

"Where is Darkbow?"

Eel did not bother taking the time to answer. He could see right away this woman was out for blood.

He spun and dove for the window, cursing himself for having closed the shutters.

The woman roared, and there were more sounds of wood breaking and cracking.

Eel ducked his head and threw a shoulder into the shutters, the latch popping, the wooden slates splintering and spraying.

Then he was outside, in the alley, falling.

<u>18</u>

"Finding everything comfortable?"

The words were filled with sarcasm, and for the first time in several hours they had not come from within Kron's head. He opened his eyes and stared at the speaker standing at the foot of the plush bed the size of a wagon.

Kron grinned. "Yes, thank you. Everything is to my liking."

Lalo grimaced. "I did not realize upon entering this ... alliance with you, that you would be confiscating the best room in the house."

Allowing the covers to fall down from his bare chest, Kron sat up in the bed. He rubbed his eyes then glanced about the large room, scarlet tapestries on the walls, thick rugs on the floor, a kindling hearth on the other side of the chamber. "It looked as if no one had been using Belgad's old room, therefore I believed it available. Was I mistaken?"

The Finder's frown showed no sign of turning into a smile. "No one has utilized this chamber in months, since Lord Belgad's departure. The only person who has entered here has been myself, and that was to gather personal effects my former master wished shipped to him in Kobalos."

"Was this a shrine to the great Dartague, then?" Kron asked, *his* smile still strong. "Please, if I've overstepped my bounds, allow me to rectify the situation." A naked leg slid from beneath the covers, the foot landing on a rug.

Lalo raised his hands to ward off the other man's nakedness. "No, no. By all means, use the room."

The leg withdrew and Kron maneuvered himself so he was propped up on a pillow.

"Still," the Finder went on, "I find it interesting that not so long ago I offered you this very room, the very position Lord Belgad once held, yet you refused. Now, however, we find you stationed within the very household you had recently derided."

Kron's grin faltered. "My presence is merely a precaution. Kerjim would not think to look for me here, and I needed a place to rest. In a few days you will have the house to yourself once more. Now, may I ask why you decided to wake me?"

Lalo nodded. "My apologies, as I did not realize you would be asleep. But as you are now awake, I have given some thought to your query."

"You have a name for me?"

"Midge Highwater."

"I don't know the man."

Lalo scoffed. "I would not expect you to. Master Highwater is the chief of the storytellers guild."

"Storytellers?" Kron appeared incredulous. "How can he be of help?"

"Master Highwater might only be a storyteller, but he is no fool. Oh, the man comes off as a simpleton, I will admit, but there is a cagey intelligence behind his eyes. He is a man who pays attention, who knows things. Besides, he has not always been a storyteller."

"No?"

"No. Master Highwater has been many things over the years. Once he was a sailor. For a while a member of the city guard. He even served as one of Belgad's personal sentries some years ago. He only turned to storytelling upon his retirement from a more adventurous lifestyle."

"Very well," Kron said with a nod. "I will go see the man tomorrow. Anything else?"

"No," Lalo said, turning away. "In the morning I will have Stilp make you aware of Master Highwater's current whereabouts."

"Till then."

"Yes." And Lalo exited the room, gently closing the door behind him and leaving Kron all alone once more.

Except for the hundred undead people living in his thoughts.

We do not trust thats ones.

"Shut up," Kron said, his voice low as he eased back beneath the sheets, allowing the room's warmth to wash over him. "I don't trust him, either, but as long as I am working in his favor, he will keep partner with me."

***

The fall was not a long one, less than thirty feet, but enough to do serious damage. Fortunately for Eel, he was an experienced climber and had suffered his share of tumbles in the past. He rolled in the air, bringing his right shoulder around, his stuffed bag of belongings beneath. Better to break an arm than a leg.

He hit with a resounding snapping sound, a cry of pain thrusting forth from his lungs. Yes, the arm had broken, but it could have been much worse without the sack to ease the blow. He rolled over onto his back, his suddenly wet eyes trying to focus.

"Do not move!" It was a big voice, a hefty voice. It came from a big, hefty head sticking out the window from which he had jumped.

Then the head disappeared inside.

Nearly screaming, Eel forced himself to his feet, the weight of Darkbow's sword shifting on his back. He had to move. Mama Kaf would be upon him in a matter of moments. Thank goodness she was big and slow.

But where to go? He had no home anymore, no friends who didn't have connections somehow to his uncle. And there was the matter of his broken arm.

He turned deeper into the alley and trudged way, into the depths of the maze that made up the backstreets of the Swamps. He decided where he had to go first. He only hoped Mama Kaf would not guess the place.

***

It seemed of late all Kerjim Sidewinder was doing was waiting. Waiting for a meeting. Waiting for someone to come to him. Waiting for someone to be available. Waiting for the lies to end. He was rather tired of it.

Everything had been going along so smoothly, until Eel had lied to him. Since then, everything was near unraveling. The meeting of the guilds had had to be postponed. Darkbow still roamed the streets. Mama Kaf was on a rampage, only minutes earlier having stormed out the front door of The Stone Pony.

He smirked at that last thought. He liked the idea of the massive woman pounding her hammer down upon the idiot boy's head. Served him right for his lying. Through his single falsehood, Eel had proved he was no longer worth Kerjim's time and efforts. But it went beyond the lie about Darkbow. Eel had shown he was weak, was like his father and mother as Kerjim remembered them. Why the youth had lied was still beyond the Docks boss, but lied Eel had. That combined with his general demeanor the last couple of days showed the lad did not have what it took to be a guild leader, especially of a thieves guild. To head up a group of thieves, one had to have a streak of sensible daring, and a heart that could turn to stone at a moment's notice. Sacrifices had to be made to one's moral character, after all, if one wished to achieve. Eel obviously did not qualify.

The Pursian pushed away from the table and stood, noticing several eyes of the tavern folk glancing in his direction. He was an important person, so why not?

He paused to listen to the outside, half expecting to hear Mama Kaf on the frenzy, but he could detect nothing other than the typical night carousers.

Sighing at the lack of entertainment outdoors, he turned and made his up the stairs leading to the Pony's second level. Kerjim was tired of waiting. His nephew was being dealt with, which meant it was time for the Docks chief to get back into action. The gathering of the guilds had been delayed a few days, and he expected to be sitting in a position of strength when that meeting finally came. He *would be* the head of the Guild of Guilds. It was his fate. It was determined. By whom? By his own desire. By his own ambition. Too many chances had been taken and too much planning had been involved for Kerjim to fail now.

Which was why he came to a halt in front of a door and gently knocked.

"Come in, Kerjim," the voice of Frex Nodana sounded from the other side.

The Pursian pushed his way into the room and closed the door behind him.

The mage was laid out upon her bed, a silken robe of golden thread shielding her small body, her dainty feet curled beneath a thin sheet. "What can I do for you this night?"

The question might have been alluring, but Kerjim brushed it aside. Enough time for such pleasantries later. Now he had decided upon a mission. But first, "How did you know it was me out in the hall?"

Nodana opened her mouth to speak, but he cut her off with a wave of his hand.

"Forget I asked," he said. "You're a wizard, after all."

"Yes. And I'm guessing my craft has something to do with your reason for being here."

"It does," Kerjim said. "I want you to find Kron Darkbow for me."

Nodana sat up. "An easy enough task. I'm surprised you didn't ask earlier."

"I had my nephew to deal with first."

The mage moved to the end of her bed. "Do you want me to do this now?"

"No." Kerjim shook his head. "In the morning, after we've slept. I want to be wide awake when we hunt this man down."

19

The day's light was only a light gray haze as Eel lurched his way from yet another alleyway and trudged across the open way leading to the Swamps healing tower. It had been a long night and his head was fuzzy from lack of sleep. He had spent hours scrambling from one back street to another, his nervous eyes always on the lookout for a hulking shadow that could prove to be Mama Kaf. Fortunately he had never come across the woman. Unfortunately, he was dead tired and still suffered from a broken wing. At one point he had pulled out an old shirt and used it to make a sling for his arm, but the pain had not gone away, only dulled to a solid ache that sometimes screamed like fire until he thought he was going to pass out.

Somehow, however, he had survived the night. He could have gone to the tower earlier, but feared Mama Kaf or others might be there waiting for him, and believed he was more likely to receive immediate care during daylight when more staff was available. Now after having spent the last hour patrolling the place and seeing no signs of his uncle's thugs, Eel felt it was time for healing. He had some coin to make a donation, possibly enough to land him a healing mage, usually the best of the lot. He had heard for months about a young healer who was supposed to be the best in the city, and Eel prayed he would be lucky enough to land under this man's care. Eel needed to be whole. He still had no idea what he would do once healed, but whatever it should be, he needed his arm fixed

Approaching the nearest open door to the giant structure that was the healing tower, he was surprised to discover there was already a growing line waiting to get in, a line of people hacking and coughing and occasionally crying out. He guessed there was always a call for healing services.

At least he was early. The wait was little more than a half hour, then he was shown indoors by a boy who acted as an orderly. For a moment Eel had feared he might be turned away because of the sword on his back, but no one seemed to pay the lengthy blade any mind. He found himself placed upon a stool along the outer wall of the lengthy hall that wrapped the inside of the building. He was not alone. At least another score of people were seated every few feet along the hall, and a couple were laid out upon unfolded cots.

Eel waited again, but this time only for a few minutes. A young woman wearing the white robes of a healer soon came along the hall, stopping every so often to speak with one of the infirm. Then she would point the person one direction or other before moving on to the next person. Eel was the fourth she came to.

By that time the traffic within the hallway had increased. Other healers walked by, going from left to right and back again. More sick and injured made their way indoors, searching for a place to rest their aching bodies. A handful of others, nondescript by their casual garb, also could be seen moving about. Eel continued to watch for anyone familiar to him, but otherwise was not interested in the others.

The woman healer stopped in front of Eel and knelt next to him, gingerly pulling back the edges of his makeshift sling to look at his busted limb. "Looks like you've got a broken arm."

Eel would have laughed if he hadn't known how much it would hurt. "Looks that way, doesn't it?"

The healer stood and pointed to Eel's right. "Third door on the left. You won't have to knock. Healer Terrimand will see to your arm."

She turned to leave.

Eel grabbed a sleeve of her robe, halting her.

She looked down at him. "Yes?"

The youth looked up into her brown eyes. "If it makes a difference, I have enough for a mage."

The woman smiled. "I'm sorry. It doesn't work that way here. We operate on a first-come, first-serve basis, depending upon the severity of the patient's difficulties, of course. But if you'd like, I can recommend you to one of the mending practitioners in Uptown."

Eel's face sunk as he shook his head and stood. "That won't be necessary. Third door on the left, you said?"

She nodded and he returned her smile before leaving her to her duties.

Marching along slowly in order to keep his arm from jarring, Eel counted the doors on his left. "One. Two. Thr--"

"Excuse me."

Eel stopped and turned in the direction of the voice, his good hand casually planting itself on a dagger in his belt. Before him was a fellow not much older than Eel himself, the young man dressed in white and wearing a look of benevolence, almost priestly.

Eel did not know the man. "Did you mean me?"

The healer nodded. "Yes."

"Uh, are you the person I'm supposed to see about my arm?"

"I don't think so," the healer said, "but at the moment I'm more interested in that sword you're carrying on your back."

"No one said anything when I came in," Eel said. "If it needs to be peace-tied or something I can -- "

"No, no, it's not that," the youthful healer said. "It's just ... I know that sword."

***

Spider spun his seat around and sat with his arms crossed on the chair's top rail as if he were bored. "I'm not really sure why I am here."

Kerjim glared at the little man with gray hair. "You're to be the head of the new Thieves Guild, correct?"

Spider nodded. "That's what the licensing papers say."

"Then pay attention," the Docks boss said. "You might actually learn a thing or two."

Frex Nodana slid into a chair opposite the other two at the round table. "Are you two still squabbling?"

"I am making sure the new top thief is cut out for his duties," Kerjim said.

"I am!" Spider nearly cried the words.

Nodana's shoulders slumped. "If this is what every Guild of Guilds meeting is going to be like, I'm not sure *I'm* cut out for my duties."

Kerjim tutted. "Nonsense, Nodana. I would have never approached you about heading the Mages Guild if I did not believe you were up to the necessary tasks. Besides, this is only an unofficial gathering, though one with a specific goal."

"To find Darkbow," the mage said.

Spider nodded as he glanced at their surroundings. The room was small but solid with aged oak walls partially covered by tattered hangings with threads of fading colors revealing images from the city's past. Everything about the room had a battered feel to it, from the chipped table between them to the cracked chairs upon which they sat. Even the two doors to the chamber looked as if they had been hammered upon at one time or another, though they still appeared sturdy.

"Nice place you've got here," the little man said to the Docks boss.

Kerjim frowned. "It might not look like much, but it has served well as a meeting room for the Docks hall. You should have seen the place when I inherited it."

Spider waved a hand around the room. "I'm just saying it doesn't look like the kind of place you'd expect to find magical rituals being performed."

"What kind of place *would* you find magical rituals being performed?" the Pursian asked.

Spider opened his mouth but Nodana cut him off by slapping a hand onto the table's surface.

"Are we going to do this or not?" she asked. "If not, I have plenty of other things I could be doing."

"Sorry," Spider said.

"My apologies. Please proceed." Kerjim gestured to the mage.

"Very well." The wizard laid both hands flat upon the table and shut her eyes, immediately her closed lids revealing movement behind them.

For some time she sat there unmoving and silent, the two men in the room focusing their attention upon her.

Eventually Spider grew bored. Perhaps he could help, even with his limited education as a wizard. "I suggest trying to use your inner eye if you can't -- "

Nodana shot up a hand. "A moment, please."

Quiet returned to the room.

Minutes passed.

Finally the woman opened her eyes and smiled. "You're not going to believe this."

Kerjim leaned nearer to her. "What? Where is he?"

"Yeah, where?" Spider asked.

Nodana's grin widened. "He's at the Finder's estate."

Spider slumped. "Wouldn't have thought he'd be there."

Kerjim appeared just as flummoxed. He eased back onto his chair, his brain obviously at work behind his eyes.

"This is most unexpected," Nodana said.

The Docks boss shot her a glance. "No doubt. It seems the Finder and Darkbow have come to some kind of an arrangement. This does not bode well."

"Alright." Spider stood and moved away from the table. "Let's go get them."

"Sit down, fool!" Kerjim's face was red, full of annoyance. "It's the middle of the morning. We can't just march up to the estate, kick in the door and expect to draw no alarm from the city guard."

"Right." Spider sat.

Nodana turned to Kerjim. "How do you want to handle this?"

The Pursian paused for a moment before speaking, still thinking, no doubt. Then he looked the mage's way once more. "I'll need you to do some more scrying, find out what kind of security remains at the mansion. I know Tuxra put pressure on the guards left over from Belgad's time, but that doesn't mean there won't be a few hanging around. Also, double check for any wards, in case Lalo hired a wizard to protect the place. Once we know what we are facing, then we can put a plan into action. How long will it take you to scope out the estate and grounds?"

"I can give it a cursory look in a matter of minutes, but if you want me to get into the details, a few hours."

"Go for the full look, then," Kerjim said. "I want to know everything about the mansion you can find out. I figured Darkbow would be holed away somewhere nondescript, but this changes things. If we have to break into the estate, we'll wait until tonight to do so."

"What do you want me to do?" Spider asked.

Kerjim turned a narrow gaze upon the chief of thieves. "Go by the estate and give it a casual look, but do not be seen. Just in case."

"I'll get right on it."

**

Eel had been hesitant. The young man dressed in healer robes had wanted Eel to come back to his private quarters for treatment, but that route seemed dangerous at first. This man recognized Darkbow's sword, which meant somehow or other he knew Kron Darkbow. How well he knew the man in black was up for question, but Eel could not trust anyone with links to the person he had recently tried to kill.

Then again, Eel couldn't trust much of anyone at this point.

But the healer's face appeared serene and calm, almost beatific. If he was a friend of Darkbow, he stood out in stark contrast to that man. The two were complete opposites. This one wore white and had a softness about his eyes that resonated peace and amity without exposing weakness.

Apparently the healer had sensed the youth's wariness in the hallway.

"Here," the man in white had said. He had reached out and touched Eel's broken arm.

There had been a slight sensation of warmth, then a clicking pop, and Eel's arm was no longer fractured. He could sense right away his limb was better, was as perfect as it had ever been. He untied his makeshift sling and stretched out both arms, feeling the strength in both of them.

More jarring to Eel than his arm's miraculous repair had been the lack of preparation or apparatus on the healer's part. The healer was obviously a mage, but he had not muttered a spell nor gone through any incantations. There had been no healing potions, no rituals, nothing like that at all. He had merely touched Eel's arm and the limb had been whole. No mage in Eel's experience was that good.

"I am Randall Tendbones," the healer had said. "We need to talk. In private."

From that moment on, Eel trusted his newfound friend. Not completely, of course. Eel was no fool. But it wasn't likely Kron Darkbow would be hanging around the healing tower, or if he did he likely wasn't in much of a condition to confront Eel here and now. As far as Eel knew, Darkbow was likely alive, but in what condition? Additionally, even if Darkbow were present, it was unlikely he would launch a full-scale assault upon Eel while they were in the tower.

So when Randall Tendbones once again suggested they retire to his private room, Eel went along with it.

Once inside, the former thief found himself in a small chamber, obviously an office, a desk near the right wall, a single chair behind it, two chairs facing the desk. Across the room was another closed door. Scattered throughout the room and shoved up against the walls were several smaller tables, gurneys and folding chairs. Atop most of these furnishings were various vials and tools and bottles. Though he was on alien grounds, Eel found the place clean and restful.

Randall motioned toward one of the chairs facing his desk as he planted himself on one corner of the large table. "Please, have a seat."

Eel saw no reason not to comply. He plopped onto a seat.

The room's inner door opened and Eel almost reached for a dagger. He stopped his hand when he saw a young, plain-looking woman standing there.

Randall craned his head around to look at her. "Althurna, thank you, but I will not be needing your services for this patient."

The woman gave a single nod, took a step back into the secondary room and closed the door.

Eel didn't know who she was, but she unsettled him with her silence.

"My assistant," the healer said as way of explanation.

Eel shrugged. Fine with him. "Why did you ask me here?"

Randall leaned back on his hands. "I am facing a bit of a quandary, and I'm hoping you can help me with the situation."

"Me?" Eel jabbed a thumb at himself. "We don't even know one another, so I don't know what I could do to help you."

The healer grinned. "It seems obvious to me you were one of those involved in a recent confrontation with a friend of mine."

So this fellow *was* friends with Darkbow. Eel's mouth went dry. He tensed, ready to flee for the door if necessary.

Randall noticed the tightening of the youth's hands upon the arms of his chair. "Please, do not alarm yourself. I intend you no harm and have no plans to turn you over to the authorities."

Nice little speech, but Eel wasn't dropping his guard just yet.

"Which is part of my dilemma," Randall went on. "You have partaken in an assault upon my friend and you currently are in possession of his rightful property, but I am not sure what to do about you. If I were to attempt to arrest you myself, that would go against the protective code of ethics by which we here at the tower try to abide. It could also lead to a fracas which I wish to be no part of, but which most assuredly would end in your capture."

Here the healer's eyes grew hard for a moment, as if he wished to add weight to his words.

But then his gaze softened and he continued. "Another option would be for me to take you to Kron himself and -- "

Eel bolted from the chair and spun toward the exit.

"Please, sit."

The words were spoken without anger or malice. They were said in a plain voice, almost calm.

But Eel found he could not ignore them. The terror rising in his throat, he could but watch as his body moved in jerking motions and returned him to the chair where he sat and stared up at the healer.

Randall blinked.

Eel's body deflated, his autonomy of movement returned to him. He gasped in swallows of air, his fear not deflating despite his freedom as his eyes broadened and he stared up at the mage.

"My apologies for having to do that," Randall said, a slight frown at the ends of his lips. "In fact, I hated doing that. But I need you to hear me out."

Eel sucked in more air, his heart beating like that of a rabbit. He was powerless before this seemingly innocuous fellow, and there was little he could do to change the situation. They sat but inches apart, but was he fast enough to pull a dagger and plunge it into the other man before magic could erupt once more? Eel thought not, though he knew himself to be faster than most. This Randall Tendbones was not fool, and he wouldn't be seated so near if he felt threatened.

"Here." Randall reached out.

Eel flinched.

Once more the healer laid a hand on the younger man's shoulder. Immediately Eel's heart began to slow and the sweat upon his brow cooled.

Randall removed the hand and sat back. "Better?"

Eel nodded.

"Good. Then we can continue our conversation."

Eel nodded again. What else was he going to do?

"As I was saying," Randall continued, "one possibility would be for me to turn you over to Kron himself."

The healer halted his speech, watching the former thief as if to make sure Eel was not going to try to dart off again.

Upon seeing the younger fellow seemed nailed to his seat, Randall went on talking. "Of course that could bring further complications. Knowing Kron the way I do, it's not impossible he would want to beat you into unconsciousness, perhaps even kill you. That I will not allow. And I do not wish to cross my friend. On the other hand, of late he has shown restraint that is uncharacteristic of his former self. I would like to think I've had some small role to play in that change of demeanor, but not enough time has passed for me to be convinced it is a permanent adjustment of his character. So, do I take you to him or not?"

The healer had stopped talking, his soft eyes staring at Eel.

Who could only respond with, "Uh?"

Randall grinned once more. "Allow me to put this another way, since I am not completely familiar with your interactions and your relationship with my friend. If I were to promise you my personal protection, would you be willing to go with me to Kron Darkbow?"

***

"You are not going to believe this."

Kerjim looked up from behind the desk where he was using an iron stylus to fill out various guild papers.

Nodana stood in the open doorway, Spider lurking behind her. Both wore grins.

183

The Docks boss used his pen to point to a pair of chairs in front of him. "Come in, and close the door behind you."

The two entered, Nodana slipping into one of the seats, Spider shutting the door then leaning against it.

Kerjim looked from one to the other. "Alright, what did you find?"

"Nothing," Nodana said, her voice almost giggling. "There are no guards, no wards, nothing."

Kerjim looked to Spider. "And you?"

"The same. I detected no magic, and there wasn't a sentry in sight. The front gate isn't even locked."

The Pursian set down his stylus and leaned back in his chair, placing his hands behind his head as he stared at the ceiling. "They expect nothing. How can it be this simple?"

"They've underestimated you," Nodana said. "Apparently they didn't think you would have a mage at your service."

Kerjim's eyes shot back to her. "Is the place empty?"

The woman shook her head. "I detected three people there, one of them Darkbow. I assured myself none of them were guards, but I didn't check the identities of the others, figuring they were Lalo and perhaps a servant."

"Good, good." The Pursian lowered his arms to the desktop, then glanced to Spider "It's time you announced your presence as thief master. Get a team together. Have them ready to act tonight."

"What about Mama Kaf?" Spider asked. "She won't be happy if this goes down and she isn't a part of it."

"Include her," Kerjim said, "and don't bother hiring a mage. Mistress Nodana and I will be going along to make sure nothing goes wrong this time."

***

The sun warming his bare back, Kron hefted the curved sword in front of him in one hand. It had a decent weight, but the balance was different from his familiar weapon. He preferred a larger weapon, a tool that could be utilized in one hand or two, and for the extra power that could be put behind blows. Of course he had been trained with many different types of swords, but he still had his preferences.

Preferences for killings, we ares sure.

Shut up! Or I'll find that river bridge.

Inner silence.

Kron flipped the sword around, caught it by the back of the blade and tossed it to Stilp.

Who cried out and ran.

The saber fell onto the grass.

Kron chuckled at the other fellow. "You were supposed to catch that."

"Yeah? Where? In my lungs?" Stilp had stopped running and now stood with his hands on his hips in front of the mansion's entrance.

Lalo laughed in the open doorway. "You did look rather silly."

Stilp glared at his employer. "I don't see you out here sparring with him."

The Finder straightened. "Of course not. I'm no combatant."

Kron walked toward the other two, retrieving the sword along the way. "Actually, Lalo, it wouldn't hurt you to have a little training. Your work has been somewhat precarious over the years."

Lalo sniffed. "Lord Belgad was always around for that sort of thing."

Kron handed the sword off to Stilp, then brushed at his buckskin leggings and high leather boots. "If you haven't noticed, Belgad is no longer here."

The Finder did not appear to appreciate the obvious. His face soured. "Well, if the guilds hadn't suddenly become so haughty, I would still have my guards. Besides, there's always Stilp."

Kron and Stilp glanced at one another. Then both burst out laughing.

Once the mood settled, Kron picked up a soft tanned shirt to one side of the entrance and pulled it over his head. "That saber is a fine weapon, but if you don't mind, I'd like to take another look at your armory. Maybe I can find something more suitable."

Lalo looked past Kron down the hill to the iron gate at the estate's outer walls. "Perhaps you will not need to."

Kron and Stilp turned.

A pair of young men were working their way through the gate, then closing it behind them. One was the healer Randall Tendbones, the other was dressed in typical plain street clothes except there was a big sword with leather wrappings hanging on his back. Kron recognized the lad, and the sword.

Randall waved as they approached.

Stilp waved back. Lalo and Kron merely stood their ground.

When they were within talking distance, the healer put out a hand and grabbed his companion by an elbow, pulling him to a stop.

"You must be Eel Sidewinder," Kron said to the newcomer with Randall.

Eel nodded.

Kron glanced over the youth's shoulder. "You have my sword."

Eel reached for the weapon's hilt.

Kron took a step.

"Wait!" Randall moved between the two, his heavy glare on Kron. "There will be no confrontation here, do I make myself clear?"

Kron nodded and stepped back.

"I was just going to return the sword," Eel said.

Randall held out his arms. "Give it to me."

Eel did as he had been told, slinging the large weapon around and placing it into the healer's hands.

Randall turned and offered the weapon to its rightful owner.

Takes its and kills thems all!

Kron flinched but managed to force down the ghosts within. He reached for the sword and unsheathed it, staring along the familiar blade. "No nicks. Still oiled. It's in good condition." His flat gaze rose to glare over the healer's shoulder to the young man standing there. "It is a good thing."

"Eel has come here in peace," Randall said.

Kron drove the sword into its leather sheath and lowered it to his side. "That is fine with me. I have never attacked the boy nor gone out of my way to make him an enemy."

Randall seemed to soften at those words, his shoulders sinking. "I am glad to hear it."

"Did you only bring him here to return my sword?" Kron asked.

Eel stepped around the healer. "He brought me here because he didn't want to turn me over to the city guards, and I came because ... well ... "

"Spit it out," Kron said.

The boy lowered his head in shame. "I came here to apologize. I wanted to say I was sorry for what happened the other night."

"You mean when you and your crew tried to kill me?"

"And me!" Stilp piped in.

Eel nodded without looking up. "Yes. I ... I was following my uncle's lead, but I don't mean that as an excuse."

"Kerjim."

All heads looked up and around. It had been the Finder who had spoken the single word.

"Yes," Eel said.

Kron looked to Randall. "What do you expect me to do with him?"

The healer's eyes went wide with puzzlement. "To tell the truth, I'm not sure. I wanted your sword returned to you, but beyond that I don't know. I wasn't going to turn him over to the guards, but I didn't want to just let him go. I guess I was thinking you would decide what to do with him."

Kron eyed the lad once more, then offered a brief chuckle. "Does your uncle know you are here?"

Eel shook his head.

"I don't suppose he would approve, would he?" Kron asked.

Again, Eel shook his head.

Kron sighed. "If your uncle would not approve and does not know you are here, that leads me to believe you are on the outs with him. Is that the case?"

This time Eel nodded.

Kron snapped his fingers. "Have you lost the ability to speak?"

"No," Eel said.

Kron chuckled. "But single words are all you'll say?"

Eel shook his head, then stamped at the ground, frustrated. "No, I can speak just fine. And yes, I've parted with my uncle. I want nothing more to do with him or his ways."

Kron's dark eyes narrowed. "Interesting."

"What is?" Stilp asked.

"This young fellow has had a change of heart, for whatever reason," Kron said, motioning toward Eel, "and now he has allowed himself to be lead to the very person who by all rights would want to see him punished. That takes bravery, and a certain level of moral fortitude. *That* I can respect."

Eel's face screwed up in confusion. "You mean you're not going to do anything to me?"

Kron grinned. "You would not be the first person to change their ways for the better."

Now Eel smiled. "I thought I was a dead man."

"A year ago and you likely would have been."

The others had a chuckle at the truth of Kron's words.

"There is something I would like to ask you, though," he said to Eel.

"Yes?"

"Why does your uncle want me dead? I don't even know the man."

"Oh." Eel blinked as if the answer should be obvious. "He doesn't want you dead, he wants to kill you, personally, or at least be in charge of the men who do."

"But why?" Kron asked.

It was the Finder who answered. "Because you are Kron Darkbow. Because you are the man who drove Belgad the Liar out of Bond."

Kron snickered. "There's little truth to that, and all of us know it."

"Yes," Lalo went on, "but those of the street believe otherwise. All they know for sure is Belgad was here and now he is gone, and you had something to do with that." He looked past Kron to Randall. "However, the truth is Prince Kerwin here was mostly responsible."

Kron looked to the healer and saw the pain in his friend's eyes. Randall had given up his official title and claims to the throne of Kobalos. His secret and true identity were known by few within the city, all of them present. In fact, Kron had not been aware Lalo had known the truth, but the Finder must have learned during one of his correspondences with his former master.

Randall looked to the current head of the estate. "I no longer use that name."

"My apologies," Lalo said. "I did not realize my social error. Perhaps if -- "

Randall interrupted. "Perhaps we should continue this discussion indoors."

"Good idea." Kron grabbed Eel by an elbow, the lad looking more confused than ever, and lead him toward the entrance.

"Kron?" Randall asked. "Can you hold on a moment?"

Kron handed Eel off to Stilp, turned back to the healer and waited.

Randall watched as the others went inside, and only then spoke. "I've been meaning to ask how you are feeling."

"I am fine. Why?"

The healer stared into his friend's eyes. "You are not fooling me, you understand? I know you are not alone in there."

Kron blinked. "I am ... keeping them under control."

"For how long?"

"As long as it takes."

"To what end?"

Kron grinned but remained silent.

Randall shook his head. "I should have known. You've got something twisted planned, something *evil*."

"I promised Gris I would not kill anyone," Kron said, "so you can rest assured about that."

"You wouldn't *kill* anyone? That makes me feel, oh, so much better. You forget I've seen what you can do with your fists alone."

Kron smiled. "Your sarcasm goes without appreciation." He gestured toward the building. "Now, may we join the others?"

"Might as well." Randall shook his head as he moved toward the door.

"By the way, what lead you to find me here?" Kron asked out of the side of his mouth as they neared the entrance.

The healer smirked. "How do you think?"

And they entered.

20

Though the mansion that had once belonged to Belgad the Liar was quite spartan by standards of the wealthier classes of Bond, to Eel it was a landmark to extravagance and opulence. Upon entering the main room, everything seemed to be made of marble. Two curving stairways, one to the right and the other to the left, curled to a walkway above. Straight ahead were a pair of open doors that revealed a lengthy chamber beyond, at the end of which could be seen a dais upon which set a heavy chair that looked to Eel's young and inexperienced eyes much like what he would expect a king to sit upon.

"This way." The Finder directed them to the stairs on the left. "We can speak freely in the library."

The others followed, Kron pausing long enough to close and lock the front door behind them.

Upstairs Eel soon found himself within a room much longer than it was wide. A hearth at the far end lit the chamber, revealing two doors in the wall facing the rest of the house. A trio of windows on the far left wall were shuttered but obviously looked down upon the estate's grounds. Atop a thick rug in the center of the room was a massive desk, behind it a large chair and before it two smaller chairs. Around the room were scattered a few more sitting spots. Most impressive to Eel were the rows upon rows of books and scrolls that lined the walls. He had never imagined there were so many books in the world, let alone in one room.

Lalo rested himself in the chair behind the desk and motioned for the others to sit wherever they wished. Stilp took a reclining seat near the fireplace. Randall eased into one of the chairs facing the Finder. Kron remained standing near the door. Eel looked around, feeling foolish, then plopped down next to the healer.

It was Randall who spoke first, staring at the Finder. "My past is not relevant to the current situation. I see little reason to bring it up."

"Again, my apologies," Lalo said. "My curiosity got the best of me. I will not approach the subject again without your suggestion."

Randall nodded. The matter was closed.

Kron spoke up. "But we do need to know what Kerjim has planned."

All heads turned on Eel.

The youth glanced over his shoulder to Darkbow standing behind him. "What do you mean?"

The Finder spoke before Kron could open his mouth. "It is obvious, young man, your uncle has been behind the riots that so recently brought tumult to our city. From what I have heard, it also seems obvious he is behind some major moves within the guilds environment of late. We merely wish to confirm from you if this is true, and perhaps you can enlighten us to anything else that could be pertinent."

Eel licked his lips. These people knew a lot, or they had been able to figure out much on their own. None of them seemed stupid, after all. Okay, well, maybe Stilp didn't seem the brightest flame in the candle shop, but Eel had yet to speak much with the fellow. Regardless, they were asking him to betray his uncle more than he already had. But why not? Kerjim had only ever used Eel, never really caring about him. That much had become obvious during the last few days.

"He plans on making himself master of a Guild of Guilds," Eel said.

Several eyebrows raised throughout the room.

The lad continued. "The original idea was for me to be head of a new thieves guild, with a woman named Nodana to be boss of a mages guild."

"Frex Nodana?" Randall asked.

Eel nodded. "You know her?"

"I've heard of her," Randall said. "She was a student at the university some while back."

Kron strode over to Lalo's desk and sat on one end, a leg dangling over the side, his sheathed sword hanging from one hand. "All of that is fine, but what about this Guild of Guilds? And these new guilds? What do they have to do with Kerjim?"

"It gives him a stronger power base," Lalo said.

Kron glanced at the man, as did the others in the room.

The Finder explained, "If he is running for master of the Guild of Guilds, the thieves and mages would give him two more votes, as well as provide him backing on the street levels. It's actually quite sly on Kerjim's part."

"But why would the other guild masters vote for him?" Randall asked. "Wouldn't they each want the position?"

"Of course," Lalo said, "but the smaller, less powerful guilds are going to follow the lead of the stronger. It helps that Kerjim is already a known quantity, and a powerful one within the guilds. That combined with his vote as Docks Guild master, and the additional votes from the thieves and mages, gives him a strong boost. At this stage, it would be possible but not likely the lesser guilds would vote against him, or to be more proper, that they would vote for other candidates. Only major guild powers would even try for a position as master of Guild of Guilds, and it would seem Kerjim is already ahead of the pack."

Kron craned around to look at Lalo. "Who else could run against him?"

The Finder held up a hand and counted on his fingers. "Captain Tuxra with the guards guild, for one. Then there's Kadath Osrm, head of the Merchants Guild. The master of the beggars guild often holds much sway as they are the eyes and ears of the streets."

"Anyone else?" Kron asked.

"Perhaps Scurvy Nob, master of the sailors," Lalo said, "but that guild tends to have more power outside of the city than within, and Nob is somewhat new to his position. I doubt he could drum up enough support to threaten the Docks chief."

"What of this storytellers guild you told me about?" Kron mentioned.

Lalo grinned. "They are a small guild, without much funding. Midge Highwater can be a formidable individual and is apt to go his own way, but he presents little power within guilds politics."

"Still, it would seem Kerjim would face several possibly formidable opponents in an open election," Randall said.

"True." Lalo nodded to the healer. "But he already has strong backing from the Docks, and with these new guilds."

Eel cut into the conversation. "He's counting on Tuxra and Osrm running for the title, maybe The Gnat, too. He thinks it would split the vote, give him an opportunity."

"Your uncle is correct, and a shrewd one," Lalo agreed. "At this point the only thing likely to stop him would be a triumvirate of those three guild masters, which is not likely to happen. None of them would want to see the other in power over their guilds."

Kron rapped a knuckled against the desk. "But why did he drag me into all this mess? I realize killing me might give him some support on the streets, but I've never been directly involved with guild politics."

"The guilds operate on the streets, Master Darkbow," Lalo explained. "Few truly understand that. The power plays might go on behind closed doors, but that is nothing if one cannot control the streets and the beliefs of the commoners. If Kerjim shows himself as the man who slew Kron Darkbow, then he gains all the votes of the lesser guilds. It would be a major conquest for him."

Kron looked to Eel, who nodded back in agreement with the Finder's words.

Randall reached over and tapped Kron on a knee. "Don't you think it's time to bring Gris into this?"

His friend shook his head. "No. I want to tackle this on my own."

The healer held up his hands. "But why? Let the authorities handle it."

Kron's gaze narrowed. "This city is my home. If I am to remain here, I cannot go running to the city guard every time there is a ... situation. As Lalo said, the power is on the streets. That means the people on the streets need to know I will not tolerate those who will threaten me."

Randall threw his hands higher. then sank back onto his chair. "Honestly, Kron, it sounds like so much bravado."

"Perhaps it is, but I do not plan to run and hide every time some brute decides he wants to make a name for himself by killing me. I won't live that way."

Eel moved forward to the edge of his seat, once more drawing the room's attention. "I don't blame Kron for feeling that way, but at this point, what can be done about it? I mean, the election probably won't be for a week or two, but my uncle isn't going to give up trying to kill Kron before then."

Lalo chuckled, motioning to the man sitting on the edge of his desk. "A year ago, my guess would be Master Darkbow would have torn a bloody swath across the city to get to Kerjim, but it seems he has had a change of heart concerning his former ways, and has decided upon a different path."

"I want to beat him at his own game," Kron said.

"But you're not going to kill him?" Randall asked, almost unbelieving.

Kron shook his head. "No. Unless he forces my hand."

Lalo laughed again. "It seems Master Darkbow has decided to take a role in politics."

The room went quiet. Everyone stared at Kron.

Finally, it was Stilp who opened his mouth. "What? Darkbow is running for office?"

Another moment of silence.

Then followed plenty of laughter, the Finder and Randall adding most to the joviality, though Kron himself added to the crowing.

Eventually the clamor died down and Kron spoke again while wiping tears of hilarity from his eyes. "Let me make it clear, I have no plans to run for any election, but I do have an idea for turning the tables on Kerjim."

"What is it?" Randall asked.

Kron glanced to Eel, then back to the healer. "Allow me to keep that to myself for the time being."

Eel looked up. "If you want me to leave so you can talk some more, just say the word."

"No," Kron said. "I want you right here where we can keep a watch on you."

The youth slunk back in his chair, looking sheepish. "Sorry."

"No need to apologize," the Finder said to Eel. "It just so happens I am a short on manpower at the moment. How would you like a position?"

Eel looked up again. "Why would you want me after everything I've done?"

"Yeah, why?" Stilp asked.

Lalo and Kron traded looks, then Kron nodded.

"It would appear you have cut ties with your uncle," Lalo said.

Eel agreed with a wave of his hand.

"In that case," the Finder went on, "you are going to need employment and a place to stay. Food, shelter, the basics in life."

Eel nodded.

"You need all of that," the Finder said, "and I am in dire need of employees. It only makes sense for me to offer you a position. You can be in charge of security. How does two gold a week sound?"

"It sounds like robbery," Kron said with a grimace.

"Alright, three golds a week."

"I'll take it!" Eel nearly shot out of his seat to interrupt anyone else before they could speak. Three golds a week wouldn't make him rich, but it was more money than he had honestly earned during a week in his life.

More than a few chuckles followed the youth's enthusiasm.

Once the laughter drifted away, Kron slid off the table and straightened. "Since we have all that settled, I need to be off. I've got preparations to make before meeting with Master Highwater."

"Do you still need to go?" Lalo asked. "What more is there to discover?"

"The mood on the streets," Kron said. "I want an impression of what we are up against."

"My uncle is going to be looking for you," Eel pointed out.

Randall added, "And if he has Frex Nodana working for him, he's going to be able to find you."

"I'll take precautions."

The healer stood, closed his eyes for a moment, then opened them. "There. I've placed a misdirection ward about you. It should keep magical eyes from finding you for a few days." He turned to the Finder. "And since you have no guards, before I go, would you like me to place protective wards around the perimeter of your estate?"

Lalo grinned. "Ask my chief of security."

Randall looked to Eel.

The youth appeared sheepish once more. "Uh, sure. But we'll be safe going in and out, right?"

Randall nodded. "Everyone in this room will be fine crossing the border. Only strangers who enter the grounds will face any difficulties."

"Very well." Kron gave a salute to the room, then he was gone, exiting into the hallway.

Silence rolled over the library once more as the others stared at Kron's wake.

Stilp stood and stretched. "Not much for goodbyes, is he?"

It was less than an hour later when Randall opened the door leading to what had once been the master bedroom of Belgad the Liar. He entered, pausing long enough to take in his surroundings and to notice Kron on the other side of the room standing next to the bed. His friend looked up while buckling a thick leather sword belt about his hips, his returned weapon hanging heavily from his left side.

"Randall," Kron said as way of acknowledgment while he continued tightening the belt.

The healer glanced around the chamber again. "So this was the great man's private room?"

Kron nodded, retrieving a pair of sheathed daggers from the end of the bed.

Randall faced his friend. "I must say, you seem more and more yourself."

Kron slid one of the daggers into the top of his right boot and looked up, confusion in his features. "What are you talking about?"

"Those ... spirits swirling about in your head."

Kron grunted and went back to work, the other dagger finding a home stuffed within his belt. "My controls grows stronger all the time."

"For how long?"

Kron stopped what he was doing and eased back on the bed, exasperated. "Alright, Randall, you have concerns. I'll admit they are legitimate ones, but I am keeping everything under control. It won't be much longer, I promise."

"You don't know what you are trying to dominate, Kron. If they should get the upper hand on you, there is no telling what might happen."

"Such as?"

Thinking, Randall wrapped his hands together within the folds of his robes. "For one, some of the spirits could try to take control of you."

"They already attempt to do so on a daily basis," Kron said. "Thus far it has been manageable."

The healer nodded. "Much like with magic, force of will can play a major role in something like this. But what about others around you? Do you realize what will happen if the ghosts were to be released all at once?"

Kron grinned. "Not exactly. But I have my ideas."

Randall did not looked pleased. "This is not a laughing matter."

The grin fled. "I never said it was. Just trust me on this. When the time is right, I shall release my guests. Until then, I might have use for them."

"You are playing a dangerous game."

"When have you known me not to?"

"True enough, but recognize this, considering the number of spirits rolling around within your skull, once they are released, it will be impossible for me not to notice. It's possible a handful of other powerful mages within the city will also notice, but they are not likely to become involved. At that point, I *will* become involved. Do you understand?"

"I do," Kron said, "and I thank you for your concern."

"It's not just you," the healer said. "If those ghosts are released without vessels for containment, they could very well latch onto others, men or women or even children without the fortitude of one such as yourself. It would drive people mad, perhaps even damage their very souls."

"As I said, Randall, you'll have to trust me for now."

The healer sniffed. "As you say, very well. For now."

Kron shoved away from the bed and reached for a leather sack near his feet, rummaging through it. "Anything else?"

"One last thing," Randall said.

Kron looked up as he pulled a thin cord attached to a grappling hook from the back and looped it around the hilt of his sword. "What is that?"

"I've warded yourself and the house," Randall said, "but that won't keep you from prying eyes on the streets."

Here Kron grinned. "You've known me long enough to appreciate I can disappear when I want."

"So you'll take precautions?"

Kron nodded. "Don't worry, old friend. I'll wait until dark falls, then exit over a back wall. I'll stick to alleys and rooftops as much as possible, at least while in the Swamps."

"Where is it you are going?"

"Southtown," Kron said, "not far from the Scabbard. Lalo tells me this Highwater character usually works out of The Gilded Pony."

22

Evicting the old couple from their tenement had been a simple matter. All it took was one look at Mama Kaf, and the old man grabbed the old woman by the hand and the two fled down Beggars Row.

"You can have the place back tomorrow!" Spider yelled at the couple, then followed up with a chuckle.

Soon enough Kerjim and his crew had the apartment to themselves, and the others living in the building were smart enough to become scarce.

Wrapped in one of the old woman's cloaks, Spider was placed on the doorstep to keep an eye on the Finder's mansion just down the road; from his position, the thief boss had a direct line to the entrance gates and could spy the front door to the building atop the hill behind the walls.

The rest of the party took over the main room of the apartment, other than Mama Kaf who remained out in a hall and acted as sentry while also keeping an eye on Spider.

Kerjim planted himself in a comfy chair, likely the old man's personal favorite, and put his feet up on a small, padded but threadbare stool. Frex Nodana sat opposite him in a similar chair, the two almost looking like a home-bound couple themselves. Stationed with Mama Kaf were a pair of young toughs in light leathers, each carrying knives. In the kitchen behind Nodana and Kerjim were another three fellows, each burly, wearing studded leather mail and hefting maces and short swords; they took their time tearing into the pantry, scarfing down whatever looked edible.

Now all they had to do was sit and wait. The sun would be going down sooner or later, and then it would be time to make their move.

"Do you want me to study the mansion again?" Nodana asked at one point.

"Wait until the sun goes down," Kerjim said.

So they waited.

***

There were once two cousins who decided to go into business running a pub together. They opened their establishment in the middle of the Swamps, a part of town not nearly so seedy in their day, and hung a shingle outside naming the place "The Stone Pony" after a recalcitrant mule they had owned. Why they didn't name the tavern "The Stone Mule" is a subject lost to history. As the tale goes, business went along well for some years, but then one of the cousins caught the other in bed with his wife. A family feud began. After some months of bickering and quarreling and fighting, each cousin decided he could not spend another day living in the same world as the other and thus a duel was called for. Not being gentlemen, these fellows knew next to nothing about the art of the duel, but they did not let that deter them. A date was set, as was a place, a dry shingle on the southern shore of the Swamps near where Frist Bridge now crosses over to the Southtown. Since neither cousin could afford a proper dueling weapon, each showed up with the best he had on hand, one with a wooden club, the other with a big, mean dog. Then the two let at one another. When it was all said and done, one cousin limped away with a torn pair of breeches while the other strutted home with a dog knocked stupid. Yes, stupid, because that dog was never worth a darn after being thwacked about the head by that stick; in fact, that dog was so stupid from that point on it wouldn't even chase rats around the tavern any more, let alone earn its keep as a sentry. Anyway, the two cousins had reached an impasse. Neither was brave enough or smart enough to try to kill the other, so eventually they decided to go their separate ways. One moved across the river to dryer land that later was dubbed Southtown; here he opened his own little establishment, a place known as The Gilded Pony. Where the wife ended up, nobody knows to this day.

This is how two taverns within the city came to be named after a worthless mule.

Why is this information important? It is not, to tell the truth, but this little piece of history was revealed to Kron Darkbow as he sat in a corner of The Gilded Pony listening to the tale as it was spun out by Midge Highwater.

What was most surprising to Kron was every so often the grizzled old storyteller would glance over the heads of those seated around him to look directly at Kron himself. Their eyes met on several occasions, but the storyteller showed no outward signs of recognizing this newcomer to the tavern.

Once Midge was finished with his tale, he passed around a floppy, weather-beaten hat and a few coppers and a silver were dropped into it by the dispersing crowd, most of them also older fellows who looked as if they had lived rough lives and had likely heard old Midge's stories a thousand times. When the hat returned to him, the storyteller frowned at his earnings but did not hesitate to pocket them before plopping the hat atop his gray head.

He turned briefly to warm his thin fingers before the hearth, then picked up his jack of ale from the edge of a stool and walked directly to Kron's table.

"Don't you normally wear black, young fellah?" the old man asked.

Kron blinked. "Do we know one another?"

"Not so as you'd know it."

Kron blinked again. *What the hell had that meant?*

"I was at Belgad's little shindig last year when you busted in," the storyteller explained. "In fact, you landed right on my table when you came crashing through that window. Ruined a perfectly good roast duck and busted my mug of Nebrarian ale. If I'd had my knife with me, I'd probably have done the Liar a favor and skewered you myself right there on the spot."

Kron couldn't help himself. He grinned. He liked the old man.

"Stop that. It makes you look like a crazy person."

Kron forced down his smile. "My apologies."

The storyteller tossed back the last of his drink, then slammed the leather mug down on Kron's table before sliding onto a seat. "So, you here to make amends?"

"Amends?"

"Sure. You could start with paying for my dinner."

Kron had to force himself not to smile again. "Very well. Order whatever you want from the menu."

"This is The Gilded Pony, pup. They ain't got no menu. They got soup and moldy bread. Stew on holy days. That's it. And cheap drinks."

"Well, order as you see fit. And add your drinks to my tab."

"I plan to."

The old fellow turned in his seat and waved over a serving woman who looked as if she weren't much younger than Midge. He ordered the soup and the moldy bread, and told her to keep the drinks coming until his friend finally left the establishment.

All the while Kron rubbed at his face with a hand, hiding the smile that kept creeping to the surface.

"Something wrong with your face, boy?" the old man said after the server went away.

"Not at all." Kron lowered his hand, nearly causing his jaw to spasm as he fought laughter.

Midge tapped on the table as if enumerating a point. "Alright, out with it. You been watchin' me for the better part of a half hour, so you must be wantin' something. To what pleasure do I owe the presence of the great Kron Darkbow?"

Kron nodded. Straight to the point, more or less, after the food and drink was ordered. He could appreciate this. So why not speak the truth? "I want to talk to you about the guilds."

The old man grinned, showing a few of his teeth were missing. "I thought it might be something like that. Rumor was you was dead, then rumor was you was alive. Now rumor is you won't be for long. Seems someone wants you in the ground."

"That someone is Kerjim Sidewinder."

Midge cackled. "Well, you ain't no fool, that's for sure. Got that much figured out already, do you?"

Kron nodded. "As well as a few other details."

The storyteller rubbed his hands together again, then leaned into the table as if enjoying the subject. "You know about this Guild of Guilds, then?"

"I do."

"In that case, you'll know Sidewinder wants to be master of it."

"I do."

"And killin' you will give him loads of clout on the streets."

"I know that as well."

"Then what the hell you comin' here wantin' to talk to me for?"

Kron choked down another grin. "I came here to seek your advice."

"Me? I'm just an old man who likes to run his mouth. What good can I do you?"

"You are a man who knows things," Kron said. "You are a man who keeps his eyes and ears open."

"What makes you think that?" Midge asked.

"Because you are a storyteller."

The old man stared from a squinted eye. "You're smarter than you look, you know that?"

"I had to be to survive Belgad the Liar."

"And Lord Verkain," Midge added.

Kron's eyes went wide.

"Oh, yes, I know all about it," the storyteller said. "How you and that ... let's call him a healer ... went up north and got yourself into a gods-awful mess in Kobalos."

This could pose a problem. What had the old man meant concerning Randall? If the fellow knew Randall had been a prince of Kobalos, that alone was dangerous information to be floating about, but if somehow he knew more than that ...

Midge gave a sad grin and eased back in his seat as he waved a hand toward Kron. "I see by the look on your face you'd rather I not know what I know. Don't worry. I'm not one to blab others' secrets."

Kron gulped. How could he be sure of this?

As if reading the man's thoughts, Midge said, "Besides, if I was gonna blab about your business, don't you think I woulda done so by now?"

He had a point, Kron had to admit.

Midge tapped the table again. "Enough about that. It's the past. You came here to talk about the guilds. What is it you want to know?"

At that moment the old woman came forward, placing a bowl before the storyteller along with a wooden spoon and another mug of ale. The two men held their breath until she was gone, then Midge went to work eating.

"I need to bring down Master Sidewinder," Kron said.

Midge swallowed a tablespoon of his soup and wiped at his lips with a sleeve. "Figured a fellow like you would just go and kill 'im."

"I am ... trying to change my ways."

Midge set down his spoon. "What, you get religion or somethin'?"

This time Kron couldn't help but grin.

Midge lifted his spoon. "Stop it. You look crazy."

Kron gave the old man a few moments of silent feeding before he spoke again. "I can't allow Kerjim to become head of the Guild of Guilds. If someone else were to take the position, I believe Kerjim would lose interest in me."

"Well, that would sure take the wind out of his sails, that's for sure."

Kron nodded. "That is my hope."

"But what's to stop someone *else* from comin' after you? I know Belgad is fine and well up north there, but on the streets it's a different story. People believe what they want to believe, and most of 'em believe you killed the great man. That puts a big target on your back. You got an answer for that?"

"Fear."

The lone word gave the old man pause, his spoon stopping halfway to his lips. He looked away from his meal into the eyes of the man seated next to him and shivered, spilling the contents of his spoon. "You mean that, don't you?" His words were barely more than a whisper.

"I do," Kron said.

Midge glanced at his empty spoon and placed the utensil next to his bowl. "Well, I don't see how you can pull it off since you ... changed your ways."

"Maybe I have new ways," Kron said, his words chilled.

Tells him! Tells him and see the fears in his face!

But it was plain there was already a touch of dread in the old man's features. Kron saw no reason to add to it. "I plan on killing no one. I do not want you to be concerned anything you tell me will bring others to harm."

The fear in Midge's eyes was replaced with pain. Old memories lingered behind those orbs. "Killing a man isn't necessarily the worst that can be done to him."

Kron nodded again. "I agree. However, I can assure you no physical harm will come to Master Kerjim or those in his employ, not unless they force it upon me."

The storyteller blinked, those old memories slowly fading away. With a shaking hand, he reached for his drink. "Alright. What can I tell you?"

22

The group assembled on the street a half hour after the last of the day's glow had faded from the sky. Frex Nodana counted their numbers. Nine altogether. She wondered if it would be enough against the slayer that was Kron Darkbow. Of course he might still be suffering wounds from Eel's attack from earlier in the week, but the mage believed the man in black would have found a healer by now.

"Let's get on with it." The gruff voice was that of Mama Kaf, the humongous woman standing in the middle of the street like some giant tree that had taken root, her massive sledge hammer hanging from a hand the size of large ham.

"Proceed," Kerjim said.

As a collective they began a slow march toward the outer walls of the Finder's estate, the iron gate of the residence in their sight all the while.

Her nerves getting the best of her, Nodana glanced around as they walked. There were few people on the street, which was odd. Though night, it was yet early. There should have been plenty of traffic. Perhaps Kerjim had spread some coin to keep Beggars Row empty. More likely, word had flowed forth that the west end was not a safe place to be after dark on this night.

Once they were within an arrow's shot of the walls, the hair stood up on the back of the mage's neck. Another step and she gasped.

The party came to a halt, all eyes turning to look at Nodana.

"Is there something wrong?" Kerjim asked.

The wizard looked to Spider and saw his eyes were wide. "You sense it, too, don't you?"

The little gray-haired man nodded.

Kerjim sighed. "What is it?"

Nodana pointed to the walls ahead. "Wards have been placed."

The Docks boss glanced toward the estate, then back to the mage. "But they were not there before?"

"No," Nodana said. "I only now detected them."

Kerjim frowned. "You did another scan of the grounds?"

"That's just it," Spider cut in, "we *weren't* looking."

The Pursian's face screwed up. "But --"

"We did not use any magic," Nodana tried to explain. "Neither of us. We *sensed* the wards."

"I do not understand the distinction," Kerjim said.

"We did not cast any spells. We should not have been able to detect the wards without doing so."

"Which means?"

Nodana and Spider traded glances, then she looked back to the Docks chief. "For these wards to trigger our senses without us actively searching for them, it means whomever placed them is powerful on a scale that is ... frankly, it's quite frightening."

Kerjim looked to Spider. "You, too?"

Spider nodded.

The Pursian looked back to the walls. "Can you take down these wards?"

"Possibly," Nodana said, "but it will take time."

"How much time?"

"Hours. If we can manage it at all."

Kerjim sighed. "*Hours*. Which would give those inside plenty of time to notice us standing out here, or for a city patrol to come waltzing past."

Nodana looked up to the sky. "There's a cloud cover tonight. Little moonlight and no stars. That helps. I could cast an aura of darkness around us that would shield us from view."

The Pursian stood there in the street, surrounded by his associates. He looked from one to the other, pausing only at the heavy gaze of Mama Kaf, then he threw up his arms. "Do this, then. The sooner we get started, the sooner we get inside."

***

Twirling the short sword in his right hand, Eel had to admit it had a better heft than those belonging to his uncle. The blade also looked newer, and of a better grade of steel. He grinned as he slammed the weapon home into the scabbard at his waist and glanced around the small room. Racks of spears lined one wall, round shields of wood and iron hanging behind them. In the center of the room was a long wooden framework sporting numerous slots from which swords of various sizes and styles protruded; a similar but much smaller frame, this one holding daggers and knives and other lesser blades, was next to the sole entry. A dummy in one corner wore a long chain shirt and shoulder pads of bronze. Belgad the Liar had known his weapons, and had spent a small fortune securing his own personal armory, an armory the Finder had placed at Eel's disposal in the young man's role as head of security for the household.

The former thief strutted over to the rack of daggers and looked over the dozen or so blades. His fingers wrapped around the dark leather hilt of a heavy curved hunting knife and he lifted the weapon free, eying its simplicity and quality while feeling the perfect balance in his palm.

A crack like lightning caused him to jump as the ground shook beneath his moccasins. That was the warning sign of which Randall had warned them.

As soon as the floor became still, Eel slid the knife into his belt and turned toward the door, throwing it open and pounding up stone steps. The sound had come from outside, he was sure. The healer's wards had just been set off.

***

Frex Nodana lay on her back in the road, black steam drifting up from her motionless form.

"Spider, check on her," the Docks boss said.

The little man dropped to a knee next to the mage and placed two fingers against her throat. There was a pulse, hearty and strong. He looked up. "She's alive. Just out of it."

Kerjim nodded, then glanced to the iron gate in front of them. "Now we have to question ourselves as to whether the wards have been dispelled."

The group stood in silence for several moments, all eyes staring at the gate.

Then, "Bah!" Mama Kaf shoved her way through the group, her big hammer already swinging.

Kerjim threw up an arm, ready to cry out.

The hammer's head slammed into iron, clanging loudly and crunching the lock, bending back several bars.

But no more balls of blue lightning shot forth.

Kerjim grinned. "We are in luck."

The hammer flew again, banging into the gate.

***

He was moving so fast, Eel nearly stumbled as he came out into the main hall of the mansion. He slid to a stop on the cool marble, looking in all directions. There was no one to be found. "Stilp! Lalo!"

The library's door opened on the second floor and Stilp rushed out onto the balcony, his features full of panic as he stared down at the younger man. "I heard it! What do we do?"

"Is the Finder still up there with you?"

Stilp nodded so quickly it looked as if his head might crack.

Eel waved toward the long hall where the throne-like chair still revealed itself through open doors. "The two of you get to the back of the house. Stay near an exit. If you hear combat, get out right away. I'll find you."

"You can't fight them on your own," Stilp said.

He was right, of course. But what difference did it make? Eel figured his life had been one long mistake after another, and this night might bring another one, a fatal one. Perhaps, though, he could make amends for some of his mistakes. At the least, he could slow down those invading the house, and he had a pretty good idea who they would be.

The young man shook off his thoughts. "I'll do what I can. Just go. I'll catch up."

Stilp nodded and charged back into the library.

Eel glanced down at the hilts of his new sword and knife. It seemed he was going to get a chance to test their mettle, and their metal, sooner than he had anticipated.

Ah, well. Such is life. And sometimes death.

The weapons came free of their scabbards as he approached the estate's front door.

***

Mama Kaf led the ensemble up the hill toward the mansion, and Kerjim showed no inclination in stopping her. Why not? If she wanted to be the first to encounter Kron Darkbow, then so be it. If she could finish the man without Kerjim's personal involvement, all the better. Or, if she should fall, at least she will have weakened their mutual opponent before the rest of them entered the fray.

The Pursian had to grin as they trod along the gravel path. The big woman in front was becoming experienced in breaking through iron gates. This time it had only taken three swings of her hammer, the lock destroyed and a few bars bent out of shape. From what Spider had told him, the gate at the Asylum had fared much worse.

Speaking of Spider, Kerjim turned to the mage-thief at his side. "Now that the wards are down, can you tell how many are in the house?"

Without pausing his stride, Spider closed his eyes for a moment. "There are still three."

"Is one of them Darkbow?"

Spider shrugged. "That would take more time to discover."

"Forget it, then." Kerjim trudged ahead. There had been three earlier. There were three now. Likely one of them was Darkbow.

***

He had put out the few lamps and candles that had been burning in the foyer, leaving mostly darkness. From behind a window, Eel watched an approaching monstrous figure of black blocking the view of the city and sky beyond. It had to be Mama Kaf with those big, wide steps and that steady stride. The others would be behind her.

He backed away from the window as the big woman neared the front door, his hands shaking as his right tugged out his new sword and his left removed the hunting knife from his belt. Back stepping across the room, he planted himself in the opening to the long chamber beyond, torches there revealing the lengthy red carpet that lead up to the big chair on the dais, tall windows to the sides showcasing gardens of multicolored plants. At any other time it would have been an elegant view, but Eel didn't bother to notice.

If he was smart, he would have run. That much he realized. Lalo and Stilp had already headed to the back of the mansion, possibly had even already fled out a back door. Eel knew he should have done the same. There was no way he would survive the next few minutes.

But he was not the Eel of even a few days ago. He was no longer his uncle's boy, a puppet to be used and discarded. He had to prove himself to himself. If that meant death, then so be it.

There was a banging at the front door, a crunching of wood. The door visibly shook, even beneath the darkness of the room.

Eel slid one foot in front of the other, turned slightly so his right side faced the entrance and readied his weapons. It occurred to him he could try and tell Mama Kaf it had not been Darkbow who had killed her son, but he didn't think it would matter at this point. Besides, it would not likely improve her mood or his chances if she found out it had been one of Lalo's men who had done the deed.

***

The hammer struck again. Splinters of wood rained upon the air as the door slammed open and Mama Kaf filled the doorway.

She took one look across the entrance room to where Eel stood, the lad's knees quivering, and tromped in his direction.

The others filed into the room behind her, pausing to take in their surroundings before moving forward.

Kerjim caught a glimpse of his nephew around the big woman's side. He smiled. "Oh, this is a pleasant surprise."

Mama Kaf slung her weapon up on a beefy shoulder, steadying it for a strike.

Fear plain on his face, Eel stood his ground, his curved knife held in front and his short sword out to one side.

The woman roared, shaking the ground. The hammer swung down from upon high as if an angry god were unleashing fury. There was a swishing whistle through the air as Eel darted back, then the cracking of the steel mallet upon marble. The hammer's ringing jarred the nerves, sending shivers along the spines of all present with the exception of Mama Kaf herself.

Who tugged back on her weapon and brought it up to her shoulder once more.

Eel's feet remained planted, but his shoulders shifted from side to side, readying him for a lunge one way or the other. It was obvious to everyone all he could do was try to avoid the mad brute, for there seemed no way his little blades could put a stop to his attacker.

Kerjim sighed and stepped forward. "Hold!"

Mama Kaf stood motionless, her hammer gripped in both hands in front of her heaving chest. Her massive head twisted slightly to one side, a squinting eye staring at the Pursian.

"We are here for Darkbow," Kerjim said. "If my former nephew will inform us as to the man's location, we might allow him to live."

Mama Kaf's head rolled around to stare at the young man before her.

Eel glanced around the big woman's shoulders to his uncle. "Go to hell."

The hammer came up.

***

Kron was still more than a block away when he heard the thudding noise. At first he paid it little mind. He was in the Swamps. There were lots of noises in the Swamps. Though night, it was yet to be late, and lots of people were still out and about, carts passing by, even the occasional horse or mule or oxen.

But as he sauntered forth from an alley onto Beggars Row, it occurred to him the sound had come from the direction of the Finder's manor.

He took off at a run, unslinging his sword as his boots crashed again and again onto cobbled stones, carrying him forward.

As he neared the estate, he slowed, cursing because the wall's outer lamps had not been lit, diminishing his view in the darkness. Still, he could tell the gate's lock had been busted and several of its bars were leaning back. This looked all too familiar.

He was just about to charge through the open gate onto the grounds when something brushed against his left boot. He stopped and looked down to find a figure little larger than a child laying there.

Kron dropped to a knee and felt the neck for a pulse. The person was alive. He brushed back the short dark hair and leaned closer to the face, barely able to make out smooth features. It was either a woman or a young man. Kron could not tell more without further light or feeling along the person's body.

Another sound from the main building of the estate, this one like the crack of thunder and followed by a scream which was quickly cut off.

Whoever this was at his feet, he or she would have to wait. Kron took off at a sprint.

Barreling his way up the front driveway, he was surprised to find most of the place in darkness, only a few lights burning on the upper levels and toward the back of the main building. His boots skidding on the stone stoop as he neared the battered entrance, Kron slowed to listen to the inside. He heard nothing of consequence.

He darted forward, shifting to one side, lowering himself to make as small a target as possible. A quick swivel of his head revealed there were no immediate threats. He was about to move up the stairway on his right when the light from the open doors to the hall ahead revealed a small pool of red to one side.

His sword at the ready, Kron slid forward, his eyes shifting from one place to another, always on the lookout for danger.

When he was halfway across the entrance chamber, he could make out within the hall a slumped figure to one side of the open doorway. It was Eel. The youth was unmoving, his back against a marble column, his head hanging almost between his knees. The blood had pooled at his feet, having streamed from between his legs.

Kron rushed forward, pausing only long enough to ascertain there was no immediate threat. Then he crouched next to the boy, lifting Eel's jaw to look him in the face. Kron nearly flinched at what he saw. The youth's left cheek was crushed inward, the bone shattered and the skin ripped open in a ragged tear that left a flap of skin hanging and blood oozing.

Kron allowed the head to droop and once again felt for a pulse. It was there, but weak. Eel would not live long, probably not until morning, without the benefit of magical healing. The extent of the damage was too much for the lad to survive otherwise.

A scuffing of leather upon stone brought Kron away from the lad. The sound had come from behind and above. He moved into the front room once more, his sword out at his side.

"There he is!" The shouted words came from behind the balustrade on the second-floor balcony. Two men stood there, bulky fellows in studded armor, each gripping a sword.

"Don't move!" one of them yelled.

Kron showed no inclination of moving, the light from the hall outlining his figure.

The other fellow stuck his head in the library's door. "It's him!"

Then the two made their way down the stairs, coming to a halt in front of the manor's entrance, blocking the most obvious route to freedom.

Kron gave no sign of caring. He stood motionless. His gaze followed the two fighters, and only shifted away when another figure appeared above outside the library.

Even in the near darkness of the room, Kron could make out the bulky figure squeezing its way through the door. The thing still hefted that big hammer, just as it had the last time they had met on a rooftop. Only now Kron was not wounded.

Kill thems! Kill thems all!

Kron gave a brief nod. If death was what it took, then he would be glad to deal it out. He might be trying to pacify his own darker side, but that did not mean he would run from a fight, especially with the young man unconscious and seriously hurt on the floor behind him. If he left Eel, only death awaited the youth.

"He is mine!" The voice of Mama Kaf boomed from the second level, jarring the ears of all those exiting the library.

Kerjim rubbed at his ears as the big woman thundered her way down the stairs, her iron gaze locked onto that of the man in leathers holding a bastard sword in the middle of the foyer.

The Docks boss had to give Darkbow credit. The man showed no sign of fleeing, nor of any fear at all. He stood there with his legs slightly apart, watching as Mama Kaf reached the bottom of the stairs, passed in front of Kerjim's two men there and slowly approached.

"I've got to see this." It was Spider who had spoken, his words little more than a whisper as he and the others filed down the steps toward the entrance.

Kerjim sighed from relief. So, finally, Kron Darkbow was to fall. It had cost him enough, including his only nephew. He winced thinking of the single blow from Mama Kaf's hammer that had laid Eel low, but the boy had gotten what he deserved. Kerjim could hold no regrets there.

As the massive figure of the woman huffed and puffed to a stop within striking range of her enemy, the Pursian slipped down the stairs. He, too, did not want to miss what was coming.

***

Up close and now in the borders of the light, the monster before Kron was revealed as a woman, and easily the largest woman he had ever seen.

She hefted her hammer, readying to slam it down upon his head. He could not allow that.

He waited.

Silence stretched forth.

Then a cry from the woman and the hammer whirled.

Kron dove to his right, hitting upon a shoulder and rolling up on one knee.

An explosion of marble chips erupted where he had stood a second before.

He chopped to his left, the steel of his sword singing. Metal cleaved leather and flesh and muscle and fat and bone and out the other side, severing a thick leg from the colossal figure that was Mama Kaf.

Yessss! Blood!

The woman swayed for a moment, suddenly off balance and in shock. Then with a groan she crashed forward, slamming down with a resounding blast that shook her body and the floor. She lay writhing in pain, rolling over and moaning, her forgotten weapon lonely to one side.

Kron kicked away the big hammer and stood away from the woman.

Two of Kerjim's men rushed forward.

"I would not do that!" Kron shouted.

His assailants came up short, at the foot of their downed comrade, and glanced to their boss.

Kerjim shrugged. "Finish him."

The two big fellows charged around Mama Kaf, their swords already swinging for their target.

Kron remained unmoving until they were right on top of him. His sword flashed to his left, slicing along an arm and causing an enemy to drop his weapon as Kron's right boot kicked low, crunching into the other attacker's groin.

The cut man retreated with fear in his eyes. The other fellow slumped to the floor crying.

Before anyone else could move, Kron pointed his sword at Mama Kaf. "This woman will bleed out within minutes if she does not receive care. The longer we fight, the less her chance of survival."

As if to accentuate his remarks, the woman cried out and rolled over into a growing lake of her own blood.

"She needs a healer, now," Kron added.

Kerjim sighed. "Very well. Bentus, Chess, grab hold of her and we'll take her to the Swamps tower."

The next two men nearest Mama Kaf gave the dark swordsman a leery glance, then they moved forward with wariness, tugging on the large woman's arms and sliding her toward the exit, leaving behind a trail of gore. The man with the slash along one arm helped his crying companion to his feet, then they headed for the exit.

When the party reached the front door, Kerjim snapped his fingers. Spider and another man helped lift the big woman outside.

Then the Docks boss turned to his enemy. "This is not finished."

"It is for tonight," Kron said.

Then Kerjim spun away and his crew made their way down the hill.

Kron watched their back for long moments, making sure they were indeed retreating, then he turned back to Eel.

A head stuck out from behind one of the hall's doors. "They gone?"

Kron almost skewered the man. "Stilp, where have you been?"

Lalo's employee stepped out from behind the door. "I helped the Finder get out a back exit, then I've been here all the while watching your back."

Kron grimaced. "Is there anything like an infirmary here?"

Stilp shook his head. "Just some bandages and salves down in the basement."

Kron waved the man on. "Find your master and bring him back here, then head to the healing tower and collect Randall. Hurry!"

23

If what he was experiencing was the afterlife, Eel decided he was better off dead. He had never felt so relaxed in all his years. A sense of warmth pervaded his being, as did a feeling of floating upon clouds. Everything was dark, but the lack of sight did not bring concern. Here he was at ease. He suffered no pain, and his belly was not tight as it often had been during his youngest days. There was no fear, no anger, no betrayal. There were no expectations to be met, no hearts to break, souls to crush, others to disappoint.

Yes, this had to be heaven.

"Get your ass out of bed."

The voice was jarring, and somewhat familiar.

"The healer says you're fine, so get up!"

There was a jerking sensation and suddenly Eel felt himself flipping through the air. In mid-flight his eyes popped open but everything was awhirl, only brief images flashing before his eyes.

Then he landed with a thudding noise, the air forced from his lungs as pain was reintroduced to his flesh. He groaned, his eyes closing once more as he felt a hard wood floor beneath his naked body. He rolled over on his side.

Where he was gently prodded by a boot. "Get up. The others want you."

Eel opened his eyes again. Stilp was standing over him.

"Tendbones got you right as rain, didn't he?"

The youth blinked away the last of his confusion and rolled back onto his stomach, glancing about at his surroundings. He was in Kron's bedroom, the chamber that had once belonged to Belgad himself. A small fire burned in the hearth and a few candles were lit throughout to provide light.

Groaning again, Eel pushed himself off the floor. Cold swamped over his skin and he suddenly realized he was without clothes. He spun for the a sheet from the bed, but Stilp was standing there holding out a silken robe.

"Put this on," Lalo's employee said. "No need for you to run around with your backside hanging out."

Eel grabbed the robe and pulled it around his shoulders. "Thank you. But did you have to toss me out of the bed like that?"

Stilp smiled. "Nope, I didn't. Just wanted to make sure you know where things stand."

"Which is?"

Stilp kept right on smiling. "You might be the new boy around here, and head of security and all, but I'm the one who stuck with Lalo through thick and thin. I'm the last of Belgad's old clients who remained loyal. Got it?"

A dull ache was creaking up the back of Eel's skull. He wasn't sure if it was caused by a ghost of his recent wounding or Stilp's words bashing away at his head. Either way, "Uh, sorry. No, I don't get you."

Stilp jabbed a finger into the young man's bared chest. "You don't order me around, right? I'm the number two man around here right after Lalo himself."

Eel blinked. Okay. Sure. Now he understood. Poor Stilp was feeling threatened and trying to throw around what little weight he had. Now it was Eel's turn to smile. "You don't have to worry about me. I won't be telling you what to do."

"Fine."

"But ..."

"But, what?"

Eel kept right on smiling. "It seemed to me you needed someone giving orders when Mama Kaf showed up."

Stilp's eyes narrowed. "Yeah, well, it wasn't me who got my head caved in from the woman, now was it?"

"Nope, it wasn't," Eel said. He decided then and there it was time to set things right. If he were to keep his position within the household, he couldn't have animosity between him and the head servant, or employee, or client, or whatever Stilp was. "Look, I'm not your boss, and I know that. You answer to Lalo, just like me. At times I might need your help with something, and as I'm head of security, sometimes I might have to work fast, maybe even be a little gruff. I don't mean anything by it. At the same time, I realize since you're the head of ... well, whatever it is you do ... I know there might be times when you'll need me as well. I plan on being there for you as long as you're there for me. We're both here to protect Master Lalo, after all."

It was a fine little speech. It might even have gotten through the hard-headed skull that belonged to Stilp.

Eel would never know for sure, though, because at that moment the door to the room opened and Kron entered.

"We need to talk."

***

The kitchen of the Finder's estate was relatively small for such a sizable house. A large table with a slab of thick, white marble atop it took up the center of the room. Cabinets and counters lined the walls except at the two doors, one to the rest of the house and the other to the outside, and where a large stone hearth took up nearly an entire wall. Glass windows on the sides of the hearth and the outside door revealed the blackness of night beyond.

Stools had been pulled from somewhere and placed about the room. A wooden platter covered with sliced fruit and cheeses rested in the center of the table next to several slim but lengthy kitchen knives and steaming bowls of what smelled to be some kind of strong tea.

"Please, have a seat." The Finder motioned toward an empty stool as Eel, Stilp and Kron entered the room.

Eel glanced about the chamber and found Randall seated upon a stool in a dark corner next to the outside exit. Then the young man sat on the offered stool, placing himself across from the Finder.

The healer nodded recognition to Eel, then moved his chair closer to the others, within a ring of light brought about by a small chandelier hanging above their heads.

Stilp snagged one of the knives and began poking at apple slices and popping them into his mouth, seating himself only after his third slice.

Kron approached the table but opted to stand. He glanced about at the others present. "I suppose most of you think I'm about to go on some rampage, hacking limbs and spilling blood across the city."

The knife, with a chunk of pear on its end, paused halfway to Stilp's mouth as he stared at Kron. Lalo and Eel remained silent, watching.

It was Randall who shook his head. "No. I've seen you in action too often before. If you were going to do something like that, you wouldn't be here now. Which impresses me, honestly. It means you have changed."

Kron grinned. "Perhaps, but I still wish to have my vengeance for this night."

"Why?" Eel suddenly asked. "You weren't hurt. It was my face that was smashed in. If Tendbones here hadn't come along, there's no telling what condition I would be in."

"You would be dead," the healer offered. "And you can thank Stilp for your life. It was he who woke me and brought me here."

Stilp lowered his knife. "That's right. And I did it with a fair share of danger, too. Kerjim and his boys were at the tower. I had to skirt around them without being seen."

"Alright, my thanks to both of you," Eel said, pointing to Kron, "but I'm still curious why Kron wants to go after my uncle."

"Yes, I finally met this uncle of yours," Kron said, "and he only came here because he wants me dead. I don't want to be dead. I see little reason I should not try to stop him."

"Guess I can't blame you there," Eel said, "but if you're not going after him with swords flying, what are you going to do?"

Kron's grin widened as he glanced to the Finder. "That is a matter I'm still working on. I'm hoping to end your uncle's plans without harming anyone else."

Stilp snickered.

Kron looked directly at the man. "You have something to say?"

Stilp froze, his eyes wide. "Uh, no, sir. Just, well, there's a leg and a hammer out in the front room, and they didn't get there by themselves."

"You can clean up that mess when we are finished here," Lalo said.

Now Stilp looked aggravated. "Why me?" He pointed his kitchen knife at Eel. "The boy here is just as --"

"The boy here is head of security," Lalo interrupted, "and it would seem he has already performed his duties for the night."

Everyone looked to Eel, who shrunk on his seat as if not wanting the attention.

Kron patted the youth on a shoulder. "You did a brave thing tonight. Brave, but stupid. You should have fled."

Eel didn't know what to say.

"Speaking of which," Randall said, looking to the lad, "how are you feeling?"

The youth glanced at the healer. "I feel fine. Whatever you did, it worked."

Randall smiled.

Kron tapped the table. "To the business at hand. We need to find a safe place for all of you tonight, perhaps even for a couple of nights. I don't think Kerjim will visit here again, but you never know."

"The healing tower is out," Randall said with a shrug. "I wouldn't mind, but a group this size would draw attention. Besides, we already know Kerjim took his wounded there, where they're likely to stay for at least a few days, especially the one who lost a leg."

"What about the Asylum?" Lalo asked.

"No," both Kron and Eel said at the same time, then looked at one another.

"Kerjim might look there," Kron went on. "Plus it is in no condition for living quarters."

The Finder sighed. "There are still a few small estates that belonged to Lord Belgad out in the countryside. I rarely visit them, but they are sitting empty."

"What is the closest one?" Kron asked.

"A couple of days to the south on the road Dailentown," Lalo answered.

Kron shook his head. "Too far. I want all of you fairly close in case we should need one another."

"What difference does it make?" Eel asked.

Kron looked to the youth. "If your uncle thinks I have gone with you, he might try to find you. I want to be close so I can help if I need to."

"You're not going with us?" Eel asked.

"No," Kron said with a shake of his head. "I need to remain in the city."

Randall leaned forward, placing his hands on the table. "Speaking of which, you have yet to go into detail about your plans. You say no bloodshed, but where does that leave you? Yesterday Lalo here mentioned politics, but that doesn't make sense."

Kron glanced toward a darkened window. "It'll be morning in a couple of hours. Once the sun rises, I have a few contacts to make, people I hope will help me take Kerjim Sidewinder down a peg or two."

"To what end?" Randall asked. "You still have told us nothing."

Kron sighed. "Let me put it this way, I am working to erase temptation from Kerjim's thoughts."

"Temptation?" Stilp asked between chews of fruit.

"Temptation to become master of the Guild of Guilds," Kron said. He then looked to the others, his gaze falling on each of them. "My talk with Midge Highwater opened my eyes to the procedures, rules and laws concerning the guilds, providing me with details which perhaps even the Finder here is unaware."

"I doubt it," Lalo said, "but please, do go on."

Kron grinned again. "In the morning I will meet with a few individuals who will hopefully remind Master Kerjim of some of these rules."

"That's it?" Stilp said. "That's all you've got?"

"That's all I'm telling you, for now," Kron said. "All of you will be safer, as will I, if my secrets remain my own. The timing has to be precise with what I have planned, and I cannot take a chance on word leaking."

"So you don't trust us?" Eel asked.

Randall chuckled. "Kron doesn't trust anyone."

A general laughter went about the room.

Then Kron held up a hand. "But we still don't have a place for the rest of you to stay. I need to know you are safe before I can move forward."

"I'm not connected to any of this, not directly," the healer said. "I believe it will be safe for me to return to the tower.

Kron nodded. "I won't disagree."

"I could rent some rooms at the Rusty Scabbard," the Finder suggested. "It is not secretive, but it is far too public a place for Kerjim to attempt another attack."

"That is not a bad idea," Kron said, "especially since a number of city guardsmen frequent the place. And I have a room there already, which I could put at your disposal."

Lalo looked around the room. "Any objections?"

None were voiced.

"Very well, then," the Finder said. "The Rusty Scabbard it will be, as soon as the sun rises."

24

The sun was just coming through the hall's windows as Randall approached the door to his office.

"Excuse me, but are you Randall Tendbones?"

The healer turned to find the speaker was an older man with deeply tanned skin, dark hair going gray around the edges and narrowed eyes as black as the night.

"Do I know you, sir?" Randall asked.

The man came closer, glancing about as if to assure no others were near. His concerns were unfounded, as the closest patients and other healers were around the bends of the curving hall.

The stranger stopped within arm's reach of Randall. "May I ask where you have been this early in the morning?"

Randall stared at the man, trying to remember if he had seen the face before. Perhaps during the riots? No matter, he had an idea of who this fellow might be. " Master Kerjim, isn't it?"

The Pursian nodded. "I am, sir. But you did not answer my question."

"I was away on a personal matter," Randall said. Which was the truth, even if he had been called upon to perform his duties as a healer.

Kerjim's thin eyes grew into full slits. "Would that matter concern a man named Kron Darkbow?"

Randall sighed. "What does this pertain to, Master Kerjim?"

The Docks boss gestured down the hall. "I have several wounded, one seriously. When I arrived I asked for the best healer, which rumor has it is you. After a search by the orderlies, I was informed you were not available. Then I see you walking in the front door, and I ask myself where you have been this past night."

"As I said, it was a personal matter. My whereabouts are my own concern."

Kerjim's eyes almost closed. "Then you will not answer my question?"

"Master Kerjim, if you still wish me to work my magics upon your companions, then by all means lead me to them," Randall said, "but my duties as a healer in no way entail me having to account for my personal location at any given time."

The Pursian grunted. "I don't suppose you were up at the Finder's mansion, now where you?"

Randall glared at the man, then reached into a pocket of his robes, pulled out a key and turned toward the door. "I believe this conversation is finished, sir."

"Alright, alright," Kerjim said to the healer's back. "But one of my people has lost a leg. Can you heal them?"

Randall paused as he slowly turned around. Actually, he probably could grow back the leg, but such power he did not wish to display as it would draw attention to himself. He looked to the Pursian. "I will see what I can do."

Breakfast was salted minnows spritzed with lemon juice, baked flat breads and a bowlful of violet-colored berries shipped on ice all the way from Bidia, more than two thousand miles distant. The simple meal cost more than the typical annual household income for those who lived within Bond, but to Kadath Osrm the cost was not even a second thought. Being master of the Merchants Guild had its perks, as well as a hefty salary. And why shouldn't it? In essence, Osrm was in charge of all goods that traveled to and from the city, and she was the representative of those who managed the transport of those goods.

Along with money came power, and with power came security, proof of which came with the half dozen stalwart fellows she had hired, all through the bodyguards guild, of course, to provide her with security while enjoying her breakfast on the covered veranda of her estate in Uptown.

Curious, then, that there was a stranger marching toward her across the vast verdant expanse that made up the enclosed grounds behind her home. Instead of fear, Kadath Osrm was filled with curiosity. The fellow was tall and broad of shoulder, handsome with his dark hair and nearly chiseled jaw. His eyes, however, were too dark, too weighted, revealing depths that should likely not be plumbed. His clothing was nothing special, dusty soft leathers that would be familiar to any woodsmen or traveler, but the lengthy sword hanging from his belt was the sign of a professional man of one military stripe or another. Osrm realized the sword should have represented a warning to her, but she did not scream for help nor jump up and flee. If this man were here to do her harm, would he appear in the open in such a manner? Would he boldly stride across her backyard? No, a killer would have tried to sneak up on her, perhaps striking in the night instead of appearing here beneath the brass glow of the morning sun.

She did not have time to voice such thoughts to the two armored men who suddenly announced themselves upon her veranda with the swishing of steel drawn forth from scabbards. These were a pair of her personal bodyguards, and they did not waste time before rushing out onto the lawn.

The approaching figure did not hesitate in his steps, but kept right on walking toward the woman.

Her two guards rushed in, one directly, the other from a side.

Warnings were shouted.

To little effect.

The stranger dropped to the ground and spun, one leg catching the foremost guard beneath a knee and toppling him to the ground. The other guard jabbed with his sword, but the stroke was ignored as the mystery man rolled away and came up on his booted feet, his fists up and ready for striking.

Interesting that he had not drawn his sword.

Osrm jumped to her feet. "Enough!"

The standing guard glanced her way, as did the stranger. The fellow on the ground groaned as he rose to one knee, his sword in front of him as a shield between the newcomer and his mistress.

"Allow him to approach," Osrm ordered. "If he meant me harm, I doubt he would appear so in broad daylight."

The tumbled guard stood and he and his partner back toward the patio, their weapons out and pointing at the other man who came forward slowly.

When the boots of her men reached the bottom of the few steps leading up to her, Osrm held up a hand. "Far enough."

The guards stopped. The stranger stopped.

"It seems you are intent upon speaking with me," she said to the handsome, mysterious figure.

The man nodded. "My apologies for approaching in this manner."

Osrm smiled. "You could have asked my secretary for an appointment."

"I have not the time for such," the man said.

"In a hurry?" Osrm asked. "Very well, say what you will."

The stranger straightened. "Though we do not know one another, it might be you have heard my name."

"Which is?"

"Kron Darkbow."

Osrm's eyes flashed. So this was the fellow all the fuss was about. This was the man involved in Belgad's leaving town, and who was apparently the bane of Kerjim Sidewinder's existence. She was impressed by his audacity in coming to her as he had, and she was more than a little attracted to his physical charms. Though those eyes, they spoke of an intricate bleakness Osrm did not wish to welcome.

She finally nodded. "I am familiar with the name."

"Good," Kron said. "Then you know who I am. It may make all of this easier."

"Make *what* easier?" Osrm asked.

"My dismantling of Master Kerjim's goals."

He had said it so straightforward, so dauntlessly. Who would voice such out loud? With Belgad's departure, Kerjim and a handful of others had become the most powerful individuals within the city, Osrm counting herself among that group. And with the Pursian's designs upon the Guild of Guilds, he was perhaps a step ahead of the others.

Despite the heaviness of his gaze, she stared directly into his eyes. "I am listening. Tell me more."

"It has come to my attention the vote for master of the Guild of Guilds will not take place for approximately two weeks."

Osrm nodded. "Yes, as is stipulated by city law."

Kron nodded. "But there is also a clause allowing for an immediate vote."

Osrm's interest grew. Yes, Darkbow was correct. There was such a line within the laws concerning the governance of guilds. The clause had rarely been invoked, but it was there. It allowed for members of a new guild to push ahead with electing its representatives. Such expedience was generally only necessary when important matters pertaining to the new guild were coming to a head, such as when a vote was nearing for city or national legislation that could affect such a guild. In theory, other emergency situations could also be a stimulant for such measures.

Like the riots.

The master of the merchants grinned. "You know your law, sir."

Kron shook his head. "I am but a recent student."

"Tell me, then," Osrm went on, "how does this legal clause apply to Master Kerjim."

"It is no secret he is vying for master of the Guild of Guilds. As things stand, he is likely the most dominant candidate, and two more weeks of posturing would only help to solidify his position."

Osrm couldn't disagree. "Yes, but what good would it do to move up the vote?"

"None," Kron said, "unless there was another appropriate candidate."

Osrm blushed. Did he mean her? Possibly, but not likely. If she were to step into the battle for the Guild of Guilds, she would find herself confronting not only Kerjim, but also Captain Tuxra and perhaps others. As things stood, Kerjim was the only strong candidate. If Osrm should enter the race, the floodgates would open for others to do so. While this might not be unexpected, it would most definitely complicate matters and tear open wounds within the future Guild of Guilds, wounds that would take years to heal. No, the only candidate who could enter at this point and not draw immediate rancor would be someone who was an unknown, an outsider, but then that person would stand little chance of winning the election.

She frowned. "Another candidate serves little purpose at this point."

"Unless it is someone experienced yet with no direct ties to any of the current guilds," Kron said.

Osrm threw up a hand in mock disgust. "It would take a coalition of the stronger guilds to back such an outsider, and that is not likely."

"What if it were someone with the guilds' best interests at heart, someone who was non-threatening?"

The woman smiled once more. "That would nearly be the perfect candidate, a person who could work for the guilds without trying to control them."

"I know of such a person."

Who could it be? Osrm ran over a list of names in her mind, but there was no obvious choice. She motioned for the man in leathers to come closer. "Please, sit. Have some breakfast, and tell me of this potential candidate."

***

Mama Kaf was stretched out upon a heavy table, the big woman moaning softly but otherwise insensible to her surroundings. Whomever had given her a sedative had done a proper job, Randall surmised, probably giving triple the normal amount because of her size.

The other two wounded had been treated and allowed to leave but moments earlier, the one with a fresh wrapping upon his arm and the other with a goat bladder filled with ice held to his groin. Those two would be fine within a matter of days, perhaps sooner if they were careful.

Mama Kaf was not so lucky. Staring down at her within the enclosed chamber reserved for surgery, Randall realized this woman would never walk again without support of some kind. And he hated it. He could heal her. With a touch he could grow back her leg, or return to the Finder's estate, retrieve the dead limb there and reattach it with renewed life. But he would not. Such an act would draw far too much attention, and he already received too much notice for his renown as the best healer within the city. It was not so much he was concerned with himself or his own privacy. No. He was concerned with the general well being of others. Randall was a god. Sort of. But he remained so in secret. If the truth were revealed, there was no telling the outcome. But Randall did not believe it would be a happy one. Wars would sprout up. Men would kill men, all in his name, believers and unbelievers alike. Ashal had once walked among men two thousand years earlier, and it had lead to generations of misery and bloodshed. Randall vowed not to make that mistake again.

"I am sorry," he said, his words soft as he stared down at the large, contorted face. "I can heal her wound, but she will have to learn to walk without the appendage."

Kerjim snarled from behind, seated in a chair near the room's only door. "So much for the greatest healer in the city."

Randall turned, bristling at the disparage comment. "Most healers would fare no better than ointment and a bandage."

"And you?" The question came from Frex Nodana, the mage leaning against a small table on the opposite side of the exit from the Docks boss.

The healer glanced to the woman. "I will make sure to cover the stump with a new layer of flesh. Still, that will take some little time."

"How long?" Nodana asked.

Randall shrugged. "Some few hours."

The woman blushed. "That *is* impressive. I've never known a healing mage so powerful."

Randall offered a lopsided grin at this, then turned away to his patient.

Kerjim shoved out of his chair. "Frex, let us go. There is nothing we can accomplish here, and there is much yet to do."

The two parted, Randall pausing as they left to watch their backs disappear as the door closed behind them.

***

Captain Tuxra grunted with surprise as he crossed the corridor leading to the back of Osrm's mansion. A servant had pointed him in the right direction, but had failed to mention The Gnat was also present. The two guild leaders gave a brief bow as they neared the door to the veranda and yard beyond.

"What brings you here, Master Gnat?" the captain asked.

The little greasy-haired fellow tittered as he held up a scroll in one hand.

Tuxra withdrew a similar sheet from beneath the folds of his uniform. "It seems we have both been called forth."

The Gnat cackled and put away his paper before pushing open the door.

Revealed to the two was Osrm seated at a table some distance away on the patio. Two guards stood at the sides of the door, stiffened as if awaiting trouble. The person who drew the most attention, however, was a young man with dark hair and serious eyes. The stranger was sitting next to the merchant guild boss but stood at the opening of the door. Tuxra studied the man as he and The Gnat approached, noting the sword on his hip, his aging but serviceable leathers, his stance, his size. This was a warrior born if not bred.

Nearer the table, the captain turned his attention to the host and held up his scroll, crumpling it in a fist. "Osrm, why have you called for us as if we are one of your petty clients?"

The Gnat remained quiet at the captain's side, his head bobbing up and down, his big eyes remaining on the figure of the man standing next to house's master.

Kadath Osrm smiled. "My apologies Captain Tuxra, and to you Gnat, if my dispatch was blunt."

"As well as mysterious," the captain added.

Osrm motioned for the two newcomers to come closer. "Please, have a seat." She looked up at the man next to her. "And you as well, Kron."

Tuxra's face grew flush. "Kron Darkbow?" He traded a fixed stare with the younger man.

The Gnat clucked and slapped at his knee, the grin on his face nearly stretching from ear to ear.

Osrm rapped the edge of her table. "Please, everyone, sit. We have much to discuss."

With his eyes never leaving those of the captain, Kron edged into his chair, keeping his sword free to one side.

The Gnat tittered some more before moving ahead and sliding out a seat.

Tuxra huffed then did the same, planting himself between his host and The Gnat so he could look across the table at Darkbow. "This is most irregular, Osrm."

"Yes, again, my apologies," the woman said, "but I did not go through regular channels because I wish this meeting to remain confidential."

"You speak and act most abstrusely, Osrm, not a habit I appreciate," the captain said. "Adding to your mysteriousness is this man across from me."

Darkbow raised his head better to look at Tuxra. "Does my presence give you apprehension, captain?"

The older man barked out a laugh. "If you are trying to frighten me, pup, you had better show more fang."

There was a moment of tense silence, but then Kron grinned. "Not my goal here, captain."

Tuxra returned the smile before turning to Osrm. "So what *are* we doing here?"

The merchants chief gestured toward Kron. "Master Darkbow has made a rather unique proposal, one that involves all of us, all the guilds."

The captain sat back in his chair, once more glancing across the table. "What could he offer that's so important?"

"A candidate," Kron said.

Tuxra's brow narrowed and his face darkened. "A candidate for *what*?"

"Master of Guild of Guilds."

Tuxra looked to Osrm. "He can't be serious. The guilds would never approve him."

"Not me," Kron said. "There is another."

Osrm placed a hand on the captain's arm. "Listen to him, Tuxra. He has a devilishly intriguing idea for dealing with Kerjim and his lot."

The burly man turned his eyes once more upon Darkbow. "This had better be good."

The Gnat cackled again.

***

Frex Nodana shifted uncomfortably in her seat as she watched the hustle and bustle of the inner hallway of the healing tower. "This is silly, Kerjim."

The older man in the next seat turned his harsh gaze upon her. "He was up at that mansion."

Nodana sighed. "How can you be so sure?"

Kerjim counted off on his fingers. "He is the most powerful healer in the city. He was missing at early hours of the morning. *And*, when I asked around to some of the orderlies, it seems this Tendbones has a common visitor in a young fellow who always dresses in black."

The woman's eyes widened. "He knows Darkbow?"

"It sounds so."

Nodana clucked. "Still, sitting here in the tower isn't doing us any good."

"He'll have to leave sooner or later," Kerjim said, "and when he does, I want to be right behind him. I want to know where he's going, if he'll lead us to another of Darkbow's hiding holes."

"What difference does it make?" Nodana turned to look directly into the Pursian's eyes. "Kerjim, this has gone on long enough, and has cost you far too much. Give up this obsession of yours with Kron Darkbow. You only wanted the man dead to score political points, and now it has gone beyond that. You're going to look a fool to the guilds and everyone else."

"All the more reason to kill him," Kerjim said, "to show everyone I don't fear a few ... difficulties."

The mage sighed again, crossed her arms and sat back in her chair. "This is becoming foolish. Besides, whomever set those wards last night is far more powerful than I can face, even with Spider's aid. We are outclassed, Kerjim. It is time to let the matter drop."

The Pursian was about to speak, but the opening door to Randall's room closed his mouth.

The healer stepped out into the wall and turned to stare directly at the two seated figures.

"Oh, no," Nodana said.

Kerjim stood and pulled his companion up with him as the healer approached, orderlies and patients and other healers making their way around Randall.

"How is Mama Kaf?" the Docks boss asked.

Randall's voice was low enough those moving along the hall behind him could not hear. "You are not here for concern of that woman."

Nodana gasped. The Docks boss merely blinked.

"Master Kerjim," Randall said, "I highly suggest you leave me be. I will not lead you to my friend, nor will I provide any information that could be potentially harmful to him."

"So you admit it?" Kerjim asked.

"That I am friends with Kron Darkbow? Most heartily."

"Then you must be listed among my enemies."

Randall's shoulders slumped. "I had really wished it had not come to this."

The healer's left hand darted forward and a single finger brushed against the Pursian's garments.

Kerjim blinked, then looked from Nodana and back to Randall. He smiled at the healer. "Hello. Do I know you, sir?"

Then the Docks boss patted off down the corridor, his head bobbing around, his eyes looking here, there and everywhere.

The woman grabbed Randall by an elbow. "What did you do to him?"

"You know exactly what I did," Randall said, staring back into her eyes.

She released the arm and looked to the Pursian. "Did you clear *everything* from his mind?"

"No," Randall said, watching Kerjim's back as the man wandered from one side of the hall to the other. "That would have been too dangerous. I merely made him forget my existence."

"And your friend? Darkbow?"

Randall looked back to Nodana. "I allowed that to remain. I feared removing any more of Master Kerjim's memory as I was not sure what it would do to him. That, along with the fact our two associates seem intent upon confronting one another, stayed my hand from further excesses."

Nodana blinked. "It was you, wasn't it? You were the one who placed the wards at the Finder's."

"Oh, dear," Randall said. Then his hand launched again, touching the other mage's wrist.

Nodana's eyes glittered. Then she smiled at the stranger before her. "Hello?"

***

Kron stood away from the table. "We are in agreement, then? It will be the Bodyguards Hall?"

Osrm and Tuxra looked up at the man. The Gnat was busy chewing on a slice of fruit that dripped juice down his grizzled jaw, but he paused long enough for a brief nod.

"I will send the appropriate messages," Osrm said.

"I, too," Tuxra added. "I have to hand it to you, boy. I didn't think you could convince me, but you have. Siding with the counterpart to an old enemy, it doesn't make sense on the surface, but you made a strong case. You might consider politics someday."

Kron grinned. "I thank you, but the political arena holds no love for me."

"Until tonight," Osrm said.

With a wave Kron turned and sprinted back the way he had come across the yard and into a line of shrubs.

"I didn't know you had a back gate," Tuxra commented.

"I don't," Osrm said.

25

Scribes were called for and soon enough servants of Guildmaster Osrm were distributing several dozen missives throughout the city to the appropriate individuals. Blacksmiths calmed their hammers long enough to read the delivered note, and so too did others halt their daily labors to peruse the short letter from the powerful woman, a letter containing the signature not only of herself, but that of Captain Tuxra and The Gnat, as well.

Seamstresses set down their needles. Butchers put aside their knives. Poets, their pens. All to read the scrawled words.

Only Midge Highwater had no utensil to set aside as his labor's tool was his mind. He grinned at the note as he sat on the stoop of The Gilded Pony.

The old man's smile grew wider. "Kerjim is going to soil his pants."

***

"That bitch!"

Kerjim stared at the paper in his hand as if he could not believe what he was seeing.

"I received one as well," Nodana said from the open door to the Pursian's office.

He looked up at the mage, anger clear in his red eyes. "I should kill her for this. And Tuxra, too."

Nodana gave a sly grin. "Don't forget The Gnat."

The Docks boss wadded his paper into a ball and flung it into a corner of the small room. He stared at the top of his desk, trying to find answers. "What could be the meaning of this emergency meeting? It can't be Osrm running for the Guild of Guilds master. Tuxra wouldn't back her, neither would Gnat."

Spider suddenly appeared behind the woman in the doorway, his face flush and full of excitement.

Nodana glanced over her shoulder. "I take it you received a notice from Master Osrm?"

"Yes." Spider held up a scroll. "Anyone know what this is about?"

"Haven't a clue," the mage said.

Kerjim looked up, his anger turned to a smoldering hate. "Whatever it is, I want us to be prepared. Spider, put together another team. Have them ready at The Stone Pony a couple of hours before this meeting."

"Have you lost your mind?" Nodana's words were heated. "We can't go rushing into the Bodyguards Hall with a bunch of thugs. Tuxra's men will squash us flat."

The Pursian turned a harsh gaze on the mage, but then he softened and motioned to Spider. "She is right. But go ahead and assemble a group. This has the stink of our friend in black about it, and I want to be prepared."

Before he could react, Randall was thrown back across the room to slam into the stone wall. The wind knocked out of him and a cut to the back of his head bleeding, he dropped to his knees and looked up with blurred vision as the monstrous figure of Mama Kaf roared once more and lifted herself from the makeshift bed of sturdy lumber that been made for her.

Standing there on one leg, a pudgy hand gripping a small table next to the bed, she glared across at the healer. "Where is Darkbow?"

Randall blinked away the last of the haze and forced himself to raise his head, rubbing at the back of his head. "I have no idea, my dear, but you need to be back in bed."

"Bah!" The big woman gripped the table with both hands and lifted it, then planted it several inches in front of herself. She hopped forward on her one leg.

Leaning against the wall, Randall pulled himself to standing. "I must insist you --"

"Shut up!" The words were bellowed with force as Mama Kaf lifted the table once more, slammed it down and hopped forward.

Soon enough she turned and headed out the door.

"I did my job too well this time, it seems," Randall said to himself.

***

The black thread pulled tight, the needle dug into the cloth once more, over and around, into and out of. It went on and on like some worm burrowing into the ground briefly before sticking its head up again, then returning to its dig. When he reached the end of what had been a tear in his cloak, Kron pulled the thread tight once more and bit into it with his teeth, freeing the needle. His fingers went to work securing a knot, closing up the tear.

Setting aside his work, he glanced at his dark garb displayed atop his bed in the Rusty Scabbard. Shifting on his chair, he lifted the black leggings and eyeballed the hole where a crossbow bolt had protruded but days earlier. Turning the pants inside out, he reached for the spool and thread and went to sewing once more.

For tonight's work, he would wear his black. The garb might be needed for blending into shadows. It might not, but he was taking no chances. There was also the consideration that his darker wardrobe tended to unsettle others, and this, too, could be used to his advantage.

His fingers found the hole and he dipped the needle into the cloth, pushing it through and wrapping it around as he had done a million times before. In the Prisonlands, far from civilization of any size, wardens learned to tend their own gear. Some few had spouses for such tasks, but the border towns of the Lands were not places to raise a family.

Soon enough there was no longer a break within the black cloth and Kron set this aside, too, before glancing down at his legs wrapped in buckskin. Days earlier there had been a hole there as well, a piercing of the flesh that had run deep but without breaking bone. He should have been crippled for some while, if not for life, but he had his ghostly guests to thank for his healing. They had wanted him healthy, using the power of their own souls, the very essence of magic, to rebuild that which had been broken. Their reasons for doing so had

221

been obvious. The dead had wished to take control of his body, to put it to use for their own ends. The dead, after all, wish to be alive. But Kron had been too strong for them. Admittedly, he had had help. Not all those tumbling about within his mind were the madmen of the Asylum. There was also the protectors, the men who had kept the madmen locked away.

Soon it would all come to an end. One way or another, the spirits would be set free before the sun rose once more. Kron had held onto them in order to make use of them, so in that respect he thought himself little better than the dead who had wanted to use him. At least he was willing to give them their freedom eventually, though he was not sure what all that would entail. His hope was it would be a simple process, no more difficult than had been the one that had tied the ghosts to his own soul.

You will finds out!

Kron grinned at the rare words. Yes, he would. Until then, he kept the dead forced back, tamped behind the walls of his mind as would a mason laying bricks. Every once in a while they spoke up, the maddest of them, but he had managed to keep them in check, even quietening them. How long he could continue to do so, he had not a clue, but the task had seemed to become easier instead of more difficult. That bothered him, causing him concerns that perhaps the dead were merely lulling him into a false sense of conviction. Ah, well. It was too late now. His plans had been laid. The dead were part of him, and they must be released one way or another eventually.

Dropping the leggings back onto the bed, he glanced toward the shuttered window and took note the outside light was fading. He then stood and retrieved the weapons belt hanging from the back of his chair. It was time to prepare, to sharpen his blades and dress. The guilds gathering was growing near.

***

Spider's hands visibly shook as he held out the carved wooden appendage.

Mama Kaf hovered over the little man and stared with one eye squinting. "This is the best you could do?"

The shaking grew worse, Spider's hands jarring up and down. "It was the best I could find on short notice. The cabinet maker said if you want to come by for a proper fitting, he could make something more ... uh, comfortable."

"Bah!" The big woman grabbed the wooden leg from his hands and dropped herself onto a chair, her weight causing the seat to groan and crack loudly as she went to work with the leather straps to bind the artificial limb to the bulky stub at the end of her knee.

Kerjim stood near the door to the woman's room. "Are you sure you want to go through with this? We have enough men as it is."

A pair of dark eyes looked up at the Docks boss. "He owes me for a son, and now a leg."

Kerjim nodded. "Fine. We will be leaving in a half hour."

"Good." The woman went back to work, grunting at her labors and cursing the smallness of the wooden leg.

<u>26</u>

A dozen men stood at attention in front of the home to the Bodyguards Guild. Four were stationed at the paved entrance to the building's grounds, two men to a side. Four more, two to a side, stood sentry at the open door to the guild building itself. The other four were also split into parties of two, each group centered in the yard on either side of the walkway leading to the door. A dozen torches lined the front of the building, as well as another half dozen atop tall, iron stands throughout the yard, revealing the freshly oiled chain hauberks the men wore as well as the heavy swords on their belts and the long ax-headed halberds each gripped at the ready. It was an overstated display of force, one that might be laughable under different circumstances and in a different place. But this was the Bodyguards Guild, and Captain Tuxra felt no compunctions about demonstrating the power at his command. The dozen men he had hand picked for the night's assignment were all veterans, their faces often showing scars from blade and sun and frost. The captain wanted those attending to know a touch of fear, to think twice about causing any foolishness this night.

The alarmed, pale faces of the guild masters proved Tuxra's goals had been accomplished as the men and women filed through the front door, some singularly and others in pairs or small groups.

The view within the main hall was little better. Another half dozen men stood guard duty against the right wall, their twins ranged along the left wall. The black stone floor had been recently polished, revealing a mirror of the long chamber above. The high, arched ceiling added to the ominous aspect, giving the room a feeling like that of an ancient morgue or one of the older, more astringent churches.

Unlike the earlier meetings Kerjim had called together at The Stone Pony, here there was enough room and seats for everyone. Several long tables had been placed together lengthwise down the center of the hall, chairs lining all the way around.

Tuxra himself stood just within the entrance, a pair of his lieutenants at his side, greeting each guild boss as he or she came through the door. The captain was smiling this night, an unusual affectation on his part, adding all the more to the nervousness of those gathering.

At least there were plenty of vessels of wine upon the table, though no signs of food.

Soon enough everyone present was seated, though several chairs at the far end remained empty.

Tuxra claimed the end seat nearest the door, Kadath Osrm settling in to this left and The Gnat on his right.

The merchants boss glanced down the table, smiled at a few familiar faces, then turned to the captain. "They are not here."

"They will be," Tuxra said. "Would you be in a hurry to your execution?"

Osrm grimaced and spoke in a low voice. "I would hope Kerjim has no idea what is to occur here this night."

"Of course I do," the Docks boss said.

The Gnat snickered as all heads turned toward the entrance.

Kerjim stood in the center of the open doors, bolstered by Frex Nodana and Spider at his sides. He stared about the room as if he had a sour taste in his mouth, then strode forward toward an empty chair on one side of the long table.

The Pursian glanced down at two young men sitting on either side of the vacant seat. "Move."

They moved, relinquishing their chairs and shuffling back toward the wall behind them.

Kerjim motioned for his partners to approach, then planted himself into the middle of the three chairs. Spider slunk forward and captured his seat. Nodana took her time, her cloak flapping about her diminutive form as she sauntered to her chair.

In silence the Docks Guild chief glanced around the table from one end to the other, his heavy gaze finally falling on that of Kadath Osrm.

"You have much to explain," he said to the woman.

Osrm raised an eyebrow. "I do? Pertaining to what matter?"

The Pursian slammed a fist onto the table. "You know damn good and well! You called for this emergency meeting of voters for the guilds collective, and I can only imagine one purpose for it."

The rest of the room remained silent, like a group gathered to watch a pair of famous duelists going at one another.

"Really?" Osrm asked. "What would that be?"

Kerjim nodded to Tuxra and The Gnat. "Collusion. You have partnered with these ... villains ... in an effort to win master of the Guild of Guilds."

Osrm tutted. "I have done nothing not within city or guilds laws."

Ignoring her for the moment, Kerjim turned to Tuxra. "What did she promise you? It had to be something *big*. I can't imagine you giving over your vote for Kadath. It makes no sense."

"I'm not voting for Kadath Osrm," the captain stated, his face blank.

Kerjim sat back alarmed. He glanced about, finally looking to The Gnat. "And you?"

The little old man shrugged and laughed, holding up his hands at his sides.

Osrm chuckled. "Kerjim, you are correct that I called this gathering for an emergency vote concerning the Guild of Guilds. And why not? What with the riots bringing about a lull in trade, drastic measures must be taken. However, your assumption that I am running for master of the new guild is a false one. I do not try for that seat."

"Then who?" Kerjim glanced about the table. "Who but me is viable for this position?"

Osrm raised a hand and snapped her fingers.

A door opened on the other side of the table from Kerjim and his pair of comrades. Into the chamber stepped the tall, slender figure of Lalo the Finder, behind him following Eel, the young man standing to one side as if on guard.

The Pursian pointed to Lalo. "*Him*?"

"Yes, Master Sidewinder," Osrm said. "The Finder has come forward as a candidate."

"You can't be serious," Kerjim said, spittle flying from his lips. "Lalo was Belgad's boy, the enemy to all the guilds represented here. Besides, he isn't even a guild member."

"I am as of today," the Finder said as he slid forward to stand behind Captain Tuxra.

"*What?*"

"That is correct," Osrm said. "The Finder's dues were paid this afternoon, his signature given. He is now represented by the Merchants Guild."

"This is insane!" Kerjim shot out of his chair and turned his back on the table. He paced toward the wall where the pair he had unseated moved out of his way. He smacked a hand against stone and spun around. He gritted his teeth as he spoke. "This makes no sense whatsoever. The Finder has been our enemy for years."

"No, I was not," Lalo said. "I was merely in the employ --"

"Of the man who tried to ruin us all!" Kerjim completed with spit flying once more. "For fifteen years Belgad's boot was on the back of our necks, and you were right there with him, hiding in the shadows behind his shoulders."

Osrm stood. "Master Kerjim, I understand your --"

He spun upon her. "You understand nothing! You are handing over all I ... *we* ... have worked for, and you are giving it to the very man who kept us down for so long."

"The Finder is no threat," Osrm pressed on.

"No threat? *No threat!* Are you insane?" Kerjim held up his arms and presented himself to the rest of the chamber. "Are the rest of you truly going to stand for this?"

A lone figure stood toward the far end of the table.

All heads turned once more.

"It seems to me the woman is right," Midge Highwater spoke. "The Finder is as experienced as anybody here at runnin' things, and he's got no army and, rumor has, not a heck of a lot of money. Who else better to head up this Guild of Guilds but someone who knows what they're doing but isn't a threat to the rest of us?"

Quiet. Dust settled.

Kerjim's eyes grew big. The man could not believe what he was hearing.

His fist banged onto the table. "*Fine.* I call for a verbal vote, here and now, to determine who shall be master of the Guild of Guilds."

"The Merchants Guild votes for Lalo the Finder," Osrm said.

Kerjim winced.

Tuxra stood, his chain shirt jingling beneath his uniform. "The Bodyguards Guild votes the same."

The Gnat rapped the table with a knuckle and pointed to the captain while nodding.

Nodana rose from her seat next to Kerjim. "The Mages Guild votes for the Finder."

The Pursian's head cracked around. "Traitor!" he snapped.

Nodana kept her voice low. "We have lost here, Kerjim. It is time to move on, to put your personal vendetta aside."

The Docks boss looked down the table. "Anyone else?"

"Storytellers vote for the Finder," Highwater said.

Another man stood. "As do the scribes."

225

Then a woman. "And the street cleaners."

And another. "The poets go with the Finder."

One by one those within the chamber climbed to their feet, voice after voice asserting its decision for Lalo the Finder. It took several minutes for each member of the crowd to speak, but eventually it was down to the last two, Kerjim himself and Spider.

The gray-haired fellow next to the Pursian pulled himself to standing. "Well, the thieves go with Kerjim Sidewinder for Master of the Guild of Guilds."

No one said a word. Kerjim slowly planted his knuckles on the table and seethed as he stared at a spot between his fists.

"Master Kerjim?" Osrm asked.

The man did not move.

"Very well, then." Osrm raised her head and looked along the table. "As the Docks Guild is not to voice a vote, I call this election at forty-four to one, the title of Master of the Guild of Guilds going to Lalo the Finder, who may begin serving his first term at the end of two weeks from this day."

Kerjim growled and shoved away from the table, stomping toward the exit.

Spider flushed, looking afraid, then shrugged and fled after his boss.

More than a few chuckles followed them out of the room.

"My goodness," the Finder said. "I hope the man is not considering anything drastic."

The Gnat cackled as Tuxra and Osrm traded knowing smiles.

***

Storming out of the guild hall, Kerjim promised himself blood would be the price of the night's treachery. In his mind he formed a list of those who would suffer. Darkbow and the Finder, of course. Then his nephew. After that, he would have to be more careful. Osrm would make the list, as would Tuxra. Even The Gnat. That loudmouth idiot, Midge Highwater, would also suffer a terrible fate. When Kerjim was finished, there would be no one left to head the Guild of Guilds. Hell, there might be no one left to head *any* of the guilds.

Tromping down the marble steps between guards, Spider in his wake, the Pursian brought himself up short when a cloaked figure stepped into his path in the yard.

Kerjim looked up to find the object of his hate. "You."

Kron nodded. "Yes."

"It was you!" Kerjim pointed. "You are the one responsible for this!"

"Remember," Kron said with a wag of a finger, "you came after me, Master Kerjim. I had no clue you even existed until you tried to kill me."

The Docks boss roared and grasped the two sword handles on his belt.

Four of Tuxra's guards sprang forward, the points of their halberds lowered and pointed at the Pursian.

Spider planted a hand on Kerjim's right shoulder and whispered into the man's ear. "Not now. Not here."

The guild master glared at the man in black. "Watch yourself, Kron Darkbow, because one of these nights -- "

Kron interrupted. "What? You will try to kill me again? You've failed miserably, so far."

Kerjim gritted his teeth hard enough to draw blood.

Kron waved a hand. "But why not settle this tonight?"

"Name the place," Kerjim stated with hate in his voice.

"The Asylum. Midnight."

The Docks master was taken back for a moment, but then the humor, the irony, collapsed upon him. He could not help himself. He laughed. Lowering his hands to his side once more, he tossed back his head and roared his laughter to the heavens. Then, "As you wish, Darkbow. I hope you say your prayers to Ashal before then."

Kron grinned. "I might just do that."

Then the man in black stepped to one side and gestured for the other two to be on their way.

Kerjim spat at the ground in front of his enemy's boots, but then strutted past, Spider looking sheepish at his back.

When the two were gone, Kron turned to the nearest guard. "That went well."

Then the man in black made his way into the guild hall.

27

Stone struck steel. Sparks flew, igniting tinder. Within a matter of moments Kron Darkbow was parading along the walls of the Asylum's main chamber, one arm upraised with a burning ember extended, lighting ensconced torches as he advanced. There were soon a dozen lights burning, and Kron extinguished his brand within the ashes of a pot in one corner. The spirits had not bothered to provide their own lights this night, yet the man could feel their anticipation.

Freedom was looming for the ghosts of the dead.

Soons. Soons.

Yes, soon. But Kron was not sure they would long enjoy the liberty that was to come to them. Part of him almost hoped they would, as it might make things easier. Either way, he would proceed. He knew he had aid, spiritual protectors. His mind was not alone with only souls of the mad, but there were the others, those who had remained silent. The guards from the Asylum. Many of whom Kron had known personally for some short while. They had a role to play, but would they? Kron could not be sure. Their silence caused him concern, but knowing these ghosts when they were alive, he could not imagine them wanting the dangerously insane to run free in this world or any other.

Kron's plan had formed by happenstance. He had had no idea what would occur when he had bared himself, opened himself, to the ghosts of the Asylum. Anger had been his motivator. It had been those most deadly who had sought him out first, who had tried to clamp down upon his own being, to take control of him. They had lured him, the maddest of them, with the lights within the Asylum the night he had been wounded, his weakness having urged them to try him. It had been a struggle, a fight he might have lost if the other spirits had not waded in, those ghosts who sought to retain order among the chaos. In the end, Kron had found himself with control of his own mind and body. And though quiet, he could still feel the spirits of the guards pressing at the back of his thoughts, keeping at bay those who would use Kron to their own dark, bloodthirsty purposes.

Tonight Kron would test the boundaries of his own mind, of his own inner will, and that of the spiritual world itself.

He chuckled as he approached the Asylum's open main door and stared out into the darkness beyond. A year earlier the building had been flooded with water that had become host to the bodies of the dead. Tonight it would be flooded with the dead once more.

Kron only hoped he would survive.

***

There were an even dozen of them, three with crossbows. Kerjim had wanted more, but word had spread on the streets and among the Docks Guild of the fate of those who had recently done the Pursian's dirty work. Men had been scarred, crippled, a number killed. There was not enough gold to pry loose the fear that gripped those formerly compliant with the guild master's wishes. Kerjim had become unlucky of late, the rumors went, and Darkbow had proven himself not a man to cross. It did not help that news had spread quickly of Master Kerjim's failure to win the vote as boss of the new Guild of Guilds.

The Pursian had much to prove to regain the trust he had once enjoyed. That would begin with killing Darkbow, he swore.

The dark-skinned master of the Docks glanced around at the group standing with him outside the twisted gates of the Asylum. A lamp held up by Spider revealed the monstrous figure of Mama Kaf standing next to the much smaller man, the woman leaning to one side to ease the displeasure obviously caused by wearing her new wooden leg. She huffed as she lifted her new weapon, a wooden two-handed mallet that until recently been used to knock senseless large fish and other creatures pulled from the rivers by sailors. Of the others, all were burly fellows, men who wore the scars of having lead rugged lives on the streets of the Asylum.

Kerjim trusted none of them, especially after the betrayals by his nephew and Frex Nodana, but he needed these people. He would use them to wipe away the stain that was Kron Darkbow. Would it be enough? Darkbow had proven himself a reliant opponent, physically and in the arena of guild and street politics. The Pursian shook his head. The dozen here would have to do.

He scanned their surroundings. The night was quiet, as expected. A handful of silver coins had cleared the streets and the tenements across the way. The only possible interruption could be that of a random patrol of the city guard, but Kerjim had even lessened the chance of that. The cost had been more than a few silver, and more than the Docks boss had wished to relinquish, but it had bought him at least an hour of protection. No, the city guards would not be patrolling this corner of the Swamps for some time.

Mama Kaf huffed again and glared at Kerjim. "Why are we waiting?"

The Pursian looked to the big woman. "Merely giving you a moment to catch your breath."

"The moment is over. Let us move."

Kerjim nodded and waved his party forward. The going was slow, mainly because they had to wait for Mama Kaf to thump forward one step at a time. The woman was frustrated at her sluggishness, cursing under her breath constantly, but Kerjim would not move forward without her presence. As slow as she might be, the woman was a powerhouse, a tool that might be used to blunt the edges of Kron Darkbow.

They had not moved far when the entrance to the Asylum began to glow with a faint light beyond. It was difficult to see much from their distance, but for a moment the luminescence faded as if someone was standing in the doorway. The moment passed quick enough. The group did not halt. Darkbow was expecting them, after all.

As they made their leaden track up the hill to the building, all eyes darted here and there as the group spread out. Kerjim had warned them to be on their guard. Darkbow was a canny enemy, and there was no telling what tricks he might attempt to play upon them.

But nothing greeted them but the slight wind, the distant noises of a city at large in the middle of the night, and the grunts and huffs of the massive one-legged figure hopping forward a step at a time.

Nearing the open door, Kerjim realized he was an idiot for walking right up to an enemy's stronghold, but he was beyond caring. Darkbow had to die. The Pursian's rage boiled deep beneath his flesh, giving away most thoughts of caution.

Still, he would not allow himself to be a total fool. Before the doorway, he motioned for his crossbowmen to go ahead.

The three looked to one another, then warily made their way forward, one in the center, the others at the sides. The central figure took the lead, jolting ahead through the doorway with his weapon raised to his shoulder. His two comrades fell in behind.

From outside, Kerjim watched as the men heatedly transferred the aim of their weapons from one spot to another over and over again, showing their nervousness.

After several moments of nothing, the middle of the three turned toward the doorway and shrugged.

"Bah!" Mama Kaf pushed ahead, turning sideways to fit through the door.

The rest followed, spreading out around the entrance once inside.

Kerjim paused to stare up the three stories of landings housing barred cells, then at the crater in the center of the large room. He glanced up to a similar hole far above in the ceiling.

"I was here right after it happened," Spider said, pointing with a dagger at the roof. "Belgad said he thought it was the healer did it."

The Docks boss looked to the thief. "Tendbones?"

"That's what the boss believed," Spider said.

"Yes, it *was* Randall," a voice spoke from nowhere, "and he has regretted it ever since."

Crossbows were raised and further weapons drawn as the room went tense. All eyes beneath the torchlight shifted from corner to corner.

"Show yourself," Kerjim commanded. "Let us finish this."

The soft clopping noise of hardened leather upon stone flowed from a darkened hallway far to the left. The crossbowmen switched their positions to aim into that black.

"I suggest you tell your men to lower their bows." Kron appeared out of the hall's gloom, one outstretched gloved hand gripping a clay orb the size of an apple. "Otherwise, an accident might occur."

Several heavy breaths were sucked in, but none of the party moved as Darkbow came to a halt, holding up the clay ball.

"Is that a grenado?" Kerjim asked.

"It would appear so," Kron said, bouncing the object in his hand. "A rather large one, at that. I would hate for it to hit the floor."

The Pursian stepped forward and threw up his arms in front of his archers. "Alright, boys. Lower them." Then he turned eyes of hate upon his foe. "Though I have my doubts it is a real grenado."

Kron tossed the ball into the air over his head and caught it with his other hand. "Would you care to find out?"

Kerjim yanked his two short swords free of their scabbards and hefted the weapons, ready to move forward. But was shoved aside by the mass of Mama

Kaf hobbling forward, the woman screaming at the top of her lungs.

With a grin, Kron flung the grenado.

Fearful cries went up throughout the room as weapons were tossed and the party as a whole dove for protection. Spider and another man flew out the door. Kerjim rolled beneath a heavy desk against a wall. The crossbowmen panicked and ran back before diving in a huddle behind the open door. Mama Kaf and those remaining had fewer options and flung themselves flat on the floor.

There was a small cracking sound, but nothing followed.

Kerjim looked up to find the clay ball rolling to a stop in front of his nose, the orb now showing a thin crack running through it.

He roared and shoved himself out from beneath the furniture.

But Darkbow was gone.

"Find him!" The Pursian yelled, waving his swords toward the dark hallway.

***

Fighting the urge to laugh, Kron remained unmoving on his back on the floor of the second-floor landing in front of rows of iron bars that fronted the cells beyond. In their haste and rage, it was unlikely his foes would bother to look up or to begin their hunt in the cells. He had intentionally not lit the torches along the upper levels of the prison walkways, allowing him to better blend with the darkness to be found there. That combined with the brightness below, a brightness that would shield viewing beyond the torches, almost assured his momentary safety. Still, he gripped a knife in each hand just in case.

He listened to the curses and the thumpings of their feet below, the sounds quickly fading along the hallway with the gruntings of the big woman with the mallet. Only the soft breathing of a pair remained beneath.

Easing his cloaked head to the ledge, Kron peered down to spy Kerjim and Spider near the entrance, the two men facing the darkened hallway. Kerjim was not a complete idiot, but he was allowing his impatience and anger to get the best of him. Kron would never have believed an enemy unseen had taken the most obvious route. He almost laughed again. If not for his quick reflexes and his black silk rope hanging unnoticed above the steps leading up to the higher cells, he would not have made it in time to hide. Also, the railing of black iron bars running along the edge of the walkway had helped, and offered some little protection from viewing. He had had but seconds to act, fear keeping down the heads of his opponents.

But the moment was passed.

He closed his eyes and pulled deep within himself. *Hear me, those who have been trapped, those who have been held back. Now is your moment. Now is your freedom.*

A hissing noise came to his ears, like that of a thousand snakes, though he realized it was but illusion brought into his own mind. Then he felt more than heard a jarring, a hammering, as if the iron bars next to him were being battered down by the big woman with the wooden hammer.

At lasts! We go frees! Frees!

Kron grimaced at those voices. These were the depraved, the deviants, rapists, killers and torturers all. These were the voices of souls seeking only the pain of others, as they had done in life. These men had felt nothing for themselves or for others, and Kron could detect their icy fingers clawing at his thoughts.

231

You others, he sent out in the void, *you protectors, you must help me now. It is all up to you. One prison cell is to be traded for another, if that be possible.*

There was a screech from the darkest of those within him. *Betrayal! Lies!*

Yes, Kron thought, *and you are deserving of no better.*

With nary a sound, he slid his knives into their leather sheaths. There had been no words from the inner guards, those Kron hoped would help him to ensnare the others. This was not a good sign, but the ghosts of the Asylum guards had yet to speak to him, and he was not sure he should put much emphasize on their silence now.

Whatever the outcome, he had committed himself. If worse came to worse, he could hide once more or fight his way out of the Asylum. He knew these halls. His enemies did not.

It was time.

He stood, planting his hands on the railing before him.

***

Kerjim and Spider looked up at the same time.

"In here!" the Docks master shouted.

Shouts rang out from down the Asylum's halls.

Kron vaulted over the metal banister, landing in a crouch on the other side of the ragged-edged pit that lead to the lower level.

Pointing a sword at Kron, Kerjim turned to Spider. "Kill him!"

Spider gulped and stood motionless as he stared across to the man in black.

Deep, dark chuckles sprang from Kron, echoing throughout the massive chamber.

The Docks boss cursed and used the flat of a blade to slap Spider about the shoulders. Then Kerjim turned and marched toward the edge of the crater.

The racket of those in the hall drew louder.

A black-garbed hand reached up and tugged back Kron's hood. He stared with hard, unblinking eyes at the man across the pit from him. "Kerjim, this is your last opportunity. Leave here now, drop this personal war against me, and I swear not to seek vengeance."

The Pursian spat. It was his only answer. Then he shifted to his right, beginning to make his way around the lumber and stones and iron beams sticking up from the center of the room.

Kron's shoulders slumped, his disappointment clear at the actions of the guild master. He lowered his head and closed his eyes. "Then let what comes be upon your head."

***

Now.

It was but a single word, a single thought, in the man in black's mind.

Yesss! At lasts! Freedoms!

A warmth welled up within Kron's chest, followed by a pressure from within. For a moment it felt as if his breast would burst, his beating heart to explode outward in a rain of red mist. Just as he could stand no more, his eyelids snapped open and his legs buckled, crumbling beneath him.

He tumbled to the floor, managing to land upward on his knees despite the shudders that rippled through his body, forcing his head back and howling a scream from his throat.

Through eyes filling with water and ears filled with a growing roar like that of an ocean rampaging against a stone shelf, Kron could make out only vague impressions of his surroundings. Kerjim had come to a halt not far from him, the Pursian's face suddenly drained of anger that was replaced by fear. To Kron's right, the opening to the hallway was suddenly filled by the rest of the Docks chief's crew, the large woman pressing through to take the lead, but all coming up short at what they witnessed.

An invisible maul slammed into Kron's stomach, forcing him to drop forward, catching himself on his hands.

Now we shalls be the betrayers! We shalls turns upons you!

***

Spider had not moved from the open doorway. He was in as much shock as the others, his boots feeling nailed to the floor, his eyes unable to turn away from the image of Darkbow on the floor.

An unseen force jerked the man in black upright onto his knees once more, the pupils of his eyes rolling back to white, his mouth agape and voicing a silent scream. A scarlet glow scattered from within that open maw, followed by pale vapors that sprang forth, dancing in front of Darkbow's withdrawn features before expanding higher and higher, a thin line of brume stretching from the larger cloud back to the man in black's gaping mouth.

That cloud grew bigger and bigger, expanding from within like smoke bellowing from unseen flames. Outlines formed, screaming faces with lips parted in silent howls, sunken eyes pleading for an end to torture. Then the features vanished as if blown away upon a wind.

A throaty chuckle sounded throughout the chamber, followed by others joining it. The noise grew and grew, those present darting nervous eyes at one another.

Then an outburst of mist from the cloud of faces expanded, growing the vapors to twice their former size. Moments later long, snake-like appendages shot out from the haze and hovered over the heads of those in the chamber.

One of the misty arms sank slowly like a fog drifting toward the ground, then it sprang forward at one of the crossbowmen, its slinking end swelling into a clawed hand that wrapped around the man's head. A scream from the fellow was cut off as that vaporous snake tore apart his lips and forced its way into his mouth. The man's cheeks puffed out and his eyes rolled back in his head. He fell to the ground on his knees, his weapon clanging down next to him, his body quivering as his head was thrown back.

The other misty arms shot out toward those watching.

Spider had seen enough. One foot already out the door, he gyrated to the outside and fled down the hill in front of the Asylum, not once looking back.

***

Enthralled by the enveloping vision before him, Kerjim had not had time to react when a limb snaked out from the giant ball of gray fog and wrapped itself around his head. He dropped his swords as his body arched back then forced him to his knees. A cold like that of an ice knife stabbed into his mind, forcing him to scream in silence to the ceiling. He felt his thoughts fracturing, tumbling away into nothingness, cracking and breaking. His memories were pulled from him, supplanted with those of others. Images of blood and flesh laid open skewered his inner eye, repeated over and over again before being followed by gut-wrenching visions of rape and mutilation. He saw a man chop away an arm of a living child, then the man began to gnaw on the arm as if it were a piece of raw meat. Another image appeared of a woman hanging from an iron hook through her chest, though somehow she still lived; a shadow stepped forward, sliced across her stomach, her intestines disgorging into a bucket. Murder. Rape. Vivisection. Blood. Skin flayed. Lips severed. Fingers crushed.

It was all too much. Too much. The horror dissolved the Pursian's self, plunging what little was left deeper into an abyss of blackness that seemed bottomless. His face became a cracked mask of anguish.

Throughout the room, the others were on their knees. Their bodies shook. Their mouths raged in silence. Their eyes were nothing but balls of white.

Then all slammed forward like marionettes with their strings cut. More than a few heads slammed against the floor, bringing fresh blood to the scene.

For a moment, all lay unmoving. Then slowly, so slowly, heads were lifted. Their eyes were red, completely red, with no pupils. From those crimson orbs dripped tears of blood, crawling down cheeks, leaving behind trails of red lines.

Only Kron appeared normal. He rocked back on the floor, sitting up on his booted feet. He shook his head as if to clear away a dream, then looked about the chamber, his eyes going from face to face.

The others in the room stared back at him. Their faces were now snarls of hunger and hatred and madness.

He grimaced as his hands went to his daggers.

***

If you are still there within me, Kron pleaded to the spirits, *know that your job is not finished, but has just begun. The prisoners are released, freed, and their wrath shall be awful. Now only* you *can end this, can build new cells for them. Only you.*

Silence. As was typical. As was feared.

Then, Kron's stomach heaved and he dropped his weapons to thrust his arms forward once more to hold him upright.

We shall do what is necessary.

The words were different, more solid, than those that had come before, and Kron was thankful for their presence.

His body shook again, spasms racing up and down his limbs, entrenching within his gut, forcing him to shake and cough.

His mouth forced open once more, another glowing fog sprang from within, this one quickly building into a whirling cyclone above the floor's pit.

Those with red eyes began to climb to their feet, with jerky motions pushing themselves off the floor. They moved awkwardly, as if drunk, barely able to stand. Their limbs did not seem to want to cooperate. All the while, their crimson stares were locked onto the man in black.

Kron cried out, then collapsed forward, his chest slamming into the floor.

The red-eyed killers jerked and moaned as they made their way toward the downed figure, their shambling steps carrying them forward one slow step at a time. The one that had been Kerjim paused long enough to bend and lift the fallen short swords, then stumbled ahead toward its prey.

The storm of vapor continued to rumble and roil, turning around and around within itself. As before, there were faces to be seen for brief moments, but there was no one now looking. If there had been, they would have found stern features, but not ones of insanity and brutality as had been before.

It was Kerjim's bleeding figure that reached the man in black first, the undead thing within the Pursian's body bringing up the retrieved short swords for a blow.

"*We hates its*," the thing whispered, the swords dipping in for the kill.

A serpent of mist shot out from the glowing storm, wrapping itself around Kerjim's body, pulling it back toward the pit.

Other arms sprang from the cyclone, tethering themselves to the others, their bodies jerking.

Only Kron remained free.

The ground shook, followed by a distant sound not unlike thunder. The storm grew in intensity and size, sucking in the bodies of those it had grasped, twisting and turning and throwing the mortal forms around and around.

Kerjim was flung, his body slamming into the floor near the entrance and rolling to a stop against the wall. Other figures were tossed, some landing hard with crunching noises, other barreling across the floor until a wall or piece of furniture brought them to a halt.

When there were no more bodies within the storm, the cyclone twisted and built itself higher and higher, reaching for the opening in the ceiling. The moon rained down its glow, touching the mists that seemed to vie for the outside world.

Then silence, and a collapse. The storm fell within itself, in upon itself.

And was no more.

Dust settled.

Weak groans could be heard from one corner or another.

Weak, battered, Kron slowly raised his head. He glanced about at the others, finally finding Kerjim's face next to the door. The Pursian's eyes were locked up, flat, unmoving, unblinking; the man's lips quivered, as did the tips of his fingers.

Kron tried to push himself up, but he had not the strength. He collapsed once more, the side of his face landing against the cold floor. He stared across the room to Kerjim once more, and still saw only a dull, numb madness.

Then the man in black's eyes closed and he knew no more for some little while.

28

"I don't want to know."

At the words, Kron glanced over his shoulder as the sun winked atop the walls to bring the morning's warmth to the Asylum grounds. Gris was there, a half dozen orange-garbed soldiers behind him at the remains of the front gate.

The captain approached as a trio of young people dressed in whites moved past carrying stretchers of cloth and wooden poles. He flashed a look towards the healers as he neared his friend, ignoring others wearing pale robes working their way through the gates and around his guards.

"I don't want to know," Gris repeated, shaking his head.

"I kept my word," Kron said. "Not one of them is dead."

"Yes, but maybe you delivered worse than death."

"I won't argue your point."

Gris spat off to one side. "At least that's something. From what the healers tell me, Kerjim and his crew have lost their minds. They're little more than husks with nothing inside."

Kron nodded. "I gave him an opportunity to end this, but he pressed on."

The clatter of hooves and the rattle of wheels drew their attention back to the street where a dark carriage was slowing in front of the gate. Stilp climbed down from the driver's seat, handing off the reins to a near city guard before opening a door on one side. Eel stepped down from inside the cab, Lalo right behind him. The trio spoke a few words with the guards and healers there, then began the climb up the hill to the captain and Kron.

"Impressive," the Finder said to Kron as his party came to a halt. "Word has already spread on the streets. The Asylum is haunted, its ghosts having driven poor Kerjim mad. How did you do it?"

Gris groaned and threw his arms up with disgust. "I need to see what's taking those healers so long." He tromped off in the direction of the Asylum entrance.

Stilp cackled.

"My uncle?" Eel asked Kron. "Is it true?"

The man in black looked back toward the retreating captain and the Asylum beyond. "Kerjim lives. That is all."

His head swinging low, Eel backed away from the group. After a moment, he turned and marched back toward the carriage.

"He will be fine," Lalo said, watching the boy leave. "He just needs time to reconcile all this. Master Kerjim brought his troubles on himself."

"Yes," Kron said with another nod. "It is not easy losing one's family."

"Speaking of Kerjim," Stilp said, "what did you do to the man?"

Now it was Lalo who nodded to Kron. "Yes, that is the question. You're no mage, after all. What stunt did you pull this time?"

The man in black grinned. "Allow me to keep my secrets."

The Finder chuckled. "Very well, but tell me one thing about last night."

"Yes?"

"How did you know the guilds would approve me as master of the Guild of Guilds?"

Kron shrugged. "I didn't know, not for sure. You were qualified, more than qualified, and you were somewhat of a neutral party. You had a past with Belgad, true, but you were known as a solid administrator, without ties to violence. I made my case to the guilds as best I could, and once Osrm was interested, I realized the rest would follow. They did. And now the guilds can move on. The city can move on."

Stilp sighed. "*All* of us can move on."

"What now for the great Kron Darkbow?" Lalo asked.

The man in black laughed and pointed up to the Asylum building. "I've still got a roof to mend, and a floor that needs fixing."

"No second thoughts about coming to work for me?" Lalo asked. "I could use you. Eel needs experience and training, after all."

Kron's eyes shined. "I'll work something out with the lad, make sure he can do his job properly, but no, thank you. I prefer to remain an independent."

The Finder laughed. "You still haven't learned, have you? *No one* is independent."

Stilp opened his mouth to speak, but the approach of a pale-garbed young man from the Asylum caused him to close his mouth.

It was Randall. He walked up to Kron and held out a cracked ball of clay. "I found this inside. I suppose it belongs to you?"

Kron lifted the ball from his friend's palm, glanced at it while grinning, then tossed the orb over a shoulder.

Stilp cursed as he and Lalo ran for their carriage.

A solid chortle burst from between Kron's lips as he watch the two flee.

"I take it that grenado was a dud," Randall said.

"Just river mud. I made it down at the bank yesterday."

A pair of orderlies from the healing tower came tromping by from the Asylum, between them a stretcher bearing the quivering form of Kerjim Sidewinder, the Pursian's mouth twisted to one side, his eyes flat and motionless, staring into the sky. The carriers did not stop, but kept moving toward the street where a wagon waited to take the infirm to the tower.

"Do you think anything can be done for them?" Kron asked as he watched his former enemy vanish through the estate's gates.

Randall shook his head. "Their minds have likely been destroyed. I could release the spirits trapped within, but there would be nothing left but a shell of a person. They probably wouldn't live long. At least as things stand, there is a chance the displaced souls of Kerjim and his gang might eventually find their way back to their bodies. It's unlikely, but I suppose possible."

"My apologies," Kron said. "I realized this morning when I called upon the tower I would be placing a terrible burden upon your colleagues."

The healer sighed. "We will do the best for them we can." Then he turned slowly to look up the hill to the Asylum where a group of tower workers were huffing and groaning as they worked a heavy two-wheeled cart through the entrance, the bereft figure of Mama Kaf filling the small wagon. "I have another concern, however."

"Which is?"

Randall was quiet for a moment, watching the orderlies as they finally forced their cart through the door. Then, "There are still ghosts within the Asylum. You know this, do you not?"

Kron nodded. "Their freedom was the price I paid. Without them, I could not have contained the others."

"I could send them on. I could show them the gates to the ... beyond."

The man in black shook his head. "I think not. They have earned their freedom, at least for now. They accommodated the transfer of those in their care from one prison to another, after all."

"Do you believe it will bring them peace?"

"I do not know. I hope so. They showed a willingness to perform their duty, and to return to familiar tasks. That has been granted."

Randall sighed again and offered a lopsided grin. "Kron, you might be the only person in existence who has spirits of the dead as his personal sentries. I hope some arrangements can be reached with them."

"I've already done so," Kron said, then he walked away, heading toward the Asylum as the orderlies carried out the rest of the helpless, muddled figures.

Randall turned his head to one side and watched his friend climb the hill. "Now what's that supposed to mean?"

Book II:
DEMON CHAINS

Part 1:
Bond

1

1,995 years After Ashal (A.A.)

A thick fog drifted across the boardwalk, working with the dark of night to ensure little could be examined beyond an arm's reach. The moon could not be seen, nor the stars. The only light was a vague glow low among the clouds north of the river, revealing the presence of The Swamps, the innermost recesses of the city of Bond.

Flint struck against steel and sparks shot forth, soon followed by dancing flames at one end of an oiled torch.

"You sure that's a good idea?" Bentus asked, shivering as he hunkered down behind a row of stacked barrels.

Kneeling, Chess looked over at his partner, a big man like himself, but they did come smarter. "I told you, there aren't any wharf guards here. This quay is old and wobbly. Nobody hardly uses it anymore, and that Khadiran cog has spooked the dock master's staff. We've got it all to ourselves."

Bentus looked from side to side, nervous as if expecting someone to jump out of the fog. "Maybe, but no captain leaves his ship unwatched."

A frown crossed Chess's lips as he shook his head. "Look, I've been watching this ship ever since it came in two days ago. The only people that got off was some fancy foreigner, this weird kid he had with him, and a small crew, no more than a dozen. Nobody else was here. Nobody. There aren't any guards. I looked over everything earlier today. We're safe."

"Then what happened to the crew? And this foreigner?"

Chess sighed. Bentus always had been a worrier, even when they had been working as bully boys for Kerjim, back before the guild master lost his mind and had to be locked away in a healing tower. One might think such a big fellow as Bentus, who not only had size but some training and experience with the sword, would have a sturdier gut than what he usually showed. But no. Chess had to get stuck with a street thug with butterflies in his stomach and rocks in his head. Still, they didn't come much more loyal, and it was true they needed work. Emptying the Khadiran craft of whatever they could haul away counted as work.

"The crew disbanded, hired only temporary, I guess," Chess said to answer his partner, "and the foreign guy got some rooms somewhere. I'm telling you, we're not facing any trouble here."

Bentus still didn't appear convinced. "Didn't they unload anything from the ship? Doesn't make sense for a cog like that to come all the way from Khadir with only two passengers getting off."

Chess growled in the back of his throat, growing tired of his companion's weakness. "Maybe the foreigner is rich. Maybe he could afford the passage, or maybe it's his damn boat. I don't know." He used the torch to point further down the boardwalk. "But I do know there's a ship sitting out there with nobody watching over it. Even if it's not stuffed to the gills with merchandise, they'll be sailing gear and stuff we can swipe."

The other fellow frowned.

Chess slapped him on an arm. "What are you afraid of? This'll be an easy job. We can sell whatever we get, then be on down the road. This Khadiran isn't going to come looking for us. Hell, he's rich, he probably won't even notice a missing quadrant or telescope, or whatever we find."

Bentus held to a silent, stubborn firmness for a moment, staring back at his partner, but then he let out a breath of misty air, wrapped his cloak tighter around his shivering arms and stood. "All right. Let's do it and get it over with. The sooner we get back to The Stone Pony for some warm soup, the happier I'll be."

Chess grimaced and stood next to his accomplice. "You sure? You don't want me to hire a couple of bodyguards to make sure you don't get hurt or something?"

A large knife sliding forth from the folds of his belt, the other man straightened and sneered while nodding further down the boardwalk. "Let's just get this done with."

Chess nodded in return, then pulled out his own blade, shaking it out to one side. "All right."

The two thugs shifted and tromped into the dark mist, their torch leading the way but only revealing the gray boards of the wharf inches at a time. After they had traveled some distance, the sound of water slapping against posts at their sides, a wide plank appeared on their right, beyond it the vague outline of a large vessel gently bobbing up and down in the water.

"Here we go." Chess didn't hesitate, but turned to strut up the slightly inclined piece of lumber, Bentus right behind him.

At the top they came to a rope across their path, but a swish of steel had the cord falling in two pieces. They stepped onto the flat deck of the cog, the large stern-mounted rudder off to their left.

Chess eyed the dark oak wood of the smallish craft, its single mast and lone square sail. "Never liked these Khadiran vessels. You'd think after all this time they'd make use of proper ships, like a caravel or something."

Bentus glared at his partner, but kept his voice low. "You want to scream out for the city guard to hear us?"

A sneer was the only answer. Chess turned away and headed toward a closed door beneath the stern castle, his soft leather boots causing the deck to creak beneath his feet.

As his hand touched the door's handle, a cold chill ran up his arm. But that wasn't enough to give Chess pause. It was an abrupt, metallic clinking noise followed by a thud that cause him to straighten as fear ate its way along his limbs.

"Bentus?" he asked without turning around.

There was no reply.

Slowly, with wide eyes, Chess spun around and stared back the way he had come, his knife and torch leading the way.

Through the mist rolling across the deck he could barely make out the dark lines of the ship's railing, but it was obvious his partner was no longer with him.

"Bentus? Where are you?"

Again, no reply.

His knife hand shaking, Chess eased forward into the fog, his feet sliding him haltingly toward the gang plank. After a moment his flame burned away the thickest of the gloom, exposing the opening to the pier where the two pieces of cut rope still hung from the sides of the railing. Of his partner there was no sign.

"Bentus?"

A snap of metal, then Chess was enveloped, a gigantic weight landing on him and forcing him to the ground. His knife went skidding away. The torch fell to one side but managed to stay ablaze. He tried to roll away from whatever was embracing him, but it was like fighting with a thousand weighted snakes. No matter what move he made, he was wrapped by unseen threads that pulled and forced him down. His own strength was as nothing to this vaporous enemy.

Realizing nothing he was attempting was working, the fight quickly died away from the man, and he was held, pinned facing the deck boards, several splinters thrust into his chin. The fallen torch burned a few feet away, revealing the rough wood of the ship's deck and nothing more. Chess could not even crane his head around to see what held him.

The stomping sound of boots soon came to his ears, revealing someone heavy taking their time crossing the plank from the pier. Each step was louder than the one before, making Chess suddenly wish he had listened to the guarded words of his partner.

The boot steps came to a stop not far from the thief, but he could make out no shadows or anything else that might be revealing.

"I usually prefer boys," a tilted but rough, foreign voice sounded, "but one must not refuse a free treat. It was a good thing we remembered to place warding alarms."

There was movement along Chess's legs. He could not budge an inch, but the cool of the night clambered over his backside and he could tell that whatever had been covering his legs had slid away but still gripped him by his ankles.

The hefty fumblings of a belt being unbuckled came to the downed man's ears, quickly followed by the brushing noise of trousers dropping about one's feet. Chess was familiar with the sound. He had heard it a thousand times before, had been the cause of it a thousand times before, in whore houses throughout the city.

There was a grunting, then a shadow was leaning over the thief. A tearing sound followed, and suddenly Chess's legs were colder than before, the night's mist chilling his bared flesh.

"Please, no," he managed to whisper.

There was a titter of laughter. "Oh, he begs. How precious. And our night is only beginning."

2

The morning frost crunched beneath the sergeant's boots as he trudged his way up the slight incline, the orange tabard of the Bond city guard enclosing his shoulders and keeping back the worst of the chill that still lingered with the remaining fog. As he grew closer to the giant shadowy outline of the stone building that was the Asylum, the clanking and grunting sounds of men at work came to his ears.

He paused as a motionless wagon rose out of the mist on his right, several burly fellows there unloading lumber from the back while another man steadied a pair of hitched bulls.

At the sight of the sergeant, one of the workers came forward, a younger man than the others and dressed in better rags, almost as if he were some noble down on his luck. He paused long enough to remove his dark floppy hat and wipe the sweat from his face before speaking. "Something I can do for you, officer?"

The sergeant came to a halt. "Sorry, sir, I'm just a sergeant, not an officer."

The young man grinned at his own mistake. "Very well, then, sergeant, anything I can do for you?"

"I'm seeking Kron Darkbow"

The worker gestured further up the hill. "Master Darkbow is within the Asylum."

The sergeant glanced in the direction, but then looked back to the young man. "May I have your name?"

"Why, yes, sir. I am Montolio, head architect for the repair of the Asylum. Is something amiss?"

"How long have you been here this morning?"

Montolio frowned. "All night, sir. You can't see because of the thickness of the fog, but we have tents on the grounds."

"Your workers were with you as well?"

"Some of them," Montolio answered. "Others live close by, and they go home at night. The rest of us bundle up here."

"When did you first see Master Darkbow this morning?"

The young architect appeared confused. "Several hours ago, I suppose, when he exited his own tent. He stays here most nights himself. May I ask what is the problem, sir?"

The sergeant ignored the question. "So, as far as you know, Darkbow was here all night?"

"Yes, sir. He entered his tent late last night after meals had been served, and did not leave until early this morning."

The sergeant pointed up the hill. "And you say he is now inside?"

"Yes, sir."

"Thank you. You have been most cooperative." The sergeant shifted away from the younger man and trod toward the shadowy building.

A pair of workers, bald, rough men, approached their boss. "Something wrong, Montolio?" one of them asked.

The architect stared at the back of the retreating soldier. "I don't think so. Either way, it's not any of our concern. Back to work."

As the grunts of labor returned to his ears, the city guard sergeant approached the front entrance to the Asylum. Now near the building, the dark edifice rose out of the fog like some ancient, long-forgotten castle along the hinterlands. Rumors were the place was haunted. The sergeant could well imagine how such stories had begun, especially considering the property's current owner.

A shadow loomed from the doorway. "Corporal Rogins, forgive me, but I overheard your talk with my men below."

Rogins hesitated, as he always did when facing this one. Kron Darkbow was tall and broad in the shoulders. Everything about him reeked black, including the buckles of his garb and the handle of the large sword he wore over his shoulders. His hair, too, was black, but most disturbing were those dark, impaling eyes in the middle of pale features.

The sergeant shivered, but then got control of himself. "Uh, I'm a sergeant now, sir."

"Ah, yes," Darkbow said. "With Gris's rise in rank, so goes your own. How is my friend fairing these days?"

"Um." Rogins did not know quite what to say. He was here on official business, and had little experience in personal pleasantries with this man.

"My apologies," the dark-garbed figure said. "I should have realized upon hearing you below. You are here in your official capacity as sergeant of the city guard. What may I do for you this day?"

Rogins blinked away the fog spreading dew upon his lashes. "Captain Gris would like a word with you, sir."

The cloaked head of Kron Darkbow inclined forward. "Concerning my whereabouts of last night?"

"Among other things, sir."

"Am I to be placed under arrest?"

"I have no such orders, sir."

"But you *were* interested in my location last night, were you not?"

Rogins hesitated. This man was a sly one. What to tell? "Sir, my questions were merely procedure. I wanted to ... uh, to make sure of a few things before proceeding."

An eyebrow was raised. "Questions concerning what?"

"There is a situation, sir. Two men are dead."

Darkbow straightened, his sizable figure looming in the mist like some dark giant. He nodded. "Very well, sergeant. Lead the way."

3

The two bodies were laid out next to one another. That on the left was garbed but soggy, slightly bloated, with blue rings around the eyes. The other was naked from the waist down, dark bruises running up and down the back of the legs, and sporting a callous, red line around the throat; half of the face had been burned away, leaving behind a charred blackness that in no way resembled a human appearance.

Kron stood from kneeling, his eyes roaming over the two corpses resting in the center of the boardwalk. The initial revulsion continued to lurk in the bottom of his stomach, but it was not as if he had not seen dead men before. He had even been known to leave behind a few in his wake on occasion. These two were different, however. No slash of a sword had felled these men. The one appeared drowned, which was a common enough occurrence in a city surrounded by three rivers, but the other had suffered an unusual death. There had been more than simple fire in the torched fellow's suffering. He had been battered and abused, then something thick and hard had wrapped around his neck. It was obvious from the blood welling beneath the flesh the fire had been applied at the last. The poor man had still been alive, though possibly only barely, with any luck no longer being conscious.

Torture had been involved. What confounded Kron, however, was he could not characterize what had happened to this second victim, what had been the means of torture. The wound around the neck might have been caused by some kind of heavy rope or cloth, but there were no threads left behind as evidence to this. It did not help that the burning had blurred much of the neck marks, the coal that had been flesh reaching down beneath the chin and around the throat. Also odd were the bruises along the back of the dead man's legs.

Kron leaned down once more and used a gloved hand to gently press aside one of the burned man's knees. A slick like that of faint oil glistened upon the inside of the thighs.

The man in black stood straight. "He was raped. Brutally."

"And repeatedly."

Kron turned at the words to glance at the rugged, stern features of Captain Gris, head of Bond's city guards. Behind the officer stood a half dozen of his orange-clad soldiers, each pale in the face and blocking the pier from any citizens curious enough to want to investigate. There was little need for the sentries, however, as this was a mostly empty part of the city, a wasteland of rotting, forgotten warehouses and piers jutting out into the South River. The Docks, a newer and more well-kept part of the city to the east and north was the mainstay of the city's economy and had been for a century. Here, in this gray place, there was nothing.

Kron grimaced and looked back to the bodies. He recognized these men.

"I understand now why you asked for me," he said.

Gris nodded. "You knew Bentus and Chess."

"Only in passing," Kron said. "I had not seen them in months, since their ... intrusion at the Finder's estate."

"Yes, you were enemies, at least then."

The man in black glanced to the captain once more while motioning to the bodies. "You can't believe I had anything to do with this."

Gris sighed and shook his head. "Of course not. It's not your style. When you kill, you kill swiftly."

"Not always." Kron stared off into the murky waters of the river, remembering the fate he had brought upon the leader of a group of cannibals only a year earlier. The flesh eater had been deserving of his slow death, but Kron had paid a price. His mind had nearly snapped, and his atrocities had cost him the woman he loved. But that was then. Another place, another time. He was no longer that man.

Kron snapped back to the present. "They don't appear to have been dead long, perhaps a day or two. I'm surprised they were found so soon."

"They likely wouldn't have been," Gris said, "but the new Docks boss came down this morning because of a rumor about an anchored Khadiran ship. No captain had visited the river master's office, so the Docks chief was thinking piracy or smuggling. He didn't find the ship, but he did find these two dead."

"So you brought me here to identify the bodies."

The captain shook his head. "No. I realized who they were as soon as I'd heard the description from Rogins. I called on you because I want to hire you."

"Officially?"

"Yes," Gris said. "The city guard isn't a policing force. We don't have the authority or the manpower to go looking into every crime. If anything, we clean up the messes after they've been committed. On a good day we can prevent something before it happens, but that's rare enough. We have no investigative officers. That's where I can use you."

Kron nodded in agreement. It was no boast for him to admit he was one of the best trackers of men in the city, if not the country. Before returning to his home city of Bond, he had spent years as a border warden in the Prisonlands and had never lost an escapee.

"I'll put you on the payroll as an adjunct officer, a lieutenant," Gris said. "That's if you can spare the time away from the Asylum."

A cold wind blew in from the river, ruffling the edge's of Kron's dark cloak and knocking away the last of the morning fog. "I can manage. Montolio is a good man. He won't need me to continue the construction. Besides, I can use the coin you're offering."

"Good."

"However, for the future, you need to consider creating a scouting agency or some such," Kron suggested. "And why you've not hired squad mages since you've become captain is beyond me."

"No coin for it," Gris said, "but I've been pushing the mayor."

The man in black looked to his friend. "Has she made you a full captain yet?"

"Goes into effect next week. She was only waiting for Captain Chambers's retirement papers."

"Good." Kron nodded again and turned his attention back to the corpses. "Benton and Chess were strong and experienced swordsmen, yet it looks as if they put up little fight. If I didn't know better, I would hazard a guess there was magic involved here."

"I won't disagree."

"I'll ask around some mages to see what they can discover."

"The university?"

"No." Kron shook his head. "They're too scholarly for this work. I'll look in on Nodana. It's the street mages who will be of help here."

"What of Randall?" Gris asked.

Randall Tendbones was a healer and, unknown to the general public, the most powerful wizard in the city. He also happened to be a friend to Kron Darkbow and Captain Gris.

"Randall has his own concerns. I'll only bother him if I must." Kron pointed to the dead men. "Where were these two originally found?"

"Bentus was floating just off shore, caught on some rocks. Chess was on his back pretty much where you see him now."

"Where will they be if Nodana needs to see them?"

"Until I can find the next of family, they'll be laid out in the main Swamps temple."

Kron's gaze shifted to the waters lapping at the edges of the wharf. "And what of this missing ship? Can you tell me anything about it?"

"It supposedly came in a couple of days ago and the crew disembarked," Gris said. "Other than that, I know nothing. But if you want, I can put out word in the taverns."

"I suppose it could not hurt," Kron said. "I'll do some hunting myself."

"Hunting?" Gris asked with a sly grin. "Just make sure you bring the prey to me. We don't need another street war."

4

Frex Nodana was a small woman. She stood no taller than the average ten-year-old child. Still, she was shapely, and despite nearing her third decade she could still pass for a young woman half her age. At least when she wore coal around her eyes and painted lips. Her short, dark hair also added to her youthful image and somehow made her diminutive size appear even more so.

There were those who might call her a dwarf or a midget, but in truth she was neither. She was merely a small woman. She was also an intelligent woman. She was not above making use of her feminine wiles when necessary, but she had found much more personal success through use of her intellect.

Frex Nodana was the head of the Mages Guild for the city of Bond. She was the first such master. The guild itself had existed only a matter of months. Before, magic had been thought to be a tool of only the educated, and to some extent the wealthy. The *intellectuals*. Before the guild, there had seemed little need for a cooperative, a gathering of wizards, within the city. The university had filled that function with its College of Magic. It had taken Frex Nodana and several others to realize this was an error. There had been, and continued to be, a number of street mages throughout the city, men and women of various levels of skill who had never been a part of the collegiate circles. Nodana herself was an educated woman, but she had grown up from the poverty that had plagued her childhood, and she had had more than a little help in attaining her current position. Years of working beneath various low-level politicians had finally paid off.

It had all been worth it, however, the kowtowing, the bowing, the bending. She had worked her way from the lowest rungs of West Ursian society up to a position of no little power and envy. But being the master of the Mages Guild was not simply about power for her. She did not adore others fawning over her, nor did she have a lust for gold. For Frex Nodana, her station in life was all about freedom. No longer did she have to grub for food as she had done as a child on many occasions. No longer did she have to stare into the bleary eyes of her parents, Ashal rest their souls, after they came home from drudgery but still with little more than a handful of grain to show for their labors. No more of being at the very bottom levels of society, of living among the rats, the roaches, the slime.

Education, skill and luck had fulfilled her desires. She had no wish to further herself beyond her attainment as leader of the street mages, but that did not mean she would not be open to further opportunities. Only a fool would settle for less when more was offered, and Frex Nodana was not a fool.

Though she did look rather foolish as a tall, dark figure entered her office and she looked up from behind her desk. Her eyes went wide at recognition, and for a moment she felt her heart flutter. Not a woman to fall easily for a man, Nodana had to admit if there were a man who could take away her soul, it would be Kron Darkbow.

He nodded as a sign of acknowledgment, but remained standing behind one of the two padded chairs facing her.

She smiled. "It has been some while. To what pleasure do I owe the great Kron Darkbow?"

He did not smile. "Two of your friends are dead."

Nodana blanched. Who could he mean?

"Chess and Bentus," Kron said as way of explanation.

The guild master's brows furrowed. "I have not seen them in months, since leaving Kerjim's employ. And I would never claim them as friends. Co-workers, at best."

"Either way, they are dead."

"You came all the way from the Asylum to Uptown to tell me this?"

Kron shook his head. "It appears they were murdered. The city has hired me to look into it."

Frex Nodana leaned back in her chair. For a moment her heart beat even faster, out of concern she was to be considered a suspect in the crime. But that was foolishness. If she was suspect, a squad of city guards would have apprehended her. Darkbow would not have been sent to shepherd her into a jail cell.

"What can I do for you, Master Darkbow?"

"You can begin by cutting out that 'master' nonsense," Kron said. "I am no one's master."

"My apologies."

Kron placed his gloved hands on the back of the chair before him. "It seems Bentus was drowned, perhaps after being hit over the head or possibly throttled. Nothing too unusual about that, except Bentus is not one to stand still for an attacker. There were no signs of a struggle with him."

"And poor Chess?"

"Beaten. Choked. Raped. Burned."

Nodana blanched again, her face turning as pale as a dead fish's belly.

"I believe magic might be involved," Kron said. "Little else makes sense."

The guild master's eyes lowered to stare at the top of her desk where scrolls and papers were arrayed in a seemingly random cluster. Darkbow likely spoke the truth. She had not known Bentus and Chess well, but they were a familiar sort of man, brutal but not necessarily hostile unless provoked. Neither would have allowed himself to be mistreated in a harsh manner, definitely not to be worked over and raped.

She looked up into Darkbow's midnight eyes. Her voice was small. "I know of no street mages who would do such things. There are a handful who might have the sheer power to accomplish it, but the will or inclination? No."

"One can always be fooled."

"True enough," Nodana said, her voice growing in strength, "but if that is the case, I will admit to having been fooled when the time comes. Still, to the best of my knowledge there are no mages of any sort within Bond who would take part in such barbarity."

"I won't disagree with you," Kron said. "My thinking is there might be a new element within the city."

"What makes you say so?"

"The bodies were found at an old dock on the southern shore of the Swamps. Days earlier an unmarked Khadiran vessel had been spotted there."

"The ship is likely gone, taking with it the murderer," Nodana surmised

"Possibly," Kron said. "A crew was seen leaving, but none was noted to have returned. It is not impossible a small crew could have joined with the ship late at night. That part of the Swamps isn't overly crowded to begin with, but it does not feel right to me. Magic is likely involved with the actual murders, which leads me to wonder if magic was used to do away with the ship."

"To transfer it through the very air?"

"Or hide it. Or perhaps call up a wind to move the ship on its own power."

Nodana nodded. "Such is possible, but it would take a powerful wizard to do so. The easiest path would be to camouflage the ship."

"Are you suggesting it might still be sitting on the river right in front of us?"

"It is possible, yes."

Kron frowned. "That had not occurred to me."

"If I came down to this dock, a simple spell would reveal the truth, that is if the ship is only hidden away," Nodana offered.

"My thanks." Kron nodded. "I would appreciate as much."

Nodana stood. "Would now be an appropriate time? My schedule for the day is rather light."

"I can escort you there," Kron said. He turned toward the door, then brought himself to a pause, looking back at the woman. "There is one more thing, however."

"Yes?"

"Would you be willing to look at the bodies?"

5

Liquor was a gift from the gods of the ancients. At least that's what Corporal Talend of the Bond city guard believed. Nothing could clear up a ringing headache like alcohol. Nor could anything else quench the fires of a burning crotch, sometimes the harsh liquid applied directly and sometimes down the throat. Finally, in her estimation nothing could blot away memories like that most precious of gifts, alcohol. And Talend had a lot of memories she wanted blotted, the most recent of which was that charcoal face of the dead man down by the river earlier in the day. Just her luck she had drawn duty in the Swamps the very day a disfigured corpse and its soggy partner were pulled from the shore. The drowning victim she could stomach, like she had a hundred times before, but that other fellow had had a face like beef chopped and cooked for too long.

She placed a hand against an alley wall to hold herself upright before bending forward. Her throat gagged for several seconds before a natural reflex kicked in within her stomach and her dinner of potatoes and pigeon stew erupted forth to paint the rust-red bricks beneath her feet.

The ejection of food was short-lived as luck would have it, and soon enough the corporal was swaying her way further down the alley.

It was seven bells in the evening, past dark by only an hour, and Corporal Talend was already feeling the delicious nectar of Nebrarian whiskey flowing through her veins. It had not been the liquor that had made her sick, but the image of that burnt dead man in her mind's eye. Even sober she would have thrown up. At least that's what she told herself.

The woman had spent the hours since she had gone off duty in the Gilded Pony tavern in Southtown. She had not even bothered to travel home to remove her bright orange tabard nor the leather armor she wore beneath. Her duty sword still hung on her hip as did its matching dagger on her other hip. Swaying as she was, she was lucky the weighted steel on her belt did not drag her into a wall face first, but then she also still wore her kettle helmet which afforded some protection.

Reaching the end of the alleyway, she paused once more, leaning against a wall. Across her path stretched a dirt road, one familiar but which she could not name in her condition. A few folks passed by, but none seemed to pay her any mind. That was fine with Corporal Talend. She just wanted to get home and fall to sleep on her nice, warm bed.

Trying to figure where she was, she looked up and down the road. There was a butcher's shop on the right and several cheese shops on the left. Talend shook her head. She still didn't know where she was. She could be just about anywhere in Southtown.

Across the way from her, the black opening of another alley beckoned. The corporal stared at it. She could just make the street lamps at that alley's far end and a few more people walking by. Perhaps if she made it across that alley she would recognize where she was.

Lurching ahead, a few pedestrians gasping and rushing out of her way, the armored guard crossed the dirt path one drunken step at a time. Her only thoughts were of reaching that next alley, because that alley would lead to home. It had to. Or, at least, it had to lead to somewhere, which was better than not knowing where she was.

Nearly tumbling into the shadows, Corporal Talend finally reached the shelter of the new alley. Once more she was forced to lean against a wall to keep from falling over. She belched, glanced around, then sauntered forward.

She had gone no more than a few steps when her left boot caught on something. The woman cursed and lifted the boot, a tacky fluid sticking to the bottom of the hardened leather sole.

"Damn vagrants," she said. "Pukin' and pissin' in a perfectly good walkway. I oughtta arrest every last one of 'em."

Talend twisted her lifted boot to one side and placed it down again. Once more her foot came into contact with something tacky, gummy.

"What the hell?"

She had had enough. She wanted to know what it was she was stepping in, then she would find who had placed it there, and *then* she would place *them* under arrest. She turned back toward the well-lit road and stumbled in that direction. On packed earth once more, she paused to catch her breath, then stretched and reached up for an iron lamp hanging atop a post. It was a good reach, but she was a big woman.

Soon enough the lamp was in her hands and likely would have singed her fingers if not for the thick leather gloves she wore and her intoxicated condition.

Talend swung around and lifted the lamp, angling its glow to shed light upon the alleyway with the sticky stuff on the ground.

She suddenly wished she had not.

The lamp fell from her fingers, crashing onto the ground and going out.

She bent forward once more and a new outburst forced its way between her teeth and lips. By the time she was reduced to dry heaves the woman was on her knees.

More sober than she had been in days, she fumbled at her belt. Her fingers raked against a small brass cylinder, tugged it free and lifted it to her lips.

The whistle called out into the night with a shrillness that hurt the ears of those who heard.

Within five minutes a squad of city guards were on the scene.

More lamps were lit.

Unveiled was a scene even alcohol would never erase from Corporal Talend's mind.

6

"A child."

Kron wanted to look away, but he would not allow himself to do so. He sought to burn the image before him into his mind. The boy likely had been no more than ten years of age. A child. Someone had done this to a child. *This*.

The corpse was layered in ragged cuts, some so large as to reveal the inside workings of the body. Bruises and caked, drying blood streaks were more prevalent than any unblemished flesh. A pool of red had grown around the remains but had cooled, showing where Corporal Talend had stepped.

The worst were the eyes, small and hooded and empty, staring off into horrors that should not be known by anyone, let alone a child. This boy had suffered untold pain to the body and the spirit.

Rage was swelling within Kron Darkbow. He had fought this darkness for the longest of times, knowing full well the penalties of his own wrath. He had slain innocents, but at least they had been grown men capable of fighting back. The error of his ways had finally been shown to him, and he had forced himself along another path, one that he had hoped would lead to less violence in his life. But now *this*. There was no sanity in what he saw. There was no reason. It was simply evil. Vile men had performed the most awful of acts, torturing and slaying a child. Kron had once been naive enough to believe men killing for money were the worst of sorts, but his eyes had been opened over the years. And now he had been reminded.

A gagging noise caused Kron to finally turn away. He swung around to find Frex Nodana crying in the arms of another, much larger woman, the corporal. Talend's face was stunned, as was that of the other dozen guards standing in a half circle around the end of the alley, but the mage's features were cracked, broken.

Sergeant Rogins stood off to one side, his back to the alley and its awful scene. The few citizens who wandered by saw little through the line of guards, but the three lamps that had been placed about revealed enough scarlet and gore to rush off even the most inquisitive of onlookers.

"Someone must pay," Kron said to himself, barely above a whisper.

Rogins glanced over his shoulder, making sure his gaze went no further than Kron's face. "Did you say something, sir?"

Kron strode forward to stand next to the sergeant, both facing outwards, their eyes not lingering upon any one particular sight. "I'm taking it you've already called upon a church caretaker?"

"Yes, sir," Rogins said. "He should be here anytime now."

"I don't suppose anyone knows the family of this boy?"

"No family, sir," Rogins said. "One of the other guards recognized the lad. His name was Malk. He was a street urchin."

The rage continued to boil behind Kron's eyes. This was a boy who had not known the loving touch of parents, a boy who had raised himself on the streets of the city, who had likely fallen prey to the worst types of people more than once, finally succumbing to tragedy. Was there no justice in this world?

No, Kron had to admit, there was little justice to be found. Justice had to be fought for, won at the end of a sword. Men were weak and cowardly, too afraid or lazy to step forward and do what was right. Perhaps if they would not protect their own, someone would have to show them the way.

Nodana groaned to one side, her body racked with near convulsions. Kron sympathized as he watched her. It was a small twist of fate they were even here. He and the mage had been traveling to the church in the Swamps, preparing to see the bodies of Chess and Bentus, when Sergeant Rogins had arrived, expecting to find them at the temple.

"Nodana," Kron spoke, the word soft.

The woman continued to cry, impervious to the outside world, streams of black running down from her eyes.

"Nodana." The word was louder, stronger.

No response.

Enough was enough. There was no time for grief. Killers of children were on the prowl. "Nodana!"

The woman's head snapped up. She wiped at her eyes with the sleeve of her robes and moved away from Corporal Talend. She looked to the man in black.

"Can you tell me anything about this ... crime?" Kron asked.

Grief rolled over her features once more, but she did not shed new tears. "Give me a moment, please."

Kron nodded as the sergeant and other guards watched.

The wizard faced toward the body but did not look at it, mumbling ancient words beneath her breath and waving her hands in the air before her closing her eyes.

It was not long when she gasped and was thrust back as if an invisible force had hammered against her chest. The woman would have tripped on her own feet if Talend had not rushed forward and grabbed her by the shoulders again.

The mage stood there in shock, her eyes red and wet.

Kron stepped forward. "What did you find, Nodana?"

"You were right," the woman said. "There was magic involved."

Kron nodded. "But there is more."

"Spells were used for silence and concealment, but ... the worst was not from a human source."

The man in black's eyes narrowed.

"There is demon magic involved here," Nodana said.

"Demon?" Rogins asked.

"Or a caster in alliance with a demon," the mage said. "The monster captures the prey, then the wizard, he ... he rapes. It is the demon who then slays."

"That ties in with the Khadiran ship," Kron said.

The sergeant looked to the man next to him. "How so?"

"Khadir is one of the few places known to be home to dark mages," Kron explained. "Outside of Kobalos, it is a rare thing for a wizard to be in league with demons."

"So you think the killer in the Swamps is the same as here?"

Kron nodded. "I believe so, yes."

"I don't know," Rogins said, not quite convinced. "It was dark when this boy was slain, but it happened pretty early in the night. The other attack likely happened after midnight."

"True enough. But as Nodana has told us, magic shielded the killers from outside view. It's possible this attack could have happened in daylight, and yet no one would have seen. Still, it's likely this horror happened after dark, otherwise someone would have come upon it before Corporal Talend here."

Kron turned toward the mage. "Nodana, are you still willing to see Bentus and Chess?"

The woman nodded in silence.

"And will you go to the shoreline and investigate?"

Again, the woman nodded consent.

Kron looked to Rogins. "Would you provide an escort for Guild Master Nodana?"

The sergeant blinked. "Of course, sir. But I thought you would be doing so."

Kron glanced at the shredded body once more, his fists quivering at his side. "The inclusion of a demon has changed things. A man I can arrest. A demon can only be destroyed, and temporarily at that. I have a task to perform before confronting such a beast. But I *will* find this killer."

7

Rumors abound that the Asylum was haunted. No one would come near the place. Montolio had been forced to pay double wages to the workers he had managed to scrounge together, though fortunately they had proven to be a solid crew so far.

The tale of the Asylum was not completely known by the Lycinian, but he had put pieces of it together here and there. Apparently the place had been a hospital of sorts, more like a prison, for the dangerously insane. A magical accident of some kind had flooded and slain those within the main building, all three stories and the basement. Kron Darkbow had somehow been involved in that incident, and soon after he had purchased the building for his own uses, whatever those might be. The rumors went on that only months earlier Kron had somehow drawn the ire of one of the more powerful guild masters within the city, and assassins had been hired to kill Kron. A confrontation had taken place at the Asylum. Kron had walked out unscathed. The assassins and the guild master were now shells of men, wasting away like clams in some healing tower somewhere.

As he had only arrived in the city a month ago, Montolio did not know if the history of the Asylum was true, but he could confirm the place was haunted. The spirits of the dead did not show themselves to the architect nor to the workers, but still, they were there. Montolio could sense them, could *feel* them, just on the edges of shadow. More than once he had spied something out of the corner of his eyes, but upon looking directly had found nothing.

The ghosts did not concern him, however. So far they had not proven to be any sort of threat. If that should change, if the dead should decide to make a nuisance of themselves, Montolio believed he could deal with the situation without drawing too much undue attention, perhaps even without letting his employer or his employees know. Besides being an architect, the Lycinian was a mage, having studied glamour and sorcery and even necromancy within the gilded halls of the famed University of Salvino on the island nation of Lycinia. Here in West Ursia none of his history meant much of anything, but in Lycinia, Montolio would have been considered an up-and-coming gentleman. He was educated, intelligent, and well traveled, having spent much of his life in Brome, Trode and Salvino before coming to Bond. He was still young, in his mid twenties, and though not overly handsome, he was by no means unpleasant to look upon.

Unfortunately, he was not wealthy. He had grown up in a family of some little money, but a father with a thirst for drink and a sibling with gambling ambitions had wiped out what fortune there had been. Which was why Montolio had not remained in Salvino, a city he had loved, and had moved north and nearly across the continent before settling finally in Bond. For some reason unfathomable to the Lycinian, his family's debtors had felt he was responsible for paying back everything and anything owed. After completing another season of schooling, Montolio had been broke. Thus he had fled.

A man of his wide education and talents could fare well, however, and he had paid his way during his travels by utilizing various of his skills. In Bond he had settled upon a career in architecture, seeing a need for such. His true love was painting and drawing, but there was little money to be found in such artistry here in the West. Montolio hoped to change that some day, but until then he would continue as he had.

He was thankful to have decent employment and a profession. Though no longer wrapped in the arms of his lovely Lycinia, he had still found a civilized home, though Bond and West Ursia were proving to be a bit more rough around the edges than had been life among the islands.

Kron Darkbow was a prime example.

Standing in the shadows of the Asylum and staring up at the three stories of murky brick, Montolio pondered that the building was much like its owner. Dark and large, but silent and draped in shadows. This building held a history, and secrets. When Montolio had first taken on the job, the first task had been to drain the basement level of water. The second task had been to remove several dozen bloated corpses from within the maze of that basement, this costing a fair amount of coin because the workers would not do so on the cheap. Again, these thoughts reminded him of Kron Darkbow. Were their bodies in the basement of Darkbow's soul?

"Good evening, Montolio."

The young architect nearly jumped at the sound of the voice, the brass lamp hanging from one hand bouncing up and down. He turned and found the master of the property standing on the sharp edge where the black shadows from the building ended and the moonlit ground continued. Further down the hill could be seen the tents where the remaining workers were finishing their late dinner and beginning to bed down for the night. Sounds of their chattering drifted across the air to Montolio, but he was surprised to have not heard the approaching steps of his employer.

He nodded to the man in black. "Good evening, sir."

Kron approached, staring up the nearest wall and the scaffolding of iron bars and lumber that fronted it.

Montolio followed the gaze. "We just about have the new roof completed. Placing the beams was the difficult part. The rest of the tiles should be laid down within a day or two."

Kron nodded but was silent for the moment.

"Then we'll get to that hole in the floor in the main hall," Montolio continued. "I've already had the debris removed and a portion of the edge cut away. So far we are on schedule. We should be finished before the first snow."

The shadowed face beneath the black hood looked to the architect. For the first time Montolio noticed there was a change in his employer. He had known Kron Darkbow little more than a month, and the man had always been somewhat distant, even cold at times, but this was new. There was something almost mechanical in Darkbow's simple motions, as if he moved with certain intent, a ruthlessness.

The hooded head leaned back and for a moment the moon raked across the face. It was all Montolio could do not to gasp. Yes, this was Kron Darkbow, but he was a different man. This was a side of his employer the architect had yet to see, and what he saw sent a shiver along his spine the autumn nights were not cold enough to produce. It was the eyes, more than anything. There was a hardness there, like cold, black iron dug from the center of the world. Yet there was also almost a physical change in the set of the jaw and the face's cheeks. Darkbow's features appeared more angular, chiseled. It was like he was made of stone.

The man in black seemed not to notice his employee's perusal. Yet he spoke. "Montolio, when you first came to work for me, I was under the impression you held a rather wide education."

The architect nodded. "Yes, sir."

"Artistry, architecture, mechanics and such."

"Yes, sir."

"What of alchemy?"

Montolio breathed in the cool night air. There was nothing wrong with being an alchemist, yet that particular field had a reputation next to that of magic, which was far from the truth. Alchemy was merely a study of the natural world, and of making use of nature. Still, as one did not advertise being a mage when walking certain parts of the world, it was also not common to let it be known one had skills in alchemy. Was Montolio about to lose his job? Something was wrong with his employer. Did Darkbow have something against alchemists? It was not as if Montolio touted alchemy as a profession, yet he did have experience in all the sciences.

He decided then and there he would not lie. Montolio was not a man who made a habit of not telling the truth, and he saw no reason to now. If the truth cost him this job, then so be it. At least he had saved enough coin to survive until he could find more work.

The architect opened his mouth.

Kron cut him off. "I noticed a worn satchel among your gear when you moved into your tent. It appeared to me to be a basic alchemical kit."

Montolio was brought up short again. His employer was a shrewd man, and watchful. There was little he seemed to miss. All the more reason not to lie.

"I have some training in the natural sciences," he explained, "but I would never consider myself a professional."

Kron nodded. "How adept are you at working with sulfur?"

Sulfur? "The element has a variety of uses, some of them curative."

"And others not so."

Where was Darkbow going with this? "Yes, it's true, sulfur can be used in other fashions."

"Do you have any experience building grenados?"

Montolio's eyes popped. Grenados. Deadly weapons of flame. Rare here in the West, even somewhat in the lands with which he was familiar, they were generally believed to be more common in the far southern lands, Pursia, Khadir, even the furthest of foreign lands, Hipon.

The Lycinian turned his eyes to the ground. He would not lie. "I have some little experience forming grenados, yes." His education had been well rounded, after all.

The moon revealed the glint of a smile. A hard smile. All teeth. "That is good. Do you have a supply of sulfur?"

"Some little bit."

"How much?"

Montolio paused. Where was this going? He knew grenados were illegal in this land, and he had no wish to become a criminal, even for his employer. "Enough for three grenados." It was his first lie, but not by much.

A gloved hand extended from the darkness of Kron's cloak, holding forth a glass bottle. "Can you use this to make a special type of grenado?"

Montolio glanced at the the corked top of the offering. It was too dark to tell what was inside the bottle, but it sloshed when moved. "What is within?"

"Holy water."

Montolio blinked.

"I visited a temple before coming here," Kron said.

The architect took the bottle and held it up in the moonlight, staring at the bouncing liquid within. "I do not understand. How can one make grenados with water?"

"I do not expect an explosive," Kron explained, "merely clay grenados that will crack upon contact, splashing the fluid from inside."

The bottle lowered. Montolio looked to his employer again. "Holy water? What good would it do except against ..." His words trailed off.

Kron nodded. "Yes. Demons, or walking dead. Can you do it?"

"I believe so. There is enough here to make at least three."

"Can you still make for me burning grenados?"

"Of course. How soon do you need them?"

"As soon as you can have them finished. I am willing to pay extra."

It was Montolio who nodded now. Things were beginning to coalesce in his mind. He had heard Darkbow was hired by the city guard to investigate at least one murder, and now here the man was seeking not only grenados, but weapons of holy water. Was the killer a walking dead man? Or something worse?

"I will have the weapons for you by morning," he said. "I will remain awake all night, if necessary."

"Thank you," Kron said. "Lives might depend upon it."

The man in black turned to walk away.

"Sir?" Montolio said to Darkbow's back.

Kron paused and glanced back. "Yes?"

"Why me?" Montolio asked. "Why did you seek me for this task? Surely there are other alchemists within the city."

Kron nodded again. "True enough. But it is late, and their shops will be closed. Also, I need these tools soon, and have other tasks to perform before the night is through. Besides, you strike me as a man who can be trusted."

"Where can I find you when I am finished?"

"I will find you, in the morning."

With those words, Kron Darkbow shifted away and sauntered down the hill.

Montolio watched the receding back, then followed, heading toward his tent and his alchemical gear. It was to be a long night. He needed to get started.

8

It would not be midnight for a couple of hours, yet the twinkling of frost combined with the moon's glow made the lanky boards across the top of the pier look like ancient bones laid out in a long row. Frex Nodana shivered beneath her dark cloak, but she could not tell if this was because of the autumn night's chill or the image before her.

She looked to her right where the armored form of Corporal Talend stood between her and the river. The city guard stared straight ahead along the pier as if she, too, did not like the view, all the while her hands gripping the handles of the sword and dagger on her belt.

They were alone, and it felt as if they had been transferred to some far off, alien world. Around them was darkness but for the moon and its light sheening off the smooth river. Across the water could be spotted lights along the shore there, but the sounds of the city were distant, making it difficult to believe they were surrounded by hundred of thousands of people.

It was a spooky place, and Nodana suddenly wished her escort had included more than the lone guard.

Talend huffed out a breath, the warm air turning to fog before her face. "I suppose we should get this over with. Is this close enough, or do you need to go out on the pier?"

Nodana glanced at the dirt beneath her feet, then looked once more upon the forlorn walkway stretching out before them. "It would be easier if I were to go out some ways."

The corporal wrapped her own cloak tighter around her. "Mind if I wait here? It'll be colder out there on the water."

The mage saw no reason not to comply with the other woman's wishes. There was only one way onto the pier, and the corporal would be guarding that. Also, it was not as if Nodana were expecting trouble. This killer, this sick person, might have once been on this spot, but she no longer believed they were in evidence. If something as large as a ship were hiding in plain sight just off shore, she would have picked up on that even while remaining on land. No, it was obvious the ship was nowhere to be found immediately, but magic often left a trail and it was not impossible Nodana could pick up on that.

She nodded. "Remain here and I will be back in a few minutes."

"Do you need a torch?"

"No, no thank you," Nodana said, then made her way forward, crossing onto the creaking bones of the pier.

The wind picked up once she was out over the moving water, the cold air playing with the end of her cloak and slapping it against her legs. The mage entwined her arms for warmth as she walked forward, staring at the second, murky moon hinted at on the river's surface. It was more than the weather making her chilled, however. Who could be responsible for such atrocities as had occurred in the city? Especially against a child? Frex Nodana had on occasion walked a fine line between what others considered right and wrong, but she was no beast. She could not imagine a mind so evil as to do harm to a child, let alone the horrors she had witnessed just off a street in Southtown.

She stopped more than halfway along the pier and glanced back toward the direction she had come. It looked far, but she realized she could not have walked such a long distance in so short a time. Still, she could barely make out the bulky figure of Corporal Talend stamping her boots along the flat of the floodplain.

Nodana turned her attention to the river, allowing her gaze to flow with the waters, up and down, east to west, in the direction of the distant ocean many hundreds of miles away. She gradually reached out with her mind, searching for any hints of lingering magic. A proper casting would allow her to better focus, but first she wanted a feel for the area.

There. To her right. That was where the ship had been.

Yes, it had the barest stink of the sulfur about it. Whomever the caster was, he or she was powerful, able to summon forth a full demon. No imp or lesser creature from hell had been here, but a true monster. Nodana wondered what type of demon. War demons were generally the most common, but other types were available for summoning, if one were fool enough to do so. Demons never played fair, thus it was usually only the most powerful of mages who dealt with them.

All right. The ship had been here. That much she had already known, or could have guessed at from the words of others. But a demon had also been here. What had happened to the ship?

Her slender arms slipped out from beneath the cloak and raised facing the river where the Khadiran cog had once bounced up and down. Nodana whispered words of a language unknown to most.

An image snapped into her head, hard, darting and painful. She stepped back, her arms dropping at her side. She reeled for a moment, gasping.

Then her blood settled and the pain worked its way out of her mind. She stood still, breathing in slowly.

There had been powerful wards placed upon the ship, wards that shielded it from being found easily. A wizard casually observing would not have felt the spike of that ward, as Nodana had not. It was only when she had purposefully gone looking for the vessel that she was attacked. She had been fortunate, lucky. Though Nodana did not count herself as the most powerful of mages, she was no novice, and a novice might very well have been killed by the warding around this ship.

She nearly turned away, believing her efforts had been fruitless, but then paused while recalling her casting. There had been an image in her mind, brief but sharp. It had not been enough for her to pinpoint a location of the ship, but it did hold some clues. The view had been murky, shifting, as if Nodana had been looking through a glass of water. Much had been dark, though there were hints of a light glow high above. Perhaps the moon? Also, there had been something moving past her vision, something long and stringy, almost like rope. *Kelp.* The word popped into her mind. To her knowledge kelp was an underwater plant located only in oceans or seas, but surely there was a similar cousin to be found inland, perhaps even beneath the rushing surface of a river.

Nodana narrowed her eyes and stared outward. Could the ship be right here in front of her below the water's surface? Powerful magics could accomplish such, she knew, but it would take tremendous willpower to keep that level of power ongoing. Too, a craft of any size could not be close to shore or it would be seen. So if the ship was out there, it had to be out some little ways.

Could she discover the truth without facing the dangers of that ward again?

Her shoulders dropped. The easiest way to avoid the wards would be for her to swim out there and dive. It would be foolish for most to attempt such, quite dangerous, in fact. The cold and the undertow would prove deadly. But Frex Nodana was a wizard. She could layer herself with spells that would protect her from such.

She groaned as she tore away her cloak and dropped it to the deck of the pier. "Corporal?"

"Yes!" The woman had to raise her voice to be heard.

"I don't want you to worry," Nodana said, "but I'm going in for a brief swim."

Silence for a moment, then, "That doesn't sound like a good idea to me, ma'am."

"I'll be fine," Nodana said.

The tromping of hardened leather on wood grew closer and the corporal soon appeared beneath the moon. "Are you sure about this?"

Nodana bent and tugged off her shoes. "I think the ship is under the water."

Talend glanced out at the river. "Why don't we wait until daylight? Then we can get a diving crew out here."

"It might be gone by then," the mage said, straightening. "Don't worry. I have spells to protect myself."

The corporal looked back to the wizard and shrugged. "I'll wait here for you, if that won't mess up your magic."

"That's fine," Nodana said.

Then she mumbled more magic words and slipped over the edge.

The water here was not deep, barely up to the mage's chest, but she pushed out and angled downward, forcing her way below the surface as soon as possible. She could still feel the cold nipping away at her, but her protecting magics kept the worst at bay. Her vision was dim, but much stronger than it should have been, thankful to a second spell she had cast.

Right away, though, as her kicking legs and scrambling arms took her deeper and deeper, she knew she was on the right path. As yet she had seen no signs of the vessel, but the view in front of her was much the same as she had seen above. Gray plants washed against her, streaming from below toward the surface where a bright blot revealed the moon. Some few fish swam past, most of no size.

Nodana brought her legs beneath her and allowed the magic to hold her in place against the current. She wanted to pause to look around.

There was a tightening of her chest from lack of air, but that did not overly concern her. She had minutes of safety left. While above she could have cast a spell allowing her to find air under the water, instead she had chosen to extend the period she could go without breathing. Still, she could feel the weight pressing upon her lungs.

A glint off to one side.

She twisted and waved her arms, floating around for a look.

Yes, there was the ship, resting on the river bottom as if it had done so for a thousand years. The vessel appeared whole and in good condition, not at all like a sunken ship. Nodana briefly had thought the killer and the demon might have sunk their cog, believing it of no more use, but the evidence before her told otherwise. They were merely hiding the craft, keeping it here under the protection of magic until they would need it again. Thinking of the power it would take to do so, even with the help of a demon, was astonishing to the mind. Nodana could count on one hand the number of wizards she had personally known who might have been powerful enough to attempt such magic, and most of those had been old and were no longer living. Whomever this spell caster was, he or she was worth avoiding if possible. All the worse, this person had to be dangerously mad to have tortured and killed and raped.

She had seen enough. Nodana now knew the location of the Khadiran ship. What that meant, she did not know. Perhaps Kron would want the vessel raised, or would send down divers to investigate. Whatever he decided, Nodana would provide a warning and what aid she could. This killer must be caught. Perhaps she could find more magical help from the university, an older professor or someone who was more powerful than herself.

The mage kicked toward the top, nearly a minute later her head breaking the surface.

There were voices from the shore.

"I thought I had smelled magic." The speaker was unknown, though there was a heavy foreign accent, possibly Khadiran.

"Do I look like a wizard to you?" The words came from Corporal Talend, and sounded panicked.

What could Nodana do? She stared into the darkness, but she was near the middle of the river, only her magic sustaining her in the swift current. She could see nothing and was too far away to be of help to her escort. Even her spells were limited considering she was floating along the river; possibly she could cast, but it would weaken or outright dispel the magics protecting her from the elements.

The foreigner spoke again. "I have no need of this woman. Slay her for me."

There was an explosion of motion from the pier. Crackings as of wood and bone. Then a wet sound and a scream, cut off as swiftly as it had started. Something black blossomed into the night's sky for a moment, blocking the stars beyond, then sank down to disappear along the shoreline.

Nodana nearly cried out but caught herself. Shock rolled over her and she became nearly motionless, only her magic keeping her afloat. Corporal Talend was dying slowly, agonizingly, not a hundred yards from her. The poor woman.

Slurping and struggling noises found her ears, as did an anguished mewing like that of a tortured animal.

Then nothing. Silence.

Finally, soft footsteps moving out along the pier.

Nodana kicked with her legs, forcing herself toward the further shore. Her heart and mind were filled with sorrow for the fate of the corporal who had seemed a decent woman despite smelling like a brewery, but the mage knew she could do nothing here. She had hesitated, which might have cost Talend her life, but if this evil was as powerful as she was beginning to believe, there was little she could have done anyway.

After a few seconds, Nodana twisted around and forced her arms to splash forward and back, taking her toward Southtown. Each second she expected to be pulled down or enveloped by some unseen evil, but there was nothing to do but keep moving.

The salty tears from her eyes went unnoticed as they mixed with the river.

9

The old man sat on the edge of the stoop in front of The Gilded Pony tavern, watching a few customers come and go as he casually raised a brown earthen bottle to his lips. A broad-brimmed hat shadowed his eyes, but it was obvious he was a man who paid attention. He nodded to those he apparently knew and kept a sharp focus upon those he did not.

Kron watched this as he approached along the alley that fronted the entrance to the tavern. Any other time he might have smiled at the sight of Midge Highwater, a feisty fellow Kron liked despite himself. But not tonight. Crimes of the worst sort had been committed, and now was no time for joviality.

"I hear you've been busy this day," Midge said without looking up as the man in black came to a halt in shadows created by the two lamps hanging above the tavern's entrance.

"I have." Kron eased to the edge of the shadows, just to make sure he could be seen.

"Nasty business," Midge said, setting his bottle on the board next to him. "Word is Captain Gris hired you to do somethin' about it."

"He did."

"Good." Midge crooked back his head, light falling upon the deep lines surrounding his eyes. Those orbs were like ice. "Somethin' as nasty as this, someone needs to pay."

"They will," Kron said."

"Good," Midge repeated, lowering his head. "What brings you here?"

"You do."

The old man looked up once more, surprise in his features. "Me? What can an old storyteller like myself do for you?"

"You see things," Kron said. "You watch people. Better yet, you *know* things."

"Knew you wasn't a complete fool," Midge said with a chuckle. "All right, I'll help if I can. What do you want to know?"

"There was a Khadiran cog anchored off the south shore of The Swamps until this morning. I seek the crew."

"Heard about that," Midge said. "Sailed in a few days ago, didn't sign with the river master. Usually means it's smugglers, but sometimes pirates. They got something to do with these killings?"

"I do not know," Kron admitted. "The first bodies were found on the very spot where the ship had last been seen. Two dead were left behind, but the ship is gone."

Midge nodded. "So you're thinkin' they either shipped back out or switched crews. Is that it?"

"Something like that. If any of the crew is still in Bond, perhaps they can tell me something."

"If they're smugglers or worse, they're not likely to stay in the usual places," Midge said. "Fact is, they likely skedaddled with the ship, or else they're holed up somewheres safe."

"What would they consider a safe haven?"

Midge paused, obviously thinking. Then he nodded once more. "Possibly with the thieves guild. Other than that, I'm not sure. Maybe split up, spendin' their time and coin on whores or some such."

Kron raised a gloved hand and snapped a two-fingered salute. "Thank you." Then he swiveled into the shadows once more.

"Darkbow!" the old man called out.

Rustling in the darkness came to a halt.

"Find whoever did these things," Midge said. "Find them and punish them."

There was a brief breeze, then silence, and the old man realized he was alone.

10

Sergeant Thag grimaced as he tromped his way down the steps from the entrance to the city guard barracks in Southtown. His usual station was to the north of the rivers in Uptown, but an illness here and there had meant there were too few sergeants for the schedule to cover the whole city. Double duty was called for, and now after midnight, Thag was into his second shift of the day.

He paused at the bottom of the steps, looking over a shoulder at the massive building that housed the main command of the city guards. Hanging lamps above the entrance and torches lining the path ahead kept the dark at bay, and a handful of lesser officers and soldiers were coming and going, though Thag was surprised there were no prisoners being carried along. That meant it had been a slow night so far, and the sergeant hoped things remained that way.

Turning back the way he had been going, he followed the path between the torches to a broad dirt road that fronted the barracks building. Thag tugged his cloak tighter around his arms, feeling the chill of the autumn air biting even through his tabard and leather armor. For a moment he thought of returning to the barracks for warmth, but then decided against it. He had been setting out for the Rusty Scabbard just down the way, intent upon a warm late meal if it could be found; for civilians the tavern and inn was closed this time of night, but its doors always remained open for the city guard and was used frequently.

Just as the sergeant's boots scuffed onto the dirt path, a distant cry came to his ears. He stopped, listened, but heard nothing else. Shaking his head, he moved on.

"Help! Please, help!"

That voice was louder now, intelligible, and could not be ignored by a man with a conscious.

Thag turned to his left, the direction the sound had come. Emerging from shadows between a row of houses was a small figure slightly bent over. At first the sergeant thought the person a boy or young man, but the street lights soon outlined the figure of a diminutive woman. She was soaking wet, her dark clothes sticking to her body.

The woman straightened as she noticed she had caught the sergeant's attention, then scurried toward him. "Oh, thank Ashal!"

She ran right up to him, nearly bumping into the man. Thag put out a gloved hand and gripped her by a shoulder. "Steady yourself, ma'am."

Now they were closer he could make out her eyes were red and there was fear and concern on her face.

"You're city guard," she said is if just taking in his uniform.

"Yes, ma'am."

"I need to see Sergeant Rogins," she blurted.

Thag stared into her bleak features. What had happened to her? "I'm sorry, but Sergeant Rogins is not on duty tonight."

"Captain Gris, then."

That was a mighty big expectation. "My apologies, ma'am, but the captain is also not on duty."

The woman's eyes cleared and she stepped back, straightening further as she got hold of herself. Thag had to admit she showed steel in her backbone despite whatever had befallen her.

"Corporal Talend has been murdered," she said.

Now it was the sergeant who took a step back. His eyes went wide. His black mustache puffed out. "You are sure of this?"

"It was dark," the woman said, "but I heard it happen."

"Where?"

"The other side of the river."

"The Swamps?"

"Yes."

"You mean you swam across the river in the middle of the night?"

The dark-headed woman hesitated, then, "Sir, I am Frex Nodana, master of the Mages Guild. I had ... aid ... in crossing the river."

Magic. Thag understood that much. He had also recognized her name, and as boss of the mages, she would have some power.

"I was on official duty when the attack occurred," Nodana said. "I was working under Lieutenant Kron Darkbow."

Darkbow. Thag barely knew the man, though he was familiar with the name and face. At the beginning of his shift, his *first* shift, he had been informed of the adjunct position given to Darkbow for investigation of the grisly murders that had hit the city that day.

The woman sounded like she knew what she was talking about, and this appeared serious business, especially considering a city corporal had possibly been murdered. He half turned and gestured toward the barracks. "Guild Master Nodana, if you would accompany me, we will get you warm clothes and a fire. Then I can see to waking Sergeant Rogins or Captain Gris."

<u>11</u>

As the hardened leather of his right heel snapped against the door, Kron realized this was what he needed. Violence. It had been building within. And now here it was. Release.

Wood cracked and splinters flew and Kron Darkbow charged into the hall. He was greeted by two burly ruffians in soft leathers, both men wearing looks of surprise and eyes fighting the sleep they had so recently enjoyed. Each also wore a knife on a belt, but they had not the sense to draw their weapons.

Gloved fists hammered to the left and right, and both big men slumped to the ground.

Kron gave no one else the chance to fully wake. He waded into the larger room, kicking aside trash and jumping over waking figures sprawled out upon the floor. It looked as if there had been a party. A dozen men and as many women were strewn about the dirty room, empty and half-full bottles of wine sitting up or rolling across the floor.

At the end of the room was an old wooden altar, one of the few reminders this had once been a house of holiness years in the past. Now it was a den of thieves, and the chief thief was sprawled across the top of the altar, the man's gray head rising, his eyes blinking.

"Spider!" Kron roared.

Many winced, including the gray man on the altar.

Kron darted forward, bounding over more revelers who showed signs of headaches and worse, sores around their mouths, grime covering their thin garb, rats and mice scurrying among forgotten food, spilled wine and no few pools of urine.

Rubbing away the last of his sleepiness, Spider sat up fully.

Only to have a fist glance against his jaw.

The boss of the thieves cried out and rolled back, falling off the altar to land face first on dusty wooden floorboards. His jaw cracked loudly and a tooth went flying as a spot of blood layered his top lip. Before the man had a chance to act, a hand grabbed him by the back of his shirt and pulled him to his feet where he swayed.

Spider blinked again, then stared into the dark, hardened eyes of Kron Darkbow.

These two men had history. Spider had tried to kill Kron on more than once occasion. Obviously he had failed. It was luck and the lack of his own significance that allowed the thief to remain alive. So far.

Ignoring those rising behind him, Kron glared into Spider's reddened eyes. "A Khadiran ship struck shore in The Swamps a few days ago. The captain didn't sign with the river master. The crew went ashore. Where are they?"

Spider blinked, shaking his head. "How would I know?"

Kron slammed the thief on his back onto the altar, jarring the floor. "Where are they?"

Spider paused long enough to catch his breath. "I don't know, I swear."

A black gloved fist raised higher.

The thief held up his shaking hands. "Look, honest, a few of them came to us day before yesterday. They were pirates from down along the coast. Said they were looking for a new job and didn't want to sail with their old ship no more. Said everyone had quit, even the captain."

The rustling of weapons being drawn did not deter Kron from pushing. "That makes no sense. Why would they leave their ship? Especially this far inland?"

Spider shook his head. "They said the owners were mages, and they frightened everyone. The captain and crew signed on in Lobaldo, so there's no telling what kind of dark wizards they'd been sailing with."

Kron had to agree. Spider might be little more than a lowly chief of thieves, but the man had some little magical talent and education. Lobaldo was one of two sizable cities among the island nation of Lycinia, itself relatively near the main continent and sitting right in the middle of the shipping lanes from Pursia and Khadir, two countries with vastly different customs concerning magic than here in the West. Dark mages were not unknown among those lands.

The man in black gripped Spider by the shirt. "Where are these pirates now?"

"Honest, I don't know," Spider said, near pleading. "I couldn't line anything up for them, so they said they were heading to the Docks to find work."

Kron gave one last push on the smaller man's chest, bringing a wince to Spider's face, then he eased away. Looking up, he found himself facing a room full of thugs, each now carrying some sort of cheap or makeshift weapon. The looks on the thieves' faces ranged from sneers to thin smiles.

Shifting his shoulders to remind those in the room of the large sword hanging from his back, Kron moved to one side of the altar and stared out into the crowd. "All of you know who I am. You know of what I'm capable. It's entirely likely the lot of you together could take me down. But how many of you will I take with me?" He lowered his head, his dark eyes staring from beneath a heavy brow.

Silence ruled the chamber.

Spider coughed and rolled over, his feet slapping onto the floor. He waved a hand. "Let him go."

No one moved.

"Let him go!" Spider shouted.

The room parted, an open space appearing from the altar to the exit.

Kron glanced down at the rumpled boss of the thieves. "My thanks."

Then he walked down the corridor of flesh and steel, not once looking to the right or left at the hardened eyes staring back at him.

He reached the exit without interference.

"Darkbow!"

The man in black halted, turning his head to one side.

"How did you find us?" Spider asked.

Kron yanked his hood up, shielding all but his pale chin and a growing, white smile. "I've kept tabs on you, Spider. I always know how to find you. Remember that."

Then he disappeared into the night.

12

The plan had been for Kron to meet up with Nodana outside the Rusty Scabbard tavern well after midnight, giving both of them time to complete their appointed tasks. There had been no thought to sleep. Those with a conscience did not sleep when children were being butchered.

After waiting a half hour, Kron decided he had to hunt the woman down. Not known for patience, he headed out on foot toward Frist Bridge which would take him across a river to The Swamp. Once past the bridge, he turned to his immediate left and then left again, following a cobbled street that ran along the southern shore of this section of town.

Nodana and Corporal Talend had been heading to where the first bodies had been found. Their job had been to search for the Khadiran ship. They had had plenty of time. Hours had passed. Something was wrong, and Kron's concern was growing.

Still blocks away, he could make out the glow over the rooftops of abandoned and crumbling warehouses. He picked up his pace, jogging ahead.

Darting between two old buildings, he came out on a strip of dead grass that fronted the shoreline proper. Still at a distance, he could not help but see the dozen torches and lamps that had been formed into a ring around the site where the Khadiran ship had last been seen. Kron could make out no faces, but with the number of lights, even this far away he could spot at least a dozen bright orange tabards of the city guard.

Yes, something definitely was wrong.

He charged ahead, the cold night's air cutting into him.

Only near the glow of the torches, when two soldiers stepped across his way with their swords drawn, did Kron slow to a crawl.

"Let him through," rang the familiar voice of Captain Gris.

Kron nodded to the two who had barred his path, an acknowledgment they had only been doing their jobs, then shoved his way through to the inner circle of light.

His first view of the inner scene revealed much, but not all. Gris stood to one side in a small group with Sergeant Thag and several other lesser officers with whom Kron was unfamiliar. Nodana sat on the ground on the opposite side of the ring of light, her arms wrapped around her knees pulled to shield her face.

In the center of the area was a red smear on the end of the pier still over land. Here and there broken bones protruded from the scarlet mess, mingled with gelled sacks and snakes Kron recognized as the inner organs of a person. He had seen enough bloodshed in his day to know a heart, stomach and liver. The rest of the organs were indiscernible, flattened, squashed. There appeared to be some ripped and torn sheets or cloth among the gore, but there was no telling if it was clothing or something else. To one side rested an iron helm splashed with blood.

Kron walked over to the mage and knelt next to her, resting a tender hand upon a knee. "Talend?" He didn't have to ask the question. The answer was obvious. The corporal was the only person missing who should have been there, and she had been the one to set out withe Nodana.

The wizard raised her head. Her eyes were crimson and wet, leaving streaks down her face. "It was horrible." Her voice was little more than a whisper.

"Can you speak of it?" Kron asked with pity and concern in his words.

"She's already told me," Gris said from behind.

Kron turned away from the woman, allowing her to lower her head once more.

The captain motioned for his friend to move away with him. The man in black followed, the two striding toward the edge of the light where the water slapped at the shoreline next to the boardwalk.

"She was out in the water when it happened," Gris explained. "Said she didn't see much."

"The water?" Kron asked. "It must be freezing."

Gris shrugged. "She's a mage."

"Did she hear anything?"

"A male voice, foreign, likely Khadiran, speaking with Talend. The speaker mentioned magic, and sounded as if there was someone else with him."

"The demon," Kron said. "He was speaking with the demon."

"Rogins and Nodana told me about your theory, that there's a mage with a demon running loose in the city."

Kron nodded again. "Nodana detected demon magic at the sight of the child's murder."

Gris turned slightly to face the pool of blood and carnage that had been his corporal. "I can't disagree with your assessment."

"Any signs she was raped?" Kron asked, pointing to Talend's remains.

The captain shook his head. "We have no reason to believe so, though obviously there's not much here we can use to tell. Nodana seemed to think it happened too fast."

"*What* happened?"

"She couldn't tell for sure," Gris said. "It was too dark. She could only make out shadows against the sky. Something large loomed up, then engulfed Talend. There were ... sounds. That's the best description we could get of the event."

Kron gestured toward the river. "What of the ship? Did Nodana mention it?"

"She said it had been out there hidden beneath the surface," Gris said. "That's why she was out in the water, looking for the boat. Unfortunately, by the time we arrived it was gone, and Nodana doesn't know to where."

"They've moved it," Kron said. "They know we're on their trail."

"Maybe so, but we still don't know who they are or why they are doing this. Have you discovered anything?"

"I've been trying to find the crew," Kron explained. "No luck so far, but I've had a tip some of them were headed to the Docks to look for work."

"That's as good a place to check as any," Gris said with a dip of his head. "Do you want a squad to go with you?"

"I don't think so. I can keep a lower profile on my own."

"I'll be going with you," another voice sounded.

The two men glanced over. Frex Nodana stood near them, the woman wrapped from her neck to her feet in a wool cloak supplied by one of the guards.

"Go home and get some sleep," Kron suggested. "You've done enough this night."

The mage's eyes flared. "Do not tell me what to do, Kron Darkbow. This is a powerful wizard and a demon you are tracking. If you run into them, you will need all the help you can get, especially from someone with my skills."

"She has a point," the captain said, glancing aside at his friend.

Kron gave a short bow to the woman. "Very well. I will not argue the point."

"Because I'm right," Nodana said, her teeth gritted.

"In fact, you are," Kron said.

"Good."

Gris rubbed his gloved hands as if to warm them. "That's settled, then. The two of you are off to the Docks?"

"I'll report to you as soon as we know something," Kron said.

Nodana edged closer, nearly between the two men, looking from one to the other. "There is one more thing. I think I have figured out why he kills so frequently."

"Yes?" from the captain.

"Even a madman doesn't spill blood so often," the mage said, "though I won't vouch for the sanity of our prey."

"No disagreements here," Gris said.

"I believe he rapes and tortures for the sheer thrill of it," Nodana said, "but the number of killings, and their proximity in time, make me believe he has a purpose."

Again, "Yes?"

"He is using low magics," the wizard said.

Kron and Gris traded glances. What Nodana had told them made sense. Outside of those experienced in the world of wizards, magic was magic, but the truth was more complex. There were two different types of magic, high and low. With high magic a spellcaster utilized the power of his or her own soul to accomplish eldritch feats. With low magic, the souls of others were used for castings. The most powerful low magics were accomplished with the death of the one whose soul was being used. Low magics were not common, at least not in West Ursia.

"It makes sense," Nodana went on. "I've been wondering how this wizard is so powerful, but why he kills so often. I can think of no other reason. It also helps to explain the demon."

"How so?" Gris asked.

It was Kron who answered. "Demons thrive on souls, feed on them. They can even take them back to Hell, if they wish."

Nodana nodded. "Basically correct. The wizard uses up the souls, weakens them, then the demon swoops in to steal the remainder."

The captain turned a dazed look upon the mess that had been Corporal Talend. "Are you telling me not only did they do this to her, but that her very soul is imprisoned in Hell?"

"Most likely," Kron said, "at least until the demon is destroyed."

Gris looked to his friend. "And the torture?"

"It will be unending," Kron said. "This wizard is a madman worse than any I dealt with in the Asylum."

"Unless we do something about it," Nodana added.

Gris held up his hands. "What can be done against such?"

"We find the wizard," Kron said. "We kill him. Then the demon."

"Easier said than done, I'm sure," the captain said.

Now it was Kron who gritted his teeth. "Let them try and stop me."

13

Most things just never turned out right. Of that, Turnip Boyle was convinced. He had spent seventeen of his thirty-two years on the high seas, and not once did his luck hold true longer than a day or two at a time. He had sailed all corners of the continent, from Jotsland in the far north all the way to Hipon in the far south. He had witnessed much, most of it bad. Blood spilling out on a wet deck, storms carrying men off into the depths, slaves pushed overboard when the authorities appeared on the horizon. And worse. A lot worse.

But nothing matched what the aging pirate had seen in the last weeks since he had signed onto that Khadiran ship out of Lobaldo. Men torn to pieces, literally. Little strips of bloody flesh were all that was left at times. Children, almost always boys, beaten and tied and gagged, then raped and finally murdered.

Turnip Boyle was lucky to be alive himself. He and another dozen swabbies. If they hadn't been able-bodied seaman necessary to sailing that cog, he was sure all of them would have faced the same fate as the other dozen unlucky souls who had been aboard the ship, some crew but most of them passengers.

Thank Ashal the ship had finally settled. It had been a long trip from Lycinia to the southern coast of West Ursia, then up the South River to Bond. Again, Turnip Boyle knew himself lucky to be breathing. They had been low on food and water, and that was the only reason he could guess the cog had finally made to shore. A few stupid bastards had tried to jump ship when they struck the river, but none of them had made it to land. Fhaland and his *ward* had made sure of that.

Now here Turnip was in another tavern in another foreign land, far from his home in East Ursia. It wasn't that he was homesick. No, no. But he was broke, not a copper to his name. Fhaland hadn't paid anyone, only saying they would receive their coin upon returning to the ship in a few days. Well, a few days had passed and no one was likely stupid enough to return to that Khadiran craft, especially not Turnip Boyle.

If Turnip hadn't been wanted in half the ports of the known world, he might have considered reporting what went on aboard that cog to the authorities, but as he *was* wanted, he would keep his mouth closed. Probably why Fhaland had hired on only pirates and other crooks in the first place.

He huffed, staring into the dregs that remained of his drink. He didn't even know how he was going to pay for this. That worthless thieves guild had proven a turd's bucket, and the morning was still hours away before Turnip could speak with the Docks guild master. Something had to break. A man had to eat, after all.

A cold wind channeled its way across the floor, causing the sailor to look up from his table. Other than the barkeep, Turnip had had the place to himself for an hour now, so it was a surprise that someone would be strolling in at this late hour.

Turnip's mood worsened upon spying who had entered. Chantal and Whiskey stood in the open door, their beady eyes taking in the room of the tavern before finally pouncing upon Turnip himself.

Turnip groaned. The last people he wanted to see was anyone from the cog.

"You gonna shut that door?" the barkeep asked, his voice a tad surly.

The two sailors entered, the lank figure of Chantal slamming the door closed behind them.

"You still open?" Whiskey asked the barkeep.

The man behind the bar nodded. "What will you have?"

"Him," Whiskey said, smiling between his thick gnat-filled beard as he pointed to Turnip.

Turnip groaned again.

"Skinflints," the barkeep said barely above his breath.

But the two newcomers didn't seem to take umbrage. They made their way across the room, striding directly up to Turnip's table.

"Figured you'd be in the bar closest to the Docks," Whiskey said, still smiling as he took a seat next to Turnip.

From another table, Chantal pulled over a chair and turned it around, sitting in it backwards, hanging his arms over the top rail. "Planning to look for work in the morning?"

Turnip frowned and shoved his empty mug away. "Somethin' like that, yeah. What's it to you two?"

"We thought we'd join in with you," Whiskey said, brushing at his whiskers with chubby, grease-stained fingers.

"You're not going back to the cog?" Turnip asked.

"Hell, no," Whiskey said. "Nobody's going back to that hell trap."

"Not even for our pay," Chantal added.

The entrance door slammed open, hammering back against the wall. A furious breeze of cold night air flung itself through the opening, trailing about the chamber like invisible fingers.

"Didn't close the damned door tight!" the barkeep yelled before rushing out from behind his station. He grabbed one edge of the door and pulled it toward himself, fighting against the storm-like winds but seemingly to little use.

The light died. There had been a half dozen candles burning throughout the establishment. They all died.

The only light was a murky blush from the moon outside the door.

Turnip Boyle stood, drawing an old fishing knife from his belt. "You fools. You've brought him here."

The barkeep cursed, then finally slammed the door closed, killing the last of the outside light. In the dark he spun upon his remaining customers. "What the hell are you talkin' about?"

"He was speaking of myself," a new voice answered.

Turnip wet himself, the warmth flowing down both legs and dampening the inside of his trousers. And he did not feel less the man for it. Death was here, and he doubted he could survive it this time. In fact, it might be best if he just cut his own throat.

Chantal and Whiskey were suddenly moving, jumping up from the table and shoving their chairs behind them. The sound of steel sliding against leather came to Turnip's ears, and he imagined his two companions bringing forth their own knives.

A chuckle filled the air.

"Who the hell is that?" the barkeep asked from the entrance.

His answer was a metallic snapping noise followed by a grunt and a squeal. Then a thudding.

The barkeep spoke no more.

Every limb of Turnip's body quivered. The only reason he hadn't killed himself was because he was too much the coward. At least everything was dark and he wouldn't have to watch what was going to happen to everyone else before he died.

"Gentleman," a voice familiar to the surviving three said from the darkness, "I find myself once more in need of a crew."

Whiskey's voice stuttered. "You've yet to pay us for the last trip, Fhaland."

That raucous yet almost feminine laughter filled the air again. Then halted. "Who said anything about pay?"

"We don't work for free," Chantal bravely said, "especially considering ... well, what we have to put up with on board."

"I am not asking," Fhaland said from shadows.

Silence. The sailors knew not what to say. To return was death. To refuse was death. There were no options.

"Bah! I tire of waiting. Kry'lk, slay these fools."

A blast of movement in the darkness. Furniture being overturned, chairs and tables tossed aside. Whiskey screamed out, his cry cut short by a rattling and wet noise.

Chantal grabbed Turnip by his shirt. "Save me!"

But it was too late.

Turnip Boyle felt the cloth of his garb rip as Chantal was pulled away from him.

There was a thunking sound, as of something heavy slamming into meat.

Then dripping. Dripping. Dripping.

Turnip breathed in slowly. He had not moved. He was too frightened to move. His knife slipped from his fingers and clanked onto the wooden floor.

"Oh, yes, Turnip," Fhaland said casually, as if three men had not been slaughtered in the room within the last few minutes. "You proved yourself on the ship. Last chance. Will you return?"

Turnip never considered himself a brave man, though he also knew he was not a coward. To survive, he should go along. Perhaps there would be another opportunity to escape somewhere down the river, or perhaps back out to sea. But he had seen what happened to those who had tried to flee. Even now, here, away from the vessel, Fhaland showed no signs of allowing his servants to go about their way.

No, there would be no escape. Never. Death and torture would always be looming.

So, the final act of Turnip Boyle's life was one of sadness yet also denial and valor.

He licked his lips. Then spoke one word.

"No."

14

"I do not care what time of night it is, wake the man," Kron said in the house's foyer.

The robed servant woman glared at the man in black for a moment, then slammed her lamp onto a small table near the entrance and turned away into the darkness.

Nodana stood in the corner opposite the door from Kron. "Do you think she will wake him?"

She was answered moments later as thumping sounds could be heard from a hall to their right.

A moment later a second glow appeared from the hall, then around the corner arrived an old man with a shaggy head of white. Other than wooden clogs on his feet, his only clothing was a thin nightgown. In one hand he held a small lamp made of a hardened yellow gourd.

He lifted the lamp and stared at Kron. "*You!*"

"Yes, me," Kron said flatly.

The old man used his lamp to motion to Kron. "It was you who caused me to be hauled out of retirement. I should be spending my days napping and playing with my grandchildren. Instead, I've been bamboozled back into the Docks Guild."

"At least you are the master of the guild," Kron said.

"Yes, of course," the old man went on. "What else was the guild going to do after you killed their last Docks master?"

"I did not kill the man," Kron said.

"You might as well have!" the old man shouted, stamping a foot. "The poor fellow doesn't have a brain left in his head, sits there and jibbers all day in the healing tower. There's no oars in his boat, no ale in his jack, no hooves on his horse!"

None of which made sense.

The fellow seemed to notice Nodana for the first time. He turned to the mage and gave a short bow. "Please forgive a cranky old man, my lady. The name is Ritters. I'm at your service."

For the first time in a long while, Nodana allowed a thin smile as she bowed back.

Ritters rolled his attention back to Kron. "Now what's the meaning of waking up an old man in the middle of the night?"

"We're looking for a crew who landed on a Khadiran cog a few day ago," Kron said.

The Docks boss grinned, showing a few teeth missing. "After some pirates, are you?"

"Not for reasons you might think," Kron said. "But you're familiar with them?"

"Sure, sure." Ritters nodded. "A few of them came to me yesterday looking for work, told me others might be coming along. Knew what they were as soon as I seen 'em. Acted kind of odd, though. It's strange enough for pirates to be this far inland, and you'd think they'd be signing back on with the cog, but when I asked about it, their eyes got spooked. Just said they needed a new transport. I told 'em I'd find something for them. It's kind of late in the year for the merchant crafts, but there's always a logging ship or three running from here down to Port Harbor ."

"The men you spoke with, do you know where they are?" Nodana asked.

Ritters shrugged. "There's hostels all over town."

"No place specific?" Kron asked.

"These fellows seemed down on their luck," the old man said, "so likely they picked the cheapest spots they could find to stay in. Could be they shacked up in one or another of the taverns here along the Docks. Chump's Squall and a couple other places let sailors sleep on the floor or in a back room for just a few coppers a night."

Kron looked to Nodana. "You up for a visit to this Chump's Squall?"

Ritters interrupted. "Might not be open this close to morning."

"We'll open them," Kron said.

The old man chuckled. "I just bet you will."

The man in black and the mage turned toward the door to leave.

"Hold on a moment," Ritters said. "What's this all about, anyhow?"

Kron glanced back. "Have you heard about the murders?"

It was as if the light died from the old man's eyes. Any semblance of a smile fell away from his lips. "You talkin' about the two found down by the South River, and that boy?"

Kron nodded. "And they've added a city guard to their victims."

Ritters licked his lips as if thirsty for a drink. "You think one of these sailors did all that?"

"Doubtful," Nodana said, "but we believe they might know who did."

The Docks chief held up a frail hand. "Chump's Squall isn't far, but give me a few minutes and I'll ready my wagon."

Before Kron or Nodana could voice another word, the old man had vanished into the depths of his house.

The two did not have long to wait. Within minutes Ritters returned, now dressed in gray leggings, moccasins, and a pale shirt. A thigh-length cloak of a rusty shade gripped his shoulders. From one hand extended a lamp. Held tight in the other was a cane of gnarled oak.

"I'll be going with you," he said. "One of my servants is out back hitching up the team as speak."

Kron lifted a flat hand. "Thank you, but there is no reason for you to involve yourself."

Ritters raised the cane and shook it. "A lad died today, and men as well. If there's justice to be done, I'm not going to shirk from it."

Kron frowned, appearing flustered. "After the death of a city guard, we have to assume these villains know we are searching for them. I mean you no offense, Master Ritters, but I do not want your death on my conscience if we should run into trouble."

A slim hand rested on Kron's right elbow. He turned to find Nodana.

"He can help identify the sailors," she said, "and if they are not there, he could tell us where to go next."

The man in black looked to the old man.

Who grinned once more. His teeth hadn't grown back.

"Fine," Kron said, turning and exiting.

Two gangly horses hitched to a wagon awaited them on the gravel lot out front of the Docks master's home. A yawning manservant in a nightgown stood to one side holding the ends of a harness.

With only a brief wave to his servant, Ritters clambered up onto the flat board seat. Kron aided Nodana climbing in the back, then hauled himself up beside her where the two sat on a small pile of hay.

The servant handed the reins to his employer, then wandered back toward the house.

Ritters wasted no time on words, snapping the leathers and heading the animals north along Dock Street.

Kron was thankful for the ride. Fatigue was beginning to set in with him. He had been awake nearly an entire day, and more than once he had crossed the city back and forth on foot. Reminding himself he needed to purchase a new horse at some point, he looked to Nodana.

The woman dozed with her eyes closed.

Kron grinned at her, reminding himself he was not the only one who was tired.

Their respite was short lived. In less than 10 minutes the old man was hauling in on his horses' reins, pulling the animals and the wagon to halt in front of a row of small warehouses with their backs to the North River.

"We're here," Ritters said, tying off the reins on a near post, then dropping down from the wagon, the lamp once again in one hand while his other clutched the cane.

Prodding Nodana awake and helping her down from their ride, Kron paused while still standing in the back of the wagon. "I see no tavern sign."

"There isn't one," Ritters said. "Burnt it for firewood years ago. But the place is just down this ways a bit. Odd, though. No lamps burning in the window. Normally Chump's Squall stays open all night for any late ships coming in."

Kron's jaw tightened and he jumped down from the wagon. Approaching the Docks chief, he took the light from the old man's hand. "Which building is it?"

A crooked finger pointed.

"Stay here," Kron told the others. "I will be back in a moment."

Then he moved off into the night.

Ritters looked to Nodana. "I get the feeling he does this a lot."

"What?"

"Goes about in the dark by hisself."

The woman shrugged.

Ahead of them, Kron withdrew a dagger from his belt and made his way forward with wary steps. Ritters had said the place should be open, should be lit. The darkness and silence told there was something amiss.

For the first time since seeing those two men dead by the river the morning before, Kron felt he was growing closer to his quarry. He could not say what told him this. Perhaps it was only a feeling. Perhaps he was beginning to be able to smell demon, as Nodana had seemed able to do. Perhaps he simply recognized danger when it loomed.

At the swinging doors to the place Ritters had pointed out, Kron paused and listened. He heard nothing but the chilled wind.

Always expecting the worst, he squatted low to make himself a smaller target and moved to one side of the door. A quick spin and a kick, and the door burst open. Kron forced his way through, the dagger pointing the way, the lamp held out to one side so as not to ruin his vision.

The sight would have been enough to shake a lesser man, a man not as experienced in violence.

The glow of the lamp revealed four corpses, all men of size. The nearest body lay almost at Kron's feet. A wicked red slash ruined the dead man's throat, and a pool of drying blood encircled his head. The next two lay halfway across the room amid a tumble of tables and chairs and spilled drinks. These men bore the now familiar neck wounds, as if a heavy whip had wrapped itself around their throats and squeezed. Spots of blood littered the floor around them.

Worse, by far, was the last victim. There was barely enough for Kron to tell this person had been a man. Arms had been ripped from sockets. Legs had been torn from the trunk. The head had been pulled away from the body and now rested atop the bar, its wide lips frozen in a permanent scream of terror. Everywhere around the bar there was wet red. Kron could barely believe so much blood could be contained in one person.

The man in black nearly gagged as he turned away, rushing back into the street and almost dropping his light.

"What is it?" Ritters asked as he and Nodana rushed forward.

Kron lifted the back of a gloved hand to his mouth as if were about to expel his last meal. "Don't go in there."

The old man glanced over Kron's shoulders to the door but showed no sign of ignoring the suggestion.

"It is ... bad." Kron looked to Nodana. "Can you detect anything from out here?"

The mage closed her eyes briefly, then they popped open wide. "They have not been gone long, perhaps only minutes."

Kron turned to the old man. "Where is the next closest place some of the sailors might sleep?"

The Docks boss nodded down the road. "Not far. A couple of minutes by wagon."

"Take us," Kron ordered.

The three climbed aboard the wagon once more, Ritters snapping the reins and getting the horses going. He pushed the beasts as much as he could, but they were old themselves and not built for speed.

Hunkering down next to the mage, Kron rested a hand on one of her shoulders. "It would appear they know we are on their trail."

"Or at least that someone is after them," she agreed. Her face grew tight. "How many were there in Chump's Squall?"

"I saw four."

"They were -- "

Kron cut her off. "As bad as the others. One was ... worse."

Nodana's face went white, but the man in black did not think less of her for it. In fact, he had to give her credit for remaining with him and for staying up all night helping him to track down this killer or killers. Most others would have been in bed this early in the morning with the sunrise only hours away. Even most with a conscious would have decided to put off the search until the morning. Kron was not such a person, especially with the bodies stacking as fast as they were. To his growing comfort, Nodana was also proving determined. He had made the right decision in going to her for aid. It was almost difficult to believe they had been enemies not so long ago, the woman having been part of a band seeking his death.

"We're here." Ritters tugged the reins to one side, slowing the animals and the wagon to a creaky halt.

Ahead on the right was a two-story structure of brick, it the only building on the block with lights still burning inside.

Kron rolled off the back of the wagon, helped Nodana down, then moved toward the old man climbing down from his seat.

"I want you to stay here," he said to Ritters.

The Docks boss didn't appear happy to hear the words. "I'm not useless, you know."

"I realize that," Kron said, "but I want you with reins in hand ready to fly in case we need to leave in a hurry."

Ritters raised his cane and used it to scratch the side of his head. "Makes sense, I suppose."

Nodana walked up to them and motioned toward the tavern. "It's not dark like the other place. Perhaps they have not been here."

"Perhaps," Kron said, "but it is too quiet for my liking."

Ritters glanced about. "Can't say I disagree. Even for this late in the night, the street's awful empty. Haven't seen another soul since we left my house. Almost like everybody can smell danger on the wind."

"Which proves those in hiding are smarter than we are," Nodana said with a light grin.

"No. They're just frightened." Kron swished away, heading toward the tavern, the lamp extended before him.

Nodana was about to follow, but Ritters tapped her on a shoulder with the end of his cane.

She looked back at him.

"I don't know about you," he said, "but I'm plenty frightened myself."

"As am I," she said before turning to follow Darkbow.

She found him standing in front of double doors, a sign facing outward above the entrance reading, "The Jaded Mermaid." A bright glow of natural firelight exuded from the windows, revealing plenty of lamps or torches inside, as well as a working fireplace that continued to disgorge gray smoke from a chimney on the right of the building. There was no movement from indoors, no sound.

"Eerie," Nodana said.

Kron handed her the lamp. "Wait here for me."

"No." But she took the light.

He looked to her. "If something should happen, I want you out here to protect my retreat."

"If you confront this demon, you're not likely to live long enough to retreat," she said.

Now it was Kron who grinned, but there was little mirth in his lips. "I have fought demons before."

She stared into his dark eyes for a moment, seeing he was intent upon going ahead alone. Finally, after several quiet seconds, she lowered her gaze. "Very well, Kron Darkbow, I will wait here for you. But do not get yourself killed doing something foolish."

"Never," he said. Then he was gone. Through the doors.

Nodana looked back to Ritters, who only shrugged.

"He likes to do these things on his own, I take it," the old man said.

15

Patience was not a virtue that came naturally to Kron Darkbow, but now, striding through the front door of The Jaded Mermaid, he allowed his training to take over and slowed himself, glancing about the front room of the inn. It was a rugged place, but there were worse within The Swamps. Across the way was a pair of swinging doors over which could be seen a kitchen. Against the wall on the right was a bar, behind which a cracked mirror ran the length of the room. Here and there throughout were the expected tables and chairs. A few empty tankards spotted the bar and tables. To Kron's immediate left was a dark stairwell which hooked to the right after only a few steps, obviously taking climbers to rooms upstairs.

However, there was not a person to be seen.

Several lamps along the walls were burning as were a handful of candles at tables around the room. The room was well lit, perhaps even more than it should be. Ritters had mentioned the place stayed open at night for any sailors who came in from late ships, but there seemed no one was here. Why waste the tallow and oil?

The silence more than anything caused Kron to restrain himself. His impulse was to charge ahead to the kitchen or perhaps up the stairs, but he realized that might get him killed. The man in black was not facing ill-trained thieves with rusty weapons. If he was to meet a foe in the tavern, it would likely be a mage and a demon, opponents worth taking serious. His uncle Kuthius had been responsible for most of Kron's training back in the Prisonlands, and the older man had often been flummoxed by his nephew's lack of levelheadedness. Now, however, he would be proud of Kron.

Murmuring from above caught his attention. The voice was not loud, but he could make out its cadence from the stairwell.

Three small throwing darts were slipped from the back of Kron's left glove as he took the stairs, keeping his boots on the outer edges of each step so as to lessen any chance of squalling wood.

Revealed at the top of the stairs was an unlit hallway, a line of a glow emitting from beneath the first door on the left.

The voice came from behind that door.

"Others have already died tonight, Korick," an odd, male voice spoke. "I only spare you now because I am in need of a crew."

"Go with you and likely die out at sea, or die here and now," a rougher voice said. "Some choice you're offering."

"At least I am offering."

A brief, dark chuckle. "That much is true. But why such a hurry?"

"I have what I came for," the foreigner said. "It is time to leave."

Movement downstairs.

Kron glanced around but saw no one. Was someone trying to sneak up behind him?

The man in black made no sound as he slipped down the steps. He had heard enough above to make him believe he was on the right track. The killer was upstairs. But was it the mage who had spoken? It did not seem the voice of a demon, so where was the beast?

Reaching the landing in the turn at the bottom of the stairs, Kron found Frex Nodana standing in the now open entrance.

"Nodana?" he asked.

She did not look at him. Her attention was focused within the room, almost as if she were mesmerized.

Kron descended the final steps and turned to look at what the woman was watching.

The sight was so unusual, it took several seconds for Kron's mind to make sense of what he was seeing. Standing across the room in front of the kitchen doors was a boy. He appeared about ten years old though small for his age, standing not as tall as Nodana. His head was bald, his flesh an odd dusty pale with gray undercurrents, as if he were from a far southern climb yet had endured darkness for a long period. His eyes were wide and dark, his lips thin and almost nonexistent. A high, stiff collar holding his head high and straight topped a white robe that snaked down his short frame and fanned out upon the floor, hiding the youth's feet. There was undulating movement beneath the robe, as if a living animal were underneath, struggling to claw its way out, yet the boy showed no signs of discomfort or even acknowledgment. If anything, a slender grin played about the edges of the youth's lips.

The man in black took a step forward. "Boy, are you all right? What has --"

One of Nodana's hands shot forward, grabbing Darkbow by an elbow. "Kron, that's no --"

The boy's robe burst outwards as if a high wind were unleashed. For the briefest of moments, Kron witnessed the youth's secret. There was little flesh to be seen. What there was were thin, spindly arms and legs that were little more than flesh stretched across bone. But those limbs were lost in a blink of an eye, for hanging from them and stretching forth from them were linked chains of all sizes and metals. There were so many chains, the body was instantly hidden from view beneath them.

A cackling filled the air.

The chains came alive, stretching and flying forth from the boy as if living serpents starved and finding a meal. They filled the air, there were so many of them.

Kron had little time to react, the threat was so swift. He threw out an arm to shield the mage behind him and thrust a hand toward his own face in an effort to keep the chains from entwining his neck.

Then the links were upon him. They pervaded his senses, blocking his sight and bringing a scent of oil and sulfur. The metal coils wrapped around his legs and arms, dragging him down. A strand encircled his head, tightening around the arm there and squeezing against his face.

He was pulled into a sea of iron and steel and gold and brass links. He could not catch his breath, drowning beneath the wave of metal.

There was a shout and a flare of light.

287

A squeal followed, like that of a stuck pig, and suddenly Kron could see and breathe again.

The chains retreated across the floor, writhing back the way they had come.

Kron sucked air into his lungs and blinked away the wet in his eyes caused by the near suffocation. The boy-thing stood hunkered over, the robes now having fallen to the floor again, the last of the chains twisting and twining their way beneath. The youth gripped at his chest where a blackened smear sent up trindles of smoke.

Hate filled the youth's eyes, now nothing more than black orbs that glared over the prostrate Kron Darkbow.

Rolling on to a knee, Kron glanced behind himself to find Nodana standing there, one hand outstretched and pointing at the robed figure.

Movement to one side. A tall, heavy man appeared at the bottom of the steps. He was robed in red and gold, his meaty features holding golden eyes wrapped in black ink above a bulbous nose and thin beard.

"Kry'lk!" the man shouted, looking with concern to the youth.

The boy hissed, then spun away, disappearing through the kitchen doors, his garment sailing out behind him with a generous clanking noise.

"Bitch!"

There was another flash of light, this time from the newcomer, and Frex Nodana was sent hurtling across the room to slam into a wall.

Kron had still been recovering and too surprised to react, but now, as the wizard on the steps turned his attention to the man in black, he remembered the three throwing darts in his hand. Thank Ashal they were still there.

He cast out his hand and the darts sailed.

All three found purchase in the target's chest, sprouting circles of red. The wizard shrieked and swiped an arm across his breast, knocking away the tiny javelins, then turned and tromped up the stairwell.

Forgetting his fleeing enemies for the moment, Kron hustled to where Nodana had been thrown. The woman lay unmoving, a spot of red marking the wooden floor beneath her head. One of her arms was twisted back beneath her at an unnatural angle, one of her legs bent at a place where it should not.

Kron knelt and pulled off a glove, holding a finger beneath the mage's nose.

Nothing.

He placed an ear against her chest.

A thumping. Barely.

He took a moment to glance at the top of her head. What he found did not please him. A bump the size of a berry was growing there, cracked and draining scarlet fluid.

Kron pulled back from her and pushed his way out the front door. "Ritters!"

The old man sat above his team of horses, his cane raised as if a club, fear written in his features.

"Get the wagon ready!" the man in black shouted, then spun back inside.

In her condition, Nodana would not survive long without aid. This much Kron knew. He also knew there was only one place to take her.

<u>16</u>

Cursing as he rolled into a sitting position on the end of the cot, Kron berated himself for falling asleep. His boots hit the floor and he sat up straight, rubbing the last of the sleep from his face before staring about the small, familiar round chamber. Stone walls and a single oak door greeted him. High upon the wall across from him was an open window, sunlight blazing through to warm the room.

The door opened, around its edge appearing a young man in white robes.

Kron's fists tightened upon seeing the other man's garb, but then he realized this was not the youth from The Jaded Mermaid.

"Glad to see you finally woke," Randall Tendbones said, pulling a chair into the room and slipping onto it.

Kron stared into his friend's eyes. Those eyes were steady and ancient, older than any man alive, but the face was that of a youth who had few years as a man. How old *was* Randall? Twenty two? Twenty three? He was at least a few years younger than Kron, that much was known. Randall's age, however, was only a physical trait pertaining to this, his current lifetime. The young man was in spirit at least two thousand years old, which was another reason he was the most powerful magic user in the world. Or, at least, there was so far no evidence of anyone more powerful. It was fortunate for the world Randall was the most benevolent of men, but it was also fortunate for Randall the world knew nothing of his true potential; to those who came and went in the life of Randall Tendbones, the young man was only an exceptional healer. Kron new otherwise. He knew the truth.

He only hoped Randall's magic had been enough to save Frex Nodana.

"She lives," the healer said, reading the question in his friend's eyes.

"What is her condition?"

"Her skull was cracked slightly, but I have been able to mend it. Fortunately her arm and leg suffered clean breaks, nothing too nasty from a remedial point of view. There will be a raised lump on her head and some bruising for some time, but I have given her something for the pain."

"Will she be all right?"

"She needs bed rest for the next several weeks, but she will be fine," Randall said. "She is a strong one, and your quick actions saved her life."

The healer chuckled. "Old Man Ritters gave me a fright, however. He was so afraid and concerned for the two of you, I feared he might have a heart attack on me."

"Where is he?"

"I shooshed him on home. I saw no reason for him to stay."

Kron nodded then stood, stretching, loosening the muscles of his body. "What is the hour?"

"Three bells in the afternoon."

Kron cursed again, but lowered himself to sitting on the bed once more. "You should not have let me sleep so long."

"You needed the rest," Randall said. "Your reserves were low, your stamina weakened."

A glare accosted the healer. "There is a killer out there."

Randall nodded. "Yes, two of them. Truth be told, there are probably a hundred or more killers in the city, though none as bloodthirsty and diligent as the pair you have been chasing."

Kron sat up straight again. "You know of my targets?"

"Not directly. But I have picked up a few things here and there."

Of course he had. Little happened in the city without Randall's notice, especially when concerning people and events of a magical nature.

A sneer crossed Kron's lips. "Yet you've done nothing to stop them."

To anger Randall Tendbones was no easy task, and it was a sight rarely witnessed, but Kron's words caused those ancient eyes to harden and narrow. The mage sat forward in his chair, his chin pointedly aiming at the man in black. "You have no right to judge me, Kron Darkbow."

A scoff. A laugh. "Judge you? Why should I not? Here you are, the mightiest wizard in existence, practically a god, and you do *nothing* to waylay these murderers, these killers and rapists of *children*!"

Randall sat back, allowing his own ire to drift away as with unblinking eyes he watched his friend's heaving chest.

"Do you want to know where I have been while you were hunting these killers?" the healer asked.

"I know where you were!" Kron nearly spat. "You were here in the healing tower!"

"That's right! I was here in the healing tower."

Kron jumped to his feet and began pacing to keep his eyes averted. "With a snap of your fingers you could have captured this wizard and his demon at any point. You could have saved lives, saved that child and the others who were killed."

Silence was the response.

Kron kept walking for several seconds, then he paused, glancing to his friend. Randall was sitting there, his face plain and unemotional.

"Have you no nothing to say?" Kron asked, his voice now calm.

Randall looked to the bed. "Kron, please have a seat."

Darkbow hesitate, but then he returned to the cot.

The healer sighed and moved to sit on the edge of his chair, to be closer to his friend. His voice was low, though not a whisper. "You judge me, but you do so without knowing what it is like being me. Powerful I might be in the eyes of men, but Kron, even my magic knows limits. I cannot be in all places at all times. I cannot stop the hurts of the world everywhere at once. Believe me, if I could, I would give serious consideration to doing so."

"But why not help me catch these killers?" Kron asked. His words were like those of a pleading child.

For a moment, Randall stared at the stone floor, then he looked up. His face was pained. "You ask where I was, and I tell you I was here in the healing tower. That is the truth. But while you were out there hunting, I was upstairs, removing a cancer from a baby's chest. A *baby*. Do you understand that?"

There was no answer.

"Before that I had to heal the spine of a farmer," Randall went on. "He had fallen beneath the wheels of a wagon, and his wife had loaded him into the very same contraption and spent the last three days driving him here to Bond because this was the only place she knew to get help. The man is the provider for his family. Without him, they would starve."

Kron's head drooped.

Randall continued. "Early this morning, before you arrived, a woman was brought to me, stabbed by her husband because he believed she had been unfaithful. She hadn't, but she still suffered a liver cut nearly in two."

Kron's head lowered further. He would not look up.

"Without me, those people would now be dead," Randall said, "as quite possibly would Nodana. You sit and judge me for not helping in your cause, but where have you been while I was here cutting out a cancer or mending a spine?"

Silence.

"It's not easy to answer, is it?" the healer asked.

"No. No, it is not."

"Kron, you and I are very different people, but I do not begrudge you or your dark bearing. We simply have different approaches, and despite your demeanor, you do just as much to help others as I try. Can you not give me the same acceptance?"

Kron finally looked up. "I do, but ... it is difficult."

"I realize that," Randall said. "Your skills and drives are ones of action, whereas mine are more of reaction."

Kron stood and thrust forward a hand. His eyes were sheepish. "My apologies."

The healer grinned as he got to his feet. "A simple handshake will not do." He clasped the other fellow about the shoulders, hugging him tight.

After a few seconds, the two parted. Kron would not look Randall in the eye.

The healer backed toward the door. "Do you wish to see Nodana?"

"Yes," Kron said. "She was a ... a true hero. If it had not been for her, I would likely be dead."

"Ritters explained some of what happened."

"I should have told you," Kron said.

Randall brushed off the comment with a swipe of a hand. "You needed your rest. I allowed you to have it."

Kron looked up, his expression one of anguish. "I told Nodana to stay outside."

The healer chuckled. "Believe it or not, not everyone follows your orders. And like you said, you might be dead if she had not intervened."

"She recognized the demon for what it was," Kron said. "She tried to warn me, but ... that thing, it was so fast."

"It sounds as if it were an *ashashi kul kanon*."

"What did you say?"

"An assassin demon."

"You have experience with such?" Kron asked.

Randall snorted. "Do you forget I was raised in Kobalos? My father used to make me play with the things when I was a boy."

Kron's gaze drifted off to one side, as if he were staring into the past. "I've never seen anything so fast. It ... exploded out at me. I barely had time to react."

"I'll do something about that," Randall said. "I am needed here, but I will make sure the next time you meet up with this demon, you will be better prepared."

Kron's head craned up to face his friend. "I have grenados awaiting me, some infused with holy water."

The healer chuckled again. "Holy water. How coincidental, considering ... ah well, considering. Did you retrieve the water from one of the local temples?"

Kron nodded.

"As is, it would do little against the demon," Randall said. "However, I will make sure to sanctify it before you leave. That should help. The water will burn the beast, but is not likely to seriously harm it. Also, I will enchant your weapons. That should give you an edge against the creature."

"I can't match its speed," Kron pointed out.

"The holy water will help to slow it, and my enchantments will allow you some small level of resistance against the thing's legerity."

A cloud moved across the sun to shadow the room, causing the healer to glance up at the window. "It will be dark in a few hours."

"I should be going soon," Kron said, "but first I wish to look in on Nodana."

"Do you know where you are going?"

"To retrieve my grenados."

"And after that?"

"The search begins anew, I suppose," Kron said. "I have no clues as to where these villains are in hiding, that is if they are still in the city."

A smile crossed Randall's lips. "I believe I can help you there."

17

Seven gray balls of clay were lined up on the table. Three were the size of apples. The other four were the size of large berries.

"The larger ones contain the holy water," Montolio explained. "The others are for fire."

"I had only asked for six total," Kron said.

The architect nodded. "True enough. But I had enough powder and clay to make the extra." He grinned. "I thought you might need it."

Kron returned the smile. "I will."

Montolio lifted a leather sack from next to his feet and began to scoop the grenados into it. "The ones with the water are larger than what you are probably familiar, so you'll have to carry them in this bag. The others I suppose you can carry however you normally do."

"Hidden pockets within my cloak," Kron commented.

Montolio stopped his work and stared at the other man. "That's dangerous, isn't it? What if you fell down and landed on one of them?"

Kron smirked as he retrieved the lesser grenados from the table. "Life is full of dangers."

Drawing the string around the top of the bag, Montolio handed it off. "Just be careful."

"I will." Kron hid the smaller explosives within the folds of his cloak, then tied the offered bag onto his belt. "And my thanks. These are much appreciated. I have had a difficult time getting my hands on grenados since arriving in Bond."

"It's not a craft many know this far north, probably because they're illegal," Montolio said, "but if you need more, you know how to contact me."

"Again, my thanks."

"Don't worry," the architect said with another grin. "I'll just add it to your bill."

With those final words, Kron turned away and exited the tent, tromping out onto the Asylum grounds as the sun began to wind down to the west. He paused long enough to stare at the large dark structure that was to be his home once the work for it was completed. For a moment he thought he could detect the moanings of the dead spirits who still drifted within those brick walls, but then realized it was the chattering of workers he was hearing, the group of men high on a scaffold on one side of the building.

Hearing Montolio getting back to work behind him in the tent, Kron made his way down the hill toward the iron gate in the wall that fronted the property. Beyond he could spy citizens coming and going about their daily tasks, many slinking off to their homes this late in the day.

For Darkbow, his day was only beginning, and he still had a pair of killers to find. Initially he had been at a loss as to what direction his search should take. A brief return to The Jaded Mermaid had revealed empty rooms, the proprietor informing Kron there had been only one sailor in the upstairs rentals, a fellow by the name of Korick who had skipped out without paying. Where Korick could be found, and the wizard Kron had heard him speaking to, was anyone's guess.

Fortunately, Randall had been of aid before Kron had left the healing tower.

"While you were asleep, I did a little magical searching of my own," the healer had explained. He went on to inform Kron the killers' vessel, the Khadiran cog, was no longer within the borders of the city, though likely still hidden beneath one of the rivers somewhere not too distant. Next Randall mentioned detecting powerful magics within a home along Mages Way in Uptown.

Kron had recognized the address. "I have been there. Kadath Osrm lives there."

"No longer," Randall had said about the master of the merchants guild, a known wizard herself. "She moved some months ago. I heard a jeweler purchased the property, and I fear he and his family reside there."

Both men had frowned. It was not likely the family was still alive if the murderers had intruded upon them, but Kron would endeavor to discover the truth.

The healer also revealed another fact to his friend in black. "For some little while I have noticed a magical ... emanation from the property. It was small, not powerful, but ancient, possibly hundreds or even thousands of years old. I did not investigate earlier because Master Osrm had owned the property, and her being a mage, I had believed what I detected was likely only a ward or some such about the place. Now I am not so sure."

"You think this is why the wizard and his demon could be there? Some old artifact maybe?"

"Perhaps."

Randall had not been sure, and that had not made Kron more confident about tackling these two enemies on his own. Still, he was not one to shirk a task, and bringing justice in this case was a task needing done. If he had wanted, he could have contacted Captain Gris and had the place surrounded by a small army of city guards, but that would alert the dark mage and his beast. Better to let them think their trail had been lost. Besides, Kron feared such a direct approach might lead to a number of innocent deaths.

No, he would go alone. It was how he preferred it, and others would not be put at risk. If he could ascertain the location of his prey, then he could take in the situation and make a final decision on whether or not to involve others.

In the end, as Darkbow had been exiting the healer's chamber, Randall had offered to go with him.

Kron had looked back. "You are needed here, my friend. Remember, our talents lie in different areas. Think of me when you are saving lives."

18

The house that until recent had belonged to the leader of the merchant's guild reminded Kron of the home where he had grown up, the place he had lived with his parents until he was ten years of age and they were slaughtered in front of his young eyes. Unlike his parents' home which had been in Southtown, this structure was in Uptown, the northernmost district of the city where the wealthy resided. Like Kron's childhood home, it was made of stone and wood and stood two stories tall. The front of the place faced the wide road of Mages Way and to its immediate right was a yard nearly an acre in size surrounded by a wall higher than the average man was tall.

Kron had once climbed that wall and found a spacious garden that led up to a patio sporting furniture, lamps and servants.

Staring at the place from down the street, it looked deserted. The night had not ruled the air for long, but there were no lights from within the house. The only lamps were those lining the broad street, with citizens roaming here and there, and a pair of carriages rolling along. Being somewhat early yet, the street would not be empty, and likely would not for several more hours. Interference was not likely, but also was not impossible. The wealthy had a habit of calling for the city guard at the first sign of disturbance in their little world. Kron had nothing to fear from the guards, especially as he was an adjunct officer currently in their service, but he did not wish to be detained from his work.

He would have to remain unseen. Which was not a problem for one at home with the night.

Waiting until there was no one near, Kron made his way across a darker patch of the road, angling his path so he passed between the extreme limits of two of the street lamps. He approached the front stoop of a near house, then glanced about to make sure he was not being watched.

He was not.

He darted to his left into darkness, shoving through a shrubbery until he was up against the wall lining the former property of the merchant's chief. Pausing for a moment to listen and detecting no alarm, he slid down the length of the wall, edging his way further from the road and into deeper shadows.

Once satisfied he was far enough away from potential prying eyes, a jump placed the ends of his fingers atop the flat wall. For a moment he considered using the grapnel and rope hanging from his belt, but realized this would be a simple climb. Pulling himself up, he chided the owners for not installing spearheads or fencing along the top of the barrier.

Again Kron paused, staring about for any who might be spying upon him. He then turned his focus to the yard and the large house beyond. There were still no lights in the building or within the grounds, and the windows on the bottom floor were shuttered. All was black. Only a moon buffeted by clouds allowed for any vision, and little of that reached within the walls.

Kron could make out nothing other than a sea of ebony stretching before him. From his memory he drew forth images of tall bushes beneath the inside of wall, directly below where he now perched. Would the plants still be there, or would the new owners have removed them?

Only one way to find out.

He dropped.

And landed in the bushes, nearly crying out as he lost his balance and was flung forward. A quick hand grabbed onto a branch and halted him from landing on his face.

Catching his breath, the man in black stared out from behind the hedge. There was still little to be seen as the clouds were not cooperating.

The silence and darkness of the house disturbed Kron. He was beginning to fear the worst for the inhabitants. Obviously the house could not have remained quiet for long without drawing outside attention, but if the wizard and his demon had been here it would have only been during the last few days.

Glancing up, he waited for the clouds to move past the moon, and reminded himself to speak with Montolio or Randall about a spell that would allow him to see in the dark. Several minutes passed and the clouds did not appear to be moving fast enough. Kron cursed under his breath. At least he could not be seen, but he also could not tell what lay ahead of him in the yard. Memory would have to suffice.

He took a step forward. His front boot bumped against something yielding.

Drawing the leg back, Kron wondered what it could have been he had touched. He could recall nothing beyond the hedge to the back patio.

Kneeling, he reached forward into the dark, his unseen fingers playing about in grass, searching for whatever he had touched.

It was a little time before he found it. The thing felt of cloth. His gloved digits searched further. There. Something beneath the cloth, something spongy but with weight.

There was a squishing sound as one of his fingers plunged into wet.

And the moon drifted from behind the clouds.

Kron's hand rested on a butchered corpse of a man, the one finger inserted into an open wound. The sight was not completely unexpected. Kron withdrew his hand and stared at the body. The poor fellow had been lashed repeatedly, deeply, the wounds long and open. The chains, of course. Blood layered the figure but had been dry for some while. This man had not died recently, and from the looks of the remains of his silken garb, he was someone of wealth. Likely the home owner.

The moon retreated and Kron stood. One person was dead, and other corpses were likely to be found on the grounds or within the house. He swore to himself there would be no more killings. He had the evidence he needed to prove his enemies had been here. More than likely they would return at some point. He had a decision to make. Should he leave to find aid, knowing he might miss his prey if they should return then leave, or should he wait for them?

Such a decision was an easy one for Kron Darkbow. He would wait. Randall had enchanted his blades giving him some protection, and hidden here in the dark among shrubs meant he was safe for the time being.

His wait was not long.

A light sparked into existence in the house, shedding a glow from a second-story window. At the distance Kron could not make out who or what was within, but the flickering luminescence and dancing shadows revealed movement.

Time to go.

Overstepping the dead man at his feet, Kron shot forward into the darkness. One, two, three strides. A dozen. Cold air slapped against his face. The house grew in his sight.

Then there was nothing beneath his feet. He was falling. Plunging down.

Not knowing into what he dropped, not able to see, Kron wrapped his arms around his head and pulled his legs in to shield his stomach.

The fall was not far.

He landed hard on his side, ribs cracking but not breaking as the breath was forced from his lungs. Restraining himself from moving, he lay there curled nearly into a ball, his cloak falling over his downed form. He could smell fresh earth, and what he could feel through his garb was like grit.

A hole. Someone had dug a sizable hole in the back yard. He had not seen it when the moon had been out earlier because his attention had been focused upon the dead man.

A hole? Or a grave? It was obviously a sizable pit for it to be big enough to take his whole body into it when he had fallen.

Catching his breath, he reminded himself other dangers might be lurking about. He listened. No shouts or cries from the house, which was a good thing.

He blinked and uncurled his limbs as moonlight once more filtered down. Looking about, Kron found he was indeed in a hollow in the earth not unlike that of a grave. The indention he was in was longer than it was wide, and was deeper than he was tall. He glanced about as he sat up. The wall nearest the house was not of dirt, but of pale stone. There was an opening not unlike a small window. The top of the stone was several inches below the ground level.

So, an old building or tomb. Someone had been digging for it, that someone likely the dark mage or demon. Kron's notion of an ancient artifact was sounding more plausible. Items containing magic were not common, and were often sought after for their potential power and even monetary value. What could it be this dark wizard sought? More importantly, had he found it?

All questions that could not be answered while sitting on the ground.

Kron shoved himself off the dirt and glanced toward the back of the house. A light still burned there. No alarm had been thrown up. Good.

He pulled himself out of the pit but lay low in the grass, the moon now working against him as the clouds seemed to have drifted away. He could not stay unmoving forever, though, and slowly began to crawl his way across the grass toward the patio at the back of the house. At least he was trained in the arts of silence.

Halfway to a set of iron chairs and a table outlined against the back of the main building, he halted as shadows moved across the light in the upstairs window. Kron sucked in air, holding his breaths.

Nothing untoward happened.

He crawled on.

Within minutes he was at the back door. Again he hesitated. Though he had visited here once before, he had not ventured within the main building. The lay of the rooms was unknown to him, and he did not enjoy the idea of chartering foreign territory in the dark.

Still, there was nothing to be done about it.

He gently tried the door, found it locked. His left hand reaching out, he ran fingers around the door's handle until he discovered a lock. His other hand pulled from his belt a small leather package from which he took a pair of small tools. Not being able to see, his work was difficult. It helped that he was experienced. Within a minute he felt and heard the slight movement of the inner latch.

Returning the tools to their hiding place in his belt, Kron withdrew a dagger and made his way indoors, all the while trying to be as quiet as possible.

Once inside, he stopped and gave himself time to catch his breath again. Glancing about he could make out little more than shadows from window lattice, though there was a stench of something burning upon the air. No, not burning. *Burned.* Something had been burned within the house recently, and there was a slight reek of cooked meat. None of this pleased him.

His eyes adjusting as well as they could, and the moon providing some light between shutters and outside doors, Kron moved deeper into the house. As best he could tell, he had entered some kind of hallway with closed doors in each wall. Ahead was an open area with more moonlight streaming through windows from the front of the house which he could not yet see.

Movement above, and a voice, cursing.

Kron stopped again, waiting to see if whomever was up there was coming down.

Silence returned.

He edged forward, his boots sliding along the wooden floor.

At the end of the hall he came to the bottom of a stairwell on his right. The staircase climbed into darkness.

Then a flare of light at the top of the steps. Shadows moved along a wall. Someone was moving around with a candle.

A grunt from above. Then a sigh.

Tromping of heavy footsteps coming nearer.

Kron slid back around the corner from the bottom of the steps, holding his breath as he heard someone plodding down the steps, each movement bringing a creak of wood beneath.

A large, balding man came into view. He was a rough-looking character with a jaw that had not seen a razor in at least a week, and his clothing was rough and torn in no few places. His breeches stopped between the knees and ankles, and his feet were layered in new but cheap leather shoes.

A sailor fresh to the shore, Kron surmised.

The big stranger held out a simple tin lamp with a candle stuck in its middle. Beneath his other arm was a bundle covered in burlap rags. He turned away from Kron, heading toward the front of the house.

Darkbow shoved off the wall, drubbing forward the pommel of his dagger. The rounded steel connected with the back of the big man's neck. There was a crack and the fellow went to his knees, dropping his package and the light.

But he remained conscious.

He grunted again as he pulled a curved knife from behind a rope belt. He brought up one leg, trying to stand.

Kron stepped in and hammered twice with a fist.

The big fellow swayed on one knee for a moment, then he slammed down on the floor.

Kron kicked away the knife, then stood there staring, waiting.

His opponent did not rise.

The man in black slid his own dagger into his belt, then pulled out his climbing cord as he straddled the unconscious figure. "Let us see if you are willing to talk."

19

Tying up and gagging the thug was the first order of business. After that, Kron made secure the bonds, then he lit the candle once more and spent the next several minutes making sure there was no one else in the house. As he had expected, he and the unconscious fellow were alone with each other.

Upon dragging the tied fellow into a front room, Kron made a startling discovery. The source of the burning tint upon the air became obvious. The room had been torched, at least in part. It was obvious the chamber had once been a sitting room of sorts, with several padded chairs of fine red wood lining the wall and a roll top desk and a short book shelf huddled in one corner. All these furnishings were marred now, and a sizable black circle was centered on the thick red Nyponese rug in the middle of the room.

Kron slung his weighty companion onto one of the chairs, heard the seat groan, then held up the candle to glance about the room. It was not only signs of a fire that raised the hairs on the back of his arms, but something else. For long moments he could not pinpoint what it was, but then it struck him. This had been a controlled fire. More than that, it had been directed. Charred lines stretched out from the center of the room, wrapping around the legs of the furniture and climbing the walls.

There was a mystery here.

Only one way to find answers.

Now that he was closer and in the light, Kron could make out his prisoner was an older man, likely in his late forties or early fifties. He had broad shoulders, but years of good eating had added girth to his belly. A scar climbed down one side of his head, reaching from above an ear to the lower jaw. He smelled of rum and fish. Definitely a sailor.

Tugging the cloth from the unconscious man's mouth, Kron dropped it to the ground, then gently slapped the fellow across his left cheek. Nothing happened.

Kron placed the candle on a table and slapped the captive again.

Eyes snapped open.

Kron held up a knife. "If you wish to live, I suggest you not yell out."

A narrow gaze stared back.

"Do you understand?" Kron asked.

A nod.

"Good." Kron looked the fellow over from head to toe. "You don't look like a house servant."

The other man's lips grew into a sneer, but he said nothing.

"Going to play it tough, then?"

Another nod.

A slash.

A wince and a hiss.

A line of red widened on the captive's left cheek.

Kron sat back on his heels, his dagger bouncing in his hand. "I can do this all night."

The prisoner chuckled. "You go ahead and do what you want. Nothing could be as bad as what *he* can do."

"The dark mage?" Kron asked.

No answer other than a flat stare.

The man in black grinned in return but did not use his small blade again. Instead, he sheathed the weapon and reached into a shadow to one side, pulling forth the cloth-laden bundle the other fellow had been carrying when down the stairs.

The prisoner's eyes darted to the package.

"What do we have here?" Kron asked, pulling a cord from around the burlap wrappings.

The packet unfolded by itself.

Kron stared in surprise. Inside the bundle were several long yellow and cracked bones, obviously from a human, as well as most of a skull, the jaw missing.

The parcel placed on the ground before him, Kron lifted a leg bone and held it up to the light. "Someone you know?"

"Never met him."

Now it was Kron who chuckled. "Do you know who it was?"

The man leaned his head to one side and spat onto the blackened rug. But he said nothing.

"Fine." Kron hammered the bone against the floor, cracking it further.

"Stop! Don't!"

Stopping for the moment, Kron held up the bone. "And why should I?"

Sweat was now dripping down the prisoner's face. His lips twitched.

An arm raised as if to slam down the bone once more.

"All right! I'll talk to you. Just put the bones down."

For a moment Kron stared into the other man's eyes. He saw true fear there. Then he placed the package and the bones to one side.

"Thank Ashal," the other said. "If anything happened to those ..." His voice trailed off.

"What?" Kron asked.

The prisoner gulped. "Let's just say I would be better off if you killed me here and now."

The man in black grinned. "Why don't we keep this simple and start over? What is your name?"

"Korick."

"Where do you hail from, Korick?"

"Originally? East Ursia."

"How about your last port of call?"

"Salvino in Lycinia."

"What about between there and here?"

Korick shrugged. "Brief stops in Dailentown and Port Harbor, the usual ports along your coast."

"Tell me about the dark wizard."

The sailor's lips slammed closed. It wasn't so much that he had decided to be silent again as the fact he had been caught off guard by the change in questioning.

301

"What's his name?" Kron prodded.

Korick licked his lips as if biding for time.

A black glove slapped against the pommel of the dagger at Kron's belt.

"Fhaland," Korick said. "I don't know any other name than that one."

"What about the demon?"

"You mean Fhaland's ward?"

"I'm talking about the bald-headed lad with all the chains."

Korick gulped. "Didn't know he was a demon."

"He is."

"Fhaland calls him Kry'lk. Said the boy was in his care."

Kron chuckled. "Could be, I suppose. So what can you tell me about those two?"

"Not much," Korick said. "I signed onto their cog in Lycinia. Seemed like a simple enough cruise at first, me and another score deck hands. Plus there were a half dozen kids or so."

Kron's eyebrows rose.

"Don't look at me like that, judging like," the sailor said. "The south ain't like here. Slavery is common, and kids in chains or cages can be found in any marketplace. A man has to make a living, so don't you judge me. I do what I gotta do to get by."

"Tell me about the cruise here."

Korick closed his eyes and lowered his head. "It was pure hell. At first it seemed like any other jaunt, just with a ship master who was kind of odd. Then third day out, sailors started showing up dead. Not just dead, but torn to pieces. There wasn't even enough left to give them a decent burial at sea. We tossed the remains overboard, which was why a line of sharks followed us all the way to Dailentown."

The man stopped speaking but did not raise his head or open his eyes. It was obvious there were memories swirling around behind his hidden orbs, memories he would prefer to forget.

"Go on," Kron said.

"The children were the worst," Korick said. "We could hear the screams each night. The thrashings, the tearings. Each morning there was a new body to dispose of. They were as bad as the dead sailors. It never seemed to end. Always death, and brutal death at that. A week out, almost to Dailentown, the crew decided it had had enough. The captain was with them. We tried to take over the ship, but Fhaland unleashed Kry'lk on us. Weren't much of a fight. A sword or two was drawn, then all those chains sprang out and ripped a pair of men to pieces right in front of us, sending strips of flesh and body parts flying all over the deck, spraying everyone in a red mist. From then on, there was little trouble from the crew. From then on Fhaland and Kry'lk were out in the open with what they were doing. At night they'd pull one of their slaves right out on deck and Fhaland would ... he would have his way with a lad, then Kry'lk would finish the boy off. It was a pitiful thing to see."

"I bet it was," Kron said, gritting his teeth. "Why didn't you escape when you reached the next port?"

"A few tried. All of them were slain. Even when we reached the river, a few attempted to swim to shore, but Kry'lk tore them to pieces. We learned quick to keep our mouths shut and the ship moving. Even that wasn't always enough, especially after they ran out of slaves."

The sailor finally lifted his head, and tears were streaming down his face.

Kron showed no signs of letting up. "Why did they come to Bond?"

As the line of blood dried on his face, Korick pointed with his chin to the bundle next to Darkbow. "The bones."

"What of them? Who did they belong to?"

"That you'll have to take up with the dark mage," Korick said. "All I know is the bones were important enough to sail halfway across the ocean for. Kry'lk dug a pit in the back yard there to find them."

Kron glanced around the room, his eyes following the marks of burning. "What happened here?"

Korick shook his head. "Not for sure. My guess would be the demon had his way with someone. First time I entered the house was tonight."

"You expect me to believe that?"

The sailor shrugged beneath his coils. "Matters little at this point. Whether you kill me or not, I'm a dead man if I don't bring Fhaland those bones. Hell, even if I do take them to him, once he finds out I've been talking, he'll likely kill me anyway."

"Not if I get to him first."

Korick grinned. "You've got to be joking. Sonny, you've got a good punch, I'll give you that, and you seem to know what you're doing carrying around that big sword on your back, but if you think you can take on a pair like those two, you are living in a dream."

"I survived the demon at the tavern," Kron pointed out, "and Fhaland didn't exactly fair well against me."

Korick's grin widened. "So it was you who threw those little darts at the wizard. He screamed and howled all the way out the back door, swearing he would hunt down the man who had ruined his undershirt."

"I would have gone after him then," Kron said, "but I was ... distracted."

"Your mage friend?"

Darkbow's eyes narrowed. "What of her?"

The sailor shrugged again, wincing as the cords pressed against him. "Nothing, just Fhaland said she got what she deserved for interfering."

Kron said nothing to this, only stared with hard eyes.

Korick slumped in the chair. "So what now? You going to kill me?"

"I'm not finished with you yet. Where is Fhaland and his demon?"

Korick gave out a weary sigh of resignation. "Somewhere out in the city. I don't know where."

"Doing what?"

The sailor locked gazes with his jailer. "Finding children."

Shaking his head in near disbelief, Kron grimaced. "To what end?"

"You know what end."

Kron raised his head and their eyes engaged once more. "Will he take the children somewhere?"

"To the ship," Korick said. "He wants enough of the kiddies to last for another journey. And no, I don't know where he plans on going this time, probably back to wherever he came from once he's got those bones."

"He doesn't have a crew."

A thin smile crossed Korick's lips. "That was my job, finding a crew. I'm supposed to do that in the morning, then meet up with Fhaland tomorrow night."

"Where?"

"The ship."

"Which is where?"

"Down the river, near a little town called Hommel."

"Hommel?" Kron's eyebrows crumpled. "That's going back toward the ocean."

Korick opened his mouth to say something more, but a cracking noise from behind closed his lips. His words would never be known.

20

The wall behind the sailor exploded, sending forth a rain of splintered wood and plaster dust as iron tendrils like that of a hundred hungry octopods sprang forward.

Korick had but a moment to look at Darkbow, terror in the sailor's eyes. Then the man was gone, enveloped as if by a giant maw clamping down, smashed, crushed, smothered. A red spray upon the air was the only evidence he had ever existed, and it quickly mixed with the falling detritus to create a crimson smear on the floor.

Flame blossomed in one corner of the room, the fallen candle having lit upon the rug.

Kron had had no time to react. There was nothing he could have done to save Korick.

He threw himself back, rolling away from the demonic arms flailing and lashing about, flipping his cloak across his face to shield him from flying debris. Expecting death at any moment, Kron came up on a knee and twisted to face a wall of living chains snaking across the floor toward him, a red smear all that remained of the sailor. Thrusting a dagger out before him, Kron's other hand searched at his belt for the bag of grenados.

The wall of chains hissed and screeched, links of all sizes digging into the floor and tearing up the burning rug and strips of wood as the beast's limbs clawed closer and closer.

Just as the chains were inches from his face, the cables extended taut toward his eyes, Kron gripped the sack of grenados.

Then he was engulfed.

A sea of iron and bronze wrapped him from head to toe, entwining and encircling every inch of his body. He had no time to scream as the air was forced from his chest. The weight was instant, pressing into his clothing and upon his flesh, pushing to the point of nearly tearing him limb from limb.

The dagger in his right hand saved him. His wrist twisted, scraping the blade across a dozen metal tentacles and sparking. There was a cry from within the mass of the writhing demon, then Kron was dropped, bouncing onto the floor. Sucking in air, he had a moment to thank Randall for layering magic upon his bladed weapons.

The chain links pulled back and rose like a thousand heads of snakes ready to strike.

The respite would be only temporary, Kron realized. Korick had been slain for telling what he knew, and Kron had to die not only for his new knowledge but for his tenacity in the hunt.

But Darkbow was not a man to go down without a fight. He flung his dagger into the midst of the swirling monster, the thing sissing and baying as the small blade entered the depths of its core, then he rolled to his feet. He jerked the bag of grenados free while his other glove unslung the bastard sword from over his shoulder, the heavy weapon's black blade shining in the light of the flames now growing upon one wall.

The demon's limbs sprang again, this time in a solid mass as if a giant hammer angling for its prey.

Kron slashed out with his sword, connecting and sending up another array of sparks that lit up the chamber. The monster within all that metal roared, but this time did not withdraw. Instead, the mass of chains splintered once more into singular bands, thrusting out and around the sword, reaching for warm flesh.

The blade came up, metal scraping metal, and more screeches filled the night.

The army of links lifted and rained down, slamming aside Kron's sword arm. The man in black cried out and attempted to withdraw toward the door, but was again drowned in a sea of iron.

This time he was not simply engulfed, but was tugged and pulled toward the center of the monster. Blinking back tears of pain as a hundred links tightened on his arms and legs, Kron stared into the belly of the beast, and for a moment caught a glimpse of a massive maw, a round portal lined with rows upon rows of serrated teeth the size of daggers.

There was a growl from the demon, then flame erupted within the beast's center, spreading forth along the lengths of chains as if chasing a streak of oil toward the man in the thing's grip. The monster had come up against a worthy foe, and was unleashing all its powers in a bid to prevail.

Kron watched as the flames darted closer and closer, jumping from link to link, narrowing in upon his twisted and entwined form. He was going to die here. Of this he was certain. Snarling, he swore to take his tormenter with him. The fingers of his left hand worked at the drawstring atop the bag he still gripped. His hand plunged into the sizable pouch and he felt the cool roundness of one of the larger grenados.

Fire raged over him, coursing over and burning away the black cloth shielding his arms and legs. His cloak lit aflame but was quickly snuffed by the metallic limbs roiling and squeezing. His flesh turned red and swelled in places as if near blistering.

Screaming at the anguish tearing into his flesh, Kron lobbed a grenado into the center of the maelstrom of gnashing teeth, fire and flailing chains.

There was a thudding sound as of something heavy being dropped on the floor, then a hissing and sizzling noise. The iron and bronze links went mad, lashing and flogging at the air like a million worms in a dance of death.

Kron felt himself plummeting, but not far. He struck the floor on his side, shouted in pain and surprise, and rolled away from the demon, the beast roiling and bucking on the other side of the room, its tentacles withdrawing, sucking back in towards itself.

There was another howl, then a flash of light.

And silence.

The demon was gone, fled back the way it had come through the wall.

Kron lay there on the floor, the singed remains of his hood falling almost into his eyes. He stared at the scorched rug and the large hole in it that now revealed a blackened floor beneath. Beyond that site was a breach the size of a war horse in the wall. Beyond that hole, another wall and another aperture. Through all this, with dust and soot snowing down from above and flames licking at the side walls, Kron could spy the outside yard he had crossed not so long before.

Then he collapsed into unconsciousness.

21

The world became a combination of mayhem and misery. Shadows drifted in and out of Kron's vision, along with unpleasant sensations like that of ants nibbling at his flesh and tearing away small strips of skin. His ears were filled with a dull throbbing that would not abate, giving rise to dreams of jungle drums beating time and time again against the inside of his skull.

There was a shout and cry, followed by the noise of cracking wood.

Smoke rolled. More yelling. A perception of floating, of being lifted.

Coughing. Spasms to the chest. Warmth. Heat. Flame.

Then cold across his face. The coldest of colds. A chill to stab at the soul.

Drifting, falling, a thumping din. Movement. Wheels rumbling. Horses.

A face. Familiar. Stern. Then a grin.

Darkness.

Followed by a sense of motion, of rolling. The cold had not abated, but lay upon his skin, bringing uncontrolled shivers.

Rolling. Rolling forever.

Was this death?

Kron thought not. He had visited death, or nearly so, and it had not been like this. Then there had been a new world opening before him. Here there was but shadows and a clammy sweat dripping from his brow.

His stomach churned and bile rose to pass through his lips. A cough. A rocking movement.

Then all motion came to a halt.

Lifted once more. Other faces. He knew not these men. Shouts.

Movement.

Light, then dark.

The cold lingered. It bit into his arms and legs like angry starving mice.

Then warmth flooded over him, easing him into waters clean and pure.

"Kron?"

It was a voice he knew.

"Will he survive?"

Another voice, also familiar.

"If he can make it through the night, yes. His fever is high. He is warmer than anyone I've ever seen."

"Do what you can."

Mist moved across his eyes, his thoughts, his mind. He was floating, swirling. Then nothing.

22

"You keep almost getting killed."

It was a voice unknown to Kron.

"Maybe you should find a different type of work."

He opened his eyes. Before him was a slender face with thin, pale features, brown eyes and long, straight hair. The woman was leaning over him, lending a shadow across his eyes, her face almost touching his own.

Who was she? Then it came to him. Althurna. Randall's assistant. He had not known she could speak. The woman had always been mute in his presence, and she had never shown him much regard.

She gave a single, brief nod, then retreated out of his sight. A clatter told him she had gone through a near door.

He gently raised his head and found his surroundings familiar. He was stretched out on a cot in one of the inner chambers of the healing tower where Randall cultivated his craft. Lamps along the curved walls revealed the door, another cot and a bed on the far side of the small room. Sticking above folded sheets atop the other bed was the dark-tressed head of Frex Nodana, gentle snores telling the woman slept.

He glanced down at himself. There was no sheet here, but he had been dressed in a thread-bare gown.

Resting his head back upon a pillow, Kron marveled that he was feeling no aches and pains. Randall had been at work here. Kron knew he should have been a quivering mass of ruined flesh. The demon had nearly torn him apart. The beast's flames had only added to his suffering. At the least there should have been scorched flesh or scars, but none of that was in evidence.

How did he get here? He did not know. Luck? Likely not. Randall was quite powerful and had likely sensed Kron's situation. Or perhaps not. It was difficult to tell with one who was a god walking the world.

The sound of the door opening came to him again. Kron looked up.

"Glad to see you are back among us." Randall was smiling as he approached.

"How long have I been out?"

The healer paused next to the downed man and reached out to grab one of Kron's wrists, feeling at the pulse. "Don't worry yourself about that. But I'm glad to find your heart is strong."

"*How long*, Randall?"

The healer blinked. "I don't know exactly. You were brought to me in the middle of the night."

"What time is it now?"

"Morning. Nearly nine bells."

Kron cursed and sprang up to a sitting position. He would have jumped out of the bed, but a restraining hand held him firm.

"You need rest," Randall assured.

"You don't understand," Kron said. "I have to go."

"Go where?"

"Hommel."

"Hommel? That little town west of the city?"

"The dark mage is supposed to be there tonight."

"Wait." Randall backed off, raising a flat hand for Kron to remain seated. "No need to explain all of this twice. Gris is here, and he wants to see you. I'll fetch him."

The healer turned and exited the room, giving Kron time to search his surroundings once more. No signs of his clothing, or whatever would be left of them, nor his weapons. Nodana continued to sleep, probably induced by magic or drugs because otherwise she would likely have woken by now.

The solitary door creaked open, through it marching the gruff figure of Captain Gris in an orange tabard beneath a tan cloak, a long sword in a leather scabbard slapping at his left leg. Behind him came the healer, Randall closing the door behind them after entering. Before the portal was sealed, Kron caught a brief glimpse of a half dozen other city guards milling about the outer room.

Gris glanced around, then pulled the other cot over in front of Kron. He plopped down with a grunt, the healer coming to a standing rest behind him.

The two warriors stared at one another, their faces grim and brooding.

"What do you remember?" the captain asked.

"Enough."

Gris glanced over a shoulder to the healer, a questioning look in his eyes, then he faced his friend once more. "What is that supposed to mean?"

Kron sighed. "It means we do not have time for an interrogation. There are children in danger."

"Our killers still roam the streets, then?"

"Yes," Kron said. "A dark mage named Fhaland, and a demon called Kry'lk."

"Tell me what happened last night."

"We do *not* have time for this!"

Gris sat back exasperated, raising his hands to ward off another outburst. "Kron, I'm just trying to make sense of what has happened. There were reports of fire and some kind of altercation in a house on Mages Way, then when the guards investigate they pull you unconscious from within. I've been told there were dying flames and plenty of signs of combat, including several walls with holes big enough for an elephant to charge through. Apparently you were in bad shape, your arms and legs burned nearly black. Randall here tells me you have been mostly healed, and we can all be thankful for his skills. But none of this tells me what has happened, nor what is going on with your hunt for our killers."

Kron's gaze bore into the floor. There was too much to tell. He had already lost hours. He glanced up. "Hommel. I need to get to Hommel. Immediately."

"The village?"

"Yes."

"Why?"

Kron cursed. Time, time, time. He had not enough, and wished he could summon it from the very air. There was no telling if Fhaland had slaughtered more innocents, or how many he had captured to be slaves for his next voyage.

He would have to explain in as few words as possible. "Randall suggested I search out the house as he had recently detected a magical disturbance there."

A glance from the captain to the healer showed there was no embellishment.

"Not knowing what I would find," Kron went on, "I decided to investigate on my own."

"In other words," Gris said, "you decided to play the hero."

Kron glared. "I decided not to waste the time of city guards when I had no real evidence the killers were at the house."

The two sitting stared at one another with harsh eyes for a moment. Kron's recklessness was an old matter between the two. It would not be solved this night. Gris nodded for the other to go on.

"I came across a sailor who was working for Fhaland, the dark mage," Kron explained. "He told me much, including he was supposed to meet with the wizard and the demon tonight in Hommel, where the missing cog is hidden. It's likely Fhaland will still be there, probably trying to find a crew for his ship."

"What happened to this sailor?"

"You saw the house?" Kron asked.

Gris nodded.

"Then you saw what happened to him."

The healer and captain traded glances again.

"A little holy water is all that saved me," Kron said, "and perhaps some luck."

"What about the children?" Gris asked. "You mentioned there were more in danger."

"The sailor seemed to think Fhaland was out scouting for more ... targets. Apparently the plan was to hire on another crew, meet tonight at Hommel, then sail back down the river to the sea."

The captain shook his head. "None of this makes sense. What were they doing here in the first place?"

An image appeared in Kron's mind. "The bones! Did you find them?"

"Bones?" Gris asked. "What are you talking about?"

"There were wrappings, a bag of sorts. Within were several bones, including a skull."

Gris appeared confused. "There were no bones found at the house. What do they have to do with anything?"

The demon must have collected them before fleeing. "I'm not sure why Fhaland wanted the bones, but the sailor told me that's why they came to Bond in the first place."

The captain sighed and slapped one of his knees before standing. "We will talk further, by Ashal, but first I'll get a squad on the road to Hommel."

"Your men will only be killed."

"What do you expect me to do, then?" Gris asked. "Hail the entire army and have them march down to Hommel? That's out of the question."

"I'll go alone," Kron said.

Gris chuckled. "I don't think so. You've already nearly been killed fighting this demon."

Now it was Kron who sighed. "If you send a squad, they'll be slaughtered before they can even find the ship. At least I know how to remain hidden."

The captain pulled a pair of gloves from his belt. "I am not sending you alone to chase down this mad wizard and his pet demon."

"Then allow me to put together a special squad," Kron suggested. "Hand-picked men. Those I can trust not to be fools."

The captain stared at his friend for long moments, his mind working behind his eyes. Finally, "I'll be going with you."

"You can't be spared," Kron said. "You are a captain now, Gris. Your duties are here within the city."

"Then who?"

"I'll need a mage."

Gris looked to Randall.

"Not him," Kron said. "In his own way, Randall is as important to this city as are you yourself, perhaps even more so in some ways."

The captain grinned. "Thank you for the vote of confidence. But you need magic to back you on such a mission."

Kron glanced from Randall to the still sleeping Nodana. "What is her condition?"

"She will be out for at least another day," Randall said. "Her wounds were caused directly by magic, which slows her recovery."

Kron's eyes screwed up in confusion as he glanced down at his bare arms and the pale flesh there. The skin looked as if it could belong to a child, it was so pink. Why had not the monster's magic done more harm?

"The demon is a magical creature," Randall explained, "but his fire is of the common variety."

A face appeared in Kron's thoughts. His head snapped up. "I have someone in mind, a mage of many talents."

Gris tugged on his gloves. "Good. Go fetch him, or her. We'll get you some men and have you outfitted once more. There's no garrison in Hommel, but I'll make sure to give you a letter to the local constable, just in case."

Randall moved around the captain to be between the two. "One thing, though. Hommel is thirty miles away. Can you make it there by night?"

Kron stood. "We'll have to ride as if dragons were after us."

Part 2:
Hommel

23

"Sheriff, you're going to want to see this."

Micklewhite groaned as he dropped his boots from the edge of his desk and lifted his prodigious self from the rasping chair. He shifted the studded mace on his belt to one side and approached the open window where stood Deputy Ollie staring out.

Despite the chill of the early winter morning, the sun was bright and revealed a carriage pulled by a half dozen horses coming to a halt in front of the structure that served as a jail and billet for the sheriff and his deputy. The horses were the most beautiful Micklewhite had ever seen, dark and full of muscle, snorting out puffs of air that misted away to nothing. The carriage itself was also impressive, an oily black like something that would belong to an undertaker, its lines and curves showing influence in its owner and extraordinary skill in its maker.

The town of Hommel was familiar with strangers and others traveling through. The place was only thirty miles from Bond, the largest city this side of the mountains, and rested along a main road not far off the South River. The wealthy and indigent alike were common, but rarely did they stay longer than a day or two, just enough time to rest themselves and their steeds or pulling animals before moving on to places elsewhere.

Every once in a while there would be a true oddity stopping in Hommel. Micklewhite could still remember two summers earlier a pair of traveling duelists, a man and young woman, who had spent a night in the town. Their loud bawdiness and eagerness to fight had nearly sent the townsfolk into a frenzy. Torches and pitchforks had been prepared. A few soft words from the sheriff, as well as an offer to cover the costs of the couples room at the inn, had healed things over long enough for Micklewhite and Ollie to shepherd the strangers out of town and on their way to Bond.

Since then there had been few bizarre characters to be found within the town, but it seemed there was always somebody coming and going. Burly drovers with a penchant for hard liquor and punching. The occasional huckster or swindler looking to cheat the yokels out of their few coppers. A traveling mage who scared everyone whenever he or she rose an eyebrow.

It never ended.

Yes, there had been few oddities of recent, but that was changing.

As of today.

The carriage and the horses were slightly unusual with their signs of wealth, but there was something more, something disturbing about the whole setup. Those horses, when the light hit them just right, their eyes flamed red for a moment. And the carriage itself almost seemed to seep unease, as if all that oiled wood and iron gave off hints of smoke here and there. But surely that was just a trick of the morning sun.

The animals and the craft, however, were not what stood out as most eerie to the sheriff. It was the person atop the contraption, the driver. He appeared to be a boy of no more then ten or twelve years. That alone was not enough to draw Micklewhite's eyes into a furrow, as he had seen plenty of young wagoneers and such in his day. No, the boy and his youth weren't what stood out. It was that bald head, those blank eyes, the pale but smoky skin, and that spotless white robe that held the youth's head high with a stiff collar yet floated down to cover the body whole. Standing out on the lad, almost as an abomination to that smooth flesh, was a fresh scarlet whelp across one side of his face, as if he had been lashed or burnt of recent.

The image of an undertaker and a funeral returned to the sheriff's mind. The boy looked as if he were to be laid out on a deathbed.

Despite his deathly demeanor, the lad moved, dropping the carriage's leathers before hopping down onto the far side of the vehicle where he could no longer be seen from the window.

Deputy Ollie shivered at the sheriff's side. "I expect nothin' good to come of this."

Micklewhite shrugged. "Probably a wizard or some other oddball. They'll be on their way soon enough."

"Kind of weird they're pulling up here, though, instead of down at the inn."

The sheriff sighed again. "Well, I'll go out and see what they want."

With that Micklewhite rolled his shoulders and shifted his weight, heading out his office's lone door. Outside he jotted down the few stone steps in front of the building and stepped into the sunlight. He paused long enough to look up and down the main brick road to see a few locals milling about or walking one place or another. The road ended in a triple intersection in front of the sheriff, one leg of the path heading north to the river, another going south, the path directly before Micklewhite the road back to Bond from which it appeared the carriage had come.

Stepping nearer the dark contraption, the sheriff brought himself up short. Now that he was nearer the horses, he could feel a soft heat rolling off them, and then there was the gentle sound of sobbing coming from within the carriage. The noise was like that of a woman or child, and best he could tell, it seemed there was more than one person.

Micklewhite glanced around for the driver but saw no signs of the odd youth, not even his legs or feet beneath the other side of the carriage.

The sheriff was about to knock on the vehicle's door when it snapped open. Within was complete darkness. Nothing could be seen.

Until a fellow with girth, nearly as wide and tall as Micklewhite himself, appeared in the doorway. The man wore long robes of the brightest colors, and his eyes were painted like those of a whore. A line of a beard rode along the edges of his chin below a large, round nose. He did not appear happy as he glanced up and down the street, but he wasted little time before gingerly climbing down onto the bricks.

"Hello, sir," Micklewhite said, not approaching closer.

The stranger's eyes darted to the sheriff as if noticing him for the first time, lingering for a moment upon the mace at the official's belt. "Are you the constable?"

"Sheriff Micklewhite at your service, sir."

A sly grin crossed the stranger's lips. "I am in need of a crew for my ship. A dozen or so men should do."

The sheriff's brows rose in confusion. He glanced up the north road past the inn and the few houses there to the wooden dock fronting the river. The dark blues and golds of the moving water glittered, but there were no boats or ships to be seen.

Micklewhite looked back to the newcomer. "I'm sorry, sir, but there's no vessels docked at the moment. Are you expecting one?"

The grin broadened. "It is there, good sheriff, merely unseen."

Which did not make sense to the sheriff, who was deciding he did not care much for this stranger.

Micklewhite tugged his weapon belt higher, as much to keep it from sliding down his girth as to show the man before him he was someone of importance. "Sorry, sir, but if you're looking to hire a crew, you would be better off in Bond." He pointed east along the road the carriage had just traveled. "Few sailors here this time of year. Most of them hole up in the city."

The odd man with the painted face stepped closer, as if to share in some conspiracy. His eyes grew the size of large coins and his grin parted to show teeth filed to points. "I never said anything about *hiring* a crew, sheriff, only that I was in need of one. A dozen of your little town's hardiest fellows should do. What they don't know about sailing, I can bypass with the use of spells."

Micklewhite gulped. No, he definitely did not like this person.

"In fact," the stranger went on, "you can be the first to join my crew."

A gold swirl swam forth from those painted eyes, and the sheriff felt his chest go cold as warm liquid flowed down his legs. He could not move. He could not breath. All he could do was stare into that twirling madness that filled his mind.

Then Micklewhite's eyes rolled over white, and he stood motionless.

"That's a good lad," the stranger said to his zombie.

Oblivious to what had happened, Deputy Ollie suddenly appeared at the sheriff's side. "What's going on here?"

The newcomer continued to smile. "Hell has come to your village, little man, and it shall feast before it departs."

24

Six horses. The best that could be found on short notice. Froth flew from their quivering mouths, their riders driving them hard. The day was bright but not overly warm, allowing the animals a retreat from a hard sweat but bringing a harshness to their breathing. Each was well muscled, built for speed and riding, and they proved this as they galloped west along the brick road, passing by carts and wagons, the occasional other rider, and peasants on foot.

At the head of the pack, Kron glanced back to make sure the others were keeping with him. They were, proving their reliability. Of sergeants Thag and Rogins he had had little concern, having known the men in some little measure and having witnessed them in action before, but the big woman that was Corporal Makeshift was an unknown to Kron, as mostly were Montolio and Dolk, the burly worker who was the architect's assistant.

Gris had talked well of the corporal. The woman spoke few words, but she had size and allegedly some experience. Besides, she would not have made corporal in the Bond city guard without showing a certain level of brightness and dependability. There was also a smoldering fire behind her gray eyes, and this had drawn Kron to accept her. Where there was heat there was rage, and the man in black could use rage. He had built his life upon it, though of late he had tried to temper his own wild side. At least until children were being raped and slaughtered in the streets. For that, the flames of retribution and justice could not burn hot enough as far as Kron was concerned.

Montolio had been the only other mage known to Kron, at least the only one who would be available for traipsing across the countryside in search of a killer and his pet demon. The foreigner gave an impression of being familiar with high society, but he was well educated, intelligent and an experienced wizard. He had also not hesitated upon being asked to take part in hunting down these criminals. That alone had raised Kron's estimation of the dark-haired wizard.

Dolk appeared to be a simple man, though not a simpleton. Short but showing muscle and scars, he had been one of the workers at the Asylum site. Trusted by Montolio, upon hearing what was asked of his employer, he gladly volunteered himself to join along. Claiming to be a veteran, he too had shown a flame behind his look, though an older one that kindled. Of those in the party, Kron knew this man the least, but Montolio had spoken well of him and Dolk had given an impression of knowing what he was doing.

Kron only hoped it would be enough, the six of them. Captain Gris had sent another party straight across land, those half dozen riders to block the road south of Hommel. Another dozen had been sent down the river on a pair of boats, heading toward the small town. Kron and his group were expected to arrive first, but the major exits from Hommel would be watched and, if necessary, blocked. The man in black had his doubts about the other soldiers being able to survive against the demon, let alone having the ability to defeat the beast, but the truth was those men were not expected to take part in the coming fray. Kron and his small squad were to be the head of the spear, were expected to confront the monster and its mage directly.

The road passed in a blur beneath the horses' hooves. Brown and gray trees along the road whipped past so swift they could barely be seen. Yet it was not enough. It seemed as if time were standing still for Kron Darkbow.

Vengeance needed serving, but more importantly, children needed saving. Perhaps even the town of Hommel itself was in danger.

25

Tears streaming down her face, Leesa ran and ran and ran until her lungs hurt and her legs felt like they would collapse beneath her. She darted through the open doorway of the crumbling tower to the south of Hommel and fell to her knees, holding her sides to keep from breathing or crying too loudly. If she were heard, she might soon join the fate of the others.

It had all happened so quickly, before the men of the village had been able to put together any kind of defense. That evil wizard had slain a dozen with little more than a wave of a hand, raining down lightning from a clear sky to skewer and jolt women and men and children who had been doing little more than walking the streets of their own town.

But that had been only the beginning.

Then the monster had appeared, shooting forth arms of chain links from beneath its pale cloak, stabbing and slashing, rupturing and eviscerating all it came across. Smoke was soon upon the air, followed by fire and screams.

The wizard and his creature had rampaged through the center of the village, slaying nearly all who dared to show themselves. Only a handful of men and children had been spared, corralled into the jail to await a fate unknown to the crying girl.

Leesa herself had come close to capture. Only her father and mother had saved her, stepping in front of the girl as the wizard had approached from down the street. The evil man had slapped at the air as if swatting flies, then blood had erupted from father's eyes and he had dropped to his knees screaming while clawing at his own face. From the folds of her dress, mother had pulled out her largest kitchen knife.

Then mother had looked down at her. "Run," the woman had said.

And Leesa had run, not daring to look back, not even when she had heard her mother screaming. Darting between two houses, the girl had come out in the barren field just to the west of the town. There had been nowhere to hide, so she had run to the south, following the back of the village's buildings until she had come to the end.

By this point, lines of black smoke were belching from half a dozen of the houses. And still the screaming had not abated. Sticking her head out from behind the last house before the open road stretched south, she saw horrors she would never forget, people ripped in half by unseen forces, decapitations and disembowelings, flesh flayed from arms and legs, bones broken and shattered into a thousand tiny pieces layered in gore. She had also witnessed a collection of men and children being herded into the sheriff's building. Why some were spared and others not, she did not know, but she had to wonder if the dead were not the lucky ones.

Fear had tugged at her again there behind the house. Leesa had charged across the road, hoping not to be seen. She had come to the old tree that legend said had once been the home of a powerful wizard hermit. She had tried the door in the center of the large tree, but it had not budged. Glancing up, she had spotted the lower level of the house built amongst the gray limbs, but it had been too far for her to reach and there was no rope nor ladder. Still, she hid beneath the shadow of the big tree for some little while, resting and catching her breath.

The day had waned. The screaming continued in the distance. Leesa eventually ran again.

Once across another dead field and up a hill, she had come across the old keep tower that had been there all her life. Tales were that the tower had been used in days long past to protect the village, but it had been in ruin as long as anyone in Hommel had been alive. It was rumored to be haunted, but the girl and her friends had never witnessed anything unusual there. It had always been a silent skeleton of dark stone on the horizon, often seen but never approached.

Until now.

Her breathing slowed and her body stopped shaking. There was only so much horror a person could suffer before drying up inside, and Leesa was dry nearly to the point of becoming a desert within her own mind.

She sat in the darkness, moonlight seeking through the open doorway but not finding her. She sat and sat. For a while she had prayed to the mighty Ashal for a savior, but such thoughts had long sailed away. Her parents were dead. Her friends were dead or enslaved. Such things did not happen in West Ursia, a nation of freedom that had known peace for generations. But they *had* happened, here in her own home, in the small, quiet little town of Hommel. And nothing would ever be the same.

26

A mind could only live with so much horror before breaking, snapping. In those situations, the sufferer became either a raving lunatic or nearly comatose. Sheriff Micklewhite had experienced both sensations in a matter of hours.

What was worse, he had been forced to watch horrors and not been able to do anything about them. He had not even been given the privilege of turning his head away, of closing his eyes. His body had become alien to him, nothing more than a husk within which he resided. He had watched, listened and felt, but his body had not responded to him. Flight was not an option. Fighting was not an option.

The first death had been Deputy Ollie. The man had sauntered up casual like and asked a simple question. The dark wizard had uttered some kind of response, then had snapped his fingers. Ollie had coughed and a froth of red had protruded from between his lips. The poor fellow had turned questioning eyes upon his boss, then he had fallen over twitching. Within seconds even the twitching had stopped, and Ollie would never move again.

The door to the carriage had then opened once more and out dropped the boy in the white robes. Micklewhite caught a glimpse of the inside of the vehicle. Shrouded in near darkness were a half dozen young bodies, all nude and sprawled out along the floor.

At that point the wizard had chuckled and worked his fingers in the air as if he were a puppeteer. Against his will, Micklewhite had turned to face the town, his home of years and years, and the true horrors had begun.

The wizard and his pale, hairless companion had sauntered down the street as if on a holiday jaunt, taking their time going from house to house, pausing here and there to unleash some particular abhorrent fate on those who dared to try and fight or who had simply not run fast enough. Magical spells of the vilest sort were unleashed, painful and torturous to all victims before finally slaying them.

By the time the deadly pair had walked from one end of Hommel and back, a task that took not a half hour, several homes were smoking, a few in flames. Bodies lay here and there, and the remains of bodies. Torn limbs. Sprays of blood. Twitching corpses.

The sheriff hoped some few had escaped, but it was soon made clear to him there was nowhere to hide. After scouring the town, the wizard and his beast seemed to confer, then they spent a lengthy period of time rooting out those still alive and in hiding.

It was nearly dark by the time they had finished, and almost all two hundred of the citizens of Hommel were dead or missing.

Some dozen men had been spared, and four children. All the survivors, including Micklewhite, had been herded into the jail. They had had no choice in the matter. The evil pair told them what to do and they did it, as if they were some kind of automaton.

Once everyone was locked behind bars, the big wizard with the painted face had sighed as if tired and eased himself onto the sheriff's chair in the front office. At that point, those imprisoned had regained the use of their bodies. They had screamed, shouted, threatened.

The wizard had turned the chair to face them, and sat there with flat eyes staring back at those who would slay him if they could. He appeared weakened, and remained quiet for some little while as the sun went down.

Then the child in the white robes had returned. With him was a young man little more than a boy. He was the village priest's son, a student of his father's since the lad's mother had died when he was young. It was obvious this young man was still in the swoon of a spell, forced to walk around the sheriff's office until he stood next to the desk, his eyes white with no pupils.

At this point the wizard had stood while his companion backed into a corner and gave off a devilish grin.

The wizard turned to those behind the bars. "As we have some hours to spare while our vessel rises from the depths and drains itself, and because it would be taxing to have to bridle all of you every minute of the day, I feel a lesson is in order." He snapped his fingers, and once more Micklewhite and his companions were locked into place, unable to move, even to blink. "Pay close attention, because your fate could be thus."

Micklewhite had believed the worst terrors had already been presented to him, but he was soon proven wrong.

With the wizard's words the priest's son had disrobed there in front of everyone, revealing the innocence of his young, pale flesh. Then the wizard removed his own clothing, showing a heavy body of golden skin layered in rolls of fat with muscles in the legs and arms, every inch of him covered in a thin layer of greasy sweat. What followed made grown men in the jail weep in silence as they were forced to watch.

But that had not been the end of the horrors.

When finished with the lad, the wizard had shoved aside the bruised youth. Then the white-robed figure had stepped forward.

Micklewhite could not contemplate what happened next. It had been so horrific, his mind had rebelled and blocked the memory from him. When the orgy of blood had finally been completed, the priest's son was in pieces, his head and limbs slung throughout the room. Blood covered the walls while the trunk of the body remained planted on the desk as if a stuffed pig prepared for a meal. What had happened to the youth had meant no more to the wizard and his beast than what children do to flies or frogs. The two had reveled in their abomination.

And none of those jailed had been able to turn away from watching a boy they had known all their lives raped and torn limb from limb by the man and his demon of chain tentacles.

Yes, it was enough to drive one mad, and Sheriff Micklewhite had retreated so far into the darker recesses of his mind, he would not have believed he could ever return.

27

The riders could not spare much time to slow down, but there were signs they were drawing nearer the village. At first it was the look of fear in the eyes of those they were passing. Kron eventually pulled the group to a halt to give their mounts precious moments of rest, and Sergeant Rogins had taken the opportunity to question those aboard a passing wagon. These folks had not come directly from Hommel, but lived not far from the town. They told of screams and fire and smoke. They told of fleeing, figuring it was time to pay a visit to relatives in Bond.

The next sign of trouble was the hint of burning upon the air. At first it was a heavy scent of smoldering wood, but then had followed the taint of cooking flesh. It was enough to churn the stomachs of the riders, Montolio having to slow his animal and lean to one side to empty his stomach of its contents.

Daylight was fading as they drew nearer to Hommel, and darkness reigned once they reached a hillside looking down upon the town. From their spot on the road there were no signs of movement within the village. Everything was quiet. Few lights burned on the streets or in windows, but several lingering red glows outlined the remains of burned buildings that had suffered earlier during the day.

Sergeant Thag pulled his horse up next to Kron. "How do you want to do this?"

Standing on his stirrups, the man in black shook his head and surveyed the land. There was little to see as the moon was behind clouds this night, but here and there he could make out shadows and darker outlines against the sky. "What is that?" he asked, pointing to a looming structure in the distance.

Corporal Makeshift rode up next to the two men. "Old tower," she said. "Fallen into disrepair."

Thag turned his head to the corporal.

She looked back. "I grew up near here," she said as way of explanation.

"Is the tower defensible?" Kron asked.

"The upper levels are a mess, fallen in," Makeshift went on, "but the floor level should be usable."

"How far would you estimate it is from the village proper?" Kron asked.

Makeshift shrugged. "About a half mile. A little more maybe."

Kron turned in his saddle to look at the others behind him. There was little to see on the darkened road, but he wanted to make sure he was heard. "We'll head for the tower. Once inside, possibly we can start a light, if the conditions are safe enough. There we can leave our horses and move into the village on foot. I'm thinking we'll split into two groups of three, one entering from the north of town, the other from the south. Anyone have suggestions?"

Dolk's rough voice came from the night. "What about sending in one man first to get the lay of the land?"

Good man. Good question. "I've considered it," Kron said, "but I feel timing is important here. Since we are dealing with a wizard of some power, my guess would be he will be aware of us quite soon. If we can get in there and hit him before he can prepare for us, I think we stand a better chance against him. Anything else?"

No one said a word.

"All right, then." Kron turned his steed toward the distant tower, then kneed the animal in its side.

The others followed.

28

Even fear must bow before the weight of exhaustion. The body and mind can only support the turgid emotions following sheer terror for so long before giving in to physical limitations. There comes a point when flight is no longer an option, when the legs and arms become too heavy to carry one further, when the mind tumbles in upon itself and surrenders to dread and weakness.

Twelve-year-old Leesa had reached that point huddled in the darkness of the remains of the crumbled tower. She had long ago caught her breath, but she had run so long her body no longer had the strength to carry her further, at least until she rested.

Huddled on the dusty floor, spiders crawling around her, arms wrapped around knees, she swooned into a numb dreamworld. Before her were the faces of those she had loved, mother and father and the kind people of Hommel she had called friends all her life. These faces smiled down at her and she felt a longing, as if they were beckoning to her. But how could this be? Even in sleep she recognized her friends and family were no more. A cloud of rank vileness had settled upon the village, sweeping away all she knew and all she held dear.

The heavy sound of approaching hooves stirred her awake, but she did not move. Her body remained stiff, and her mind felt drugged. The horses drew nearer, and she thought she could detect muted voices speaking outside the tower's remains.

Then the sounds drew closer, right behind her. There was a spark, then a light brought shadows to the curved wall before her unblinking eyes.

"Kron! There's someone in here."

Shuffling of feet. Muted talking. The wispy shiftings of cloaks. The slaps of hardened boots upon stone and packed earth.

A dark figure appeared before Leesa. She did not look up, but stared at the black leather boots before her. Were these the boots of the one who had slain all she loved? She did not know if she cared. If she were to die, so be it. Perhaps those smiling faces would be waiting for her.

The dark figure dropped to a knee, the man leaning forward until the girl caught a glimpse of a pale face topped by black hair surrounded by a dark hood.

"Girl?" the man said.

She did not respond. There was no need. He was not the slayers from the village, but what did it matter? This man could not change the past.

He leaned closer, placing a gentle arm around her. She did not flinch. She barely breathed.

"Can you speak?" he asked.

Only then did she tilt back her head and turn her eyes directly upon his face.

"Please," she said, "please, kill me."

It was *he* who flinched.

29

"Has the girl lost her mind?"

Kron looked around to find Montolio had asked the question standing in the doorway, a lantern outstretched in one hand. Outside behind the mage the others were using ropes to hobble their horses.

"I don't know," Kron said, being honest.

A small hand reached up and clasped at the man in black's cloak. "Who are you?" her weak voice asked.

Kron's gaze shifted down again to stare into those flat, unmoving eyes. They looked like a doll's eyes, or of something dead. Whatever atrocity had happened to this girl, it had affected her mind. While he could feel pity for her, he wished she were cognizant enough to provide them with information about what had been happening in Hommel. There were too many signs Fhaland and his demon had spread their hell to the town, and any knowledge Kron could gain would help to put an end to the fiendishness.

He removed his arm from around her shoulder and sat back on his heels. "My name is Kron Darkbow. We have come from Bond to ... to end this madness."

She blinked, finally. Her eyes dilated as if she were waking from a dream, or a nightmare.

"Mother," she whispered. "Father."

"She's in shock," Montolio said, moving further into the tower. He glanced up to find most of the floors above were missing, rotted away or removed by the locals for building material. From inside he could see the stars winking high above the ruins of the tower's circular wall. "Explains why she didn't pick a very good place to hide. This tower sticks out on the horizon, and would be the first place they would look outside the village proper."

"They don't seem interested in anyone outside of the village."

It was the girl's voice, a fresh voice, young and weak. Both men looked down at her.

"They haven't left there all day," she said.

"The wizard?" Kron asked.

"And his monster," the girl said, nodding.

It was not in his mood, but Kron forced a gentle smile. Any sign of kindness would do the girl a wonder at this point. "What is your name?"

"Leesa."

Montolio eased closer and hunkered down next to Darkbow. "Leesa, we are here to help. Can you tell us anything about what's happening in the village?"

Her head turned to one side and her eyes drifted away. For a moment it seemed she would return to her fugue, but then her lips moved. "They killed everyone."

Kron and Montolio traded concerned looks.

"Everyone?" the mage architect asked.

Leesa gave a brief tilt of her head, almost a shrug. "There were a few people forced into the sheriff's office. Maybe they are still alive."

Kron looked to the other man again. "He's rounding up a crew for his ship."

Montolio rested a hand on the girl's shoulder, surprised she did not jump away. "Can you tell us where is this office?"

Another voice spoke from behind. "It's in the center of town. The main road runs right up to it."

Kron looked back. It was Corporal Makeshift who had spoken, the big woman in chain armor now standing in the open doorway.

"Like I said, I grew up near here," she said.

"Can you draw us a map of the town?" Kron asked.

Makeshift moved into the light and knelt next to the others. With a gloved finger she began to draw in the dust off to one side. "It's basically a T-intersection. Our road runs right into the center of Hommel. The other road runs north from the river to the south, toward the coast and Port Harbor."

Leesa's head twisted around and she watched the image of her home town as it came into view upon the floor. She nodded again, showing the corporal spoke the truth.

Kron looked back to the girl. "Leesa, are you okay with horses?"

Her face grew confused.

"Can you ride?" the man in black asked.

The girl nodded yet again.

Swiveling to face the others directly, Kron pointed toward the door where the two sergeants and Dolk were now waiting, listening. "Sergeant Thag, I want you and Montolio and Makeshift to come in from the north. The rest of us will skirt down and come up from the southern route."

"Will we meet up somewhere?" Thag asked from the door.

"Our goal can be the sheriff's office," Kron said, pointing at the corporal's map in the dirt, "but tread with caution. If you make contact with our targets, I'm sure the rest of us will be able to hear it when it happens. Try to hold on until all of us can get there. It's probably best to hit them from a distance, if possible. I suggest Dolk and the soldiers take our crossbows. I've got my longbow, and Montolio can use his spells. The northern group can take one of my water grenados, but save it until necessary. Since Randall magicked our weapons, don't waste the grenado, at least not until you're in close and know you won't miss."

"I take it we will be sneaking in?" Sergeant Rogins asked.

Kron grinned again, but there was no cheer in it. "I don't suggest walking down the middle of the street. Just remember we have to keep a look out for one another and for any civilians who might be in hiding. We don't want anyone wounded because of our nervousness."

The man in black shifted his attention back to the girl. "Leesa, you should be safe here. Can you watch the horses for us?"

"I can," she said, "but there's no reason."

"Why is that?" Kron asked.

"Because none of you will be coming back."

<u>30</u>

The village was as silent as a graveyard. In fact, there was a cemetery in the northwest corner, and it showed as much life as did the rest of darkened Hommel. Clouds still stretched across the sky, blocking most of the stars and the moon's glow, and the usual street lamps were dead. Even the houses that had been burned were reduced to smoking bones against the sky. The only light came from a glow behind the two windows of the sheriff's office.

The river at their side a stone's throw away, Montolio, Sergeant Thag and Corporal Makeshift stooped low as they hurried behind a stone fence lining the north side of the cemetery. For a moment starlight flickered off the soldiers' chain shirts, but soon enough they joined the wizard in hiding behind a clump of trees and shrubs near the dirt road that ran from the water into the village.

For the third time in the last several minutes, Makeshift checked to make sure her crossbow was in working order with an arrow at the ready. Then she knelt and stared down the familiar lane toward Hommel proper. It had been at least five years since she had ventured along this road, back before she had become a member of Bond's city guard. In those days she had simply been a regular, one of hundred of heavies who had the job of taking the front lines. Of course there had not been a major war involving West Ursia since before she was born, but like most of the nation's soldiers she had spent her share of time rounding up bandits and facing down enemies in minor border tussles in one place or another, most often in the mountain range that separated her homeland from East Ursia.

The last time she had been in Hommel had been when she was passing through from the old homestead, the little farm her parents had worked before the two of them had passed away, Ashal rest their souls. Her father had just died, leaving her the property, but she had had little use for it. Despite her strength and bulk, the farming life was not for Makeshift, who had gone by another name back in those days before a drill sergeant had labeled her upon joining the guard. The sergeant had said she had a knack for making use of anything and everything as a weapon during tight situations.

Now memories came rushing back upon the woman, not all of them kind ones. That brought forth images of her friend, her fellow soldier and sometimes companion, Talend. The two had known one another since basic training over near Pinsonfork, nearly a decade back now. Talend had been there when Makeshift had killed her first man and when the two had become corporals together under Sergeant Thag himself. But no more. Talend had been killed, slaughtered by this madman and the demon.

Makeshift spat, thinking about the disgusting pair. She would be happy to kill them not only for all those who had suffered, not only for the poor villagers of Hommel, but for Talend and the memory of the woman.

They had been friends. Now that had ended. The wizard and demon were at fault. They would pay the price. Makeshift's only regret was she doubted she would be able to deal out the pain Fhaland and his monster had caused to Talend and the others.

Thag hissed at her side, causing the corporal to glance in his direction.

"You ready with that holy grenado?" the man asked.

"If needed." With her free hand she patted the bag hanging from her belt.

"Just be careful with that," Montolio said from behind. "We don't want to risk damaging it before we need it."

The corporal glared over a shoulder at the mage. She barely knew the man, but hoped she wasn't going to have a reason to dislike him. He seemed anxious enough to take part in this business, but he also came off as a little on edge.

"I'll do my part," she said. "Just make sure you do yours when the time comes."

The wizard had no response other than an awkward shrug. Sergeant Thag smirked at Makeshift's side.

Ignoring the mage for the moment, she turned back to watching the road. "What do you think, sarge? You want to sneak up or charge straight down their throats?"

Thag shifted his crossbow from one arm to the other, then glanced across the road to the other side where there was a line of ragged bushes, thick but little more than dried twigs now that winter had started. The dead-looking plants ran right up to the nearest house, or what was left of it. A leaning wall that was little more than blackened lumber faced the bushes but appeared whole enough to offer protection.

"I don't think charging down their throats would be what Darkbow meant by treading with caution." The sergeant pointed across the road using the head of his crossbow bolt. "I'm thinking we trot across, jump those big weeds and head for that wall, planting our backs against it."

"We'll be in the open for a few moments," Montolio commented from behind, "but there's plenty of cloud cover. We should be okay."

The two soldiers glanced back. "You right behind us, then?" Thag asked.

The wizard nodded.

The sergeant slapped Makeshift on a shoulder. "Take lead."

The corporal was off running, her heavy boots slapping hard upon the ground as she chugged. Being so large, Makeshift was not the fastest runner, especially wearing armor and carrying a sword and iron crossbow, but she made it across with no trouble and dove over the plants, landing on a shoulder and rolling over onto her feet. As trained, she did not look back to make sure her comrades were with her. They had to be. It was part of the plan. She took off again, heading toward the wall. Only when she was directly beneath it did she drop to a knee again, planting her back against blackened lumber while raising her crossbow.

Thag and Montolio were only a moment behind, the sergeant dropping down next to the corporal, the wizard off to one side and breathing heavy from the jog.

Makeshift stuck out her shaggy head and stared around the edge of the house's remains. There were no signs they had been noticed and no one had appeared on the street. In front of their temporary shelter was a small yard which fielded several bumpy objects. For a second the moon worked its way between the clouds and the corporal could make out the objects were body parts. A leg and two torn arms were strewn across the flattened grass.

She pulled her head back.

"How's it look?" Thag asked.

Makeshift sucked in air, trying to steady herself after what she had seen. "Quiet."

"What do we do now?" Montolio asked.

The sergeant moved around Makeshift and took his own swift look down the road. Then he pulled back. "We make our way across the yard and to the next house. I'll go first with you two watching my back, then Makeshift next and finally the wizard. We keep skipping along like that until we get to this sheriff's place. If anyone gets in our way, we take them down."

The three traded glances.

"Ready?" Thag asked.

31

For a moment Kron thought he saw a flicker of movement on the far north side of the village. Shadows flitted across the road. Had he caught a glimpse of Thag and the others moving in? He could not be certain, but hoped he was the only one who had witnessed it. So far there had been no other movement, and no signs of life came from the sheriff's office, the only lit building. Then again, Kron's viewpoint was limited from the ditch that ran along the eastern side of the brick road on the south side of the village.

He glanced right and found Dolk and Sergeant Rogins huddled, checking their crossbows. Reaching up to retrieve his own longbow from over his shoulder, he also grabbed an arrow and placed it along the bow.

"Now?" Dolk whispered.

Kron's hood nodded.

The sergeant rolled over the top of the ditch, came to his feet and took off at a trot. Soon enough he reached the other side where he plunged into a thicket, no trace of him to be seen.

Kron nodded again.

Dolk shifted his wide shoulders and pulled himself up onto the road. He was clumsier than had been Rogins, but he made good speed crossing the bricks and disappearing into the bushes.

A heartbeat passed as Kron waited to make sure the situation would not explode. When it did not, he jumped and ran after the others, a moment later diving through the thick plants to land on his knees.

The three traded glances to assure each was fine, then as a group edged toward the nearest house, fortunately one not destroyed by flame. At the house's closest wall they came to a halt once more, giving themselves time to rest. Kron stuck his head out around the corner and looked up the street. There was nothing to see ... then there was. Movement on the opposite side of town. Not much, just a few shadows edging along a yard in front of one of the far homes. It had to be the northern group.

Kron eased back behind the wall. "The others are on the move."

Rogins opened his mouth to speak but a noise like that of wood slapping wood shut him up.

Confused looks were traded.

Kron stuck his head out once more.

The door to the sheriff's office was now open halfway between the two groups of infiltrators. Light shed upon the steps and the road in front of the building, and soft mumbled voices could be heard from within.

It was too far to run without being noticed. The distance was within the extent of their bows, but not so much to make Kron comfortable about a ranged assault. The dark of night did not help.

"On me," the man in black said, then he skirted the front of the house, hoping the others would follow.

They did, which Kron soon discovered as he planted himself behind the next building, a two-story structure with a sign out front proclaiming it was a shop of some kind. Rogins and Dolk nearly bumped into him as the group crowded, their weapons ready.

Kron looked again. Further movement up the road near one of the houses. The other party was moving in.

Shadows appeared in the doorway of the sheriff's place, then a heavy figure stepped into the street.

Raising his bow, Kron aimed down the arrow at the target. The person appeared about the general size and shape of the wizard. Kron paused. He could not be sure. There was not enough light. The big person might be Fhaland, but it might also be someone else. Had that been a robe flapping about the person's legs? Kron couldn't tell, and he wasn't familiar with the local residents to know if any could be this person.

He lowered the bow and cursed under his breath.

Sergeant Rogins tapped Kron on a shoulder. When the man in black looked around, the sergeant held up a questioning hand.

Kron held up his own hand, a flat one to request patience and silence. Sounds of movement brought his head around the corner again.

There was a line of people shuffling their way out the front door of the sheriff's office. They moved slowly, mechanically, one step at a time. Each was in unison with the other. It was as if they were being controlled; Kron realized they probably were. After the execution of Korick, Fhaland needed a new crew. It seemed he had found it. When finished exiting the building, the line appeared to contain nearly twenty individuals, all lined up like a snake ready to slide forward. At the group's head were two burly figures, then a dozen or so men. Toward the back, those there were small. Children. More children.

One of the two at the front had to be Fhaland. Likely one of those at the back was the demon.

Kron cursed again. He and his partners were still too far away.

There was a shout from ahead, and suddenly the line began to turn, heading north toward the river.

And straight for Montolio, Thag and Makeshift.

32

"Oh, hell, they're making a break for the river," Sergeant Thag said.

With a double thump, Makeshift and Montolio landed in crouches behind the sergeant against a house, this one appearing whole. The two breathed heavily for a moment after their brief run from cover to cover.

Thag waved them toward the back of the house. "Go. Go!"

Without questioning, the corporal and wizard retreated, jogging toward where the house ended behind them, open fields beyond. Thag wasted no time and followed. At the end they rounded the corner, then all three dropped to their knees, the sergeant's head probing around the corner to where they had just been.

Slowly, the line from the sheriff's office appeared on the road at the front of the house.

"Too dark to take a shot," Thag whispered to the others. "Can't see who is who."

A slap on his back brought the sergeant around to face Makeshift.

"I'll go around to the other side, come up behind them," the big woman suggested.

Thag didn't like the idea of splitting their small group even further, but Makeshift could take care of herself. Plus, it might help if they had a better view of their potential targets, and Makeshift could get that if she was closer to the road behind the line of stilted, emotionless walkers.

He gave her a nod and she was off, her armor jangling about her shoulders. After a moment she disappeared at the far end of the house, covering its corner to head toward the front on the other side.

Thag looked to the wizard and tried to give a cheering smile, then realized his face probably couldn't be seen in the dark. He turned back to watch the road, the walkers filing past slowly, gradually.

33

His boots splattered with dried blood after walking through the remains of the priest's son, Sheriff Micklewhite marched at the head of the line. Ahead lay darkness, the vague glint of the river ahead and Fhaland's reassurances a ship would now be there waiting for them. Behind lay death and slaughter unbelievable. The sheriff's body was not in his own control, and his mind continued to retreat further and further. Part of him realized this way lay madness, but he saw no other option. There was no fighting this wizard's theft of Micklewhite's frame, and to think of vengeance or justice was absurd at this point. The best Micklewhite could hope for was a quick death, and there was little evidence such would be allowed.

Fhaland himself was at the head of the pack, with his little monster in charge of the children somewhere behind. If there was true remorse left within the sheriff, it concerned the children, but there was no hope for them nor for anyone else. The worst the world had to offer was now here, and nothing could be done about it.

They had not walked far from the jail building when the large wizard in the sashaying robes stepped to one side and held up a hand. The group came to a halt.

Micklewhite could barely make out the bulging face as the mage turned to him.

Fhaland's voice was a whisper. "It seems we have visitors. Not wholly unexpected, but nonetheless it is not impossible they could retard us reaching of our goal. Sheriff, I give you charge of the situation. Return to your weapons and deal with these meddlers."

Micklewhite's glazed eyes turned almost normal, the pupils rolling down and staring back at the wizard. For a moment the sheriff almost believed his freedom would be returned to him, but then he felt the muscles in his arms tighten and move, his legs twist and turn, marching him back toward the place that had once been his office.

34

Movement in the shadows. Someone big. A few houses ahead. Kron grimaced. Fhaland and his slaves were on the move, and it appeared at least Makeshift or Thag were moving in closer to the group. Not an optimal situation, but that was to be expected.

Without looking back, Kron said, "I'm heading in. Leapfrog two houses ahead, then watch my back. Anyone comes at me, pepper them with arrows."

He didn't wait for a response, but took off at a jog across the front of the nearest building, slapping boot steps from behind telling him Rogins and Dolk followed.

Halfway to his next hiding place, a large figure separate from the line of mesmerized slaves moved toward the back of the group and headed back to the sheriff's office. For a moment the figure crossed into the light spilling from the still open door and Kron could make out a burly man with gray chin whiskers. The fellow's eyes were dazed but he seemed intent upon a mission, tromping up the steps and disappearing into the office.

Kron dropped to the ground behind a house and heard his partners finding their own hiding places behind him. Ahead, the man in black could just make out a heavy figure in the shadows of the house the other side of the sheriff's office. Movement again. A glint of light on iron. A crossbow was being raised.

The line of slaves was suddenly moving again.

And the big man with the beard appeared in the doorway once more, this time hefting a large studded mace in one hand.

<u>35</u>

As the large fellow with the gray beard had shuffled past Makeshift's hiding spot, one of the children at the end of the line had turned to watch him. On second glance, the big woman realized that child was no child. The corporal had listened intently to Darkbow's description. The demon, it had appeared like a bald-headed boy, dressed in white robes from its neck to its feet. Of course that had been before it had exploded into some kind of monster made out of chains. Makeshift couldn't quite understand how a demon could be made out of chains, but none of that mattered at the moment. The demon was there at the end of the line.

She raised her crossbow and aimed down its length, lining up the end of the bolt with that pale, round head.

Just about to press the bar that would loose the arrow, a clatter to her right drew her attention. She glanced in that direction. There was the bearded fellow again, not a dozen yards away on the stoop of the sheriff's office. He stood there motionless, staring into the night, in one hand gripping a big mace with iron studs. Somehow he seemed familiar. He kind of looked like a man Makeshift had known years earlier when she had been a child. His name had been Micklewhite, and he had been a soldier. He had also been a family friend. It had been his tales at the kitchen table that had given Makeshift the notion of becoming a soldier herself. But that couldn't be him, could it? Micklewhite would be an old man now.

Her mind had wandered.

She shouldn't have let that happen.

She turned her gaze back to the demon.

And found it staring right back at her.

<u>36</u>

The demon exploded, covering the distance to Corporal Makeshift in a blink. One moment the beast appeared as the young boy in white, the next that vision was gone, replaced by a thing the size of a wagon sprouting iron tentacles dripping oil and flames. The chains shot out, engulfing Makeshift. The woman had just enough time to shout and loose her arrow, the bolt disappearing in the storm of links that enveloped her. The demon seemed not to notice the arrow. It melted over the large woman, chains upon chains drowning her.

It had all happened in a moment, in a flash. Kron had not had time to move.

Sending out an unheard prayer for the corporal, the man in black raised his bow.

The big fellow with the mace was suddenly standing in Kron's line of sight, blocking the path to the demon, the beast now sending forth crunching and slurping noises.

Kron almost let loose with his arrow. Almost. Then he lowered the weapon. Whomever this man was standing between him and the demon, he was not to blame for his being under the wizard's spell. Kron would not slay him without just cause, and it was already too late to save Makeshift.

A loud cracking sounded from the roiling demon, followed by a hiss. The monster screeched then pulled away from its meal, the blob of chains sliding back toward the unmoving line of children and people. The beast had come upon Makeshift's grenado of holy water. Kron grinned. At least the damned creature had paid some small price.

A shout went up from the front of the line. It was too dark to see what was happening, but Kron could sense much motion. Likely Montolio and Thag had entered the fray.

The demon recoiling in pain, and Fhaland seemingly occupied, it was time to act.

Kron dropped his bow and arrow and charged for the man with the mace. He might not be willing to kill the fellow, but if he presented a threat, Kron would have to disable him.

The mace came up, slowly, mechanically. It was hardly worth Kron's time, yet he slid to one side and snapped out a fist, whacking the man's wrist. There was a brief cry, then the studded weapon was falling.

Kron swung away toward the line of prisoners.

A bright, explosive light erupted like fireworks sparking against the night sky, outlining the unmoving figures ahead.

But suddenly they were moving. Their eyes blinked and their jaws fell. Their limbs shook and a tenseness in their shoulders collapsed. There were screams and shouts and tears. These people were no longer in Fhaland's thrall.

Kron skidded to a stop in the road and glanced back to the man he had disarmed. The fellow looked back, confusion in his eyes.

Which quickly turned to rage.

The man dipped and retrieved his weapon.

Kron would not wait to see if the coming attack was meant for him. He tugged at the sack on his belt and switched around to face the line and the demon once more.

The demon was gone. It had been there a moment earlier, but had vanished. The remaining townspeople were running around frightened, like chickens with their heads cut off. Quickly they disappeared into the night, most fleeing away from their homes, some few running one way or another down the street as if looking for loved ones. There was no need to search, however, because their loved ones were dead. Those who did not realize the truth would do so soon enough.

Kron's head swiveled from side to side. Where had the demon gone?

The man in black felt a presence at his side and shifted away, expecting an iron mace to come swerving in his direction. But there was no attack. Kron completed his spin and looked toward the heavy man with the beard. The fellow stood where Kron had a moment earlier, hate filling his red eyes as he stared into the night, the sounds of screams coming to them across the dark.

"Kill them," the man muttered under his breath. "Kill both of them."

Kron grabbed him by an elbow. A maddened face full of wrath glared back.

"You can't slay them on your own," Kron pleaded.

"I can try," the man said, "and after what I've seen today, death would be welcome."

Then he shrugged off the hand and charged into the night.

37

Makeshift was probably dead. Montolio was pretty sure of that. He hadn't seen what had happened on the other side of the house, but he had heard the woman's cry followed by all those crunching noises. He reminded himself to say a prayer for her if he lived through the next few minutes. As things stood, that was not looking likely, especially since Sergeant Thag had been split in two down the middle from head to crotch and the two pieces of the man were at Montolio's feet. A man split in half, yet somehow still blubbering. It was enough to draw one into madness.

Soon after that big fellow at the front of the line had disappeared down the road, that was when something bad had happened to Makeshift. That was also when Thag had had enough and charged ahead toward the road. Montolio had heard a spell muttered, then a flash of light and a meaty tearing sound. The architect had been too far behind, and blinded by the flash, to see exactly what had happened, but the evidence of the sergeant's fate was now at Montolio's feet.

He had stepped directly into the mess that had been Thag, the architect's shoes sinking into intestines and blood and who knew what other kinds of gore. There was nothing Montolio could do for the sergeant or the corporal, but he was a mage himself, and he could go down fighting this Fhaland.

His eyes had raised and through the darkness he had seen the massive robed figure standing on the road at the end of the alley between the two houses. There was steam strewing upward from one of the figure's chubby fists. That was the mage, Montolio was sure. That was his target.

He let loose with a spell of his own. A wave of magic rolled forth, hissing and smoking, tearing apart the edges of the walls lining the alleyway.

The shadowy, bulky figure on the road had shrugged. Then a wave of a hand had dissipated one of Montolio's most powerful spells, knocking it aside as a child would swat a fly.

The two stood there staring at one another across the darkness.

And that was when Montolio realized he was truly in trouble.

He was about to retreat when a chorus of cries went up from the road. The bulky figure of the wizard there turned to face the line of prisoners, shock plain on his face beneath the ashy light of the moon.

The slaves were now free.

So, Montolio's spell hadn't been a total waste of time. At the least, he had interrupted the other wizard's hold upon the last of the townspeople.

But soon enough they would be under Fhaland's spell again unless someone did something. As everyone else appeared to be dead at the moment, Montolio decided that someone had to be him.

He rushed forward, raising his arms for a spell. His enemy was no longer facing him, distracted by the chaos of those running to and fro on the street.

Montolio let loose with a blast of light.

The bolt caught Fhaland in the side, sending the big man reeling back into shadow.

Then the man with the beard was there once more. He no longer looked like an automaton. No, his emotions were quite clear on his face. Rage and hate. He moved into the shadows where Fhaland had fallen.

"Could it be over?" Montolio asked himself as he ran forward. If the dark mage was down, no better time than to hit him again.

He reached the edge of the street, a hint of light streaming to him from the sheriff's office several buildings down. Chaos was everywhere. The surviving townspeople were fleeing for their lives, and here came a flapping, cloaked figure in black charging right toward Montolio.

The wizard raised his hands for a strike, then realized it was Kron running at him. Montolio sighed. He had almost blasted the man.

There was a crunching sound to his left in the shadows, followed by a squeal and a grunt. Seemed the angry man was having his way with the wizard.

Until the night filled with fire.

38

Kron could make out Montolio straight ahead. The fellow with the mace had disappeared into the darkness on the other side of the road. Why he had gone that direction, Kron could not guess. But suddenly that fellow was no longer his concern.

The night lit up, a wall of fire springing forth from the very shadows where the angered stranger had run. The shadows disappeared as if the sun had risen early and the light burnished so strong Kron had to throw a hand up in front of his eyes as he came to a halt near Montolio.

The architect wizard cried out, shielding himself with an arm, then the fire was raining down upon them from on high. Kron grabbed Montolio and pulled him into the alley between two houses, dropping and throwing his cloak over the two of them. The thick black cloth was not much, but if the fires did not last long, perhaps it would be enough.

There was a groan and a scream, then a shout from the road.

The light died. All was black again.

A heavy huffing noise came from the street.

Kron was alive, so that much was still good. He lifted his cloak and allowed his eyes to adjust to the near darkness, tiny flames dancing upon the side of the house providing some view. Kron found himself face to face with Montolio, who stared back.

"We're alive," the mage said with a grin.

Another groan from the street.

Kron rolled over and pushed himself to his feet, the bag containing the largest of his grenados raised over his head and ready to strike.

But Fhaland and his demon were not to be seen. Instead, swaying in the middle of the street was the older man with the gray hairs and the mace. His clothes were singed and smoke rolled off his shoulders. His head hung low as if he were barely on his feet, but he had kept a hold on his heavy mace, the big weapon hanging from a beefy hand to one side.

Seeing the immediate menace was gone, Kron took a leery step forward. "Are you all right?"

Blackened eyes snapped up. "I will never be *all right* again."

Kron lowered the bag and held up a flat hand to show he meant peace.

The big man with the mace swung around to stare up and down the street. "Bastard got away from me."

Kron eased up nearer to him, but kept a distance. "The wizard?"

Dark eyes once more glared upon the man in black. "I almost had him. Got a couple of good blows in. Likely cracked some ribs. But now he's gone."

"Powerful," Montolio said, coming up to the pair. "Only the most powerful of mages can do such things, transporting themselves away like that."

Kron nodded agreement. He had witnessed such before.

"He likely isn't far," Montolio went on. "It takes concentration for such a spell, and I don't think he had time for that."

Their eyes darted everywhere, glancing into shadows, looking for Fhaland.

Sergeant Rogins and Dolk came trotting up at that time, their crossbows hoisted to their shoulders and ready to launch.

"Get the wizard?" Rogins asked as he and Dolk came to a halt.

Kron shook his head. "But Montolio thinks he's around somewhere. Probably licking his wounds at the moment."

Again, nervous eyes shifted in search.

"What of Thag?" Kron asked Montolio.

The wizard shook his head. "Makeshift?"

"Damn demon got her," Rogins said.

Kron turned to the remaining sergeant. "What of the demon? Did you see where it went?"

"Slipped down a lane between two houses," Dolk said, shivering. "Eerie thing. Slithered like a mound of snakes."

The big man with the mace stepped in front of Kron. "Just how many of you are there?"

"Four of us left," the man in black said.

"*Four?*" the man said. "I'm taking it your from Bond. Why didn't someone send an army?"

The four squad members looked at one, but it was Kron who spoke. "An army wouldn't have accomplished anything but gotten a lot of people killed."

The mace was swung about, motioning toward the town's remains. "If you haven't noticed, a lot of people were killed anyway."

"A lot more *then*," Kron said, his teeth gritted. "We wanted to hit the wizard and his demon before they knew we were here."

The mace lowered as the big man spat into the ground. "A lot of good it did. He knew you were here. Told me so while I was still under his spell."

Rogins stepped forward. "Look, the mage is hurt and so is his pet. It seems to me we've got them on the run. We can stand here and argue about what should have been done, but I'd say it's time we finished this."

Dark stares were shared. Finally, Kron spoke, "They know we're here, so no need to hide. We could use some light."

The big man pointed his mace toward the open door to the sheriff's building. "There are lamps and torches in my office."

"You're the sheriff?" Kron asked.

"Micklewhite," the big man said, "and I ain't the sheriff of anything anymore. There's not enough town left for a sheriff."

39

As the group made their way indoors, the enormity of the events of the last few minutes crashed over Montolio. Poor Makeshift was dead, and Sergeant Thag had been ripped apart before the architect's very eyes. His breath caught in his throat and he eased onto a chair near the door.

As he crossed the small front room to a desk, Kron paused and glanced at Montolio. "Are you going to be all right? You've gone pale."

The mage nodded and slowly sucked in air. For a moment his head swam, but he sat up straight, forcing himself to remain calm and alert.

It was true he was more an intellectual than an adventurer, and it was true bloodspilling was not common to his experience, but Montolio was not without some small acquaintance with the darker sides of the world. He shook his head to clear away his concerns, his fears. Another time. Now he had to focus. The full weight of the deprivations of Fhaland would have to wait, as would any tears for the dead. There were citizens of this town out there running scared, and a murderous wizard and demon were still on the loose.

He sat straighter and leaned back in the chair, his breathing coming normally.

The others had gathered at Micklewhite's desk where the sheriff was lifting a pair of bronze lamps from the floor and removing a handful of short torches from a drawer. The gray-headed man placed the items on the top of the desk next to his mace, then turned to face the others.

"You knew about this wizard?" the sheriff asked no one in particular.

"We followed him here from Bond," Kron explained. "He left behind a trail of tortured dead."

Micklewhite shook his head as he stared at the floor, and for the first time Montolio noticed that floor was caked in dried blood. There were torn, severed body parts piled in a corner. Legs. Arms. A head. A torso.

The wizard coughed and gagged.

A hand landed on his right shoulder. "Are you sure you will be all right?"

Montolio looked up into Kron's dark blue eyes. He winced. "I'll manage." His voice was weak.

Kron didn't look as if he believed, but he stood back and turned his attention to the others. How the man could ignore the carnage around him was beyond Montolio. For that matter, the others seemed to pay the blood and body parts little attention. The mage figured they were all soldiers of one stripe or another and had witnessed such devastation before.

"There's a squad watching the road to the south and another headed this way along the river," Kron told the sheriff.

Micklewhite looked up. "You were right outside there. An army would have been worse, charging in and a bunch of men getting killed. My apologies for my heavy words."

"None needed," Kron said. "You've ... been through a nightmare."

Straightening to stand at his full height, Micklewhite lifted his mace from the table and slid it into a loop on his belt. "Well, we've hurt the bastards, so I know they can be killed."

"Only magic will work against the demon," Kron pointed out. "Our blades have been touched by a wizard, and I have with me some holy water."

"I hope it's enough," Micklewhite said.

"It will be," Kron said. "Right now they're likely hiding out somewhere, one of the houses, or perhaps out in a field. We'll have to flush them, then finish the job. It won't be easy, but they're not going anywhere unless the wizard can sail his ship on his own."

The sheriff nodded. "I'll be going with you."

Kron looked to the man, then nodded. "One other thing. Did you see the wizard carrying any kind of bag or package?"

Before the sheriff could answer, Montolio was on his feet, horror dawning on his face. He had heard Kron's words about Fhaland and the demon searching for a place to hide. Then he remembered the broken tower where they had left the girl. The place had stood out on the horizon, making it the most logical place to draw their enemies.

"Oh, no," he said, drawing the looks of the others.

40

Death.
Death.
Death.
It was all that encompassed Leesa's thoughts as she sat there and rocked back and forth on the cold ground of the tower. Everyone she loved was dead. Everyone. No longer would she stare into the warm face of her mother as the woman stoked the stove to bake bread in the mornings. No longer would her father smile down upon her as he came in from a day's work. No more would she play with her friends, nor chat with the old lady who lived next door, nor eat pies from Hommel's lone inn. No more. No more anything. It was all gone.

The warriors who had come brought no hope. They were only men, like those of her village. They could not stand against the evil that now overran her home. And if by some miracle they could stomp out this vileness, what difference would it make now? Everyone was dead. Leesa had no family, no future.

She sat there, her arms bare as the night's cold wrapped around her, stealing her warmth. Her eyes were unblinking, locked upon a spot on the decaying wall opposite her. The girl's back was to the open door. The sound of the hobbled horses came to her ears, but that noise did not reach into her mind.

New screams came to her from the distance, but she seemed not to notice. Following soon after were the huffings and puffings of people outside, running past, not even stopping long enough to investigate the horses, if they even noticed the animals in the darkness.

Then silence returned. It was not the time of year for crickets, and the wind was not strong enough this night to spread its ghostly sound upon the land.

Leesa rocked and rocked, staring at nothing.

Eventually there was another sound, the shuffling of feet followed by heavy breathing. A gleam of light suddenly grew behind her, shedding its glow upon the dusty chamber. The horses neighed and whinnied, nervous.

Then a stilted voice sounded at the girl's back. "My, my. What is it we have here, Kry'lk?"

<u>41</u>

The plan was a simple one. If Fhaland and his monster were at the tower, the most logical direct point of attack would be from the village down the hill. And that was exactly what Kron Darkbow would give them. Only Montolio would use his magic to provide a bit of distraction, to make their enemies believe they were facing foes from the opposite direction, from the road and the woods to the east of the tower. Coming from the village might be the most direct approach, but Fhaland would realize this, and would expect his pursuers to advance from another direction. Or so everyone hoped.

Kron took the central point position, an arrow from his bow leading the way. The others fanned out behind the man in black, keeping some distance so as not to offer Fhaland a single, larger target for his spells. Unlit lanterns hung from belts, darkness having been decided as the key to any chance of success.

Halfway up the gradual hill to the tower, the leaning structure taking up most of their view ahead, Kron brought the group to a halt. They paused and listened, hearing and seeing nothing from their former hiding spot. Not even the expected horses ahead made a sound, which did not speak well for the animals' survival but gave some proof the wizard and demon had likely been there.

Silently, Kron eased back into the pack and patted Montolio on a shoulder.

The architect wizard's head bobbed in the darkness as he turned to face the bare outline of trees along the horizon on the far side of the tower. He muttered a few ancient words as his hands rose and waved.

A small burst of light among the trees, enough to provide a glow around the base of several of the stark oaks, enough to look like a torch burning in the distance. Montolio flicked a finger toward the light, then another luminous point joined the first, then another, and finally a fourth. Then followed a series of noises, gentle pattings as of men marching through the woods.

Montolio looked back to Kron, who nodded, then the five men continued their climb up the hill.

They had not gone far when Kron held up a gloved fist sketched against the backwoods glow. All halted. Kron motioned for the others to remain while he moved ahead, soon disappearing into the night.

Silence and stillness followed. Feet began to shuffle as the nerves of the others were stretched.

But then Kron appeared out of the gloom, marching straight toward the group.

"The horses are dead," he said, stopping as the four gathered around him, "their throats torn open. No sign of the girl."

Sheriff Micklewhite spat into the grass. "The bastards. Poor girl. No telling what they'll do to her."

"All the more reason to find them soon," Kron said.

"But where do we go from here?" Dolk asked.

Kron looked to Montolio. "Can you find them?"

The mage nodded. "I can, but my searching will draw Fhaland's attention, let him know where I am."

Kron hesitated, obviously weighing the situation, then, "Do it. If they are near, we will deal with them. If they are not, then they're no immediate threat."

Sergeant Rogins stepped forward, nearer to Kron. "Perhaps we should take this inside the tower, just so we are not so out in the open. I hate to think of them close by, and us vulnerable like this."

The hood of the man in black's cloak nodded. "Makes sense. Let's go."

The party turned as a whole and trudged toward the open door to the tower. While walking, Montolio snapped his fingers and his distant spell of distraction faded away, but not before the light had given him a grisly image of their dead steeds laying around the entrance. The poor animals had not stood a chance, hobbled as they had been.

As they reached the door, it was Rogins who entered first, pausing long enough to light the wick of his lamp. The others followed him, and soon they had a circle in the center of the room.

Kron glanced around. "No blood. She might still be alive."

The sergeant lifted his lantern to allow a better view upon the curved wall. Still no signs of violence.

Then he raised the light over his head and glanced upward. What he saw made him look again, this time with eyes full of awe and despair. His hands shook and he almost dropped the lamp.

No words were spoken. None were needed. All eyes saw the sergeant's reaction and all eyes turned up.

To find a web of thick, oily chains hanging spread across an upper level of the tower. The chains were thick enough to almost block out the night's sky.

There was a moment to curse.

Then the chains dropped.

With a horrible hissing noise.

<u>42</u>

Montolio was the most fortunate. He was closest to the door. Without thinking, he dove for the outside, landing hard on a shoulder and wincing at the pain.

The others were not so lucky.

Rogins and Kron were in the center of the room. As the chain demon fell, there was little time to react. The sergeant swiveled his crossbow so it pointed upwards and squeezed the weapon's lever. The arrow darted into the metallic mass, screeching as metal grazed metal. Kron tossed his long bow aside, the weapon useless in such tight confines. The man in black's hands went to his belt, one for the dagger on his left, the other for the bag holding the largest grenado.

Micklewhite and Dolk were between the door and the others. At first the burly workman was too surprised to do anything but stand there and watch doom fall from upon high, but then he lunged for the sheriff, landing atop him and taking him to floor. Micklewhite cursed and attempted to throw off the man, then realized the futility of such and raised his mace to one side as if to shield off the oncoming demon.

Then all but Montolio were enveloped, buried beneath weighted chains of all sizes, colors and metals. They were swamped in an ocean of swirling iron and bronze and brass.

43

Dolk was going to die. He knew that much. It had been a shit of a life, barely getting by on the streets of Bond from an early age, turning to the bottle when he got older, whoring, busting other men's bones for pay, all in the name of survival. He had eaten cat on more than one occasion, and had even stooped to rat soup when necessity had raised its ugly head. A couple of times he had killed men, just for a few extra coppers, just to be able to put food in his mouth.

But then things had changed, and not so slowly. He had lucked into a bricklayer's job with old Felton Keldaris. Felton had been a tough one, but somehow he had seen promise in Dolk's eyes. For the first time in his life, Dolk had actually had someone else who depended upon him, even if it was only to show up for work on time and to put in a day's labor. It had been enough. The bottle had been tossed aside, life on the streets had been pushed back. Dolk didn't have much, a room above a whore house, a bag full of silvers stuffed beneath a mattress, but it was a start, a start to a future he now realized he would never have.

When that thing had fallen from above, when that wide expanse of iron links had looked him in the eye and then plummeted, Dolk had briefly thought of himself. What to do? How to survive? But he had quickly surmised there was no survival from this, not for him.

Perhaps, however, he could save someone else.

That sheriff, Micklewhite, had been the closest. Dolk didn't know the man, but he seemed an okay sort, a little tense perhaps, but what man wouldn't be warped by all the terrors that had been going on? Dolk couldn't blame a man for being a little rough around the edges, especially after all he had seen in the last day.

With those final thoughts, Dolk had gripped the sheriff and taken him down onto the dirt floor. Their faces almost touching, Micklewhite's cry caught the worker in the face, spittle raking his nose. Then their eyes locked onto one another, and Dolk only hoped the old man realized what Dolk was doing for him.

Before Dolk could explain, before he could hope to explain, he was swimming in metal seemingly almost molten. It wrapped around him, devouring his limbs. An iron snake wrapped around his neck and squeezed, misting blood and separating his head from his body. The pain was brief, then Dolk knew no more.

44

The arrow had been useless. Despite the added magic from the healer in Bond, the corporal's crossbow and its quarrel had done nothing to stem the plunging demon.

Before Rogins could act further, the monster's chains consumed him, taking him to the floor hard enough to knock the breath from the sergeant's lungs.

His thoughts turned to Jenna. Two years it had taken him to rise to corporal, then another to make sergeant. Only three years since he had enlisted. He was the youngest sergeant the city guard had ever known, not even in his mid-twenties yet. He had saved his coin, as had Jenna with her position as a sewer of gloves with that seamstress in Southtown. They were setting it all aside, to buy some little place on the edge of the city, someplace not quite in the country, a place where they could have a little girl or a little boy, maybe a dog or a cat. Rogins would raise squash and pumpkins in their garden, and Jenna would sow beans upon the hillside behind their place. Then after his twenty years of service, he could retire in his early forties and the two of them could spend their days together forever, living off his pension and raising their children, feeding the cat and kicking the dog from time to time.

It would have been a life.

A life that never came.

But still, it all flashed before the young man's eyes as tendrils scored across his body, curling and embracing him as if he were a meal.

His vision went dark, and he tried to reach out with a grasping hand as rage filled his soul.

Jenna!

I will be coming home to you tonight!

I will *ask the question! Finally, after your years of pleading.*

I will not die like this!

I love you! I love you! I have always lo --

45

As much of a surprise as the demon's ambush had been, it paled into comparison with Dolk's actions. The big man had grabbed Micklewhite and pulled him to the floor, the burly worker planting himself on top of the sheriff. Micklewhite had struggled, sensed the futility of it, then raised an arm to one side and lifted his mace as if it could ward off the falling monster.

Micklewhite had stared into Dolk's eyes for a moment, just before the demon thing had enveloped them, ensnared them, folding them within a sea of rasping metal. Then a blackened, steaming coil had twined around Dolk's neck and squeezed. Blood had sprayed, covering the sheriff's face so he could barely breathe or see, and Dolk's head had popped off and rolled to one side into the maelstrom of links.

One more horror, one more tragedy, in a day of horrors and tragedies.

A brief moment of regret for a man he did not even know, then the rage flowed back into Micklewhite's bones. He screamed and kicked and lashed out with his mace, suddenly wishing he had taken one of the offered weapons from the soldiers from Bond. They had said their blades had been enchanted by some wizard, and perhaps that would make a difference. Instead, Micklewhite was left swinging iron against iron, a futile effort at best. But Dolk's body was still atop him, the open neck pouring blood all over him, slicking his chest and hands. The body provided some few moments of protection from the worst of the demon, and it still carried Dolk's weapons, the ones that had been touched by the wizard.

Micklewhite let go of his preferred weapon and plunged a hand down between himself and the flopping corpse that held at bay the swarm of iron and bronze. His fingers brushed against a wooden handle, a sword or knife, and he gripped the pommel, tugging the blade up and up until it was before his face.

A short sword.

It would have to do.

Screaming, he tried to push aside Dolk's body, but the weight of the writhing chains atop them was too much.

Ah, well. He could still stab out at his sides.

Which he did.

To an impressive spark of fire and a howl from the demon.

46

I will not die here. There is the girl to think of, and oh, so many others.

Those were Kron's thoughts as the monster descended. His dagger came free of its sheath, but the grenado bag caught on his belt as he was hammered to the floor by the weight of chains.

Forgetting the holy water for the moment, Kron punched up with the dagger, glad to hear metal barking against metal.

Then he could breathe no more. Hundreds, thousands, millions of steel appendages layered him, wrapped around him, pressing in upon him.

There was a splash of blood somewhere to Kron's right, followed by a scream that sounded as if it came from Micklewhite.

Kron could barely move as entwined as he was, the chains tearing at his clothing and pressing his flesh, but he managed to twist the dagger in his hand from side to side, scouring the links in some little fashion.

Let there not be fire this time.

It was his only true fear.

He punched with the dagger again. A hiss from the demon.

He could fight his way free of this, but only if there were no flames.

He felt the warmth, the chains growing heated.

Soon there would be fire.

And death.

<u>47</u>

Ignoring the pain in his shoulder, the architect rolled over onto his back and stared at the mass of metal links dipping and diving repeatedly within the confines of the tower. It looked like a giant soup of iron, boiling and bubbling. Arms of chain kept rising and falling, slashing and burrowing into itself. Montolio had heard a cry, perhaps even a roar of rage and a hiss, but he could no longer see any signs of his comrades.

The architect discerned he was the only hope any of them had, if they were even alive. Only seconds had passed, but was that too long? He forced himself to his feet, hoping the precious moments it took to do so would not cost others their lives.

Words of magic, ancient words, words discovered and first written down by a race older than men, spewed from Montolio's lips. He spoke quick, so quick he feared he might mismanage the pronunciations, though he knew the truth was the words themselves were nearly meaningless, little more than an interface to draw forth the magic of the soul. A flare glowed from the ends of his fingers, shot forth, tearing into the waves of chains dancing through the crumbling doorway.

<u>48</u>

I know of you, Darkbow, spoke the voice in Kron's head. *Word of you has spread among my brothers and sisters. Tales of you have riven hell, bringing trepidation. And here I find you nothing more than the others, the puny mortals, flesh and bone to be stripped and sucked dry. Know this, fool, here you do not face a war demon, a creature of mere might. No, you are in the arms of* ashashi kul kanon, *an assassin demon! And I will enjoy spending centuries devouring your soul.*

Kron grunted and stabbed out with his dagger. "Then shut up and get on with it!"

49

Shimmering lines of magic continued to roil forth from the ends of Montolio's fingers. At first there seemed to be little effect upon the demon, then smoke began to rise from the mass of undulating chains.

A scream of pain, a throaty bawl, and the chains were more active than ever, rising, climbing, moving away from the floor of the tower, reaching up the inside walls, tearing at brick and wood and stone and air in a sudden burst to escape, to flee the anguish caused by the wizard's magic.

A pale, outstretched arm gripping a mace was the first sign of any survivors. Montolio blinked, realizing that had to be the sheriff's arm, then he rushed forward, grabbing at the thick wrist and pulling. The demon cooperated, its thousands of chain links sliding away, crawling up the insides of the tower to seek escape. Micklewhite's blood-splattered face became visible, the man's cheeks puffed and blue, his eyes glazed.

Montolio tugged on the heavier man. The architect was the smallest of the group, but adrenaline was running high in his blood, making him the strongest. With a noise of metal rending, he pulled the sheriff free from the few remaining chains, Micklewhite spilling out on the ground as Montolio fell next to him.

There was a final screech and cry, then the last of the demon could be seen through the doorway.

Montolio glanced at the sheriff, saw the man was breathing, then moved forward once more. The others had not been engulfed long. They had to be alive. They had to be.

What he found inside the tower brought him to his knees.

Dolk was in pieces, torn limb from limb. Montolio shed a tear for this one, knowing some of the fellow's rough past. Dolk had been looking to start new, to start fresh, and had proven himself to be a smart, talented and assiduous worker. Despite his past, Dolk was a man who would be missed.

Movement caused the architect's eyes to rise. Across from him sat the man in black, a blonde head resting in his lap. Sergeant Rogins was splayed out upon the ground, his body crushed, little more than bruised flesh beneath bones of dust. Kron stared unblinking down into the still face, the skull within the only remaining portion of the skeleton seemingly intact.

A scurrying noise caused Montolio to look up. The moon revealed the final snaky limbs of the monster disappearing over the broken ledge of the top of the tower, the demon fleeing to its master.

The mage sighed and realized he had been holding his breath. He took in air and lowered his eyes to look back to Kron.

Darkbow gently placed the sergeant's head on the ground, then rolled his shoulders and lifted to his feet, his gaze locked onto that of the dead man now at his feet.

Montolio stood, glancing behind to see Micklewhite slowly rising onto his elbows.

"What do we do now?" the wizard asked.

Kron's eyes snapped up, causing Montolio to flinch. There was so much hate, so much rage, that look was enough to shiver the architect's knees.

"We find them and we kill them," Kron stated.

50

Beneath quivering torchlight the three survivors went to work covering their dead comrades with blankets and retrieving what gear they wanted from the remains of their horses. Each realized proper burials would have to wait for all the dead, as time was important. A little girl might still be alive, might be in need of them.

Rubbing at his strained shoulder while hefting the freshly loaded crossbow that had once belonged to Rogins, Montolio turned to Kron. "Where do we go now?"

There was no question of not continuing. There was no question of waiting for others. They had a task to accomplish.

Kron stared off into the darkness that was the town. For a moment Montolio thought the man in the dark, tattered garb might not have heard his question, but then Kron turned to face the other two.

"The ship," Kron said. "Without a crew Fhaland might not be able to move the ship for any length of time, but he has gorged himself on souls this day."

Montolio nodded agreement. "That's how he brought it here from Bond, after ... feeding."

"So it's to be a direct assault, then?" Micklewhite asked.

"I'll take the center of the road leading to the dock," Kron said. "Sheriff, if you would take the left side, off in the treeline, then Montolio can take the right. I want each of you with a crossbow."

"What are you going to do?" the mage asked.

Kron stared off in the distance for another moment, then he looked back to the others. "I'm going to walk right up to them and cut them down."

51

Would Fhaland wait for them? Kron believed so. Micklewhite had told them the wizard had been waiting for the ship to rise from the river's depths, but that had been some little time ago, perhaps hours. It did not matter, however. Kron and those who had fallen around him had proven themselves more than a simple thorn in the sides of the mad mage. Fhaland would want vengeance, especially after his demon had time and time again proven less than a challenge.

Marching down the center of the dark street where the bricks ran into the dirt path heading to the river, Kron could make out glimpses of Montolio and the sheriff moving at his sides, the two men forcing their way through scrub and around taller bushes and trees. Straight ahead the river rolled beneath the moonlight as it likely had for thousands of years. The wooden dock could be seen in the distance, resting along the shore, but of the Khadiran cog there was no sign.

It did not matter. The ship would be somewhere close by, and thoughts of this assured Kron the girl Leesa would still be alive. Fhaland would want her to ensure Kron and the others would be drawn to him. After the coming confrontation, Fhaland would save the girl for future use. The notion caused the man in black's shoulders to shudder.

As he trod forward, the width of the river growing in his sight, he unfurled the bag from his belt and withdrew the sizable grenado Montolio had prepared for him in Bond. This weapon had been created only a day earlier, but it felt as if hundreds of years had passed. Castles had been built, empires had grown and crumbled, whole peoples had risen from the dust only to disappear beneath the tramping boots of history. It was not the truth, but it felt as if such.

Kron gritted his teeth. Too many had died by Fhaland's will. Who would be the last? Would it be Kron himself? Or Micklewhite or Montolio? Perhaps the girl Leesa? Or would these two beasts ahead survive the day and escape to other climes, to places where they are unknown and could spread their pain with ease?

No. It would end here. It *had* to end here. There had been enough death and torture and rape. At times it seemed the world thrived on such anguish. But Kron Darkbow would not stand for it, not today.

He tossed aside the now empty bag and with his free hand reached up to grasp the handle of his sword. The heavy blade came free and he swung it around in front of himself, the grenado gripped tightly in his other fist.

Almost to the river, the ship made an appearance. The vessel bobbed in the moving waters slightly to the west, just on the edge of where the dock ended. The trees had hidden the ship until now, but moving forward Kron gained a view straight at it.

He paused in his steps, as did the two hiding in bushes at the sides of the road, and allowed his eyes to linger on the floating craft. A lantern hung low from the single, thick mast, shedding a blush of light across the deck. There were no other signs of their enemies.

"It seems we are expected," Kron said of the light.

There were no answers from his companions. None were expected. They were not fools, and would say nothing to give themselves away so soon.

Trusting the others to follow, Kron marched on, moving ahead with the grenado gripped to his chest and his sword stretched out to one side. His boots scraped wood as he crossed onto the dock, continuing casually, slowly toward the gently rocking ship.

Halfway to the vessel, a thin, tinkling sound caused him to balk at going further. He halted, straining his ears. The metallic clinking din came from the ship. His sword shifted around in front and he moved forward one wary step at a time, his shredded cloak hanging behind like something dead.

He stopped before the gangplank, staring across the narrow gulf to the cog's deck where the source of that hesitant sound was revealed. Individual links of chain were rolling about on the wood, sliding across the deck toward one another, binding with one another, building upon one another. Within the blink of an eye, several small chains had been completed. Another blink and the chains were longer and growing. Popping and chinking noises pervaded the air as link met link.

Behind the man in black, Montolio and Micklewhite exited the trees by the road and approached, keeping their distance out to the sides.

The chains were a pile now with more links being added all the while. The tiny iron and bronze circlets rolled and skidded from the gunwale where they appeared from over the side, as if they had been climbing from the water.

Kron glanced beneath the boarding plank, saw only the rushing river, then boldly took several steps across to the vessel itself. As he stepped foot onto the deck, the chains erupted into a column nearly as tall as himself. From behind, Montolio and Micklewhite raised their crossbows.

Before an attack could be made, a thick, soupy fog folded over the chains, covering them in entirety. The little links no longer floundered about, but had all disappeared within that monument of smoke. There was a popping sound, soft, and the smog rolled away, trailing down the figure now standing where the chains had recently been. Floating across the deck, the smoke drifted away as if a light breeze has assaulted it.

Standing before Kron, only yards away, was the figure of the small, pale-headed boy wrapped in white robes. The image was a lie, and why the beast had chosen such a visage Kron could not fathom. It was a travesty upon the mind. The monster stared back at him. Its eyes flared, and a thin smile cracked its lips.

Kron smiled back and lifted the grenado directly over his head, but not as if for a toss. His sword followed on the other side, the weapon's grip now adjacent to the throwing weapon.

"Let us finish this," the man in black said. His few words were filled with hate and bravado. This creature was no fighter, but a mere butcher. It had showed itself time and time again to flee at the first hint of injury caused by an opponent. All it was good for was killing those who would not fight back. There was little reason to fear this thing in Kron's mind.

Yet the demon's smile grew wider.

As did Kron's.

The man in black glanced upward, at his weapons, then he raised the sword slightly higher and smashed it against the grenado. A crack appeared in the clay, growing and growing.

Kron closed his eyes as the cool holy water washed down upon him, splashing his face and drenching the top of his shirt.

His chin lowered and he stared across at the demon as the remains of the grenado were discarded.

The demon no longer smiled.

Kron charged.

52

Two crossbows twanged and their bolts slammed into the pale figure of the boy. The creature grimaced and hissed, the magic-enhanced arrows harming the beast but not taking it down.

Kron gave the demon no time to attack. His assault was brutal and wild. He bound across the distance separating the two and waded into the monster, his bastard sword now gripped in both hands, the heavy blade chopping into the youth's left shoulder and sinking deep as if burrowing into meat.

The demon threw back its round head and let loose with a roar that shook the boards beneath Kron's boots.

But Kron did not relent. He tugged back his sword, spraying black oil that appeared to be the creature's blood.

Before he could swing again, the demon exploded, the vision of the boy vanishing as the thing's many arms of chain links discharged, shooting toward Kron and all around him.

The heavy sword came up, across Kron's chest, knocking aside several of the reaching limbs, but others made it past his defenses. A trio of iron tentacles wrapped Kron's arms. Another pair tackled his legs, pulling him down.

"Do something!" Micklewhite shouted to the mage.

Montolio dropped his crossbow at his feet and pointed at the demon while long chains drove through the air for himself and the sheriff. There was a cold flash of light and those approaching arms halted as if stung, then quickly withdrew toward the mass of writhing chains that was the body of the beast.

Within the maelstrom of tentacles, Kron found himself on his back being pulled toward a gigantic maw of teeth. His legs were pinned as were his arms. He realized there was little hope for him unless Montolio cast another spell and soon. Then hope returned. A chain snake twirled itself around the black figure and began to squeeze. For a moment Kron felt the breath forced from his lungs and the creak of his ribs, but smoke began to rise from the encircling appendage.

The demon hissed again and the many arms suddenly withdrew, dropping Kron onto the deck once more.

The holy water had done its work.

The man in black spun around to his feet, facing the retreating creature. As he had predicted, the monster was rolling itself toward the railing on the far side of the ship, the many arms of metal flashing out, grabbing hold of the mast and anything else it could find to pull itself away from danger.

Not this time, Kron swore to himself. The creature could not be allowed to escape again. This must end.

Black boots thumped against wood and carried Kron forward. His sword rose high above his head then slammed down, steel scraping into iron and bronze and all the metals of the chains. Sparks illuminated the deck and links flew through the air. From somewhere deep within the swollen object that was the demon's body, the monster howled its pain. It was not enough for Kron. It would never be enough. He hacked and hacked, his sword biting again and again into softer metals.

Montolio added to the melee, sending forth streams of magic that blasted at the flailing chain tendrils, forcing them to withdraw as they melted at their ends.

Sheriff Micklewhite huffed as he crossed the gangplank onto the ship, his hands busy at loading his crossbow. Once on the deck, he dropped to a knee and took aim. His arrow sailed straight, diving into the center of the mad beast.

In the middle of the chaos of combat, Kron Darkbow stood with legs apart, his sword rising and falling, rising and falling. As he did, the demon seemed to withdraw before his eyes. The thing from hell was losing its seemingly endless arms of metal. One by one those tentacles were cut through, their ends falling useless to the deck before turning into a black mist that sailed away upon the night air. Steel and magic combined again and again to tear into the monster, slicing through to its core.

When the beast was little more than the size of a man, the last of its chain arms snapped back toward it, into it. Appearing before its attackers was the form of the boy in white robes, its bald head now covered in red, bleeding scars as it lay on the deck.

The assault ended for the moment. Kron stood over the creature, his chest rising and falling. Behind him, Micklewhite moved to one side and aimed his weapon again while Montolio busied himself preparing his own bow.

The eyes of the boy-thing were muddled, rolling around in its head. Then it blinked and looked up at Kron. Its eyes pleaded, asking for mercy, for protection. It was just a boy, those eyes said, harmed and lonely and in pain, needing someone to comfort it, like a child needing a mother. All it needed was love, and then the world would be all right. Love would make it all better. Love would end the pain. Love would bring them all together.

It was a lie. Not for everyone, not for all times and all places. But here, love was being used for a lie. This much Kron knew.

He flipped his sword around over his head in a double backwards grip so the long blade pointed at the demon. Then he thrust, the man in black putting all his weight into the blow, leaning over the sword's pommel and pressing down, forcing the sword to slide into the chest of the beast and deeper, into the wood of the ship.

That small, round head craned back to one side. The lips parted wide in a silent howl, tiny, pointed teeth revealed in the depths of the mouth.

The chin fell to the chest.

Wisps of smoke drifted up from the body. The remains convulsed, shook, then went motionless. The smoke drifted higher and grew in darkness until fully black.

By the time Kron tugged his blade free, there was no more body. Even the white robes had vanished.

The man stared at the incision his weapon had made in the deck He swayed on his feet as if exhausted, then turned to face his companions. "Now for Fhaland."

53

Micklewhite approached cautiously, his crossbow still at the ready. "Is the demon dead?"

Using the back of a glove, Kron wiped the sweat from his brow and nodded. "Or as near. I've had other dealings with the like. My understanding is they are banished to where they cannot return, at least for some while."

The wizard came up to the others. "That is my understanding as well."

The sheriff glanced about. "Where to now? Where is this mage?"

His sword returning to its sheath on his back, Kron gestured around the deck. "The two of you wait here. I'll look below." He drew forth a dagger.

Micklewhite stepped in front of him. "We can't let you go alone. That madman could slaughter you."

"I concur," Montolio said. "Our weapons were charmed against the demon, but if you face Fhaland alone, it will be only your steel against his sorcery."

A smirk formed on Kron's lips. The grin was dark enough, disturbing enough, to cause the others to take a step back. "I expect close quarters below," Kron said. "He will not have room to avoid me, and little room to get off a spell before I can plunge a knife into his heart."

Micklewhite frowned. "That's *if* he is below."

"If not, then I have nothing to fear," Kron said.

Then he turned toward the quarterdeck, his boots carrying him to the closed doors leading to the lower levels of the vessel.

"For some reason," Montolio said, watching the back of his dark-garbed friend, "I doubt he fears anything either way."

<u>54</u>

A wall of darkness greeted Kron as he proceeded to the levels below the main deck. Not even wan light from the open doorway intruded upon this domain of ebony. It was unnatural. Most men would have known fear upon entering such blackness, but Kron Darkbow was not other men. He believed long ago he had witnessed the worst the darkness had to offer, and he had survived it. At a young age he had claimed the night, prowling about the streets of Bond, crawling the forests of the Prisonlands. There was nothing he feared in the dark. The lack of light was his friend, his companion, his lover.

Though he did not fear the dark, he was no fool concerning it. The enchanted dagger leading the way, he slipped a glove against one wall and moved forward, the tips of his boots searching out ahead to save him from a stumble.

The blackness seemed to grow heavier, almost thick as if made of wet sand. There was sorcery here, evidence the wizard was near. It seemed Fhaland was as much a coward as had been his demon. There was proof enough in this in that he had allowed his monster to fight alone, unaided. Now, somewhere here below decks, another monster sheltered, a monster possibly with a little girl as hostage or worse.

Pressing into the inkiness, Kron felt his limbs stiffen. It was as if he were wading through mud. His legs became weighted and could barely move. His arms slumped beneath an unseen burden, unable to lift above even his belt.

He allowed himself to come to a halt to give himself time to comprehend. Fhaland had placed a ward of some type, likely an enchantment. Kron was familiar with such, had been trained in the Lands how to deal with such. Mostly it was a matter of will. Who was the stronger of mind? Kron or the dark mage?

There was little doubt in the man in black's mind. Fhaland was vicious, a killer and rapist, but he was also pathetic for those very same reasons. Kron himself was a killer, but to his mind there was a chasm between what he was and what Fhaland had become. Kron did not enjoy killing, though he did revel in the thrill of combat. He killed only when necessary, only when justice was served, though that had not always been his mindset. Kron had killed in the name of vengeance before, numerous times, but that was no longer his goal. He was a different man now.

Yes, there was a difference between himself and Fhaland. The mind of the mage could not hope to strangle that of Kron Darkbow.

Kron shook off the spell and moved forward once more. It was as simple as that. With the failure of Fhaland's magic, the blackness seeped away. There was still little light, though a glow peeked from behind Kron through the hatch where he had entered. He found himself in a narrow passageway with a door at the end.

With the release of the darkness also came new sounds, a soft thumping and a weak cry ahead on the other side of the door.

Kron rushed ahead. He did not bother to try the door but bashed into with his shoulder. Wood splintered and the portal burst open.

Before him was what appeared to be the quarters of a sea captain or some other officer. A heavy oak table was bolted to the floor in the middle of the room. The wall to the left was covered with pinned vellum maps. The wall to the right was bare other than a closed porthole, beneath a small bed also bolted down.

Lying in the center of the bed was Leesa, her eyes wide and full of fear. Her arms were at her side and her legs were tightly together as is she were tied. She was nude, her clothing in a huddle on the floor beneath her feet.

Kron would not look at the girl, not as she was. Her torment had been enough, and there was little reason to raise her shame further. He raised his head and found himself staring into the black, hollow eyes of the wizard.

Fhaland stood over the girl. He wore no clothes and his fat body glistened in the candlelight from the table. He did not appear human, but like some giant slug ready to pounce upon the girl. In one hand was a slim dagger of bronze. His other hand was between his legs holding his own member. Sweat dripped from his face.

The wizard opened his mouth to speak.

Kron would have none of it. There was nothing Fhaland could say he wanted to hear.

He charged the short distance, punching out with the pommel of his dagger. Steel connected with bone through flesh and there was a crunching sound. Fhaland crumpled to the floor, dropping his stiletto and laying unmoving.

Kron stood over the massive body for a moment, his breast heaving, his eyes full of hate. He lifted his dagger and his hand shook as his fingers tightened their grip. He could do it. It would be so easy, and justice would be served. Fhaland deserved to die, deserved worse than death.

The hand holding the dagger shook harder and harder.

Then slowly lowered. No, Kron would not kill a helpless figure, regardless of how horrible a villain this wizard was.

His gaze shifted to that of the girl. She still lay on the bed, her body stiffened but her eyes moving. Those eyes, they beseeched, they begged.

"Can you move?" Kron asked.

She said not a word. The spell must still be in effect while Fhaland lived.

Kron reached down to his belt and grabbed the silken cord there attached to a hanging grapnel. The cord was strong, able enough to carry his own hefty weight, but could it hold someone as large as Fhaland? He did not wish to take chances. He glanced about the chamber but saw no sign of another rope. With an eye remaining on the downed wizard, he twisted his head to face the ceiling. "Micklewhite!"

"I am here!" came the muffled yell from the deck above.

"Bring a rope!" Kron shouted. "Plenty of it!"

There was a shuffling and stomping above, but Kron knew the two would have little trouble finding a rope aboard a ship. He returned his attention to the girl.

"Can you say anything?" he asked.

Still not a word, not a move.

The heavy figure of the sheriff bounded into the doorway, a coil of hemp over one arm. "Gods, man, is he still alive?"

Kron looked to Micklewhite then back to the curled up figure of Fhaland. "He lives. Tie him fast so we can be done with this business."

The sheriff tromped forward and dropped to his knees next to the wizard. He spit on the floor next to Fhaland, then began to uncurl the rope. "We should kill him now for what he's done."

"I won't disagree," Kron said, "but there are questions needing answered."

Micklewhite's thick fingers worked fast, binding the wizard's hands and feet. "There are no answers worth the lives of those he tormented."

"True," Kron said, "but there was a bag of bones dug up and taken from Bond. In and of themselves they might be nothing, but I would hazard a guess Fhaland had some use for them. If we can discover what he had planned, perhaps we can save lives by finding these bones."

The sheriff huffed and puffed and sat back on his heels. "All right. I'm finished with him. What now?"

"Can you carry him?" Kron asked.

"Nope," the sheriff said, "but I'd be glad to drag him."

"Good enough." The man in black slammed his dagger home and turned toward the girl. "I'm going to lift you now, then I'll carry you upstairs. Do you understand?"

Nothing from her other than a flicker of her eyes. At least she was conscious, meaning she likely understood. Kron hoped so. The poor thing had been distressed enough.

He bent and cloaked a sheet over the girl, then wrapped his arms around her, lifting. For a moment she was heavier than he expected, but then he managed to bear her in his arms as if she were a baby.

"I'll be right behind you," Micklewhite said.

Kron moved ahead into the hallway as the sheriff grunted behind him and began to slide the massive wizard toward the door. Pausing to watch Micklewhite for a moment, Kron was surprised the man was having such an easy job of it. True, the man had size and muscle, but Fhaland was a monster of a man, easily weighing at least as much as two normal men.

"Go on," the sheriff said as he pulled the unconscious figure to the door. "He's out of it and tied. I can manage."

Kron nodded and turned into the darkness of the passageway. He worked his way through by memory and soon enough found the exit to the deck above.

He clambered into the flickering light of the torches and found Montolio standing near the gangplank, a crossbow cradled in the mage's arms.

Montolio's eyes went wide. "Kron! That's not --"

The words were not fast enough.

The bundled girl in Kron's arms convulsed and suddenly seemed much heavier, so heavy the violently shaking figure bore the man in black to the ground. Before the dark warrior could react, the girl's body bubbled, growing twice the size it had been, then again, and again.

Kron found himself under a pile of ever-growing, quivering flesh, sweaty and covered with short, prickling hairs. Where Leesa's face had been there was now a distorted monstrosity, a bulge with a mouth stretching wider and wider.

Montolio raised his crossbow to a shoulder.

A heated blast of air shot forth from the giant, shapeless thing, catching the wizard in the chest and hurtling him backward off the ship between the cog and shore. A splash followed.

Meaty weight continued to press upon Kron, forcing his lungs closed and nearly smothering his face. He snarled and grimaced as the stinky flesh grew and grew, coming closer and closer to his lips and nose. Barely able to move, fortune had been with him once more. He could not reach the dagger on his belt, but his hands were near one another. If he could adjust his fingers just enough ... there, he had hold of one of the small throwing darts from the back of his left glove.

He jabbed.

What followed was a howl of pain. The giant blob of flesh twisted and rolled, trundling away from the warrior it had covered.

Lovely air suddenly filled Kron's lungs, and he gave himself a moment to breathe in more and more.

By the time he looked up, the monstrosity was gone, replaced by a naked, limping Fhaland, a red hole draining blood down his left leg.

"I have had *enough* of you!" the wizard spouted, pointing a hand at Kron.

Suddenly Micklewhite was in the open doorway. "What the hell is --"

A cold wave smacked against the sheriff, knocking him into darkness once more.

It was the distraction Kron needed.

The throwing dart hastened across the distance between the two, impaling the mage on the back of his outstretched hand. He howled again, cursed and turned toward the gangplank.

Two more darts sailed after him, one tearing at a shoulder before flitting on into shadows, the other planting itself directly between the man's shoulder blades.

Fhaland cried out and lurched forward, shuffling away into the night.

Kron gyrated onto his feet, grabbing a near torch and holding it just inside the entrance to the lower decks. Micklewhite was sitting there on the floor, rubbing and shaking his head.

"How do you fare?" Kron asked.

The sheriff's head turned up, hate in his eyes. "I'll be fine. Get after him, man."

"The girl?"

"She appeared just as you reached up here. She's quiet, but otherwise appears whole."

Kron nodded and twisted around. He trotted to the edge of the ship and looked over the rail.

Montolio was down below treading water. His face was upturned. "Did you get him?"

"No, but he's in bad condition."

"Finish it," the mage said. "I can wait."

Looking back to the sheriff, Kron dropped his rope and grappling hook on the deck. "Micklewhite, if you please?"

The big man came rumbling out of the hatch. "Go on, go on. I'll pull him up."

Kron nodded his thanks, then almost jumped across the gangplank, his sword coming out and directing the way next to his torch.

55

The man in black did not have far to go. He came upon Fhaland only a hundred yards from the ship, the limping mage now covered in a gray robe as he passed down the street between the empty houses that had once been homes to the villagers of Hommel. From where had the robe come? Likely magicked, but that was of little concern to Kron Darkbow.

The wizard's back was to him as Kron came up behind the man, hanging back just out of sword reach but keeping pace with the lumbering villain. Fhaland's breathing was heavy, and despite the chill winter air, perspiration stood out on his neck beneath the dark curls bouncing atop his head. The man took a step and hitched, took a step and hitched. It would have been pathetic if Fhaland were not so evil and twisted.

Eventually the mage sensed the torchlight behind him and he stumbled forward, catching himself with his arms outstretched before spinning around.

The end of Kron's sword stuck against the flesh of Fhaland's throat. The wizard went still.

"Give me a reason," Kron said between gritted teeth, "and I spill your blood here."

Weary eyes looked up from beneath sweaty locks hanging in the mage's face, and now Kron could see the man's wounds continued to bleed.

Fhaland's gaze lowered. "If you are going to kill me, then do it."

The sword tapped the chin, raising it, and Kron's steel gaze glared into the mage's face. "What makes you think you deserve a quick death?"

Fhaland shrugged. "I do not. I know this."

Kron thrust his torch forward, spraying sparks, and the fat man yelped before backing a step.

The sword kept pace, always below that sagging chin.

"Good," Kron said. "You still fear pain. I can use that."

"In what manner?"

"Tell me about the bones," Kron said. "Why were they worth the trouble?"

Fhaland's head hung low again. His shoulders sagged. His voice was soft. "Perhaps they were not."

Kron dropped the torch, his free hand darting forward to grab his enemy by his head of hair. As he leaned in closer, he tugged the chin up, bringing a wince to the wizard's face. The torchlight at their feet glinted along the length of the sword. "I *want answers*."

Drooping eyes stared back, then drifted off to one side.

Kron smacked him. Hard. Fhaland reeled, but the man in black kept up with him, the sword always at the ready to strike. Before the mage could catch his footing again, Kron kicked out, connecting with the wounded leg. Fhaland cried and dropped to the ground, blubbering like a child.

The sword descended from above, the point resting against the wizard's chest, pressing and pressing, nearly to the point of breaking through the thin cloth and the flesh beyond.

"Tell me," Kron spoke.

New hatred poured from the mage's eyes, replacing the weakness and defeat of a moment earlier. "Why should I tell you *anything?*"

"Because I can make the rest of your short life very painful," Kron said.

"Ha! Do you think you can do worse to me than I've done to others?"

Kron shrugged. "I can always try."

Fhaland smirked.

"Have you ever been raped by a branding iron?" Kron asked. "Or perhaps a steel rod wrapped with jagged wire?"

The wizard's face went still. "You would not."

"I would, with glee," Kron said, leaning forward just enough to put weight on his sword. The point dug further, tearing the cloth but not quite skin. "You underestimate me, Fhaland. You don't know who I am, and that is your mistake. I have traveled to Kobalos itself and returned, defeated that nation's lord, bested war demons and now assassin demons alike. I was raised in the Prisonlands surrounded by men who forced themselves upon other men, who feasted upon other men. I have witnessed all this, taken part in much of it, and yet I stand here today ready to slay one more cretin who thinks to end his pain by forcing it upon others. Would I not spend hours upon hours torturing you? Of course I would. For me, it would be a delight. I would enjoy every minute of it, hearing your screams howled into the night."

The man in black's eyes were as cold as the moon and as hard as diamond. He pressed further and a drop of blood swelled at the end of his sword.

Fhaland gasped. "*Who are you?*"

"I am known as Kron Darkbow. That is all you need know. It should be enough."

The sword went deeper and the drop of red became a small pool.

The wizard grunted and winced. "Please," he begged.

"Tell me about the bones."

Something drained from within the wizard. The last of his defiance was slaughtered and hoisted from the mage's soul. Kron could see this with the man's eyes. Fhaland knew defeat, true defeat.

"They were from a god," the Khadiran said of the bones, "a god born millions upon millions of years ago, a creation of the Zarroc themselves." He glanced up at Kron. "Do you know of the Zarroc?"

The man in black nodded.

"With those bones, I had hoped to draw forth the power of this god," Fhaland went on, "to make myself the most powerful mage in all of Majkir. Only then could I return, to bring vengeance upon those ... those who had forced me to flee my homeland, forced me to surrender my ... my ..."

"Your predilections," Kron added.

The mage nodded, tears streaming from his eyes. His voice lowered to a whisper. "They hunted me, the other sorcerers, the enchanters. They were jealous of my power, of how I harnessed the souls of others to draw further might."

A grimace formed on Kron's lips. "In other words, they would not abide your appetites."

Fhaland blubbered, spittle flying from his lips. "I learned of the god's resting place from ancient tomes I had heard of in Lycinia. All that travel, all my labors, for nothing. Nothing!"

"All those souls," Kron said, "all those bodies. Broken, butchered, for your lust."

Fhaland's hands welled up before his face as he hid his features. "I just wanted to feel something."

Kron showed no sympathy. "Where are the bones now?"

Sniffing, the mage lowered his hands. "If not for my wounds, I would have spelled myself away from here. I could have blasted you from the ground. Set your soul aflame."

The man in black said nothing to this. He merely gave his sword a slight twist.

Fhaland yelled out in anguish, then his features grew more twisted, red and sweating as he glared up at his tormenter. "The bones will go with me to my grave! I will never tell you their location."

Movement from behind caused Kron to shift to one side. Montolio and a limping Micklewhite were making their way toward the downed wizard and the swordsman standing over him.

"Kill him!" the sheriff spouted.

Kron looked down at Fhaland. "The bones?"

"Never!"

Montolio stepped forward. "If the bones are of magic, I can find them."

Kron looked down upon Fhaland and saw no reason to spare the man further.

The sword bit deep, pressed by gloved hands from above. The mage squirmed as the steel blade sliced through him and into the dirt road beneath. Fhaland was impaled upon the ground. His chunky fingers reached and reached, finally grasping at the sword. Metal cut into the thin flesh of his hands, dripping blood down the blade and the wizard's grip.

Kron grunted and twisted his weapon, bringing a new convulsion to the foreigner. Then another twist, and more squirming. Then Fhaland's hands fell back at his side and he lay unmoving.

Micklewhite stood leaning against the architect, the larger man's eyes unblinking and wide with anger as he stared upon the fate of his town's torturer. Montolio also stared, but his expression was pained, almost one of guilt.

"It is done." Kron's words were soft as he planted a boot on the dead man's stomach and tugged his sword free.

He slung the blade out to one side, sending blood cascading across the road, then leaned forward to use the end of Fhaland's robe to wipe the weapon clean. Once the sword had returned to the sheath on Kron's back, he turned to the other two men. "Montolio, you are sure you can find these bones?"

Montolio shifted beneath the weight of the heavier man leaning against him. "Did he tell you what they were for?"

"Fhaland believed they were of some ancient god, and that they would allow him to grow in power."

The architect mage nodded. "Not an impossibility if he was right. Regardless, if he was correct, then they should give off a sheen of magic."

"Can you find them?"

"It should be a simple task."

56

A dry warmth settled over the land as the sun glinted above the horizon, washing away a thin layer of fog that had built up along the shore of the river. A second vessel, smaller though just as long, was tied behind the cog, and a dozen men in padded leather armor were gradually climbing from the boat onto the boards layering the dock. From the south a half dozen fellows in chain and riding sturdy animals trotted into Hommel, the helmets atop the riders' heads shifting from side to side.

Soon enough the newcomers from both directions spotted the lone figure walking away from the Khadiran craft. It was Montolio, the young mage in dark garb carrying a bundle of rags beneath one arm. Officers came forward to speak with the man, and he pointed them in the direction of the sheriff's office in the middle of the village.

As the soldiers made their way to the open door of the building, they walked around a dozen butchered bodies, mostly men. One of the dead was a large man in gray robes, in the center of his chest a sizable circle of red, at one shoulder and on a leg smaller blemishes drying upon his clothing.

At the doorway, a tall, muscular man with a big sword tied to his back exited the building. Questions were asked, plenty of questions. Kron pointed toward the ship, then nodded toward the broken tower on the hill to the southwest. Eventually the man in black and a pair of officers retreated indoors and the soldiers began the work of retrieving the remains of the dead.

Slowly, one by one, people began to appear. They were the survivors, the lucky few, if they could be considered lucky. They had hidden in near fields or further away, over hilltops. Some few had managed to make it to the houses of relatives several miles down one or another of the roads. Now they were coming home to face what was left of their lives, and to face those they would never hold or speak with again. Tears were found in abundance, and more than a few men stomped forward to kick at the bloated figure in the gray robes. Some few others who appeared were ignorant of the recent events of Hommel, being travelers prepared to stop in the town; they moved on without a word.

Eventually there was a team of townsfolk and soldiers working together to bury the dead in the village's cemetery. One of the sergeants managed to get a fire going near the shore and meals were handed out to those in need and those who were simply hungry from the work they were doing. Through all of this, Montolio walked with that bundle under his arms. The mage appeared in shock, without a word as he watched those around him busy at their labors. The light of day had brought to the young architect's eyes the full reality of what had transpired within the town.

It was afternoon when the officers and Kron exited the sheriff's building, Micklewhite close behind. The group paused on the stoop, watching the last of the bodies being carried toward the cemetery.

The man in black looked up to the sheriff standing slightly above him. "Will the town survive this?"

Micklewhite shrugged. "I do not know. There's not much town left. But those of us still living ... we've got nowhere else to go. We'll do the best we can. Start over."

Kron glanced over his shoulder to the shadows within the building. "What of her?"

Glancing back, the sheriff saw Leesa curled up in a chair. The poor girl was pale and dirt still spotted her face from the events of the night before. At least she had found some retreat within the bounds of sleep.

"She's speaking and eating some," Micklewhite said, "so hopefully she'll come around."

"What will happen to her?" one of the officers from Bond asked.

"I'll take care of her," Micklewhite said. "She and I, we were the only two locals here at the last. I'll make her my niece or god daughter. It's the least I can do for her."

"What about you?" Kron asked. "How will you fare?"

The sheriff shrugged again. "I'll survive, I suppose. What else is there?"

Kron stared at the man for a long moment, but then he looked away to find Montolio slowly approaching, the architect looking unsure of himself.

"I think it was all too much for your friend," Micklewhite said. "Better see to him."

Kron approached, holding out a hand to the mage. "Montolio?"

The young man shook his head as if waking, or as if to ruffle away memories he would rather not have. He blinked and his features became more warm, more alive. "I wish there was more I could do."

"You did all anyone could ask of you," one of the officers said from near the sheriff.

Montolio looked to the man and winced.

Reaching out a gloved hand, Kron patted the mage on an arm. "I can't promise you your nights won't be filled with terrors for some while, but eventually it grows less. It'll take time, but you'll find a way to live with the guilt."

"The guilt?" Montolio asked.

"Of surviving," Kron said.

The wizard nodded. "Yes, there is that." His eyes locked on those of his companion. "You are ... familiar with this?"

Kron thought back to his parents, dead more than half his lifetime. "Yes," he said with a nod, "I am familiar with the guilt of enduring."

Before the gathering could become more maudlin, Micklewhite limped forward. "What about those bones? What's to happen to them?"

Montolio glanced down at the package in his arms. For a moment his face was confused, as if he had forgotten his burden. Then he looked up with clear eyes. "I'm not sure, to be honest. They give off some little magic, but I don't know how useful they would be."

"You mean Fhaland might have come all this way for nothing?" the sheriff asked.

"Possibly," Montolio said. "I can't know without further studies."

Kron and Micklewhite traded a knowing glance, then the man in black spoke. "I'm not sure that's a good idea."

"I understand," Montolio said. "Believe me, I have no wish to carry these artifacts any longer than I have to. I just don't know what to do with them."

"I have an idea," Kron said, reaching out. He took the burden from the mage's hands. "I'll take these to Randall and see what he suggests, but my feeling is they should be buried once more, someplace deep and far from the civilized world."

A grin spread across the wizard's lips. "I won't argue against it."

Micklewhite pointed toward the river. "What of this Khadiran cog? What's to happen to it?"

Kron transferred his bundle from one arm to the other as his gaze followed the sheriff's finger. "As you are the only surviving member of the town's officials, I believe you can make claim to it for purposes of the village. Is that correct, sergeant?" He looked to one of the soldiers standing near.

The man nodded back. "Sounds about right to me."

"You can keep it for whatever purposes," Kron said to Micklewhite, "or you can sell it, use the proceeds to help rebuild."

The sheriff seemed to be deep in thought for a moment, his eyes hard upon the craft, then, "Or we could burn it down to the water."

Kron stared unblinking at the man. "If that is what you wish."

Micklewhite shrugged as he turned back toward his office. "There will be time to decide upon that later."

With those words the group broke apart, the officers returning to their men to oversee the remaining work. Kron and Montolio retreated to the cooking fire, their bellies growling after a lack of food for nearly a day.

By the time darkness settled upon the village of Hommel once more, the dead were no more to be found and the soldiers were gone. The smaller vessel from Bond had withdrawn, and even Kron and Montolio were missing, having sailed back with the river squad. There were few lights in the houses of Hommel, but at least there were a few. A handful of chimneys belted smoke into the night's sky and every so often the sound of crying drifted upon the wind.

Through all of this, the cog continued to float up and down next to the dock, the ship standing out as something foreign, something *wrong*, in these lands. Upon a hill south of the vessel, a crumbling tower stood as a sentinel on watch, one bare window staring down upon the water in the distance as if keeping an eye for the return of evil.

Book III:
THE COMPANY OF SEVEN

Part 1:
Sparks

1

1,996 years After Ashal (A.A.)

The ground cracked. It should not have cracked. Several months of a harsh, dry winter had left the earth packed, seemingly solid, and it should have remained so until the temperature had risen. The temperature had not risen.

The ground cracked from *beneath*. One moment the surface of the light brown soil was flat and smooth. The next moment a slight bulge rose from below. Then followed the cracking, initially a single, straight line that slowly ripped through the soil, growing in length but not yet width. Nearly two feet long, the black line splintered, a dozen smaller lines branching away from it, each crooked and narrow.

The bulge grew. The original line grew. The lesser cracks, each of them grew. Then a minor eruption.

Crumbles of dirt shuddered and rolled away from the center of the implosion. The central crack itself grew further in length, then it widened. The lesser lines sprouted tendrils, spreading out along the surface of the ground.

The earth shuddered, then the bulge in the soil tumbled in upon itself, forming a ragged, shallow pit.

Pressing up through the dirt in the center of the pit appeared a singular stony, vaguely cylindrical object. It was crooked and cracked in multiple places. Its color was indistinct beneath the moonlight, but appeared to be of a pale shade, a dirty white or gray.

This entity crooked around like a snake's head searching for a meal. Then more dirt erupted around the thing and it was joined by another, similar object. For a moment there were the two, then the pit widened yet again and a third crooked, cracked cylindrical object pressed up from beneath nature's floor. A second later a fourth pressed up from the earth, shorter than the others but of a similar kind. Finally a fifth pale object pushed its way from beneath the soil to join the rest.

Five. Five fingers. Skeletal. Lacking flesh. Waving around, seeking. Each so dried and decimated it barely seemed able to remain as a whole. It was as if some unearthly paste held each together.

Up thrust the full hand, bony and wan as it sent another spray of dirt flying from the crust of earth. The hand itself was little better than the fingers, though some few strips of hardened sinew and crumpled cloth showed themselves. The hand spun around, reaching and clawing at its surroundings.

Another push and an arm up to the elbow appeared. The limb gave evidence of more stringy flesh, but none of it living, only hardened like that belonging to a corpse dried in the sun for a lengthy period. Dirt continued to roll away, and

379

what had been a line in the earth grew more broad and stretched forth.

The hand twisted around and pressed itself upon the ground, pushing down as if trying to lift itself from below.

An explosion of hardened soil rained into the air and a dark figure blossomed within the night's light, propping itself up with the sides of the small ditch it had created. There were now two claw-like, skeletal hands, and they flattened against the sides of the hole, pressing down.

The earth rumbled gently as the figure pulled itself further from its grave. The thing rolled to one side and fell on what remained of its stomach, little more than pale ribs, its fingers scrambling at the ground, finding purchase a couple of feet away in cold, dry grass. Those fingers pressed through the weeds and impaled themselves into the dirt, pulling its own weight, drawing itself from the pit.

Soon the skeletal monstrosity was crawling forth, now free of its subterranean confines. For a moment it perched upon its knees and elbows like a prey animal ready to spring, then it rolled over onto its side, then onto its back. It lay there, empty sockets for eyes staring up at the moon far above. It was like a man out of breath, pausing to catch its air.

After several minutes it sat up on its rear, the remains of a faded and torn robe slumping down from its shoulders. The thing found itself sitting next to its hole in a small grassy field surrounded by a high wall. Straight ahead was a structure of some kind. A building? The edifice appeared large enough for a small temple, or perhaps some king's summer home, but the dark windows and the moon's glow revealed nothing other than general size and shape.

Glancing around, the skull noted a faint, dancing light here and there atop the wall. The glow of flame, torches or perhaps lamps. There were no lights upon the wall itself, so the sources of luminescence were beyond, on the outside.

Every so often sounds would reach the inside of those walls. Distant voices carried, though no particular words could be discerned. The clatter of wooden wheels upon stones, the occasional punch of boots and shoes rapping upon a cobbled street, the moans of animals, the crackling of small fires, all these and more lingered upon the air and visited the skull that had no ears yet could hear.

A city. This was a city.

It was sure of that.

No, not *it*. He. *He* was sure of that. He was a male, after all, wasn't he?

His memories remained vague, recalled as if seeing through a cheese cloth. This city, was it the New Salvino he had known hundreds of years earlier. No, not New Salvino. The city had a new name. What was it? In more recent times there had been soldiers, men and women in uniform, and they had told him the name of the city. When had that been? How many years? Centuries? Decades?

He could not remember. He had slept so much and so long, there was no way of knowing how much time had passed. But time had indeed passed. There was no wall on these grounds, not in his memories, but the presence of a large house, that felt familiar.

Bond.

His head jerked to one side at the memory. Bond. That had been the name of the city, the name provided to him by the soldiers. Those damned soldiers. Kicking at him, punching at him, using his own magic against him. They had beaten him down until he had been practically nothing but dust. Only the strength of his magic had brought him back together, made him whole again. That and the protective wards of the temple far below the surface, the temple that had stood above the ground thousands of years in the past and was now little more than a ruin, a few tunnels connecting with this city's sewer system.

So long ago.

Or was it?

Not that it mattered. Time was of little concern for him. His goals were ever the same. What difference the name of a city? Centuries careened by, empires rose and fell, whole peoples flourished then withered into nothingness. One city? It was less than important.

But what of his own name? He had had a name once, hadn't he?

The skeleton stood, its robe snaking down its spare frame to rustle against the ground. The skull twisted around, those empty eyes taking in the wall and building and the yard yet again.

His name? Yes, he had had a name. His parents had called him Sadhe Teth, and that name had risen to power and had sought more power, unimagined power, the power of the gods. Power *over* the gods.

He was Sadhe Teth, and his ambition had yet to be fulfilled. He still had need of ... of what?

Teth swung around, his sightless eyes searching the horizon along the top of the wall. He drew open the old pull of magic from deep within himself, from the well of power he had stored at the cost of thousands of lives. For a moment he noticed nothing, then his attention was brought to the east.

The building stood there. The house? He could smell the rot of violence upon the place. A small group of people had died there most atrociously, and fairly recently. What he sought, it had been there for a short period. Those people had died in part because of it. That much he could sense.

But his immediate goal, his want, it could no longer be found within that place. It had moved on.

His sockets returned to the top of the wall, searching, seeking. His mind reached out like a thousand fingers in all directions. He had to find ... something.

There. That was the new resting place. The ... what were they? Sticks? Spears? No. They were bones. Yes. Bones. The bones had been taken from the temple beneath his feet and transferred to a location somewhere else within this new city. He could sense the bones, their magic no longer shielded by the protections of the temple, their presence noticeable by any with the skill and the will to look for them.

He had to have those bones. It was a new age, a time to live again. A time to kill again. This time it would be different. This time he would take what he wanted. No one, not even gods, would stand in his way.

He strode toward the nearest gate in the wall.

***

A sigh pressed its way between Malin the Quill's lips as he stood, pushing the stool back from his work table and lifting his arms to stretch. A yawn followed as the distant tolling of a church bell reminded him it was well past midnight. He should have been in bed hours earlier, but such was the life of a student assistant to a professor of the University of Ursia's College of Magic. Malin only wished he spent less time doing menial work, such as grading the latest batch of exam papers piled on the table in front of him, and more time delving into the more mysterious aspects of magical research.

He sat again, lifting a cooling cup of tea to his mouth for a sip. His other hand reached over to a glowing crystal ensconced atop a brass candlestick. He gave the crystal a gentle tap, then returned the cup to its place to one side while the magical glow grew brighter, providing his weary eyes with much-needed light for continuing his night's mission.

Halfway through grading the exams, he still had another hundred or so to go, all by morning before he was due to attend his first class of the day.

Another sigh escaped him as he picked up a quill from a bottle of red ink. Staring at the quill for a moment, he gave the simple tool a simple smile. He had been named for the item because from a young age he had shown a strength in reading and writing, unlike the other children of the village where he had grown up in northern West Ursia near the border with Caballerus. Nearly twenty years of age now, he had moved beyond his simple beginnings. Recalling the traveling hedge wizard who had first discovered Malin's talents, the youth supposed he had the man to thank for keeping him from a life of toiling away in fields and barns.

Yet Malin wasn't feeling very thankful tonight.

He returned the quill to its bottle and half turned on his stool. He stared down the length of the narrow room, work benches and tables lining both walls to create a narrow walkway that ended in a tall window looking out upon the night. His back now to the chamber's only door, his eyes shifted as if in search for a particular item.

He looked for some minutes, then his gaze stopped upon a leather sack folded in on itself on top of the bench to the right of the window. What was within that sack represented the very mysterious nature of magic that Malin wanted to explore.

Standing, he crossed the room with delicate steps, as if someone in the hall outside the room might be listening. Only when he was standing over the folded leather did he stop, his hands lingering in the air over the bundle.

A grin formed on his lips. Yes, this was what continued to draw him to magical studies, despite the long, boring nights and the tedious classes taught by old men with old ideas.

His fingers brushed back a section of the sacking to reveal a pair of bones. The bones appeared human, somewhat long though cracked and jagged at their ends. Malin was no expert, but he guessed the bones were femurs, though maybe the shorter of the two was a humerus.

He blinked and stretched out with his thoughts. Even though only a student he still had enough training to detect the faint glow of magic coming from the bones.

His fingers neared the package, but he did not dare to touch. It was a mystery he yearned to uncover, but a mistake might find him kicked out of the university. He could not allow that to happen, not while he was still in training to be a wizard. Malin had grown too appreciative of life in the big city of Bond to want to return to the village of his parents, and he would do whatever it took to keep that from happening.

Even if he had to keep this particular mystery at a distance.

He flipped the sacking over the bones once more and returned to his seat. As a hand rested on the quill in the bottle, his mind scrambled, thinking back upon the bones within the leather confines.

The package had come to the college through a meandering route. Rumors had been rampant the year past about a mad wizard and his pet demon causing all kind of atrocities throughout the city. Malin had been too busy to follow the news, but he had heard word of torture and rape. Apparently the madness had even stretched outside of Bond into one of the outlaying villages. A contingent of the city guard had been sent forth and had apparently dealt with the situation, the bag of bones being one of the few items left from the now-dead mad wizard. Another rumor was that the wizard had dug up the bones from someplace within the city, perhaps from an ancient temple hidden beneath the ground. Somehow or other a local healer, a minor mage who was not even a graduate of the university, had been handed the package of bones, and after some study had handed them over to the college for examination.

Malin the Quill had no idea if any of this was true. His professors supposedly knew the truth, or some version of it, but had not deigned to pass that information along to a lowly student.

He glanced down the length of the room once more to the leather sack, wishing he could crack this secret. To whom did the bones belong? They appeared human and were obviously ancient, nearly stone in their hardness. If they had been buried in some underground temple, a temple to whom? Some ancient god? An early temple to Ashal?

Many questions. Too many. And Malin would never be allowed to answer them because he was only a student.

Maybe one more look wouldn't hurt. Who knew, perhaps he could stumble upon a secret or two? Perhaps he might notice something about the bones that no one else had? If that were to happen, he would be the hero of the college, and then maybe he could spend his time with things more interesting than doing professors' work for them.

He set down his quill and stood, facing the back of the room.

Skritch.

Malin stopped. What had been that sound? It had been slight, barely audible.

He looked up and down the length of the room. Nothing untoward presented itself.

Shrugging, the young mage took a step toward the leather package.

Skritch. Skritch.

He stopped again, and turned around. The noise had come from the front of the room, somewhere near the door. It had sounded like something scratching, like maybe a cat or mouse at a window. Or at the door.

"Is someone there?" he asked.

He didn't expect an answer. At this hour there were rarely any students or professors moving about the college's main building. Every once in a while a steward or custodian might be about, possibly even another assistant, but that was rare enough. But the scratching noises he had heard hadn't sounded like a person trying to knock at a door. The thought of a cat returned to him, and he wondered if some mage's familiar was running loose, or perhaps if there were rats within the building.

He opened his mouth to speak.

Skritch.

And promptly closed it.

Thoughts of the horrendous events surrounding the bones intruded upon his mind once more and froze him in place, but then he gave a soft laugh. He was being silly. The university was a safe place. Nothing bad ever happened on the grounds, other than maybe the occasional drunken prank.

Was that it? A prank? Some under grads trying to frighten the late-working assistant?

Well, he could play at that game himself. He might be a student, but he had some skills and training. Magic was his tool, after all, and if anyone was hiding on the other side of the door he would be able to find out without opening the door itself.

He muttered a few ancient words, words which would allow him to ascertain if anyone living was on the other side of the closed portal.

When nothing appeared to his magicked senses, his head jerked back in surprise.

Skritch.

There it was again.

Malin pondered the situation. Okay, no one was out there, of that he could be sure. But *something* was making that noise. Had someone hung an item on the other side of the door, something that could make sound? Or had one of the mechanician students put together a little toy that made that scratching on the door?

Fear was being replaced with anger. Someone was trying to make a fool of Malin the Quill, that much he was sure. He would show them. Whatever he found outside that door, he would blast it into a million pieces. The thought made him grin again, thinking about the sight of some apprentice tinkerer's downturned face over his or her eradicated knickknack.

Malin tromped across the room, ready to cast a spell at whatever lay beyond the door.

His left hand grasped the door knob, twisted and pulled.

A wall of blackness greeted him.

He took a step back. The outer hall was always dark at night, but this was beyond mere darkness. It was as if a wall of ink confronted him.

After a moment, the surprise melted away. Obviously the wall of black was magic, a relatively simple spell Malin could perform himself, or he could do away with it.

He opened his mouth to do just that.

A skeletal arm shot forth from the darkness, grasping the student by the throat. The Quill fought back, slapping against the pale, cracked limb, but all he managed to do was knock away bits of dirt layered upon the bones.

Malin found himself struggling to breathe, his throat tight, his vision going blurry. He tried to kick away from the door with his feet, but that hand at his neck held firm as if made of stone.

A visage loomed from the darkness, a face without flesh. Black orbs for eyes stared out of a skull into the student's face.

"*The bones are here, yes?*" hissed a crackling voice.

Malin could not answer. He tried to flail again, but his arms were weak, his legs tired. His fear had given away to a drowsiness, which if he had been in his right mind he would have recognized as magical in nature. His eyes fluttered, yet he fought back, remaining conscious just barely.

The skeletal figure pushed its way into the room, holding the student up by the neck. The door closed of its own accord as the tall form robed in rags glanced about the chamber. Its sockets came to rest on the bag of bones.

It was impossible to tell, but Malin thought he saw a grin form among the thin layers of remaining skin stretched across the skull's lips.

"*Yes, you have the bones,*" the unearthly thing said, answering its own question. Then its empty eyes turned upon the hanging youth. "*And you have something else almost as important to me. You have your body.*"

A skeletal hand rose toward Malin's face.

2

Not the most religious of individuals, Frex Nodana still found herself praying at least once nearly every day, usually early in the morning. It was silly really, a notion that had stuck with her since childhood. She did not ask Ashal for anything. She merely offered her thanks. Thanks for warm toes. When she thought about it, she would giggle, remembering how she had prayed for warm toes when she was a little girl. She had called them "toasty toes." Now older, near thirty and much more affluent, she still prayed in thanks for warm toes. Being a child of the lowliest section of Bond, the region called the Swamps for its likelihood in flooding during the rainy season, she had grown up often without warmth. For some reason her tiny little toes had always represented that warmth or the lack of. She chilled first in that portion of her body, there at the ends of her feet. Waking with warm toes wrapped in a blanket, that was a luxury she had rarely known during her youngest days, but now it was a common occurrence every morning.

Below closed lids, she allowed a smile to form on her lips.

Thoughts of warm toes reminded her of the warm spot in the bed next to her. One of her hands snaked over, but she felt nothing. The place was still warm and held Kron's shape, but he was not laying there where he had been the night before.

Her eyes creaked open. She stared at his back revealed by the morning sun shifting through the windows of her apartment.

He sat on the edge of the bed to the left of her warm toes, his pale, muscled back presenting itself, his dark head dipped as if staring at something in his lap. Nodana's eyes followed the lines of his muscles, surprised yet again that a man of such misadventures did not find himself layered in scars. She supposed it paid to be friends with one of the most powerful healers in the city.

Yet the lack of physical scars did not mean there were no emotional ones. Kron Darkbow was a good man, Nodana told herself, and he was a good lover. A *delicious* lover. Still, though he gave all of his body into their lovemaking, there was a part of him never present, always ... elsewhere. She had tried to reach through to him, but there was a wall around the man's core. He rarely spoke of his past, though she knew some of it from mutual acquaintances and the little things he had let slip here and there. His parents murdered before him when he was a boy, he grew up among the border towns of the Prisonlands, raised by an uncle who had been a warden. After his uncle's passing, Kron had given up being a border warden himself and had returned to the city of his birth to find vengeance for his slain kin. The details were lost upon Nodana, but apparently had involved Kron fleeing far to the north to the land of Kobalos, along with his healer companion Randall Tendbones, both running from the notorious Belgad the Liar. Whatever had transpired there, no one was telling, though Kron and

Randall had returned to Bond while Belgad had remained, somehow crowned king of Kobalos.

Little of it made sense. It was like something from one of the great, old sagas.

Of more recent events in Kron's life, Nodana was well aware. She had been a part of them. There had been the riots of the year before, when Kron had become an officer with the city guard, followed by a struggle among the city's various guilds for new leadership. During that time Frex had managed to rise to chief of the new mages guild. Following those events, there had been the rampage of a mad wizard and his pet demon. Kron had hunted down the deadly pair, and upon returning to Bond had fallen into a relationship with Nodana.

It was as if he had something to burn away, as if he needed some kind of release. In this case a sexual release, one which Frex most appreciated. Perhaps his past or his soul troubled him. Never a shaken man, a broken man, there were still at times a lifelessness behind those eyes, as if he was not always there.

She felt that deadness inside herself while watching the gentle rise and fall of his back, the breaths escaping and flowing into his lungs. She sometimes tried to pry from him his thoughts, his emotions. He would freely answer her questions, but rarely did he go into any depth.

A gentle scraping sound came to her ears from him. What was he doing?

"I know you're awake," he said, standing to reveal a sheet wrapped around his hips.

He took several steps forward and turned, sitting in a cushioned chair in a corner. In his hands was a sizable book, old and bound in tattered leather. Not once did he look up, his eyes remaining locked on the pages before him. He did not even spare a glance to his sword, the lengthy scabbarded weapon leaning against the back of the chair

"You've been reading a lot lately," she said.

He gestured toward the wall behind him where shelves housed row upon row of books she had collected over the years. "My formal education is lacking. It is time I amend that."

"We've never talked much about your education," she said.

Kron placed a finger on a page, then looked up. "Little proper schooling. My youngest days were spent on the roads with my parents, both of them traveling merchants. We ventured to a lot of different lands, and I picked up quite a bit, but most of my basic schooling came from marms in the Prisonlands."

"Yet I know you to speak and read several languages quite well," she said, "and you seem well acquainted with alchemy, philosophy, even magic, which is odd for a non-practitioner."

He gave a grin, but it was not filled with warmth. "One learns much growing up around the Lands. Every year there are more men from far lands arriving to work as wardens. It is part of the original treaty. With them they bring much knowledge, practical knowledge. Unfortunately, more than a little of what I learned is not found on the written page. For instance, my understandings of ancient history and military tactics are quite amiss."

She raised a thin arm and pointed at him. "What are you reading now?"

He hefted the heavy tome with one hand as if to show it to her. "A history of the Brimming Horde. Written nearly seven hundred years ago."

"How is it?"

"The writer lacks grace."

Nodana grinned, thinking of Kron as a critic.

He snapped the book closed and held it up. "But I think it time I put aside my reading material for now. We need to be going."

She grinned and sat up in bed, pulling a quilt around her. "Is there any hurry?"

"It is only a formality, but I want it finished." He stood and placed the book on a shelf. Turning away from her toward the exit, he paused as the cover encircling his waist slipped and dropped to the floor. He bent and reached for the sheet, then stood once more, wrapping the cover around him. "Get ready. I'll find us some breakfast and hail a cabriolet."

She couldn't help but stare at his solid frame hinted at by the folds of his covering. "Are you *sure* we couldn't spare a few more minutes?"

***

To the casual eye, not much looked different about the place. Kilchus could admit this, though he did not have the casual eye, and until five years earlier had been quite familiar with the mansion or fortress, call it what one would. Standing at the corner across the street, he took in the high stone wall which surrounded the grounds, the closed double gate of black iron, the path of crushed rocks which rose gradually up a hill to a circular drive in front of the main building, the mansion proper.

All of this was familiar, though perhaps a little age showed here and there.

Stomping his feet and pulling closer his wool cloak, the swordsman breathed out warm air that formed into mist in the early morning cold. There were few people out yet on the streets of the Swamps, which was fine with him. He had no wish to draw undue attention, and standing in a casual manner on a street corner was not likely to draw much attention, even when across the road from the estate that had once belonged to the famed underworld figure of Belgad the Liar.

Kilchus blinked. Upon second thought, yes, much had changed. There were no longer guards stationed at the gate. For that matter, there were no guards strolling the grounds nor camped out near the mansion's main entrance. Belgad would never have allowed such laxity in security. Kilchus knew. He had once been chief of the big man's security forces.

At least the grounds had been kept well. What patches of grass could be seen through pockmarks in the snow showed signs of having been cut before cold weather had arrived. The few shrubs near the front of the building appeared in a condition pleasing to the eye.

Someone was in charge. It just wasn't Belgad.

So, it seemed the rumors were true, or at least some of them.

The only way to find out would be to knock.

He stamped his feet again, looked both ways across the road for any oncoming horses or carriages as well as to make sure no one was paying too close attention to him, then trotted across to the black gates.

He pushed.

Not even locked.

Which caused him to shake his head in disbelief.

Once through, he closed the entrance behind him and made his way up the gravel path someone had been so kind to shovel either the night before or earlier that morning.

As Kilchus tromped his way up the hill, he glanced around, expecting at any moment a hidden guard to spring out of the bushes or to appear at the house entrance. Yet nothing happened. He could but shake his head again.

At the top of the hill he paused in the circular driveway, giving anyone inside plenty of time to see him. He didn't want to surprise any sentries napping on the other side of a window. Not a curtain moved. No alarm went up. No one presented themselves. If not for the landscaping, the fresh curtains, and the shoveling job, Kilchus might have believed the place was empty, maybe even abandoned.

But that didn't appear to be the case, at least according to the evidence presented to his eyes. That and the fact the few people he had seen on the streets had steered clear of the place. *Someone* was here. But who?

He sighed out another warm breath and allowed his cloak to fall open as he stepped up to the front door. The sword and dagger on his belt would be revealed to anyone answering, but hopefully no one would be too excited upon seeing him. It wasn't as if he was brandishing the weapons, after all. Besides, he needed answers, and as far as he knew there was no reason for him not to reveal his presence within the city. At least for now.

He lifted a gloved fist and gave three hard knocks on the door.

Lowering his hand, he waited.

For the longest time there was nothing. Then he thought he heard steps approaching from somewhere deeper within the house.

Kilchus kept waiting.

The sound of heavy bolts being drawn came to his ears, then the thick wooden door creaked open. Beyond was a young man in light leathers, a belt around his hips sporting two short swords.

The sight of the weapons brought a grin to Kilchus's face. Two swords? Only a fool would dare carry two swords. The youth probably thought it made him look dangerous.

But he had to admit, the heavy gaze on the lad's features at least gave the appearance of someone experienced with the blades. That could be but gruff performance, however.

"What do you want?" the young man asked.

"Tch. How confrontational." Kilchus grinned, showing teeth. He meant it to look disturbing, dangerous. "Do you treat all guests this way?"

"Only strangers wearing weapons," the youth said, placing a hand on the pommel of one of his weapons.

Kilchus's grin grew wider. Then he blinked upon a sense of vague recollection. "Don't I know you?"

The young man's eyes narrowed. "I don't think so. We've never ... wait. Yeah. I remember you. You used to be called the Sword."

Kilchus couldn't help but chuckle. "I'd almost forgotten. That's a name I've not heard in some while."

"Yeah," the youth went on. "You were Belgad's body guard or something back in the day."

The laughter and the smile vanished. "I was a hell of a lot more than a body guard," Kilchus said.

The youth shrugged. "That was then, this is now. If you came here looking for your old job, you're out of luck. Belgad's no longer here, and I'm head of security now."

A twinkle of the laughter returned to Kilchus's eyes. "You? You're a boy. What would you know about guard work?"

"Enough." The other hand came up, both gripping the pommels of the youth's swords.

The pair of short blades brought back a memory. "I remember you now," Kilchus said. "You were Kuthius's kid, right?"

"I'm not his *kid*," the young man said. "He was my uncle."

"*Was*? What happened to him?"

For the first time, the youth lost his look of defiance. He glanced down at the ground, then back up, his lips fumbling for a moment before he spoke again. "He's in one of the healing towers. He had a ... seizure or something."

"Or something?" None of this made sense to Kilchus, but then he hadn't come here to catch up on the past. "Okay, well, you're the head of security, so who is master here now? I guess with Belgad gone that puts Lalo the Finder in charge."

The young man nodded.

Kilchus grinned once more. "Tell the bastard Kilchus the Sword is here to see him."

"Can't," the young man said. "He isn't home at the moment."

"What about ole Stilp? I bet that slinker is still around."

"He is with the master."

"Where are they?"

The youth's eyes grew to slits again. "If Master Lalo wanted everyone to know his constant whereabouts, he would have it posted on the front gate."

Kilchus couldn't help but laugh. The kid showed backbone. "All right. Is there anybody else I could see?"

"Just me," the youth said. "I'm the only one here at the moment."

"You mean to tell me the master of the house went out without his chief guard?"

"He wasn't expecting any trouble. You *have* been away, haven't you? Things have changed since Belgad left."

A burst of laughter sprang from Kilchus's lips. "Changed? They surely have changed if a rich man can walk the streets of Bond without his guards."

"They can and they do. Besides, Master Lalo is chief of the Guild of Guilds. No one would dare touch him."

"Guild of Guilds?" That was a new one. Five years gone and Kilchus barely recognized the street politics of his own city. "What about Spider? Surely he's still around."

"Nope," the youth said. "He's head of the thieves guild."

Thieves guild? There hadn't been a thieves guild in ages. Belgad never would tolerate such. Always said it was bad for business, stealing from everyday folks. So, there was a thieves guild, but the streets were safer? That hardly made sense.

"Tell me this," Kilchus went on, "since you're head of security, what kind of guard jobs are available?"

"We don't have any openings."

"I don't mean here. Anywhere in town. Have you heard of anything?"

The kid shook his head. "No private jobs that I know of, but the city is hiring on, putting together some kind of new squads."

"Good to know. I'll have to look into it."

"Talk to Captain Gris if you're interested."

"Gris?"

"That's the man. You know him?"

"He left the border wardens soon after I joined up."

"In the Prisonlands?"

"It was ages ago," Kilchus said. "We never worked together, just shared some of the same officers."

"Well, check with him. If he knows you, that'll probably work in your favor."

That's what you think, came to Kilchus's mind.

"Anything else I can do for you, Master Sword?" the young man asked. His voice wasn't nearly as polite as the actual words.

Kilchus shook his head. "I guess not. Tell Lalo that Kilchus came by to see him. He'll want to catch up, I'm sure."

"Where you staying?"

"Got a room at The Stone Pony."

The youth reached to close the door. "I'll let him know. He'll send a runner if he wants to see you."

"Hold on a second." Kilchus held up a delaying hand.

"What is it?"

"Your name. I can't remember it."

Now it was the young man who grinned. "Eel. Eel Sidewinder."

And the door closed.

Kilchus stood there for a moment with a smirk on his face. Eel Sidewinder. Yeah, he remembered now. Little brat had run around behind his uncle, a thief and a thief in the making. Weird that. Eel's uncle had been head of the thieves guild years and years ago, but now he was waylaid and Spider was in charge. Spider. The gray-headed fool had never seemed a take-charge kind of guy, though he had had his uses. And the kid? How old was he? Was he even twenty yet?

No sounds from beyond the door, so the kid hadn't moved on. Thinking it best not to raise any suspicions, Kilchus turned and walked his way back down the pathway between the snow.

Anyway, he had learned what he had wanted, and a few other things as well. Now he just had to report.

3

His high dark boots crunching into snow as he stepped down from the carriage, Kron pulled back the edges of his cloak to hold out several coins to the driver. Their transportation paid for, he lifted Nodana from the back of the small black vehicle and placed her on the ground next to him.

He towered above her as the pair of horses, driver and cab clunked away in the near-freezing slush of the city streets, but that was to be expected. Kron was a big man, his arms and chest and legs filled with muscle, though he was no oversized brute. And Frex, she was small, at a distance appearing as a child to those who did not know her.

Much about the pair did not match as he lifted his cloak and brought her within its confines for warmth. He wore black from his toes to his neck, even the buckles of his garb were painted dark. Frex Nodana sheathed herself in a gray cloak, but beneath she wore bright padded pantaloons, a tan jacket with slashed sleeves over a white blouse, and soft leather leggings that rose to her knees. From his hip hung a large sword, a matching dagger on the other side of the belt, and those who knew him would not have been surprised to learn there were half a dozen other small weapons and tools hidden away within the confines of his clothing. She, however, showed no outward signs of being armed. His face was flat, nearly impassive if not for a grimness to his eyes and lips. She was all smiles, open to the world.

Where they matched was in the blackness of their hair, his short nearly to the point of a military cut, hers a curt bob with bangs that ended barely over the tops of her ears.

They stood out from one another, but the old saying that opposites attract seemed to hold true for them.

Turning around, they faced a high stone wall that stretched to their left and right and encircled ten acres of land beyond. On the other side of the wall, the snow-draped grounds loped to a slight hill where sat a dark, three-storied structure encompassing a tower in the southwest corner. The Asylum. Once a place of madness and death, now it belonged to Kron Darkbow.

"I never understood why you purchased the place," Nodana said over the street traffic behind them, the comings and goings of wagons and carriages and the trampings of the underslugs of society. The Asylum sat in the northwestern corner of the Swamps, the poorest and often most dangerous section of the city, and those rambling the streets were not always to be trusted. Still, most of the common folk seemed to steer clear of the Asylum's walls.

Kron ignored Nodana's remark for the moment. He stared from the main building on the Asylum grounds to a pair of much smaller structures on its left, a stable he had had built as well as a tool shed. Looking down and further to his left he saw the open black iron gates that led onto the grounds. Standing at attention on either side were a pair of armored figures, each holding halberds and wearing the bright orange tabards of the city guard, four guards in all.

"What is this?" Kron asked, nodding to the guards.

Nodana couldn't help but smile. "A little something special."

Squeezing her tighter beneath the folds of his cloak, he looked down into her features. "What have you done?"

Her grin grew wider. "Just you wait and find out. Besides, you still have to answer my question."

"You never asked a question."

"About the Asylum?"

He looked to the four guards once more, each of the men staring straight ahead into the street. Gris trained his people well.

"You made a statement, but there was no question."

She sighed. Sometimes Kron could be overly literal. "Okay. What about the Asylum? Why did you buy it in the first place?"

He wasn't sure he had a good answer. The place had been a wreck when he had purchased it, the main building badly damaged by flooding and a magic spell gone awry. Many had died there, perhaps hundreds. The final death count had never been confirmed. Kron felt responsible for those deaths. He had been a guard there at the time. He had been the one to open a door in the basement level, a door which unknown to him opened up onto the flooded North River. The waters had poured in, filling the basement. A young wizard had made use of magic in an attempt to thwart the flooding, but the situation had only exploded. Kron had been lucky to survive, one of the few who had.

Why had he bought the Asylum? Why had he spent all his money and the last year having the main building rebuilt?

"Originally, it was to be a shrine to the fallen," he said to her as he nodded up at the building. "The mad and the deadly alike died there, but so did a lot of good men, men who I worked beside."

"Originally?"

"Yes. Now, I'm not so sure."

"But you and Gris ..."

"Yes, we've found a use for it. I just hope the results are worthy."

He turned his chin away from her, looking once more up at the Asylum's main structure. Not for the first time, he pondered on the similarities between the grounds here and those of his former foe, Belgad the Liar. Belgad's mansion, now Lalo the Finder's mansion, was laid out in a similar fashion to the Asylum grounds, towering walls and iron gate included, and the buildings were of similar size and shape. The two were also the only such grounds in all the Swamps, and two of the largest buildings other than the one healing tower and a number of the warehouses along the shores of the rivers.

A clattering of wood on stone and the snorting of a horse caused Kron and Frex to glance around. Approaching was another carriage, this one enclosed and driven by a middle-aged fellow stooped over in the front seat, much of his face hidden by the wool trim of his jacket's hood pulled around his face.

"Stilp," Kron said.

The carriage swayed to a stop in front of them as the driver pulled on the reins and the pair of horses snorted again. Without looking, the driver tossed the leather straps to Kron, who did not bother catching them, then the older man jumped down onto the side of the street where his shoes sank into slush.

"Damn it all," the man said as he opened the door to the back of the carriage.

"Tut, tut, Stilp," a man's voice said from the shadows of the vehicle. "We are in public society today. One must comport oneself likewise."

The voice belonged to a thin, white face that appeared within the carriage's darkness. Beneath the nose was a black mustache as thin as a needle.

"Lalo," Kron said with a curt nod. Holding Nodana next to him, he moved neared the carriage and held out his free hand.

The newcomer smiled and accepted the gloved hand which helped him climb down into the snow while avoiding the worst of the slush.

"My thanks," Lalo said.

Stilp closed the carriage door, retrieved the fallen reins and climbed into the driver's seat. "What time you want me to pick you up, boss?"

"Give me an hour," Lalo said.

With that the carriage trundled away into the busy streets of the Swamps.

Kron smirked. "Same old Stilp."

Lalo couldn't help but grin. "Yes, a silly little man, but he has his uses. And he's as loyal as a well-fed hound."

A burst of laughter escaped Nodana's lips. The Finder had described his employee well.

Standing tall, his gray cloak flowing down from his shoulders, Lalo the Finder's height more than equaled that of Kron himself, though the newcomer was nowhere near as broad. There was a regality, however, to Lalo, one which Kron nor few other men wore, an unusual trait in that the man was not of the noble classes but apparently had come up on the streets.

He turned to glare at the four guards stationed near the entrance to the Asylum grounds. "I did not realize this was to be a formal event."

"Neither did I," Kron said. "Ask Nodana. She's worked up something, and I'm just finding out about it."

The Finder looked to the woman. "Well, my dear?"

She blushed. Before she could answer, a dark head stuck its way out the open iron gates.

"There you are!" a young man called out.

"Montolio!" Kron hailed. "What goes this day?"

The young man with the black hair grinned. "You'll have to ask Nodana, or come inside and discover for yourself." He stepped out the gates to stand between the guards, shuffling his boots in the snow as his coat shook from shivering shoulders.

Kron glanced to Lalo. "Shall we?"

"You may proceed," the Finder said.

With one last squeeze of the woman in his arms, Darkbow stepped forward, making sure his footing found the safest places to land before falling. Lalo the Finder right behind him, he and Nodana rounded in front of the four guards, Montolio stepping aside to give an open view of the Asylum grounds beyond.

What Kron found before him was mostly unexpected.

A path of gravel had been laid down to create a road from the wide gates up to the large building's entrance, though this he had ordered made some months back. This day the way was clear of snow, a not altogether unexpected condition. More surprising were a half dozen riding beasts tied to a post off to his right, the animals sending up plums of warm air as they stamped the snow beneath them into mud. To the left was something else new, a sizable tent large enough for at least a dozen to feast comfortably, which appeared to be exactly what was in the waiting.

The heavy tent's flaps tied back, within was a long table surrounded by a dozen hardback chairs. Atop the table had been placed plates and silverware along with cloth napkins. At the far end of the temporary structure was an iron stove with piping running up to a hole in the roof. Another long furnishing had been set up near the stove, this table covered with dishes of steaming food. In front of the table of food stood several servants, young men and women in white obviously hired for the day's tasks. The floor was covered with clean straw, and warmth rolled forth from the makeshift chamber to show it was quite comfortable within.

For a moment Kron did not know what to say. He came to a standstill, his eyes pouring over the scene. Finally, he found some few words. "This ... this is too much."

"Nonsense," added a new voice.

Kron turned and discovered his friend Gris approaching from the far side of the horses, the captain of the city guard decked out in his dress uniform, an orange tabard emblazoned with the markings of his office.

"Well met this day," Gris said as he gave a two-fingered salute, the gesture of a Prisonlands border warden.

Extricating himself from Nodana, Kron returned the salute, then stepped forward to grip his friend by the hand. "I knew you would be here for initial inspection, but I didn't expect all this. Nodana has been busy."

"Yes, she has," came yet another voice.

A young man dressed in a bright robe walked in from the street, trailing behind him a dour-faced woman whose eyes never left the ground, much of her slender features hidden beneath the lengthy straight hair hanging in her face.

"Randall," Kron said, moving forward to shake the hand of his friend.

The healer returned the warm handshake, then motioned to the young woman with him. "You remember Althurna?"

"Your assistant, of course," Kron said.

Althurna gave a curt nod, but she did not look up.

"My apologies for being late," Randall said.

"No need to apologize, I think," Lalo said. "A healer has his duties, after all."

His hands free once more, Kron gave a slow spin, taking in all his friends, though his relationship with the Finder was more cordial than truly friendly, the two sharing some financial and political past. A rare smile appeared on Kron's lips, but then it was a rare thing for all of them to be together like this. He seemed uncertain of how to proceed.

Gris chuckled. "Nodana has been planning this for weeks, Kron. She would have had more people here, but I insisted we keep the gathering rather small. There are official functions to be performed, after all, and there's no need to bore half the city with the details."

Kron looked to his lover. "This was just to be an inspection."

"I know that," Nodana said, her smile broad, "but you and Montolio have been working on this place for a year. The two of you deserve a little fun. Besides, all your work is worthy of some celebration. Nothing wrong with mixing business and pleasure."

The captain chuckled again. "Have you had a tour yet?" he asked of Nodana.

Kron answered for her. "She won't go inside the place."

"Why not?" Gris asked. "It looks just like it did before the accident."

Nodana shivered. "That's the problem. The history here is so ... unsettling."

Now it was Kron who chuckled. "I think she's just afraid of the ghosts."

"Ghosts are no laughing matter," Nodana said. "Wizard I might be, but any mage with sense won't cross the dead."

Montolio stepped forward and placed a gentle hand on the woman's arm. "No worries, m'lady. The place is truly haunted, but the spirits rarely show themselves. And when they do, they've caused no harm. In actuality, they seem to protect the place, guarding it now as they did in life."

"You're sure about that?" she asked.

"I am," the architect went on. "I've cast a few espial magics myself, and I've found nothing dangerous within the Asylum. Some disturbing memories, perhaps, but nothing to harm anyone now, at least nothing to harm any of us."

"I concur," Randall added. As a healer, he was also a noted mage. "I've done my own investigations and the place seems safe."

"See," Gris said to Nodana. "You should have Kron give you the tour sometime. Montolio and I have spent the last few days going over the building and the grounds, and I must admit it is comparatively homey from what it used to be."

"You've already been on tour?" Kron asked.

"I have," Gris said with a grin. "I wanted it out of the way before today's festivities. In fact, I've already signed the official documents. They're in my saddle bags only awaiting your mark."

Appearing confused, Randall asked, "What is all this about? Is the city buying the Asylum?"

"Not exactly," the captain said. "More of a temporary lease."

Nodana eased up next to Kron and nudged him with an elbow. "Yes, it's about time you told us the details."

"Perhaps inside?" Lalo questioned, pointing toward the open tent, warmth and the waiting meal.

Several laughs spread throughout the gathering.

"Of course," Gris said. "We can talk while we eat. And no need to stand out here in the cold."

As the group filed into the tent, they discovered their dining room was quite toasty, so much so they began to remove their coats and cloaks, turning them over to the waiting staff who folded the garments and placed them on top of a crate in a corner. The party then took their seats, Nodana leading Kron to the head of the table at the back of the tent, the stove and the rows of food behind him. She took the seat to his right where she could occasionally grip him by the hand. Being the closest of Kron's friends, Randall took the seat to the man's left, Althurna quietly slipping into position next to the healer. Captain Gris sat to the right of Nodana, Lalo the Finder to the right of him, with Montolio finding a spot across from them next to Althurna.

Which left a handful of empty chairs.

"I told you Nodana wanted more guests," Gris said, "but I persuaded her otherwise."

"Who else could there have been?" Montolio asked.

"My body guard is quite fond of Master Darkbow," Lalo pointed out.

"Eel?" Nodana asked.

"That's the one," Lalo said. "He would have come, but ... well ..." His voice trailed off.

"It was my doing," Gris cut in. "Some of today's talk will not be for all ears, so I weeded out the guest list. I'm sure Lalo would vouch for Eel, as might Kron, but I didn't want our party to grow too large. The fewer ears, the fewer mouths, so to speak."

"So this isn't going to be all fun and games?" Kron asked.

Captain Gris smiled. "This little gathering is for you, my friend, but we still have official matters to discuss. Plus, something else has come up."

"Can it wait?" Nodana asked. "I'm famished, and the food looks fabulous."

General laughter was her answer, then the serving staff came forward with wooden platters and bowls of food.

The meal was mostly simple but quality fare, in respect to the guest of honor. A goose was served, as was a small ham. Several varieties of rolls were available next to a steaming bowl of mixed vegetables, mostly cabbages, beets and onions with a few legumes. All of this was washed down with a weak mulberry wine.

One side dish stood out from the rest. It appeared to be made up of small slivers of some kind of meat covered in a red sauce.

"What is that?" Gris asked at one point, targeting his fork at the dish.

"I believe it is thrush tongues covered in a raspberry jelly," Lalo the Finder answered.

Montolio gave a nod of agreement. "Though not common, I used to see it from time to time in Lycinia. I believe it was quite expensive."

Nodana squeezed Kron by the hand and smiled at him. "I wanted something unique for today."

"It is quite tasty, I'll admit," Kron answered.

Lalo let out a little laugh. "With all the festivities, I'm almost surprised there's not a ribbon cutting ceremony."

This brought further laughter from around the table.

"Speaking of which," Gris spoke up, "perhaps it's time we consider changing what we call the place. It's no longer an asylum, so why not give it another name?"

"I suppose it depends upon what use the city is putting it," Randall said.

"No." The single word came from Kron. It was spoken in a low tone and there was a menace to it, his eyes hooded as he stared out across the table and allowed Nodana's hand to slip from his own. The room seemed to chill.

No stranger to that gaze, Captain Gris did not allow it to stop him from pressing. "What do you mean?"

"It remains the Asylum," Kron said. "I bought it with that title, and it will remain with it."

The captain gave a shrug of indifference. "As you wish. After all, it's your property, and I suppose you might take it back from the city after a while."

Silence rolled over the table for a moment, but then the room warmed as Kron gave a nod of the head and a weak grin.

"Of course," he said.

The meal was soon finished, the table cleared and the waiting staff allowed to go about their way with promises from Nodana that she and Montolio would see to any of the party's remaining needs and that they would clean up any mess. During the hustle and bustle, Kron noted a few odd looks from Nodana, but she said nothing and he let it go. Plates of warm food were then taken to the four guards waiting outside the gate, the city's finest thankful to have their belly's filled on a winter's day. While with his men, Captain Gris gave orders for the tent and stove to be removed by the day's fall.

After that the party retired to the tent once more, the flaps pulled closed and wooden mugs of cider passed around, though Lalo and Nodana continued to sip at wine.

Randall spoke up first. "So now that we are alone, what is with all this secrecy concerning the Asylum?"

"I'm not sure 'secrecy' is the right word," Gris said. "They are more like simple precautions being put into place."

"That still doesn't tell me anything," the healer said.

"The ghosts gave me the idea," Kron said. "Not directly, of course. They never speak with anyone, at least not directly. But it occurred to me any man who could live with such ... entities ... also would have the nerve to face down magic."

Randall appeared none the wiser, and his face screwed up in displeasure at what he was hearing. "So the Asylum is to be some kind of testing ground?"

"No, no," Gris said. "Not exactly, anyway."

Nodana sighed. "Leave it to these two to make use of a bunch of words while never saying anything."

Althurna let out a giggle, drawing more than a few curious looks.

Nodana turned to Randall. "Let me try and explain. I realize you're not from Ursia and might not be aware of all the intricacies, but magic has only been legal here in the West for a few generations."

"I'm well aware of that," the healer said.

"But have you noticed over time that magic's use has become more and more common? Events of recent years have shown magic has the potential to disrupt public life, in a manner of speaking. Understand?"

Randall nodded. Of course he understood. It had been his magic gone awry which had been part of the disaster of the Asylum's recent past.

"The city had to do something," Nodana continued. "The government had to do something. Yet politician after politician has been elected without any public recognition of the troubles on the streets. Despite its legality, magic has never been a popular topic for Ursians. Though split from the East, the people here still have a long distrust of all things having to do with the arts of glamour. Finally, Captain Gris and Lieutenant Darkbow approached Mayor Karn and talked her into doing something, and First Councilor Menoch has not only given his blessing, but has provided a certain level of financial and political support."

Gris cut in. "It was Kron's training which really clinched the deal. Without that, we might not be sitting here today."

The healer still did not appear to know what was going on. He turned to Montolio. "Can you tell me what they're talking about?"

"Kron and Gris are putting together a special unit to deal with magic-related crime in the street," the architect explained.

Lalo chuckled. "Finally, a straight answer."

"But what does this have to do with the Asylum?" Randall asked.

"The Asylum will house this new unit," Gris said. "It includes training grounds and living quarters."

"I converted all the old cells into private sleeping chambers," Montolio said, "and made a few other modifications. The warden's office has been converted into Kron's personal quarters, and the basement now includes an alchemist's workshop. There is even a small library and a chamber for magical testing and applications."

"I helped oversee that," Nodana said. "If special members of the city guard are to be trained in thwarting magic, they need to become familiar with experiencing such."

"And then there will be the squad mages," Montolio added. "This was Kron's idea, too, something they apparently do in the Prisonlands. The unit will be broken up into various squads, each having at least one wizard. Nodana here proved herself invaluable in rounding up potential squad mages."

Randall held up a hand. "Hold on a second. Who will be doing the training?"

"I'll handle most of it early on," Kron said, "but Montolio will take care of the squad mages, with the occasional aid from Frex."

Randall appeared more confused than ever. "But I thought you were turning the Asylum into a private residence. Where are you going to live?"

"I'll have my personal chamber here," Kron said, "but I've still got my apartment above the Rusty Scabbard. And of late I've spent much time at Nodana's."

The woman-mage allowed a slight blush.

"I'll always be in residence here," Montolio said. "Gris has hired me as some kind of lower-level officer."

"You'll be second lieutenant under Kron," the captain said.

"I'll also be in charge of the grounds," Montolio went on. "It's perfect for me. I was only in the construction business to help make ends meet."

The healer pointed to Gris. "You mentioned Kron having some special training. From his days as a warden?"

"That's correct," the captain answered. "He worked with knights from the East who were specifically trained in combating wizards since they don't take kindly to magic over there. I received a little of the training myself, but Kron gained far more experience than anyone else I know of in the West."

Randall gave Lalo a questioning look. "Where do you fit in all this?"

Gris answered for the Finder. "Honestly, Lalo did all the *real* work. I'm still new as captain of the guard, and I'm no politician. Neither is Kron. The Finder smoothed the way for us with most of the bureaucratic nonsense. And if it weren't for him, we likely wouldn't have received funding from the state. He impressed First Councilor Menoch so much that not only did we get the money needed, but our special unit is considered a testing ground for the regular army. If all goes well, within a few years there could be squad mages throughout all West Ursia."

"East Ursia will just love us for that," Nodana added with a snicker.

Kron turned to Randall. "My apologies, old friend, for not including you in any of this. But I know you've been busy at the healing tower. Besides, Frex and Montolio have take care of all our needs concerning magic."

"No apology necessary," Randall said. "A healer's work is never done, after all. I'm just surprised by all this. The lot of you have been busy these past months."

"You can say that again," Gris said.

Laughter erupted from the group.

The Finder sat forward in his chair and stared at the captain. "One thing I've been curious about ... you do realize this will change the position of the city guard quite drastically, don't you?"

"Obviously," Gris said. "Until now the guard has been an arm of the national military. Starting with our new special unit, and perhaps eventually the rest of the guard, we will become a wing of city government, answerable to myself and the mayor, ultimately to the city council. Frankly, the time is right. The city is big enough and complex enough that a policing force of some nature is necessary. Historically when the city officials have not set up some sort of law-enforcement group, the locals take it upon themselves, usually through street gangs and the like."

"And we don't want that," Nodana said.

Lalo nodded in agreement. "I understand. It would be a return to the days of Belgad."

"True," Gris went on, "and the city can no longer afford that much power in the hands of one individual, whether a private or public individual. We broke from the East in no small part because of such a situation, and now is the time to firm all this up. It helps that Kron and I are border wardens and have some training in matters more appropriate for a policing force than for the military."

"To be clear, this transition will go beyond your special squads into the rest of the guard?" Lalo asked.

"Some of it, perhaps," Gris said, "though that will probably take some while, perhaps a few years. It will all depend upon the success of the initial squads."

"Which becomes official when?" Lalo asked.

The captain chuckled. "As soon as Kron here signs the papers in my saddle bags and officially leases out the Asylum and its grounds to the city. The first training sessions begins tomorrow morning."

Darkbow pushed away from the table and stood. "With those words, I think it time we got about our business. This has been a most pleasant feast and gathering, but there is work to be done."

"I'll be right back," Gris said, standing and exiting.

Lalo also stood. "It has been a most pleasant, and informative, gathering, but guilds business awaits. If you will excuse me?"

A few pleasantries passed among the group, and then the Finder made his way out.

"I suppose I should be getting back to the tower," Randall said, rising from his seat, Althurna standing next to him.

Gris returned, pushing his way through the tent's flaps, a stack of papers in one hand, a small iron bottle and a pair of quills in the other. "Randall, you leaving?"

"I thought it time," the healer said.

Placing his load upon the table near Kron, the captain motioned for Randall and Althurna to sit. "If you would, please. There is one other thing I would like to discuss with those of us here."

With concerned looks, the healer and his assistant returned to their chairs.

"Should I retrieve Lalo before he gets too far?" offered Montolio.

"I don't think so," Gris said with a shake of his head. "I passed him coming in, said my good-byes. And this is a matter I don't believe needs to occupy him."

"Well, get to it, man," Kron said.

Taking a seat, Gris looked to Darkbow. "Remember those bones you and Montolio retrieved from that wizard and his demon?"

"Of course," Kron said.

"They've gone missing."

"Missing?" Randall asked. "From the university?"

"Yes," Gris said to the healer. "After you looked them over and couldn't find anything out of the ordinary about them, I had them taken to a group of professors at the College of Magic."

"I wouldn't say there was *nothing* unusual about them," Randall said. "There was some latent magic within, but I detected nothing else."

"Neither did I," Montolio added.

"Whatever they might truly be," the captain went on, "they've disappeared. Two nights ago. But that's not the weirdest thing."

"What is?" Nodana asked.

"There was a student working late in the very room where the bones were stored," Gris said, "and he has gone missing as well."

"Stole them?" Kron asked.

"Maybe," Gris said, "but I don't think so. The young man has no such history."

"I'm guessing you asked some of the schools' wizards to search for the item, and the student?" Nodana said.

"I have," Gris said, "but they've turned up nothing. I thought some of you might want to give it a try."

"The university has some of the strongest wizards in the city," Randall said. "I can't speak for Nodana and Montolio here, but I'm not sure I could add anything to the search, though I'm more than willing to make the attempt."

"Normally it should be a fairly simple matter of a location spell," Nodana said, "which makes me think one of two things has happened. Either the bones have been sent far away, which would make it much more difficult to find them, or else someone has placed a protective shielding ward upon the bones to keep them from being found. It would take someone fairly powerful, however, to thwart a search of the university's finest."

"I don't think our missing student would have had such skill," Gris said.

"But someone could also be hiding him," Nodana pointed out.

"Or they've killed him," Kron said.

The grim words brought around all heads to stare at the man at the head of the table.

"Merely the most likely outcome," Kron said.

Gris nodded. "A possibility, but I won't give up hope for the young man just yet. We've had two days of searching, both the wizards at the school and my men on the streets, and nothing has turned up. I'm thinking someone must have stolen the bones thinking they could sell them, and this student was simply in the wrong place at the wrong time."

"But who would have even known about the bones?" Randall asked. "True, their existence wasn't kept secret, but it also wasn't as if the bones were common knowledge."

"Word gets around in the underworld," Kron said. "The horrors last year with that wizard and his demon, they were public enough. All it would have taken was one city guard, or even one of us, inadvertently passing along word of the bones. Stories travel, and eventually they get to an ear that can make use of the information."

"The thieves guild?" Gris asked.

"Always a good place to start when something is missing," Kron said. "Perhaps some sorcerer seeks the bones and hired them. If you want, I can drop in on Spider."

"But we don't know the location of their latest hideaway."

Kron smirked. "*You* might not know."

For a moment the captain of the city guard looked nonplussed, then he let out a slight chuckle. "All right, all right. Speak with Spider, but try not to rough up too many of his boys."

"Depends upon how I am received," Kron said with a dark grin.

"Enough." Gris slapped the stack of papers on the table. "Let's get these signed, then everyone can be about their day."

4

Midge Highwater couldn't help but grimace as he slurped at the mug of warm ale before him. The drink tasted like bilge water as far as he was concerned, though it had been many a year since he had spent any time at sea. He nearly chuckled as he returned the clay vessel to the top of the bar. He was becoming too snooty, he figured. *Been living too long down in Southtown where a man can buy a decent brew for a few coppers.* Not that he thought he was too good for the Swamps, nor The Stone Pony, where he now sat facing the bar. He had been raised in the Swamps, at least in a manner of speaking, having called the place home at one point for longer than he could remember. It was just that his tastes had changed along with his change of address some decades earlier. His move to Southtown, the portion of Bond across the South River from the Swamps, had not been an easy one to make, but it had been necessary. He had been growing old, was older now, and the only way he could find to make a living was as a storyteller. And unfortunately, few hands in the Swamps could afford to pay for something as nonsensical as a story. Now the Southtowners, those fools parted with their gold far too easily. The rich folk in Uptown? Those rich bastards were skinflints. Thus Southtown had been Midge's home for more than a decade.

In fact, he rarely crossed Frist Bridge back into the Swamps. He hardly ever had a need. No family living, few friends. All he had left was a small room in the back of the Rusty Scabbard tavern and the thousands of tales roaming around within his brain. That and the fact he kept abreast of all the news there was worth knowing, and even some that *wasn't* worth knowing, because a man never could tell when some little piece of information could prove important.

Such news was what had brought him over to the Swamps for the first time in years, specifically to the tavern and inn known as The Stone Pony.

Slowly turning around on his bar stool, he looked across the heads of the dozen or so patrons to the subject of the recent news, not that one man normally drew much notice in a city the size of Bond. This man, however, the one Midge now watched, stood out from the crowd.

The fellow was a knight, which was obvious by the tarnished steel plate covering his breast, the padded leathers beneath and the lengthy sword leaning against his table not far from his right hand. Knights weren't all that common any more, especially a knight from another country, and plate armor was out of fashion, even if just a chest covering. This man was a knight of Caballerus, the nation north of West Ursia, as revealed by the emblem of a horse etched into his chest's armor. Knights of Caballerus were not known to leave their homeland, not unless they were in escort to their king.

Which was a sad tale in and of itself. The king of Caballerus was dead, murdered this past year by his own brother who then took the throne for himself. Which meant Caballerus had a new king, Midge supposed, though how someone could call such a traitorous, murderous swine a king was beyond the storyteller.

It occurred to Midge this might explain why the knight was sitting in a bar in a nation foreign to himself. It might explain the nearly empty bottle of Ursian brandy resting in front of the knight upon the table there. It also might explain the blank, forlorn, unblinking stare the unshaven fellow consistently wore.

Another storyteller, a man of lesser skill, had brought word to Midge of this armored stranger. At first Midge had been suspect of the description, but now he saw it fit quite well. The swordsman drinking over there was a man with problems, a man with a soul burned to ashes. That much was obvious, which was probably why the rest of The Stone Pony's clients gave the knight's table a wide berth.

It also occurred to Midge that perhaps this fellow wasn't a knight. Maybe he was just a skilled fighter, a mercenary who had had some luck in combat and had slain a knight of Caballerus. Maybe this mercenary simply wore the armor and weapons of his fallen foe. But Midge did away with this notion rather quickly. That sorrowful drinking fellow, there was still something vaguely noble about him. He was down on his luck, obviously, but the few movements he made, usually bringing the bottle to his lips, still contained almost a regal sense to them.

No, this man was definitely a knight. Or had been a knight.

He probably had a hell of a story to tell. *If* Midge could just wheedle it out of him.

The storyteller stood, half turned towards the nearest bartender, planning to order a bottle of Ursian brandy, a gift for a potential new friend.

Then the front door opened and in tromped a face Midge had not seen in five years.

Kilchus the Sword.

Midge eased back onto his stool and reached up to tug down the wide brim of his hat to hide his features.

Kilchus was scum. The worst sort of man. Oh, he wasn't an assassin or some crazed killer, no. That would be too precise for Kilchus. He was a bully, through and through. And Midge knew his story, too. Sent off to the Prisonlands as a border warden, when by all rights he should have been a prisoner. Kilchus's connections with Belgad the Liar had saved him from that. Which was too bad, Midge believed, because the world would be a better place with the likes of Kilchus locked away somewhere. The Sword had beaten half a dozen men senseless, nearly to their grave, in this very tavern. Two of the men had been little more than boys, not even twenty years of age. None of them had deserved what they got, just good hard-working dock laborers minding their own business while sipping a beer or two. For some reason, Kilchus had taken a disliking to one of them, which had led to blows and broken bones. Kilchus, a trained fighter in light armor against six fellows who hadn't even served in the military nor been brought up on the rougher side of the streets. Every now and then Midge would spot one of those boys on the streets. Neither of the younger ones could walk, reduced to begging because their legs were crippled, tied up beneath them as they shuffled along with crutches. And the other four men hadn't fared much better, one of them rumored to be a permanent guest at the Swamps healing tower because of his constant pain.

Thankfully Midge knew of no reason he could be in Kilchus's disfavor, but he did not want to test those waters. That fight here at The Stone Pony had not been the Sword's first troubles.

The storyteller started to turn fully away.

Then halted again, his eyes hooded but watching from beneath the brim of his hat.

Kilchus was walking to the knight. Oh, the Sword tried to hide it, kind of, by meandering about a bit, but there was no doubt where he was headed.

Kilchus barely stopped as he reached the armored man's table. He muttered a few words, the knight nodded and muttered some speech of his own, then Kilchus sauntered on past as if he had never been there. Midge's eyes watched as the Sword made his way up the stairs to the second level of the Pony. The knight appeared unchanging, unblinking, barely aware of his surroundings.

Funny, Midge hadn't even realized until then that the stairwell was almost directly behind the knight, as if the armored figure was keeping a watch, possibly even keeping guard.

The storyteller turned back to the bar, tossed down the last of his nasty ale in its mug, and promptly exited. He had seen enough. Kilchus the Sword was back and he was up to no good. Midge Highwater was sure of that, and he wanted no part of it. The knight's tale would have to wait. Whatever Kilchus's plans might entail, Midge could find out the story later. From the survivors.

If there were any.

***

Only when he reached the top of the stairs did Kilchus stop and glance into the main room below. Midge Highwater. There was no mistaking those grizzled features, even with that big floppy hat on top of the old man's head. The storyteller was making his way out the swinging front doors, and he was wasting no time about it.

Kilchus almost laughed. Let the old bastard fear him, and let his tongue wag for all the Sword cared. It wasn't like Midge was any kind of real threat, and Kilchus wasn't exactly hiding his return to the city. Sure, he had left under a bit of a cloud, but five years was a long time in city life, and Kilchus could easily provide an excuse for no longer remaining in the Prisonlands, even if that excuse was a lie. By the time anyone could check on his story, Kilchus would be long gone. Or at least that was the plan.

Grinning to himself at thoughts of old Midge, he turned and walked the length of the upper floor until coming to a halt in front of a door to one of the Pony's sleeping rooms.

He knocked.

There was no answer.

Good.

Kilchus retrieved a key from a pocket of his pantaloons, then unlocked the door. In one swift move he pushed his way through, closed the door behind him and turned the lock from his side.

The chamber was nearly in darkness, no candles or lamps burning and the only light a haze pouring through a window covered by a reddish curtain.

"Falk," Kilchus said.

"Over here," was the return answer.

"Where? Damn it, man, I can't see a thing, you keep it so dark."

A thin, bony hand reached up from the shadows of a bed and grasped at the curtains, pulling them aside to allow the day's light to flood the room.

"Better?" said the voice belonging to an old man sitting on the bed.

Kilchus nearly blanched. Falk looked worse every time he saw him, far worse than that old bastard Highwater below. Falk's head was nearly bereft of any hair, only a few white strands remaining to flutter around above his skull; his skin was tight, giving his face and hands almost a skeletal appearance. The gray robes covering the old man's frame enveloped him, though Falk was not small in height.

"Damn, you're a sight," Kilchus finally managed. "And why are you sitting here in the dark?"

An eerie grin crossed the old man's lips. "The same reason I didn't answer the door when you knocked. In case it was someone besides you. Anyway, you'd look this bad, too, if you were dying."

Kilchus smirked. "You ain't dying. You're just old."

"Same thing."

"Yeah, maybe so at your age. But that don't mean there's still not work to be done."

"True enough," Falk said. "Tell me, did you speak with Lalo?"

"He wasn't home," Kilchus said. "Don't worry, I told his boy where to find me. If I don't hear something by tonight, I'll drop in on him again."

"We can't proceed until we talk with the Finder."

"I understand. Still, the visit wasn't a total waste."

"How is that?"

"I found out a few things," Kilchus said, "a few surprises, to tell the truth. You remember Belgad's boy Spider?"

The old man shook his head.

"I suppose Spider would have been beneath your notice," the Sword said. "Anyway, he's the boss of the thieves guild."

"Thieves guild? Impossible."

"That's what I was thinking, but you know, without Belgad around, anything could have happened. Whatever the case, it seems the streets of Bond ain't the same as they were a few years ago."

"Can this Spider prove of any worth to us?" Falk asked.

"Maybe," Kilchus said. "It wouldn't hurt to pay a visit. If Lalo turns us down, maybe Spider can help somehow. If nothing else, he might be able to lend us a little muscle, if it should come to that."

"I think not. We've enough between you, the twins and Curval downstairs. By the way, how did he look when you came in?"

"Same as ever. Still moping. And since you mentioned them, where *are* the twins?"

Falk waved a hand toward the window. "Out. Scouting. I told them it was a waste of time, but they insisted on learning the streets of the city. 'Just in case,' they said."

"Not a bad idea, them being strangers here," Kilchus said. "It always pays to have an escape route and a back-up plan. Speaking of which, Lalo's boy told me the city guard might be hiring."

The old man glared at him. "You would consider this?"

The Sword shrugged. "Why not? I never place all my money upon a single card, and I might learn some things. Besides, it's not as if you're promising anything solid."

"That's true," Falk said with a nod, "but if I should fall, you are likely to fall with me. It is not as if we do not share some history."

"Maybe, but there are other options. You might not get what you came here for, but that doesn't mean Lalo or anybody else will turn you in."

"Let us hope it does not come to that."

Kilchus gave a dark grin. "Yes, let's."

***

The person who had been Malin the Quill nearly stumbled as he made his way along yet another alley. It had been a long, long time since Sadhe Teth had walked with mortal legs, and even after two days he was not quite again familiar with the sensation. The same with thinking. His mind was a whirl of patterns and thoughts and memories. At first upon implanting his soul within Malin's body he had not been able to tell the difference between himself and the young man. He had spent hours within that strange room at the college, huddled in a corner with his arms wrapped around his head. Slowly, ever so slowly, his thoughts had formed a semblance of sanity.

Sadhe Teth lived again, even if in a stolen body. Malin the Quill wasn't quite dead, not yet. A piece of the youth's soul still swam at the center of the mind Sadhe now controlled, and this was why the long-dead wizard continued to struggle from time to time with simple tasks such as walking. Malin was stronger than Sadhe would have thought, likely because of the youth's minor training in magic, and every so often that little piece of soul flexed and pushed, trying to retake what had once been his.

That would never happen. Sadhe Teth was far, far too strong to relinquish the body he now considered home.

Coming to the end of the alley, he straightened, the momentary wave of dizziness passing as he mentally pushed Malin the Quill back down, deep down. Leaning against a wall to rest for a moment, Sadhe stared out at the traffic crossing his path along a street.

It was a busy road in a busy city. That much he had learned. It was by far the largest city he had ever experienced, though memories from Malin seemed to think nothing of it. The name of the city was Bond, which struck Sadhe Teth as odd. Cities were usually named after a person or perhaps another place, or even a feature of the land. Perhaps there had been someone named Bond in the city's past, but that seemed unlikely and did not fit with what little history he could pull forth from Malin's mind.

Pushing off the wall, the man that was part Malin the Quill and part Sadhe Teth reached inside his cloak, a garment almost left behind at the university. The sensation of cold had been forgotten over the centuries, but a part of Malin had suggested the cloak. Snow had also been forgotten, and upon seeing it for the first time in eons Sadhe had stood in awe at the white powder drifting down from the sky. Now in his new body for a couple of days, and with his memories returning, he was less fond of the snow, much of it stained brown and full of animal excrement, especially near the roads. Yet he still found potential in all that white.

For a moment he panicked. Feeling around inside the cloak he could not find that most precious of items. Then his fingers landed upon the wrappings of bones tied to the back of his belt. Gripping those rolled-up leathers, relief flooded through him and his head swam. He grinned. His goal was the same, always the same, and the bones were his key to triumph.

Yet there had been recent moments of doubt.

He still knew too little of the current world, especially concerning magic. Sadhe had been more than surprised by learning of Malin's studies in sorcery and of the actual existence of a school that taught magic. This seemed not preposterous, but definitely unusual. Had magic become so common anyone could learn to harness the eldritch powers?

That seemed not possible. Sadhe had lived long enough to know magic waxed and waned in the world, more due to the interest or lack of from mankind than anything, but he had never before experienced such seeming casualness concerning magic. Even though he had only Malin's memories to go on, it seemed magic flourished within the world, at least within the city. This was nothing like what Sadhe recalled of earlier times in which magic had been quite rare, made use of only by the elite, the rulers, the priests, those powerful in their own right. Still, the majority of magics produced in this new world were of a weaker level, not containing the strength of the ancients.

What was so maddening was that everything was new to him, far different than the old days.

There were ways to discover more of the city, of the world. He frowned thinking about such. He could open himself up, could open his soul to the world, to magic, and thus garner much information, even if for only a moment. But there were dangers.

Any use of magic, or any person skilled in magic, could be noticed by other spell casters, even from some distance. It was a simple trick in fact. And the more powerful the magics and the more powerful the caster, the more they stood out to others. Generally all it took was for a wizard to be paying attention, but specific spells could be cast which would allow a search of the world of magic, only limited by the caster's own abilities. There were ways around this, however. Always the sly one, Sadhe kept his presence shielded with wards, a constant that drained him tremendously but he felt necessary and worth the risks considering his own considerable level of power. However, he would have to drop those wards if he were to do a serious scan of the city.

Such seemed to be proving more and more necessary. He simply did not have enough knowledge. While Malin's memories proved helpful, there was still so much to learn, and the young man's soul and mind did not always cooperate as well as Sadhe Teth would have liked.

He eased back into the griminess of the alley. Here he was alone. Here he could take but a moment to reach out into the world of magic to discover what he would discover.

It was time.

Shuffling even deeper into the alley, he finally stopped and placed his back against a wall. Then he closed his eyes.

It was simply a matter of dropping walls and reaching out.

A thousand pins impaled him.

A hammer slammed into his stomach.

Sadhe Teth cast up his defenses again as he nearly collapsed onto the dirty floor of the alley. He huddled and shivered, his arms wrapped around his legs.

The wind had been knocked from him. It took several minutes for him to recover. When he finally found himself once more, standing and shaking off the dizziness, he realized he had much to consider and much of concern.

Someone with power was out there in the city. Possibly this individual was a wizard, but they had seemed stronger than any mere mortal, as strong as one of the gods of old.

There was also matter that magic was prevalent in the city, especially in the northeast corner where the university sat. For that matter the northern portion of the city seemed to hold a majority of the magic, mostly individual spell casters, but there were lesser spots of the old arts here and there throughout nearly all of Bond. Such knowledge nearly knocked the wind from Sadhe's new body. Magic had existed since the earliest of times, but it had never been this common. How the world had changed.

Far more important, and far more chilling, was the existence of that one particular, powerful being. Sadhe Teth did not know who this person was, if it even was a person, nor did he know exactly where they resided within the city. What he did know, however, was that they were out there somewhere to the west of him and they were powerful. *Very* powerful. Possibly as powerful as the god who had supplied the bones Sadhe now carried. Could it even *be* one of the old gods? Not impossible.

This knowledge was enough to shake him, and it was enough for him to close himself up once more in a protective shell by doubling his defenses. Now no other user of magic would be able to know of his existence within the city. But would it be enough? One of the old gods could have broken through Sadhe's protections, so it was not impossible this other figure could do the same.

He hoped he had not been noticed during his brief exposure, but there was nothing to be done about that now.

Sadhe had to be careful, which was one reason he had wandered the streets for nearly two days. He did not know what to do, where to go, how to begin. Now there was fear, an emotion little known to the ancient mage. He needed time, time to acclimate himself to the modern world.

He sagged, his shoulders quaking. The pool of souls within him was deep, giving him the ability to call upon the strongest of magics, yet he was still befuddled in the mind and body.

He berated himself for having dropped his defenses, for being weak of will, in having the need to know more of the world. But just as quickly he realized that blaming himself was silly. Knowledge was power, and he had had to know.

Now he knew.

He would have to remain hidden. Malin's pockets had contained some few coins, enough to provide meals for a few days, so there were no worries there, and Teth could provide himself with warmth at night through his magic. Shelter was the only thing wanting, and that he could survive without for a few days. If not, then he would have to change bodies again. His old bones now rested at the bottom of a river where he had tossed them upon leaving Malin's university, but a new body could always be found.

He straightened, gathering his strength. Time to move. Standing still for too long could draw unwanted attention if someone should glance down the alley. He had to stay on the move. That was the way to avoid detection.

Nearing the street once more, he saw a sign that informed him he faced Rovers Road, or at least that's what Malin's memories of the local language told him.

Another road, more faces. He was learning, slowly but surely. Eventually, once he felt he had the lay of the land, it would be time to get on with his work.

Then a lot of people would die. A lot.

He grinned at the thought.

But then he frowned.

There was that *other* out there. That individual posed a threat. Of that Sadhe Teth was sure.

He would have to do something about that.

***

Randall winced. He couldn't help it, though the sensation was more one of surprise than actual pain. Then he swayed on his feet, his vision blurring for a moment. He put out a hand, placing it flat against the door in front of him, the door to his hospitaler rooms in the Swamps healing tower. It seemed that hand and that door were all that held him on his feet.

Behind him, the hall was filled with the comings and goings of the sick and dying and other healers, none of them as skilled as Randall himself, most of them not even mages.

A hand grabbed the healer by an arm.

Randall blinked and looked around. The features of Althurna stared back at him, the dark eyes filled with concern behind those long bangs.

The moment had passed. Whatever had happened to him, it was over. No. Not *whatever*. He knew what had happened. He had not felt such a sensation in years, since before the vanquishing of his father.

He forced a smile at Althurna. "I am fine," he said, grasping her hand and squeezing.

She did not let go, her eyes staring hard into his. She knew something was wrong, even if it wasn't something directly wrong with *him*.

Randall glanced around. There were too many people. He could say nothing to Althurna here. It was too public a place. But to push on into his rooms, that was out of the question. Time might be of the essence.

"I need to see Kron," he said, "or Captain Gris."

Confusion filled Althurna's features as she glanced back down the hall the way they had come.

"Yes, I know it has not been that long since we left them," Randall said, "but this ... it could be important."

5

A wave of a hand, a few magic words, and the front steps of The Frog's Bottom had a thin sheet of ice layered upon them. Which was the way Spider wanted it. Just let those drunken fools wander their way up to the whorehouse's front door. It was the Swamps, and no one would notice a few ruffians rushing forward to empty the pockets of drunken, fallen fools. Not even the whores would say a word. Why should they? They were in on the deal, and at least for the rest of the day few of them would have to spread their legs to get paid, maybe even into the night if things worked out well.

Spider bundled his coat around him and squatted and waited behind a wooden crate at the head of an alley a couple of blocks from the entrance to The Frog's Bottom. His job was done, the casting of the little spell. Now all he had to do was wait. His three men would do the rest of the work. They were waiting closer to the whorehouse, the trio tucked away in another alley. As soon as some drunken idiot came trotting up those steps, then fell on his ass, the three would make their move. Easy coin. Spider was glad he had thought of the idea.

It was enough to make him smile.

Until he felt a heavy grip upon one of his shoulders.

"I wouldn't run if I were you," said a familiar voice.

Spider felt his heart sink.

"I've already sent your three goons upon their way," said Kron Darkbow to the thief's back. "Count yourself lucky I don't haul the lot of you in and drop you in jail."

The grip tightened, then lifted Spider to his feet and pulled, dragging the master of the thieves guild deeper into the alley. Spider did not fight. He knew better.

Once they reached the further coolness of shadows, Kron pressed the much smaller man against the alley's wall.

"I suppose this is where you beat me now," Spider said, glaring up at the man wearing black as was his custom on the streets.

Surprise of surprises, Kron dropped his restraining hand and retreated, grinning. "I think not. I'm trying to reform myself."

That was nearly enough to make the thief snicker.

"But I see you have not changed *your* ways," Kron added.

"We weren't doing anything," Spider said. "Just keeping a watch out, like our city charter says."

"Your city charter gives your guild permission to watch the Docks in order to halt outright pilfering," Kron added. "Yet I see you are nowhere near the Docks."

Spider gulped.

Kron grinned again. "Don't worry. I'm not here to cause you any trouble."

"The last time we met you gave me *this*." Spider raised his top lip to show where a tooth was missing. "And you expect me to believe you aren't going to cause me grief?"

"If I remember correctly," Kron said, "you lost that tooth when your jaw hit the ground."

"Which wouldn't have happened if you hadn't punched me."

"True enough," the man in black said with a shrug. "My apologies. I'll admit you were kind enough at the time to call off your dogs, but it would have been one hell of a fight."

Yes, it would have been. A dozen or so of Spider's thugs against Kron Darkbow. Kron probably would have lost. Probably. But by then there would have no longer existed a thieves guild, just a bunch of crippled fools. Then again, there was barely a thieves guild now.

"All right, all right," Spider said, his eyes falling to the cold alley floor. "What is it you want this time?"

"Two nights ago something went missing from the university," Kron said, "and someone along with it."

Spider looked up and shook his head. "We don't operate at the university. You know that. Too many wizards."

"You spent some time there as a student," Kron added. "You know the territory."

"That was a long time ago. No, we don't go near the university. And that's in Uptown. You know we don't cross Coin Bridge. Not only wizards, but too much security up there."

"So you've not heard anything on the streets?"

"Not a peep."

"Nothing about anyone missing in Uptown? No one trying to sell something unusual?"

"Nope, not a thing."

"You're sure?"

Spider sighed. "Yes, I'm sure. I can keep my ears open, but if you won't tell me what it is you're looking for, I've got no way of helping you."

"You think I trust you to help me?"

"Look," Spider said, "I get it, okay. You're mister law and order around here. I'm the boss of the thieves guild. We're enemies. Have been since we first met back in Belgad's day. But if someone else is operating in town, then we've got a mutual enemy. So, yeah, you can trust me to help get any crooks off the street who aren't valid members of the guild."

Kron reached forward, causing the shorter man to flinch, then he patted Spider on a shoulder. "Perhaps you're not such a bad fellow after all."

"Just like anybody else," Spider said, "trying to survive, make a coin here and there."

The black gloved hand fell away. "Okay, Spider. I'll trust you this time. There's a student of magic went missing two nights ago from the university, and along with him some magical ... items. You don't need to know the details."

"Has it occurred to you this student probably pilfered your magic rings or jewels or whatever they are?"

"Of course," Kron said, "but from what little I know, it seems out of character for him."

"Maybe, but people can do funny things when they've got gold coins in their eyes."

"True enough."

"And with wizards, it's even crazier. Those bastards will do anything if they think it'll gain them some small amount of power or that they'll learn some ancient rites. It's why I left the college. Got sick of it all."

"Yet you spend your nights scrounging for coin?"

Spider nodded. "It might not be honest work, but it's more honest than whatever wizards get up to."

Kron couldn't help himself but grin. He half turned away. "If you hear anything, let me know."

"I will."

"You know where to find me."

"Everybody knows where the Asylum is."

"Good." Kron gave a nod, then walked out of the alley into the street, disappearing among the crowd.

Spider let out a sigh of relief.

Another hand fell on the thief's shoulder.

"So who was the bloke in black?" a voice asked from behind.

Spider did not need to turn around. He recognized that voice.

Kilchus the Sword

The mage thief felt his heart sink again.

***

The captain of the guard for Bond had an office in the city's official government building in Uptown, but Gris had never felt comfortable there. In fact, he rarely set foot in the building, only when attending to some official matter or having been called there by the mayor. Most of his days were spent in the Southtown barracks, the large building housing the majority of city guards whether on or off of duty; many guards lived there, the majority of them being single and relatively young, few older than thirty. The barracks in Southtown represented the face of the city guard to the general public, what most people thought of when they thought of the orange-garbed soldiers who walked among them. There were a few other, much smaller barracks buildings within the city, but those were rarely home to more than a half dozen guards at a time, used mainly as neighborhood offices.

Captain Gris preferred Southtown to Uptown. It was that simple. And he did not enjoy politics. Which was another reason to stay out of Uptown and away from the city government building. Some might consider him a down-to-earth fellow. Others saw it differently, that Gris was somewhat uncouth. The truth was probably somewhere in the middle.

He had kept his old office, the small, cluttered chamber he had used for years as a sergeant of the guard. The room fit his personality and his purposes. Other than it was too small to hold all the paperwork he dealt with on a daily basis. To help with the paperwork, he had had a shed built onto the back of the main barracks building. The paperwork was stuffed in there when he was finished with it. When the shed was full, he had another shed built next to it, and planned to do so yet again once that shed got full. Eventually he might have all those papers and scrolls and other nonsense hauled up to be dumped into his empty office in

Uptown, but for the time being he found the growing piles not worth the trouble.

If he had his way, there would be a big fire. But that would be courting trouble he did not desire.

So, the paperwork kept piling up.

As it currently had upon his desk in his office where he was squeezed behind the only large piece of furniture, the room so small his back was practically shoved up against the wall.

Gris sighed as he looked over some of the papers he had watched Kron sign that very morning. Everything seemed in order, but the captain wanted there to be no mistakes. It was a touchy matter, the city leasing private property for its own use.

A knock came to the door.

Glancing to the candle at his side, he saw it had not burnt much. What time was it? Late afternoon? No matter. He was needed.

"Come in," he said, looking up.

Randall Tendbones entered, his white robes swishing around as he closed the door behind him.

"This is a pleasant surprise, healer," Gris said, standing. "We just saw one another this morning. Something I can do for you?"

The two had a friendly relationship, though they weren't exactly friends themselves. They shared a mutual relation through Kron, and often they had worked together officially.

"I hope I'm not intruding," Randall said.

"Not at all," Gris said, motioning toward a chair in front of his desk. "Anything to get away from all these scrolls and papers. Please, have a seat."

"I'll stand, if you don't mind."

The captain smirked. "You've been friends with Kron for too long."

Randall couldn't help a smile of his own.

"So, what can I do for you?" Gris asked.

Randall's grin turned into a frown. "Something has happened, and I'm not quite sure how to explain it."

"Has a crime been committed?"

"It might be related to the missing bones."

Gris's eyes widened.

"But I'm not sure," Randall added. He hesitated to speak further as if unsure of his words.

"Randall, is it something bad?"

The healer shook his head. "It's just ... I'm not aware of how familiar you are with the workings of magic. I looked for Kron before coming here, but Nodana told me he was out."

Gris nodded. Kron was no practitioner of spellcasting, but for a lay person he was relatively well versed in the subject matter. "Try me," he said. "I spent more than a little time working with squad mages in the Lands."

"Do you understand that wizards can search an area for magical effects? Even for other wizards?"

"I'm familiar with the general notion. I don't know how it works, but I figure you cast a spell and you can see a glow or aura."

"It's more of a feeling, and it's not really a spell," Randall said. "It's kind of like the sky at night."

"How's that?"

"The stars and the moon, they are always there," Randall explained, "but walking along, you don't really notice them unless you look up."

"I guess I can understand that," Gris said. "This magic sensation, or whatever you want to call it, is always there, but you only notice it if you're looking for it."

"Exactly." Randall grinned again. "However, mages can hide themselves from being found. They can even hide the effects of their spells and those of magical objects. It's a fairly simple process."

"Okay, but what does this have to do with the bones?"

"I'm not sure it does," the healer said, "but earlier today ... well, I felt someone searching across the city. They were searching for magic."

"Across the whole city?"

"Yes, sir."

"I didn't realize wizards could search such a large area."

"Only the most powerful can do so," Randall said. "Like my father."

The captain grimaced. He was not personally familiar with Randall's father, the former king of Kobalos known as Lord Verkain, but he had heard the stories. Even Kron had let slip a few details here and there. The possibility of such an individual being loose in the city was more than a little disconcerting.

"I don't believe it was my father," Randall added.:

"That is a relief, however, you can't know for sure."

"No, I can't. But, my father ... let me just say that I think it would be too soon for him to come looking for me, if he should even want to do so."

"What does *that* mean?" Gris winced and held up a belaying hand. "Don't answer that. None of my business, and I'm not sure I want to know. But if it's not him, who else could it be?"

"Someone powerful."

"I don't like the sound of that."

"I didn't think you would," Randall said. "On my walk over here I did my own search and found nothing out of the ordinary, the usual street mages, the more powerful wizards at the college."

"Anything specific you can tell me about this person?"

The healer shook his head. "All I know is he or she is quite strong with magic, stronger than that murderous mage last year, stronger than any other wizard in the city."

"With the exception of yourself," Gris added.

"I didn't say that."

"You didn't have to," the captain said. "It speaks for itself. If every wizard from here to the Old Road knew about this ... person ... then there would be such a mess half the city would be knocking on my door, at least the mayor's office. Instead, only you showed up. That makes me think this wizard or whatever he is is powerful enough to hide his presence, except from you. Which tells me you are at least as powerful as he is, or maybe even stronger."

"I wouldn't want to test your theory," Randall said.

"I hope it doesn't come to that. But tell me, what makes you think this has something to do with the missing bones?"

"It might not, but it seems too much of a coincidence. It's also not impossible the person I sensed isn't normally so powerful, but perhaps the bones have made them so."

"Could that happen?"

"Maybe." Randall shrugged. "Low magics feed off the souls of others, and if the bones truly belonged to someone who was believed a god at some point in the past, that god or wizard or whomever could have been quite powerful. Enough of their soul might linger around the bones, enough to be drawn off by someone with the right skills."

Gris visibly shivered. "Sounds ghastly."

"It is. Eventually the soul would be destroyed."

"You sound as if you know a little of this."

"My father had tunnels beneath his castle filled with slaves just for such a purpose, to drain for his own magics. It is a fate worse than death, a painful destruction of the last threads of ourselves."

The captain gulped. "What do we do?"

"I'm not sure there is anything *to* do," Randall said. "I can keep scanning the city, but I'm fairly certain this individual detected my presence. They will hide themselves well now."

"Could you break through whatever is hiding them?"

"Possibly, but it will take time."

"Would you be willing to give it a try?"

"Of course."

"Good, then please get to work as soon as you can," Gris said.

Randall opened his mouth to speak, but the captain cut him off.

"Believe me, Randall, I understand how busy you are at the tower," the captain said. "And I understand the importance of your work. Your reputation is growing, though you might not appreciate that and possibly might not even care for it. There are those who claim you are the most powerful healer in all West Ursia, perhaps even beyond, and there is no doubt you save lives. But this could be important. Finding this person, whether they are the ones who took the bones or not, could also save many lives. I don't think anyone wants a repeat of last year, nearly a whole village wiped out."

"I understand."

"And I thank you for your patience. I realize those you help are important to you."

"They are."

Gris nodded. "Good. Unless you've something else to tell me, the sooner we can find this wizard, the sooner you can get back to your patients."

"What about Kron?" Randall asked. "Do you want me to tell him?"

"I think there's little need at this point," Gris said. "I'll see him in the morning and can inform him then. That's unless something happens during the night, or you can think of some reason he would need to know."

"None I can think of."

"All right, then. Dismissed."

Randall stood motionless, his features uncertain.

Captain Gris chuckled. "My apologies, healer. I'm so used to giving orders, I forget half the time when I'm talking to a civilian. Is there anything else?"

The healer allowed a small smile. "Nothing else. I'll report to you as soon as I find out anything."

"Good. Thank you."

***

The hand on Spider's shoulder tightened and twisted, forcing the small, gray-haired man to turn and face the person holding him.

"You didn't answer my question," Kilchus said.

Spider appeared flustered, his lips working but saying nothing.

The hand tightened further, causing the small man to wince.

"Sorry!" Spider blurted out. "I was just surprised to see you."

The hand loosened its grip, but Kilchus did not remove it from the shoulder.

"The guy in black?" he asked.

"Darkbow," Spider said. "He's just a guard officer."

"Darkbow? That names rings a bell."

"It might," Spider said. "He was a border warden. Speaking of which, when did you get back?"

Seeing his old companion didn't look as if he was about to run off, Kilchus finally withdrew his hand. "A few days ago. Darkbow, you say? Yeah, that was a name I heard a few times in the Lands. Was a son or nephew of some sergeant. Didn't expect to run into anyone from there here in Bond."

"The captain of the city guard was also a warden."

"Yeah, that I knew," Kilchus said. "Gris, he and me passed one another a few times in the Lands."

Spider went quiet then. Fear kept his lips closed, but so did a spark of intelligence. Kilchus had sought him out for a purpose. Spider knew of no reason to hide anything from this man, but it was always safer to find out what someone like Kilchus wanted before running one's mouth.

The Sword glanced down the alley toward the street where pedestrians passed by every few seconds. "You alone?"

"As far as I know."

Kilchus turned his hard eyes on the much smaller man. "What's *that* supposed to mean?"

"I had a few guys with me down the street," Spider said, "but Darkbow told me he ran them off. I didn't have time to look into it before you showed up."

"What were the four of you up to?"

Spider didn't answer.

A finger jabbed into his shoulder.

"I already heard you're boss of the thieves guild," Kilchus said with gritted teeth. "So spill it. Now."

"We were watching The Frog's Bottom," Spider said. "I iced the top steps. Sooner or later somebody would've taken a tumble."

"Then you and your boys would have swooped in?"

"Something like that."

Kilchus took a step back, removing the jabbing finger and placing his hands on his hips. "What kind of bottom-dwelling guild you running here, Spider? Does that sound like something a guild boss should be involved in? Where the hell are your plans for pilfering cargo at the Docks? Or breaking into some rich guy's house? Anything besides this petty crap you're involved in."

"This isn't the old days," Spider said, wincing again, this time at the accusations. "There ain't no Belgad around, and the city guard, they're a lot more on the mark than they used to be."

"This Darkbow, I suppose."

"Him, yeah, but Gris as much as anybody," Spider said. "The man has reworked the guard, and has some new powers or rules or something from upon high. I don't know all the details, but I know they've got their act together, at least since the riots last year."

"Riots?"

"Yeah, you remember Kerjim?"

Kilchus snickered. "The old thieves chief? Yeah, I saw his cub this morning."

"Eel? Forget him. He's just running security for Lalo. It was Kerjim who brought the thieves guild back, and it was him involved with the riots. He was making a play for Belgad's old spot, but it fell through on him."

"This Eel hinted as much."

"It wasn't pretty," Spider explained, "and it was all Darkbow's doing. Kerjim, he and a bunch of his guys are ... well, I don't know. It's hard to say what they are. They're breathing but not much else. Don't talk, don't move, don't even blink. They got them squared away up in the Swamps tower."

"Darkbow did all that?" Kilchus asked. "The man didn't strike me as a mage."

"He's not. At least I'm pretty sure of it. Believe me, I've been studying him for a while now."

Kilchus the Sword leaned back but lowered his head, bringing up a finger to rub at his chin, a sign he was deep in thought. Then, "So nobody took over for Belgad?"

"Nobody."

"What about Lalo?"

"The Finder? No. He took a stab at it, a little one, but he didn't have the clout."

"But he's still in Belgad's old place."

"That's more a matter of convenience than anything. Lalo still has plenty of pull, but not on the level of Belgad. He's head of the Guild of Guilds, this new collection for all the guild bosses."

Kilchus rocked back on his heels. "That sounds ... interesting. But nearly unbelievable."

"Ask the man himself if you don't believe me."

"I intend to. But let me see if I've got this right ... the city, it's ripe for the taking?"

Spider shook his head. "That's old thinking. Things aren't what they were just few years ago. I told you, the city guard have their act together nowadays, and the guilds are a lot more equal and united than ever. They don't *want* another Belgad running things."

"They split the pie up among themselves, and threw Lalo a bone."

"Sort of. Kind of. Sure."

A grin appeared on the Sword's lips. "This could work."

"*What* could work?" Spider asked.

Kilchus didn't answer for a moment, glancing again toward the street. "There's somebody I want you to meet, Spider, but first I need to talk with the Finder."

"You know where he's at. Go see him."

"I stopped by this morning," Kilchus said. "That's when I saw Eel. I got the impression he gave me the runaround, but maybe Lalo really wasn't there."

Spider shrugged. What else was there to do?

Kilchus smiled again and turned away, then halted, looking back at the mage thief. "This has been a most educational talk, old pal. Let me try again with Lalo, then I'll get back to you."

"Do you know where to find me?"

"I can find you."

Then Kilchus the Sword turned and walked away.

For the first time in at least a half hour, Spider could breathe easily.

***

As the light of day faded to the dark blue of early evening, Sadhe Teth stared with stolen eyes out upon the circular road that ran around the outside of the large, rounded building. He had nearly forgotten how the darkness came on early during the coldest time of the year, and nearly did not remember to pull his cloak closed in front of him.

Shivering people walked up and down the road. A few horses or other animals trotted along. A carriage passed him by.

Yet he did not move.

He stood with his back nearly against a building and he stared across the road.

Malin's memories told him this was a healing tower, one of two in the city. This one was the larger of the two, located in the district known as the Swamps. Here the poor and destitute came to have their pains and ailments discarded.

Like those mortals passing in front of him, Sadhe Teth also shivered, but not because he felt the growing chill. A minor casting kept him warm beneath his outward garb. No, he shivered because of fear, a sensation not overly familiar to him.

His ramblings, his wanderings, they had brought him here. Walking the streets, learning the streets, he could not get out of his mind the knowledge that someone of power was out there, and that they likely knew of his presence.

His mind was still not fully his own, Malin's soul continuing to fight back from deep down within, but Sadhe Teth had known to go west. From Southtown he had crossed Frist Bridge into the Swamps, his feet taking the lead more than his mind. It occurred to him this was his second visit to the Swamps, but early on he had not known the city, had not gained enough knowledge of his whereabouts. Now he was growing in knowledge, the mental map of Bond taking semblance within his thoughts.

Once in the Swamps, his feet had taken him west, in the direction of that presence he had detected. More than once he had thought of doing another search for magic, but had deemed it too dangerous to attempt. The *other* would be on guard now.

Sadhe Teth had allowed his feet to carry him, his subconscious showing him the path of where he needed to go.

After walking for what felt hours, sometimes going in circles, he had discovered this healing tower. The moment he had seen it he realized this was where he needed to be. For some reason he had felt the place to search for *the other* would be of size. There were a lot of large buildings in the Swamps. There were warehouses along the rivers, buildings of three and four stories filled with sleeping chambers, a solitary mansion in the far western end and an eerie place Malin informed him had been an asylum for the mad. Yet none of them had felt right. Not until he had seen the healing tower.

Now he had been there for a half hour, watching and waiting. For what, he did not know.

Besides the pedestrians passing by, people came and went from the tower. Many of those going in showed signs of sickness or injury. A number of those leaving wore bandages. In amongst these people were a handful of men and women dressed all in white. Malin's memories told him these were healers, those who tended the sick and the injured and the dying, and that some of them were wizards while others were surgeons or apothecaries or sometimes simply a person who cared and knew how to wrap a bandage.

Sadhe Teth scoffed at their humanity. Let them help these worthless mortals. He would have no part of it. Such was beneath him.

Yet it struck him as odd that the individual who potentially posed a threat to him could be found within. Why would someone of such obvious power resort to utilizing such an establishment? Surely he or she could not be one of these healers. Or could they?

No. It was impossible. This *other*, they had to be someone in charge, someone with political power. Anything else was impossible to imagine.

Until his eyes fell upon a solitary figure, a young man dressed in white. This young man, only a handful of years past being a true youth, he sauntered forth from the tower to help others carry inside a hobbling old man dressed in rags.

Sadhe Teth ignored the old man and the other healers, but he could not ignore the young man in white. As soon as he saw that face, he *knew*. This mortal was the one he had sensed. He did not know how this knowledge imparted itself upon him, but of it he was sure. Teth cast no spells, nor did perform a search for magic, mainly because he did not need to. This young man, he was the true danger here. Until this healer was dealt with, Sadhe Teth could not get about his plans.

He watched as the last of the healers entered the tower. Then the door closed, cutting off any view of the young man in white.

It was time to act.

Sadhe strode forward, directly toward the tower.

No.

He stopped himself after a few steps.

He did not know enough. He did not even know the identity of this danger. He could not challenge this young man without more knowledge. Perhaps it would even be best if he did not challenge this entity on his own, or at least not face to face.

Yes. That sounded wise.

He would not do this himself. He would find someone else. Somehow.

But first he would identify his enemy.

He walked forward once more, heading toward the door to the healing tower. He had not made it but a few steps when the big wooden door opened again.

Out stepped another healer, a young woman in white robes with a white cloak wrapped around her. She turned away from the tower and headed toward a side street.

"Excuse me!" Sadhe Teth called out.

She did not take notice of him.

"Excuse me, miss!"

At the corner to her street, she paused and looked back. Their eyes met. He rushed to her.

"May I help you?" she asked.

Sadhe Teth grinned, calling upon Malin the Quill's memories in order to say the right things, to lie and make it sound believable.

"I'm sorry to detain you, madam," he said, "but my brother was sick a few days ago and I brought him to the tower."

The woman nodded, thoughtful and caring. "Yes?"

Teth brought out a wide smile. "Thank the gods he is doing much, much better."

"Gods?" she asked.

He had said the wrong thing. There was only one god now, and in his rush had forgotten this.

"My apologies," he said. "I meant to say, 'thank Ashal."

She brightened at this, obviously a believer. "I am glad to hear he is well."

"Oh, yes," Sadhe Teth said, "but the reason I called upon you is I wanted to personally thank the healer who helped my brother."

"I'm sorry I don't recall your brother," the woman said, "but I help a lot of people. What was your brother's name?"

"Oh, no, it wasn't you. You weren't his healer. Sorry, no offense was meant."

She smiled, understanding.

"It was a young man," Sadhe Teth went on. "Probably about your age. Light hair. Average in height."

"That sounds like Randall," she said.

"Randall?"

"Yes, Randall Tendbones. I just saw him if you want to step inside and offer your thanks."

Teth motioned toward the door. "Was he one of the ones who was just outside here?"

"That was him," the healer said.

"Thank you for your time," said Sadhe Teth.

6

She sat and she waited. The thought of doing so amused her. Frex Nodana had never waited for any man, not unless there had been something in the waiting which would benefit her. Money. Power. These were things she had sought all her life. She had not wanted these things for themselves, nor because she felt some sense of entitlement, that she was better than everyone else. She had simply wanted wealth, and to a slightly lesser extent power, because they shielded her from the childhood she had known.

She sipped her wine and shook her head. No reason to think about all that now. It was behind her, the past. The future lay ahead. Possibly a future with Kron Darkbow.

Feeling silly, she stood and drained the wine from her glass, then turned from the small couch in the vestibule of her apartment and marched down the short hall to the kitchen where in the center of the room was a small oak table topped with a silver platter. On the platter rested a porcelain bowl heavy with various berries and slices of fruit, a smaller plate of rolls off to one side.

Nodana stopped at the table and stared down at it, placing her empty glass next to the plate of bread. A proper supper had not been in the works, not with Kron out doing whatever it was this night.

She popped a berry in her mouth and slowly chewed it.

Denial was not a trait common to her. She shook her head again. No, she would not start with denial now, and it was not fair to Kron. He had a reputation for being a night owl, but she had to admit that had not been her experience since they had been together. Oh, he was more than willing to stay up until all hours of the morning, but he did so with her, usually at her place. There was never any question to his location at night. This night, she knew what he was doing, though she had no clue as to his exact whereabouts.

He was going to see Spider, the boss of the thieves guild.

Nodana sighed. She had been one of those involved in the creation of the modern thieves guild. Did she regret such? Not exactly. Spider was not the most competent of individuals, and the modern guild was far less a danger than had been the old one, though she had been a child during those days. Still, she held some memories of those times, the pit fights, the street wars, Belgad's rise to power. It had been he, the foreign barbarian with a fist of iron, who had ended the fighting among the guilds. Since his leaving Bond, the city's underworld had collapsed with one minor power seeker after another hoping to take Belgad's place.

Nodana had been one such person, but she had finally seen another way. Captain Gris, along with the help of others, including Kron, had managed to keep sanity on the streets, all while allowing the guilds to operate freely and independently while still bringing money into the city. In many ways, things were more stable than they had been even under Belgad. At least there was more freedom among the guilds, and to some extent for those who toiled within the guilds.

The klack of the front door caused her to turn around, leaning against the table. She could not see the hall from her position, but she could hear the soft thumpings of his boots as he made his way to her.

"You did not have to wait for me," Kron said as he stopped in the entranceway, taking in the food and the empty glass of wine, his dark eyes finally coming to rest on her own.

She shivered at his look. It was both frightening and astonishing, thrilling and nearly overwhelming. "I only had a berry and a glass of wine."

He nodded and unclasped his cloak, reaching back to hang it on a hook in the hall. Then he unbuckled his sword belt and hung it with the discarded cloak. "It is not late yet. We could still have a proper meal. Perhaps at the Scabbard."

She shook her head. "I'm not in the mood to travel all the way to Southtown."

"There's The Twelve Chairs," Kron offered, mentioning a closer tavern there in Uptown.

She shook her head again and gave a short laugh. "I'm not in the mood to be around other mages, especially the younger ones who will pester me with a thousand questions."

Now providing his own smile, Kron reached toward the table and pulled away a chair, turning it around and sitting with his arms crossed atop the chair's back. He stared up at her. "So what would you like to do for dinner?"

"Something simple," she said. "Maybe stay in for the night."

The idea seemed to meet his approval, and he grinned. "Fine with me."

"Randall stopped by. He was looking for you."

"Did he say what he wanted?"

"No, only that he would go on to see Gris."

"Must not be an emergency," Kron said. "Otherwise they would have sent for me."

"Probably."

"Anyway, I'll see Gris in the morning," he added.

She shuffled her feet, glancing down at the floor. "Did you find Spider?"

"I did."

"Did you at least take him to the healing tower afterward?"

His smile vanished. He lowered his arms and sat back on the chair. "Is that what you think of me?"

"I only know your history with Spider."

He grimaced and closed his eyes, rubbing at his temples.

"I'm not judging you," she said.

"You are."

"No, I am not. I realize in your line of work sometimes you have to do things that are unpleasant."

Opening his eyes, he sighed as he stared up at her. "Frex, I'm not that man, okay? I'm not the sort who goes around beating on innocent people."

"Spider isn't exactly someone who is innocent."

"No, he isn't," Kron said, "but that doesn't mean I look for reasons to pound on him."

"You did before."

He opened his mouth to speak, then seemed to think better of it, his lips pressing closed.

She turned away from him and moved around to the other side of the table where she pulled back a chair and sat. "I'm sorry. I didn't mean to cause a fuss."

"What brought all this on?" he asked.

"All what?"

"Your questioning me about Spider."

Now it was she who sighed. "I just worry about you, that is all."

"Are you concerned about the violence in my life?"

She nodded. "There is that. I can't help but think about the danger you place yourself in."

He stood and moved around to sit on the edge of the table next to her. Reaching down, he used a finger to lift her chin so they could look in one another's eyes.

"You didn't know me before I went to Kobalos," he said.

"No, I did not."

He grinned, but it was short lived, showing no real humor. "It seems so long ago, but it was only a couple of years. I was a very different person then."

"How so?" she asked.

"I was eaten up by a sense of vengeance," he said. "It ruled my life, controlled every action I took. Had since I was ten, when I watched my parents' murder."

"And now?"

"Now ... well, since coming back from Kobalos, things have been different."

"In what way?"

He lowered his hand and shrugged. "That thirst for revenge, it's gone."

"Then you killed the person responsible?"

"It's more complicated than that," Kron said. "I thought ... I believed this one individual was responsible, but it turned out not to be the case ... sort of. And the person who was responsible, he was already gone by the time I learned the truth."

"You were denied your chance for vengeance."

"Something like that." He shook his head. "Not exactly. I'm not sure."

"So what changed within you?"

"I was a husk," he said. "An empty, dry husk. I lived for vengeance so long, there was nothing else to me. I sputtered around with little purpose, surviving more by luck than anything. If I hadn't been friends with Gris, I don't know what I would have done for a living. I suppose I might have drifted back to the Prisonlands. But the Lands was part of my problem. Years of being surrounded by brutal men who wanted nothing more than to kill you, and the job ... you hunt, and if the prisoners do not surrender when found, you slay them."

"But you've done well," Nodana said. "You became an officer. You purchased the Asylum and turned it into something useful. You have filled your time in a most honorable fashion."

A rarity occurred. Kron Darkbow blushed.

She laughed at him. "See? You know I'm telling the truth."

"All of that was accidental," he said. "The Asylum ... I'm still not sure why I bought it. Maybe guilt. As for me being an officer, that happened only because I wanted to help an old friend."

"What more do you need?" she asked.

He sighed again. "I don't know. I feel like I've been floundering around, floating on an ocean of events, as if things are happening *to* me instead of doing anything myself."

"What do you *want* to do?"

He had no answer. At least not an immediate one.

"Think about it," she said. "If you could do anything, what would it be?"

"I ..." his voice trailed off.

"Maybe you don't need to do anything," Nodana said. "Maybe there's nothing wrong with things happening *to* you. Your life was guided by this sense of revenge, but then it was gone. You have a new life now. Like you said, it's only been a couple of years. You're still young. *We* are still young. There is time to find the answers."

"Answers to what?"

"To whatever you want."

He stared down at the floor. For a moment he did not move, then he slid away from her and around the table once more, finally sitting in his chair, his back now to her.

"I'm sorry," she said.

"Nothing to be sorry about," he said. "I'm not hurt or offended, if that's your concern. You've simply given me a lot to think about."

She rushed around the table, stopping to kneel next to him. "No, no, no. I want just the opposite. Don't think about all this, at least not now. We have time. There is no need to rush."

Grinning, he raised a hand and caressed her chin. "Sometimes I wonder if you are too good for me."

Now it was she who blushed. "I could say the same thing."

They shared a laugh.

When quiet again, he shook his head as if to clear it. "So tell me once more, what brought all this on?"

She hesitated, then, "The party today."

"The feast at the Asylum?"

She nodded.

He couldn't help but grin again. "That was your doing, my dear, and I've been meaning to properly thank you for that."

"That's just it," she said. "I'm not sure you should thank me."

His face screwed up in confusion. "What do you mean?"

"Kron, it was obvious you did not enjoy yourself."

"What do you mean? It was a fine meal, and it was good to see everyone together in one place, and for once without a sword or worse hanging over our heads."

"I'm sure you appreciated it," she said, "but it's not the same. You didn't exactly jump for joy."

He stared off to one side, then glanced sideways at her. "Frex, I'm not the sort of person who finds enjoyment in such things."

She opened her mouth but he cut her off with a wave of a hand.

"Give me a second here," he said. "I didn't mean to be insulting, and I don't mean to belittle what you did today, bringing everyone together and putting the feast before us. I'm sure it was a lot of work. But ... I'm not exactly what you might think of as someone who enjoys being around people. I find I prefer to work alone."

Her eyes flared and she stood, stepping away from him. "That is such bullshit."

He reared back, away from her. "What do you mean?"

"You sit here and tell me you don't like people, while in the same breath you go on and on about this sense of vengeance you had. It doesn't add up, Kron. It's bullshit. Whether you like it or not, others care for you, and while you might not ever admit it, you care for them, too. If you didn't, why all this talk about revenge? If you weren't seeking vengeance *for* someone, then who the hell were you seeking it for?"

"For myself," he said, his voice cracking, nearly broken, "for the loss of the little boy who watched his parents felled in front of his eyes."

For a moment she could but stare at him, stunned at the pain in his words, in his eyes. Then she leaned into him, wrapping her arms around him.

They stayed there, her standing, him sitting, until their eyes were dry.

Eventually she removed her arms and turned away, giving him a moment to recover from any embarrassment.

He was not embarrassed.

"I have changed," he said. "I was a different person when I came back from Kobalos, and after last year, I've changed further."

She turned again and looked at him. "The demon."

"The demon," he agreed. "The atrocities that beast and its master unleashed upon this city, and then upon that village." He quivered. "At the time, I simply did what I had to do. I pushed through it. But afterward ... there were some rough nights."

"That's about the time we got together."

"I admit it," he said with a sideways grin. "You helped me escape the nightmares. I don't know what I would have done without you. And to think, we almost lost you to those monsters."

"But you didn't."

"No."

"Kron, promise me one thing," she said.

He looked up at her. "What?"

"If ... if anything should ever happen to me ..." She hesitated.

"What is it? What?"

"I don't want you going on some rampage," she said. "I don't want you spending one single minute seeking vengeance for me. Morn me, that I would ask, at least for a while, but then move on with your life."

He stood, reaching for her. "What are you telling me? Are you suspecting something? Are you in danger?"

"No." She shook her head, taking his hands. "Nothing like that. But in the type of work we do, the type of work in which we sometimes find ourselves facing danger, it's to be expected. I plan to live a long life, but just in case, if something happens ..."

He pressed forward, wrapping her in his arms. "Don't say that. Don't even think it."

She nested against him. "We have to, from time to time. There is no denying it."

Leaning back, he stared down at her. "Yes, there can be denial. You simply don't allow it."

She appeared confused. "Allow what?"

"Death," he said. "You fight it with every breath you've got. You never give in."

She smiled. "I'm not planning on going anywhere, you silly man."

"Good."

And they hugged.

***

Another knock at the door. Gris finished signing the bottom of a scroll, shuffled the paper to one side and glanced at the candle on his desk. The wax was melted nearly to the iron plate it sat upon. Damn the winter for its early nights.

"Come in," he said, repeating his words from earlier in the day.

The door creaked open and in walked a man the captain felt he should know. The fellow had some size, though he was not unusually tall or muscled. A hauberk of hardened leather barely hid itself beneath his dingy cloak, and a broad sword swung from one hip. His face was the most striking thing about him, however, full of pock marks and a week's beard. It was a cruel face.

"Can I help you?" Gris asked.

The stranger smiled, but it was an awkward smile, that of a killer.

"I take it you don't remember me," the man said.

"I'll admit you do seem familiar."

"The Prisonlands," the newcomer said, giving a two-fingered salute. "I went by the name of Saber."

Saber. Yes, Gris recalled that name. The border wardens did not use their real names, at least not when interacting with the exiles. Gris himself had been called Griffon. He did not have many memories of Saber, but the two had crossed paths a few times during one detail or another in the Lands.

Gris stood and stuck out a hand. "Yes, I remember. Kilchus, wasn't it? You were stationed on the Eastern border, weren't you?"

Kilchus took the hand and shook it, his grip strong. "Yes, sir. That was me. Served under Captain Lutellus."

Their hands parted.

"Please, close the door and have a seat," Gris said.

"My thanks." Kilchus did as he was told, taking a chair in front of the desk.

"You arrived not long before I left the wardens, if I recall correctly."

"A matter of months, sir."

"Are you from Bond, then?"

"I am," Kilchus said.

"Well, Saber, what can I do for you?"

"I've heard the guard might be hiring on," Kilchus said. "I just came home a few days ago, and I'm in need of work. To be blunt, sir."

"What kind of work did you do before the Lands?"

"Mostly body guard work and house security."

"Do you have any references?"

"Possibly Lalo the Finder, sir," Kilchus said.

Griss's eyes went wide. "So you worked in the house of Belgad?"

"Yes, sir. I was head of his house security for several years."

"That must have been a well-paying job. What made you decide to become a border warden?"

For the first time, Kilchus looked down at the ground, appearing sheepish. "Well, sir, it's not something I'm proud about." He looked back up. "But the truth is, I got in a bar fight over at The Stony Pony. A few boys were seriously hurt, though no one killed. I never even drew a weapon."

"So a magistrate sent you to the Lands as a border warden?"

"Yes, sir. That's how it happened."

Something about the story didn't sit well with Gris, though he had little doubt the man was telling the truth, or some version of the truth. City magistrates often sent to the Prisonlands swordsmen and the like who found themselves in trouble. The Lands was for serious crimes, murderers and the like, but often enough the place also served as a home for those who had committed lesser offenses. Of course such fellows were border wardens and not exiles, and often enough the job of a warden called for men who were a bit rough and tumble. Back during his days in the Lands, Gris had known more than a few wardens who were nearly as bad as those they kept from escaping.

Still, it seemed foolish to pass on an experienced man, one who had spent time as a warden.

"Do you have your discharge papers?" Gris asked.

The Sword offered a lopsided grin. "I was afraid you would ask that."

"Why?"

"Do you know about the troubles year before last in the Lands?"

The captain nodded. "I heard about the break outs, and how Kobalos had something to do with it. Seems war was barely averted."

"It was a mess," Kilchus said. "Exiles, *armed* exiles, they fled by the dozens. Everything was in tumult for the longest time. And we lost more than a few good men. Even some of the villages were overrun."

"I'm guessing you're telling me you don't have any discharge papers."

With a hint of disdain, Kilchus glanced at the piles of papers and scrolls on the edges of Gris's desk. "There were more important considerations at the time."

Gris sighed. "Can you get the papers?"

"I can write to my captain," Kilchus offered. "I've been gone for a while, but the last I heard things had settled down. I'm sure he could send me something."

This sounded odd to Gris. "How long *have* you been gone?"

"Nearly a year."

"A year?" Gris could hardly believe what he was hearing. "With all the problems they were having?"

"I didn't bail on them, if that's what you mean," Kilchus said, his eyes and nose flaring. "By the time the worst of the mess was cleaned up, there were a lot of ... frankly, there were a lot of deaths. A lot of bodies. Exiles and wardens alike. I lost more than a few friends. And I wasn't the only one. The Voting Council discussed things with the officers, and they decided it was best to bring in some new blood and let some of us old timers go, for our own sanity, if nothing else."

"I hadn't heard any of that," Gris said. "We've received no notice from the Council seeking new men."

"Doesn't surprise me. Things had settled down when I left, but a lot was lost in all the attacks and escapes. Officers had to be replaced, villages were burned. The mail hasn't been a top priority. Most of the new recruits were taken from Caballerus or East Ursia, them being closer."

"So where have you been for the last year?"

Kilchus gave a dark grin. "All around bad luck, that. I'd heard Belgad was no longer here in Bond, so I figured my old job was dead. After I left the Lands, I decided to try my luck in Caballerus. Wasn't as far to travel, you see?"

Gris nodded.

"Bad timing for me, though," Kilchus explained. "The king got himself assassinated, then his brother took the throne. That didn't sit well with a lot of the nobles, so a minor war broke out. Nothing overly nasty, but there was some fighting in the streets and more than a few necks stretched by the time it was all said and done. I barely made it out of there myself."

"And you came here?"

"Yes, sir. Looking for a job."

It all still didn't seem to fit for Gris. Something was missing. Something was wrong with this story. Yet he couldn't lay a finger on exactly what disturbed him. Then, upon further reflection, he realized what it was. He did not like this man, Kilchus called Saber. He had not known Kilchus during earlier times in Bond and had barely registered the man in the Prisonlands, but none of that mattered. Gris didn't like the look of the fellow sitting across from him. But if he never hired a person because he didn't like their looks, then he would have damn few guards.

Before making a decision, there were a few more things Gris wanted to know.

"You say you worked in the East?" he asked.

"Yes, sir."

"I understand they do things a little different in those districts, and I suppose you never had the chance to work with any squad mages."

"I did during the clean up," Kilchus said. "All bets were off at that point. Everything was such a jumble, we took what help we could wherever we could find it. And we were moving around so much, Eastern squads mixing with the others and all."

If everything the man said was true, he would be perfect for the job, Gris had to admit. And if everything *wasn't* true, time would tell.

"Okay, I'll tell you what," the captain said. "We're putting together a special unit, guards and mages working together in squads. Not dissimilar from the way things were in the Lands, at least in the West."

"Sounds good."

"We're just starting out and could use experienced men like yourself," Gris said. "In fact, the first training session is tomorrow. That's if you're interested."

"I'm interested."

"Good. Then show up at ten bells at the Asylum."

"The Asylum?"

"You do know it, don't you?"

"Of course," Kilchus said. "But why there?"

"That's to be the training ground," Gris said. "Remember, ten bells."

"Yes, sir." Kilchus stood and extended his hand. "I'll see you there."

Gris stood as well and shook the hand. "Perhaps, but Lieutenant Darkbow will be in charge of your training. He'll get you squared away."

"Darkbow?"

Their hands parted.

"You know the man?" Gris asked.

"No, but I've heard of him."

The captain chuckled. "I hope most of it was good."

"Neither good nor bad, but he does seem to have the reputation."

"Truer words were never spoken," Gris said with a grin, then, "Meanwhile, write to your old captain and get those discharge papers. Even if it takes a few months."

"Yes, sir."

***

The night was still early, yet Randall was as tired as if he had been awake for several days. After the lunch-time feast at the Asylum, he had spent the rest of his day in a manner most familiar to him, making use of his healing talents. Unlike the majority of healers in Bond, Randall's skills were mostly based upon magic, though he had picked up a few things here and there from physickers, chiurgens, even alchemists and wisewomen.

He eased into the chair behind the desk in the front room of his working quarters. The lamp on the desk burned low, giving the room dancing shadows upon the wall.

Closing his eyes, he leaned back in the chair and rested, thankful to be alone for the moment.

Yes, it had been a busy day. Two broken arms, a mysterious rash, a tumor growing out of an old man's neck, several cancers. The cancers sapped his strength the most, yet he was glad to help, especially as he was the only healer who had the power to do away with the cancers completely, and without surgery of any kind. A few mumbled words, a passing of his hands over the body, then a laying on of the hands, and the cancer was gone. Often it took only minutes, sometimes as long as a half an hour depending upon how tired he was and the extent of the disease.

Unfortunately his talents meant he was quickly becoming known as the best healer in the city, a reputation that brought him more fear than it did pride. If his true nature became known, the consequences could be monstrous.

Such were the concerns of the god Ashal, He Who Walked Among Men.

Only Kron knew his secret, though there were perhaps one or two others who had suspicions. Still, Randall would be surprised if those others guessed anything near the truth. There had been Adara, raised from the dead by his own hand, but she had never said a word other than her thanks, and she was far away in Kobalos the last Randall had heard. His own father was out there somewhere, and he knew the truth, yet the seemingly immortal wizard would likely be in no condition to challenge the son, at least not for some while.

And then there was Althurna. Did she know the truth? Randall did not think so, but she was perceptive in her quietude. The young woman had approached him out of the blue, offering to be his personal assistant. He had seen her a few times before around the Swamps healing tower, always tending to those who were the most in need, but he had never taken any special notice of her. Why she had come to him was beyond his knowledge, yet she had proven herself helpful time and time again. She even had some minor magical talents of her own, and though he had never heard her mutter more than a handful of words, she did an excellent job in dealing with patients, filling the right healing herbs and lotions, and with general duties necessary in a healer's office chamber.

Randall opened his eyes at the sound of the main door opening. As expected, it was Althurna herself. She gave a slow, almost sad smile to his nod, then moved across the room to the second door, which she pushed her way through. The inner chamber was where Randall did the majority of his serious work with the sick and injured. This time every day Althurna gave the room a good cleaning.

She made his job so much easier, he had to admit. He would have to do something special for her.

But now, at the end of his work day barring some emergency, he had a more important task to complete.

Closing his eyes again, he brought his elbows up to his desk's top and rested his chin in his hands. He allowed his thoughts to wander for a moment, still building what strength he had left. Even a god had his limits, as Randall had discovered.

After a short rest, he focused his mind, reaching outside of himself into the world beyond his room, beyond the healing tower. His presence stretched across the city, his view like that of a bird in flight but faster. He looked in one spot, then another. His gaze shifted from Uptown to the Swamps, then to Southtown. He followed the rivers, all three of them, until they came together in the Docks district. He looked in the temples, the office buildings, the apartments, the taverns, even the private residences.

Nothing.

No, not nothing, but not what he sought. As was always the case, there were hints of magic here and there throughout nearly all of Bond, especially around the university. But none of them seemed worth his extended attention. None of them were overly powerful. None had struck him as unusual.

Which meant his target was in hiding, or had fled the city.

Randall could stretch himself further to look into the countryside, even across West Ursia and into other lands, but he saw little need for such. He could also attempt a forced viewing, pushing past the defenses of any powerful mages shielding themselves from being found. At the very least, this was considered rude. At the worst, it could provoke someone with power into action.

Randall was not sure he wanted that, to face such a response. He had little doubt he could deal with it in one fashion or another, but the results could be quite traumatic. Two powerful magical entities fighting it out in the middle of a city could prove disastrous.

But Randall needed to know, as did Captain Gris and perhaps the rest of the city.

He pushed ahead with his thoughts, with his mind.

He pressed. He probed. For the faintest moment there was ... something.

Then it was gone.

Randall nearly swooned, his chin falling between his hands. He snapped back, sitting erect.

The door to the inner chamber opened and Althurna stuck her head out. Her brows were wrinkled in concern.

"What is it, my dear?" Randall asked.

She stepped into the room, a frown forming on her lips.

"Did I cry out?" he asked.

She nodded.

"My apologies," Randall said. "I was taking a nap. I suppose I had a bit of a dream."

She stared at him for a moment, then she nodded again and retreated to the back room.

Randall let out a sigh and slumped in his chair.

Yes, someone was out there. He had felt it, just barely. He had not been able to determine their location, but they were near, within the city. And anyone strong enough to cause him such trouble, they had to be powerful. Perhaps even stronger than his father.

The thought did not sit well with the healer, and he shuddered.

***

Sadhe Teth jerked awake, sitting up in a pile of hay he had discovered on the second story of a barn just outside the northern walls of the city.

For a moment he did nothing. He waited, knowing full well what had roused him from his slumber. Someone was searching for him. That healer.

When nothing untoward happened, he leaned back in the hay, allowing himself to drift toward sleep. He had not been discovered, of that he was sure, and there were enough protective spells around him to make sure of his safety from interlopers and even the weather.

Tomorrow he would have to do something decisive about this matter. Until then, he would remain guarded, even in sleep.

Snuggling beneath Malin the Quill's cloak, he soon drowsed once more, assured of his protection.

***

His feet dragging as he crossed the front room of The Stone Pony, Kilchus the Sword was too tired to enjoy the patrons swiftly moving out of his way, giving him a straight line to the stairs to the second level. Normally such fear would bring a smile too his lips, but the day had been filled with walking from one end of the city to the other and back again, and he was ready to get off his feet.

At the bottom of the stairs he stopped and turned to face the nearest table where sat the knight who had seen better days. Curval sat alone, as he always did, his sword at his side. The beard on the knight's cheeks had lengthened, giving him a darker complexion, and the front of his chest plate appeared stained as if food and drink had dribbled down his chin.

Curval took no notice of Kilchus. Instead, he swigged at the earthenware bottle before him.

"Anyone come calling for me?" Kilchus asked.

For a moment, nothing, then a heavy hand rested on the bottle on the table. Curval did not look up, but he did shake his head.

Kilchus cursed.

No response from the armored figure.

"Are the rest upstairs?" the Sword asked.

Curval nodded.

Kilchus sighed, then made his way up to the second floor and to the room he had visited that morning.

He knocked on the door.

Which opened immediately.

Gazing out at him were a pair of faces, almost identical. The same flat eyes the color of a stormy ocean. The same tawny hair, approximately the same length, just down to the tops of the ears. Each dressed in dark leathers and sporting several daggers on their belts. Each the same age, somewhere in their mid-to-late twenties. The only obvious differences were the one on the left had the lump of a male in his throat and the one on the right had a jaw slightly more sleek.

The twins.

Kilchus tried looking over their shoulders into the room beyond, but he could make out nothing but the flickering light of a lamp prancing upon the far wall.

"He awake?" he asked.

The male of the two nodded.

"Can I come in?" Kilchus said, his voice showing frustration. "I'm tired."

"Allow him entrance, you two," came Falk's voice from the room. "It is late, and we need to discuss much before sleep."

There was hesitation, but then the young man and woman parted, giving Kilchus just enough room to slide through their opening into the chamber before one of them closed the door behind him.

The Sword gritted his teeth, fighting the urge to backhand someone, smart enough to realize his present company had the skills to stand against his threats or bullying.

"Rest your feet, Kilchus," Falk said from his bed.

It appeared the old man had not moved. He sat in the exact same place Kilchus had seen him that morning.

Grunting his tiredness, Kilchus crossed the room and sat on a lone chair next to the window. He glared at the twins who took guarded positions, one on either side of the door, their backs to the wall.

"Have you heard from the Finder?" Falk asked.

"Not a word," Kilchus said, holding up a delaying hand when the old man sat up. "But don't worry. First thing in the morning, I'll pay a visit. And I won't take no for an answer."

"You had better not," Falk said. "Everything depends upon the Finder. And the longer I remain in hiding, the higher our chances of being found out."

"Understood," Kilchus said.

"Did you find anything else of interest today?" the old man asked. "You've been strolling all over the city it seems, so I hope your work hasn't been for nothing."

"I saw the boss of the thieves guild."

"Oh?"

"Spider," Kilchus said with a dark grin. "I don't believe he will be of much help to us."

"Then why are you smiling?"

"Because he's a fool, and this whole city is apparently filled with fools."

Falk tilted his head to one side. "What do you mean?"

"I realize a lot of Bond's street politics was beneath you back in the old days," Kilchus said, "but remember, this *ain't* the old days. There's a Guild of Guilds running the show, with Lalo at the head."

"That's good," Falk said, nodding. "That could work for us."

"Maybe," Kilchus went on, "but best as I can tell, he's got no muscle to back him. All the guilds are playing nice with one another, and there's nobody like Belgad to stir things up. Even the city guard have their act together, and that's a first."

Falk shrugged. "So? What does this mean?"

"It means there is a void to be filled," said the male twin by the door. "It means we can move in and take over, if we want."

Kilchus glanced over a shoulder at the fellow. "That's right, Jarin." He looked back to the old man. "There's no street boss, and there's nobody vying for the position. Lalo is weak, and most of the guilds are easy pushovers, with one or two exceptions."

Falk sat up straighter, huffing, his eyes going narrow. "You think I have interest in ruling over some street rabble?"

"It would be a start," Kilchus said, "and it could give you some leverage. That's if things don't work out with the Finder."

The old man spat into a corner.

"You can scoff all you like," Kilchus said, "but remember Belgad? The most powerful man in the city? That could be yours, with a little luck and if we play the game right."

"My goals are much higher."

Kilchus held up a flat hand. "Yeah, yeah, I've heard it all before. Honor and title and family name. Yes, I understand. But you have to start somewhere, and sometimes you to fight with what you've got."

"Why me?" Falk asked. "Why not you, or even the twins?"

"Because right now you've got the best chance of getting your hands on some money and power," Kilchus said. "It all depends upon the Finder, and the pope."

"And if one of them should shun me?"

"Then we reconsider. But still, you've got some clout. Your name is known. I'm sure there are political interests within Bond that would give you some backing. It might not be much, but it could get things rolling."

"And what if they try to arrest me?" Falk asked.

Kilchus grinned again and glanced once more back at the twins. "That's why you have us, and Curval. If you have to, you go into hiding somewhere else."

"It sounds thin to me."

"It *is* thin," Kilchus said, "but it's the best any of us got at the moment. Look, I'll be straight with you, if things go bad for the great Lord Falk, *all* of us are going to be on the run. Or we'll have to go into hiding, or both. I'm fine playing things the way you want, but it might reach a point where we gotta try something desperate."

The old man sighed, his shoulders drooping, making him look even older. "I'm not sure I understand you, Kilchus. What exactly is it you are suggesting?"

"If worse comes to worse," the Sword said, "we make a play for boss of the streets. You've got muscle in me and Curval, and I can't think of anybody better to head up a guild of thieves or assassins than Jarin and Rgia. We're lacking in coin at the moment, but we can deal with that."

"It would be dangerous."

"Yes, very much so, but it might be our last hope. If it comes to it, all we've got to do is find a place to lay low, which means you'll have to call on some old friends, if you've got any left, and I'm betting you do. After that, we just keep one step ahead of the city guard."

"Yes, the city guard. You really think we can avoid them?"

Kilchus's grin grew wider. "Let me tell you where I'm going after I see Lalo in the morning."

7

The temperature had risen considerably during the night, so when Kilchus the Sword stepped out of The Stone Pony that morning his boots sank not into snow, but mud.

"Damn the Swamps," he said, scraping his heels on the edge of a low windowsill.

At least the early traffic was slim, allowing him to walk in the middle of the streets instead of the murky, mucky gutters nearer the buildings.

He made straight for the mansion that was now house to Lalo the Finder, and once more he could not help but smirk as he saw no guards and found the outer wall's gate unlocked.

Climbing the hill to the main building, he looked for any guards or other security measures upon the grounds, but he found nothing. Lalo obviously felt not threatened. Belgad the Liar never would have allowed things to become so lax, especially when Kilchus had been running the show here.

At the front door he moved to one side to scrape his boots clean yet again, this time on the sides of a sizable stone with an iron ring embedded in its top, a place for tying off horses.

Shifting his sword further back on its belt, he stomped up to the door and knocked. Hard. Three times.

Then he waited.

And waited.

He knocked again.

This time he did not have to wait so long.

But he did have to wait.

Eventually the door opened. Standing beyond was the same young man he had met the day before. Eel Sidewinder. The youth wore the same soft leathers and the same two short swords on his belt. His hair was a mess, as if he had just crawled out of bed.

"What do you want?" Eel asked.

"Lalo didn't come calling," Kilchus answered.

"He was busy yesterday," Eel said. "I'll tell him you came by again."

The door began to close.

Kilchus stuck out a boot into the entry, halting the door.

"Hey!" Eel called out, pulling the door open again, a hand falling to a sword hilt.

Kilchus kicked out, hardened leather cracking against wood. The door slammed inward, catching Eel in the chest and sending the youth reeling. The Sword moved inside, slamming the door shut behind him. For a moment he could not see, little of the early light filtering through the curtained windows, but once his eyes adjusted to the gloom, he could make out Eel sprawled on the marble floor several feet in front of him. The boy was confused, shaking his head, placing one hand flat on the floor in an attempt to push himself to standing.

Kilchus never gave him the chance. He jumped forward, landing with his boots on either side of the youth, his fists flailing out like hammers.

The first blow caught Eel across the temple, knocking his head to one side. The second hit caught him in the jaw. His head snapped to the other side. Then his hand slipped from the floor and he dropped back, his head cracking on the marble.

Taking a knee next to the youth, Kilchus raised his fists for another barrage.

"Back away from the boy," a new voice commanded.

The Sword looked up to find a familiar face.

"Stilp," he said.

The small man with brown hair stood a dozen yards away in front of a pair of open doors that led to a large hall beyond, a crossbow in his hands, the head of the weapon's bolt pointed directly at Kilchus.

"I said get away from him," Stilp said, staring down the length of his weapon.

Kilchus grinned and stood, his fists unclenching and falling to his sides. "It's been a while, Stilp."

"Not long enough," Stilp said. He glanced down at Eel and saw the lad was not moving. "Now back on out of here before I pin you to the wall."

"I'm not leaving until I see Lalo."

"Then we have a problem," Stilp said, "because I'm not letting you take another step in this house."

Kilchus's left hand grasped the handle of his sword. "You've only got one shot, old buddy. Do you really think a single arrow can take me down before I can get to you?"

"Want to find out?" Stilp asked.

"Enough!" The shouted word came from above.

Kilchus and Stilp looked up a curving stairwell on one side of the entrance room to a second-level walkway above. The tall, slim figure of Lalo the Finder stood behind a railing, his dark eyes blazing with anger.

"Kilchus, come up and let us be done with your business," the Finder said. "Stilp, see to Eel. If you have to, take him to the healing tower. And leave a decent donation while there."

"Boss, you trust being alone with this madman?" Stilp asked, not yet lowering his crossbow.

Lalo glanced to the Sword. "If he meant me any harm, I doubt he would have knocked at the front door."

"Twice," added Kilchus.

"Yes, twice," Lalo said. "Now come along, Kilchus, and Stilp, put away that crossbow before you end up skewering your own leg."

For another moment the little man did not move, his eyes hardening as he glared at the smirking Sword. Then he backed a few steps and aimed the crossbow at the floor.

"My thanks," Kilchus said, spinning toward the steps.

Stilp grimaced before moving to Eel.

At the top of the stairs, Kilchus stopped in front of the Finder. The Sword was all smiles. "I have to admit, I didn't think the little guy had it in him."

Lalo said nothing. He turned to one side and motioned toward an open door.

Kron found Randall waiting for him at the gate to the Asylum grounds. The healer stood by as Kron retrieved the key from a cloak pocket and unlocked the gate, allowing them entrance.

"Frex told me you stopped by last night," Kron said as they made their way up the hill to the main building.

"I saw Captain Gris instead," Randall said. "Have you talked with him this morning?"

"Just came from his office. He told me what happened to you. Do you really think it could be connected to those bones?"

"I don't know," Randall said, "but whomever it is, they're still out there."

"What makes you say that?" Kron asked.

"I searched for them again last night. They're still in the city, and they're hiding from me, or from someone. And they're powerful."

Kron stopped halfway up the incline and looked to his friend, who stopped next to him. "Your father?" Kron asked.

"I don't think so."

"But you can't be sure?"

"No. But it doesn't feel right. And I'm thinking it's too soon."

"Could it be a demon?"

Randall shook his head. "As frightening as it is to contemplate, Kron, this person or entity, they are far more powerful than any demon."

That was indeed disturbing. Kron nearly shivered at the thought.

"Another wizard, then," he suggested.

"That would be my guess," Randall said, "but I've never heard of anyone this strong. Even the famed Markwood was nothing like this."

The news did not make for a cheery mood in Kron Darkbow that morning. "What can we do?"

Randall shrugged. "Hope they're not up to something. What else *can* we do? I know they're out there, but I can't pinpoint exactly where or who they are. Maybe it's someone just passing through."

"When are we ever so lucky."

"Never." Randall sighed. "Look, I've a busy day, but I'll give it another search this afternoon."

"Do you think it's worth your time?" Kron asked. "For that matter, could it cause you some trouble? If this wizard knows you're looking for him --"

"He will."

"-- then he or she might decide to lash back at you."

"Maybe," Randall said, "but they'll be cautious. And if they mean no harm, then they'll realize I'm only being careful."

"You hope."

"Yes, I hope. It's all I know to do in this situation."

Kron started walking again. Randall did not follow.

"Will you see Captain Gris again today?" the healer asked his friend's back.

"I will," Kron said, still walking. "He'll want to know how today's training session goes. I'll let him know you did another search."

"Thank you," Randall said. "If anything changes, I'll be in touch."

Kron stopped, turned and stared at his friend. "Be careful, Randall. You don't know who this is we're dealing with."

"I'll do my best," the healer said.

Turning away once more, Kron asked, "Do you want me there with you?"

There was no answer. After several steps, he stopped and turned around again.

The healer was gone.

Kron stood there in surprise. "So that's what that feels like."

***

It had been at least five years since Kilchus the Sword had stood in the room, and he was surprised how little it had changed. It was a lengthy chamber with a row of windows facing the door in which he entered, a similar door in the same wall further to his right, both exits allowing access to the railed walkway surrounding the second floor of the mansion's entrance room. Thick rugs padded the dark wood floor, and shelves of books and scrolls and knickknacks lined the walls. Set into the far right wall was a sizable fireplace, a decent blaze now roiling and bringing a toasty feeling to the room. Directly in front of the Sword were a pair of leather-bound chairs, in front of them a large desk layered with more books, papers and scrolls.

Belgad the Liar might have just stepped out of the room.

In fact, the only thing that seemed out of place was Kilchus recalled a silvered mug that had always rested atop the desk; the mug was now gone, probably with its owner.

Lalo sighed as he moved past the swordsman and around the desk, where he slide into a high-backed leather chair. When he looked up, his eyes were filled with menace. "All right. Let us finish this. What is it you want?"

Kilchus ignored the question, his eyes still roaming about the room. "You've not changed a thing."

"Which makes sense because I designed the room in the first place," the Finder said. "It fit Belgad's need to appear the wealthy, educated fellow, and it fulfills my needs as a working office.

"But none of that is of import at the moment. I repeat, what is it you want?"

Kilchus continued to stare for a few more moments, then he eased around and plopped onto one of the comfortable seats. He leaned back as if to raise his boots onto the desk.

"Do not press your luck," Lalo said.

A grin sprang to the Sword's lips. "And what would you do if I did?"

"Me? I would do nothing," Lalo said.

"I know you can't depend on the boy downstairs," Kilchus said with a smirk. "What is he? Twenty? Twenty-one?"

Lalo sighed again. "Eel has received training by the best this city has to offer."

"Then I feel sorry for the city."

The Finder glared into a corner for a moment, biting his bottom lip, then, "He suffers from youth and inexperience. Those he can outgrow. Today will be a lesson for him."

"One too many lessons like that and there'll be nothing else to learn."

A hand smacked onto the desk. "What is it you want?" Lalo nearly shouted.

Kilchus eased back in the chair, allowing the soft, cushioned leather to wrap around and enfold him. He couldn't help but grin. "I'm back."

438

"I can clearly see that."

"And I notice that things have changed."

"They most assuredly have."

Kilchus looked up at the ceiling, fingers rubbing at his chin as if deep in thought. "It seems to me you don't quite have the clout of your predecessor."

"My predecessor?"

"Belgad."

Lalo snickered. "You misconstrue how things stand. I have not replaced Lord Belgad. The ... arrangement, shall we call it? Yes. The arrangement is quite different now, yet satisfactory to all."

The Sword's gaze dropped to stare at the Finder. "You're kidding me, right?"

"No."

Now it was Kilchus who sighed. "Lalo, I know we've been out of touch, but I remember you. Always the king maker, never the king. This can't be what you want."

"I am satisfied with how things stand at the moment."

"Bowing and scraping to the guilds?" Kilchus asked.

The Finder's eyes flared. "You truly have misjudged things, haven't you? There is no bowing and scraping here. I am Master of the Guild of Guilds. The guilds as a whole answer to *me*."

"On paper maybe," Kilchus said with a snicker, " but I've had my ears open. You can deny it all you want, but you don't have the muscle or the money to run this town."

"I am not trying to run this town," Lalo said. "I am not Belgad. I have no intentions of being Belgad. Believe it or not, but the way things stand in this city are to my preference. I never entertained otherwise."

Kilchus smirked again. "That sounds about right. You always were a bit squeamish."

"I did what I had to do when it was necessary."

"And nothing more. Yes, I remember."

Lalo threw up his hands in frustration. "We are going around in circles, Kilchus. I am busy, so tell me what it is you want, or get the hell out."

Right away the Sword could see he had broken the Finder's calm demeanor. It was enough of a small victory. Time to get down to business.

"There is someone you need to meet with," Kilchus said.

"Really? Who did you meet during your five years at the Prisonlands who could possibly be of interest to me?"

Kilchus did not answer directly. Within, he steamed. How dare this skinny man speak to him as if he was some common thug. Business was business, but when this was all over, the Sword might have a few things to say to the Finder. And Kilchus often let his fists do his talking.

For the time being, he checked his anger. "Lord Falk," he said.

The two words brought several sudden changes to Lalo the Finder's face. Initially there was astonishment, quickly followed by confusion, then a dawning, and finally distrust.

"Oh, I see," Lalo said.

"You do?"

"Oh, yes. I see quite clearly. Your coming here after the Prisonlands nearly fell apart, and you bring with you, of all people, Falk."

"I never said I brought him with me."

"No, but you said I need to meet someone, and then you mentioned Falk."

The Finder had him there. Kilchus could not deny it.

"I'm guessing you helped Falk to escape," Lalo said. "So, tell me, what has the great Lord Falk promised you in return for your service?"

The truth hit far too close to home. Again, Kilchus was too stunned to say anything. His grin had died.

"Allow me to hazard a guess," Lalo said, then continued without waiting for any response. "He must have told you about certain investments he made with Lord Belgad prior to Falk being arrested. Perhaps he even mentioned certain properties he purchased through Lord Belgad, properties with a high financial value and held in Belgad's trust."

The fingers of the Swords hands gripped and dug into the arms of his chair. He should have remembered how intelligent and how shrewd the Finder could be. The man guessed at every word he spoke, but he spoke them with conviction.

Lalo went on. "Perhaps Falk even convinced you I would return to him these properties, and that I would square away with him any and all monies owed him due to his investments."

Kilchus could but stare in silence and awe at how much the Finder guessed.

"Does that about sum it up?" Lalo asked.

Ambition. It drove a man. It kept him up at night, caused him to skip meals, brought him to do things he otherwise would never contemplate, even horrible things. Yes, Lalo the Finder had guessed much, nearly all, but he had not revealed any foreshadowing of Kilchus's own ambitions, and those ambitions rose rather high.

The Sword pulled his fingers free of the chair's arms. He fought back another grin in an attempt to remain steady, to remain seemingly passionless. For the moment, let the Finder think he had won.

Lalo snapped two fingers in front of the swordsman's face. "Do you have anything to say, Kilchus?"

Kilchus snarled. "Snap those fingers at me again and I'll cut off your hands."

Laughter was the response. Lalo eased back in his padded chair and patted at his slender stomach as if he had just finished a fine meal. "I see you are not amused. But do you know why I was labeled the Finder?"

There was no answer except a glare.

"Not because I can find people or things," Lalo went on, "but because I can find out things *about* people. Some consider this quite the talent. I myself think of it as little more than common sense combined with a study of my fellow man. Talk with a person for some little while, get to know them and their personality, and one can learn much. However, in your current situation, I must admit one thing confounds me."

"What?" The single word was stated with near hate.

"I do not understand why it has taken you nearly two years since the troubles in the Prisonlands for you to show your face in Bond."

"We got caught up in the mess in Caballerus," Kilchus said. He saw no reason to lie.

"Ah, the assassinations, the change in government." Lalo nodded. "That makes sense."

"There were a lot of killings," the Sword said. "I'm beginning to understand why."

The Finder snickered. "Don't be a fool, Kilchus. Yes, I've played with you, and I've no doubt damaged any notions you have of working with Falk, but that doesn't mean I don't recognize your talents. You are one in a thousand, in a million. You are a man with no compunctions about harming another living being. That is an ability quite useful, perhaps more so than you can imagine."

"Is that a job offer?"

"No," Lalo stated. "I merely point out the benefits of your company."

Kilchus grimaced. "You should still talk with Falk."

"You insist?"

"What could it hurt? Let the old man down to his face. Then when it's over, I can get around to doing whatever I end up doing."

Lalo stared off to one side for a moment, then, "Bring him around for dinner tonight. Make it fairly late, nine bells. The fewer people on the streets the better."

"I will do it." Kilchus stood. "Until then." He nodded and turned away and marched out the door.

Lalo watched him go without saying another word.

Outside on the second-floor walkway, Kilchus paused for a moment after closing the door. There was no sign of the others, so he figured Stilp had taken Eel to one of the towers.

His left hand grabbed at the end of his sword's handle and squeezed. He wanted the Finder dead, but realized that was only his momentary anger getting the best of him. It sounded as if Falk's was a losing cause, and Lalo might prove necessary to increasing Kilchus's fortunes. He would let the Finder live.

For now.

***

It had taken time, a few days, longer than he had expected. Slowly, gradually, his will had come to dominate that of the lesser man, the far younger man, the man who's body he now controlled. Malin the Quill still existed, but only in the most distant reaches of his own self, buried far under the weight of Sadhe Teth.

And it was about damn time, Teth told himself as he worked his way along yet another grungy, grimy alleyway, kicking aside clutter and stepping from one swampy puddle to the next. He had spent days rambling about the city, two minds fighting for control of one body. There had never been a question of who would triumph, but Teth had known he could not safely take the next step along his destiny until Malin had been imprisoned forever.

Now the transition was complete.

The only question was about the healer, the Randall Tendbones person he had discovered looking for him, or at least looking for this new powerful, magical force in the city.

No. In truth, there could be no question, Sadhe Teth told himself as he came to the end of the alley and stared across a busy street to the multistory tavern known as The Stony Pony. There was no question because there was only an answer. Tendbones had to go. He had to die, be destroyed, be removed.

Only then Sadhe Teth would feel safe enough, confident enough to do what needed done.

But how to go about it? Tendbones was obviously quite powerful and aware of another powerful presence in the general region. Direct confrontation would be foolish, with the outcome uncertain.

During his nights of sleeping in hovels and his days of wandering, he had given much thought to how best to deal with the healer. It would have to be a surprise assault, and someone other than Teth must do the job, someone unexpected, preferably someone unknown to Tendbones. More importantly, it would have to be someone with no ties to Sadhe Teth himself, which was easy enough to accomplish since he had no ties to anyone living, not unless one counted the poor, unfortunate Malin the Quill, and for all intents and purposes poor Malin was no longer living.

It would have to be an assassin, a professional. Someone with no qualms about killing, someone experienced in such tasks. Teth knew he did not have enough money to purchase such a person's talents, but there were ways around that, and he would deal with such matters when the time came.

Malin's memories had told him the Swamps would be the place to look.

Earlier that morning he had dared to use some little magic, nothing too powerful, nothing that would draw attention of other mages. He could not cast a spell that would point him in the exact direction to a professional killer, but he had been able to send out an emotional web across the city, one that allowed him to detect surface feelings and general characterizations.

Teth had been surprised at how few individuals there were who could prove themselves useful to him. Professional killers? Perhaps a half dozen. Maddened murderers? Perhaps another half dozen. There were plenty of soldiers and warriors and the like, and more than a few burly fellows who enjoy a bit of punching and pounding, but men or women who had no trouble slitting a throat and walking away with no qualms? Rare. Teth had to admit such talents had always been rare to some extent, but this? It seemed humanity had weakened during his long sleep, no longer with fire in its belly. He supposed such was natural considering how much more civilized mankind had become in the last several thousand years. Cities bred laziness and weakness.

But that did not mean there was *no one* of possible benefit to Sadhe Teth.

Street traffic passed him by as he watched The Stone Pony. He did not know the faces of the persons he sought, but he was assured they could be found within, and he was assured there was more than one of them. His casting had informed of as much. He had felt their emotions, even a few of their thoughts. They were killers, had killed before, were looking forward to killing again. They killed for money, or for gain of any kind. And it was best they were not complete lunatics, murdering at random or in a frenzy. No, they were practical, studious, protective of themselves. They were *professional*.

The thought kept Sadhe Teth warm beneath his cloak.

All he had to do was wait and watch. He would know them when he saw them, of that he felt positive.

***

On the tenth tolling of the distant temple bells, the front door of the Asylum's main building opened and out stepped an imposing figure in black. He was tall and well built, with enough muscle to provide him prodigious strength while not so much as to reduce his lithesomeness. His face was like stone, hard with angles, yet handsome beneath short, dark hair. Upon his back hung a large sword, big enough to be used with a double grip but still capable of being utilized with a single hand. From his shoulders draped a black cloak that seemed to snake away from him where it touched the ground.

A sense of menace hung about this person, even beneath the morning daylight.

He was Kron Darkbow, and his appearance caused more than a few knees to quiver at the bottom of the hill in front of the gate leading to the streets.

Kron paused for a moment, glaring down the hill to take in the five individuals standing in line before the gate. He did not appear pleased. Three men and two women, all of them with decent bulk, all of them wearing the orange of the city guard, and all of them with swords on their belts. Their hair hung down beneath their helmets as they sweated with the growing warmth of the day, and the men looked not to have shaved in a couple of days.

Kron glanced back at the still open door to the Asylum. "Gris said there would be six of them."

Montolio exited, coming to a halt behind the man in black. The former architect and sometimes mage and alchemist wore dark himself, black breeches tucked into knee boots, a dark gray jerkin fronting a white doublet. Smashed atop his dark head was a darker cap, soft and round.

He frowned. "You're right. Gris did say there would be six."

Kron grumbled, then turned away and marched down the hill. Montolio followed.

As they neared the line of men and women, it became apparent none of them were at ease. Each stood straight, rigid, with widened eyes. One or two had shaking bottom lips.

"What the hell is wrong with them?" Kron asked as they walked.

"You're kidding?" Montolio said.

Kron glanced aside to him.

"You're the great Kron Darkbow," Montolio said, "the slayer of demons, the man who sleeps among ghosts, the one who charged into last year's riots without a weapon in hand."

"All nonsense."

Montolio raised an eyebrow.

Kron grimaced and looked ahead once more. "All exaggerated, then."

A grin crossed the second lieutenant's lips as they finished their stroll.

The five shuffled their feet a little as the two officers came to a halt in front of them, everyone's boots sinking into the muddy ground.

Kron stood there, Montolio at his side, staring up and down the short line. He opened his mouth to speak.

And a creaking noise stopped him.

Everyone looked in the direction of the gate.

Coming through from outside was a rugged-looking fellow with a hauberk of hard leather beneath a gray cloak, a sizable sword on his belt. Closing the gate he turned to the others, then stopped, seemingly embarrassed.

"Sorry for being late," he said.

"Your name?" Montolio asked.

"Kilchus."

A few of the guards shared glances, and Kron took note of this.

"You're late," the man in black said to the newcomer.

"Sorry," Kilchus said.

Kron pointed to one end of the line. Kilchus came forward and stopped.

Lowering his finger, Kron sneered. "Captain Gris tells me you were a border warden."

"That's right, sir," Kilchus said.

"Then I expect you to understand discipline," Kron snapped.

"It won't happen again, sir."

Kron had nothing more to say on the subject. He turned away to Montolio. "Anything to add?"

His second shook his head.

"Good." Kron turned back to face the six. He stared once more up and down the line, now four men and two women. "Some of you I recognize from the barracks, though I do not know you personally. But whether I am familiar with you or not, none of that matters. Captain Gris has picked each of you to take part in a new experimental unit of the guard. How much he has told each of you individually, I cannot guess. I have known Captain Gris for some while now, and I trust him, which means I trust his judgment in deciding upon each of you."

Here Kron glared at Kilchus. "But that does not mean you do not have to prove yourselves to me in the days and weeks to come."

The man in black turned away again, pausing for a moment to point up the hill at the Asylum proper. "In a month's time, after your initial training, each of you will come to reside within the Asylum. It will become your new home, your new barracks."

More than a few nervous faces quivered.

Kron turned back to face them. "I am well aware of the rumors, and let me inform you right now, the truth of the matter is worse than the stories. The dead remain within this place, moving about, sometimes speaking, sometimes moaning. They rarely show themselves or interfere, but their presence can be felt and it can be intimidating."

He glared up and down the line again. "This intimidation, it is part of the point, part of the reasoning behind your staying here. You are meant to become familiar with the unknown."

Besides the speaker, the only sounds were the trompings of passers-by on the street outside the walls and the occasional screeching of wagon wheels.

"This new special unit of the guard," Kron went on, "if things work out, will eventually be broken up into several squads. How many, we do not yet know. You lot, you are the first. For now, you will incorporate not only one squad, but the entire unit itself."

Here Kron looked to his aid. "Second Lieutenant Montolio and I, working with Captain Gris, have come up with a training regimen we believe will prepare all of you for dealing with wizards and other magical elements."

"What type of elements?" one of the guards asked.

Kron looked to the man. "Demons. Magical weapons. Who knows? Maybe even dragons."

The guard who had spoken turned pale.

"It will be our jobs to be prepared to deal with such," Kron said, taking a step back so he could see the group as a whole. "It will not happen overnight. Our estimation is it will take roughly a month before any of you will be ready for serious work on the streets. In that time you will schooled in the basics of magic from a layman's perspective. You will be taught how to detect magic, how to thwart it, how to know when it cannot be avoided altogether. Eventually the individual squads will have their own wizards, squad mages. We're not going to send you out on the streets without any protection."

One of the women raised a hand.

"Yes?" Kron asked.

"Sir, will we be training with these squad mages?" she asked.

"Not for a couple of weeks," the lieutenant answered. "We have yet to decide upon the wizards for the unit. Until then, Second Lieutenant Montolio here will act as squad mage. He is a skilled wizard, and has experience in alchemy and other matters which will be part of your training."

Kilchus took a half step forward.

Kron glared at him. "You have a question?"

"Yes, sir," Kilchus said.

"Ask it."

"Why is the city doing this?"

Kron continued to glare for a moment. It was obvious he did not like the looks of this recruit. "It is time for the city to make some changes," he said. "Magic is becoming more and more common in Bond. The city must protect itself."

"Against what?" Kilchus asked.

"Against any magic-related threats to the city itself or its citizens, whether such threats be criminal, clandestine or other."

"And the local mages are standing still for this?" Kilchus asked.

Kron's eyes grew to slits and his hands formed into fists.

Seeing this, Montolio stepped up front and gave a reply. "This is not the East," he said. "Magic is not being outlawed, nor is it being curtailed any further than the current laws already allow. But the use of magic is not as rare as it once was, and the city would be foolish not to deal with this. Criminals, or worse, can make use of magic just as they could any other weapon or tool. Do you understand?"

Kilchus nodded and stepped back in line.

Kron's fists unclenched His voice was like stone. "Montolio will give you a tour of the Asylum and provide you with a schedule for the coming weeks. The rest of today will be spent with him in orientations. Then be back here tomorrow at ten bells."

Kilchus smirked.

Kron glared at the man. "Ten bells, or don't show at all."

8

Jarin and Rgia knew they were being watched as soon as they set foot out of The Stone Pony.

Breakfast had been late as they had slept in, up much of the night before as was their custom. The late hours were often enough spent prowling about the city, learning its back passages, rooftops and gutters, as well as the wealthier districts in the north and the merchant shops to the south. Falk balked at the unceasing travels back and forth across the city, but to the twins it was important to learn as much about Bond as they could. It might even prove to be a matter of life and death.

Such were the ways of assassins.

Neither made any showing of the knowledge they were being watched, no more than a mere glance at one another before Jarin's boots touched the mud of the street and turned to the left, Rgia following for a moment before coming up beside him. They stared straight ahead as they moved, keeping their pace slow enough so their watcher could follow.

And follow he did, darting forth from an alley across from the tavern to mingle with the flow of the day's crowded street. A person unfamiliar with the twins might have believed they had eyes in the back of their heads to be able to notice their follower, but the truth was much more mundane; though this was not a wealthy part of the city there were still glass sheets in some of the windows, and with a studious glance one could see in all directions.

The pair continued as if they had not a care in the world, their features unmoving. They made daunting figures as they walked down the street, each in their soft leathers beneath sturdy jerkins, the daggers lining each of their belts causing more than a few eyes to flinch away in hopes of having not drawn attention.

Still, the stranger followed, keeping his distance but always there.

Normally Jarin and Rgia would not have remained in the open so long, each preferring the shadows of alleys or the lonesomeness of rooftops, but they did not want to make it difficult for their follower to keep track of them. They had not had much fun since coming to Bond, Falk's orders being strict, and each looked forward to a little adventure.

The two remained walking straight for some while, pedestrians moving out of their way with wary glances. Only when they reached a corner where a side road led to the bazaar in the center of the Swamps did the twins come to a halt.

Rgia glanced to their left at a rundown cobbler's shop, then she looked to her brother, who nodded. A moment later the woman crossed in front of her twin and made her way inside the shop. Jarin stood there waiting next to the road, his head never turning, his eyes never seeming to move, rarely to blink, though he remained aware the whole while their follower had also stopped several buildings behind them, that the stranger was watching and waiting.

Jarin remained there motionless for several minutes, then he slowly turned.

Their shadow no longer appeared down the street, though Jarin showed no surprise at this. He walked back the way he had come, traveling directly to where he had last noticed the man who had followed them.

When he reached the exact spot, Jarin paused, then turned to his right to stare down a dark alley between two three-story tenement buildings. There was little to see in the shadows, but he could make out some small movement in the depths of the alley.

Then came a whimper, barely audible over the street noise of walking feet, carriages, wagons, horses and mules.

Jarin slid a hand onto the handle of one of his daggers, the largest one on his belt, then marched into the alley.

He did not have to go far. His eyesight soon adjusted to the gloom and he could make out a pair of figures, the man who had tailed them now unmoving with his back against a wall, Jarin's sister in front of the stranger, a knife at the man's throat.

Jarin came to a stop next to his sister. He stared at their prey. She stared at their prey.

The stranger was young, barely more than a boy with his dark mop of hair and slender frame, but there was something about his eyes which spoke of age. He was not afraid, even with the edge of Rgia's knife against his throat, but was smart enough not to move. Odd. Even more odd were the fellow's clothes; his cloak and simple leggings and shirt appeared to have been fairly nice, not expensive but nice, though recently rumpled and dirtied. Upon second glance, the youth's chin sported a few hairs and his hands looked grubby in a new manner, as if they were not used to work but had recently been faced with toil.

It was a mystery. Especially as to why the lad would be stupid enough to trail after two assassins.

"What do you want?" Jarin asked.

The youth said nothing for a moment, then he grinned as if there was not a knife at his neck. "I want to hire the two of you."

The twins looked at one another, then back to the ragged figure against the wall.

"To do what?" Rgia asked, her knife pressing deeper against flesh.

The youth's grin broadened. "To remove someone."

***

There was no such thing as a typical day for the chief of the city's Mages Guild. Some days Frex Nodana found her hours spent among the leaders of the other guilds, usually trying to iron out minor details pertaining to relations among the guilds. Other days she spent going from one business function to another, explaining to merchants and moneylenders the importance of the Mages Guild and what the guild could do for the city. There were days at the university where she met with professors and students, most who considered themselves above what they thought of as the petty concerns of her guild, though it was up to Nodana to change their minds and to foster a working relationship between those she represented, most often street-level mages, and those at the university who thought of themselves as *real* wizards. There were days of paperwork, and days of working with Captain Gris on the safety of the city. There were days meeting with other government officials, looking for new ways magic could be utilized to better the city.

And then there were days like today in which she found herself embroiled in the nasty disputes among those she represented. Evan the Cage was a known street mage with a penchant for using his magic to tame small animals. Rorius the Cleaner was also a street mage, one who generally frequented the Docks and was employed by various ship captains in ridding their vessels of rats and other unwanted critters. Until three days earlier, Evan and Rorius had not known of one another's existence even though they were both members of the Mages Guild; an unfortunate meeting had occurred when Rorius made use of a poisonous gas spell to kill a group of young rats living in a hole in the wall of a warehouse along the Docks. It had turned out Evan had been training the rats to perform little shows, jumping through hoops and the like, apparently a modest but important source of funds for the minor wizard dubbed the Cage. All-out war had nearly broken out. Evan had cast a spell growing warts all over Rorius's face. Rorius had cast a spell turning Evan's pet pigeons into baked hens atop beds of rice. It had taken the entire day, and all of Nodana's patience, to come to an agreement between the two street mages.

Tromping home through mud, she wondered if it wouldn't have been easier for her to have simply blasted the two fools into nothingness.

Such was her day.

Thus she was tired when she arrived home.

But she was also happily surprised to find Kron there waiting for her.

"You're early," she said as she entered the front hall, removing her cloak and satchel from around her shoulders.

"It was only an orientation day," he said, taking her things and hanging them on a hook. "My real work begins tomorrow."

They briefly hugged then moved down the hall toward the kitchen.

Upon entering the small room, she marveled to see a large wooden bowl atop the center table, and within the bowl a mixture of greens, sliced onions and tomatoes. Off to one side was a glass jar filled with a cloudy, creamy sauce of some kind.

"A pleasant surprise," she said, her shoulders dipping as if a weight had been removed from them.

"I knew you would be too tired to cook or go out, and I'm not much beyond basic fare, so I thought of this."

Nodana laughed as she retrieved smaller wooden bowls and wooden utensils from a cupboard. "Wherever did you find the greens and tomatoes this time of year?"

Leaning against a counter, Kron couldn't help but grin. "Montolio. He's been experimenting with some kind of ice magics to freeze foodstuffs and store them. He even mixed the dressing, some vinegar and cream and herbs. I thought all of this was one of his better successes."

"It all looks so fresh." Nodana used a large fork to separate the salad into the smaller bowls. "My compliments to the wizard. It seems he has his hand in a little bit of everything."

"That's Montolio," Kron said. "Willing to experiment with anything."

They shared a chuckle as she went back to preparing their salads.

"You've never seen him with a woman," Nodana said.

"Montolio? That's true, but I've only known him a year or two. For that matter, I've never seen Randall with a woman, and I've known him longer."

"Pfah!" Nodana finished with the salads and poured the dressing over them. "I've seen how that little Althurna follows him around. Assistant, my foot. She's infatuated with the man."

"You think so?"

"I do." She turned and handed him a bowl and fork. "A woman knows these things."

"I've seen no signs of it." He took her offering and they retired to the apartment's central room where the both of them sat on padded chairs around a small table. "She's so quiet. Barely says a word."

"Can she speak?" Nodana asked. "I've never heard her say a word."

"She can speak," Kron said, "though I admit I've never actually *seen* her talk. I heard her once, but I was coming out of a rest at the time."

"Interesting," Nodana said, then took a bite of her salad. She closed her eyes, savoring the texture and the taste, a rarity in winter. Eventually swallowing, she added, "Perhaps it's time the two of them became more than work acquaintances."

Kron nearly choked on a slice of tomato. Once it was down, "I'm not sure Randall thinks of her that way. But I don't know. Randall and I have never discussed women."

"Never?"

"No."

"Not even during your trek to Kobalos and back?"

Kron hesitated, chewing another forkful of salad, then, "On our way there, it would not have been appropriate. Coming back, we had plenty of other matters to discuss."

"Why not appropriate on the way there?"

Kron hesitated again. It was obvious he did not want to continue the conversation, or at least that he was unsure of how to continue it.

"Kron?" Nodana asked. "What is it?"

"There was a woman who traveled with us to Kobalos."

She snickered. "Well, so? Did the two of you share sleeping tents?"

He almost sneered, as if something in the food was of distaste to him. "It was nothing like that."

Setting aside her meal, Nodana reached out and touched one of his hands. "Kron, it's all right. It's not as if I expected you spent all your nights alone before we met. We're not exactly boy and girl, and I had my share of dalliances during my younger days."

"I'm not sure I want to hear this."

She removed her hand, sitting back from him. "I'm not planning on going into detail, if that's what concerns you, but you can't possibly be naive enough to think I had never been with another man. I'm sure you had your share of women."

He said nothing, but stared at the floor in front of him.

"You did, didn't you, Kron?"

Again, he said nothing.

She sat up even straighter. "Are you telling me I was your first?"

For a moment he continued to do nothing, then he nodded, his head ducking as if ashamed.

A grin slid across her face, but then Nodana removed it, recognizing it would hurt him. "How can this be? You came to me so easily, almost hungrily. There were no signs of hesitance." She grinned again, unable to help herself. "And let me tell you, that first night, I saw no signs of an amateur."

He added a grin of his own, but he would not look her in the face. "There were opportunities, but I never took advantage of them."

She giggled. "I bet somewhere out there are a handful of women who kick themselves every day for missing out."

His grin kept growing. "Perhaps."

"I know you're a couple of years younger than myself, but you're not *that* young," she added. "What about when you were growing up in the Prisonlands? Were there no women there?"

"Few," Kron said. "No female exiles are allowed, and even if there had been, they would have been off limits, by the laws and by my own ... rules. There were a handful of women in some of the villages, mostly wardens' wives and daughters, but I was too intense to draw the attention of those available. Village whores could be found, but they held no interest for me. As for other wardens, we didn't have a lot who were women, and of those who were, most of them were too intense for *me*."

Nodana snickered. "What about when you returned to Bond?"

"Never had the time," Kron said. "Early on I was engaged with nothing but revenge, then I was busy helping Gris or working on the Asylum."

"But you took the time to come to me."

He had no response, but merely sat there staring ahead.

"What about this woman who traveled with you and Randall?" Nodana asked.

"We kissed," Kron said. "Once."

"Just a kiss?"

He gave her an accusatory glare.

"I'm just asking," she said. "I'm sorry, but it's difficult to believe you never knew a woman before me."

"It is the truth."

She lifted her bowl and fork and went back to eating.

"Does this bother you?" he asked.

She chewed, took another bite, chewed some more, then, "No, it doesn't bother me. I'm just thinking."

"About what?"

"I find it baffling, how you were never with a woman before me."

"I told you I --"

She cut him off. "I know, I know. And I believe you. It's just difficult to imagine." She looked to him. "Kron, you're quite the handsome fellow, even if you won't admit it or aren't aware of it."

He gulped, glanced aside, then back to her. "That may be, but much of my life I have been somewhat ... emotionally distanced."

"I can see that." She took another bite of food.

"You do?"

She swallowed. "Of course. Which is another reason I've been surprised we ended up together."

He grinned. "Well, we started off as enemies."

She couldn't help but laugh. "So true."

"You probably tried to kill me on more than one occasion."

Nodana stopped and set aside her meal once more. She grabbed him by a hand and looked directly into his face. "Never," she said. "Yes, we were enemies, and yes, there had been the possibility of us crossing blades or worse, but it never happened, and I'm no killer. If it had come to it, I would have tried to knock you unconscious."

He grinned again. "You mean you would have tried."

"Yes. Tried." She went back to eating.

***

The hood of his cloak shielding his features, Falk shuffled along, a cane in one hand tapping against the road every few steps to help him keep his balance. Every so often his nose would peek forth as he glanced around, staring at others making their way about the Swamps at night. No one came close to him, nor showed any interest in doing so. Not once did he look back at Kilchus and the twins following him several yards away.

When the old man halted in front of the gates to the mansion of Lalo the Finder, he motioned toward the others. The Sword rushed forward, opening the gates.

Falk still do not look at them. "Kilchus, remain here. Allow no one entrance."

"Are you sure you want me to hang back?" the Sword asked.

Falk cursed. "Yes, I'm sure. You caused enough trouble this morning. Showing your face will only antagonize the Finder. No more need of that."

"What about the twins?" Kilchus asked.

For a moment the hood of the old man's cloak shifted as if he would look to the brother and sister, but he did not. "Have them patrol the outer wall. If anyone leaves, let them go, but I want to know about it as soon as I exit."

"*If* you exit," Kilchus said with a snort.

"Lalo will not try to detain me," Falk said. "There is too much for him to gain here."

"It did not sound that way this morning."

"So you said, but you have no way with words." Falk went quiet at that point and trudged on through the gates.

Kilchus stared at the man's back for a moment, then turned away. The twins disappeared into shadows.

It took Falk some while to make his way up the hill, and every so often he cursed his old age. Someone such as he should not be sputtering along in the cold at night, should be ensconced before a warm fire with a glass of Ursian brandy in one hand. Not for the first time, he promised himself such would be his future.

Slowly moving forward, he looked over the front of the mansion. The place was lit well on the lower level, but on the second floor there was only a row of connected windows showing signs a life, his memory telling him that would be the library, likely with the fireplace sporting flame. He had been within the room a few times, but it had been more than a decade since his last visit. Belgad had been running the show then, but Falk was grateful it was Lalo in charge now. The Finder wasn't as quick to dramatics as his former lord, and Lalo had a shrewd mind that could work out matters in a matter of moments. Belgad had shown smarts in hiring the Finder in the first place, and Falk couldn't help but wonder if someday he might do the same, at least if Lalo ever found himself facing hard times.

As he reached the entrance the front door eased open slowly, light spilling out causing Falk to shield his eyes with a hand.

"I can't hardly believe it," said a voice from the past.

Falk lowered his arm and squinted, his eyesight not what it once was, especially at night. "Is that Stilp?"

"Yes, sir, it is. Let me help you." With that the small man with brown hair stepped out and took Falk by an elbow, helping the older man to cross the threshold into the mansion's front room.

"It has been a long while," Falk said, brushing back his hood. He couldn't help but smile. By nature Stilp was a clown and a coward, but the man knew his place and how to treat his betters, and Kilchus had told a surprising tale of the little man's fortitude from the events that morning. "You are no longer the young man I once knew."

"We've all gotten a little older, my lord," Stilp said, removing his hand from the elbow as they came to a stop in the entrance chamber.

"Stilp, help Lord Falk up to my office," came another familiar voice.

The old man glanced up, his eyes straining through the brightness of the multitude of candles in a chandelier above his head. He found Lalo the Finder standing at the top of the stairs leading to the open walkway around the second floor, a railing following the outside of the path, every so often a door. One particular door stood open.

"Belgad's old library?" Falk questioned as Stilp helped him climb the stairs.

"Still a library," Lalo answered. "Or, more properly, my personal office."

Falk glanced up at the Finder as they approached. "It has been a while."

"Yes, it has, Lord Falk," Lalo said.

The old man almost smiled again at the recognition of his past life. Lalo was being quite kind with him, but then Lalo would, the man always having showed deference to those above his station, and no matter how far he had fallen, Falk considered him above the station of most men. It irked him to have to depend upon those so far below him, but he believed time would provide, and his revenge would know no bounds once unleashed.

"This way," Lalo said, pointing as he stepped aside to watch Stilp proceed with Falk in his grip.

It took a few minutes, but eventually Falk found himself comfortable in a dark leather chair with a padded seat and a strong, padded back. He faced Lalo's desk, the fireplace to his right throwing light and a fine warmth across the room. It had been some while since the old man had known such niceties, but he had not forgotten, and he swore such would be his again. Soon.

"Please leave us, Stilp," Lalo said to his underling as he sat himself on the seat behind the desk.

"Want me to bring anything to eat or drink, boss?" Stilp asked.

Lalo looked to Falk. "Will you partake, sir?"

"No, thank you."

"That will be all, Stilp," Lalo said.

The servant nodded and backed out of the room closing the door behind him.

The two remaining waited until the pattering of Stilp's shoes faded away.

"Many thanks for seeing me, Finder," Falk said.

"It seems I am seeing a lot of old faces of late."

"My apologies for the way Kilchus acted this morning. He always was a hot one."

"Yes, he is," Lalo said, "and his intentions were clear."

"Again, my apologies. I did not mean for that to happen."

"Yet you knew what kind of man Kilchus is, and you sent him to represent you."

Falk shrugged. "I had to send someone, and I wanted that person to be familiar to you."

Lalo stared for a moment. When he finally opened his mouth to speak, Falk cut him off.

"How is your bodyguard, by the way?" the old man asked.

"Sidewinder is fine," Lalo said. "He will spend the night in the Swamps healing tower, and should return by morning."

"Unfortunate."

Lalo appeared flustered, as if unsure of what to say. Then he sighed. "Lord Falk, I saw you out of curiosity and recognition of the title you once held, but I must admit my patience is being tested. Kilchus placed your demands before me, and I see very little I can do to appease you. His actions this morning showed the level to which he will stoop, whether by your command or not, but I must inform you, threats will accomplish nothing here. Even if I should want to help you, I do not have your money nor control of your former properties."

The old man bared his teeth, seething inwardly. If he had been facing any lesser person, he might have lashed out with his cane, but he knew Lalo was one who rarely if ever told a lie. Threats and violence would indeed accomplish nothing here.

Swallowing his pride, Falk said, "It was my understanding Kilchus told you next to nothing, that you made a series of assumptions."

Lalo blinked, then tilted his head to one side. "In actuality, that is the truth. I supposed you were seeking a return on your old investments, and that you continued to hold interest in properties that had once belonged to you. Am I mistaken, or are you not interested in these things?"

"Pfah!" Falk had to fight back the notion to spit on the rug. "Of course I'm interested, but I know you. If you say it's not possible, then it's not possible."

Lalo nodded. "I am glad we have an understanding."

"But I still want to know *why* it isn't possible."

For the first time since Falk had appeared at his door, the Finder appeared surprised, his eyes going wide. Then he composed himself once more and his gaze narrowed.

"Time," he said, "and your particular ... circumstances."

Falk snarled. "In other words, you and Belgad figured you'd never have to pay me."

Lalo held up his hands. "You would have to speak with the former master of the house concerning the details. All I know is all Lord Belgad's properties were sold off and all investments divested when he left the country."

"Don't give me that! I know he's off in Kobalos now while you remained here. What you tell me might be true, but Belgad would have had you do all the work for him. Hell, even if he *had* been here, you would have been the one to handle everything. Don't try and play me the fool, Finder."

Lalo nodded. "Very well. Believe what you will, but whatever the case may be, I am in no position to return to you lands and monies which I do not own and which are not in my power."

The old man snarled again, twisting his head to one side to stare with hate at the fire. Falk himself burned, burned with hatred. He wanted to smash something, to break it, burn it. He had known things would not go easy, but had believed the Finder would still have control of all Belgad's old investments and contracts. Otherwise, why was Lalo still in the mansion, why was Lalo the master of this Guild of Guilds, as he had heard?

Pushing back his anger, Falk found his voice again. "You expect me to go all the way to Kobalos to find Belgad? To beg like some dog for what is rightfully mine?"

Lalo held up his hands again. "I cannot tell you what to do. I simply am not in a position to help you myself. As for what is or is not rightfully yours, you would have to discuss the matter with a solicitor, and I am not sure the courts would decide in your favor."

Falk almost pushed himself out of the chair. Almost. He gritted his teeth yet again, lowering his head so the Finder could not see so much of his anger.

"Speaking of the courts," Lalo went on, "you have put me in a most precarious position. If the local authorities learn of your presence here, I could be charged with harboring a wanted man."

Falk raised his head, glaring. "What makes you think I'm wanted?"

"Oh, come now. Ten years ago you were shipped off to the Prisonlands. No one returns from the Prisonlands."

"No one except Belgad."

Lalo nodded. "Yes, that is true, but his circumstances were quite different than your own."

"You mean he had money. He paid off the church to make him a knight, freeing him."

"That is one way to see it."

A wrinkled hand smacked onto the desk. "That is the *only* way to see it!" Falk shouted. "Belgad had millions secluded away from his raiding days, then bribes the pope to set him free. It's monstrous! The man was a barbarian!"

"His roots were rather ... rustic, I admit."

"Rustic? The man wouldn't have known nobility if it had ridden him down! What's worse, a true knight like myself has his title stripped from him."

"These are different times, Falk, than those of our fathers and grandfathers," Lalo said. "The nobility isn't revered as it once was. We live in a republic now, and the few remaining nobles are only tolerated. Besides, the crowd wanted your blood after that little incident on Frist Bridge."

"Little incident?" Falk said. "Are you afraid to say the words, Finder? Are you afraid to call it what it was?"

There was no answer, only a blank, almost bored stare.

"The courts called it murder," Falk nearly shouted with a dark laugh. "The fools! I was glad to batter the man. Some little scrub of a peasant blocking my path! He should have gotten out of the way! I yelled at him, then when he wouldn't move, I rode him down like the scum he was. The bastard got up, tried to pull me from the saddle. I took the pommel of my dagger and bashed his brains in."

"And you're lucky the crowd didn't do the same to you," Lalo added.

Falk fumed in silence for several seconds, then he jabbed the end of his cane into the rug. "Ashal be damned!"

Lalo raised an eyebrow. "Cursing god now? That is unlike you. You have changed, Lord Falk."

The old man grumbled for a few moments, then, "Yes, god. And his miserable, damned church. If only the pope hadn't removed my knighthood. Hell, by all rights I should have been a duke, like my ancestors, but then the damned war and all. Freedom! Pfah! What do these peasants know of freedom?"

Lalo sat up straight. "Speaking as one who would have been a peasant, I believe I have done quite well for myself. If not for --"

Falk cut him off. "That's *it*. Yes, I see it know."

"What are you talking about?"

Raising his head, Falk stared straight into Lalo's eyes. "The pope is the key."

"I am afraid I do not understand you."

"The pope," Falk said. "He can perform an annulment."

"Annulment?" Lalo asked. "Have you been married?"

"No, no, you fool," the old man nearly screeched. "He can annul the taking of my knighthood, restoring to me my title."

The Finder couldn't help but give a sorrowful look. "I am sorry, Lord Falk, but I am not sure that would work. It's not even the same pope, and it would probably be quite the unpopular move to return your privileged status."

"I don't give a damn which pope it is," Falk said, pointing a finger at Lalo. "You owe me, Finder. You owe me for my lands and my investments. You owe me for the ten years I spent in that forested hell up north. *You* will do this for me."

"Me?"

"Yes, *you*!"

"But I hold no sway with the church," Lalo said, his face screwed up in angst and confusion. "I'm not even a member."

"But you are a powerful man," Falk said. "You have high connections, the highest, throughout the city and the country. And you have a silken tongue, Finder. If anyone can do this, it would be you."

Lalo let out a sigh, his shoulders dipping.

Falk stood, leaning against the chair while pointing his cane at Lalo. "Do this. Speak to the pope. Return to me my knighthood. Once the annulment is completed, the state will have to give me my old holdings, Belgad be damned. Then I will see to recompensing you for your aid in my most trying of times."

There were no words or actions from the Finder. He sat staring off into a corner, brooding, contemplating.

"Speak!" Falk shouted.

Lalo sighed again, then pushed back from his desk. "Very well, Lord Falk, it will be as you wish."

The old man quivered, almost as if doing a little dance of joy.

"Give me a few days," Lalo said, "and I will see what I can do, but I make no promises."

"You can do it, Finder. I know you can."

Lalo nodded. "Very well. Tell me where you are staying so I can contact you."

The joy seemed to vanish from the old man. His eyes narrowed. "There is no need for that. I will contact *you* in three days' time."

"As you wish." The Finder came out from behind his desk and motioned toward the door. "I believe our business here is completed for the night, and the sooner I get to work on your situation, the sooner you can have returned to you what is rightfully yours."

"Oh, yes." Falk allowed his elbow to be taken as Lalo led him toward the door, which was swiftly opened, the pair exiting the library for the walkway.

As they made their way down the stairs, Falk's hampering movements slowing their descent despite the use of the cane, Stilp appeared from somewhere and moved to the front door, which he promptly opened.

At the door, Falk cackled and reached out to pat Stilp on a shoulder. "It is good to see old faces."

Stilp smiled. "Perhaps we'll see one another again soon, my lord."

Falk cackled again. "Oh, I am sure we will."

"Good night, Lord Falk," Lalo said, his face impassive.

The old man turned to the Finder, once more pointing a finger at him. "Remember our business, and what you have promised."

"I cannot forget," Lalo said.

"Good." Falk spun away, then limped out the door, his cane leading the way.

Stilp and Lalo watched the old man's back disappear into the night, then Stilp closed the door.

And turned to Lalo. "Boss, you want me to go get Captain Gris?"

"No," Lalo said. "Falk will likely have someone watching the house and watching us."

"What do you want me to do?"

"For the moment, nothing. But tell me, did you see anyone with Falk when he arrived?"

"There were a few people hanging around the front gate," Stilp said, "but it was too dark to tell who they were, or if they were even with him."

"How many, would you say?"

"Three, maybe four."

"So he has put together a crew," Lalo said. "Kilchus is obviously one of them."

Stilp sneered. "That bastard. If I see him again --"

"You will report to me," Lalo snapped. "If you see Falk or Kilchus again, come tell me immediately. Understood?"

"Yes, sir."

"Good." Lalo turned away, then stopped and looked back. "Is someone from the tower bringing Eel in the morning, or are you going yourself to retrieve him?"

"I thought I would take a wagon and get him."

"Good." Once more Lalo turned away, but again he stopped. "See me in the morning before you leave."

"Whatever you say, boss."

"I need time to think," Lalo muttered, then he made his way back up the stairs.

9

The warmth of earlier in the week had done away with most of the snow, but the cold of the night before had frozen the mud of the Swamps into a hard crust that stabbed into the sole's of the feet. Fortunately for Jarin and Rgia Oltos their soft leather boots had hardened bottoms that kept the worst from their flesh as they tramped about the large, round building known as the healing tower.

The night had been long for the pair. Trading shifts, each had slept only a few hours while the other kept watch on the mansion atop the hill behind walls and a gate. Kilchus was now taking a turn at watching, which would have given the twins a few hours to rest or sleep if not for the mission they were considering taking on.

They had not told Falk or the others about the commission they had been offered to kill Randall Tendbones. To the twins' way of thinking, the assassination was a separate matter from Falk's reasonings for being in Bond. There was also the matter of sharing the payment, which neither Jarin or Rgia were interested in doing with Falk or Kilchus or Curval.

The pair turned around, marching back across the cobbled courtyard surrounding the tower. They had been doing this for some minutes, watching the comings and goings of limping citizens, some few being carried in arms or on stretchers by friends or family.

Reaching the other side of the area, the two split up, Rgia sliding into a dark alley where she turned around to keep a view of the tower's main entrance, Jarin continuing on to the outside circle of buildings that surrounded the tower, his right shoulder nearly brushing the apartments and other structures found there.

All the while, people came and went. The sky was not even yet a pale blue, and people came and went. Every so often someone in a white robe would appear from within the tower, raising eyebrows of the twins, but the individual never matched the description of the Tendbones character.

At no time did either of the twins give thought to the morality or lack of behind their possible mission. They had a job to do and would do it, at least if they felt the target was not unduly dangerous or presented some kind of unusual obstacles. They always checked out a target before agreeing to a job. It was their way, as long as the offered pay was worth their while. In this case, the pay was definitely worth their while. The strange, young wizard who had called himself Malin had offered ten thousand in gold for the death of the healer, an extraordinarily high amount of money for a target who appeared to hold no political power.

The twins weren't fools, however. The size of the payment coupled with the seeming insignificance of the target made them wary, as did the odd way Malin had looked, disheveled with eyes fluttering all over the place, as if he were not right in his mind. Still, the youthful mage had showed a handful of gold coins, with a promise of much more to come.

If Jarin and Rgia had been back in their hometown of Provenzano, they likely would have turned down the job. The guild would have had to approve, first of all, and there were too many concerns to set aside without investigation. But here, now, in Bond, the twins were wanted fugitives, and they had need of money. As Kilchus had pointed out on more than one occasion, it was not wise to put all their faith in Falk and his goals. The old man was wanted himself, and his plan for retrieving his past seemed somewhat farfetched, now more than ever since the twins had arrived in Bond and gotten a feel for the locals, a people who held little regard for nobility.

The door to the healing tower opened again, another white-garbed individual coming forth, this time to guide a mother carrying a baby toward the entrance. Jarin and Rgia stared at the figure in white, but a moment's examination told them the man was too old.

Just as the healer disappeared inside with mother and child, two ancient-looking horses pulled a creaking wagon in front of the door and came to a shuddering halt. The poor animals were so thin and gray with age they drew attention from the driver, a small nondescript fellow bundled up in a coat, his features hidden by a hood.

But as the driver jumped down and tied his beasts off to a hitching post, a wind knocked back his hood.

Jarin strode straight over to his sister. "Is that the man from the mansion?"

"The Finder?"

"No, the other one. The one we saw open the door."

Rgia stared from the darkness of her alley into the weak light of the gray morning, then stepped forward for a better view. She squinted, then gave a slow nod.

"I believe you are correct, dear brother," she said.

Jarin looked back at the man with the wagon. "Should we do something?"

"There's nothing *to* do," Rgia said. "Falk told us the boy Kilchus gave a beating would be returning to the mansion today." She pointed ahead. "This one is probably here to pick up the boy."

A moment later, the little man made his way through the growing number of sick and injured at the door. Without hesitating and without calling for a healer, he entered the building.

***

Stilp had visited the healing tower in the Swamps many times, so he had no troubles making his way along the curving outer corridor that ran around the building's central core where most of the healers' work chambers were located, the wards for those convalescing overnight and for longer periods on the higher floors. He worked past healers in their white robes, through knots of the ill clustered together with their families, and around those who lay suffering on stretchers. Not once did he look at anyone else. He was a man on a mission.

Outside the door to Randall's room, he found Althurna kneeling, wrapping a bandage around a little girl's arm.

"Is he in?" Stilp asked as he approached.

Althurna shot him a glance, nodded, then went back to work, the little girl smiling up at Stilp.

He smiled back down at her. "How you doing, kid?"

The girl lifted her arm just a little, which caused a grimace. "I fall down off steps."

Stilp kept smiling. "You and me both."

Althurna finished with the bandage, then turned her head to glare up at Stilp. "What about Eel?" he asked. "Is he ready to go?"

She nodded again.

"Thanks." He pet the little girl on her head. "See you later, kid."

Then he slipped past the two and entered the outer chamber.

He found Randall sitting on the edge of his desk, a stack of papers in his hands. The healer shuffled the papers from one hand to another, quickly scanning the words written there.

Randall glanced up at the sound of someone entering. "Morning, Stilp." He nodded toward the chamber's other door, which led to an inner room. "He's getting dressed. Should be good as new."

Stilp walked right up to him. "We've got other business. Important business."

Setting aside his paperwork, Randall gave his full attention to the little man and was surprised to find him all serious. Stilp was known to be a bit of a buffoon, but he showed no signs of it now. "I hope everything is okay."

"That's yet to be seen," Stilp said, "but things aren't looking good."

"What can I do for you?"

"Do you know the name Falk?"

Randall peered off to one side for a moment, thinking, then shook his head. "Can't say I do."

"Before your time in Bond," Stilp surmised. "Probably better the less you know. Anyway, the boss sent me to ask you a favor."

"I thought you were here to retrieve Eel."

"I am," Stilp said, "but this is more important. Lalo needs you to deliver a message to Gris."

Randall's face screwed up in a mix of curiosity and bewilderment. "I have no problems doing your lord a favor, but why can't you deliver it yourself?"

"We might be being watched," the little man answered. "In fact, I'm *sure* we're being watched."

"By whom?"

Stilp opened his mouth to answer, then shook his head. "It's too much to explain. Maybe Gris can tell you later. Anyway, we need you to deliver this message."

"Me?"

"Yes, you personally. Nobody else."

"All right. What is it?"

"Tell Gris that Lord Falk is back in town," Stilp said, "and that he's been in contact with Lalo."

"And Gris will understand?" Randall asked.

"He'll get the seriousness of it, yeah."

"Anything else?"

"Yes," Stilp went on. "Tell him not to do anything until he's sent someone to talk with Lalo. And tell him to make it someone who won't draw any attention, definitely not a member of the guard."

Randall gulped. "Sounds important."

"It is."

"Anything else?" the healer repeated.

"Nope, that should do it," Stilp said. "And I hate to take you away from your work, but if you get the chance, the sooner you deliver that message the better, as far as I'm concerned."

"Lord Lalo will be at home then?"

"Be there all day," Stilp said with a nod. "He's canceled all appointments."

The inner door opened, standing there the youthful figure of Eel Sidewinder in soft leathers, his sword belt unbuckled and hanging from a hand.

"Did I hear the name of Falk?" he asked.

"Yep," Stilp said. "He's back in town."

"Oh, hell."

"Can someone tell me who this Falk is?" Randall asked.

"He's trouble," Stilp said. "That's all you need to know for now."

***

"There he is again."

Jarin looked to where his sister nodded, and indeed, she was correct. The little man from the mansion had exited the healing tower, trailing behind him a much younger fellow wearing a belt with two short swords.

"That must be the one Kilchus said he punched," Jarin said, nodding at the youth.

A moment later the little man and his young partner were aboard the wagon. The reins snapped and the old horses began to pull as if they carried the heaviest weight in the world.

The twins watched until the wagon turned around, slowly making its way through the growing number of morning pedestrians before finally vanishing down a street.

"Should we wait here?" Jarin asked his sister.

"We can't," his sister said. "We have to relieve Kilchus."

The two stared in the direction the wagon had gone, the morning traffic building all the while, the line of those needing tending growing in front of the tower.

Finally, Rgia said, "You remain here and keep a watch for the healer. I'll relieve Kilchus."

"Good." It was all Jarin had to say.

Then his sister walked away from him in the direction the wagon had traveled.

***

It was practically unknown for a stove to exist on the second floor of a building, mainly because such was considered dangerous. In most homes of the rich and poor alike, and even in larger structures such as castles, stoves were built of stone or brick either in a separate building altogether or into an outer wall on the first floor, usually with a large stone or packed earth beneath. Thus it would have appeared strange to anyone who saw the bricked stove in the kitchen of Frex Nodana's apartment for the first time. Being a wizard had its benefits, and Nodana had applied special wards around her kitchen, spells which protected against accidental fires. Few knew of her stove and her special kitchen, only herself and Kron and the landlord, a wizard himself. If word had spread, it might have caused some panic in others who lived within the building, perhaps even in those who merely lived close by. Thus Nodana's stove was a secret of sorts, one which her landlord was glad to share as he was an inquisitive fellow and more interested in the experiment than in safety.

All of this explains how that cold morning Nodana was able to boil oats in her own kitchen, then mix the oats with milk and butter and honey to form a sort of oat porridge. She was not a breakfast person, but Kron was, and he had insisted she take part in the early meal for her own health. Until they had begun spending their nights and then mornings together, Nodana had eaten breakfast only a handful of times in her life.

Now her life had changed. Breakfast was prepared and served every morning in some form or other, most often her playing the role of kitchen maid, though Kron was not above lending a hand or even working at a meal himself. This particular morning Nodana had thought she would handle the chore as Kron had provided dinner in the form of salad the night before.

When he arrived in the kitchen, dressed from head to toe in black as he often was, his sword slapping against his left leg, he found two bowls at the center table, one for each of them, iron spoons resting next to them.

They smiled at one another, then sat and ate in silence for several minutes, enjoying the company of one another without words between them. Kron was not much of a talker, as Nodana well knew, but of late she had had a little more luck in pulling his thoughts from him. Their growing familiarity with one another seemed to slowly pry away at his emotional defenses, allowing him to open up a little at a time. There was no rush for Nodana, but she was happy at the trust he was beginning to show in her.

As if to prove her point, he finished first and said, "I've been meaning to tell you more about Adara."

She placed her spoon in her bowl. "Who?"

"The woman I mentioned last night," he said, "the woman I kissed."

Nodana smiled and touched his left hand. "Kron, you don't have to tell me anything, not unless you want to."

He smiled back. "There's not much to tell, really, at least not about any relationship she and I might have had."

"What do you mean?"

"I mean we were never a couple, though the potential had been there."

"You are sure of this?" she asked. It was a forthright question, but one she feared might hold hidden meanings for Kron. By his own admission, he was not experienced with women, at least not sexually, and Nodana could not help but wonder if he had seen something in Adara that had not been there, that it had all been one side on his part.

But he nodded. "I am sure. Believe me, we had more than one conversation on the subject."

"What is it you want to tell me about her?"

"It's not specifically about *her*," Kron said, "but more about me, and it relates to what you were saying the other night about the violence in my life, in *our* lives."

She stared straight into his eyes. "I do not understand."

He grinned, sheepishly, a rare look for Kron Darkbow. Then he pulled back his hand from her touch and rubbed at his face. When his hands came back down and tangled with her fingers, he was no longer smiling.

"It was my fault things went bad between Adara and myself," he said.

For a moment Nodana did nothing. Then she shrugged. "It happens, Kron. We all have our faults. Sometimes even love isn't enough."

"No, that's not what I mean," he said. "At least not exactly."

"So what *do* you mean?"

He hesitated as if afraid to go on. Then, "When we were on the road to Kobalos, we came upon the Prisonlands during the troubles a couple of years back. The prisoners had been armed and were breaking free with outside help. What I saw of the Lands, it was in shambles, unlike anything I'd experienced during all my years growing up there. Most of the border wardens we found were dead, butchered by the exiles."

"I've heard a little of this," Nodana said. "It was Kobalos that armed the exiles, wasn't it?"

"It was," Kron said, "but that situation eventually settled itself."

"With your help."

He nodded. "I was involved, yes, but things were more complicated than they might have seemed, and to tell the truth ... there are things I can't tell you, that I can't tell anyone."

Her head tilted to one side, curious. "Why not?"

Kron said nothing for a few seconds. He looked to one side as if making his mind up about something, then nodded, and said, "There are secrets that are not mine to tell, and I would not betray the trust of others by giving them up, even to you."

"You mean Randall?"

"I did not say a name."

"You did not need to."

"I hope this does not come between us."

Now it was she who glanced off to one side, but only for a moment. "No, I can respect your decision. If Randall has something he wants to tell me, he can do so any time."

Kron lowered his eyes in gratitude. "Thank you for understanding."

"But what does this have to do with Adara?"

"When we were in the Prisonlands, we became separated. Randall and Adara went one way while I chased after some exiles. It turned out the exiles belonged to a family of cannibals, and I --"

"Cannibals?" she asked. "Did I hear you right?"

He nodded. "You did."

Nodana shuddered. "Go on."

"I fought my way through a number of them," Kron said, "but eventually I came to the leader of their clan. And in doing so I stumbled through what I suppose was their main feeding grounds."

Now it was he who shuddered, closing his eyes as if to block out the memories.

Nodana brought around her other hand and grasped one of his wrists. "You don't have to tell me all this if you don't want to."

He glanced up at her. "No, I need to tell this."

Her fingers tightened upon his hands.

"There is no need for you to imagine what I saw," he said. "Just know that it was ... awful. I still have nightmares from time to time."

"Understandable."

"What happened next ..." His voice trailed off. His eyes lowered. He would not look at her.

"What? What happened?"

Still he would not answer. His face screwed up in pain.

"Kron? What is it?" she asked, her voice rising.

When he looked up, his eyes were red and wet. "I did unmentionable things to that man, their chief. I spent hours at it. And worst yet, I enjoyed every second of it, every second of stripping his flesh from his body, and from --"

She jerked back from him, bringing her hands to her side of the table. "You don't need to tell me this." Then she stood.

For a moment he lowered his head again, then he leaned back and stared up at her. "I am sorry. I will leave."

Her face was contorted with confusion and fear, but there was no anger. She sat again, but she did not touch him. "You do not have to leave, Kron. It's just ... it's shocking to hear your story."

"You don't want me to leave?"

"By no means."

"You don't hold this against me?"

Finally she reached out and held one of his hands in both of hers. "How could I hold it against you? You had been traumatized. I can't say I wouldn't have done the same thing in similar circumstances, though I'd have used magic instead of steel. Besides, this thing you fear, this dark side of you, I do not see it."

He raised an eyebrow.

She grinned. "Okay, yes, there is a dark side to you, but not to *that* extent, not like in the Prisonlands. I just don't see it."

"So you're not concerned I might became that man again?"

"Of course not. We're all damaged, Kron. All of us. You have your past, a lot of it having to do with your parents, and I know you've done a lot of things of which you're not proud. But remember how we met? I wasn't exactly what one might think of as a nice person."

He chuckled.

She grinned some more. "Yeah, we talked about this just last night, you and I being enemies. Believe me, I don't see a bad person in you, and I hope you don't see one in me."

"Never."

"Good. Then kiss me."

And they kissed, leaning across the table into one another, their lips touching, then seeking, hungry for one another.

Finally she pushed away, her head swimming.

"I've got to get to my office," she said, shaking her head.

"And I've got to get to the Asylum," he added.

She flashed her eyes at him. "Maybe one more kiss?"

***

Rgia found the Sword hunkered down on the stoop of an apartment building several blocks away from Lalo the Finder's mansion.

The cold did not help Kilchus's mood. "About damn time," he said, standing and rubbing his hands together. "I've got to be at the Asylum in less than an hour."

Rgia walked past him a few feet then turned and sat on the wooden steps of the building. She had a clear line of sight down the road to the gates of the mansion. Despite the continuing morning chill and her lack of a cloak or coat, the only sign she showed of being affected by the weather was her pluming breath.

She had not said a word.

Kilchus gave her a look of disgust. "Where's your brother? And where the hell have you two been?"

She did not look at him, her gaze locked on the mansion. "That is our concern, not yours."

"To hell with that!" He stomped his boots in anger and hope of warmth. "We're together in this, remember?"

Finally she glanced at him, but only a glance. The single look said a lot, as filled with disdain as it was. It told him she cared little for his opinion.

Kilchus slapped his hands together for heat, then allowed his arms to hang at his side. His frosty breath came faster and faster as he glared at the woman. No one brushed him aside in such a manner.

A hand eased toward his sword.

"You would be dead before the steel escaped the scabbard," Rgia said, not looking his way.

His hand moved away from the weapon. Then formed into a fist. Kilchus stood there, still staring, still fuming.

She glanced at him again. "Don't you have somewhere to be?"

His boots stamped once more on the cold street, then he twisted and walked away from her.

Rgia snickered then returned to watching the mansion.

***

I took an hour, but the healer finally showed himself. Randall Tendbones. Watching from an alley across the street from the tower, Jarin ran the name through his mind several times, an exercise from the old days, an exercise to familiarize oneself with the target. Now finally seeing the face of his target, Jarin focused upon the healer's features. Tendbones was a young man, perhaps in his mid-twenties, short light brown hair, dressed in white robes beneath a white cloak. Just as described by the wizard Malin.

Tendbones stopped for a few minutes to talk with some of the sick and injured in a line outside the tower. While he was polite and compassionate, it was obvious he had somewhere to be. Eventually the healer dislodged himself from the mendicants and turned away from the tower, heading south down a main street.

Jarin stared for a few moments, then followed, keeping his distance but ever watchful.

Tendbones walked at a brisk pace, not quite frantic, but busy. He was in a hurry to be somewhere, that much was obvious. But where? Was it someplace important? Jarin thought that not likely, or at least it wouldn't be someplace important to himself and his sister. Tendbones was probably off to see some sick person, someone so ill they could not travel to the healing tower.

For a moment the assassin thought of the two men from the mansion, the young one Kilchus had beaten and the other with the wagon and the old horses.

Could there be some connection to Tendbones and his fast-paced stroll? It didn't seem likely. The healing tower was merely the place where Tendbones plied his trade, and it happened to be the main location for hospitalers and those who needed healing in the Swamps.

Jarin wasn't much of a believer in coincidences, but this didn't quite feel like a coincidence, more like common sense. The younger man from the mansion had been wounded, thus he had been taken to the tower, and his partner had been sent to retrieve them. If they had had dealings with Tendbones, it would have been in his vocation as a healer. If there had been something else, if those from the mansion had had something important to pass onto the healer, why had Tendbones waited several hours after they had left before making his move?

No, this was coincidence. Jarin was sure of it.

And now that he knew the face of his target, and since he already knew where the target spent most of his day, there was little need for Jarin to remain watching the healer for the time being. He needed to speak with his sister, and they needed to confirm their hiring with Malin.

Jarin slowed, allowing the healer to continue on his way, oblivious to being tailed. The assassin watched until Randall vanished into the crowd of the streets, then he turned down an alley, heading to his sibling.

Halfway down the alley he realized he was smiling, and he stopped himself. It would not do to show emotion, especially in front of Rgia. But this was a real job, their first in years, and he could feel the excitement flowing in his veins just beneath his skin.

***

Running late again, Kilchus jogged through the gates onto the Asylum grounds while pulling over his head the new orange tabard given to him the day before by Montolio. As had been yesterday's scene, he found the five other city guards lined up near the gate with Darkbow and Montolio facing them. As yesterday, the lieutenant did not appear pleased.

"Sorry, sir," Kilchus said as he rushed into his place at the end of the line.

Darkbow said not a thing. He merely stood there staring and fuming. Then he turned away, his black cloak flipping out and around him like a bat's wings before falling to hang straight from his shoulders. The man in black marched up the hill toward the Asylum itself.

Montolio came forward to Kilchus, a weak grin on his face. "We've got to talk."

"I know, I know," the Sword said. "I promised it wouldn't happen again."

"Yes, you did, and that's a promise you've broken."

Kilchus stood straighter. "Truly, it won't happen again, sir. It's just taken a little getting used to this new schedule."

"That's all right," Montolio said, still smiling as he reached out to slap a hand on one of Kilchus's shoulders. "You can make it up to me and Lieutenant Darkbow."

"How's that, sir?" Kilchus said.

That grin, it kept growing.

"Latrine duty," Montolio said, pointing toward the Asylum building.

10

His morning paperwork behind him, Captain Gris decided it was time for a break. Scrolls and messages signed, orders written and handed out, schedules checked, it was all past him for at least the next half hour, or until some runner brought another note from the mayor containing some bureaucratic nonsense, probably about how the city guard on patrol needed to shoo away pigeons in Uptown or something else as inane.

He made his way down the passage from his office to the mess hall, the large rectangular chamber where guards on duty ate most of their meals. It was not quite lunch time when Gris arrived, but already the rows of tables were beginning to fill. Most of the men and women in orange were stationed for the day at the barracks there in Southtown, as those on duty in the Swamps or Uptown rarely ate there as it was too far to walk simply for a meal; guards in the other parts of the city would make do with whatever they brought with themselves or at a local restaurant or tavern.

Gris nodded to a number of faces he recognized, returned a few salutes, but was otherwise unmolested as he trundled along between the rows of pine tables, eventually to come up to the main counter where a line of guards had formed for their food and drink. Without hesitation the captain moved to the end of the line; rank had its privileges, but Gris wasn't one to rub it into the faces of the enlisted folks, and despite his being an officer, he still felt very much like a grunt.

He had been in line only a few seconds when he saw the white-garbed figure of Randall Tendbones enter the mess hall from the other end of the room. The healer glanced around, obviously looking for someone, then backed out of the room and turned down a hallway.

Gris could think of no reason for the healer to be there at the barracks except to see him. Something had happened.

He nodded to a soldier next to him, said, "Excuse me," then made his way out of the line and across the mess hall.

He found Randall knocking on his office door.

"What can I do for you?" he asked, coming up to the healer.

"I'm not sure," Randall said, appearing flustered. "I mean, yes, there is something." He nodded toward the door. "Maybe we should go into your office."

His sense of concern growing, Gris opened the door and they went inside his small chamber.

"Please, Randall, have a seat," the captain said, gesturing to a chair.

"I'm not sure there's time for niceties," Randall said.

"Okay, well, tell me what's on your mind."

"Stilp came to me a little while ago," the healer explained. "He came from Lalo, and they wanted me to bring you a message."

"Why didn't one of them come to me themselves?"

"Stilp said something about them being watched."

Gris raised an eyebrow. "What's this message?"

"I'm supposed to tell you that Lord Falk is in town."

A chill spread through the captain's veins. Falk was a murderer exiled to the Prisonlands. He should have still been *in* the Prisonlands.

"By Ashal," he muttered.

"What was that?" Randall asked.

Gris ignored the question. "Do you know where Falk can be found?"

Randall shook his head. "Stilp said you were to take no action until you had sent someone to speak with Lalo."

"Why?" Gris asked, then shook it off. "Forget that. I'll go see him now."

Randall held up a hand. "Stilp also said you were to send someone who would not draw attention. I suppose because they believe they are being watched."

Gris let out a sigh. Nothing was never easy. Falk was out of the Lands and in Bond, where he definitely should not be. Though he had been gone a decade or so, there were still plenty of people who would recognize the former knight by sight. And if Falk was watching the Finder, that meant he was not alone, that he had allies of some kind. None of this was good news.

The captain moved around his desk and plopped into his chair. "There's got to be someone I can send. Maybe Midge Highwater."

"But there should be a logical reason for the person to go to the mansion," Randall said. "Perhaps you should send me. It would look as if I am checking on Eel."

"Not a bad idea," Gris agreed, "but if someone was watching Stilp, they might now be watching you. And you're coming here wouldn't bode well for ... well, for whatever the hell is going on. I wish there was some way I could speak to Lalo or Stilp myself, and now."

Randall brightened. "There is."

"How?"

"I could take you."

For a moment the captain appeared confused. Then he stood. "Do you mean with a spell or some such?"

"Yes," Randall said with a smile. "Markwood used to do it often enough, and I've some limited experience."

"How does it work? Do you just convey us through the air?"

"Something like that," Randall said with a wink, reaching out to grab the captain by a wrist. "Maybe it's time you found out."

And both men vanished.

***

Sadhe Teth was nearly out of money. Only a few bronze coins remained of the small sack he had found upon Malin the Quill. There was no need to panic, as Teth could easily use his magic for survival, but that might draw the attention of the healer he wanted dead.

The cold had finally gotten to the wizard, along with a dollop of common sense. The twins had told him to find them there at the Pony, so Teth had decided the most simple thing to do would be to take a room at the place. He had found his lodgings dusty, even a little grimy, but at least it was a roof over his head and a warm bed at night. Eventually he would desire much finer accommodations, but he was not a completely vain man, and his current situation would suffice for the time being.

Except he was nearly broke. And he couldn't afford his room for another night.

And then there was the hefty fee he had promised the pair of assassins.

Something would have to be done about his financial troubles.

The twins were not a problem. Once they had accomplished their task, he would merely kill them. As for lesser expenses, he could always summon up a few coins when needed, but he did not wish to do that until this healer had been dealt with.

Sitting in the front room of The Stone Pony, the wizard sipped at a cup of hot tea he had ordered. Around him at other tables were locals, most of them slurping ales even at this early hour of the day, and then there was the muscular fellow in a plate chest with a chain shirt beneath, a sword always at his side leaning against his table. Sadhe Teth ignored them all, though occasionally he took a glimpse at the big man in armor nearby; there was something unnerving about the fellow, the way he never looked at anyone, just sat and drank from a brown bottle, staring at a spot several inches in front of him on his table.

The armored figure was a mystery, but Teth realized it was a mystery that was none of his business. Earlier that morning he had watched as the twins had come down the stairs from a room above. The male had glanced at Teth with a nod, then the pair had marched out into the streets. They had not appeared to notice the presence of the armored figure, even though he had been at the same table all night, or at least he had been there the night before when Teth had gone upstairs to bed and he had been there that morning. For that matter, few people seemed to notice the armored men. Every few hours the bartender would come over to the man's table to see if anything was needed, but it rarely was, and then only a replacement bottle. A rough-looking fellow in a heavy leather hauberk had come down the stairs earlier and had said a few words to the plated figure, but there had been no response other than a shake of a head.

So, a mystery, but one not needing solved.

Sipping at his tea, he pondered another mystery, the healer, the young man in white he had seen.

Randall Tendbones. Who was he? Nothing in Malin's memories provided an answer. Tendbones was no local political figure, no known powerful wizard. He was definitely not worshiped like the gods of old. All Malin's mind could tell Sadhe Teth was that Tendbones appeared to be a healer, one of many who worked to help the sick and injured. This did not make sense to Teth. Surely someone powerful enough to detect Teth himself would have risen to a higher station within the city. If not, then times had assuredly changed since Teth's long-ago past, though admittedly he detected few wizards of any real power within the city, at least none on the level of himself or Tendbones.

Movement at the door caught his eyes.

It was the twins. It was difficult to tell the two apart, even at close range, but Teth believed it was the woman who ignored him and moved past the bar to the seated man in armor.

"Your turn." Her voice was low but Teth was close enough to make out her words.

The armored figure stood, yawned and stretched, his full height and width astonishing, even daunting. He made no sign of having seen or heard the woman, and plopped back onto his chair, picking up his bottle of spirits for another drink.

"We have other things to see to," the woman said, "but someone needs to be watching the house." She shot Teth a look as if noticing him nearby for the first time, then she leaned closer to the big man in the plate chest. Her mouth continued to move but her words no longer traveled across the short distance.

The armored figure grunted, then leaned back in his chair. His head came up, bleary eyes beneath shaggy hair. He glared at the woman. "He told me to stay here. I stay here."

For a moment she did nothing, simply glared back. Then she gave a look of disgust and turned away, making her way to the bar where she gave Teth her back. Her male counterpart locked eyes with the wizard and came to him, sitting across from him at his table.

"Well?" Teth asked.

"We have seen the man."

"You will do it?"

"We will," the assassin said. "There seems little reason not to. His ... going away ... should not be missed, at least not by anyone of consequence."

"Then we are at agreement?"

Jarin nodded. "But for one minor detail."

"Which is?"

"We do not know you," the assassin said. "This means we want a little something up front."

"How much?"

"Only a hundred."

Sadhe Teth almost winced. The twins might as well have asked for a thousand, or a million. But he quickly realized the amount made little difference. He could fool them, at least long enough for the removal of the healer.

"Very well," the wizard said with a nod. "When do you want it?"

"This afternoon. Three bells."

"That is only a few hours."

"Will that be a problem?"

Teth shook his head.

"Good," Jarin said. "We can meet in the alley out back."

"Fine."

"Three bells," the killer repeated.

"Yes."

Then Jarin Oltos stood and moved to the bar next to his sister, also giving the wizard his back.

Teth slurped down the last of his cooling tea and stood, dropping one of his bronze coins on the table. After that he marched out the door into the day. He had nowhere in particular to go, but wanted it to look to the assassins as if he was going to retrieve their money from somewhere.

Walking down the street, he had to admit he had chosen well in the two killers. From what little they had told him and what little his spells had retrieved, he understood them to be professionals, though perhaps a little out of practice. They would have no problems finishing off someone as lowly as a healer.

Then he would deal with them.

A gray blur flashed before Gris's eyes. One moment he had been in his office, the next it felt as if he had been lifted by a high wind and flung into a tornado. Then his stomach fell out, followed by the ringing of thunder in his ears, and he found himself in a familiar room, the long main hall of Lalo the Finder's mansion.

The captain had been seated when Randall had used his magic, and Gris was still in the same position. He teetered on his feet for a moment, then began to fall back. Two hands, on one each arm, was all that kept him from splaying out on the floor.

Gris looked into the healer's eyes. "Many thanks."

"Sorry about that," Randall said, pulling his companion to standing. "I should have made sure you were on your feet."

Shaking his head to remove the unease still flooding through him, Gris placed a hand against his stomach and swayed on his boots. "How about we don't do that again, by Ashal, not unless it's an emergency."

"I admit, it takes some getting used to."

"What was that godsawful sound?" Gris asked. "It was as if the heavens themselves were pounding my skull with thunder."

"Displacement of the air when we appeared," Randall explained, but quickly saw the words meant little to the captain.

Gris looked down the length of the hall, a long scarlet carpet running from a pair of heavy doors behind the captain and healer to several short steps, atop which sat a throne-like chair that had once been where Belgad the Liar had done much of his most important business, the chair empty since his absence as Lalo showed no signs of utilizing it.

"Are we at Lalo's?" the captain asked.

As answer, the doors behind him slammed open.

Spinning around, Randall and Gris found themselves facing a breathless Stilp and a panting Eel, both swords out and in the youth's hands. Looks of grim determination drained from the newcomers.

Stilp leaned over and placed his hands on his knees, catching his breath. "You know, you two could have used the front door."

"Or even knocked," Eel added, sliding his swords into their scabbards on his belt.

"Apologies," Randall said. "Time was of the essence. And I was told you lot believed you were being watched. This way, no one saw us coming."

"I suppose that much is true," Eel said with a furrow to his brow.

"Where can we find Lalo?" Gris asked.

"I am right here," came a new voice. The Finder stepped out from behind Stilp. "I am sorry for my household's response to your arrival, gentlemen, but we had not expected such timeliness in your arrival."

Still swaying slightly, Gris waved off the apology and came forward. "It was a spur of the moment decision, but one that might have been necessary. Is it true Lord Falk has returned to Bond?"

"It is," Lalo said. "I spoke with the man only last night in my library upstairs."

Gris cursed, then, "Why did he come to you?"

"He seemed to think I could be of help in reinstating him into Bond society."

"How so?" the captain asked.

"Before his arrest he made several investments with Lord Belgad," Lalo said.

Stilp smirked. "And he thought he could still cash in on them."

The Finder turned to his employees and stared at them. Stilp and Eel looked back for a moment, sheepish in their gazes, then Stilp shrugged and the pair moved back the way they had come from the front of the house.

"Was Stilp right?" Gris asked.

Lalo nodded.

"Who is this Lord Falk?" Randall asked.

"He was a knight," Gris explained, "descended from a long line of dukes. About ten years ago he murdered a man, a peasant in his way on a road. The pope dismissed his nobility and the local courts shipped him off to the Prisonlands. He was lucky he wasn't hung."

"Did you know him when you were a warden?" Randall asked.

Gris nodded. "Our paths crossed a few times. But he's old. I can't imagine he's very dangerous."

"He has others working with him," Lalo said.

Gris raised an eyebrow. "Really? How many?"

"That I do not know," Lalo said, "but at least three, perhaps more. Stilp and Eel saw them by the front gate when Falk arrived last night."

"Good thinking to wait to today to tell me," Gris said. "If you'd sent someone last night --"

"Yes, I believe we were being watched," the Finder interrupted. "I believe we are still being watched."

"But who could be helping him?" Randall asked. "If he's been locked away all this time, how could he have allies?"

"It's not impossible he has old friends here in Bond," Gris said, "maybe some older knights who feel Falk was treated unfairly."

"Perhaps," Lalo added, "but I do know Kilchus the Sword is in his employ."

Gris snapped around to stare at the Finder. "Kilchus?"

"Yes," Lalo said. "He was not here last night, but he came to me yesterday morning, had been trying to see me for a couple of days. It was he who first brought Falk to my attention. As a way of introduction, I suppose. Perhaps to lessen the blow of surprise."

Smacking the side of his own leg, Gris turned away in frustration. "By Ashal, I just hired the man as a city guard!"

"It is my understanding," Lalo went on, "that Kilchus helped Lord Falk to flee the Prisonlands, and it seems they were spending their time in Caballerus when the troubles there broke out."

Gris turned back to the Finder. "So they came to Bond. The fools. What did they think, that you wouldn't hand them over to the city guard?"

"Falk always suffered from a high level of hubris. Perhaps even more than you realize."

"What do you mean?" Gris asked.

"When I informed him I was in no position to return his investments," Lalo explained, "he entreated me to speak with the pope in his defense, to ask that Falk be reinstated as a knight."

Gris couldn't help but roll his eyes. "Madness. The man is losing his mind in his old age."

"Perhaps," Lalo said, "or perhaps he is simply reaching out in desperation. What other choice did he have?"

"He should've stayed in the damn Lands," Gris said with gritted teeth. "Either way, he can't be in his right mind. Why wouldn't he have just disappeared, been happy with a little life somewhere far from here?"

"Hubris," Lalo repeated.

Gris looked to the healer. "What do you think?"

"About what?" Randall asked.

"You're a healer," the captain said. "Could he have gone mad in his old age?"

Randall shrugged. "I have no way of knowing, not without some interaction with the man. But yes, it's possible. Anything is possible."

"I'm telling you, captain, it is merely hubris on Falk's part," Lalo said.

Turning back to the Finder, Gris shrugged. "I suppose so. Can you tell me where to find him?"

"Falk? No," Lalo said, "but Kilchus informed Eel he had a room at The Stone Pony. I would not think the Sword would be far from his master."

"Good. Good." The captain turned back to the healer. "Randall, can you take me back to the barracks?"

"You just said you didn't want to travel again by magic."

"Not unless it was an emergency," Gris said, "and this is a pretty good emergency. I've got lots to do, and I don't want to tip off Falk or any of his goons before I get a chance to set my men in motion."

"Whenever you are ready," Randall said.

Gris looked back to Lalo. "Many thanks, Finder. You've done the city a service."

Lalo gave a short bow. "I am but a humble servant."

Again, Gris couldn't help but smile. "Yeah, right." Then he turned to Randall once more. "Okay, let's go."

Randall grabbed him by a wrist.

And they were gone.

11

Stone scraped against steel. Then again. And again. A thin layer of oil protected the metal as tiny pieces, unseen by the eye, were shaved away, leaving behind a much thinner but stronger edge. It was a type of magic all its own. A pause, then the stone moved across steel once more, straight at first for much of the length of the blade, then at a curved angle near the end.

Kron held the dagger up to his eyes, staring at the one edge. He flipped the weapon over and stared at the other edge.

Perfect. Or as perfect as he could make it without a proper smithy.

Returning the small stone to a tiny bag on his belt and the dagger to its sheath, Kron leaned back on his stool and looked over the surface of the worktable in his office. A few scrolls rested on one side next to a stoppered bottle of ink and several feathered quills lined up next to it. The room was mostly dark, the windows shuttered and what little light was provided by a torch hanging near the entrance. He preferred the dark, always had, and found he did much of his best work when there was little light. The problem was, there was little work for him to do at the moment.

The six members of the new special unit were spending the next few days with Montolio learning the basics of magic. Only then would Kron take over with the mental exercises and the physical training needed in learning to thwart magic. Until then, Kron found himself with much time on his hands, which was why he had been able to arrive early the day before at Nodana's apartment, and likely would be able to do the same today.

Nodana. He had to smile thinking about her. The first couple of months they had been together had been relatively heated, their relationship based upon raw animal attraction. But they were slowly growing into a couple. She was learning him, learning *about* him, and perhaps for the first time in his life, Kron Darkbow was allowing himself to be open with another person. In all fairness, she was as open with him, but she had been so from the start, even though he had offered few questions.

Standing, he moved to the window and pulled back one of the shutters. A hundred yards away near the gate at the bottom of the hill, the six guards and the second lieutenant stood facing one another, Montolio's back to Kron as the mage gestured with his hands and his head bobbed from time to time, obviously lecturing. It was cold out there, though not quite freezing, and the six looked miserable for it, especially as they had not been offered any place to sit. It would be nearly as tough on Montolio himself, but he had the benefit of being able to move around some, and if he wanted, he could always use some minor magics to warm himself or help with any tiredness.

Kron couldn't help but grin at the current fate of his recruits, standing there in the cold, their joints stiffening, their limbs chilled and quaking. He had wanted it this way. These six needed toughening up. They needed to become more than aware, to also foster a sense of patience. Kron knew he hadn't always been the patient type himself, but he was trying, and he insisted those under his command learn such a trait. He was sure patience was one key among many in being able to fight magic without actually utilizing magic.

As he was about to close the shutter and find some kind of work to do, the gate at the wall opened and in stepped a young man wrapped in a coat. Kron recognized the youth. He was a guard in training at the main barracks in Southtown. He was also often used as a messenger.

Kron watched as the lad jogged over to Montolio. The two shared words for a moment, then Montolio half turned and pointed up at the Asylum. The youth nodded a thanks and took off at another jog, his breath coming out in cloudy spurts as he made his way up the hill.

Standing there at the window, waiting, Kron soon heard the noise of footsteps approaching his office.

"Come in," he said before a knock on the door could sound.

The youth entered, holding out a folded paper. "Lord Darkbow."

Kron turned to the young man, reached out and took the paper. "No lords here, son, just a lowly lieutenant."

"Yes, sir."

Unfolding the paper, Kron read what was written there in a familiar script. Then he read it again. He almost could not believe what he was reading, but he had no qualms with what it said.

He looked to the youth. "Tell Captain Gris it will be handled."

"Yes, sir. Anything else?"

"No. Not unless you want to hang around and watch."

***

The city guard made up a common sight in the city of Bond. Their orange tabards, leather armor and swords could be found at nearly any time upon any street. Generally the guard patrolled in pairs, sometimes one or the other carrying a crossbow or a long pole weapon. Every once in a while a group of four to six guards could be found together marching along the streets or hanging around a tavern or doing some other kind of business at a local shop usually somehow related to their vocation, weapon smiths and the like.

The average citizen saw this every day, from the poorest to the wealthiest.

But when a group marched forth in two columns of six, twelve total with the addition of a sergeant out front, four of them hefting lengthy, curve-bladed glaives and another four carrying crossbows, it drew the attention of more than a few, especially as this sizable squad wore the less familiar chain shirts beneath their orange.

Leading the way was Sergeant Adims, a relatively new member of the city guard. She was a local, having earned her stripes through several years as a grunt in the regular army before transferring into the guard. She was not a big woman, but of average size. Everything about her appeared average. Medium-length, straight brown hair. Light brown eyes. No noticeable scars or tattoos. Nothing awkward about her features or her body. She was average.

But she was also known to be one of the toughest, though fair, sergeants in the whole guard. When people saw her coming, especially with a stern look on her face, they got out of her way.

Which was what happened as the sergeant headed the other twelve out of the Southtown barracks, up the packed dirt road from the barracks to South Road, then east and north across Frist Bridge into the Swamps, more specifically the southern end of the Docks district. There the sergeant and her squad made a sharp left along Beggars Row, passing apartment buildings, warehouses, a handful of shops that appeared to have seen better times, and even past the whore house known as The Frog's Bottom and a tavern called The Royal Bear.

Along the way, despite the chill of the weather and the gray of the sky, a crowd began to form. At first it was street urchins running along behind the tromping soldiers. Then, slowly, more and more adults began to join in, many of them without work and with nothing better to do, a few skipping out on their work because whatever was about to happen seemed of more interest. Even Midge Highwater made an appearance, for the second time in a week carrying himself over into the Swamps in order to see first-hand what would occur.

Eventually the guards stopped in front of The Stone Pony. Sergeant Adims went to her people and spoke a few words. Four of the guards trotted off down an alley toward the back of the tavern. Four others approached the establishment's entrance, then split into pairs, one pair stationed on either side of the door.

The sergeant herself faced the entrance, then waved the last four of her comrades forward.

***

Curval was just sitting down to his usual spot with a fresh bottle when he heard the hubbub outside the tavern. Cursing, he popped the cork out of his bottle and took a long swallow. As the liquor burned its way down his throat, he ignored the growing sounds of the crowd. He tried to ignore the outside world completely. There was nothing out there for him but pain.

Lowering the bottle, he used a sleeve of his doublet to wipe away the lingering liquid from his lips. A few drops of the brown liquor spotted the front of his cuirass, but he paid it no mind, resting a hand next to the sword always leaning against his table.

The noise grew, as did the crowd. Individual words were difficult to hear, but there was a general racket, a mixture of unease with a carnival atmosphere. The hoi polloi were scenting trouble, and they wanted their taste of it.

Within The Stone Pony, the handful of customers besides the armored figure moved to the windows. They muttered words among themselves but not too loudly, more than a few glances thrown back toward the knight. Even the bartender came out from behind his workplace to take a look.

Joining the noise of the crowd was the clattering of boots upon the wood steps out front.

At this point the bartender had had enough. He rushed back to Curval and stopped next to the drunkard's table. For a moment the bartender stood there, his lips twitching, one hand raised as if to point toward the front.

Curval raised his head and glared with bloodshot eyes at the man.

The bartender flinched, then backed away. Once the knight's head lowered, the man turned around and rushed to the customers gawking out the window.

"Going to be trouble," someone said.

"Outside now, you lot," the bartender said, motioning toward the front door. "I don't need the headaches. All of you, out!"

There were grumbles and rumbles, but no one argued with the man. One by one, the customers made their way out the front door. With a last look back at Curval, the bartender followed, then leaving the front room of the Pony to its own fate.

The knight took another swig of liquor.

The front door opened again before the bottle touched the table.

***

Above and behind the knight, Jarin had seen enough from the second-floor landing. He spun and sprinted for the door to the room he shared with his sister and the others. He did not bother to knock as was the agreed-upon arrangement, but burst through.

Rgia whirled to face him from the other side of the room. Falk sat up in the bed they took turns sharing.

"We have to get out of here, now!" Jarin nearly shouted.

His sister wasted no time on questions but darted to a leather sack holding their few possessions and grabbed it up from a corner.

Falk sat up straighter, blinking as if rousing from a nap. "What is it? What is happening?"

A crashing din rang from below.

Jarin slammed the door shut behind him and moved across the room to the shuttered window. "City guards, a small army of them."

"Are you sure they are here for us?" the old man asked.

"Who else would they be here for?" Rgia said.

"This city is full of vile scum. They could be here for anyone."

"And send a dozen guards?" Jarin said. "I don't think so. Face it. Your friend the Finder has sold us out."

"But why would he do this?" Falk asked.

There was no answer other than Rgia's hand beneath his arm, lifting. "We have to go," she said, her voice more tame, more controlled than her brother's.

"How do we get out?" Falk asked as he was pulled to standing next to the bed.

"This way." Jarin pulled open the shutters.

"We're on the second floor," Falk cried out. "I can't climb down that way."

Rgia spun him around so they were face to face, nearly nose to nose. She grabbed his walking cane from a corner and thrust it into his hands. "I'll go first and Jarin can help you hang out the window. I will catch you."

"But it is dangerous."

Another crash from below, followed by a roar.

Rgia glanced at the door. "Would you rather try your chances down the stairs?"

Falk hesitated, his eyes filled with fear, then he shook his head.

"Let's go," Jarin said with impatience, shoving up the sash.

With one last look at the door, Falk asked, "What of Curval?"

"He is doing his job," Rgia said, urging the old man to the window.

Somewhere in the distance, a church bell tolled three times.

Huddled against a wall in the alley behind the tavern, Sadhe Teth was not aware of the commotion out front of the building. Nor was he aware of the ringing bells, or the sounds of approaching boots, or the clacking of a window opening somewhere above his head.

His focus was upon the three rocks in his hands. Each was about the size of a walnut. He had picked them up here and there during a morning stroll about the Swamps. Waving a hand over the rocks, they shimmered in his vision for a moment. Then came a slight flash and the rocks were gone, replaced by a small sack that jingled in the wizard's hands.

Teth grinned as he straightened. He was out of money no longer, and could easily afford to pay the twins and cover however many nights he wanted to spend in The Stone Pony. Of course the gold in the sack was not real, but it would hold up against the closest scrutiny, at least for a few days until the spell faded. He could have made use of more powerful magics to actually turn the stones into gold, but he had been concerned that might draw the attention of this mysterious healer.

Thoughts of the healer turned to thoughts of the twins. Where were they?

Then he had no more time to think as two things happened simultaneously.

Someone fell from the sky. The person landed on their feet right next to the wizard.

And four hefty men in chain mail and orange tabards appeared from a side alley, swords in their hands.

Surprised, Teth flinched from the person who had appeared so suddenly next to him. He had just enough time to register that it was one of the twins when one of the chain-clad men yelled out, "Do not move!"

Long daggers appeared in the twin's hands.

Then there was a blur of action.

An elbow belted Teth in the stomach, shoving him flat against the wall. Instead of surrendering or trying to flee, the twin launched into the midst of the four soldiers. Steel blades flashed and rang out. A dagger cut across a man's throat, leaving a red line and causing him to fall back. Another soldier swung his blade high, yet another swinging low. The twin jumped back a step, both swords missing, then darted forward, each dagger jabbing out, one to the left, one to the right. The two foremost guards backed away.

For the briefest of moments it appeared the twin would be surrounded by the remaining three soldiers. Then another dagger flew in from somewhere above Teth's head, the tip of the blade impaling a guard's eye and dropping him.

The twin on the ground never stopped moving, but danced around the falling man in orange and launched a barrage of slices at another soldier. It was all the defender could do to avoid or parry the smaller blades while his remaining comrade came in from the side.

The sword at the side pulled back for a hefty stab, but at the last moment the twin jerked to one side, changing direction of attack, and slid a narrow blade across another throat.

The third city guardsman died.

The last one cried out in anguish and fear, charging the smaller, leather-clad figure that had slain all his mates.

It was a dumb move.

The twin dipped low on one leg, sending the other leg out in a swinging spiral. The guard was caught in the ankles and went tumbling. He had barely enough time to fall flat on his face, the wind knocked from his lungs, and to roll over before steel plunged down into his chest, crunching aside linked metal rings to bury itself in his heart.

The last enemy dead, the twin wiped the daggers relatively clean on the tabard of a corpse. Then the twin stood and turned around to face Sadhe Teth.

It was the woman, Rgia, facing him.

Astonished, Teth caught himself not breathing. Ten thousand years old and he had not seen such swift motion in combat since the time of the old gods. The twins, at least Rgia, truly were worthy combatants, worth every ounce of fake gold he would be paying for the healer's murder.

Pushing away from the wall, he held out a hand toward the woman and allowed himself a breath again.

It would be his last, at least in Malin the Quill's body.

Jarin landed hard on the ground behind him.

Teth spun, surprised yet again.

"It was *you*!" Jarin cried out, plunging a dagger into the wizard's chest. "Traitor!"

The pain was enormous, like lightning and fire tearing into Sadhe Teth's soul. He had felt pain before, even worse than this, but it had been a long, long time since. His body went weak, his legs buckling beneath him, and he swayed but a moment before his feet betrayed him and he plummeted to the ground, cracking his head on the alley's hardened floor.

***

Inside The Stone Pony, the city guards fared little better.

When the front door opened, Curval saw right away a stern-faced woman in chain and orange. The knight's chair scraped back behind him as he stood and another pair of soldiers entered, taking places on either side of the woman, crossbows raised and pointed at him. Behind the three approached another two in orange, these with swords at the ready as they moved out beside their companions. On the street a mob of rambunctious citizens enjoyed the show, what little of it they could see.

The woman in lead reached back and slammed closed the door. She turned back to face Curval. "We are here for Falk and Falk alone."

One of Curval's hands edged nearer his weapon.

The woman scowled and pointed at him. "Do *not* touch that sword."

Curval looked to the crossbowmen, the points of their bolts aimed for his chest. There was no way he would be fast enough to grab up his sword and cover the dozen or so yards between himself and them before they could pincushion him. He moved his hand away and dropped into his chair.

"Where is he?" the woman asked.

Curval said nothing, just stared at them as he slid his hands down into his lap.

The woman grasped the handle of the long sword on her belt. "Damn you, where is Falk?"

Again, no response.

The female officer glanced aside at her troops. "Check the upstairs and the back rooms."

Two men with swords came forward.

"I would not do that if I were you," Curval said, his voice deep.

The two men stopped, looking back at their commander.

"Go ahead," she ordered, waving the men on.

The two faced forward again and hunched down slightly, readying for an attack.

Curval sat and stared.

The two soldiers took a step.

Curval still stared, not moving.

The two took another step.

Still nothing from the seated knight.

One of the two sighed, and then they came forward together as to bypass the seated figure.

Curval still did not move.

Until they were right next to him.

His meaty hands sank further below the table, grasping the heavy piece of furniture by its central leg. He lifted and thrust the table to one side as if a giant shield. The edge of thick wood caught the nearest of the two guards in the side, knocking him into his partner and sending both barreling away toward the bar and into the line of stools there.

The two crossbowmen panicked, launching their arrows.

Thunk! Thunk!

A pair of barbed steel heads sank into the the table and pushed through, one scraping against Curval's right forearm but doing no real damage.

The knight roared, lifting the table higher, almost over his head.

"Rush him!" the woman shouted.

The crossbowmen dropped their weapons and charged, bringing out swords as they moved.

Curval threw the table at them. One dodged aside the flying hunk of wood, but the other was not so lucky, his legs slammed just as the table hit the floor in front of him. A bone snapped behind the force of the throw and the weight of the table, and the wounded man screamed out and fell. The other continued his rush, his sword jabbing ahead.

Curval stepped into the approaching figure, his left hand slapping aside the blade of the sword while his right fist brought forward a roundhouse punch. The blow caught the soldier on the side of the head just beneath his round helmet, and it was as if a giant hammer had battered him, his head snapping to one side, his feet sliding out from beneath him as he hit the floor.

Her men down, the woman in charge finally pulled her sword free of its scabbard. Despite her losses, she showed no less determination.

"We do not have to do this," Curval said.

She did not answer. She should have called outside for reinforcements, but her pride had been wounded. Sergeant Adims charged.

The knight stood his ground, waiting, waiting.

At the last moment, just as the sword came chopping in from one side, he backed toward his still-standing chair and his fallen sword. His opponent's blade sliced air, the length of her swing giving Curval precious moments to grab a weapon of his own.

He opted for the chair, hefting it one handed. These were soldiers doing their jobs. He would not kill them unless absolutely necessary.

The woman came around with another swing of her sword. Curval thrust the chair forward, the heavy blade sinking into the wood, caught into the wood. A look of surprise registered on the woman's face.

Then Curval sank a fist into her throat. She choked and coughed, sputtered, letting go of her sword as her hands reached for her throat. She blinked back tears of pain and clumsily backed away from her foe.

Curval stepped forward and hit her with another blow, this one on the side of the head. She went down, laying there twitching but still alive.

The two soldiers near the bar had regrouped, their swords out as they screamed and ran at the knight.

Curval wasted no time seeking another piece of furniture or his own sword. He dipped down quick and grabbed up the sergeant's weapon, coming up with it and knocking aside the first of the blows launched at him.

The second soldier's sword came in from upon high, slicing down through air. Curval with his brawn and strength knocked aside the blade and shouldered into the man, sending him reeling. The first soldier was already bringing around his sword, this time for a stab. The knight sidestepped steel and flipped around his sword, bringing the pommel forward to hammer into his opponent's face. Cartilage crunched and blood splattered as a nose was broken, the nose's owner crying out before fainting away.

The last soldier standing swung wild, hoping for a head blow, but it was little use. The bigger man facing him ducked and the sword passed over his head. Then the soldier felt a fist slam into his stomach and he doubled over, grunting and losing his breakfast as it streamed forth from his mouth.

Breathing heavily, the knight took a step back from the carnage. There were no more immediate foes for him to face. All were down, some in worse condition than others. He tossed aside the borrowed weapon and retreated a few more steps, retrieving his own sword from where it had fallen on the floor.

A quick glance to the front showed there were no more soldiers coming in. Curval had thought he'd seen more of the orange-garbed figures outside, but the cries of the crowd must have drowned out any sounds of the fighting.

He turned, nearly rushing up the stairs to Falk's room, but then he caught himself. The twins were smart. They would have heard the racket out front and possibly the fight on the lower level. They would not have waited to see the outcome of Curval's confrontation. They would have gotten themselves and Falk out of harm's way as quickly as possible. Since they obviously had not come down the stairs, they would have gone out a back window as there were no other exits on the second floor.

Curval gave one last, almost sorrowful glance to the fellow bent over and still throwing up the remains of an earlier meal, then the knight moved away from the stairs and toward the back of the building. He had made sure of his surroundings when they had first arrived at the Pony. In the back of the first floor were a hall, a couple of private rooms and a door to an alley. The twins would be there, Curval was sure.

***

Wood cracking against wood. A door slammed open? Boots stomping and shuffling about.

"About time you showed up."

"We won't have long." This was a sturdy voice unfamiliar to Sadhe Teth. "Where is he?"

"Up there."

"Drop and we'll catch you!"

"I'll break my neck!"

"*I'll* catch you."

Teth could hear everything around him, but he could not see. His eyes squeezed tight with pain, his inner world roiled as his stolen body lay still, unable to move. Deep within his mind, Malin the Quill called out for saving, but it was no good. Even the young wizard knew he was dying with only seconds to spare, perhaps a minute. No air came to him. His lungs had been punctured. He was bleeding out.

More sounds of feet shuffling.

Then a *thump*!

"Got you!"

"See, I told you."

"Just get me out of here."

There was one chance. One. Teth would have to change bodies once more, leaving Malin to die in the bloody shell of his own form.

"Who is that?"

"He's the one who set the guards on us. I'll tell you later."

Straining, the ancient wizard opened one eye. For a moment everything was blurry, then the sights before him came into focus. He could see little, just feet. More exact, he could see two pairs of soft leather boots, probably belonging to the twins, and a pair of simple, worn walking shoes, the ends of a cloak or robe hanging around them.

Teth would have smiled if he could. It would be just and perhaps ironic if he could manage one of the twins.

"Let's go."

No! Not yet. Teth strained further, trying to force a hand to move. Nothing. Nothing! Damn the ancients! Damn the world! Nothing!

The feet in front of his eyes shifted away, the twins stepping ahead of the cloaked person.

A twitch, a spasm, then the left hand that had belonged to Malin the Quill shot forward, the fingers falling upon a shoe.

It would be enough.

Sadhe Teth felt his world change once again, and Malin the Quill screamed in his soul as he went to meet his ancestors.

***

The front door of the Asylum snapped open, cracking against the wall behind it. Out strode Kron Darkbow, behind him the youthful messenger. The man in black took his time going down the hill to the second lieutenant speaking with the line of six city guards, all in their leathers and oranges.

As Kron came up to them, Montolio caught the glances of his pupils and turned to the oncoming commanding officer.

"I was just explaining to them the differences between high and low magics," Montolio said. "Do you have anything to add on the subject?"

"It can wait," Kron said, brushing aside his second in command.

The messenger parked himself next to Montolio, a grin of delight on the youth's face. There was going to be a show.

"What is it?" Montolio asked the young man.

Before an answer could be given, Kron stepped up in front of Kilchus, less than ten feet away from him and the other five guards.

"Kilchus, remove your sword belt," Kron said.

A sly but nervous grin crossed the Sword's lips. Up and down the line of guards, similar looks were shared.

"What for?" Kilchus asked.

Kron's eyes turned to slits. "I gave you an order. Remove your sword belt."

For a moment Kilchus did nothing, then he placed a gloved hand on the hilt of the large weapon at his belt. "I think not. Not without a reason."

It seemed impossible, but Kron's eyes narrowed further, giving him a snakelike appearance. The other five guards shared nervous glances again and edged away from their obstinate comrade.

Kilchus shot a glance to the other guards and snickered. "Idiots. Never give up your --"

Kron cut him off. "Kilchus the Sword, you are under arrest."

The temperature seemed to drop further, and it was already a cold day outside. There were no more shared glances, no more shuffling of feet. It seemed even the breathing of those present had gone quiet.

The only sound was the wind flapping at Kron's black cloak, the cloth encircling one of his legs.

Kilchus's gaze locked on that of the lieutenant, and the two stared at one another for long moments.

Then, "What am I charged with?" Kilchus asked.

Kron said not a word.

The Sword tightened the grip on the hilt of his weapon. "Damn you! Tell me the charges!"

Still nothing. The wind struck slightly harder, catching the end of Kron's cloak and tugging on it, pulling it away from his legs and flapping it out to one side.

"Pfah!" Kilchus turned as if to leave.

"You will not make it to the gate," Kron said, tugging back the edge of his cloak to reveal his own heavy sword.

Glaring back over a shoulder at the man in black, Kilchus stood motionless. The two shared looks again, each stare hard, filled with cold fire, colder than the winter.

With a look of distaste, Kilchus shrugged and turned away.

Kron bound forward half a dozen feet, landing on his right boot, the cold ground crunching beneath his weight.

The lengthy steel of Kilchus's sword sprang free of its scabbard as the man swung the weapon in a wide arc around and behind him, the Sword twisting with the attack. The blade came up short, missing Kron's chest by inches, then continued on its way in its wide curve, Kilchus unable to bring the weapon to an immediate halt.

Kron sprang off his right foot, launching himself across the distance to his opponent. At the last moment Kilchus tried to bring up his free arm as a shield, but he was not fast enough. Kron dove into him, slammed into him, wrapping his muscled arms around Kilchus as the two plummeted backwards.

Landing hard on his back, Kilchus felt the air flee his lungs and his sword fall from his hand. Blinking back rage and pain, he thrust up a hand trying to grab at his foe's throat. Kron sat up, both knees on either side of the Sword, and grabbed his enemy's flailing hand with both his own, twisting.

Kilchus cried out in pain.

Kron brought an elbow around, slamming it into the other man's face.

Kilchus screamed again.

And was hit again.

The elbow cracked forward a couple of more times, then the Sword lay there on his back, a river of red flowing down from his nostrils, his breath weak and misty above him.

Kron swayed on his knees for a moment, then he pushed himself to standing and backed away. He stared down at his fallen opponent.

Silence reigned supreme. No one else moved nor said a word. The other guards were pale and wide-eyed. Montolio looked little better and somewhat gray. The young messenger smirked, already thinking of the stories he would tell to his friends.

Kron blinked, then gestured to two of the nearest guards. "Take him to a cell in the Asylum."

No one moved for a moment, then a man and woman shot forward, lifting Kilchus by the arms.

"And one of you go for a healer," Kron added. "He looks as if he needs it."

***

"Falk, what the hell is wrong with you?"

Falk? Who was Falk? He had no idea. Or did he? There was a faint memory. But memories were unreliable.

He stared through open eyes once more, but the world made no sense to him. His vision blurred, then focused, then blurred again. His sight jarred up and down as if he was being shaken. Colors bright spiraled around him, along with glowing circles and stars on the edges of his vision. People, strangers. A big man with a bigger sword, a rusting plate curaiss covering his chest. Two others, both looking almost exactly alike with their short hair and ... no, they were not the same. One was a man, the other a woman. The ... twins? Yes, they seemed somewhat familiar. But the other man, the big one, he was not so familiar. No ... yes ... in the tavern. He had seen the big man in the tavern. And who was that on the ground? A young man? With blood upon his chest. With staring eyes. Malin. Yes, that had been his name, Malin the Quill.

What else?

There was no longer the anguish, the pain he had suffered from ... what? Had he been stabbed? Was that what had happened? Surely not. Surely he would have protected himself, warded himself against something as simple as a knife. But maybe not, not if he hadn't expected any danger. The real danger, it was to come from ... whom? The healer. Yes. The man in white. That was the real enemy.

But why an enemy?

To answer that, he had to know who he himself was, and that was no easy question to answer.

Falk. Someone had said Falk. Was he this Falk? Yes. Maybe. Or a part of Falk. But there was another part of him. Teth. Sadhe Teth.

483

Yes. Yes. That sounded right. It felt right.

"We've got to get out of here. Curval, can you carry him?"

A grunt.

"Then do it!"

The swirling colors. Lifted. Floating? No, carried. Off the ground. His feet no longer touched the ground. His sight bobbed up and down once more, worse this time, like being on a ship at sea. Thick tree trunks encircled him, impeded him. No, not tree trunks. Arms. Big arms. Cold against one cheek. Cold and hard. The steel plate. The big man from the tavern was carrying him.

To where? Did it matter?

No, not as long as it was to someplace safe.

Motion. He was moving. Images flashed past his eyes, but he could barely register what they were. Shadows, then brightness, followed by deeper shadows. More movement, grunting, swaying. Shouting in the distance.

Someone said, "Where the hell are we going to go?"

A man said, "I know of a place."

"Where?"

Their voices drained away. Teth/Falk could hear no more, nothing but his heartbeat which grew faster and faster.

There was no fear, simply disorientation. He knew not where he was, where he was going. He knew not the people who carried him along, who had spoken those words. He did not even know his own identity.

Falk. Teth.

Teth. Falk.

Yes, yes. Falk, his mind was stronger than that of Malin the Quill. Though Falk held no experience with magic, he was much older than the Quill, more experienced, with a stronger will of mind. It was this against which Teth truly struggled.

Two minds competing for one body. Neither could triumph over the other, not yet. A stalemate.

It had taken time with Malin. It would take time with Falk. But Sadhe Teth knew he would triumph.

He had to. He had waited too long, struggled too much. The time was right. He had to win.

He pressed downward, forcing the piece of the old man's soul which fought against him to slip and fall and drop and plummet into an abyss, into an inward hell. Yes, Teth would triumph. Just a little time was all he needed.

Vision again. He could see. More shadows. His sight danced before him, his cheek still cold against the metal.

"Falk, what the hell is wrong with you?" someone repeated.

No, not Falk. Falk would be defeated, *was being* defeated.

His name was Teth. Sadhe Teth.

And he had a new body. An old body, to be true, but he would be more careful this time. He had been forgetful before. He had forgotten the frailty of the human body. That mistake would not happen again. As soon as he was able, as soon as his strength returned, he would protect himself from anything a mortal could throw against him.

There was only the healer with whom to be concerned.

The healer. Yes, he still had to die.

Until then, Sadhe Teth would not feel safe.

Yes. Teth. Not Falk.

Still ... there was something he was forgetting, something important.

It would have to wait, wait until his mind was clear once more, however long that would take, however long Falk would struggle against the inevitable.

He closed his eyes once more, allowing himself to be carried to a new, unknown destination.

Part 2:
Flames

12

He could hear the screams from the front gate. Riding through the open black bars, Captain Gris glanced aside at the pair of guards in orange manning the entrance to the Asylum grounds for the night. One man did not look back, his gaze locked on the Asylum building up the hill. The other guard shivered beneath his cloak, his face white beneath the light of the moon.

The terrible sound continued to rise as if it would never end, each throat-wrenching cry worse than the one before. It was enough to drive a man mad.

Wearing a frown, Gris nudged his horse around the guards. "How long has this been going on?"

At first neither said a word. Then, "An hour, maybe two," one of them said.

The captain gave a curt nod, then steered his ride up the hill. All the way to the entrance, the screaming went on and on. Gris wondered how the man's voice could hold out. Wouldn't his throat have gone raw? His vocal chords snapped? It seemed not, for the vocal horrors never ceased.

As he neared the front door, the glow of firelight behind the bars of the Asylum's windows only added to the stature of the overall structure, the three-story building not unlike a small fortress, a tower dominating the southwest end.

Tugging his reins to impede his ride, Gris brought a leg around and dropped from the saddle, tying his animal off to a hitching ring built into the wall near the entrance.

The front door opened, light beyond silhouetting the figure of Montolio. The younger man's face was hidden in shadow, but there was something about his stance which told of a man unnerved.

Gris approached, waving a hand toward the inside of the building and the never-ending screams. "Please tell me that is not my lieutenant's work."

Montolio shook his head. "No. We followed your orders. He has been placed within a cell on the third floor."

Nodding, Gris waited the moment for the mage to move out of his way to allow entrance, and then the guard captain stepped inside.

He shivered as he surveyed the now familiar room. The front of the Asylum was a long hall from right to left, openings at either end leading to rooms beyond. The chamber rose to a vaulted ceiling three stories above. Unnerving to the eyes was the wall immediately across from the entrance, three levels of walkways with handrails, beyond a series of barred rooms, a dozen per level. The insane had been kept here for years, locked away from the outside world. When Kron had purchased the place, it had been quite damaged, yet he had returned it nearly to its original working condition. There were some few changes; the cells on the lowest level no longer held doors of iron bars, and once there had been a large metal cage encircling the entrance.

Gris shivered again as the scream far above his head turned into a desperate howl. Even without the shrieks, he realized he likely would be quaking in his boots. The place was cold despite a multitude of lit torches along the wall, as if the black stones sucked away the light and heat and joy, and the fact the Asylum was filled with ghosts did nothing to dispel the eidolic sensation permeating its rooms.

Shaking off the eerie feeling, the captain asked, "Is he in?"

"Waiting for you in his office." Montolio pointed to one of the openings leading to the inner workings of the Asylum.

"My thanks." Captain Gris nodded and stomped off in the direction indicated.

The hallway was darker and colder than the entrance room, but a torch ensconced in the wall at the end showed light and promised some little warmth. To the left of the torch appeared a doorway, open and revealing more light beyond.

Stepping into the entrance, the captain found his lieutenant and friend seated behind a desk, a pair of candles providing the room's light.

"Why is he screaming?" Gris asked.

"You would have to ask him."

"Did you question him?"

Kron stood, shuffling aside some scrolls he had been perusing. "I wasn't sure what to ask."

"How much have you heard?"

"Some of the men filled me in on what happened at the Pony today," Kron said, "and they told me about Falk. I recognized his name from the Lands. Hard to believe a fellow warden betraying the trust given him."

Gris nodded, then stepped deeper into the room where the screams from the front became more muffled. "It gets even stranger." He brushed open his cloak and withdrew a familiar leather-bound package.

Kron's eyes lit up. "The bones?"

"They were found on the body of our missing university student in the alley behind the Pony," Gris said. "Poor boy had been stabbed to death."

Kron's gaze was filled with questions.

Gris held no answers. "No clue as to why the youth was there, what ties he had to Falk, nor why he took the bones in the first place."

"Maybe Kilchus will know," Kron offered.

Nodding, the captain exhaled and ran a hand through his hair. "I hope so, because this is bad, Kron. Four of my people dead, plus a civilian, and five more guards stomped down as if they were nothing. Whoever did this, these people are professionals. Falk has found himself some capable friends."

"Unusual, too, from what I've heard."

"In what manner?"

"It's strange," Kron said, "those killed were all in the alley behind the Pony, yet none inside were slain."

"I noticed," Gris said. "Either way, I'm none too pleased about what's befallen my people of late. By Ashal, all those we lost to that demon last year, and now this? Even the riots weren't so deadly. What's *happening* in this city?"

Kron pointed to the small bundle in the captain's hands. "It started with those."

Hefting the package of bones, the captain glanced down at them. "And we don't even know why, or anything else about the damned things, for that matter."

"Maybe Kilchus will have some answers."

"I hope so." Gris half turned away from the lieutenant. "Let us go and find out."

***

Cracking through a thin layer of ice into boggy water beneath, Rgia's boots sank to several inches above the ankle, nearly freezing her feet and staining the boots. She shifted the bag on her back from one shoulder to the other and held higher the bullseye lantern stolen along with the bag's holdings from a traveling peddler's camp just outside the city. Her lips tight against a curse, she was reminded how much she hated her brother, the fool having brought them to this place.

The swamp. The *true* swamp. Just west of Bond. The section of the city known as the Swamps rested higher than this region, and apparently only suffered the worst effects of flooding after heavy rains. The same could not be said for the forlorn territory Rgia found herself wading through after dark, a line of light from the lantern highlighting a forest of stunted, dead trees ahead of her, all around her. Water covered with a delicate layer of ice stretched as far as her limited vision could see, here and there dry gray scrub and limbless trees poking up from below. Each step left her toes feeling as if they were encircled by a hundred chilled worms, and the stench reminded her of raw sewage in the streets of the lowliest areas of any large city. It was enough to make her sick.

She wished she had stabbed her brother back in that alley. Better yet, she should have drowned him when they were children in Provenzano. Of course that would betray her saving him from the Prisonlands in the first place, but this was a matter of blood. No one could kill or imprison an Oltos. *No one.* Not unless they were family. Then it became a matter of feud, and that was perfectly all right within the confines of Provenzanoan street life.

Shaking off such thoughts, she pushed ahead slowly, one boot after the other, the lantern leading the way.

At least there seemed no signs of animal life, none of any size and none that were dangerous. She supposed she had the winter to thank for that.

Or maybe not. Movement to her right.

She shifted the lantern and prepared to drop the heavy bag to free a hand for a dagger. A glint off Curval's breast plate caused her to halt, then grip the bag tighter and trudge toward the big man.

His sword strapped to his back, he stood guard at the foot of a slight hill little more than a sizable bump of mud in the middle of the swamp. As Rgia drew closer, her light revealed the front of a leaning shack several yards behind the knight.

It was difficult to guess how old the shack might have been. It looked ancient, its boards warped and the color of a dead fish's belly. How it remained standing was anyone's guess. At least it had a roof, most of its four walls, and a working door nailed against the frame through strips of old shoe leather.

She slowed only feet from the knight. "Has he come around?"

Curval shook his head, his eyes never leaving from scanning the surrounding darkness, the moon and a few stars providing hints of dead plants and trees and little more.

Rgia nodded in return and slurped past the man, hefting her package up the slight incline. At least her feet were out of the water, as precarious as walking seemed on the mudslicked surface of the hill.

Pushing open the creaking door, she found the same scene she had left behind an hour earlier. Falk lay quivering atop a long, wobbly table, his cloak his only warmth other than the weak fire Jarin had put together in a corner next to his spot on a chair. It was fortunate for them she was back, as they were in need of supplies. At least the shack had an actual floor, loose boards covered in a thin rug that had become soft and mushy because of swamp water leaking through from below.

Jarin stood. "Did you find anything good?"

"See for yourself." She crossed to the table and plopped the bag down next to the shivering old man. "Has he changed any?"

Opening the sack and rummaging through its contents, her brother said, "Not much. Muttered a few words, but I couldn't understand them. Weird, him being like this. He must have hit his head when he dropped from that window."

Rgia knew that had not happened. The old man had fallen into Curval's strong, waiting arms without a mishap. Then moments later Falk had collapsed, saved from hitting the ground by the knight's quick thinking and quicker hands. What had befallen the old man, none of them knew.

"Ah ha!" Jarin grinned as he produced a lump of brown bread from the bag.

His sister kept her features impassive as she proceeded to look over Falk, checking his breathing and pulse, seeking any sign of a wound.

Moving back to his chair, Jarin sat and munched upon the bread. After swallowing, he asked, "Where did you get the food?"

Rgia ignored the question and glared over a shoulder at him. "How did you find this place?"

Jarin shrugged. "A few days ago when we were scouting. I followed a man out here, looked like a hunter. My guess is this was his hunting lodge or something like."

"What if he comes back?"

Jarin grinned. "You don't have to be worried about that, sister."

Turning back to the old man, she said, "No word from Kilchus, I presume."

"He doesn't know about this place, so we're not likely to hear from him."

Rgia sighed and turned to face her brother again, this time leaning against the table. "That wasn't very smart of you not telling him."

"Did you tell Kilchus everything *you* know?"

"Of course not, but this is different. He should have been told where to meet us if something like this happened. For that matter, you should have told the rest of us."

"If something like *what* happened?" Jarin asked. "If you've not forgotten, we don't have a clue what went on at that tavern."

"Curval said they were looking for Falk," Rgia said, "which makes sense. This Finder person must have informed the city guard."

Her brother shook his head. "Falk didn't believe Lalo would turn him in. Besides, I think it was that young wizard who was trying to hire us."

"Malin?" Rgia asked. "I don't think so."

"He showed up in the alley just as the guards did," Jarin said. "That's too much of a coincidence."

"Maybe it was just bad timing on his part."

492

Jarin snorted. "Either way, he won't be hiring us now."

"Too bad," Rgia said. "We could have used the money."

"You really think he was going to pay us as much as promised?"

Rgia thought for a moment, then, "Probably not, but anything would have been better than what we've got now, a handful of coppers."

Her brother chewed some more and swallowed. "Don't worry about Kilchus. I'll sneak into town tomorrow and find him. Maybe they haven't linked him to us."

"He was the one who introduced Falk to the Finder."

"Yeah, well, we'll see tomorrow."

From behind the woman came a groan. She looked back at the old man, who was now rolling over onto one side, his eyes fluttering.

Rgia exhaled. "We need to find Kilchus to see if there's anything we can salvage from this mess. If not, brother, I'm thinking it's time we cut our losses and left."

"I can't say I disagree."

***

Voices. They came to him as if from a long way off, as if from over a mountain. For a moment Sadhe Teth stained to hear them, but then he brushed them aside. They were not of importance. As was so often the case, he was fighting for his life and had to ignore the voices, at least for the time being.

Falk had proven a tough old man. The two had fought and fought, their minds and souls circling one another like master swordsmen in a duel. Parry, thrust, riposte. It went on for some while.

Yet there was never any question of the outcome. Teth would win. He *had* to win. There was no other option. Falk was of strong will, but he was not strong enough. Teth had known this right away, yet still the old man had fought back, his soul scrambling all its mental and emotional forces to thwart those of the intruder.

The battle was now nearly over. Teth's victory was nearly complete. It had taken hours, and the ancient wizard was looking forward to control of a body once more, even if it was not his original body which he had discarded only days earlier when becoming Malin the Quill.

Almost as important as the upcoming victory itself was the wealth of knowledge Teth had gained during his struggle with Falk. The old man's past as a knight of Ursia. The Prisonlands. The twins. Curval. Kilchus the Sword. Lalo the Finder. There had been much to learn, much of import. Teth would make use of all this knowledge as soon as his will was in control of the body. He had potential allies now, and they seemed more than adept.

The voices again. They came at him from the outside world.

"We have to go somewhere," a man was saying, his voice neither overly young nor old.

"It is still too dangerous to return home," another voice said. Was that a woman speaking? Difficult to tell.

Voices. Teth tired of not understanding, of not having context. His last true memories were of pain, the wound in Malin's body. That had been some time ago. Events were whirling past. Teth needed to make a move.

Enough.

Inside his world, he turned, twisted and found his enemy. Lord Falk.

The old man screamed his anger, his anguish. He had come close to realizing his dreams, of returning to his homeland long denied him, to returning to his rightful place as a noble.

All gone. All destroyed.

Sadhe Teth blasted away with a mental force devastating.

And Lord Falk's soul was torn apart.

There was not even time for a last scream.

Inwardly, Teth was pleased. He should have done the same to Malin the Quill. It would have quickened things. But Teth had been learning a new world, a new time. Now he had knowledge. Now he knew how to survive. He would not make the same mistakes, and would shield himself from possible unknown mistakes.

His mind reached forth again, not far this time, only around himself. His physical form, that of the late Lord Falk, mumbled a few words of power. The body that was Falk instantly became protected against most physical forms of harm, swords and daggers and arrows. The magical ward would not last forever, but Teth could always replenish it at his whim.

Now triumphant, now protected, it was time to wake once more.

"We could always continue west," a male voice said. "Perhaps Nebraria."

"Nebraria is boring. Nothing but cows."

Finding strength, Sadhe Teth opened his eyes, the eyes of Lord Falk. He found himself in a dank, dark room staring at the back of a cloaked figure. For a moment he could see little more, but then he made out the figure of Jarin Oltos seated on a chair some little distance to the side of Teth's bed. Bed? No, too uncomfortable for a bed. Was it a table? It mattered not. If Jarin was near, then that meant the other person in the room was the assassin's twin sister, Rgia.

The pair discussed leaving.

Teth let out a slight groan. No need to surprise the twins too much.

The person with their back to him shifted, revealing the face of Rgia looking down upon him.

The wizard grinned.

"He wakes," the woman said.

"Yes," Teth said with stolen lips. "I wake. And no one is leaving. We have much here yet to accomplish."

***

As Captain Gris climbed the stairs to the third floor of prison cells, he found himself entering a gloom more severe than even the murkiness of the lower levels of the Asylum. Kron and Montolio had seen fit to provide the topmost level with only a single torch hanging from the wall next to the one locked cell, that of Kilchus the Sword. Gris also found the cold nearly unbearable, practically that of the outside, and each step he took was further chilled by the screams that went on and on.

Darkbow right behind him, when Gris finally set foot on the catwalk leading to Kilchus's chamber, the shrieks faded, weakening and giving away to a mournful crying sound.

The captain stopped several feet from the cell, thankful for the width of the walkway which allowed those outside the rooms from being molested by those imprisoned. The crying continued on as had the screams, though far less loud. After a few seconds, the noise became a whimpering. It was enough to rattle the officer's nerves. Kilchus might have deserved his cell, but Gris liked not the idea of any man suffering whatever was happening to the fellow.

Gris glanced back at Kron, who offered no words nor other acknowledgment.

His fingers tightening about the pommel of the sword on his belt, the captain steeled himself for what he would find only a few steps ahead.

Then he shuffled forward.

Kilchus's back was to the cell's door, the man squatting with his head between his knees, his white-knuckled fingers entwined above his neck.

Gris took in the solitary mattress atop a wooden bed bolted to the floor, a slop bucket in a corner in the back of the chamber, another bucket, this one empty, next to the cell's door. There was nothing else in the room other than Kilchus himself and the clothes on his body. At least Kron had allowed the man a cloak to hold some of the cold at bay.

As the captain and the lieutenant's boots clicked to a halt in front of the room, Kilchus's head ticked to one side, his fingers tightening further about his neck.

"Kilchus," Captain Gris said.

There was no response other than a whimper and a quiver.

The two officers shared a look.

"The captain has questions for you, Kilchus," Kron said.

The prisoner wailed, vaulted to his feet and spun, charging for the cell's bars. The man's face was a horror of black and blue swelling beneath eyes nearly the color of blood. He thrust his arms forward between the bars, fingers clawing at the air and reaching, reaching.

Kron and Gris stood back just in time to avoid being grabbed.

"Please end this!" Kilchus shouted, spittle flying from his lips as he banged his face against the bars, his hands still outstretched, snatching at air. "They never stop! Never!"

"What in the name of Ashal is he talking about?" the captain asked.

Before Kron could answer, Kilchus drew his arms back in and grasped the bars in front of him. Then the prisoner slid down, a wound on his lip tearing open afresh to leave a crimson smear the length of the metal shafts. His screams and shouting turned to weak cries, blubbering, as he landed on his rear and flopped around, his back slamming against the metal bars.

"They're always in my head," Kilchus said, his voice barely above a whisper. "They keep telling me things, horrible things, things they will do to me, things ..." His voice trailed off into a moan.

"The ghosts," Kron said. "They're tormenting him."

Gris looked to his friend. "Has this happened before?"

"Nothing like this, but I'm not surprised."

"How so?"

"They likely consider him a traitor," Kron said. "Most of them were guards themselves here in the Asylum, and I can't imagine they look too kindly upon a border warden who betrayed the trust placed upon him."

Kilchus continued to blubber, his shoulders heaving, his head sinking into his chest.

"Is there any way to stop it?" Gris asked. "I can't question him in this condition."

"I'm not sure. I could ask Montolio to try some kind of communication."

Gris was about to speak further when Kilchus's head snapped up. The inmate no longer sniveled and cried. For a moment he stared straight ahead, then he rolled over onto his hands and knees before pushing himself off the ground to standing.

He stared between the bars at the two men, his eyes now clear but wet, his hands holding onto the bars before him but not in a frantic grip as before.

"They've given me a reprieve," he said.

The officers shared another look, one of curiosity and concern, though not as much concern for the inmate as concern for themselves. The spirits who made the Asylum their home had a tenuous relationship between themselves and Kron, and to some extent Montolio, the two mortals they suffered in their presence. Why the ghosts of the dead would do this was not exactly clear even to Kron himself, who had had the most interaction with the spirits, at one time a direct interaction, to the point of multiple possessions of the man in black's body.

None of this was known to Kilchus, and it likely would not have mattered. "Please," he begged, his head lowering, his eyes dipping, his breath panting, "do whatever you want to me, just take me away from here."

"Maybe," Gris said. "Answer my questions and I'll see about transferring you tomorrow to a cell in the Southtown barracks."

Kilchus's eyes shot up, staring at the captain. "Tonight. Tonight, and I'll tell you anything."

Gris nodded. "Very well. If your answers appear helpful, I'll have you moved tonight. But if I sense you are lying to me, Kilchus, I will leave you to rot in this place."

Unseen by the others, a sly grin crossed Kron's lips as if he were pleased at his companion's words.

Kilchus's hands tightened on the bars, his knuckles growing white once more. "Ask me anything."

"Tell us about your friends at The Stone Pony," Captain Gris said.

"Which ones?"

Gris's head cracked around to look at Kron. "It seems we are done here."

"No! Wait!" The Sword shot out a grasping hand, brushing the captain's cloak

Gris half pulled his sword from its sheath and glared at the prisoner.

Quickly realizing his mistake, Kilchus withdrew his hand. "I mean, I knew several people at the Pony. Which ones are you talking about?"

"The ones you came to Bond with," Gris said, slapping his sword back into its shelter.

"There's Falk," Kilchus said. "He's sort of the head of our little group. You know about him, right?"

The captain nodded. "We're well aware of the former Lord Falk's presence in our city."

"Former? Is he ... dead?"

"Not to our knowledge," Kron answered. "Former as in he is no longer a knight of the land."

Kilchus seemed to calm somewhat at the words. He took a step back and lowered his hands to his sides. "Then you know about his past, about where he came from?"

"We know you were a traitor to your sworn oath in the Prisonlands, yes," Gris said, "though, to tell the truth, we do not understand why."

The Sword shrugged. "Why else? Money? All hell was breaking loose, exiles were escaping left and right. It was madness. I was out with a crew trying to round up as many escapees as we could when I stumbled upon Falk. I knew him to be a big man back here in Bond, and he made lots of promises."

"What kind of promises?" Kron asked.

"The usual. Money, power. I thought it a long shot, but Falk had had high-up connections. He seemed to think he could be reinstated as nobility. Once we got here, I realized that was likely not going to happen, but I figured I'd help him until things turned sour."

Kron grinned. "And did things turn sour?"

"It would appear so."

"What of the others?" Gris asked. "There was a big man in a chest plate, and apparently another man and a woman."

"The twins," Kilchus said. "He was an exile as well, an assassin from Provenzano. His sister, when she heard about all the troubles in the Lands, she tried to sneak in to get him out. Me and Falk bumped into them as we were making our way across the border to Caballerus. Seems they had nowhere else to go, so they tagged along with us, Falk making promises all the way."

"Their names?" Kron asked.

"His is Jarin. Hers is Rgia. They're family name's Oltos, I think."

"What of the man in armor?" Gris said.

"That's Curval," Kilchus said. "He was a knight we ran into in Caballerus. Things were going to hell there, too, what with the nobles killing one another, the king assassinated and all. The whole country was torn apart, the dead king's brother claiming the throne for himself, the army and the knights split in their loyalties. We found Curval in a tavern. If you ask me, the man seemed ready to give up on life. Falk had some words with him, and then Curval joined up with us, guiding us out of the country and south to here."

"What about the wizard?" Kron asked.

"What wizard?"

"The university student."

Kilchus's face went blank. "I don't know what you're talking about."

"I think we've heard enough," Kron said, holding Gris by an elbow as if to steer him away.

The inmate pounced up against the bars, his face pressed between cold metal columns. "No! Wait! I swear, I don't know anything about a wizard."

"And the bones?" Gris asked.

Kilchus's face went blank again. "Did you say 'bones'?"

Kron looked to the captain. "Maybe he doesn't know."

Gris decided upon a different tactic. "Where could your friends be found besides the Pony?"

"Like a hiding place?" the Sword asked. "Nowhere I'd know of. The Pony was where we stayed since coming to town."

The captain sneered. "I'm beginning to think he doesn't know much of anything."

Kilchus held up a pleading hand. "Please, I don't know what's happened, why I've been arrested or anything, but you can't leave me in here. *Please*."

"You've been arrested because you helped a Prisonlands exile to escape," Gris explained, his jaw set almost as if locked. "*Two* exiles, for that matter. And I could probably come up with other charges if needs be."

"Something happened, didn't it?" Kilchus asked, his hand lowering to grab a bar once more. "Was it the Finder? Did he turn us in? I told Falk not to trust that man."

"What you need to know is irrelevant," Gris said with a sneer, "but I will tell you this much: Four of my people were slain today, along with a civilian, and *you* are connected to the people involved, which makes *you* involved. You're damn lucky to still be breathing, as far as I'm concerned."

Before Kilchus could say another word, Gris turned away from him. "Let's go," the captain said to Kron.

The two officers marched away.

"You promised I'd be moved!" Kilchus called out.

"In the morning," Gris said, tromping down the stairs.

"You promised tonight!"

The captain paused on the stairs, looking up and past his companion to where a pair of grasping hangs hung from between the bars of a prison cell.

"I said if your answers were helpful," Gris said. "You weren't particularly helpful."

"No!"

The screams began anew.

<u>13</u>

The twins spoke at the same time.

"We did not know what happened," she said.

"Thought you'd hit your head," he said.

Rgia crossed the small room to watch next to her brother as the seemingly frail figure of Lord Falk gradually brought his legs around to hang from the side of the rickety table, the old man slowly sitting up straight.

"No, I did not hit my head," Sadhe Teth said, but he stopped there for the moment. He was not sure what else to say, what else to reveal. They would likely think him a madman if he told them the truth. He would have to form his words with care, and despite all his newfound knowledge provided by Falk's memories, there were still things Teth did not know as Falk himself had not known them. "What happened at the tavern?"

"You don't remember?" Jarin asked.

"Very little."

"The city guard showed looking for you," Jarin said. "Curval held them off up front while we escaped the back way."

"How did they find us?" Teth asked.

Jarin glanced sideways at his sister. "I say it was Malin. She seems to think it was the Finder."

Rgia did not contradict him.

"Malin?" Teth said, playing off the fact Falk would not know the name.

The woman sighed. "He was a wizard trying to hire my brother and I."

"Hire? For what?"

"What do you think?" Jarin said with a grin.

Teth forced himself to frown, to appear the displeased Lord Falk. In truth, he was glad to hear the twins willing to admit to their vocation in front of him. Sadhe Teth had allies now, and he could make use of them, especially as they seemed quite capable with their talents. *How* he could make use of these people was a matter he had yet decided upon, but the time would come, and never mind the fact he had earlier planned on killing these two when finished with them.

Feeling the age of the body he now inhabited, Teth allowed himself to drop from the edge of the table and to stand. There were some slight pains in the joints and some slowness of breath, but Falk seemed to have taken relatively good care of his body despite his age and having spent much of the last decade in the Prisonlands. Falk had used a cane, but Teth did not feel the need, and allowed the useless piece of wood to remain upon the floor where it had rolled off the table.

"Tell me," he said, "what of Curval and Kilchus?"

"The knight is standing guard outside," Rgia answered.

"Kilchus we don't know about," Jarin said. "He was on guard duty when they tried to arrest us. Maybe they picked him up, too, or maybe he's wandering around the city looking for us, though I'd imagine he's heard what happened at the Pony. Who knows?"

Teth shook his head, clearing his thoughts. The ancient wizard was not yet willing to display his true nature to his new allies, which meant for the time being he would have to act as if still interested in Falk's goals, which seemed rather petty to the mage. Knighthood? That was so far beneath Sadhe Teth's own dreams as to be considered foolish. What to do, then? What should be his next steps?

"I need time to think," he admitted, rubbing at his forehead, feeling physically drained, a sensation new to him but one which he realized would probably be common in the days to come due to the age of Falk's body.

"I could maybe sneak back into town tomorrow and spy out the Asylum," Jarin offered. "If he wasn't arrested, Kilchus might be on duty there."

Did Teth still have need of Kilchus the Sword? That was the immediate question needing answered. Upon reflection, the wizard believed he probably did need Kilchus. The Sword knew the land, the people, the country, better than any of the others present, though Falk had as well, but his memories were older than those of Kilchus. Also, in Teth's opinion, though Kilchus was something of a bullying fool, he had a better grasp of the region and the people than did the late Falk and the memories provided by the dead man. Falk's sin was one of pride, and it colored all his reasoning. Teth would not fall into that trap. There was also the fact Kilchus appeared to have connections with the city's underworld, which could prove more than helpful.

The wizard inside the old man's body let out a sigh. There was much needing done.

A memory sparked in Teth's mind. There had been something he had forgotten. Now he remembered.

"What about this Malin?" he asked, still acting.

"What of him?" Jarin said. "He was a nobody. Promised more than I'm sure he could afford. I took him out when I thought him responsible for the city guard falling on us, and I *still* think he was behind it."

His sister gave him a sideways snarl.

"Who was it he hired you to target?" Teth asked.

Jarin gave a weak shrug. "Another nobody. Some healer at a local hospital. We watched him yesterday, thought him an easy enough kill. We'd planned to take the job, then see if Malin could actually afford us. If not ... well, he likely would have ended up with the same fate as the healer. Which reminds me, I should have checked his purse before we ran out."

"You didn't?" Teth said.

"We were kind of in a hurry," Jarin said.

So, they did not have the bones, which meant someone else did. Teth would have to find them, but that would take use of magic, which he was not prepared to do until Tendbones had been removed from the situation.

He felt relatively safe away from the city. Even if the healer should do another magical search for him, it was not likely the search would be beyond the walls of Bond, where Teth now was, though just barely.

"We have much to do," he said, rubbing at his head again. "Yes, Jarin, in the morning do a search for Kilchus."

"What if he's been arrested?"

"We will deal with that if it has come to pass," the old man said.

"And after that?" Rgia asked.

"Then we shall see." Teth's eyes flashed. "Perhaps it is time I took Kilchus up on an idea he recently suggested."

***

It was after midnight when he slipped beneath the sheets next to her in bed. She had not stirred when he had allowed himself into the room then changed out of his clothing, hanging his sword belt on the chair in the corner, so it was with some little surprise her eyes opened when he lay his head on a pillow next to hers.

"I heard," Nodana said softly. "It has been the talk throughout the city all day."

"I was never in any danger," Kron said.

Her eyes told she did not believe him.

"I wasn't at the Pony," he tried to explain, "and Kilchus did not pose a threat. I was never alone with him. Montolio was there, as were five of the trainees, plus two guards always stationed outside the gate."

She lifted a finger and pressed it against his lips. "If you have to explain so much, it makes me feel you have something to hide."

"I was never in any danger," he repeated.

Her eyes stared into his for a moment, the gulf between them wide at first but growing more narrow by the second. Finally she sank her head against him just beneath his chin and lay there feeling the rise and fall of his chest.

He broke the moment by speaking again.

"We recovered the bones," he said.

She did not raise her head. "The ones stolen from the university?"

"Yes," Kron said. "The poor student who stole them, he was knifed in the mess at the Pony. We don't even know why he was there. As far as we can tell, there's no link between him and Lord Falk. Gris wants you and I to meet with him in the morning to discuss the matter."

"I heard you had a prisoner."

He gave a brief nod. "Kilchus the Sword is his name."

"I've heard of him," Nodana said.

"He knew nothing about the bones."

"Do you need me to cast a truth-telling spell over him?"

"I don't think so," Kron said. "I'm fairly sure he was telling the truth on most matters. Gris is having him transported to Southtown in the morning."

"Good."

"Good?" He lifted his chin to stare at the top of her head.

"I don't want him at the Asylum," she said.

For a moment Kron had no response, then he shimmied down into the bed until they were nearly face to face once more. She refused to lift her eyes.

"Hey, this is *me*, okay?" he said. "You know I can take care of myself."

It was her turn to say nothing. Her head lay there against his side, her unblinking eyes level with his own as she stared into a corner of the room.

They lay there for the longest time until he felt her body heaving against his own and her tears landing upon his chin.

"Hey." He scooted down in a little more and lifted her chin until she couldn't help but look into his eyes.

As he had feared, she was crying, her teeth biting into her bottom lip to hold back a stronger sobbing.

Then she burst out, "I heard about all those dead at the tavern and I couldn't help but think it was you!"

There was nothing he could say. She was right. It *could* have been him. Under the right circumstances, he might have been there.

Instead of using words, he held her tighter, squeezed her against himself, using his free hand to brush back her hair.

14

Another cold morning. It was enough to make Jarin curse, the words rising in a mist from his lips. At least there hadn't been any more snow the night before, and the weak sun was slowly making its way higher in the sky.

He should have been familiar with the cold after his days in the Prisonlands where there were long winters with plenty of snow, more than a few days below freezing temperatures, and often little or no shelter. Even warm clothing had been a rare treat in the lands, and when available had been rendered useless by nights sleeping in a cold cave.

But growing up in the island nation of Lycinia, and later in the city of Provenzano, had left the assassin with warm blood, or so he believed. Lycinia had long summers with heat and sun and tanned skin.

Just thinking about it made him curse again.

His situation was made all the worse because he stood on a rooftop where the wind bowled down upon high, ruffling his cloak and reaching through the cloth to freeze his flesh and bones. The roof had been an obvious choice, the tenement building to which it belonged almost directly across the street from the Asylum, allowing him sight not only of the entrance gate to the grounds, but a direct view onto the grounds, nearly the entire walled area revealed to him other than whatever lay beyond the main building and the hill where it had been built.

So far, after an hour of watching, there had been little to see, only a pair of bundled-up guards in orange on sentry duty before the front gate. Every now and then a hawker with a wagon would stroll by, but that was about it. It was too damn cold for more traffic than that.

Glancing around to make sure he was still alone, Jarin almost wished for his sister's presence. Almost. He knew she hated him, but there also had to be some love there. She had traveled all the way from Provenzano and broken through the barriers of the Prisonlands to free him, after all. Now she was off scrounging more supplies while Curval, as always, stood guard over Lord Falk.

Falk. Now that was a strange one. Or at least he had been strange since their escape the day before at The Stone Pony. The old man hardly sounded like himself, was more assured, but also more cagey, almost as if he had something to hide. But what could he be hiding? Jarin hadn't a clue. Falk had rarely been alone since they had come to Bond, so it wasn't as if the former knight could have sneaked away without drawing attention. And the one time Falk had been alone for any length, during his visit with Lalo the Finder, the old man had not come away acting as he had the last day or so. Had something happened at the Pony to change Falk? Maybe the old man had decided to be more ruthless after his betrayal by whomever. Jarin still tended to believe it was Malin who had turned them into the guard, but he had to admit it wasn't unlikely the Finder had done the job. What had the old man been thinking, him a wanted escapee, going to a prominent local figure and asking for help? What else could have happened? Falk had made a lot of promises, none of which had come true as of yet, but Jarin and the others were desperate; a non-desperate figure such as the Finder would be less likely to follow along with Falk's words.

Movement on the street caught the assassin's attention.

It was a small, dark carriage pulled by two horses and driven by a bundled figure.

For a moment Jarin almost ignored the vehicle, but then it creaked to a stop in front of the Asylum, sliding a few inches on the icy road.

One of the two guards came forward and traded words with the driver, though Jarin was too far away to hear what was being said.

A moment later the same guard opened a door in the side of the carriage and out stepped a figure in white.

All white, from head to toe.

It couldn't be, could it?

Jarin leaned forward and narrowed his eyes in a bid to improve his sight.

The person in white moved away from the carriage then turned and spoke with the driver, the white figure's face now clear to the rooftop killer.

It was Randall Tendbones.

A moment later the carriage trundled away and the two guards opened the gate, allowing the healer access. Jarin watched as Tendbones made his way inside the grounds then followed the path up the hill to the building.

What the hell was he doing at the Asylum?

Jarin needed to talk with his sister.

He almost turned and fled.

Almost.

Then he realized he should stay where he was and watch. There had been no sign of Kilchus so far, but it was early, and the Sword usually didn't go on duty until ten bells, still hours away. More importantly, Tendbones was now somehow involved in the mix. Jarin would have to sit and watch. Perhaps Tendbones would leave again soon. Perhaps Jarin could learn something of interest.

Perhaps.

***

The front door to the Asylum creaked open and Randall found himself facing a bleary-eyed Montolio, the dark-headed wizard looking as if he had just woken, still in his night robes.

"Come in out of the cold," Montolio said, giving the healer entrance.

A loud rumbling noise caused both mages to glance down the hill behind Randall to the front gate, which once more was being pulled open by the guards. Trundling through the opening was a large, rough wagon weighted down by a giant cage of logs tied together with strips of leather, four horses pulling the rig ahead of the driver and another man next to him on the seat. Behind the wagon rode four orange-garbed figures atop steeds, each hoisting a lengthy glaive.

Randall gave the newcomers a questioning look.

"We have a prisoner," Montolio explained. "He is to be moved to Southtown this morning."

"Does this have to do with the troubles yesterday?"

"It does," Montolio said, holding the door open wider. "But please, come in. You are the first to arrive."

As Randall entered the relative warmth of the Asylum's long front room, he frowned at the sight of the wall of cells as he held up a folded paper. "Captain Gris's message said to be here promptly at seven bells."

"It seems the others are not as punctual as you," Montolio said with a grin, motioning toward a small table to one side where a steaming pot had been placed atop a ceramic plate, wooden cups with handles arrayed around. "Care for some morning tea to warm yourself?"

"No, thank you," Randall said, "but by all means, don't let me deter you. I've just come from having breakfast at the tower."

Montolio nodded his own thanks, then proceeded to sip from one of the cups, the steam rolling up his features and giving him a slight, pleasurable shiver.

"Won't you have a seat?" he asked, gesturing to one of several chairs around the table.

"Thank you, but I'll wait for the others. I don't suppose we will be meeting here?"

"Likely not," Montolio said. "I've added some chairs to Kron's office, thinking it would be best to convene there."

Before Randall could offer another comment, the door behind him clacked open to reveal Captain Gris stomping ice from his boots, Kron Darkbow and Frex Nodana right behind him doing the same.

"Good morning," the captain said with a curt nod as he entered the chamber, closing the door behind the others as they all came in out of the cold. "I see our prisoner finally quietened down."

Montolio glanced up the wall of cells. "I had to cast a sleep charm on him, otherwise I'd never have gotten any rest. Probably best for him as well."

"Probably." Gris pulled off his gloves and slapped them together, then turned to the healer. "So, Randall, have you been informed about yesterday's events, or do I need to bring you up to date?"

"I don't think that will be necessary," the healer said. "I tended to Sergeant Adims myself, and a number of your men informed me of the goings-on when they arrived with those from the Pony. However, I'm still not sure why I've been called here."

"We'll get to that in a moment." Stuffing his gloves into a pocket, the captain turned to glance from Kron to Nodana and finally Montolio. "Do any of you have anything to add before we get down to it?"

Kron shook his head.

Nodana shrugged.

Montolio pointed to the tea. "I made us a little something to warm us, if anyone is interested. And I've prepared Kron's office, thinking that would be the best place to gather."

"You have any problems with that?" the captain asked the man in black.

"None," Kron said, shaking his head again.

"Let us get to work, then." Gris headed toward the hall to Kron's office, Kron himself following right behind with Randall at his side.

Only Nodana paused long enough to retrieve a cup of tea.

"At least someone is partaking," Montolio said with a grin as he poured himself another cup. "I'm glad I didn't make the tea for nothing."

Side by side the two wizards made their way after the others, finding Kron seated behind his desk and Randall sitting across from him. Captain Gris sat on a corner of the desk facing the entrance, busy unbuckling his coat.

"Please, have a seat," the captain said as he pulled a wrapped package from the folds of his garb.

Nodana sat next to Randall, both their eyes enlarging at the sight of the bag of bones. Montolio took a seat behind them, sipping again at his steaming drink.

Placing the package upon the table next to him, Captain Gris pulled a cord to free the leather wrapping, then proceeded to untether it. Displayed were several bones of length, all of them gray and cracked, appearing brittle. As a healer, Randall had the most experience dealing with such, but most of those present were aware of what they looked upon, a pair of human femurs, a humerus, and what might have been a tibia, though it was difficult to tell as this last bone was missing its ends and had a sizable crack running its length.

"I called all of you here this morning," Gris began, "because I'm flummoxed as to what to do with these things. Each of you, especially you wizards, have had an opportunity to study the bones to some extent or other, and the supposed experts at the university have had plenty of time for examination. None of which has done us any good so far. Yet, tragedy upon tragedy keeps following these damned things around, and I want to put a stop to it. Another thing, it is my understanding the bones should have been relatively easy to find once stolen, yet that was not the case, as I confirmed with half a dozen mages at the university. I'm no expert on magic, but from what I can gather it would seem someone must have been shielding the bones from magical detection. Maybe it was this Malin person, or maybe it was someone else. Either way, I'm at a loss as to what to do."

"I could take another look at them, if you want," Montolio offered.

"Perhaps," Gris said, "but I'm not convinced we would learn anything new. We'll see how things go here today. But if we can't discover anything about these bones, we at least need to find a way to either get rid of them or keep others from finding them a temptation. We don't even know why anyone would want the bones."

He motioned toward Montolio. "Not that he hasn't given it his best, but Montolio here is officially the only wizard in the city's employ at the moment. That's going to change, especially with the new guard unit, but as of right now we are at a loss for more help."

"I could ask around to the street mages," Nodana said. "Maybe some of them have experience with foreign magics or the like."

"Foreign?" Gris asked. "What makes you say 'foreign'?"

Nodana gestured to Kron and Montolio. "They were present last year when the bones were retrieved from that foreign wizard. If I remember correctly, he was Pursian or Khadiran. Is that right?"

Kron nodded.

As did Montolio, adding, "He said he learned of the bones from some ancient texts in Lycinia."

"Magic in the far south has a much different tradition than our own," Nodana said. "Ursian magic goes back about two thousand years, to the time of Ashal, but the southern peoples have much older traditions going back to gods long forgotten. For that matter, even the more barbaric lands of the far north have some little memory of the old gods. The Dartague have no names for them, but they have been aware of their ancestors having worshiped ancient beings of power."

"Which brings up another point," Montolio said. "The foreigner said the bones belonged to a god, and that he planned to use the bones to draw out the power of the god."

"It might be possible," Randall said, "if the spirit of this god, or wizard or whomever, was still instilled within the bones, but that doesn't seem likely. All of us have studied the bones, and none of us have noticed anything unusual other than a faint aura of magic."

"Do you think it possible, if the bones belong to a god, that he or she is somehow blocking our intrusions?" Nodana asked.

Randall appeared to think for a moment, then he nodded. "It's possible, but it would take someone of great power to be able to shield all of us from learning of their nature. It would also take a certain level of sentience, and so far I've seen no evidence of that."

The three wizards stared at one another, seemingly stumped.

"What about this powerful magic you were looking for, Randall?" Gris asked. "Didn't you think it possible there was a new mage in the city, someone with strength? Could it be this god?"

"There's no link to the bones of which I'm aware," Randall said.

"Coincidence?" from Gris.

The healer shrugged. "I don't know. Anything is conjecture at this point."

"One other thing," Kron said.

Everyone looked to him.

"Fhaland was the name of the wizard who first brought the bones to light," the man in black went on, "and he told me the Zarroc had created this god millions of years ago."

"The Zarroc?" Gris asked. "What is that?"

"A legend," Montolio said. "Nothing more."

Nodana shot the young man a sharp glance. "We don't know that for sure."

The captain held up a hand. "Okay, okay. I don't want to get into some kind of historical or philosophical debate about magic, or whatever this is. Can someone simply tell me about this Zarroc?"

"There is little evidence for them," Randall answered. "A few mentions in old texts, some ruins in far flung places. The legends tell of a race of creatures who lived thousands upon thousands of years ago going back to ... well, I suppose the very dawn of existence, whenever that was."

"Creatures?" Gris said.

"There has been speculation they were not human," Montolio said with a slight sneer, "mainly because they were supposed to have existed during the epochs of the great lizards before the dawn of men. I've never found it believable."

"That doesn't matter," Nodana said. "Fhaland apparently believed it, and that might have been enough."

"Okay, so these Zarroc created this god, and now we have the god's bones," Gris said. "What does any of that *mean*?"

The three wizards looked at one another again, then in unison each gave a shrug.

"It probably doesn't mean anything," Montolio said. "Or at least it might not mean anything to our current needs of ridding ourselves of the bones."

"Hold on." Captain Gris held up a hand. "Let's take a step back for a second. This Fhaland apparently learned of the bones from some books or scrolls in Lycinia. Does that tell us anything useful?"

"Not really," Nodana said, "not unless we went to Lycinia and did a thorough search, which might take years even with magical aid. There are old texts all over the place, captain, especially in the southern climes which are more conducive to the survival of such works. And how would we know if what we were seeking were in a public library or museum somewhere, or part of a personal collection, or even somewhere else?"

"Obviously that's out of the question," Gris went on, "so we're left with no definitive answers. The question now remains, what am I to do with the things? I've kept them on my person over the night, but that is not practical.

"Despite our prisoner's seeming lack of knowledge, I have to assume Malin's presence at the Pony has something to do with these bones, and that Falk or others in his party were seeking them. It's not impossible they might make a try for them. That being within the realm of possibility, the bones need to be stored somewhere safe."

"Keep them here," Kron said.

Gris edged around on the side of the desk and glanced at his old friend. "Are you sure that is wise?"

"Why not?" Montolio answered for Darkbow. "It's as safe as anywhere. I'm almost always here, and Kron is much of the time. There are always guards stationed out front, and others coming and going throughout the day. This place is pretty sturdy, probably able to hold up to a short siege, if it had to. We've even got a strong box in the basement."

"And then there are the ghosts," Kron said.

"Yes, I've been meaning to ask about them," Nodana said. "Have they said anything about these bones?"

Montolio answered again. "They don't usually communicate with us, at least not on a level I'm able to recognize. They make sounds, bumps in the nights, but that's about it. From time to time I see a shadow move out of the corner of my eye or maybe hear a whispered word, but little else."

"Kilchus might argue otherwise," Gris said with a chuckle.

"True, but that might be a situation unique to his own circumstances," Montolio said.

"All right," the captain said. "I can see it makes some sense to leave the bones locked up here in that strong box. But what about magical protection? Is it needed?"

"I think so," Randall said with a nod.

Nodana sat up at the end of her seat. "Between Montolio, Randall and myself, we should be able to weave together protections nearly impenetrable."

"Nearly?" Gris asked.

The woman shrugged. "There's always the off chance some wizard out there is more powerful than the three of us combined."

Kron darted Randall a questioning glance, and the healer provided a terse shake of the head. There was no wizard more powerful than the God Who Walked Among Men, but none of the others present needed to know this.

Captain Gris stretched and pushed off the desk, standing between Kron and the rest of the gathering. "Okay, then, we've at least made some progress. The bones stay here. Then the rest of you can get about your busy days, and I'll make sure my people are being diligent in their search for Falk and his gang."

"Do you want help?" Kron asked, standing.

"No, not yet," Gris said, waving him off. "All of you are busy elsewhere, some of you right here at the Asylum. If Falk sticks his head up, I might come calling, but for now let's assume he is more concerned with hiding than trying to cause trouble."

The rest of the group came to their feet.

Montolio began to rewrap the bones. "I'll take these down to the basement where we can cast a ward around them in the box."

"Many thanks." The captain yanked out his gloves again and proceeded to pull them on as he headed for the room's exit. "I suppose I should give the orders to move Kilchus. Poor men are probably freezing outside, waiting for me. Kron, let's get this over with."

***

A lot of activity this morning at the place called the Asylum, Jarin thought. It was the only thing that kept him across the street on that rooftop. Otherwise, he would have given up earlier. People coming and going, mostly coming, no few of them wearing the colors of the city guards. Also more than a few riders, their horses now kept warm in the small stable building to one side of the main structure. Then there's that big cage on the back of that wagon. Interesting, that, and no place Jarin would want to be.

Stamping his feet, he was again just about to give up and head back to his comrades when the front door to the Asylum opened once more. Out strode a sizable fellow in orange, markings of an officer on his uniform. Next came a small woman, or perhaps a child, it being difficult to tell at such a distance. Then the man in white; Jarin especially kept an eye on him. Last came a man dressed all in black, and even with the length of space between them, there was no forgetting that dour face within the confines of a dark hood.

They gathered in front of the Asylum for the moment, talking amongst themselves, then they split into several groups, the woman and man in black heading toward the stable, the healer in white walking down to the front gate and the road. The officer went to the wagon where a half dozen guardsmen waited around a small fire one of them had put together; words were passed, though Jarin couldn't hear them.

A moment later the officer moved toward the stable while four of the guards entered the front of the Asylum.

Something was happening.

Where was the man in white?

Ah, yes, there at the road now, hailing a cab, probably heading back to the healing tower.

Jarin wanted to follow Randall Tendbones, still interested in the man who had almost been his next target, but there was too much of interest going on at the Asylum.

The healer soon got his cab and rolled away into the day, and the small woman, the man in black and the officer rode their animals down the hill and out the gate. It seemed the group had broken up for the day.

Just then the door to the main building opened yet again. Out came the four guards who had entered but minutes earlier. This time they carried something sizable between them.

Was that a person?

As the four neared the wagon, the driver kicked out the fire and produced a large key to open the padlock on the cage's door at the back of the vehicle. Then the four hefted their burden and shoved it onto the back of the wagon and into the cage.

For a moment the gray day cleared, just a hint of sun peeking through sour clouds. The light fell upon the figure inside the cage.

"Kilchus," Jarin whispered to himself, staring at the unmoving figure of his recent companion, the man's wrists and ankles bound by black iron shackles.

Soon the wagon was bucking its way down to the road, the four guards now on horses and trailing behind.

Jarin turned and sprinted for the back of the roof to a rope he had tied off on a drainage pipe in case of needing a quick escape. Grabbing the loose end of the coil, he tossed it over the side and climbed down after it.

He would follow Kilchus to wherever the guards were taking him. It was his task, and one he promised himself he would not fail.

After all, Bond was turning into quite the interesting place, and Jarin wanted his full share of the fun.

15

The warm breath of their steeds puffing into the air ahead of them as they rode, Kron and Nodana parted ways with the captain, who trotted off in the direction of Southtown, the growing morning traffic splitting before him.

"I've got a couple of hours before I have to be back at the Asylum," Kron said as he and the mage put their riding animals into a slow pace, "and earlier you mentioned having breakfast."

Nodana smiled at his side. "I hear Madam Fiera has opened a new bakery near the university. I thought it might be nice to try."

"As you wish," he said, the pair riding forward.

The morning traffic had not yet grown thick, in no small part due to the continuing chilled weather, but there were still plenty of pedestrians about, mostly craftsmen heading to their jobs and burly fellows walking to the Docks for their day's earnings. Few carriages or wagons were about, and even fewer riders; being the Swamps, few could afford the niceties of easy travel and had to depend upon their feet to get them around.

Nearing Coin Bridge, the riders found a logjam at the crossing, the usual morning mixture of students from Southtown having traversed the Swamps and slowing traffic to a near crawl at the bridge as the multitude of young people made their way to early classes at the university in Uptown.

As they made their way through the crowd, Kron and Nodana slowed their animals until they were barely walking.

Once over the bridge, most of the students made an abrupt right turn, heading to their various colleges, giving the riders an open street. Still, Kron and Nodana did not pick up the pace, the pair enjoying the slow ride next to one another and the warmth beneath their cloaks.

She glanced aside at him. "I've been meaning to talk to you about something."

"What is that?"

"You mentioned your parents were merchants," she said.

"That they were."

"I've been wondering," she continued, hesitation in her voice, "what happened to their estates after they were ..." Her words trailed away.

"They were slain," Kron said.

"Yes, after that."

Still riding, Kron turned his head away from her slightly, staring off at university buildings as they passed. Then, "To be honest, I'm not sure. I've never thought of it. I suppose I thought my uncle Kuthius had inherited everything."

"Your uncle was a border warden, right?"

"He was."

"What happened to *his* estate after his passing?"

"I inherited it," Kron said. "There wasn't a lot. Border wardens don't enjoy great earnings, truth be told, but it was enough to outfit myself and for me to live on for a while when I first came back to Bond."

She dithered for a moment, then, "Could it be possible your parents' estates were never claimed?"

"I suppose," Kron said. "My uncle and I never discussed the matter, but it wasn't a topic either of us wanted to broach."

"So the money might be sitting in an account somewhere?"

Kron twisted in his saddle to look at her. "Where are you going with all this?"

"I've just been thinking," she said. "If you had an inheritance, which might be fairly substantial after all these years, you would no longer have to work for Gris."

Reaching over, Kron grabbed the bit strip of her horse, pulling both of them to a halt in the middle of the street. Then he sat and stared at her.

"What is it?" she asked.

"What has come over you, Frex?" he said. "Where is the woman a year ago who tried to kill me? The woman who wasn't afraid to face off with a demon? It seems of late your only concern is with my safety."

She blushed, her eyes lowering. "Things have changed in the last year."

"What has changed? We've gone around this subject a few times, you worried about the dangers in our lives, but there have been relatively few threats of of late. Are you still thinking of my confrontation with Kilchus yesterday? I've told you it was nothing."

Her right hand snapped out, her fingers locking around the left wrist of his gloved hand. "Don't you understand? *You* have changed in my life."

"I understand I'm not as brash as I once was, and I --"

"That's not what I mean. You are the change in *my* life. Your very ... presence, it has brought about a change in me. I'm no longer the scrambling, clawing functionary I used to be. All I wanted was to rise within the power structures of Bond, first on the street level but eventually with maybe a run at the city council, possibly beyond. I'm not that person any longer. What I have found, what I have now, it is more than enough for me, and all because of you. Despite your dark ways, you are a good man, Kron Darkbow, and you've shown this by the very fact you *have* been able to change."

It was now he who lowered his head, his throat bobbing up and down as he sought words. Eventually, "Frex, I don't know. I ..."

"I know you don't feel about me the way I do you," she said.

His head came up, his eyes locking on hers.

"But know this," she went on, "I expect nothing of you, Kron. Nothing."

He gulped, sucking in cold morning air, lifting his head to stare at the buildings on either side of the road, a few members of the local foot traffic walking past with pointed glares at the pair of riders stopped in the middle of the road.

"I have no expectations," Nodana said. "Do you understand that? Can you? I'm not some silly girl who believes you will fall in love with me in time. Maybe you will, maybe you won't. I honestly cannot hazard a guess. But I do realize you are the type of man who is hesitant to unleash his feelings, who gives away his love and friendship to only a select few. I have been more than honored that you have shared with me what you have, but --"

It was now he who cut *her* off. "But it's not enough, is it?"

"What?" She appeared flustered. "No. No! I'm not trying to put conditions on you, Kron. That is the least of what I want."

"Then what is it you *do* want?"

She said nothing for a moment, glancing off to one side, then back at him. "I want you to let me do this for you. Let me find out about your parents' estates. I spend enough time at the city buildings, it would not be out of my way to look up some old papers. At least you would know, and you could claim what is rightfully yours."

"With the goal of tempting me to leave the city guard?"

"Not necessarily," Nodana said. "What was that word you used? Floundering? Yes, you yourself admitted to 'floundering,' as if you were not in control of your own life. If there are monies owed you, at the very least they would free you to decide your own destiny. You would no longer be tied to the city guard, or even to Bond, for that matter. You could go and do as you wished."

"And what if my wish is to remain right here with you and to continue in the guard?"

"Then so be it."

His free hand rubbed at his chin. "I don't recall my parents being especially wealthy."

"They were traveling merchants, right?"

"Yes," with a nod.

"And their house was in Southtown?"

"Yes?"

"Then they had a hell of a lot more than those who grew up in the Swamps."

He glanced at her, knowing her own upbringing had not been of an easy sort.

"Let me do this, Kron," she nearly pleaded.

He stared away, gathering his thoughts, pulling himself together. He had been relatively wealthy once in his life, and he had known poverty on more than one occasion, but gold had never held a temptation for Kron Darkbow. He needed enough for survival, but his uncle had also taught him how to survive without money. However, Nodana had a point, a strong one. At the very least, the money would give him options.

"Do it," he said, patting her hand atop his own.

She leaned toward him, pulling open his cloak to wrap an arm around one of his sizable forearms. "Thank you."

Soon they were riding again.

***

It had been a miserable night. A tiny fire. Holes in the walls that allowed the wind to pour through every so often. A sopping floor that occasionally froze in spots and cracked under foot. Food and drink neither warm nor hardy. A creaking, hard table for a bed.

At least none of the others had balked at Sadhe Teth taking the table for himself. They continued in their belief that he was Lord Falk, and he had yet to find any reason to dispel them of the truth. Somehow or other Rgia and Jarin had rested upon the floor, and Curval ...

Thinking of Curval brought a grin to Teth's latest features. The knight was still standing guard at the bottom of the hill outside the door. The man had been there all night, not budging once. Had he slept on his feet? Teth did not know, and he did not know if such was even possible. What he did know was that Curval's faith in Falk seemed to be quite unshakable, and Teth planned to use that to its fullest extent.

A tromping noise outside was quickly followed by the front door being pushed open, Rgia entering with another sack over her shoulder.

Teth sat up on his makeshift bed as the woman took a knee next to their dying fire and opened the sack. From within she pulled a large loaf of coarse bread and what appeared to be a round of butter the size of a small melon and wrapped in wax paper.

"Any sign of your brother, yet?" he asked.

She shook her head and stood, moving to the table and pulling out a knife to slice the bread in equal portions.

"I hope this is better than we had last night," Teth said. He did not ask from where the bread had come as he had little interest, though Rgia was proving herself more and more resourceful by the hour.

Yet the look on her face said she did not feel his trust in her.

"My apologies," he said. "I meant nothing against your skills. I was only hoping for better food."

"It is what I could find," she said, handing him a slice of the bread and the roll of butter.

As Teth went to work slathering the butter upon the crust he had been given, frustration welled within his chest, bringing forth a rising anger. He had been better off when he had been alone wandering the streets of Bond. He had been warm and fed, even when there was no roof over his head. It was not that he held a disregard for his new companions, but he was reluctant to make use of his powers in front of them.

Before he could think further on the subject, the door opened again, this time revealing a hurried Jarin.

"What is it?" Teth asked, seeing the rush in the young man as the door was nearly slammed closed.

"I have much to tell," Jarin said, then looked to his sister, "and not all of it has to do with Kilchus."

"But Kilchus first," Teth remonstrated.

Jarin turned back to the old man. "Very well. They were keeping Kilchus at the Asylum, the place where he had been on duty."

"So he was arrested?" Teth asked.

"It appeared so. They carried him out in shackles and tossed him in a cage on the back of a wagon."

"And he did not put up a fight?" Rgia asked.

"He appeared drugged or knocked unconscious," her brother said. "I barely saw him move at all, but he seemed alive, or at least they treated him so."

"Tell me you followed to where they took him," Teth said.

"Of course. They wheeled him across river to Southtown and a big building there. I had to ask around to a few street scum, but it turned out the place they took Kilchus is the barracks for the city guard. Apparently that's also where they have their jail."

"Could you see where they took him in the building?" Teth asked.

"No," Jarin said. "I couldn't get too close. There were guards all over the place, dozens of them, perhaps more."

"What is this about other news?" the wizard said.

Jarin looked to his sister. "The healer, he was at the Asylum."

"Tendbones?" Rgia asked.

Sadhe Teth was as surprised as the others. To find out more, he had to play the innocent. "Who is this Tendbones?"

"The target Malin hired us to kill," Jarin said, then looked to his sister again, "and yes, he was there."

"What was he doing?" Teth asked.

Jarin shrugged. "I don't know. He went inside, then came out and hailed a carriage to take him off somewhere, I'm guessing to his healing tower."

"How long was he in the Asylum?" Rgia said.

"Maybe an hour. At least a half hour."

"And he had no interaction with Kilchus?" Teth asked.

"None that I saw," Jarin said, "but whatever he was up to inside, I don't know."

Teth reeled back from the twins and slumped against the table with one hand on its top. "This is much news. I must take some time to ponder it."

"No." Rgia became a whirlwind of action. She scooped the food from the table and into the sack, then retreated to a corner where she had hung another bag on the wall. Taking down the bag, she slung both sacks over a shoulder and glanced around the small shack as if to make sure she was not forgetting something. "Little brother, it is time for us to go."

"Little?" Jarin said.

"Go?" from Teth.

Rgia glared at her brother. "Yes, little, by three minutes according to the midwife." Then she looked to the person she believed to be Lord Falk. "Your plans have fallen through, Falk. Your friend the Finder betrayed you, and now Kilchus has been arrested and we are wanted in yet another city. I should have done this days ago."

She moved toward the front door, grabbing her brother by a shoulder as she went.

Teth bound forward, his old knees nearly giving out beneath him as he thrust an arm between the twins and the exit. "I have need of you!"

"You are no longer my concern," Rgia said to him, her voice flat, even.

"But --"

She brushed past him, pulling Jarin with her.

Desperate, Teth lunged, sinking both hands into her right shoulder and holding her. Immediately Rgia let go of her brother and stomped to a halt, turning her head to glare into the old man's face.

"Take your hands off me," she stated. "Now."

"Rgia, listen," Teth said, pleading, "I can give you more money than you've ever dreamed of. Power, too. Anything you want."

The woman growled at him, then, "This is your last warning, Falk."

Yet he did not let go of her. "I just need you to do one thing for me. Slay the healer, and I can take care of everything else."

His words caused the woman to pause, to blink. "The healer?"

Jarin also appeared confused. "Are you talking of Tendbones?"

"He is the only thing holding me back," Teth said, leaning forward until his face was mere inches from the woman's. "I know not his true power, nor his source of power. But with him out of the way, none of that would matter."

Rgia stared into his eyes for a moment, then she shoved him away. "You have gone insane!"

Stumbling, Sadhe Teth crashed into the table, over turning it and almost spilling himself onto the floor.

"Come, brother." Rgia turned for the exit.

"No!" Teth sprang again, his arms outreaching for her.

He never made it.

In a flash, Rgia snarled and lashed out with a dagger. The blade raked across the old man's throat, but there was no cutting, no line of red. It was like a wooden spoon trying to cut into thick, heavy leather.

He stumbled back yet again, unwounded but alarmed at the attack, coming to rest next to the overturned table.

The twins stared at the wizard, their mouths hanging open. Teth could but stand there and stare back.

"What just happened?" Jarin finally asked.

"Magic," his sister said. She thrust the blade back into its scabbard on her belt and pointed at the old man. "When did you take up sorcery?"

Teth opened his mouth to answer, but she cut him off.

"You've been a mage all along," Rgia said. "You've kept it a secret so long, you even fooled those idiots back at the Prisonlands."

"It's not that simple," Teth managed to get out.

"I don't care, and I don't want to hear more of your lies," she said, spinning back to the door. "We are leaving."

Before she could reach for the handle, the door slammed open from outside. Blocking much of the sunlight was the hulking form of Curval, sword in hand.

"What goes here?" he asked.

Rgia grasped the hilt of her dagger again. "Get out of the way, Curval."

The knight looked to Teth.

"There is no need for alarm," the wizard said. "We are all friends here. Curval, please put away your weapon and come inside."

The knight stared for a moment, looking from Jarin to Rgia and finally to his boss again. The wizard nodded and Curval did the same in return, raising his sword to slide it into the sheath on his back. As soon as the lengthy steel snapped into its home, the big man pushed his way through the opening, the twins stepping back to give him plenty of room, their eyes never leaving those of his own.

Rgia glanced over a shoulder at the mage. "What now, Falk? Are you going to sic your guard dog on us?"

For a moment Teth did not say a word. He turned his back on the others and righted the table, then faced the group once more, placing his rear on the edge of the furniture. "I am hoping it will not come to that."

"Curval or not, you cannot keep us here," Rgia said. "Neither Jarin or I are afraid of spilling blood, need I remind you."

"No, you do not have to remind me," Teth said with a gleam in his eyes. "In fact, I'm betting on it."

Rgia huffed. "This is foolishness, Falk. Tell your bear to get out of the way. I have no qualms with Curval and no wish to cross blades with him, but I will do so if I must."

"There will be no need to fight," Teth said.

The wizard snapped out a hand. A flare of light, a show of power, and the door slammed shut without having been touched. From the ends of the mage's fingers drifted strands of smoke.

Rgia and Jarin moved further away, almost into a corner. Curval's eyes never left them, the knight seemingly not surprised at his master's display of magical force.

"Now," Teth said, lowering his hand and leaning further back onto the table, "no one is leaving. I will talk, and you will listen. There are things I must say."

Rgia's eyes narrowed, her nostrils flaring. "Very well, Falk. Say your piece."

He grinned at her, showing teeth. The time had come. It was sooner than he would have liked, but here it was. "First, you need to know I am no longer Lord Falk."

16

His last patient of the day out the door and his assistant Althurna headed home, Randall found himself free for the evening. He lived within the Swamps healing tower, his sleeping chamber on the floor above, but he tended to spend his waking hours in his work room. For one thing, as the strongest of the magical healers in the tower, it was common for him to be called upon in emergency situations, usually when someone was brought forth with a serious injury or a convalescent bedded on the top floor took a turn for the worse. There was also the matter of quiet and solitude. The other healers, the handful who lived within the tower, had a tendency to chat after hours, sometimes carousing about town or doing whatever it was they did. Despite still being a young man physically, and despite generally enjoying the company of his fellow healers, Randall did not often allow himself the luxury of personal entertainment.

A god rarely could.

Most nights he enjoyed studying scrolls and codices pertaining to his profession. He as often learned some forgotten lore as he did something new from a university surgeon's papers. Occasionally he would try a little experimentation himself, usually involving magic or herbs and potables purchased from a local apothecary's shop.

When not involved with such matters, even a god needed daily rest. The toll upon Randall Tendbones was not so much physical as it was mental and what some would consider spiritual. The weight of the world weighed over him every single day.

He was Ashal, the God Who Walked Among Men. He had lived some two thousand years earlier, been executed at the rope, then brought back to life in modern times. Prophecy within the exalted Book of Ashal stated that Ashal himself would rise in the end of days, that the god would return in glory to face a black figure, the dreaded Dark King of the North.

None of which had happened. Or at least it had not literally happened as of yet.

Ashal had most definitely returned, only Randall and Kron being aware of this, but there had been no great war, no great battles. Randall's father had believed himself to be this Dark King of the North, but the figure from prophecy was supposed to raise a huge army and ride down from the north in wave after wave of destruction, laying waste to all, destroying nations, slaying kings, conquering through annihilation.

That none of this had happened kept the healer awake more than a few nights. The historical and modern truth that more than a few individuals, and at least one powerful church, did outrageous, harmful things in his name, also kept him from sleep.

Then there had been the decision he had made a couple of years earlier.

Upon realizing the truth of who he was, Randall had been faced with keeping that truth to himself or in making his presence as a god known to mankind in general. Young in body and with only limited memories of his far past, he opted for his identity remaining a secret. His great fear had been that the world would tear itself apart if it was known Ashal had indeed returned.

Nothing since making that decision had changed his mind on the matter. Still, every day it was another weight hanging over him.

Now, however, at the end of the day, he would allow himself the luxury of some rest. He would need it. He still had one task to perform this night, though it was nothing related to his vocation as a healer.

He had to search for the person or magical being he had detected recently, someone or something powerful within the city of Bond. He had been too busy throughout the day to do his search earlier, and he never performed these searches in front of others because then he would be forced to come up with some explanation. Explain he could, but he felt it safer for others within the tower if they did not know what he was doing. If this unknown person or entity was as powerful as Randall suspected, his search could well draw unwanted attention, and the others in the tower would be better off not knowing anything that could land them in trouble. Randall doubted any real danger to the others in the tower, but knowledge of this entity could cause them grief.

Also, he needed to ponder how to go about this search. Over the last few days whenever he had looked, he had used a method of remote viewing, of searching with a center point emanating from himself. It was something like looking through a sea captain's optical telescope. However, that method had not proven overly effective. Randall was considering trying a different tactic. He was thinking of allowing his spiritual form to leave his body, to roam around the city in a more close examination. Randall had no idea if this would work the way he wanted, and it presented possible dangers, but he thought it might be worth trying.

Easing back further in the chair, he closed his eyes and slipped his hands behind his head. Rest for now, perhaps even as long as an hour, and then he could proceed with his search.

He snapped awake.

Blinking away his sleep and rubbing at his eyes, he wondered how long he had rested. A glance at the candle on his desk told him it had been more than an hour, possibly as many as three hours. The red wax was half the length it had been, and rivulets of scarlet had rolled down the side of the candle to build up around the edges of the brass holder.

Admonishing himself for the length of his dozing, Randall shook off the last effects of his slumber and sat up straight in his chair. He had one last bit of work to do before he could sleep for the night.

Closing his eyes again, he leaned forward, placing his elbows on his desk. Raising his hands, he held his fingers in front of his eyes and mentally counted down from one hundred. The process was not strictly necessary. There was no true need for casting of spells or muttering ancient words or going through a routine as he was now doing. None of that was needed. Yet it helped wizards, and even gods, to keep focus.

By the time he reached fifty, he could feel the power gradually building within him. At twenty there was a blossoming of magic, and Randall could feel his inner self, his own soul, working its way free of his body.

He whispered to himself the last of the count, "... four, three, two, one."

And then he was floating on the air, looking down upon his own slumped-forward figure. Despite the candle, there was now a dimness to the room, an effect of Randall's secondary state. The experience was one he had experienced a few times before, but he did not consider himself an expert in such travel. The sensation of freely floating was not one Randall found exhilarating, as some mages did, thus he did not make use of such a state very often.

He put away the thoughts. Time to pursue ... whomever.

As fast as his mind could carry him, he flitted around the city from one spot to another. He flew over the university, then along the length of Mages Way, his spectral senses seeking any sign of the powerful magical presence he had observed earlier in the week. His spirit form rooted around in the Swamps for some while, then up and down the lengths of the rivers, and finally looped in and out of Southtown.

Throughout his flight he saw many peoples and many things. Most of the faces were unfamiliar to him, though some few stood out in his memory. There near the city guard barracks limped the little boy who had suffered a broken leg after falling off the back of a wagon, Randall having re-set the bones of the lad a few months earlier. Closer at hand, just outside the Swamps healing tower was the prostitute Randall had cleansed of disease a month back, the poor fellow hobbling along with a crutch, returning to the tower as he suffered from a new disorder brought about by his profession. Then there was the old woman alone in a room in a tenement building in Southtown, her arthritis tearing at her fingers once more, the condition returning even after the best of Randall's treatments some days in the past.

And then there was Captain Gris, bedding down for the night in the city guard barracks. Midge Highwater telling a tall tale on the steps of The Stone Pony behind The Rusty Scabbard. Eel Sidewinder walking the halls of the Finder's mansion, the youth no longer showing the bruises from his beating earlier in the week.

There were others, plenty of others. Some Randall recognized, many he did not. There were scenes of pathos and scenes of debauchery and scenes of boredom and tiredness and monotony. People leading their lives.

But there were no signs of a magical presence powerful enough to draw Randall's attention.

There were the usual handful of wizards who lived along Mages Way, most of them professors. Here and there throughout the city were the familiar blips of one street mage or another. The university itself was fairly aglow with magic, most of it from students and professors, but none overly noteworthy. There also was the occasional sighting of magic so weak and dormant Randall could only surmise it came from some magical item or other, possibly forgotten, possibly lost, or simply not used often.

This last thought forced Randall to chide himself. If he had paid more attention to such seemingly minor details, all the troubles with these dug-up bones might never have occurred. But there was never any time, even as there was not now. Randall could already feel himself tiring, having spent longer than he had wanted in his search.

He jerked back into his body, which sat up again, his hands falling from his face. Weakness rolled over him. Normally he might not have been so tired after such an excursion, but it had been a busy week at the tower and his usual potent talents had been stretched.

Still, the search had been necessary, even though it had been fruitless in the end. Did this mean the magical source he sought was no longer within the city? Or was it hidden from him? He did not know, and could not know without further investigation.

It would have to wait, at least until he could report his lack of progress. He would go to see Kron in the morning, the Asylum being closer than the Southtown barracks, then decide if further action was needed.

He yawned and sat back in his chair.

He was asleep by the time his hands folded upon his stomach.

***

She was late.

Still, Kron did not let this bother him. It would not be the first time she had been late. Most often she was stuck in a meeting with some city dignitary, usually someone who believed themselves far more important than they truly were. Other times she was attending a minor but important function, a meeting of guilds leaders or the like.

Yet normally Kron would have been aware of such events. She would have told him about them beforehand. This time she had not. Which led him to believe she was probably busy wading through codices at one city office or another while searching for elements from Kron's own past.

It was nearly enough to bring him pain, to raise old wounds. He dealt with it by pushing it aside, by pushing it from his mind. If he dwelt upon the fate of his parents, the rage would roil up from deep within, and that was useless. There was nothing he could do to help his parents, no way they could be brought back, and vengeance had proven itself to be a futile undertaking.

So, he waited.

Not one to allow a wasted minute to go by, Kron kept himself busy flipping through a book taken from the shelves in her bedroom. His cloak and sword belt hanging in the entrance hall, he had settled into the kitchen, a lamp providing plenty of light and just enough warmth while he read about military tactics from a war fought centuries before he was born.

He was halfway through the book when he heard the click of the front door opening, then the clatter of it closing. There were a few moments of shuffling, probably her hanging up her cloak and satchel, then the tapping of her shoes coming down the hall.

When Nodana entered the kitchen, Kron was just closing the book and putting it aside.

"I hope you didn't wait for me," she said as she sat across from him, resting her chin in a hand. It was obvious she was weary, yet still she managed a smile for him.

"Montolio put together some soup," he told her. "It wasn't much, but it was warm, just what the squad needed after a long day in the cold."

"So you're eating with the soldiers now?"

Kron shrugged. "I thought it fitting since they moved into the Asylum today, even the new member sent over by Gris to replace Kilchus.

"What about you?"

"I grabbed a meat pie from a vendor in Uptown," Nodana said. "It kept me going."

"While?"

Her grin broadened. "While I was sorting through files at the central city building."

Kron rubbed at his face, giving him a moment to cover his eyes as a wave of fear rushed over him. When his hand lowered, he forced himself to smile. "What did you find out?"

"Apparently your uncle didn't know about your parents' will," she said. "Maybe he didn't think there was one. Not out of the ordinary, I suppose, since he didn't arrive until some six months after their ..." Her voice faded.

"Their slayings," Kron said.

She nodded. "Yes, after that."

"How did you find out he didn't come to Bond until six months afterward?"

"It was in your adoption papers."

"Adoption? What are you talking about?"

"Didn't you know? He adopted you as his own son."

Kron sat back in his chair, stunned. His thoughts couldn't help but run back to Kuthius Tallerus, the man who had raised him from the age of ten. Gruff but fair, a hard man at times, Kuthius had been one of the best border wardens to ever set foot in the Prisonlands. He also had been one of the oldest and longest serving, having passed up opportunity after opportunity to rise to the level of an officer or even beyond, to the Voting Council itself. Despite his simple demeanor, Kuthius had been full of surprises, and Kron had never known about the adoption.

Something else came to mind.

"How did you find out this information about me?" he asked.

"What do you mean?"

"I mean, Kron Darkbow is not my birth name."

She kept on grinning. "Well, I had guessed as much. Darkbow sounds like such a northern name, and I know you're not a northerner."

"So?"

"So, I asked Gris."

Kron rubbed at his face again, this time hiding his irritation. "I suppose he told you, then?"

"Why you don't want to use the name Lucius Tallerus is beyond me, but if --"

"Please do not say that name to me ever again." He winced as he spoke, his eyes full of pain. "That is a name I no longer wish to hear. It is a person who no longer exists."

Her smile faded. She sat staring at him, her confusion clear. But she nodded in the end. "Very well. I won't use the name."

"Good. Thank you."

Thinking it best to rush past the anguish, she said, "Anyway, as I was saying, there was a six-month gap before your uncle appeared in Bond to claim you. During that time, your parents' will was being held by a trustee, a solicitor hired by your father. Apparently this solicitor did not know of the uncle, and it seems obvious Kuthius did not know of the solicitor. So, their paths never crossed."

"What happened to my parents' estate?"

"The house and the goods were sold, then all monies were placed in escrow with a broker in case any relatives should ever show up."

"So my uncle was not the beneficiary?"

"Not at all."

"Then who was?"

"You," Nodana said, smiling again.

"Me? But I was only a boy."

"Nevertheless, all properties and funds were left to you," she said. "I suppose they figured your uncle or some other relative would step in to help you muddle through the estate and the finances."

"There *were* no other relatives than Kuthius," Kron said, "and from what he told me, it was months before he even learned of their deaths."

Nodana's face took on a serious sheen. "By that point the bankers and the solicitors had probably given up on any family stepping forward, and they didn't know what had happened to you. Which raises a question? What *were* you doing during the six months?"

Kron nearly hid his face again, but fought against the impulse. "I've told few of this, perhaps only my uncle. I don't even think Gris knows. Maybe Randall does. I don't remember."

"About what?"

"I lived on the streets," Kron said. "After my parents were murdered, I was too afraid to go home, which wasn't far from where ... from where it happened. Remember, I was just a boy. I thought whomever had killed them would go to the house looking for me."

Nodana reached out and grabbed one of his hands. "I'm so sorry."

He did not fight her urge. "No need to be. It was a rough life, that of an urchin, but I survived. Remember that I'd been raised by traveling merchants, after all, so I wasn't completely unfamiliar with life on the streets. Anyway, my uncle eventually showed up and took me away."

"To the Prisonlands."

"Yes."

"It does not sound like much of a childhood."

Kron shrugged again. "It was what it was. Time has moved on."

Her hand tightened on his. "At least you still have something from your parents."

Now he sighed. "Yes ... but I would give it all up for another day with them."

Tears came to her eyes. She did not blubber, but a wet streak slid down her face. He would not cry, so she would do so for him.

"I suppose," he said, "that I should claim what remains of the estate."

"Most definitely."

"What do I need to do?"

"We can go tomorrow, or whenever you want. All we have to do is see this solicitor and sign some forms. He will do the rest, dealing with the broker and the like."

"Don't I have to have some way of proving my identity?" Kron asked.

"A letter from Gris should do the job," Nodana said, "or you could write to one of the officers in the Prisonlands and request a letter, though that would take some time."

"No, I'll ask Gris."

"Don't you want to know how much it is?" she asked, her grin returning, flashing.

"I take it you already know."

She nodded in delight.

"Very well. Tell me."

"Twelve thousand," she said.

"What? In silver?"

"Gold."

Kron nearly choked. "Gold? That's impossible."

"Not at all," Nodana said. "The escrow account didn't just sit still all these years. The funds were invested, and obviously in a wise fashion. Your parents choose well in their financial protectors."

"By Ashal," Kron said, leaning back and staring off into a corner for a moment. "That's more than I came back from Kobalos with."

"More than you paid for the Asylum," Nodana added. "Quite a bit more."

He shot a glance her way.

And she kept on smiling. "I looked that up, too."

He couldn't help but chuckle. "All right, so I'm rich. Well, maybe not rich enough to be a king or some such, but wealthy enough."

"Wealthy enough to leave the guard?" she quested.

Kron looked at her out of the corners of his eyes, but he said nothing.

"Just a thought," she said.

He nodded. "I know. And I know your feelings on the matter. Give me some time to think it through, all right? At least over the night?"

Now it was she who nodded, lowering her head as she pulled his hand closer to her, almost to her chest. "I'm not going anywhere," she said.

***

It was the coldest night yet, but Curval did not feel a thing. He would not allow himself to feel anything. And the warming spell provided by Sadhe Teth did more than help.

The knight's boots unmoving for hours in the boggy water of the swamp, ice had formed around his ankles, cracking every so often when a wind would come along and brush against him, causing him to sway, his cloak flapping against his sturdy, armored form.

He had stood there for hours, and would continue to do so throughout the night, his arms crossed, his back straight, his legs slightly bowed. It was simply a matter of sleeping on his feet. As every knight of Caballerus learned during their youth, during their apprenticeship and later as a squire, sleeping in the saddle was a tradition brought down across hundreds if not thousands of years. Being able to do so while standing was a more difficult task, but it was one Curval found himself mastering. He had had little choice in the matter originally, having sworn his allegiance to Lord Falk.

Now Falk was gone.

And Curval had a decision to make.

His eyes heavy, the knight allowed them to lower. Keeping them open would have been foolish as there was nothing to see. It was the middle of the night and there were dark clouds swarming the sky, blighting the moon and the stars. Darkness ruled.

Still, his hearing worked well, even in a near doze. This was another lesson from his childhood and teen years, a trick every knight or soldier picked up in order to remain alive. There was little to hear because of the cold, the swamp animals hibernating or remaining hidden in their relatively warm dens, but every so often a bird would flap by overhead or a tree limb would crack, plummeting to the ice or chilled water below. Curval detected it all, at least all within the distance he was able to hear. Nothing unusual occurred, however. No sounds were out of place within the night and the swamps.

It was not likely a party from the city would come to the swamps in the middle of a freezing night to look for the band of outlaws who had created such a stir at The Stony Pony. Nor was it likely this healer who drew so much attention from Teth and the twins would make any kind of appearance. Yet remain on watch he did. It was always best to be prepared, to be wary of any possible enemy.

Curval's shoulders slumped as a deeper sleep approached. His mind rambled. Confusion reigned.

Falk was gone. This was a truth. And in its own way, it was a tragedy, the latest to befall the knight from Caballerus. King Alexandre was dead, slain by his own brother's men. The queen was missing, as was the babe, the true heir to the throne, both likely also dead. The brother, the last living member of the royal family, had declared himself sovereign, at his side the ever-present figure of a dark wizard and a group of formidable personal guards.

It had been enough to break Curval. He and the other knights of the realm had been sworn not only to protect that realm, but to protect the king himself, the personification of the realm. The knights had failed in their task. To be fair, they had never had a chance at saving the king. Alexandre's brother had worked in the night, behind curtains, with the worst sort of men whom had sprung from the shadows at the moment most opportune for them. The knights of Caballerus had not even been aware of their king's betrayal and murder until hours after it had occurred. By then the brother had made himself the new king.

The knighthood had fallen apart. Some had ridden away to other lands, or to seek solace in anonymity within their own country. Others had attempted to form a rebellion, to fight back against the brother, only to be thwarted at every move and eventually driven away or executed. Still others had been in shock, had fallen apart and become shadows of their former selves. Curval fell into this last group.

Penniless and no longer allowed to find succor within any of the king's castles, Curval had committed his own form of treachery. He had sold his horse. It was a crime, a sin. Oilspun had been the animals name, and it had been the most trustworthy of companions. Curval had not only turned his back on his oaths and his kin and his legacy, but also upon the best friend he had ever had.

That was when the drinking had started. Falk and Kilchus and the twins had discovered him in a tavern near the border with West Ursia. Curval had been so drunk he had barely been able to stand, but his ears had still worked fine. He had listened to Falk's promises, and they had sounded good. Falk, a knight himself, descended from dukes, had been betrayed by his own people, and now he sought redemption and a return. Even to Curval's drunk ears, Falk's plans had sounded sketchy at best, but the fallen knight had promised one thing no one else could or was willing to offer, a return to nobility, a return to sanity, a way to matter in the world, even if it was in West Ursia where the few remaining nobles were considered little more than fools.

But now Falk was gone, and Curval had a decision to make.

Sadhe Teth had promised much as well, including an eventual noble's title for Curval, but it had seemed a hollow gesture. It was obvious Teth was more interested in his own personal goals than he was in returning the nobility to its proper place, whether in West Ursia or elsewhere.

Curval could find little noble about serving such a person, a wizard who was obviously mad, claiming to have lived thousands of years ago as a high priest to some long-forgotten god. It made little sense to the former knight of Caballerus.

But what else was there? What else was he to do? Where to go? He had thrown in his lot with this band of madmen and killers, and there was nothing for him to return to in Caballerus.

The door atop the hill behind him squeaked, and Curval almost turned around. But he did not need to do so. He knew who approached.

The sound of soft footsteps upon the spongy ground followed. Then a hand upon his shoulder.

"Have you given my offer some consideration?" Sadhe Teth said in the knight's ears.

Curval gave a curt nod.

"And your decision?"

Curval still did not turn to look. He would not, not with tears frozen upon his face. "I will serve you," he said.

"Good." A pat upon the shoulder. "Good."

Then the wizard fled back to the warmth of the shack and its fire.

Yes, what else was there?

17

Morning. Cold. A rooftop. Again.

At least it was a different rooftop. Jarin had taken the bold move of climbing up the back of the healing tower in the Swamps, landing himself upon an expanse more than large enough for a jousting tournament. The building was that big.

Making his way through the maze of alleys to get to the back of the building had actually been more difficult than the climb itself, but once up top he realized right away his plan would pay off.

He found himself on one of the highest points in all the Swamps. He could see in all directions for miles, though most of what he saw were other rooftops and smoke drifting up from tenement chimneys. And though there was little sun, gray clouds dominating the sky, he could still see the occasional wink of light off the rivers to the south and north. He could even make out a few buildings across the rushing waters in Uptown and Southtown.

More importantly, he had a direct view from above of the main entrance to the healing tower. With a little walking he could even cover the other, lesser entrances, those mostly used by the healers themselves and the various staff in their comings and goings.

Looking down directly from overhead didn't give him the best of views, however, especially as it was impossible to make out faces from his angle, but that did not bother him overly much. Out front of the tower's main entrance was open ground for a good distance, other buildings and alleys and streets not overly close. Even if Jarin couldn't see a face from directly above, all he had to do was wait a bit for whomever was below to move away from the building, and then he could make out their face.

Besides, he only had to be worried about one face.

The healer Randall Tendbones. He was the target again. Actually, he had been the target all along. Only the face of the hiring client had changed, even though according to Teth he was still the original client.

It didn't make much sense to Jarin. Malin had hired the pair of assassins to take out Tendbones, then Malin had been killed by Jarin himself, and Falk had no longer been Falk but had become Sadhe Teth, who said he had been Malin all along even though he was also a powerful wizard thousands of years old.

Okay.

Fine.

At least things were more simple now. No Malin, no Falk, only Teth. At least Teth's promises were along the lines of if not better than those of Falk. Time would tell. Since Jarin had nothing else better to do and nowhere else better to go, he would stay, at least as long as his sister did.

Besides, Tendbones would be his first professional kill in Bond. His first in all of West Ursia, for that matter. The thought of such warmed him from the inside nearly as much as Teth's spell which kept his cloak feeling as if it had just come from hanging beneath a warm sun.

His first professional kill since Provenzano. How he would love to return to that city. In his mind's eyes, he saw a painting of himself riding along the streets, waving his salutations to the grocers and vendors and urchins and whores and scum. At the end of his ride he would drop down from his saddle and march up the stairs into the hall of the assassin's guild. There he would reclaim what was rightfully his, and his sister's, their proper place on the roll of assassins.

It had not been Jarin's fault, after all, that a rival had turned him over to the authorities. Such would have to be repaid, and Jarin's good name exalted once more. Along with his sister.

Speaking of his sister, where was she? She was supposed to meet him in the alley behind the tower, but she had not shown. Earlier in the morning, before sunlight, they had split, her going off yet again to find food and drink for their party.

She should have been there by now.

Jarin glanced over a shoulder toward the back of the building.

And there she was, kneeling right behind him, a sack hanging over one shoulder.

"You could have announced yourself," he said.

She said nothing in return, merely brought around the sack and opened it, pulling out and tossing him an apple.

He took a bite, his teeth chopping into the chilled flesh of the fruit. It wasn't much of a breakfast, but at least it was food. Jarin had asked Teth to magic them up a fine meal, but the wizard had balked, saying he was not free as of yet to make use of his more powerful spells.

Which was why Jarin and Rgia watched from a rooftop. For the healer. Only with the death of Tendbones would Sadhe Teth utilize his spells on a truly beneficial level.

It made little sense to Jarin. A healer? What threat could a healer be? Even if this Tendbones was a mage himself, so what? If Teth was truly as powerful as he said, why would a lowly healer in the Swamps be any threat?

"What do you think?" he asked his sister.

She ignored him for a moment, shuffling to the edge and looking down. Then she glanced back at him. "We're all fools."

He grinned. His sister could be overly wary, but often he found a certain humor in her. "What do you mean?"

She looked again, apparently seeing nothing out of the ordinary as she did not react. "We have no way of knowing if there is any truth to what this Sadhe Teth tells us."

He took another bite of apple, chewed and swallowed. "What would you have us do? Go back to Provenzano?"

For a moment she stared at him, the stare enough to mock the humor he had found a moment earlier, enough to chill him despite Teth's magic on his cloak.

"That would also be foolish," she finally said, "but there are other possibilities."

"Such as?"

"Such as we could always slink away to somewhere else, somewhere where we are not known, where we are not wanted."

"Is that what you want to do?"

She went quiet again, standing on crouched knees to lean forward and look through a crenel, one of the many running around the building's top.

"Sister, did you hear me?" he asked.

She thrust a flattened hand at him, a sign for silence.

He went quiet, and she remained with her hand out for at least a minute.

Finally, "It is him," she said.

"Who? Tendbones?"

Rgia leaned out further and pointed down. Her brother rushed to her side and stood at his full height, leaning out and forward, his head and shoulders above the roof's merlons.

She was correct. Tendbones was indeed down there, the youthful healer sauntering forth from the tower into the morning cold. There were other healers, in white as always, but none were as young as Randall Tendbones, who walked faster and straighter than the rest.

Rgia turned her head to one side and stared at her brother. For a moment he did not notice, but when he did another chill ran through him.

"What?" he asked.

"You realize it would have been rather easy to push you off, don't you?" she said.

He said nothing in return, but gulped and slipped back from the edge.

She looked from him to back over the ledge, but only for a moment. Then she pushed away and trotted toward the back of the building where Jarin had again left a rope hanging.

"What are we doing?" he asked her back.

"Following," she said, still walking.

"Aren't we going to kill him?"

At the back of the roof she stopped and dropped flat, hanging one leg over the side while grabbing hold of the rope tied tight around a merlon. "Not here. We watch, and we act only when the moment is right."

Running to catch up with her, he huffed and asked, "When will that be?"

"We'll know it when we see it."

And she dropped over the edge.

***

Walking the streets of Bond, it was not uncommon for faces familiar and unfamiliar alike to approach Randall, usually offering him a word of thanks, sometimes with a smile or a handshake or even a pat on the back. Occasionally there were even offers of gifts, food and drink and money being the most common, but Randall always refused them, suggesting to those making the offering that they instead make a donation to one of the two local healing towers.

Randall's name was known on the streets. He had treated a lot of people during the last couple of years, saved a lot of lives. He was the best known healer in the city, and the ill and injured and wounded would come from miles around to ask specifically for him and his services.

Obviously Randall could not treat everyone, but he tried his best, and often the worst cases were brought to him because other healers knew they could not do what Randall did. What that was exactly few could say, but there was little doubt the youthful healer was a mage of some power, able to heal wounds and diminish diseases like no other. Healers who were not trained in the magical arts were commonly in awe of him, but just as often those who *were* mages felt the same. Him being called upon so regularly was the main reason he often felt drained by the end of a day, even the reserves of Ashal himself having its limits.

As he made his way through the cold to the Asylum, a few pedestrians came up to him with their thanks. He nodded back, said a few words of comfort here and there, and proceeded on his journey. When traveling any distance within Bond, he usually called for one of the many cabriolets that constantly trundled the streets of the city as it was easier for him to travel without constant interruption, but it was not a long trip from the healing tower to the Asylum. Thus, Randall walked.

He was halfway to the Asylum when he stopped in the middle of the street. Someone was watching him. He felt their stare like a frozen claw gently raking down the back of his neck. He almost stopped to look back the way he had come, but realized that was foolish. Whomever was watching him was doing so from a distance.

Magic.

It seemed the person for whom he had been searching was back, or someone was. Privacy was a concern for Randall, and he nearly always kept himself cloaked behind a shield of warding which prevented him from being viewed through magic. His warding was not of the strongest sort as he normally did not wish to drain himself so much, but still, a novice could not have defeated his defenses so easily.

And there was little doubt Randall's protection had been thwarted. He could feel that cool gaze spreading across him, the viewer curious, but also perhaps a little angered.

This changed things. For one, this powerful magical unknown was no longer just sitting out there someplace, but was now actively looking for Randall. For another thing, it would change the report he was to give Kron. Perhaps he should even reconsider and go directly to Captain Gris.

But no. Kron was near at hand, or at least the Asylum was, and most mornings that was where Darkbow could be located.

He would see Kron first, then perhaps Gris. Randall would have liked to have known more information, such as the possible location of his viewer, but acquiring such was not feasible at the moment while he was in the middle of the road in public. Casting a spell, even something as simple as sending forth his spectral sight, might draw attention he would prefer not to have.

Setting out once more, that sense of being watched flowed right along with the healer. Someone was definitely interested in his movements.

Approaching the gates to the Asylum, Randall was fortunate enough to find Darkbow present, speaking from horseback to the two guards stationed there. A pleasant surprise was Frex Nodana at his friend's side, the master of the mages guild also in a saddle. Either Kron had purchased new steeds or the animals had been leased for a period, or perhaps Gris had allocated the riding beasts to the pair.

"Good morning, Randall," Frex said with a smile.

"And to you, guild master," Randall said, giving a short bow. "I did not expect you here this morning."

She blushed and gestured toward Kron. "We have business in Southtown this morning, but Kron wanted to give orders for the day to Montolio."

Kron spoke a few words to the guards at the gate, then steered his animal around to face the healer. "What brings you here this morning, Randall?"

"I was going to make a report to you, thinking you would see Gris today," Randall said, "but now I'm wondering if I should talk to him personally."

Kron could see the look of concern on his friend's face. "Has something happened?"

"Nothing too alarming," the healer said. "Just something out of the ordinary. It makes me believe our mystery wizard is still out there."

"Do you still think it has no link to Lord Falk and his gang?" Kron asked.

Randall shrugged. "Nothing tells me it does, but I have no evidence either way. I keep hoping they'll find the man. Maybe that will clear some things."

"I know the patrols have been increased," Kron said, "the extra men searching brothels, abandoned warehouses and the like. But, nothing as of yet."

"We're going to see Gris now," Nodana added. "Would you like to ride along with us?"

Kron turned in his saddle and patted the rear of his animal, a glint in the man's eye. "It's been a while since you've ridden double behind me, Randall."

The healer chuckled. "Thank you for the offer, but I'll hail a cab."

Kron also laughed. "Very well, but don't say I didn't offer. After I speak with Montolio, we'll be on our way, probably right behind you, so maybe we will see you at the barracks."

"Maybe so," Randall said, then waved a goodbye with a smile and turned back toward the street, a hand already raised to call on a passing carriage.

***

As the healer walked away, the man in black and the master of mages watched his back for more than a few seconds.

Eventually, "He would not say anything," Kron said, "but something weighs on his thoughts."

"He did seem a little apprehensive," Nodana said.

"Perhaps we'll find out more at the barracks." Kron slid down from his saddle and handed the reins off to one of the guards. "Let me talk with Montolio and then we can be on our way."

***

Sadhe Teth could not help but grin. So, his prey was aware of his presence again, and was aware Teth was watching him. Little did it matter. The twins were on the move, waiting for the right moment. It would not be long, then Teth would be free to use his magic in ways most helpful. After that, it would only be a matter of time, and once more he could return his destiny to the road upon which it had always traveled. Thousands would die, but that was the point.

He sat up on the makeshift bed, then scooted to the edge and dropped over so his feet landed on the wet floor of the shack.

"Curval!" he called out.

Barely a moment passed before the door to the shack opened, revealing the big knight.

"Pull up your hood and wrap your cloak tight so no one will recognize your features," the wizard said. "We are heading into the city."

18

The back seat of the carriage bucked beneath Randall as the vehicle lumbered along the cobbled, often bumpy streets of Bond. Between the roughness of the ride and the frigid weather, it was not the most comfortable form of travel, but Randall preferred not to rely on magic for moving around the city. His reserves were nearly limitless, at least compared to mortal mages, but tiredness still remained common to him at the end of most days after he had had to make use of powerful magics to thwart the most devastating of illnesses and injuries. Never knowing what he would face from day to day at the healing tower, he kept his magic in reserve as much as possible, awaiting the moments when a shattered figure or cancerous victim were brought to him.

The carriage jumped a few inches again as it moved past pedestrians who quickly jumped out of the way.

"Apologies, sir," said the driver from the front seat, glancing back at his passenger. "It's the weather. The cold brings up the stones from underneath, buckling the road."

Randall looked to the back of the man sitting mere inches in front of him. Shaggy gray head above a heavy woolen coat. Lined, bedraggled features when his face could be seen. It was a familiar face, one the healer had noticed at least a dozen times, yet he had never heard the fellow's name.

"No apologies needed," Randall said. "By the way, I've never caught your name."

"Scratch, sir," the driver said with another glance back and a tip of his head.

"Sorry about not asking before now, Scratch," Randall said as they trundled along. "You must've driven me across the city a dozen times before now."

"Eleven, to be exact, sir." This time the man did not look back, his attention focused upon avoiding a slow-moving wagon pulled by oxen ahead of the carriage.

Randall grinned. "Eleven? That many. And you remember them all?"

"I remember the number, sir," Scratch said. "I'm good with numbers."

"I suppose you see all kinds of customers," the healer said.

The driver nodded, his breath pluming about his head. "I've carried a little of everybody, sir. Even had Belgad the Liar as a customer once."

"Really?"

"Yes, sir. But if you don't mind my saying, you're the distinguished person I've carried the most often."

Randall went pale. "Distinguished? Me?"

"Why, yes, sir." Another nod of the head. "Everybody knows Tendbones the healer from the Swamps tower."

Allowing himself to sink back into the thinly-cushioned carriage seat, Randall's shoulders sank at the words from the old man. As much as Randall wanted to help others, his growing reputation did not bring him joy. For reasons obvious only to himself, and Kron and perhaps a handful of others who knew part of his life's story, Randall did not desire attention. He wanted a small, quiet life, one which would allow him to be of aid to others. Fame could well deny him such a life, and it could potentially deny him from helping his fellow man.

"Excuse me, sir," Scratch said from the front seat, as he reined in his two horses.

Randall looked ahead as the carriage came to a squeaking halt. "What is it?"

The answer was not so obvious. On the street ahead appeared a crowd, perhaps two dozen people, all milling around a wagon unmoving in the middle of the traffic lane.

Scratch leaned forward. "Looks as if a wheel's come off, sir. Probably due to the cold and the roads. We could be here a while."

"I'm in no hurry," the healer said.

The driver looked from side to side, showing that even though his customer might not be in a hurry, old Scratch himself actually *was*. After all, the sooner he dropped off one customer, the sooner he could pick up the next one, and get paid for it.

They were stuck in the middle of one of many streets that formed the spokes of a wagon-wheel configuration around Haven Square, a plaza and market many believed to be the oldest part of the city. Shooting off from these streets were lesser paths, often alleys of various widths and lengths, many of them crooked and twisting and surrounded by aging, nearly decrepit row houses and tenement buildings of two and three stories. There were actually a few people making their way through these alleys, but even many of the Swamps dwellers did not know all the twists and turns of this section of the city. But a cab driver wasn't just any ordinary citizen. One had to know all the back ways and back roads if one was to succeed in that line of work.

Scratch pointed to their left with his riding crop. "There's an alley over there big enough for us, sir. Comes out just the other side of Haven Square."

"If you think it best," Randall said, knowing not the path.

The riding crop smacked a horse's rear and the pair of animals pulled, their driver steering them toward the alley opening. The horses did not hesitate though the route before them was barely wide enough for themselves and the carriage. Abandoned garbage waited here and there, and the stench from the street gutters along the sides was enough to make most people cover their face, as Scratch did with a sleeve of his cloak though the healer did not seem to notice.

The carriage bucked again as it entered the alley, and as the walls closed in on either side, Randall noticed he could reach out with ease and touch bricks if he wanted. With the shadows came a stronger chill, and rider and passenger alike pulled tighter their outer garments.

With the buildings now looming above, a darker gloom spread across the travelers. The few people ahead in the alley moved faster away from the approaching cab, knowing there was not room for the lot of them in the tight confines. Rotten vegetables squelched beneath the heavy wheels, and ice cracked along with a few pieces of discarded wood, remains from a forgotten barrel or crate.

The carriage had not gone far when they came to the first side alley, a dark, narrow path to their right. Scratch slowed the horses and half-turned to glance back at his passenger.

"Not big enough for us, sir," the old man said, "but I'll have us out of here soon enough."

Randall opened his mouth to reply, but was cut off by motion from the side route.

The hooded figure moved in a blur, darting forward from shadows and barreling straight for the driver. Scratch never saw the person coming. The old man was just turning to face forward when the figure sprang from the alley's floor and landed aside the carriage, a hand gloved in deerskin snapping out to grab hold of an arm rail while soft boots landed on the foot board between driver and passenger.

Randall raised a hand as if to reach for the stranger. "There's no need for that."

But it was too late. A fist swinging wide bashed into Scratch's stomach, causing the old man to shout out and bend forward double, nearly falling from his stoop.

Before Randall could act further, another presence made itself known. It was a second person, dressed the same as the first and roughly of the same size. The healer caught sight of a white chin beneath a cloak's hood as this newcomer seemed to drop from the sky, landing beside him in the back of the cab.

In one of the figure's hands glinted the short, steel blade of a thin dagger.

The stiletto hurtled forward. It moved so fast, Randall barely saw it sink into his chest up to the hilt, nor did he feel it.

Then the gloved hand holding the blade's handle twisted.

It was as if lightning struck the healer.

Randall convulsed, his body kicking as he fell back on his seat. Pain rolled over him and his vision blurred from tears.

The dagger withdrew, but only for a moment. It punched forward again, and again and again. Stab, twist. Stab, twist. Stab, twist.

To his benefit, Randall never felt the other wounds made upon his body. He did not feel the tearing of flesh, the rending of organs, the splashing of blood.

His vision rolled and his entire self was taken up by the tragedy of that first wounding. His heart had been stuck, the flow of blood immediately cut off from the rest of the body. His frame continued to jerk for a few moments, then it quivered and finally became still.

He tried to keep his eyes open, to see his attacker, to see what had happened to poor Scratch.

But there was nothing to see.

His sight was gone.

As was the air from his lungs and the blood in his heart.

Existence plummeted into a mere pinpoint, then that blinked, and it was gone.

***

As Kron and Nodana rode onto one of the main thoroughfares leading into Haven Square, they noticed the back of a dark carriage disappearing down a side street that was little more than a wide alley. Kron had just enough time to wonder why the driver was taking such a circuitous route when his attention was caught up by a growing crowd ahead.

It was not a mob there in the middle of the road, but what appeared to be a sizable group of citizens working together at some task. Around these people were plenty of others walking past, none too few watching the goings-on but not stopping to help.

Kron stood in his stirrups, staring over the heads of the throng.

"Looks like trouble with a wagon," he said as he pulled his steed to a halt, Nodana doing the same next to him.

Then a cry of alarm and pain from the alley.

"What was that?" Nodana said.

His sword slapping at his side, Kron dropped from his saddle and held out his horse's reins. "I'll be right back."

"Be careful." Nodana took the leathers and watched as her man jogged off into the shadows.

Approaching the carriage from the rear, Kron could tell right away something was wrong. The passenger in back was slumped to one side, and there was no sign of the driver. The pair of horses were skittish. A few people in the distance were running away, their feet patting on the alley's floor a sure sign there had been trouble, no one wanting to hang around in case the situation grew worse.

Kron slowed as he came up to the carriage, now able to see over the back of the conveyance. He still could not make out the features of the passenger, but the white robes and cloak were obvious, and the driver now appeared in the front seat, the old man nearly kneeling while clutching at his stomach.

Hurrying with worry, Kron grabbed a side rail and used the driver's step to pull himself up beside the carriage. The back seat was awash in blood. The crumpled figure's face was hidden by a hood flopped forward, but the person in white was splattered in crimson, at least a half dozen dark wounds showing where a dagger or knife had been plunged again and again.

His hand shaking, Kron reached for the hood and lifted its edge.

Randall.

"Nodana!" Kron shouted, but he did not spend time wondering if she had heard him. She *had* to hear him.

Instead, his hands went to work. A dagger tugged free of his belt, he began frantically slicing away at the hem of Randall's cloak, creating strips of bandages.

The old man in the front groaned and sat up, nearly falling into his seat.

"What happened here?" Kron asked, tugging free more strips, sheathing the dagger and going to work pulling open Randall's garb.

The driver half-turned and blinked at him, then groaned again. "Who the hell are you?"

"City guard." The white cloak parted and Kron ripped open the robes beneath. Pale flesh, ruined and layered in red. Kron paid it no attention. He couldn't, or else he would scream.

"There were two of them," the old man said, shaking his head and spitting a stream of blood to one side. "One hit me from the front, the other seemed to come from above."

"Come here," Kron ordered, motioning the other man to draw nearer.

The old man hesitated for a moment, but then he turned fully and climbed into the back where he squeezed in next to Darkbow.

"Apply pressure here and here," Kron said, pointing at Randall.

Again the old man did as he had been told. "Is he going to make it?"

"I don't know." The wrapping began, but there were not enough of the makeshift bandages.

Kron raised his head to yell for Nodana again, but then found her climbing down from her saddle and tying off their horses behind the carriage.

"It's Randall," he nearly spat out. "He's been stabbed multiple times."

"By Ashal." The woman moved around to the side of the carriage, almost directly behind Kron. "Give me some room."

Kron glanced back at her.

"I'm no healer," Nodana said, "but I know a few spells which could help."

"Keep putting pressure," Kron said to the driver, then the man in black dropped the bandages and moved to the front of the carriage.

Nodana climbed up and prepared a spell, ancient words muttered beneath her breath, but then she stopped and looked at her lover.

"What is it?" Kron asked, his words frantic, his eyes furious. "Why have you stopped?"

Her voice was small. "Kron, there's little need."

"What?" He stood, looming over the pair gathered around the healer. "Damn it, Nodana, do something! Stop the bleeding at least!"

The old driver lifted his hands from the body and sat back on his rump. "I'm sorry, mister, but it's no use. Your friend is right. He's gone."

Kron stood there fuming, his hands clinching and unclenching at his side. "It can't be." But it was, or at least it appeared so. Randall was not breathing. The blood no longer flowed from his wounds. There was no sign of any movement, not even a twitching.

"Which way did they go?" he asked of the driver.

The old man pointed up. "Took to the rooftops."

Kron jumped down to the alley floor, one hand busy unbuckling his cumbersome sword belt, the other unfurling a thin silken cord from within the folds of his cloak.

"Kron," Nodana said.

He ignored her. The sword and belt clattered to the ground. The cord came free of its confines, one end attached to a small steel grapnel which was soon whirling above Kron's head.

"Kron!" she shouted.

He darted her a black look. "Get him to the tower, now. And inform Gris."

The grapnel sailed before clattering onto a roof three stories over their heads. Kron pulled on the rope, the hook above caught on something. He pulled again, testing the cord, then placed a boot against a wall.

"This is futile," Nodana said. "They'll be gone by now."

Kron's shoulders slumped for a moment as if he had the weight of a thousand worlds upon him, then he straightened and pulled himself up the rope. "There's no man I cannot track."

And a moment later he was gone, vanishing up the rope and over a ledge.

***

Having spent six months of his youth on the streets of Bond and fifteen years of his life among the forests surrounding the Prisonlands, Kron was an experienced climber, those experiences being what led him to often carry a small grappling hook and the attached silk rope. His hitting the rooftop near Haven Square was not his first venture to the world above the city, and he was almost always prepared for such.

As soon as he landed on the pebbles imbedded in tar atop the roof, he swung around surveying all directions in some minor hope of seeing a figure fleeing across the roofs. But there was nothing to be seen. Too much time had passed.

Which did not mean he would give up.

Dropping to a knee while retrieving his grapnel and rope, he studied the floor of the roof around him. He had no knowledge the persons he pursued had landed in this exact spot or even on this roof, but it did no harm to look.

Nothing unusual presented itself.

He glanced at nearby roofs, but again, nothing unusual.

Attacking from above, rooftop travel and no obvious traces left behind. These people were professionals, likely thieves or assassins, but also not likely to be locals but newcomers from elsewhere, otherwise Kron was positive he would have heard of them by now.

A thousand questions tried to imprint themselves upon his mind, especially concerning the choice of Randall as a target, but he pushed those thoughts aside. All they could do was impede him.

He swung around again, taking in his surroundings.

The west was no good, the road being busy; besides, he and Nodana would have seen anyone trying to flee that direction. The north also seemed unlikely, it being close to another road where anyone climbing down would be noticed by street traffic. The south led into Haven Square, which would be a good place to hide among the market crowds, but again, anyone swinging down from a rooftop would tend to be noticed.

That left the east, which headed toward the Docks. This time of morning there would be plenty of workers going to and fro there, but there was also a maze of alleyways between Kron's location and the Docks that would provide plenty of places to drop to the ground without being seen.

The east made the most sense.

The east it was.

His feet made the decision for him before his mind had the opportunity. Kicking off the ground, he took off at a run, less than two dozen steps away an alley presenting itself between his and the next roof. It was only a five-foot jump. He made it with ease, springing off one roof, his legs tucked beneath him with his arms out at his side and his cloak sailing out behind, then landing on the other roof. He did not falter but kept at a run, dodging a string of half a dozen soot-laden chimneys belching smoke.

As he moved he kept his sight straight ahead, his eyes scanning the rooftops in front of him for at least a half mile. There were plenty of places to hide, chimneys everywhere, water cisterns of all shapes and sizes, the occasional barrel or crate, even what appeared to be small houses but were likely storage sheds or entrances to stairwells. Fortunately for Kron Darkbow, he knew them all, had spent more than a few nights studying the above-ground world of Bond; his prey did not have such knowledge, but they were ahead of him by several minutes.

Prey, meaning more than one in this instance. He had to keep that in mind. The carriage driver had said there were two of them.

But where were they?

There.

Directly ahead. Movement. Far away but unmistakeably a running figure, legs kicking up and down. Dressed in what appeared to be soft leathers the color of deerskin. Not a small person, but not overly bulky. Only one of them. The other had probably split off or already dropped to the ground, thinking there was less chance of being caught if they weren't together.

Kron lost sight of the person ahead for a moment as he came to another alley. The next roof was not so far away, only a few feet, but it was a leg higher than his current position.

He did not slow his pace but somersaulted up and forward, landing hard, finally pausing for a moment to assure his footing, then sprinting forward once more.

Dodging aside a stack of lumber, he caught sight of his foe again. Kron was closer to the person now, but still some distance away. His prey was slowing, no longer running, probably figuring there would be no pursuit by rooftop.

That person was wrong, and at any moment he or she would become aware of this as soon as Kron grew nearer and they could hear his stomping boots.

He had to move faster, to close the gap.

His legs kicked harder.

He jumped over a small crate.

Another alley came across his path. This one was wide, at least ten feet.

He slowed as he approached the gap, then spotted a board to one side that stretched across the alley's top, probably left behind by some night prowler or perhaps children who like to play high above. Kron shot toward the board, skipping onto it and bounding across.

Halfway, the board cracked, then snapped. He had just enough time to launch himself forward. His fingers stretched and reached, the broken lumber falling beneath his feet and clattering to the ground three stories below. His leather-clad hands just managed to grab the lip of the next roof's top.

Breathing heavily, he pulled himself up and took off running again.

Once more, his prey was lost to him.

Kron kept moving.

He sidestepped a child's forgotten clay ball. He jumped a basket full of empty bottles. He grabbed a tall iron pipe sticking up from a roof and used it to vault himself across to another building.

Always moving, always watching.

Again, there. His prey. Kron was closer now. The person was sauntering along as if not a care in the world.

Kron jumped another alley, landing in a roll, coming up on his feet and moving again.

Running by a large round cistern nearly as big as a house, he saw his opponent was only two buildings away. One alley, that was all that was between him and the murderer.

Kron forced himself to run harder, faster, his legs kicking up and down along with his arms.

As he reached the end of the cistern, something flashed out at him. A leg, kicking, covered in leather and ending in a boot.

The second attacker.

Kron saw it just soon enough to swerve away to his right.

But it was not enough.

The boot caught him in his left side, bruising ribs and sending him reeling toward the edge of the roof. He thrust out a hand, grabbing at anything, finding nothing.

On the verge of going over, his back to the ground, he glanced around his shoulder and found the next roof not so far away. There was only one thing to do.

His footing unsure, his balance awkward, his cloak billowing around and nearly entangling his legs, he planted his boots on the very edge of his roof and pushed up and back with all the strength he could muster.

He soared up and over the alley, his legs extended straight up and flipping over his head. In mid-air he twisted around.

Then landed on the other side, his backwards somersault complete.

Now facing the direction he had originally been running, he spared a moment to try and spot his original target. The person was gone.

But a grunt from behind told him the other was not finished.

Kron jumped away from the roof's ledge and flipped around, and just in time. The attacker bound across the alley opening to land not far from him.

For a moment Kron had a chance to take in his opponent. Lithe, covered in soft leathers, not much bulk but plenty of muscle, the shoulders and face nearly hidden by a short, hooded cloak. The eyes flashed blue, narrow, almost feminine.

Was this a woman?

Kron backed up another step, rethinking his next actions. Experienced women combatants tended to fight with their brains, whereas men too often fell back upon their brawn, letting their bulk and muscles do all their thinking for them. To Kron's mind, this made women fighters often more deadly than their male counterparts.

He was proven correct a moment later when two daggers appeared, one in each of his enemy's hands.

For a moment Kron almost wished for his sword, but the huge weapon was much too cumbersome for climbing and rooftop fighting, which was why he had left it behind in the first place.

As his opponent moved toward him, the twin blades cutting short arcs from side to side instead of the wider swings of an amateur, Kron backpedaled, unclasping his cloak and wrapping it around his left arm as a shield, one end of the black cloth trailing down almost to the ground. His other hand sought out a dagger of his own, found it on his belt and brought it forth, gripped underhanded.

His opponent stopped, staring at him, curious, the cloaked head leaning slightly to one side. She, if a woman, was facing a trained and experienced fighter. His actions told her as much. She recognized him as a serious threat, if she had not before, and now she was looking for weaknesses in his defense.

Or she was looking over his shoulder.

Kron sidestepped and glanced around behind him.

Nothing there.

The other figure, the one who had been further away, had not reappeared.

His foe had known this.

A bluff.

He looked back to front just in time.

The hooded woman came charging at him, the head ducked low, the tan cloak billowing out above and behind in the wind, giving the fighter an illusion of size. The dagger on Kron's right swooped in from below. The one on the left dove in from above.

He flashed the hanging end of his cloak out in front of him, stalling her for a moment, giving him time to spring back another few feet.

The woman rebounded from the feint, slashing at his cloak as she did so, leaving two long tears in the black cloth.

She was fast, too fast. Also obviously well trained and experienced herself. If she got within cutting distance of him, the combat would be brutal for both of them. But she didn't seem to care. Which meant she believed herself his superior.

Perhaps she was. Or perhaps she was merely overconfident.

Kron untwirled his cloak, freeing nearly all of it to hang from a fist.

His attacker pounced again, closing the space so he could not make use of his garment's reach, her blades once more coming in from both sides, her head still low.

Instead of retreating this time, Kron stepped into the onrushing figure, his dagger punching out to his right, its steel length knocking aside her weapon there.

Her other dagger slit its way through the black of his cloak, the tip heading straight for the man in black's heart. Kron yanked the cloak overhead, the cloth still strong enough to catch her weapon and its enclosing hand, pulling her right arm up and destroying her balance for a moment.

He had her.

Or thought he did.

Her entangled hand dropped its blade, allowing the knife to fall to the rooftop as fingers bunched themselves together into a fist in the midst of the black cloth. Her other hand flipped its dagger around in a reverse grip, the strengthened attack swooping in from the side once more.

Kron thrust with his dagger, tying up her attack as their blades locked together for a moment.

But his own cloak shielded him from seeing the oncoming punch.

The blow caught him across the chin, snapping his head back and sending him reeling, his cloak still gripped by both of them and stretching taught between their fists. He twirled out several feet from her, then was brought up short as her grip on the black cloth caught.

The punch had not been the strongest he had ever suffered, but it had been enough to hurt and to dull his vision for a moment. Blinking away the pain and confusion, he happened to spy his footing.

He found himself off balance on the very edge of the building, the heels of his boots hanging over a three story drop into an alley below.

His foe's grip on the cloak was all that held him in place.

She grinned, and it confirmed to him she was indeed a woman. Only a woman's grin could bring fear and break one's heart all at the same time.

Snapping her end of the cloak, she released her hold upon it.

Kron fell back.

His boots still touching the roof, he twisted around as he dropped, spotting the next nearest roof a few yards away. He pushed from the ledge with all his might, his dagger forgotten and his cloak fluttering away as his arms lunged for the safety of the next ledge.

The distance was too far.

His chest slammed into the iron gutter running the length of the next building's roof, the warm air bursting from his lungs as his gloved hands scrambled for a grip of any kind. For a moment he thought he would hold, his fingers clawing into the gravel surface of the roof before sliding back to catch on the gutter's lip.

The gutter was cold, covered with a thin layer of ice. His fingers slid across as if touching nothing.

And he was falling again.

At least he had had a moment to clear his head, to ascertain his situation.

Twenty feet from the alley floor he snapped out a hand, sending his grappling hook spiraling toward the gutter he had just left behind. The grapnel sailed over the top and caught, the rope in his hands going tight.

Just as he hit the ground.

Kron rolled with his landing, springing away from the place of impact. The fall had not been overly long, at least not for one familiar with the ways of the rooftops and treetops. The catching of the rope, even at the last moment, had spared him a worse hit. Then his rolling, it eventually brought him up against a wall. All of these saved him from serious damage. As it was, he was bruised along his limbs and had possibly cracked some few ribs. His chest hurt as he sucked in the winter air, and for a moment he feared he would not be able to stand upon one of his ankles.

But stand he did.

Then he remembered his foes.

He looked up. The roofs were empty. There was no sign nor sound of his enemies, neither the woman or the other. Apparently they had been satisfied with escape, or believed him dead and were smart enough not to remain in the vicinity to gloat.

Glancing around, he found his dropped dagger and the remains of his cloak, the black garb now soggy as it sat wadded in a pool of icy water. At least he hoped it was water.

Retrieving the cloth, he slid the dagger home in its sheath and turned down the alley, limping his way to the nearest street.

He did not know the names of the pair who had attacked Randall, but he had a pretty good guess as to their identities. Even if Nodana had been right about the healer's condition, Kron could not admit to himself his friend was dead, not yet. Whatever the case, Kilchus the Sword would have much to answer for.

19

Word of the murder of Randall Tendbones spread through the Swamps like a hawk on the wing, even crossing the cold waters of the rivers and the cold stones of the bridges into the other sections of the city. Though the most eminent figures of Bond had barely heard of the healer, Randall was an individual much beloved by the common people. In a short span of a few years the healer had gained a reputation not only for his ability, but for his humility and his general amiability.

Old Scratch sent out the word first, leaving Frex Nodana behind with the body as he stumbled out into the streets, shouting for help in backing his nervous animals and the unwieldy carriage out of the alley. He had not had to yell long. As soon as pedestrians and the throng at the square heard the name of "Randall Tendbones," they came running by the dozens. Scratch soon had more than enough aid in reversing his cabriolet onto the street proper, Nodana all the while in the back of the vehicle, the mage busy with spells she was sure would do no good.

Once the carriage was turned around, the masses pressed in, everyone wanting a look at the pale features and blooded rags of the slain healer. More than a few hands reached forward in awe to touch the cold body, and Scratch was forced to use his riding crop to smack away straining fingers.

"Out of the way!" the old man shouted, the crop swinging wildly around him.

The crowd parted, giving the carriage room, and with a snap of the reins the horses pulled and Scratch drove forward. There were too many people for him to make good speed, but he moved the carriage as best he could through the throng, all the while making for the Swamps healing tower.

Those parting out of the way of the stomping hooves and rolling wheels soon fell in behind, and it was a swarm of hundreds who eventually settled around the healing tower as the carriage came to a halt there.

Once more sturdy arms sprang forward to steady the horses and carriage, and to carry the unmoving figure of the healer into the tower where the group was pointed to Randall's own chambers. Nodana and Scratch followed, and it was a broken Althurna they found in the front room, the poor girl a mess of tears as she wallowed in a corner.

Randall was carried into the second room where he was laid to rest upon a bed, the burly men who had carried him backing away for a last glance at the man many considered a saint.

"Thank you for your help, gentlemen," Nodana said as she rushed into the room, "but if you would, please, we need the room cleared."

No one argued with her. The men filed out, each with a last sorrowful glance at the body. Only when the last of them had fled the room did Scratch stick his head in, the old fellow's arms wrapped around the quivering, blubbering figure of Althurna.

Nodana gave the driver and the girl a mournful stare, her eyes red and wet.

Before she could say a word, a stream of healers poured into the room, the men and women dressed in white and of all ages going to work to do whatever they could.

Through all that came next, the use of minor spells and the pouring of potions and the smearing of ointments and the tearing of bandages and the sewing of sutures, Nodana could do nothing but retreat to a corner where she sat on a small round chair and cried.

***

The Asylum not being far from the healing tower, it was quite noticeable when the street traffic changed from its regular back-and-forth agitation to a general flow in one direction, toward the tower. The two guards stationed outside the front gate stood their ground as citizens strode past in a hurry, some few even running; after several minutes of this, the two guards could no longer contain their curiosity.

One of them stepped forward, laying his spear across the way of a young woman holding the folds of a cloak tight about her chest, a covered basket hanging from one arm. She ground her shoes to a halt on the frozen cobbles, turning a snarl toward the man, her look quickly softening as she recognized the orange tabard beneath the round steel helmet.

"What's going on?" the spearwielder asked, nodding in the direction the traffic was frothing.

"Haven't you heard?" the woman said. "It's Tendbones. Somebody's killed him!"

The guard was too shocked to ask anything further, and the woman brushed past him as he lifted his spear.

Stepping back to the gate, the guard turned to his partner. "Did you hear?"

"Can't hardly believe it," the other man said, shaking his head in disbelief. "He cured my boy's weak lungs just last summer. We thought we was going to lose the lad for sure."

The first guard looked through the bars of the gate. The grounds beyond were gray and quiet, the second lieutenant apparently keeping the trainees inside for the day. "Think I ought to tell somebody?"

The other guard gave a glance back at the Asylum and opened his mouth to speak.

"There'll be no need for that," another voice intruded.

The guards looked around, finding an old man in a dingy cloak standing before them, a hood pulled up to cover his head and shadow his features. Behind the stranger stood a taller, broader figure, this one's face not covered so well, the gruff face on display, but more worrisome the big sword strapped to his back.

The traffic on the street continued to flow past as if it saw not the four men facing one another.

The first guard opened his mouth.

The old man gestured with a hand, a brushing off to one side. "The two of you may leave. There is no call for you here today."

The two guards blinked, then looked to one another.

"I wouldn't mind something to warm my bones," one of them said.

"How about mulled wine at the Pony?" the other said.

They nodded at one another, then faced forward for a moment, their eyes glazed over, staring straight ahead without seeing the old man and his gaunt companion. Then the two in orange, cloaks billowing around their shoulders, turned to one side and marched away, their spears tapping the ground next to them.

Sadhe Teth chuckled. Simple minds were so easy to manipulate, and the flurry of news on the streets had reinforced what his magic had already revealed. Tendbones was dead. The wizard had more than one reason to laugh.

Curval moved around his boss and came up to the gate, resting a hand upon one of the cold iron bars while looking through to the grounds beyond. "Why are we here?"

Teth came up next to him. "I have business inside."

"I thought Kilchus had been moved to the barracks," Curval said. "You said we were to rescue him today."

Teth chuckled again. "That we will, my friend, but first I must retrieve something from within." He was lying, of course, but he would in no way tell the knight of this, at least not until the ancient wizard's quest for the day had been complete. The bones lay within, Teth's magic had revealed such, and now with the healer out of the way, there was nothing left to do but recover the artifacts. Then the deaths could begin, and Teth's power would multiply by the thousands.

His aged arms waved Curval away with a grimace while the mage felt the cold in his stolen bones. "If you will allow me?"

Curval moved back a few steps, giving his boss room.

Teth tested the gates, found them locked as expected, then waved a hand once more, this time directly across the front of the lock. There was a clicking sound and the mage pushed the gate open, entering the grounds of the Asylum, his companion right behind him, the two then making their way up the hill to the building.

All this time, not a soul noticed them from the street, Teth's magic ensuring such. There was little need for the wizard not to make use of his talents now that his only threat had been removed by the twins.

***

A gloved hand reached within the assortment of bottles, jars, tubes and small wooden cases arrayed atop the long table. For a moment the hand hesitated, hovering above a small leather sack, then it shifted to one side and flipped back the lid on a small wooden box. Reaching within, the glove grasped a hardened clay ball about the size of a large strawberry.

Montolio held up the ball and turned to face the six uniformed guards sitting atop round stools. The mage grinned at them. "Any of you know what this is?"

There was no immediate verbal response. What the teacher received were confounded stares, a single nod and one wide grin.

"It's a grenado," one of the two women finally said, the nodding one.

"That's right," Montolio said, himself nodding. "Good job, Corporal Noktl. Now, can you tell me the capabilities of grenados?"

"They're thrown weapons known for explosions and fire and smoke," the corporal answered, "but my guess is they could be used for other things."

"Such as?"

Noktl shrugged. "Maybe acid."

"That's right." Montolio beamed as he returned the grenado to its container for safekeeping. At least he had one member of the new unit who wasn't a complete dullard, though the others were not stupid, just a bit slow and not well educated. But then the expectations for the average city guard were not generally all that high.

Montolio hoped to change that, at least within the Special Squad.

He turned again to face the group and almost laughed at their fidgeting on the stools. They were bored, not overly joyed at being cooped up for the day within the Asylum's basement alchemical workshop. The wizard supposed he couldn't blame them. As cold as it had been outside, at least they had been able to move around some and there had been plenty of light, even the gray days being more bright than the dungeon-like atmosphere of the basement's halls and chambers.

The pair of torches, one at either end of the narrow but lengthy room, suddenly grew dim.

Montolio's face screwed up in confusion as he looked to the dancing flames now faded in height and brightness. A wisp of frigid air blew across his forehead, stirring his dark locks and causing him to shiver.

"*Beware yourselves.*"

The mage looked to his students. "Who said that?"

More confused faces looked back at him. The six men and women glanced at one another, then to their teacher again.

"None of us said anything," one of the men said.

"*They approach.*"

Not a mouth had moved within the room.

"Did you not hear that?" Montolio asked.

His students appeared not only confused, but worried. Was their teacher going mad?

Moving past the seated six, Montolio approached the room's only exit. He paused at the open doorway, staring into the dark shadows beyond, a hint of stone steps leading to the ground floor above only a few feet away on his right.

The cold wind blew across him again, this time stronger, playing at the hanging edges of his black jerkin.

"What was that?" one of the student's asked.

Montolio glanced back at them. "You felt it?"

Anxious nods and wide eyes were his answer.

"The dead," the wizard said. "They give us warning."

***

The air had been still until the ancient wizard and the knight had neared the heavy front door of the Asylum. As the two came to a halt in front of the closed portal, a heavy wind sprang up, whipping about them and stirring their cloaks, even forcing back the hood that had shielded Sadhe Teth's head.

Just behind his master, Curval stomped and reached up, placing a hand on the handle of his sword. "There is magic here."

"Still yourself," Teth said, grimacing into the wind cutting across his features. "There is nothing here to fear."

The hand came away from the sword, but the look on the knight's face did not show improvement.

Teth nearly snarled at the concern of his underling, but instead focused upon the door in front of them. Thick, stout wood of a dark nature, with a small, barred window inset into its center at average height of a man's face; the window was blocked from within by a smaller door.

"Open in the name of he who served the most high Onbx!" the mage shouted through the wind.

His only answer came as a howl from within that wind, distant but distinct, sorrowful yet full of warning. There were no other sounds. The clatter of traffic from the street had slipped away into nothingness, and there were no signs of life within the Asylum itself.

Teth growled and took a step nearer the door, raising a fist as if to hammer against the wood.

"*Belay that hand, wizard,*" came a spectral voice from nowhere. "*Thou are not welcome here, and are advised to return from whence thou came.*"

"Spirits!" Curval called out. The big man showed his first signs of fear, stepping away from his master and grabbing at his sword once more.

Even Sadhe Teth appeared surprised, the mage nearly stumbling back in amazement, his back brushing against the cloak and plated chest of his companion. If not for Curval, the mage might have continued his retreat.

Catching himself against the knight, Teth stood straight once more and wiped at the front of his cloak as if brushing away dust. He stared straight at the closed door, the wind growing colder by the moment, cold enough to make his bared flesh feel raw.

Launching himself forward, the wizard grasped at the door's handle and pulled. Nothing came of it. The door was not only physically locked, but barred from him by the ghosts of the dead.

He had slain thousands. Been high priest of the slothful Onbx himself. Raised the Zarroc from their endless sleep. Been the founder of the very weapons of the Gods. Keeper of the bones. Sleeper of eons. Mage beyond compare, the most powerful mortal sorcerer of all centuries. Sadhe Teth was these things, had been these things. He had known the slumber of the dead himself, though his spirit itself had never moved on, never rested, always waiting and watching and protecting the bones. Through all of this, in all that time, he had learned much, many things that were forgotten, knowledge even the most powerful mages of the current day did not know and would never know.

And one thing he had learned through all of that was magic held little effect against those dead in spirit form. Magic itself was a tool fueled by souls, but only souls of the living or the dying. Those already dead, they held no fear of magic, which was why no few wizards over the centuries had taken to conspiring with demons, creatures from beyond who held some control over the spectral unliving. Such knowledge was not necessarily a secret, but was not common, as the memories of Malin the Quill had informed Sadhe Teth. Only the most experienced of wizards would hold such knowledge.

Teth was such a wizard, but he had no demon. He had no wish to consort with a demon. All he had was his magic, as powerful as it could be, and the strong arm of the mighty figure behind him.

He roared at the door, "You dare defy me? *Me?*"

The wind screamed at him, this time stronger than ever, the freezing wisps tearing at his skin, causing the end of his nose and the edges of his lips to bleed, the scarlet fluid of life freezing solid before having time to run down his face.

"*Yes!*" a voice howled from within the nothingness of the winter. "*Yes, we defy you Sadhe Teth, and all who would stand with you!*"

It was as if a blast of air slammed into the wizard, knocking him back, his arms flailing. Again, it was the knight who caught him, halting Teth's fall to the ground. For a moment the wizard thrashed as if in a fury, his face filled with rage, his footing unsure beneath him. But then he slumped against his larger companion, the warmth Curval's body gave off comforting him as he realized the futility of further action.

"Take me away from here, Curval," he said with soft words.

"What of Kilchus?"

"*Damn* Kilchus," Teth said. "We will deal with him later."

The big knight looked up from his nearly downed master, staring into the fury of the small storm brewing between himself and the door. For a moment Curval seemed to be judging the strength of the minor whirlwind, as if he pondered his own chances against it and of making it to the door. Then he shrugged and hoisted Teth to his feet.

Without another word the two turned away from the Asylum, the wizard leaning into the armored figure as if for support.

***

The door to the Asylum slammed open revealing Montolio at the ready with a grenado raised high, Corporal Noktl right behind him with a sword drawn, the other city guards in the background, each with a weapon at hand. Below them at the front gate there was no sign of the assigned guards, but a pair of cloaked figures vanished into the stirring street traffic. A heavy wind blasted the open entrance for a moment, then it sauntered away as if drawn off by a bellows.

Montolio frowned as he lowered his throwing arm and inserted the clay ball into a pocket of his pantaloons. "Did anyone see who they were?"

"I caught a glimpse," the corporal said. "Didn't know them, but they fit the description of some of those involved with that mess at the Stone Pony the other day."

The mage glanced over the woman's shoulder to the others. "Which means Kilchus might be able to identify them."

20

Kron found everyone in Randall's outer office at the healing tower. He pushed his way through the crowd in the outside hall and slammed the door closed behind him. Her face a mirror of pain, Nodana sat behind the healer's desk, the mage utterly still, her body and mind in shock. Against the wall opposite her sat Althurna on a stool, the woman's face in her hands, her long, dark hair nearly between her knees and hanging almost to the floor, her body quaking in silence. With one arm around Althurna, the gray-headed driver of the carriage sat on another stool, his own face one of bleak astonishment. Even Captain Gris was present, the man leaning against the wall next to the door to the inner chamber, his face ashen as he looked upon Darkbow's entrance.

The captain rushed to his friend. "I was on my way to the Asylum when I heard. We need to talk."

Kron paused for a moment, looking from face to face, then he brushed past the officer. "Not now."

Gris grabbed him by a shoulder. "Kron, there's nothing you can do."

The visage turned upon the captain was so filled with rage, it caused him to remove his hand and step back, the hand lowering toward the sword on his belt. After a moment Kron shook his head, the wrath draining out of his features so his face became as cold as stone.

This time it was Kron who reached out, placing a gentle hand on the captain's shoulder. "Griffon," he said softly, using Gris's name from the Prisonlands, "we have much to discuss, but now is not the time. Let me see him, then we can speak."

For a handful of seconds the two men stared into one another's eyes, the feelings of anguish and anger shared between them. Then Gris lowered his gaze and nodded.

"As you wish," he said.

Before Kron could move away, Althurna was off her chair, rushing at him, the woman screaming as if in madness.

He saw it coming. He could have stopped her, but he did not. Her right hand slapped him across the face with a cry of wrath from her lungs, the blow a cracking explosion in the stillness of the room.

Then she stood still, one eye staring through the strands of hair hanging in her face, that one eye filled with hatred for the man in black.

Kron only stared back in return, his eyes blank. There was nothing he could do for her. There was nothing he could say, no consolation he could provide. She was right. He should have been present to protect Randall.

The old driver was suddenly there, wrapping his arms around Althurna, leading her away, mumbling soothing words to her.

Kron reached inside a purse on his belt, pulled out a few silver coins and held them out to the captain. "Gris, if you would, pay the man so he can be on his way."

Seating himself and Althurna upon the stools once more, Scratch looked up with his own brand of rage. "Nothing doing. I'm not leaving here. This child is a mess, and Tendbones, I wouldn't leave him for all the gold in the world."

Kron nodded and sheathed the coins. "My apologies. Your presence is welcome."

"It damn well better be," Scratch said, then went back to tending to Althurna as best he could.

Once more Kron looked to Gris, then he glanced at Nodana, who had made no sign of having recognized his presence. That last stabbed him in the heart more than Althurna's slap.

Turning away from them all, Kron faced the door to the inner room. He stood there a moment, staring, knowing but fearing what he would find beyond. He summoned all his courage and marched forward, reaching for the door's handle.

***

By the time they reached the squalid damp and cold of their swampy hideout, Sadhe Teth could barely walk. There was nothing wrong with his old-man's legs, but his spirit had been devastated by yet another stroke of bad luck. The healer was dead, but what did it matter if the bones were protected behind a wall of the dead. To be thwarted yet again, it was maddening, especially as Teth's powers were beyond those of mortal men. The healer had been a threat, whatever he had been, god or mortal mage, but there were no other living beings who posed a danger to Teth, at least not for the hundreds of miles he could detect. The only other possible threats were few, perhaps one of the more powerful demon lords, perhaps a dragon, if there were any still living, and a collective of dead souls working together.

The possibilities of Teth having come up against such foes in such a short span, it was unbelievable. The healer defeated, then the undead. How could this have happened?

As Curval carried him inside the shack and lay the still figure of his boss upon the wobbly table used as a bed, it came to the wizard why he had failed. He had been overconfident, and had not planned ahead for the possibility of failure. Such failure had seemed beyond believability, yet it had happened.

Shaking off his dull feelings, Teth sat up on the edge of the table, rubbing at his face to keep it warm. He promised himself he would not make the same mistakes again.

He pointed into the darkened corner where the twins had kept a fire the night before. "Warm the place, would you, Curval?"

The knight went to work with flint and steel, soon giving forth a blaze from a small pile of tinder and logs gathered the day before. Smoke floated up from the flames and out through small holes in the walls and roof, bringing a warmth to the room along with the scent of burning.

A shadow appeared in the still open doorway.

Curval glanced over a shoulder, a hand raised towards his sword.

"We're back," Jarin said with a smile of glee as he tromped into the shack, his sullen sister right behind.

The hand moved from the sword back to stoking the fire.

Jarin looked from the knight to the wizard. "Why such glum faces? And where's Kilchus?"

Rgia moved past her brother to kneel next to Curval, the woman raising her hands to the warmth of the growing flames. "Obviously they did not retrieve him."

"What?" her brother asked.

Teth snarled and stared at a side wall as if too frustrated with himself to face anyone else. "We took a detour."

The remark drew Rgia's attention. She looked over a shoulder at the mage. "Detour? What do you mean?"

"We did not go after Kilchus," Curval stated, standing, then stomping past the pair of assassins and out the door, closing it behind him before returning to his duties as guard.

Rgia now stood. Her eyes went from the closed door to her brother and then to Teth. "What did he mean?"

"He meant exactly what he said," the wizard offered.

Jarin's sister crossed the short distance to the mage, coming close enough to almost touch him as she leaned forward and glared into his face. "You told us you were going after Kilchus. What went wrong?"

His head sinking into his shoulders, Teth sulked.

"Does it matter?" Jarin said, looking happy enough to do a dance. "We took out our target, as promised."

Rgia gave him a stern look, then turned back to the mage. "What happened?"

Grimacing, Teth said, "There was something else needing accomplished before I could rescue Kilchus."

Rgia stood straight, staring down at the old man. "You never mentioned this."

"I did not think it necessary."

For a moment the woman did nothing but stare, then she backed away, resting her thumbs in the belt around her waist. "So, it's more secrets you're keeping. I should have known."

Teth snarled yet again, then twisted around on the table to face her. "There was something I had to retrieve, something that belongs to me."

Rgia rolled her eyes to the ceiling, one boot tapping the sopping floor.

"What happened?" Jarin asked.

There was hesitation from the wizard, then, "I was thwarted."

Rgia snickered, her eyes coming back down. "Thwarted? Is that what you call it, oh high wizard? First you tell us this healer must be removed because he is a threat. A healer. Not some high mage at the university or some powerful sorcerer aligned with the local government, but a healer. Then you sic us on him as if we are your personal thugs. And what do we do? We accomplish the task. Simple as that. But then we return here and find you didn't do as you told us. You didn't go off with Curval to free our one ally, the very man who can identify all of us to the local authorities. No, you went off on some side venture, some secret mission you didn't tell us about. So what was it, Falk? Oh, I'm sorry. I mean, Sadhe Teth. What was it? A magic ring? Some long lost tome of sorcery? A genie bottle? *What?*"

The wizard took her words, but he would not look her in the eye. Instead, he stared at his shoes hanging over the side of his bed.

The small room suddenly felt more warm, more confined, and tense.

"Are you going to answer me, Teth?" she asked.

His eyes flickered upward, but still would not meet her own. "Do not test me, Rgia Oltos."

"Or what, Teth?" she said. "You'll blast me into nothingness with your ancient, godlike powers? You really think you can get off a spell before I can fill your body with a half dozen stab wounds? Why don't you ask your healer about that?"

Now he lifted his eyes, looking directly into her face. "Have you already forgotten the wards of protection around me? Your mortal blades would do nothing to one such as myself?"

"Maybe not," Rgia said, glancing aside at her brother, "but one way or the other, you would find yourself without an ally, possibly two, and right now I'm thinking you need all the help you can get. So fess up and start telling the truth. Are you even who you say you are?"

Words of anger were on the mage's tongue, but he held them back. The woman was right, after all. He had been so anxious to retrieve the bones, he had not thought it necessary to mention them to his companions. His thinking had been that once he had his hands on the bones, all other things became secondary, even unnecessary, *including* his companions. But he had not retrieved the bones, and now he was in more need of allies than ever. His thoughtlessness and his hubris had been no small part in his own failure that day, and this after he had promised himself there would be no more mistakes.

His features softened. "Yes, I am Sadhe Teth, wizard and priest. And yes, I should have told you about the bones."

"Bones?" from Jarin. "As in Tendbones?"

Rgia slapped him in a shoulder. "No, idiot."

"The bones belong to a god," Teth explained. "I can draw power from them, unimaginable power."

Rgia did not appear convinced. "I thought you were already more powerful than any other mage."

Teth nodded. "Any mortal spell caster, yes, but there is always the chance of ... others."

"Others?" the woman said. "Such as the healer?"

Again the mage nodded.

"What was he, this Tendbones?" Rgia asked.

"To be truthful, I do not know," Teth said with a shrug, looking old and weak. "He was like a beacon of blazing luminescence amidst a sea of lesser lights. Of one thing I am sure. He was not one of the old gods. Of them I am familiar."

"I didn't know there was more than one god," Jarin said.

Teth stared at him. "You Ursians are so quaint. You even believe a thousand years is a long time."

"It *is* a long time," Jarin said.

"I've had longer bowel movements," the mage said.

Jarin waved aside the comment. "So, this Tendbones was a new god?"

It seemed a silly question, a stupid question, especially since it was voiced by Jarin, but there was no evidence either way.

"If a god, he bled easily enough," Rgia said to her brother.

"Again, I know not," Teth went on, ignoring the traded looks of the twins, "but he was powerful, of that I was sure."

"But he's no longer in the scene," Rgia said, a slight grin of her own.

The wizard looked up at the woman. "Yes, he is no more. I meant to tell you, good job today."

Rgia nodded her thanks, and that was all she would give him. "So, these bones. You need them. Where are they?"

Jarin jumped in before Teth could answer. "Tell him about the fight on the roof!"

"What is this?" Teth asked.

"In a minute." Rgia waved off her brother. "First, I want to know more about the bones."

"They are kept in the Asylum," the mage said. "Of that I am positive. I do not believe the locals know what they have on their hands, but they do know it has been sought by more than one sorcerer."

"So you're not the first?" Rgia said.

Teth shook his head. "There was another last year. He ... dug them up from where they had been hidden for centuries. I was to protect the bones from theft, but my physical strength was lacking. It had been a long time since I had walked the world of the living, and it took some while before I could build up my reserves."

"What happened to this other wizard?" Jarin asked.

Again Teth shrugged. "I do not know the details, but Malin's memories seemed to recall some nasty events from the past year, a mad wizard and a demon. It is unfortunate I had not the strength at the time to rise. Otherwise I would have put a stop to what occurred."

Rgia waved her brother off again. "Okay, but you said it was your job to protect the bones. Protect them from whom? And until when?"

Teth grinned. "Whom? From whomever. Until when? Until the rise of the gods once more."

***

As Kron entered the inner chamber of Randall's rooms, he averted his eyes from the figure draped in white upon the nearest cot. He turned away for a moment to close the door, all the while staring at a spot on the gray brick wall next to him. Soon enough he would have to face what lay within the room, and he was not sure how he could do so without going mad.

Randall had been more than a friend. The healer had been more than a voice of reason, had kept Kron sane during some of the darkest moments of his life. It had been Randall who had brought Adara back to them after she had been slain, executed in Kobalos. It had been Randall who stood by him against the might of Lord Verkain himself. It had been Randall, the young man's very presence, which had helped to bring Kron out of a life of rage.

Now the healer was gone, killed in a manner most awful.

Yet Randall Tendbones was more than a healer.

Kron steeled himself and turned to face the room once more. He no longer hesitated, but crossed to the shrouded body, grasping the covering by a corner and pulling it back to reveal the pale features of the man who had been his friend for several years now.

There are those who will be kind enough to say a deceased person looks as if they are sleeping. That was not the case here, nor could Kron Darkbow be fooled. The man in black had witnessed enough death to recognize it for what it was. Sallow skin, unblinking eyes, a motionless chest, no twitching or movements of the muscles.

Randall was dead.

His eyes like steel, Kron leaned over the body, staring at the still features. There had been a time when such a tragedy would have sent him off into a rage, a flight of vengeance. Randall had helped to tame such inclinations, helping to sooth the need for wrath within Darkbow's breast. Still, staring down at Randall's body, it was difficult not to froth with hate.

Perhaps it was because Randall was not like anyone else, and though no others were aware of it, there was still the possibility of hope.

Kron took to a knee, resting his gloved hands on the cot next to the corpse. "Randall."

A single word. Spoken softly.

"Randall, can you hear me?" Kron asked.

The man in black brought down his other knee, then sat back on his boots. He stared up at the ceiling, allowing his eyes to wander over the timbers there as if searching for something in the heavens beyond.

"I know you can hear me," Kron said. "Whether in body or spirit, you will know my words."

If true, there was no response.

"I have seen you look worse," Kron went on with a weak grin, his speech now little more than a whisper. "I saw you in Kobalos, remember, splayed out in your coffin, all seemingly lost. Markwood was dead, yourself gone, Adara crucified. I myself had been battered by a demon, waiting at death's door for some kind of miracle."

The only sound was the muffled noise of crying from the room beyond.

"Then that miracle came," Kron said. "It was *you*, Randall. You were our miracle. You turned the tide, saved the day. Without you, there would have been war and death. I was spent. There was nothing more I could have given, but you ..."

His words trailed off into nothingness. He lowered his head, his eyes now wet.

He lifted a gloved hand and rubbed away his tears.

"You came back to me once, Randall," Kron said. "You can do so again. I *know* you can. And not just for myself. There is too much here left for you to do. I ask you to come back not because of those who attacked you, not for any sense of vengeance within my heart. I ask you to come back because of all those you can still help, the sick and the infirm and the hurt and the lost. They need you, Randall. More than myself, they need you."

His head dipped lower, his eyes closing. A single tear burst at the corner of one lid and rolled down his face.

"I cannot do what you do, Randall," Kron said. He opened his eyes and held his hands open, staring into the leather-garbed palms. "I can only try to clean up the shambles left behind by violence." Here he sniffled. "And all too often only by adding to that violence."

He closed his eyes again, and his hands into fists. He sat there, those fists on his knees, his body rocking gently back and forth.

A thousand years seemed to pass.

Then Kron opened his eyes again. The tears were gone.

"Very well," he said, pushing himself off the ground to stand. "Perhaps it is time we mortals stood on our own."

He turned to leave, reaching for the door. Then he paused, lowering his arm and glancing back over a shoulder at the body.

"Or perhaps it is not the name Randall Tendbones I should be calling upon," he said. "Perhaps it is Kerwin Verkain. Or Ashal."

The closed eyes of the corpse stared back at him in their flatness, almost mocking.

Kron stared for a long, cold minute, then he pulled up his hood as if to ward off the chamber's chill, and turned to exit.

***

Teth smiled at the quiet that pervaded the room.

Then, "What do you mean the gods will rise once more?" Rgia asked.

The wizard couldn't help but lengthen his grin. He had Rgia hooked. Other than himself, she was the most intelligent of their group, and the most difficult to convince. Jarin was a fool, often enough following his sister but willing to lap like a dog behind anyone who would label themselves master. Curval showed signs of brightness, but rode upon a wave of melancholy nearly crippling to the knight's common sense. Even Kilchus was willing to be controlled, though he was the most shrewd of their band, that control given only at the risk of wealth and power.

No, it was Rgia Oltos who often enough provided Sadhe Teth with the strongest challenge, the most questioning.

And now he had her.

He gestured around himself, indicating the broader world. "Some are likely already out there, keeping to themselves, remaining quiet until some future time."

Rgia's eyes remained hard, though they flared with some wideness. "What of others?"

Teth shrugged. "Some are dead, their few remnants scattered across the world in one hiding hole or another."

"But you said they will rise," Rgia pointed out.

"Yes, eventually. When the time is right."

"When will that be?" Jarin asked, showing a miniscule element of intelligence.

Again the mage shrugged. "When the time is right."

Rgia grimaced and spit to one side. "That tells us nothing."

"There is nothing to tell," Teth said. "The old gods, their names are no longer worshiped, so there is no reason for them to make themselves public. Oh, memory of them lives on in some of the more backward cultures, but their aspects and names have been long forgotten. Worship of this Ashal creature has all but drowned out the old tales. The gods will rise again when there is a need for them, and not before."

Rgia hesitated, a question on her lips, then, "What kind of thing could draw them forth?"

"To be honest, I am not completely sure," Teth said with yet another shrug. "Perhaps the ascent of some ancient enemy, or maybe some power they deem dangerous to themselves. What the gods do and think is beyond mortal man, even myself."

554

The sister glanced at the brother, the two sharing apprehensive looks.

Seeing the others mum for the moment, Sadhe Teth went on. "This is one of the reasons I seek the bones. Their power is protection against the gods, and the gods and I are not on the best of terms."

"But couldn't the god within the bones rise up?" Rgia asked.

Now Teth nodded. The woman was smarter than even he had suspected. "It's possible, but not likely as long as I have the bones. I can draw power from them, weakening the god and his chances of returning."

"To which god do the bones belong?" Rgia asked.

"As if it will do you any good, but his name is Torkoss," the mage said. "He was an old enemy to my own god, the great Onbx."

"And where is your Onbx?" the woman asked.

Teth visibly gulped, his eyes lowering to the wet floor of their dank chamber. He did not wish to answer the question.

"Something else you hide from us?" Rgia asked.

Teth's eyes snapped up, fueled by anger. "Onbx was eaten alive."

"By whom? she asked.

"By Torkoss," Teth said, the words uttered with hate.

Here it was the woman assassin who smiled. "So you want the bones out of a sense of revenge."

"There is some of that," Teth admitted, "but there is also the factor that the bones contain the essence of two gods, Torkoss having ingested my old master. While the spirit of Torkoss is the most prominent within the bones, there are still elements of Onbx to be found there, making the bones doubly powerful for someone who can draw upon their strength."

"Someone like yourself."

"Yes. Exactly."

"So you want these bones in order to become more powerful," Rgia said, "just in case the gods decide to return. Am I understanding you correctly?"

"There is that," Teth said, "but I freely admit I am drawn to the dynamism of the bones. We could live like gods ourselves. Once I have the bones, that is."

Rgia kept smiling. "So this is why we should remain with you, to share in this power?"

"I do not see why not," the mage said. "What animosity could I hold toward you or your brother, or toward Curval and Kilchus? I am quite powerful already, so --"

She cut him off. "Yes, you keep telling us how powerful you are, Teth, but so far I've seen little evidence of it. You have shown evidence you are a mage, but your spells have been those any trained caster could perform. In fact, it seems to me you are constantly running into powers that thwart your own, so I have to question your claim to strength beyond that of mortals."

Teth wanted to snarl, to scream, to rage, but he held all this in check. The woman was right, after all, but he needed her and the others, at least for now. Yet it was necessary he provide an answer for her, an answer at least good enough to keep her tied to him.

"I have been conservative in my show of might," he said, "but that was before you and your brother did an excellent job in ridding me of Tendbones. Since then I have had little need to call upon higher powers."

"What about the Asylum?" Rgia asked. "Why didn't you use some of these 'higher powers' there?"

Teth saw no reason to lie. "The place is guarded by spirits of the dead, and magic has little influence upon them. Again, there was no need for a display of strength, as it would have been futile."

"So the bones you need are beyond your grasp?" the woman asked.

Again, Teth wanted to scream with fury, but once more he checked himself. "There are other ways."

"Such as?"

"We need Kilchus," Jarin suddenly said.

His sister and the wizard shot him a look. Who would have thought Jarin would have hit upon an idea?

Not dismayed by the shocked glances, Rgia's brother went ahead with his thoughts. "He was stationed at the Asylum, so he knows the place, at least to some extent. I bet he could help us get in there."

Teth had to admit, "He makes sense."

Rgia nodded. "Yes, but I've still yet to hear a good reason why we should remain working with you, Teth."

Throwing his hands up in disgust, the mage dropped down from the table and paced from one end of the small chamber and back again. "What else do you need from me, Rgia? I'm promising you power and wealth befitting of royalty, yet you want some kind of assurances. How can I assure you of anything? Is there an element of risk, of danger? Of course there is! There *always* is, but the healer being out of the scene improves our chances a thousandfold."

He stopped his pacing and turned to face her directly. "The two of you with your line of work, anywhere you go, anything you do, there will be a chance of danger, Rgia, for you and your brother. Is what I offer so bad?"

Her eyes narrowed. "Perhaps I don't like the idea of serving another, especially someone who seems more interested in their own goals than that of their comrades."

"Did Falk offer you anything better?" Teth shot back.

"Falk was not the danger you appear to be," Rgia replied.

"Maybe, but the spoils are potentially much higher."

Sadhe Teth had a point. Rgia could not tell when he was or was not telling the truth, but on the face of it, what he offered was tempting, power and wealth nearly unimaginable. Gold and sway, they were two of the oldest temptations..

The wizard sighed, frustrated but tired in his old body. "Rgia, if you have a better opportunity, something more promising, then by all means seek it out, but if not, what is wrong with what I am proposing?"

She gritted her teeth. "I don't *trust* you, Teth."

He tittered. "You, the assassin, does not trust *me*? Have you ever worked with someone you trusted fully?"

He had another good point, though Rgia could have offered that she trusted her brother to be an idiot. Not a bumbling idiot, for sure, but still an idiot. However, all in all she could not shake her distrust of the ancient wizard.

Ancient. Yes, thousands of years old apparently.

The thought gave her pause.

"All right, Teth," she said. "I will promise my services to you if you can tell me one thing?"

"Which is?"

"You say it was your duty to protect the bones from these old gods," Rgia said, "but you also claim the bones can give you unimaginable power."

"Yes."

"Then tell me, old wise one, why you waited thousands of years to make use of the bones."

For a moment it seemed Sadhe Teth had been flummoxed. He took a step back as if surprised by the question.

Then he grinned. "I told you, I only rose after the bones were stolen and I had had time to restore my strength."

"True enough," Rgia said, "but that does not explain why you did not use the bones at an earlier time. Why did you have to wait for them to be stolen?"

"I didn't," Teth admitted. "I could have risen at any point, at least after an interval of building my fortitude."

"Then why didn't you?"

"Because there was no need," the mage said. "The gods have kept themselves hidden for thousands of years, and as long as they were not intruding upon the destinies of men, there was little I could do against them since I could not so easily find them."

"But what of this ultimate power you seek?" Rgia asked. "Could you not have risen and claimed it then?"

"Of course," Teth said, "but that would have drawn the gods's attention."

"Which was something you did not wish to do."

"Obviously not. Powerful I might be, but I still would not have wanted to face the full wrath of all the gods at once, which they would have done if I had tried to seize some of their power for myself."

"Then what is different now?" Rgia said. "Why risk the chance that they will appear and come against you?"

"Because there was no other choice," Teth said. "The bones were stolen, waking me as their protector. Now I must recover the bones, and use their might in case the gods should target me."

The woman still did not appear pleased with his answer. "Why not just go back to your sleep? Why use the power of the bones if they will draw the attention of these old gods?"

Jarin thrust himself forward again, this time between his sister and the mage. "Haven't we talked enough? Isn't it time we did something about Kilchus?"

"No, no." Sadhe Teth moved around the assassin to face the woman. "Your sister has raised a good question, and I will give her answer."

"Then what is it?" Rgia asked.

The wizard grinned again, this time showing teeth appearing sharp in the room's faint light. He would not tell the truth, that the gods had likely already noticed his presence, but he would still give answer. "Because I have you lot with me now," he said, "and with such allies at my side, I see little reason to return to my eternal slumber. Now I can make my stand, and with the bones and with you at my side, no god can stand against us."

Rgia almost voiced another question, but Jarin held up a hand. "Can we go after Kilchus now?"

For a moment the female assassin looked to her brother, then over to Teth. She *still* did not trust this wizard. Everything he said could be a lie, and she had only his word that any of it was truth.

"Come on, Rgia," Jarin said. "What else are we going to do? Run back to Provenzano?"

That was out of the question. Returning would have been suicide, at least without powerful colleagues. But maybe, if Teth was telling the truth, there would be an opportunity for her and her brother to go back to Provenzano to spread a little vengeance.

If Teth was telling the truth.

Rgia had to admit, that was a very large if.

But she had few other options, other than running and hiding somewhere else, only waiting to be caught by someone, somewhere.

"Very well," she finally said, her eyes lowered. "We will work with you, Sadhe Teth, but know this, if you succeed in all you want, there will come a time when I will have stipulations."

Teth couldn't have smiled any broader. "Obviously. I would expect as much."

"Great," Jarin said. "Now can we go after Kilchus?"

The mage held up a hand. "Soon, my friends. But first, tell me about this rooftop combat mentioned earlier. Then we can help our good comrade Kilchus the Sword, and he will be able to help us in gaining the bones."

***

A new face had joined those mourning in Randall's office. As Kron came out of the back room, he found himself nearly face to face with master storyteller Midge Highwater. The grizzled old man with the floppy, wide-brimmed hat held out a sword sheathed in black leather connected to a black belt.

"I found this in the alley where it happened," the old man said, tears in his eyes. "I thought you'd want it back."

Kron gave a single nod and retrieved the belt, buckling it and the weapon around his hips. "Many thanks."

"I take it it's true," Midge said.

Looking around at the sad faces in the room, there could be little doubt. Captain Gris perched on the edge of the healer's desk in front of a seated Nodana, the mage sitting back in Randall's desk chair and looking stunned. Althurna was curled up nearly into a ball atop a chair that seemed barely large enough and stable enough to hold her, a disheveled Scratch still seated next to her, though instead of an arm around the mourning woman, he was rubbing at his face, showing his own anguish and tiredness.

"Yes, it is true," Kron said.

The entrance door opened and Montolio came into the room. He paused for a moment, looking from face to face, then his own features dropped as he closed the door.

"I heard," he said, "but I didn't believe until now."

"Believe it," Kron said.

No one else so much as moved, all of them staring straight ahead except for Althurna with her face hidden within her arms.

Montolio went pale, his jaw slackening. "Do we ... do we know what happened?"

Scratch stood. "I saw it myself. There were two of them. One came from an alley, another from the roof."

Montolio glanced at Kron, wondering about the veracity of the old man speaking to him. The man in black nodded, showing Scratch's words could be trusted.

"Why would anyone want to harm Randall?" Montolio asked.

Before anyone could answer, Althurna let out a shriek and began sobbing. Her curled-up figure shuddered and nearly tumbled from its seat. Seeing this, Nodana stood and moved around the desk to the forlorn figure, kneeling next to her and whispering words meant to be soothing.

Gris gestured towards the exit. "Perhaps we should discuss this elsewhere."

Scratch moved back to Althurna, placing a hand upon Nodana's shoulder. As the mage looked up, he said, "I'll look after her, miss, if you want."

Nodana forced a weak smile beneath her wet eyes. "Thank you." Then she stood and moved back to the desk with the others.

Soon enough Gris and Kron left the room with Montolio, Nodana and Midge Highwater filing in behind. The hallway that curved around Randall's room proved to be packed full, mourners jammed in together, all waiting for word of Randall's fate. As soon as the faces of those exiting the room were seen, a keening rose among the crowd, spreading along the length of the hall and throughout the healing tower, eventually to the outside.

Gris motioned for the others to follow, and they worked their way through the jostling crowd, finally finding an empty room to serve their purposes. Upon entering, they found it was a tight fit for the lot of them, the small chamber apparently a storage room for linens and the like, little more than a closet. Still there were plenty of shelves high and low, enough of them empty to provide places to lean against, and despite the lack of room, no one balked at Midge's presence, the storyteller being a font of knowledge.

"All right," the captain began, looking to Kron. "Tell me what happened."

"Nodana and I had leased horses and were on our way to the barracks to see you," Darkbow said to the captain. "Randall had dropped in at the Asylum earlier, and apparently was on his way to you, also. He left ahead of us, but we caught up to him just as the attack happened."

"Do you know why he was coming to see me?" Gris asked.

Kron paused for a moment, recalling a recent past that seemed a million years ago, then, "He said nothing definite, just that he had meant to check in with me this morning but then something had happened which made him believe he should see you as well. He didn't give any specifics about what had happened, but he seemed to have experienced another revelation about this mysterious powerful magic he had been sensing."

"Had he tied it in with Falk?" the captain asked.

Kron shook his head.

Montolio held up a hand. "Hold on a second. That's actually why I came looking for Lieutenant Darkbow and Captain Gris in the first place."

"What's that?" Gris asked.

"Lord Falk," the dark-headed mage said. "I believe he was at the Asylum earlier."

"When?" Kron asked, his eyes more alert than ever.

"Maybe an hour ago," Montolio said. "I didn't know him, but one of the corporals said the two men fit the descriptions of some of those at the fight at the Pony."

"Two men?" Nodana asked.

Montolio looked to her. "There was a big man in a cloak, with an even bigger sword on his back. He was bulky, like he was wearing at least partial armor underneath his cloak."

"Sounds like one of those we've been seeking," Gris admitted with a nod.

"There's more to it than that," Montolio said, his words speeding up. "The ghosts, they spoke to me."

Kron's feature showed confusion. "The ghosts?"

"They gave a warning," Montolio said. "I was in the basement with the others, showing them the alchemical lab, when the ghosts spoke. The recruits didn't seem to hear it, but I definitely did. The ghosts said something about someone approaching, then I heard moaning sounds like that of a heavy wind. It sounded strongest upstairs, so we went up to investigate, and found the noise coming mainly from the front door. When I opened it, I saw this old man and his bulky companion walking away from the Asylum as if they had just been there knocking."

"Did you try to go after them?" Gris asked.

"They vanished into the crowd," Montolio said with a sorrowful shrug.

Midge had kept quiet until then. Now the old storyteller sat up straight from his perch against a shelf. "They tried to get in the place but the dead repulsed them," he said.

Kron looked to the old man. "What makes you say that?"

Midge looked to Nodana and Montolio. "One of you tell him."

"The spirits are immune to magic," Nodana said.

Kron appeared more confused. "I thought magic fed off the power of souls."

"It does," Nodana went on, "but only of the living. A spirit freed of the body is practically invulnerable to magic."

Montolio nodded his agreement.

"That's why they were leaving," Midge said. "Falk and this other fellow, they'd tried to get in. Probably found the door locked, and the ghosts wouldn't allow them entrance. Only thing that makes sense."

"But why would they come to the Asylum?" Gris asked.

"The bones," Montolio said, his eyes lighting.

Kron nodded. "That makes the most sense."

"Unless maybe they were there to free Kilchus," Gris said. "Possibly they thought their friend was still being held inside."

"Maybe," Kron said, "but I don't think so."

The captain shot him a curious look. "Why not?"

The man in black hesitated for a moment as if trying to make sense of a puzzle. Eventually, "I can't understand it all, but things are starting to come together, at least a little. They had to realize Kilchus had been moved. Falk and his band, they've been watching us the whole time, or at least they've been watching Randall and perhaps the Asylum."

"Randall?" Gris asked.

"There were two attackers," Kron said. "I chased them after Randall was ... after he was wounded. There were two of them, definitely. I only saw one close up, but they looked roughly the same size, shape, even coloring. This lends me to believe they are these twins Kilchus told us about."

"Possibly," Gris said.

Kron continued. "That combined with Falk and his bodyguard showing up at the Asylum, it makes me think it's all connected somehow. Though I don't know why they would want to harm Randall. For that matter, I'm not sure why they need these bones, or how they were connected to that student who stole the bones."

"Most likely he was planning to sell them to Falk," Nodana added, "and he paid for it with his life."

"But if Falk wanted the bones, why did he leave them at the scene?" Gris asked. "Doesn't make sense."

"For that matter," Midge said, "Falk was never known to be a spell caster."

The rest of the group looked to the old man.

"Well, it's true," the storyteller said.

Gris rocked back on the heels of his boots and ran a hand through his thinning brown hair. "There's just so much we don't know."

"That's true," Montolio said. "Unless we can catch Falk, I'm not sure we'll ever learn the truth."

"I won't accept that," Kron said. "We have to find whomever did this to Randall."

Gris suddenly snapped down on the toes of his boots, the sound echoing throughout the small room. "There is someone who might have some answers, someone who seems to have been holding out on us."

"Kilchus," Kron said.

The captain nodded.

"Let's go." Kron turned to the exit.

***

"Curval!"

The knight slopped around in the mud until he faced up the low hill to the shack.

Teth stood in the open doorway, motioning for the big man to join him. "Come."

Curval grunted and plodded his way up to the building. Once inside he found the wizard standing between the two assassins, the old man's arms outstretched between them, the brother holding the right hand and the sister the left.

"It is time we brought our friend Kilchus back to us," Sadhe Teth said to the knight, "and since Rgia here seems rather unconvinced of my powers, I believe it is time for a demonstration.

"Come, Curval, grab one of my arms and let us be on our way."

The knight did not move for a moment, seemingly unsure of what to do, but then he shrugged and stomped forward, laying a hand upon the wizard's right shoulder.

"Good boy," Teth said.

And they vanished.

21

The bed was a slab of gnarly wood as hard as stone, layered across its surface a thin sea of rotting hay littered with tiny black bugs that had a tendency at night to come alive and bite. The floor was made of bricks the color of blood and as cold as winter. There were two buckets, one for pissing in and one for shitting in. A dented pewter plate and a dull wooden spoon served for eating. There was no table, no chair, no other piece of furniture than the bed, its iron legs bolted to the floor. The door was solid steel, several inches thick, with a small window that could be opened only from the outside, which it rarely was. The meals were served through a small slit in the door next to the floor, and only if the prisoner remembered to slide his plate near that opening; if he forgot, whomever was serving would move on past to the next cell.

At least there was a window. It contained four thick iron bars and a man had to stand on his toes to look outside, but the view wasn't so bad, the South River beyond twinkling even beneath gray of the day. Every so often a boat or barge would swing past, a bird would flap by, or even some solitary figure would stroll along the river's shore as if in search of something.

The bad part about the window was the weather. It being winter, the chill rolled right through the room, invading it. There were no blankets, no rugs, no wall hangings to cover the bricks. The cold soaked through everything like a sponge storing the chill for a warm day.

There was little sound, the chamber being on the second floor and blocked from a view of the street directly below by a row of storage sheds, though every once in a while there would come the thumpings of boots outside the door. The scent was another story, a mixture of rotting food and the stench of human filth.

This was the current home of Kilchus the Sword, and all he had to keep him warm was a short, threadbare tunic containing more than a few tears, and a thin pair of sandals made of rough rope.

And hate. He had plenty of that to warm his belly and his heart. It was all he had left, for there was no longer such a thing as hope. Kilchus had no illusions about his future. His jail cell was but a temporary abode, a wayward home until some magistrate found the time to decide his sentence, for there would be no doubt about his guilt.

As for sentencing, again, there was no hope. No magistrate would give Kilchus a simple flogging, nor time in a stockade, two common sentences for criminals in Bond. No, the Sword was bound for the Prisonlands, of that he was sure. Though Kilchus had not been directly involved, the outrages committed at The Stone Pony would warrant such a fate, at least in the eyes of the law, and no magistrate could eschew from sending a former warden to the Prisonlands.

The Prisonlands. Kilchus figured his chances there were minimal. He might last a few days if lucky. The exiles would tear him apart, and the wardens would not come to the Sword's aid. The wardens *never* came to a prisoner's aid as it was against treaty law, and more than a few of them would likely have a good chuckle at one of their own being thrust into the Lands.

Hunkered on the edge of his dank, stinking bed, Kilchus cursed his fate. He should have never helped Falk and the others escape the Lands. He should have done his duty and turned them in as soon as he had found them. Yet Falk's promises, as flimsy as they had been, had also seemed worth the trouble at the time. Then months on end in Caballerus, barely escaping the mess that was there.

Kilchus sighed. He couldn't believe it was all going to end for him this way. Yet he could not find hope anywhere.

Sitting there in the stench, absorbed in his dark thoughts, he barely registered the loud cracking noise from outside. But register it he did. He stood, thinking maybe he had heard thunder or perhaps there was something actually of interest worth seeing, and crossed the short distance to the barred window.

Before he could take a look the floor jumped beneath his feet, knocking him hard against a wall and sending his food tray skittering across the room. Sliding down the cold bricks, Kilchus flailed out for something, anything to grab hold of. His hand came in touch with a bucket. Not thinking, he applied pressure, hoping to keep himself on his feet.

There was a clatter and a splash and warm liquid crept across his boots. Then the floor jumped again, this time the whole room jarring him up and down, and Kilchus the Sword dropped onto his knees with a sloshing sound.

Crying out at the pain in his legs, he swayed on his knees for a moment. Then he dropped flat onto his back in a wet mess smelling of urine.

"Ashal damn all!" he shouted.

Laying there stunned in disgust, the echo of his voice soon filtered away from his ears, allowing him to pick out more noises outside. There were shouts, screams of agony, and then Kilchus's nose twitched.

"Is that smoke?" he asked himself.

Yes, that was definitely smoke. Something was burning. He could just hear the flickering of distant flames, and these weren't the mild crackles of torches or camp fires. Something was engulfed, the noise of the burning growing louder and louder.

While Kilchus was locked inside his cell.

He spun over, his hands sliding through his own liquid waste, and forced himself up on his feet. "Hey!" he shouted. "In here! Somebody!"

The floor jumped yet again, spilling him once more, his jaw striking the hard surface with a cracking din, a tooth sent flying from his mouth.

Laying there dazed, there was little he could do as the shaking continued this time. No longer was there a single massive quaking, but a consistent seizure of tremors that bounced the floor beneath him.

A crashing sound fractured the air like an explosion and the outer wall of the jail cell bowed in for a moment before crumbling apart, bricks raining across the floor, more of them tumbling down to the ground outside.

Coming to his senses, Kilchus rolled away as bricks clattered around him, finally stopping with his back against the cell's door, his legs splayed out in the cold wet.

When the bricks finished tumbling and his vision stopped shaking, he could make out weak daylight through the screen of mottled dust that had until recent been the outside wall to his jail.

Freedom.

If he could make it.

Splashing around in his urine, Kilchus eventually found his footing and nearly stumbled toward the new exit. The scent of burning grew stronger and now he could better hear the crackle of flames.

At the edge of the massive hole in the wall, he looked out at the river for a moment and saw several boats had pulled to shore, those aboard standing and watching whatever was happening at the jail.

"Kilchus! Down here!" a voice yelled.

Shifting his sight from the riverbank, the Sword glanced down below his feet to the grassy sward between the back of the building and the row of sheds. For a moment the dust flouted itself around his face and Kilchus was unsure of what he saw, but then he could make out the figures of Jarin and Curval, the young assassin standing with arms stretching up as if reaching for the sky, the knight motionless with his arms wrapped around one another.

"Jump!" Jarin shouted. "We'll catch you!"

Kilchus didn't think so. He might have felt a little better about it if the offer had come from the sizable Caballeran, but Curval showed no interest of providing aid.

Then again, Kilchus was only on the second floor. It wasn't that far to fall.

"Hold on," he said, dropping to his knees and turning around to face the remains of his cell.

For the first time he could hear movement on the other side of his room's door. There was someone out there, multiple someones, all hustling and bustling.

Kilchus wasted no time brushing aside fallen bricks and scooting back to the very edge of the chamber's floor which now provided a berm over Jarin and Curval below him.

A clanking sound came to his ears, the lock being turned in his door.

Holding onto the ledge, Kilchus allowed his legs to hang outside his room. Now all that was within the chamber were his head and chest and his arms up to the elbows. He hung there for a moment, perched on his elbows.

The room's door slammed open, cracking against the wall behind it.

A guard stood there with a key in one hand, a short sword in the other, surprise clear on his face. "Stop!"

"I don't think so," Kilchus said, then dropped.

***

The initial quaking could be felt as far away as Frist Bridge, churning the ground and sending pedestrians stumbling into one another, some few falling to their hands and knees. Even on horseback, the three riders could feel the quivering sensations, their animals snorting in confusion.

Captain Gris yanked on his reins to control his steed and looked to his companions abreast of him. Kron was doing the same, keeping his animal under control, while Nodana was leaning forward in her saddle and whispering to her beast to good effect.

Then Nodana's head snapped up and she stood in her stirrups, one hand pointing. "Smoke!"

She did not lie. A black ink belched forth from somewhere ahead of them and to the right.

"The barracks," Kron said, glancing to the captain.

Gris spurred his animal and shouted for those on the street to move out of his way. No one argued with the city guard officer as he rode through, observers on all sides jumping to safety, Kron and Nodana following in his wake.

The riders' path took them south at first, then the road shifted gradually to face the west. A side road of packed earth presented itself on their left and Gris took it, charging around befuddled onlookers. Again Kron and Nodana kept pace with the captain in the lead, the steady humming of their horse's hooves shielding them from sensing the worst of further ground shakings. All the while, the roiling column of dark smoke grew in their sight.

The barracks came into view, and the image caused Gris to falter for a moment, the rider tugging on the reins once more as he took in everything before him.

A rent large enough to drive a wagon through had been torn from the outside wall on the second floor facing the road and the river beyond. Flames towered above and behind the main structure, the source of all that smoke somewhere within. The front doors to the building had been thrown open, city guards in their leather armor and orange tabards spilling out onto the surrounding yard, some few of them still wearing their night dresses and underwear, those last men unfortunate enough to have been sleeping during the tumult.

The scene was one of pandemonium. No one was taking charge.

"Sergeant!" Gris shouted to a familiar figure.

A big, burly woman in orange with a round steel helmet on her head turned to face the officer. Soot streaked one side of her face and she appeared in shock, but upon recognizing who she faced, her boots snapped together and she gave off a salute.

"Sergeant Nickel at your service, sir!" she hammered out.

The captain pointed to the north past a row of houses and to the river beyond. "Get a bucket brigade going this minute, sergeant!"

"Yes, sir!" and the woman rushed off, grabbing a few other guards along the way.

Kron and Nodana pulled up next to the captain as Gris stood in his stirrups and stared from one end of the scene to the other. It looked like a battle zone, as if the large building had been struck by siege weaponry, even some of the storage sheds near the road having been flattened or knocked aside by crumbling brick

"What makes me think this is related to Falk?" Kron asked.

Gris pointed to the giant hole in the wall. "That was Kilchus's cell. I can only assume the man is either dead or escaped."

Steering her ride past the two man, Nodana glanced aside at them. "That fire isn't natural. I'm sensing powerful magic was used here."

"Can you do anything about it before the whole damn building burns down?" Gris asked.

"I'll try," Nodana said, then she slapped her horse's side and rode off in the direction of the flames, passing through stunned guards and some few civilian gawkers.

Kron went to follow after her, but a hand on his elbow from the captain held him in place.

"I'll go with her," Gris said, nodding at the fleeing mage boss. "I want to see the damage firsthand. I need you over there at that hole in the wall. If Kilchus escaped, I know you'll be able to track him."

Kron nodded, then rode fast toward the damaged wall, putting aside his concern for Nodana and his concern for Gris. There were others to consider, his friends relatively safe for the moment.

Pulling up to one side of the large opening, Kron dropped from the saddle and let his horse go. Looking up, he saw no sign of the prisoner within the shadows of the cell, but that didn't necessarily mean anything. Kilchus could be up there unconscious or dead, or simply hiding in fear.

Sidestepping fallen masonry and moving cautiously toward the building, Kron crouched, studying the ground.

There. Prints in the soil. Facing the wall.

The day was cold, but not nearly as cold as recent. The temperature had warmed some, enough for the dirt to show the prints of a heavy figure or someone who had fallen a distance.

Kilchus had jumped from above.

Spinning around, Kron's eyes sought other tracks. The area of dirt was small, soon giving away to grass, but he could still make out that there had been others present not so long ago. The grass was flattened in areas, showing a short path a couple of walkers had followed from around the storage shed.

With grass it was difficult to tell exactly how many people had been on the scene, but Kron could guess two or three. Or perhaps two *and* three? Had their been a pair waiting for Kilchus, then when he dropped the lot of them rushing away?

Quite possible.

Kron stood taller, his eyes still on the ground as he followed what seemed a possible trail away from the scene, more flattened vegetation providing clues.

He came up near the road and stopped. The trail ended abruptly. He glanced around. Another trail showed there had been others coming from different directions, as many as two, perhaps even more. All had converged upon this one spot next to the road. Then all had disappeared.

Looking to the road, Kron saw no signs of recent wagon tracks, not even marks of hooves in the chilled mud.

So, the group hadn't ridden away.

That left magic.

The man in black snarled and turned to look for his horse.

***

A raucous detonation boomed across the swampy landscape as the group of five emerged from nothingness onto the dank hillside leading up to the age-worn shack. Sister and brother swayed slightly but managed to catch themselves against one another. Kilchus stumbled before dropping on his knees into the mud, his thin breakfast spewing from his lips to darken the already sopping ground. Sadhe Teth watched all this with a demon's grin. Curval appeared unfazed, the knight glancing at the others for a moment before stomping his way back down the hill to take up his guard duty once more, his boots sinking beneath the surface of brackish water as he turned his back on his comrades and the shack, his focus upon the dead trees, frozen plants and murky scene stretching into a dull grayness at the edge of his sight.

"Teth, I suggest we not travel in such a manner again," Rgia said, pushing away from her brother.

Kilchus spat and wiped at his mouth with a sleeve, then sat back in the mud. "Teth? Who the hell is Teth?"

"Much has changed since last we met," the mage said to the Sword.

Wiping his lips once more, Kilchus sneered and jumped to his feet. "Damn straight some things have changed, Falk, and I expect some answers! First of all, when the hell did you become a mage?"

An amused look lingered on the wizard's face, then he turned away from the Sword as if dismissing the man. He pointed toward the entrance to the shack. "Jarin, if you would be so kind, the damp has probably burned out our fire by now."

The assassin entered the low building without a word.

Teth gestured toward the shack. "It is not much, but it is better than standing out in the cold."

Appearing dumbstruck, Kilchus stared at the leaning building and the holes in its walls of aged wood. "This is where you've been staying?"

Rgia let out a chuckle then followed her brother indoors.

"The Pony wasn't much, but by Ashal, it was better than *this*," Kilchus said.

"We shall find ourselves more suitable accommodations soon enough," Teth said, pointing to the door again. "Please, let us talk inside."

Kilchus hesitated, not liking the look of the place, but what other option did he have. Glancing around, there was nothing but bleakness and damp in every direction, Curval's cloaked back and the sword hanging there the only other signs of any kind of civilized world.

The Sword grimaced. "You owe me, Falk." Then he thrust his way inside the shack.

Teth merely grinned wider and followed.

***

It was hours before the blaze was brought under control. Multiple lines of city guards stretched from the remains of their barracks across the road, past houses there and to the river more than a hundred yards away, buckets empty or full of water passing back and forth all the while. Nodana provided much needed aid with her magic, causing river water to shoot up high in spouts that rained down upon the flames, but the effort tired her tremendously and she was nearly wiped out by the time Montolio managed to appear, his magic not as strong as her own but adding to the scene in ways most helpful by filling buckets with water again and again without having to be passed all the way back to the river.

Throughout it all, Captain Gris commanded the scene from horseback, riding here and there, giving orders like some mounted general on the front lines of a battle. He always seemed to know the exact place to be at the right time, directing buckets of water to most needed areas, providing words to boost the morale of his men and women, and more than once himself tossing a bucketful of water onto dancing flames.

Kron remained on the outside of the scene, the lieutenant helping to steer bucketeers in the right direction and to deal with various messages and notes from city officials and guild leaders, messages the captain did not have time to read let alone respond to, though more than a few were offers of aid.

By the time the flames were diminished to glowing coals, the southern wall of the barracks building was almost gone and the inside of the large structure had been gutted but for a few of the stronger, heavier support beams.

With the eye of an experienced architect, Montolio saw something of a silver lining in the destruction. "At least the walls still standing appear structurally sound," he informed Captain Gris.

Everyone mounted removed themselves from their saddles, their legs and rears sore from the long hours on horseback, the animals themselves needing rest. A few corporals came forward to retrieve the horses and to find the poor beasts food and water, as well as to provide a good rub down.

"Make sure to get yourself something warm to eat," Gris told the corporals as they moved away with the animals.

All around, city guards and those civilians who had come to help were collapsing from the strain of their efforts. It had been a long day, and several hundred people littered the nearby road and the surrounding grounds, most forming off into small groups in the middle of which were fires being built for cooking and warming drink. At least the day had not been overly cold.

"This is a disaster," Gris said with a grimace as the other officers and Nodana gathered around him near the dirt road.

"No one was killed," Kron pointed out.

The captain did not look as if he believed. "No one is unaccounted for?"

"There were three men missing earlier," Montolio said, then added a grin. "Turns out they were pulling duty in the ... uh, well, the Rusty Scabbard."

Even Gris's stony face showed a hint of a smile. "Remind me to give them latrine duty for a week. What about prisoners?"

"The sergeants tell me there were only a few and all of them got out unharmed," Montolio said.

Then the captain turned his gaze upon the remaining walls of the barracks. It was still a large building, two stories in height and the longest structure in Bond. The place had housed hundreds, mostly city guards but some few prisoners. It had been more than a sleeping spot for many, but a home for those guards who had no other home, a place of respite and order within the chaos of a bustling city.

"Kron, did any of those messages happen to be from the army?" Gris said.

The man in black nodded. "General Hagen asked if we needed aid. He is encamped about twenty miles north with several training units."

"Did you respond?"

"Not yet," Kron said. "His note only came recently, and I saw little need to draw him in at this point."

"Have a sergeant send him a reply," Gris ordered. "We're going to need housing immediately. Many of my people can probably find temporary shelter for the night, but that won't last. As soon as Hagen and his men can decamp and march here, the better. We're going to need tents, probably for weeks, maybe months. After I've caught my breath and things seem settled here, I'll go see the mayor, see what we can do about a new barracks."

Kron moved away to pass the message along.

"We might not have to start from scratch on the construction," Montolio said. "If clean-up crews get to work in the next few days, construction might begin in a week or so."

The captain turned to the young, dark-headed mage. "I'd almost forgotten. The city has not only a wizard on its payroll, but an experienced architect as well. Probably have to give you a raise after all this is done, maybe a boost in rank, too."

Montolio beamed.

"When the time comes, perhaps I can round up some street mages to lend a hand," Nodana offered. "It would have to be easier with the heavy moving than depending upon cranes and the like."

"Good thinking," Gris said with a nod.

As Kron returned to the group, the captain turned to him. "I don't suppose you have anything to tell about Kilchus?"

"He definitely had help escaping," Kron said, looking to Nodana, "and I think Frex was right. Some heavy magic was involved here."

"What makes you say that?" Gris asked.

"Kilchus and his group, they vanished without a trace," Kron explained. "After he jumped down from his cell, he and the others moved to the road, but their tracks end there. No sign of a horse or carriage, either. The tracks just finish."

"Sounds like instant transportation magic," Nodana added.

"Any idea who his mates could've been?" the captain asked.

"Nothing for sure," Kron said. "I asked around, but none of the guards claimed to have seen anyone. I questioned one man who witnessed Kilchus escaping, but the fire kept the fellow from pursuing, and he didn't see anyone with the Sword. Still, I'm tending to think Falk was involved. It's starting to make an odd kind of sense. They attacked Randall because they saw him as a threat, then they tried for the bones at the Asylum. Failing there, they came here for Kilchus."

Gris rubbed his jaw. "I can't argue with your reasoning, but why Randall? I mean, if they wanted to target a powerful mage, why not someone at the university, or even Nodana here? Which raises another question. *Who* is there wizard? It's my understanding Falk has no magic."

Kron shrugged. "I can't answer any of your questions." Which was not totally true. Kron could very well guess why Randall had been targeted, because Randall had been seen as the most powerful magical threat in the city, perhaps even within the country as a whole or possibly the entire continent.

"So how do we find them?" the captain asked.

"I'll have to give it some thought," Kron answered.

"I could try looking for their wizard, like Randall had been doing," Nodana said. "If it's someone working with Falk, then I could pinpoint them."

"That could work," Montolio said.

"I thought Randall hadn't been having any luck in his search," Gris said.

"Something changed there ... there toward the end," Nodana said with anguish. "Something had happened. I wish I'd asked him some questions."

"What about utilizing the Asylum and the special squad?" Gris asked.

"I admit this would be a job for them," Kron said, "but they are nowhere near ready, if that's what you're asking. They've just begun their training."

"Is it safe to keep them at the Asylum?" Gris asked.

"I don't see any reason not to," Kron said. "Falk or whomever might make another try for the bones, but you would have to have guards on duty there anyway."

"Those damn bones," Gris said. "I wish we had just dumped them in a damn river."

"I can't argue with that," Kron said.

"Okay." Gris planted his fists on his hips and looked around at the scene, the comings and goings of dozens in uniform and no few civilians. The community was coming together in the wake of another tragedy. "Nodana, you and Montolio get to looking for this powerful wizard or whatever it is while Kron and I are rounding things out here. We'll likely be busy throughout the night, but don't hesitate to let us know if you find something."

"We will," Nodana said, Montolio nodding at her side.

Then the captain looked to his lieutenant. "Come on. Let's get started. We can rest when we're in our graves."

***

Eventually Jarin went out to scrounge for food and drink, leaving the others to themselves. Except for Curval. Who stayed on guard duty at the bottom of the hill. As always.

The hours of talk back and forth, all sides telling what they had been doing, some of it truth and some of it lies, had not much quelled the rage that brewed just beneath the surface of Kilchus the Sword.

"Let me get this straight," he said, pointing at Sadhe Teth sitting on the table. "You're not Falk."

The wizard grinned. "That's right."

Kilchus looked to Rgia, the assassin squatting by the fire to feed it more kindling. "And you understand this?" he asked her. "You're all right with it?"

"I don't fully trust him, if that's what you mean," the woman said, standing to face the others, Kilchus leaning against the wall near the exit, "but as he has pointed out on more than one occasion, what choice do we have? His promises are many, though admittedly there has been little pay-off so far. Whatever the truth of the situation, Falk was no mage, and I can't deny Teth has powerful magic at his command. Besides, I don't see anyone else with a better idea than sticking with him. Someone that powerful, eventually there should be some money in working for them."

Kilchus sneered. "Yes, but those with power also tend to draw powerful enemies."

Rgia shrugged. "I've faced powerful enemies before and I'm still here."

"So what, then?" the Sword asked her. "You sit patiently by, waiting for this mage's plans to come to fruition? What's in it for you?"

"Perhaps I can answer that," Teth interjected.

Kilchus turned on him. "You?"

"Yes, me," the wizard said with a glance toward Rgia, who gave a nod of approval.

"Then say your piece," Kilchus said.

"The time for hiding is soon over," Teth continued. "As things stand now, I am by far the most powerful magic user ... anywhere."

"Anywhere? What does that mean?" Kilchus asked.

"The nation, the continent, all of existence," Teth said.

The Sword sniggered. "I find that hard to believe."

"Yet it is true," Teth said. "It is not impossible I have a powerful enemy or two somewhere out in the world, maybe an old god still lingers, which is why I need the bones, to assure myself of my capacity."

"Even if truth," Kilchus said, "what does it mean for Rgia here and her brother? Or for me and Curval?"

"For starters," Teth went on, "I think it is time to take you up on the offer you made me ... pardon my words ... the offer you made Lord Falk ... concerning taking power on the streets of Bond."

"You want to be the new Belgad?" Kilchus asked.

Teth brushed aside the words. "Or whomever. In all truth, we would be much, much more powerful than this Belgad the Liar figure, or any before or after his time. But this would be only a beginning. From there, we could stretch forth our might. Local politics at first, then beyond into the rest of West Ursia, and eventually across its borders. Nothing will be out of reach for us."

"For *us*?" Kilchus said. "You keep using words like that, and *we*, but I'm still not seeing how this would benefit any of us."

"Imagine yourself governor of West Ursia," Teth said.

"All of it?"

"All of it," the mage said. "I will need governors for my provinces after all."

Kilchus chuckled and turned to Rgia again. "Are you hearing this? Can you believe any of it? One man talking about taking over the world? Sounds like madness to me."

"He did a pretty good job getting you out of jail," Rgia said.

"True, but that's still a far cry from full-scale war," Kilchus said, "and make no mistake, that's what it would come to."

"Again, another reason to retain the bones," Teth said. "They would make me all that more powerful."

Kilchus fumed. Everything Teth said was insane, and he could hardly believe someone as intelligent and shrewd as Rgia was falling for it.

"You can't really be expecting any of this to work out," he said to her.

Again the assassin shrugged. "I'll stay until things turn sour. For the time being, I see nothing else on the horizon. If Teth turns out to be as powerful as he says, then fine, I'll be his thug or his general or his chief assassin, whatever he will have of me. But if he's lying, or if he fails, then I'm gone, along with my brother."

"It's that simple for you?" Kilchus asked.

"Fortunes are made not only in developing empires," Rgia said, "but in crumbling ones, as well. If Teth should tumble, then I might be there to pick up the pieces. Bond doesn't have an assassins guild, after all, and who else to create one than myself?"

Kilchus stared at her for a moment. There was no light of delusion in her eyes, only a moribund gaze of acceptance. Rgia Oltos was at her end with nowhere else to run, nowhere to hide. Even if she could do flee, which potentially she could, she had decided to make a stand. The Sword wondered if it was emotional exhaustion, her last years spent saving her idiot brother from the Prisonlands, then hiding in Caballerus and now this turmoil in Bond. Had Rgia given up? Or was she merely trying to make the best of a bad situation? Kilchus had to believe it was the latter, for the woman was too astute to fall for Sadhe Teth's insanity.

The Sword turned to the wizard, finally coming to a decision. "Okay, I'm in."

"Good," the mage said, rubbing his hands together to warm them in the small room's chill air.

"But I have some demands," Kilchus went on, his words loud, his face showing anger. "I'll help you get these bones back, but there's a few things I want first."

"Let us hear what they are," Teth said.

"I want Darkbow," Kilchus said, "and I want Captain Gris, and that bastard who betrayed us, Lalo the Finder. I want all of them, and I want their blood spilling out onto the cold street."

"That's quite a list," Rgia said. "Remember I fought the man you described as Darkbow, and he's no amateur."

Kilchus turned to her once more, leaning back so the fire showed the bruises still circling his eyes. "I think I know something about fighting Kron Darkbow, and I won't make the same mistake again. Next time I face him, my sword will be out."

Teth slipped down from his table and came between the other two. "I see no reason not to meet the Sword's requirements. After all, I believe it possible we can accomplish his goals while at the same time retrieving the bones."

"How are we to do that?" Kilchus asked. "From what I've heard, it sounds as if your magic is useless at the Asylum."

"Only against the spirits of the dead," Teth corrected. "I can still accomplish much there. And the ghosts, their reach only goes so far. If it came to it, I'm positive I could outlast them, or outreach them, in a manner of speaking."

"Still, there's only five of us," Kilchus said. "What with the ghosts and the guards and Darkbow and the others, that's a lot for us to take on, especially with your magic hampered."

"Are you saying we need more people?" Rgia asked.

"Yes, we need a larger crew," Kilchus said.

Teth frowned. "I'm not sure I approve. More heads mean more opportunities for mistakes."

"Well, like you told us," the Sword said, "the time for hiding is about over. Besides, I know someone I think we can trust, someone who knows how things operate in this town."

The wizard put out a hand. "Should we go to them now?"

"I'm not traveling by ... whatever that magic is," Kilchus said with a look of distaste. "Not anymore. Can't even stand up straight when you get someplace."

"You grow used to it," Teth said.

"No, I think he's right," Rgia said. "It's been a hectic day for all of us, Teth. It'll be dark soon, and we need rest."

"As you wish," the mage conceded, moving back to the table. He grinned as he climbed atop his makeshift bed once more. His body was that of an old man, and he could use the sleep. Also, what could another night matter to him? He had waited thousands of years for another opportunity such as this, and nearly every word he had spoken to Kilchus the Sword had been a lie. War? Politics? An assassins guild? These mortals had such lowly ambitions.

<u>23</u>

As the shadow of night rolled across the city, burning candles appeared in windows by the hundreds, especially in the Swamps district. Citizens of Bond honored the fallen healer as best they could, often with prayers to Ashal, more than a few mourners staring into a bottle or glass. The streets around the Swamps healing tower became empty, the multitudes grieving for Randall Tendbones having finally retreated to the warmth of their homes as the night's cold seeped along the alleys and roads.

A quiet stillness settled around the tower, usually a bustling place at all hours of the day and night. The halls were almost empty of healers and patients alike, as if fate had deemed the taking of Randall's life was enough misery for one day in Bond.

Randall's own chambers were also bereft of life, a saddened Scratch having returned to his carriage and then driven to his home, Althurna having been carried away by several healers worried about her emotional state, the hospitalers finding sleeping quarters for her in an empty room on the second floor.

The caretaker had already been called in, his measurements made, his promise given a casket befitting the healer would be ready by morning. Other healers had also already come and cleansed the body, closing the wounds as best they could. The tattered, blood-stained garments had been removed and replaced with a shroud as white as a dove.

Once everyone had completed their tasks, for several hours Randall's body was left to itself in the inner chamber of his rooms. By no means forgotten, others were busy seeing to arrangements for his body and any funeral and burial rites. The fact no one within the tower was aware of Randall's early life, including from where he hailed, led to questions and troubles. No one knew which rites would be appropriate, what ceremonies would be necessary to perform. Questions would need to be asked of those closest to Randall, but such folk were busy elsewhere that night dealing with the catastrophe at the Southtown barracks.

So Randall waited alone.

***

For Captain Gris, there was no sleep that night. Word had come from General Hagen the army would be arriving early in the morning after a forced march, but that was too late for the immediate needs of Bond's city guards. Many of the men and women in orange managed to find temporary shelter with friends or family, but more than a hundred others had no such luck. Because of the Asylum's many bunk rooms that had once been cells, Kron offered the place for general use, but the majority turned him down as they feared the ghost stories more than they did a night in the cold. A small tent city formed around the remains of the barracks, along with dozens of small fires to keep the winter night at bay.

Throughout the night, Gris stayed with his people. He owed them as much. He should have been prepared for what had happened. He should have pushed for the new squads earlier in his career as captain, for then there would be trained groups more able to deal with what had occurred in Bond that day. Since it had been legalized in the West, the use of magic had become more and more common, and now there were those with the ability to cause major disruptions in the life of Bond; the last couple of years had proven as much, and in no small way did Gris blame himself for not being prepared.

Yet others did not see it that way. During the few minutes when the captain was not giving out orders or seeing to one group or another of his people, sergeants and enlisted figures alike would approach him with their thanks for everything he was accomplishing. Even some few civilians approached the chief officer, offering him baked goods or cloaks or blankets for the night. Those people knew the captain could not have foreseen what had happened, and they appreciated his concern and his care.

Despite the double loss to the city that day, that of Randall Tendbones and the strike against the barracks, the populace was pulling together. Foodstuffs were brought to the troops sheltering in their tents. Strangers opened their homes and their beds to some of the guard. Regional eateries provided goods throughout the night, and more than a few shops opened early to bring out much needed wares, especially cooking pottery and clothing.

It was a bittersweet night for most, and candles in windows and at the entrance to tents gave indication of hurt and healing alike. Even the weather seemed to accede to the grief, the wind keeping low so as to allow the candles to burn without danger to others, the temperature chill but not dangerously so.

And through it all, Captain Gris moved from tent to tent, pausing for some few minutes here and there to collect himself, to drink something warm, to keep up his strength and his own spirits. He owed as much, he believed.

***

He did not cry, so she cried not only for herself, but for him as well.

Kron lay on his back, his arms wrapped around her so he could feel the warmth of her body against his own, her head tucked beneath his chin. Nodana quivered as the tears struggled down her face to land on his chest.

The day before had been a long one for both of them, and the night as well. The hours of darkness would end soon enough, bringing back morning and the pain of a new day, a day without Randall Tendbones in the world, a day in which the forces of law and order had been shattered, a day in which a malicious, unknown force roamed the land with jackals at its beck and call.

It was enough to drive Kron Darkbow to frenzy. Only the woman at his side, in his arms, kept him from rushing off in search of ... he knew not whom or what. Someone, multiple someones, had brought terror to the city, and Kron was determined these individuals should pay for their affront to all that stood decent.

A near sigh escaped his lips. Revenge. It was what he knew, what he had known nearly all his life since the slaying of his parents before his eyes when he was but ten. It was a tiresome business, revenge. He had tried time and time again to put it behind him, to quell the rage within his breast, but it would not die, only lay dormant for periods of time. If left to his own devices, perhaps he could ultimately splinter the wrath within himself, but the world intruded. It always intruded. There were always those willing to not only take part in the most depraved of acts, but to glorify in such acts and find glee in them.

Memories of another woman, the fencing master Adara Corvus, the lesson she had taught him, had drowned Kron's hatred for some time, and then Frex had come into his life, giving him hope. But there was no hope. Those he loved, especially the best of them, always paid a price that should never have been charged upon them in the first place.

Randall should not have been murdered. So many across the years had been undeserving of their fates, even some of those who had fallen victim to Kron himself, he could admit. But he was no longer the wild, young man who sought to still his own pain through the blood of others. Those days were gone. With age came experience. Full of rage he might still be, but he had learned to control his emotions, to guide them along a path more proper, less chaotic. He had learned to channel his rage, and only now was he beginning to realize he had pushed down that rage, denied it, for far too long. If he had been his old self, his vengeful self, he would have been more aware, and perhaps Randall would still be alive and the barracks would still be whole.

Yet that had not happened.

Someone had to pay for the suffering of the day before.

After Nodana had lay silent beneath his head for some while, she lifted her chin. "I was proud of you today," she said.

"Of me?" he asked. "Why?"

"The way you handled yourself," she said, "the way you dealt with Randall's passing. I expected something ... different."

For a moment he said not a word, then, "There was so little time to think upon it. I was always rushing from one catastrophe to the next."

"Have you had time to think about it now?"

He hesitated, but, "Yes."

"And what do you think?"

He did not answer. He would never answer the question, not then, not in the future. He simply lay there. Eventually her chin lowered, her breathing became steady, and Nodana slept.

He did not sleep. He would not allow himself to do so. There was too much to consider, too many options to weigh, too many plans to contemplate. And there were too many things left to learn.

Yes, someone would pay and pay dearly.

Even beneath a quilt, there was little warmth for Kron Darkbow.

***

The body looked cold, pale, vaguely blue, the flesh waxy. Eerie in its stillness, in the lack of muscle ticks, the lack of a chest lifting and falling. Yet there were no signs of rigor mortis having set in, and no signs of the bruising caused by motionless blood along the back and the back of the legs.

Midge Highwater stood next to the body, the door to the chamber open behind him. Beneath the drooping slack brim of his hat, beneath his bushy gray brows, his eyes stared hard into the unblinking lashes of the dead healer.

Other than the corpse, Midge was alone.

"Time to wake up, boy," the storyteller said.

Of course nothing happened. Randall lay dead, unmoving, waiting for pallbearers to come in the morning to escort him away to his final resting place.

Midge leaned back, cracking his back and feeling his years. The slight ache in his spine made him wonder if it was time for a cane or walking staff, or perhaps if it was time for something more stringent. Perhaps he should see a healing mage on his way out.

But not yet.

"I know Darkbow was in here before," the old man said. "I know he spoke with you. But you're stubborn, aren't ya?"

Still, no response.

Midge gestured around himself, signifying the ether. "I suppose you're out there floating around. But I know you're not far, not yet. I guess you figure you had as much life as you were allowed, that it's time for you to move on, that you've done all you can do here. Is that it?"

He paused as if expecting an answer, but none came.

"Well, let me tell you," the storyteller went on, "all of that is plain rubbish. You hear me? Of course you do. You can hear every word I'm saying to you, just like you heard everything your partner said to you earlier today, and just like you know everything that's going on around here."

Midge paused again, stretching his spine once more, even reaching back with a gnarled hand to rub through his cloak and tunic to the small of his back. It was a small relief.

"Let me tell you, Randall Tendbones," and here the old man's voice was grim, gritted, "there's still *plenty* for you to do. Understand? There are lots of people who still need your help, and not just the ones who come to you every day with their coughs and their cancers, their wounded limbs and their wounded pride. There's plenty of others who need you, including your friend Darkbow.

"He's not a bad sort, this Darkbow, but he's got his priorities all mixed up inside. Not all of it's his fault. He's had bad things happen to him over the years, like all of us, but he's personalized it, made it a part of himself when he didn't need to.

"You need to come back for him, if no one else, because let me tell you, the world will be a much darker place without you, and it will be a much darker place if he's allowed to run wild, which is what will happen if something isn't done. And while I think the best of Frex Nodana, I'm not sure even she will be able to keep him together when the full force of what's happened to you hits him in his heart."

Randall lay unmoving, his eyes hidden behind lids that appeared like marble.

"All right, then," Midge said, lowering his chin to his chest. "I've said my piece, so I'll let you be. You just think about all this, understood?"

The old man stared down at the corpse for a long minute, then he nodded and sighed and turned away.

At the door he paused once more, looking back.

"One last thing," he added. "Being two thousand years old, you'd think you'd know just how important you really are, and how much you're really needed."

Then Midge winked, and ushered himself out of the room and the tower.

23

Even as an urchin raising himself on the seedier streets of Bond, Spider had always been a follower. Because of this, he had never been able to finish anything on his own such as when he had failed out of the university's college of magic after only a couple of years of study and training. The university had held promise for him, especially after he had finagled his way into classes through a scholarship provided by a prominent citizen who had had high hopes for the little man with gray hair even in his early twenties. That prominent citizen had been none other than the infamous Belgad the Liar, and Belgad had sought a house mage, a wizard to be controlled by Belgad himself. There had been other prospects for the position of house mage, but for one reason or other none of them had been as malleable as Belgad had wanted. Thus, Spider, a minor street thief with some little smarts, had been talked into studying magic at the university.

Even after Belgad's leaving Bond, Spider had remained within the same household, then appropriated by Lalo the Finder. That had lasted not long, because someone more menacing and at-the-time seemingly more powerful than Lalo had come along. That person had been Kerjim Sidewinder, uncle to Lalo's personal bodyguard, Eel.

Unfortunately for Spider, and for Kerjim himself and a handful of other thugs, events degenerated and the void in street politics left behind by Belgad the Liar was not filled. Somehow in all the mix, Spider had become chief of the city's new thieves guild.

It had not been a position Spider had particularly wanted, but at the time it had seemed the thing to do, to take over the guild that had been refused by wiser heads.

For a brief time there had been an opportunity for Spider to finally make something of himself, to combine his few magical talents with his experience on the streets, but that time had come and gone. Spider had squandered his potential, and all because he had had little backbone.

And because Kron Darkbow had been on the scene, of course. Spider could never forget Kron Darkbow.

However, interestingly enough, Spider held no true animosity for Darkbow. Kron had simply been filling his role, doing his job, as Spider had seen it. Enemies they might be, but from Spider's perspective there was no heated animosity between the two, though there also was nothing like a grudging respect. Spider had no illusions that Kron considered Spider any kind of worthy opponent.

So now, after a year or so, Spider was still a follower despite the fact he headed a guild. He never attended meetings of the guild masters, and he rarely gathered to himself more than a handful of street thieves. He had tried on a few occasions to bring together a number of thugs in order to strengthen his own guild, but his interest had waned after a few days. Spider couldn't be a leader. He did not appreciate the burden that came with being boss.

His guild had been reduced to basically himself with the occasional add-on of any of the lowest street slime who had nothing to do at any given moment. Which seemed rarely, as most of the street slime were busy doing nothing, or drinking themselves into a stupor, which was practically the same thing.

Bored, weak, listless, Spider found himself alone more and more often.

Which was why he was sitting by himself with a bottle of whiskey on the end of a graying, rotting, abandoned pier that jutted out into the South River.

He was contemplating ending it all, finishing the bottle and just jumping into the cold water rushing by only a few feet beneath his shoes. It would be so nice to sleep forever, at least once the initial moments of panic and pain swept over him. On second thought, it was possible through liberal use of the whiskey and perhaps a minor sedation spell, that he could go into the afterworld without any panic and pain at all.

The thought cheered him, bringing a smile to his lips, which he promptly wetted with another slug of the brown liquor.

The stream of whiskey rolled across his tongue and he swallowed, closing his eyes at the delirium of pleasure clouding his thoughts. When he opened his eyes, he found himself staring at the bottle in his hands. The whiskey was gone, not even a sliver of it remaining at the bottom of the brown glass.

Snarling a curse, Spider pulled back an arm and flung the bottle into the river. The bottle turned end over end, winking beneath the bright of the morning, then it plopped down into the whirling currents, disappearing from view.

The master thief sat back on the palms of his hands, his eyes straight forward though he did not see the opposite shore, the houses there, the ruin of the city guard barracks. He saw only a grayness, bereft of ambition, bereft of life. It felt comforting.

"I see I've found you on the capstone of achievement."

Spider sat up straight, bringing his hands around to his front where a dagger rested in his belt. Slowly he turned at the hips to look over a shoulder.

Kilchus the Sword stood there, decked out in studded leather armor, a sword Spider did not recognize from their earlier meeting strapped to the man's waist. A dingy cloak flitted about the man's shoulders, barely holding off the day's chill.

"What is it you want?" Spider asked.

"Don't sound so overjoyed to see me," Kilchus said, sauntering forward to stand next to the sitting thief on the end of the pier. The Sword smiled as he stared out across the river.

"Quite a job someone made of the barracks yesterday," he said.

Spider looked back across the river at the distant devastation. "Surprised they haven't come looking for me yet. Seems I'm always the one they pick on first."

"And you're the one who's always innocent," Kilchus said.

The thief sprang to his feet in a flurry, turning on the Sword. "Innocent of everything they try to pin on me, yes."

Kilchus took a step back, more from surprise than fear. This wasn't like Spider.

"What's up your arse?" he asked.

"Me?" Spider said, clinching his hands at his side. "Whatever could be wrong with me? I've no money, no home, no job, and I can't even keep my own guild together. Couldn't find a woman for the life of me. And now you've shown up, I suppose to threaten me some more, maybe even throw a beating onto me to show just how tough you really are."

For a moment Kilchus's features were flat, his inner world going back and forth between rage and humor. Humor won out. It was hilarious seeing the small figure of Spider in a tizzy. The Sword couldn't help but grin.

Spider stood there fuming, his eyes glaring at the much larger man before him. If the thieves' master had known courage, he might have attacked Kilchus at that moment, but cowardice had become a way of life for the little man.

So the two stood there staring at one another as the river waters whipped past below and behind.

Eventually, "Are you here for a reason, Kilchus?" Spider asked.

"Actually, I am," the Sword said. "I'm putting together a new street squad, and seeing how your luck with the thieves guild hasn't held up all that well, I was hoping to recruit you."

Spider sneered. "With you as boss, I suppose."

"No," Kilchus said. "I told you a while back I had someone I thought you should meet, and I'm recruiting for him. I guess I'll be his second hand."

"Who is it?"

"Not anyone you'd know."

Spider turned away, glancing back at the river again. An unexpected crossroads had opened before him. Go to work with a brute like Kilchus the Sword, or jump into the river and end it all?

He looked back to the Sword. "This boss of yours, does he have any kind of street clout?"

"Not yet, not by name," Kilchus said, "but I promise, you've heard of some of the things he's done."

Spider's eyes expanded. He pointed across the river. "You mean the barracks?"

Kilchus nodded. "I was the reason he hit the city guard, me being on a temporary vacation at the barracks."

"Meaning you were in the jail."

"Of course. But that's not all my new boss has been up to of late."

"What else?" Spider asked.

Kilchus said nothing, but stared into the other man's eyes.

"What?" Spider said, then knowledge grew in his eyes. "Oh, hell. Was that you guys who did in Tendbones yesterday?"

Still Kilchus said nothing, but his head snapped a curt nod.

"I heard about that," Spider said, "but I couldn't figure who had done it, or why. Why would anyone want to hurt the healer? He was a good guy."

"There was nothing personal about it," Kilchus said. "He was a potential threat that had to be removed."

"Bloody hell." The thief turned away again, this time shock deep in his features as he stared at the river again.

"I don't have all day," Kilchus said to the smaller man's back. "I need an answer from you."

For a moment there was no response, the ramifications working themselves out in Spider's mind. Then he glanced around. "This boss, if he was responsible for all of that yesterday, he sounds powerful."

"He is."

"Then I'm in," Spider said.

Having not slept, Kron hit the streets on foot early that morning, leaving a sleeping Nodana behind with a note informing her he had gone to meet with Gris. He realized Frex was worthy of more than a note, but he promised to meet up with her later in the day at the healing tower. Besides, while it was true he did indeed need to see Gris that morning to discuss what should be done at the barracks as well as the Asylum, there was one other person with whom Kron wanted to speak.

Taking side streets and alleys to bypass much of the morning traffic, Kron crossed from one end of the Swamps to the other with relative speed. He was stymied as to where to look for the individual he sought. Normally Kron could find him at The Gilded Pony down an alley beside The Rusty Scabbard in Southtown, but that had always been at night. This time of day, with the sun barely hanging in the sky, Kron was at a loss how to proceed, a rarity for him.

Traversing Frist Bridge, he soon found himself in front of the Scabbard. He glanced down the alley toward The Gilded Pony, the small tavern in back, but there were no lights burning and no one out front around the stoop, clear signs the place was closed for the time being.

"Looking for me," a voice said.

Sliding a hand toward his sword, Kron spun to find the grizzled features of Midge Highwater only a few feet away, the old fellow's sloppy hat pulled low to his ears, his gray cloak hanging straight.

Kron removed the hand from the sword. "How did you know?"

Midge's eyes glinted. "I didn't, not for sure, but I was passing this way and saw you looking. Since the Pony is where you usually find me, I figured maybe it was me you was hunting for. And I'm a storyteller, son. I know lots of things."

Kron had to admit, he always enjoyed Midge's company. There was something comfortable and familiar about the old man, though he could be a bit gruff and off putting to those who did not know him.

"All right, yes," the man in black said. "I was seeking you out."

"What is it you want to know?"

Kron glanced up and down the street. There was no one paying particular attention to the pair in the middle of the road, but enough traffic made its way around them to be disconcerting.

The storyteller seemed to understand. He pointed down the empty alley. "Why don't we rest for a spell in front of the Pony?"

Kron looked again. There was no one in the dim passageway, with just enough pale light so the two would be able to see one another. "Fine."

The pair made their way into the alley, Midge eventually brushing at the steps in front of the tavern before plopping down there for a cold seat. As always, Kron stood.

"What's on your mind?" the old man asked.

"I'm not sure where to begin," Kron said.

"Start at the beginning."

"I don't know where or when that was."

Midge let out a sigh of deliberation. "Does it pertain to yesterday? Maybe about Randall?"

"Possibly," Kron said. "Probably."

"Then what is it?"

Kron was hesitant for another moment as if still unsure of what to say, then, "I realize as a storyteller that you hold great knowledge, but ..." His words faltered.

"You've got something you want to ask me about, but you're not sure if I'll know anything about it, is that it?"

A nod was the answer.

"Well, son," Midge said, "we'll never know unless you get the words out of your mouth."

Another nod. "There are some things that have been bothering me," Kron said. "The situation with Randall, and then the barracks, it's all a culmination of something, I'm just not sure what."

"Maybe it's not a culmination," the storyteller said. "Maybe it's a beginning. Did you think of that?"

The look in Kron's eyes grew darker, almost flat like those of a predator. "Actually, no, I had not considered such, and your words give me no great joy."

Midge gave a little smile. "Only here to help."

As the road traffic moved past the opening to the alley, Kron eased back into the shadows, a place where he seemed more comfortable. "Either way, there has been evidence of a powerful magical force within the city of late, and I have reason to believe this is related to what happened to Randall."

"And the barracks?"

"Likely, but I'm not sure."

The old man shrugged. "Your guess is as good as mine."

"I thought as much," Kron went on, "but there are still things you might be able to tell me."

"Such as?"

"This wizard, or whatever it is, has shown interest in acquiring certain objects that have been placed in safekeeping in the Asylum."

"The bones from last year," the old man said.

Kron's eyes lit up. "So you know?"

"I'm hazarding a guess, young man, nothing more. Not much gets past me. And that demon from last year, I'm still making decent coin off that tale thanks to a few city guards with loose tongues."

"Yes, then, the bones," Kron continued. "The same bones that demon and his master dug up and stole. This new force has shown interest in them, and has even attempted to acquire them directly."

"But they couldn't, right?" Midge said. "Those ghosts of yours, they kept them at bay."

Kron nodded again. "Something like that. What I'm trying to discover is why these bones are so important? What powers could they contain? I've asked some local wizards, but they knew little more than rumors from ancient history."

"The tell you about the Zarroc?"

"They did, but I'm not sure that's helpful information, a story from thousands of years ago. I was hoping you might be able to shed some light for me."

Deep in thought, Midge stared down at the alley's floor for a few moments. Then he looked up. "If my memory serves, the bones were dug up from a back yard that had once belonged to Merchant Guildmaster Osrm."

"That's right," Kron said.

"Then it all makes a certain amount of sense."

"How so?"

Midge appeared to slip off into thought once more, but he bounced back soon enough. "It was five, six years ago when a stairwell or something like it was discovered on Osrm's property. The thinking at the time was it was an old temple from the ancient times. A group of city guards were sent down, and when they came up they had some scary stories to tell."

"Such as?"

"Oh, there was talk about an undead wizard," Midge said. "Sounded like a crazy tale stirred up by some drunks, but I guess it fits knowing what we do now."

"You think this temple was where the bones were kept?"

"Most likely," the storyteller said. "And this wizard they found down there, sounds like he might be this magical whatsis you've been talking about."

"What happened after the guards came back to the surface?"

"What do you mean?"

"What happened to the temple, and the digging?" Kron asked.

"Osrm closed it back up, is what happened," Midge said. "I guess she thought it was too dangerous to fool with. Anyways, soon after that she put the property up for sale, but that being the wealthy part of town, it took a good while before new buyers came along."

"That family last year," Kron said, his eyes closing for a moment as he recalled another tragedy from the past, "the one's who were slaughtered at Kadath's former residence."

"I think that was your demon who did that one."

Kron nodded. "It was."

"So that tells us where the bones came from," Midge said. "What else is it you wanted to know?"

"Fhaland, the wizard with the demon, he told me the bones belonged to some ancient god. Could that be true?"

"I don't know why not," the storyteller said. "Most folks don't realize it nowadays, but Ashal wasn't exactly the first god ever to be worshiped. Though that's been so long ago, nobody really remembers the old gods' names."

"You do," Kron said.

The words seemed to catch Highwater by surprise. He rose his brows to stare into the eyes of the younger man. "What makes you say that?"

"Intuition," Kron said, now flashing his own grin. "I believe you know a lot of things, Midge."

"That very well could be," the storyteller said, "but I'm not able to tell you the names of all those old gods. Maybe at one time I knew, but my memory isn't what it used to be."

"Okay, but what about the Zarroc? How could they be involved?"

"I don't know, not for sure," Midge said. "Legends always tells us the Zarroc were tied in with the old gods somehow, but truth be told, the Zarroc are just barely a legend themselves, more like ancient whisperings passed down from across the ages. Even your university types, they don't know nothing about the Zarroc."

"Then who does?"

"Oh, a few scholars here and there, those willing to spend days and weeks and years shuffling through dusty scrolls in old churches and libraries. Even then, there's not much to tell."

"Could the Zarroc have created the old gods?"

Once more Midge shot Kron a knowing glance. "I suppose anything is possible."

"So these bones, they could belong to a god, a god made by the Zarroc?"

"I don't see why not, but all of this is pure speculation."

"Yes, I understand," Kron said, "but what I'm trying to get at is the importance of these bones. They apparently have some kind of power, but what could it be? What would make all this death and destruction worth it?"

Midge's face drooped, showing lines of sadness. "Could be a mage could derive power from the bones. Other than that, you'd have to ask your mystery wizard, or whatever it is he turns out to be."

***

It was a lot to take in. Compared to the commoner on the street, Spider had experienced a lot over the years, including demons and ghosts, but still, to accept a wizard thousands of years old had arrived in Bond, had practically destroyed the city barracks, had had Randall Tendbones slain, and now sought to assault the Asylum in order to gain some old, dried bones? It was difficult to believe.

Yet here stood Kilchus the Sword and his new companions, all telling the same tale. Kilchus was a bully, true, and not necessarily the brightest wick in the lamp shop, but Spider had never known the man to concoct a lie as complicated as this.

Then there were the others.

Jarin was hardly worthy of attention, even Spider could tell. The young man who looked so much like his sister might be a decent combatant and possibly a deft assassin, but he had been caught and sent to the Prisonlands, revealing a lack of care, and he showed no signs of strong intelligence. Spider recognized another follower when he saw one.

Sadhe Teth, if that was his true name, was no idiot. That much was obvious. But what was also obvious was the wizard held onto far too much ambition. It oozed from him, as if his pores gave off the stench of an appetite for anxiety and aspiration. The others seemed not to question Teth's power, and Spider himself had witnessed the rising of smoke from the barracks, so perhaps there was something truly worth the thief's time here. However, that did not mean he trusted this Sadhe Teth.

Rgia was a different beast altogether from the others. Spider recognized this right away. He had seen such a chill stare before in a handful of others, including the eyes of Kron Darkbow from time to time. Here was a woman colder than the grave, harder than steel. There was little doubt she was the deadliest of the group, Teth's magic notwithstanding. Her every move held strong intent, as if not a muscle wasted a motion, not a glance went by without knowledge gained, not a word was spoken without importance. She was always ready for action, her body poised on the balls of her feet, her hands unmoving yet being drawn towards daggers seen and those likely hidden about her body. She would be one to watch. Spider detected no duplicity from her, but he would be afraid to find himself posed against her, or simply to earn her dislike. By all rights, if not for Teth, Rgia should have been the boss of this outfit; not even Kilchus able to stand against such an opponent, Spider believed.

He pushed away his opinions. They did not matter. What mattered was what had been laid before him, the offer made to him. Still, he wasn't completely sure of what that offer entailed.

"So, tell me," he said, seated upon a bench in Chump's Squall, a tavern in the Docks district, "what kind of group is it you guys are putting together? It doesn't sound exactly like a thieves guild, but not really like an assassins guild, either."

"It is whatever I wish it to be," Teth answered from a booth next to Spider's table.

The boss of thieves looked to Kilchus and Jarin seated across from the wizard. "But what about the guilds, and the city? Won't they have something to say if there's no charter?"

It was Rgia who answered from the seat across the table from Spider. "To hell with a charter. You Ursians, you are so concerned about damned paperwork. If I decide to put together a guild of assassins, do you honestly think I would seek the approval of bureaucrats, people only skilled at deluding lesser minds?"

"That's the way it's always been done," Spider said.

"And that's why there's currently no assassins' guild," Rgia said. She turned away in disgust, glancing toward the front of the tavern where Curval sat by himself near the entrance, his sword leaning against his table and a bottle of hard liquor in his hands. "Foolishness, all of it."

"Okay." Spider stretched out the word in hopes of calming the woman. "So, as far as I can tell, Teth is putting together this faction in order to go after the bones in the Asylum, nothing more. Is that right?"

"That is only the beginning," the mage replied.

"What comes after that?" Spider asked.

"Whatever we want," Teth said with a smile.

Kilchus leaned forward in his seat. "I've already declared my stipulations."

Teth waved off the remark as if it had not been worth mentioning. "Yes, yes. There is a whole slew of individuals you wish to see dead."

"Not a slew," Kilchus said, teeth barred. "Just Darkbow and Gris and the Finder."

Spider went pale. This was the first he was hearing of this. "You want to kill them?"

"Damn straight," Kilchus said.

"It can be done," from Rgia.

The thief gulped. "Have you guys thought this through? Kron and Gris won't exactly be easy to kill, and Lalo ... well, he's Lalo. The Finder has never hurt anyone."

"He betrayed me. He betrayed *us*." The Sword nearly spat the words.

"All right, all right." Spider held up a hand as if to ward off Kilchus's venom. This alliance was turning into a touchy matter for its members. It seemed just about everyone had an axe to grind or some kind of goal to reach. Kilchus wanted a bunch of people dead. Teth wanted the bones. Rgia and her brother wanted to start an assassins guild. Curval ... here Spider couldn't think of anything.

He stared past Rgia to the knight with the plated chest. "What about him?" he asked with a nod. "What does he want?"

There was no answer for a moment, then Teth said, "A reason to matter."

"What?" Spider looked to the wizard.

The wizard waved off the question. "It doesn't matter. Leave Curval be. The question remains, however, are you to join us, Spider?"

There was no doubt about the boss thief's answer. Spider held no trust of those seated around him, and he held no joy for helping them with their various

TY JOHNSTON

goals, but he was a natural follower, and he wasn't stupid. He now knew too much. If he refused their offer, he could guess he would never make it out of the tavern alive.

Glancing around, curiosity suddenly came over the small, gray-haired thief. There were no other clients in the place, and the only worker was a tender behind the bar, the man seemingly asleep with an elbow and hand holding up his head.

Teth chuckled. "I see you've noticed we have the place to ourselves. Once again, my magic proves triumphant, and it was such a simple matter to bend the minds of a few fools, to send them on their way. The same simple magics provided Kilchus here with his new weapons and armor. He pointed out a figure wearing what he wanted, and I had the idiot disrobe and drop his weapons right in front of us. Then I expunged the poor, unfortunate memory so the fool wake up naked and unarmed in an alley somewhere."

A light laughter spread throughout the group, except for the thief.

Spider gulped for a second time. Yes, Teth did seem to have some skill with enchantments and the like, and Spider knew a little of magic.

He shot a glance to the wizard. "All right, I'm in."

What else could he have said?

Then he added, "But I think we need some more muscle."

Jarin smirked. "We've got Curval, and my sister and I aren't exactly beginners with a knife."

"No, no," Kilchus said. "He's right. We need big muscle, someone besides Curval who can do some heavy lifting if it came to it."

"Did you have someone in mind?" Teth asked the thief.

Spider shook his head. "Sadly, no. If this had been a year ago, yeah, I could have come up with a few names, but now?"

"What's changed?" the wizard said.

"A lot," Spider said. "Some of the folks I knew are dead. Others are wasting away at the healing tower."

"Really?" Teth said, curious. "From what do they suffer?"

"I think they're in a coma, or something like it."

"What brought that on?" Teth asked

"They decided to attack the Asylum."

Those seated went quiet. No one moved other than eyes looking from one to the other.

Finally, "And you're just now telling us about this?" Kilchus questioned.

"I figured you guys knew," Spider said. "Hell, I was in on it, or at least I would have been."

Rgia's eyes narrowed. "So you were there?"

"Only for the planning of it," Spider lied. He wasn't about to tell them he had run out on his companions the last time he had been part of an attack on the Asylum. The current group would probably not appreciate such information. If not for the seeming strength of Teth's magic, and Spider's current need to keep himself alive, he would have nothing to do with yet another attempt on the Asylum. But here he was, and skipping out was not an option, at least not at the moment.

Looks were traded again across the table.

Finally, Sadhe Teth gestured to the boss thief. "Spider, why not tell us what happened at the Asylum? Begin with those who had been members of your party."

585

Spider looked up to the ceiling, giving himself a moment to think. "Well, there was Mama Kaf..."

***

Most mornings there was a line of the sick and injured out the main door, often with the halls bustling from healers tending to the many needing their aid. Not this day. The halls of the Swamps healing tower remained all but empty. The few seeking help who did appear were shuffled off to private rooms where they could visit with a healer.

Outside there also remained an emptiness about the wide, round building that was the tower itself. Few came near, not out of fear but as a sign of reverence.

The only exception was the knot of silent individuals gathered near the entrance, their horses and buggies tied off on posts to one side. Captain Gris was present, as was Frex Nodana. Montolio stood leaning against the wall next to the front door, Midge Highwater standing at his side, the storyteller's eyes glued to the cobbled ground. The lanky, slender figure of Lalo the Finder strode forward from a carriage, right behind him his employees Stilp and Eel Sidewinder, the three with heads down as they came up to the captain and the boss of the mages guild.

No words were spoken. Some few glances were shared, concern and pain evident within all.

They stood there in silence for some while, the sun moving across the sky in its slow arc, providing a warmth unfamiliar the last several weeks. More than one coat or cloak was shed as the heat grew.

Eventually the door to the tower opened, the figure of Althurna standing there, as always with her dark hair hanging forward in her face to shield much of her features. She said nothing but stared out at the others.

"Is it time?" Gris asked.

The woman nodded before retreating back into the shadows.

The captain looked to Nodana. "Should we wait longer?"

"Just a few minutes," she said.

So they waited.

Just as hands and feet began to fidget, walking toward them from a side street came a tall, robust figure in black.

Kron looked up as he approached, surprise clear on his face as he noted the master of stories. "Didn't I just leave you?"

Midge Highwater shrugged with a slight grin. "I guess I know the back ways better than you."

Before Kron could say anything further, Gris stepped toward him. "You and I have been appointed pallbearers," the captain said.

The look of curiosity on Kron's face was replaced by one of gloom. "Who are the rest to be?"

Gris motioned toward the tower. "Other healers, men and women who held Randall in high esteem."

"Is there to be a service?" Kron asked.

"At the church of St. Pedrague in Uptown," Gris answered, "followed by burial rites at White Haven Cemetery."

Kron went pale. "That's next to the Asylum."

"So it is," Gris said, "but that's where Head Healer Wesler and the priest decided upon. Randall had left no testament requesting otherwise."

"Gris, Randall could afford a better burial than White Haven," Kron said with a little heat in his voice. "I know he came back from Kobalos with more than a little gold."

"I'm sorry, my friend," Gris said, patting Kron on a shoulder, "but apparently he donated all that to the tower soon after his return to Bond."

The man in black did not look happy. "White Haven is where they bury the dregs, and those without a name."

"Not always," Midge asserted, stepping forward. "Centuries ago the elite of the city were entombed beneath those grounds. There are more than a few worthy names tied to White Haven, even the name itself harkening back to when the city went by another name."

"But Randall deserves better," Kron stated, his teeth nearly bared.

It was Nodana who came to him then, resting a gentle hand on his other shoulder. "Kron, do you think it would make any difference to Randall? Do you honestly believe he would rather be laid to rest among kings and popes than those society has forgotten?"

Kron could not answer. His chest heaved, then sank in, his head lowering, his eyes wet.

Frex reached up to brush the tears away before they could fully form. As her hand drew back, he snagged it by the wrist, pulling it to his chest. Their eyes met, locked together, then he nodded.

A low rumbling came to everyone's ears, a muted, almost distant sound.

"Thunder?" Stilp asked, looking up to the gray sky.

But none of the others could be pulled away from the scene as Kron and Nodana hugged one another.

"Come," Gris said eventually, a hand indicating the open door to the tower. "He awaits us."

***

The top of the stairs held a wide landing with open double doors only a short distance away, beyond a lengthy room with a high ceiling. The light here was gloomy at best, as the tall window at the far end of the room faced upon a narrow alley and a brick wall beyond. To the immediate right of the doors sat a small table with a single oil lamp burning atop its surface, behind the table a chair holding up the weight of a young woman dressed in the white robes of a healer, the woman seemingly busy going over a scroll unwound in her hands. Past the healer and her station, a wide aisle stretched the length of the room to the solitary window and several tables beneath the window's lead frame, resting on these tables various bottles, vials, surgical utensils, a few scrolls and an assortment of other odds and ends. On either side of the aisle, again the length of the room from the front to the back, were rows of beds, each only large enough for a single individual. At least half these beds were empty, most of those the ones furthest from the nurse's station.

The beds nearest the woman held quiet patients who moved little. From time to time one of them would snore or scratch or twitch, but there were few other signs of life.

One bed stood out from the others. It was the furthest from the nurse, in the back on the left. The figure in this bed was by far the largest in the room, taking two sheets to properly cover the person's large frame. This individual, much like the others, never moved, but even more so. This person only breathed, slowly but surely, not even twitching, the eyes never rolling behind the lids.

It was this scene Sadhe Teth found as he reached the top landing above the stairwell, his shoes quiet as he stepped into the room, the ends of his cloak and robes brushing across the stone floor.

The nurse looked up, a gentle smile on her face as she closed her scroll and placed it upon her table. "May I help you, sir?"

Teth said nothing for long moments, staring the length of the room from bed to bed. Eventually his gaze fell upon the large figure in the back, and he said, "Your services will not be needed, miss. You may leave now."

She hesitated, her eyes working, her will fighting against the magic thrown against her, but after a few seconds it was the mind of the mage which overcame her own.

She stood, brushing at her pale robes. "Very well, sir. If you should need anything, you can find me on the first floor."

"My thanks," Teth said.

Then he watched as the woman came from behind the desk and walked past him. She paused at the top of the steps, her face worried as she showed strength of will, her mind fighting back once more. But after a moment her memory cleansed itself, her face grew vacant but pleasant, and she made her way down the stairs.

Teth wasted no more time with thought upon her and strolled the length of the room, heading toward the big person in back.

He stopped only once, for a few seconds. He glanced aside at a figure slightly darker of skin than the others, a man in his fifties. He stared at this person, then shook his head. "I think not, Kerjim," Teth said. One leader was more than enough, and confrontation would be wasteful.

The mage continued on his way.

As he drew upon the slumbering person in the back of the chamber, the figure became larger and larger in his sight until it became evident the individual was massive. Nearing, Teth could make out the heavy features of a woman, but by no means an attractive woman to his eyes.

Mama Kaf's face appeared to him as if made out of large balls of rolled clay, motionless and gray. Her hair was stringy and damp, splayed out in all directions around her head on a pillow. Her head itself was humongous, as large as the pair of monstrous breasts rising gently before her, each the size of a full melon. Extending down, her body was proportionally gigantic. She would tower over all but the tallest of individuals, and had to weigh at least several hundred pounds. Her arms were as wide as many a man's trunk, and her legs ....

Here Teth paused in his perusal.

The woman was missing a leg from the knee down.

The mage frowned. Spider had not mentioned the missing limb. Reflecting, the mage decided the oversight had not been intentional, but had probably been a lack of nerves, the little man having been obviously edgy when telling his tale.

Still, the lack of a leg would not be a problem for the wizard. Such could be overcome.

What was of more concern was the woman's mind. Did enough of it still remain to make her useful? Teth believed so, at least from what he had heard of Spider's story, and he believed he held the solution to her current complication.

To determine the truth, there was only one way to find out.

Teth leaned over the woman, gradually bringing his hands up to her pudgy features. His fingers hesitated a moment, flexing, then he pressed the digits into her skin.

The fingers sank into the flesh, and immediately Teth's mind was awhirl with emotion, mostly anger and frustration. No, this was deeper than anger. Hate. This woman hated.

But she was not alone within her body, within her own mind. There were others present, floating about within her brain, keeping her corralled, keeping her imprisoned within her own prominent bulk. Teth recognized them right away as spirits of the dead, and he could pull enough from them to know these haunts had once been wardens of the very Asylum he wished to enter. Even in death, these men acted as guardians of a sort, keeping the woman known as Mama Kaf from rampaging through the world, keeping her from what she considered her just vengeance.

Teth could not help but smile. The tower healers had likely feared attempting strong magics on this woman, the only possible solution to resolving her current state, but he held no such compunctions. It was possible to free her of her spectral attendants, of this Teth was sure, but such an attempt might wreck what remained of the woman's mind.

And the dead, while immune to most magics, here were ensconced within living flesh. They would not be safe from him.

Again Teth smiled. Though no easy task lay before him, it was not anything beyond his abilities. The survival and the mental state of Mama Kaf was the only concern, and here the ancient wizard had little true worry. If the woman did not survive or if she became truly mad, such did not bother the mage, but if she survived and served him, all the better. There was nothing for him to lose.

His fingers sank deeper into her flesh, his own soul reaching into her and batting aside the weaker spirits from the Asylum. He sought to find her inner self, to separate her from her caretakers.

In the outside world, but seconds passed. On the inside of Mama Kaf's mind, it seemed a thousand years crawled by as a battle was fought.

Eventually Sadhe Teth found what he sought, the soul of the woman, alone and imprisoned within the box of her own mind. The dead Asylum guards whirled about, attempting to thwart the wizard, but they were nothing as to him. Teth lashed out, his own mind cutting through the ghosts, tearing them apart, ripping them into nothingness. Again and again he did this until there were no longer adversaries to be found.

His soul stared into that of Mama Kaf, and he believed he found her willing, though not overly gracious.

"Serve me," his inner self said to hers.

She glared back at him from within, stared at him, her rage free once more and growing.

He removed his hands from her head and leaned away from her prominent figure upon the bed. Back in the waking world, all he could do now was watch and wait and hold onto his desire there would be no madness present within the woman, for he could already tell she would make a formidable opponent against his enemies.

After a few moments, her eyes fluttered. Her chest rose heavily and her lips sputtered.

"Come to me," Teth whispered.

Then her eyes snapped open, locking upon his own.

"Darkbow," she demanded, staring at the mage.

Once more, Sadhe Teth could not help but smile.

"As you wish, my dear," he said, waggling his fingers as if to prepare a magic spell, "but first, I think we need to make you a little more mobile."

***

Several stories below where Mama Kaf lay, Kron led the line of mourners through the curving outer hall of the tower. Nodana remained at his side, her left arm encircling his right. Captain Gris and the others followed, even the carriage driver Scratch who had shown at the last minute and wished to pay his respects.

Some few healers and patients passed the sombre group, all providing plenty of room for passage and staring with eyes full of pain. Randall's absence was felt beyond his personal friends, but by the community at large.

As Kron neared the next bend in the hall leading to Randall's rooms, the sound of a commotion came to his ears from ahead.

Then a shriek rang up and down the halls.

Kron glanced at Nodana, then over a shoulder at Gris.

"What could that have been?" the captain asked.

"Stay here," Kron said to Nodana, then he was off, charging ahead with a hand on his sword to keep it from banging against his legs.

As he rounded the curve in the wall, he came upon sight of the open door to Randall's chambers. Outside stood a cluster of healers, men and women all in white, most of them young, their confusion clear as they gawked into the room beyond the doorway.

Before Kron could ask a question, Althurna dashed out of the room, elbowing her way through the healers, her hands in her face as she screamed.

Springing forward, Kron grabbed her by the arms. "What is it? What has happened?"

As he tugged her hands free from her face, a surprise caught him, so much so he let go of her and stood back.

She was beaming. Sheer joy brightened her face, her eyes pouring tears of happiness.

Kron knew not what to say or do. He could only stand there and watch as she laughed at him.

"He lives!" Althurna shouted, raising her hands as fists above her head and shaking them. "He lives!"

Then she darted past Kron and ran with abandoned glee down the hall.

He could only watch her run, her words having stunned him, his own eyes going wet.

***

Rgia had to admit, either Teth's powers were growing or the mage was becoming more comfortable utilizing them with the lack of competition, especially after Tendbones's demise. Since their group's arrival at Chump's Squall, not a single person had wandered through the tavern's swinging doors, an unheard of occurrence along the Docks, especially as the Squall was a favorite dive for river sailors and other riffraff. Rgia didn't find the place all that appealing, especially the large blotches of red staining the wooden floor in the middle of the main room, but she had to admit it was far better than their shack in the swamp and provided them plenty of privacy, courtesy of Teth's magic. Not even the lone bartender had woken from his spot. Teth had warned against leaving, his influence apparently going only so far from the building, but still, how the old wizard could sustain such powerful magics, let alone perform them in the first place, was beyond the woman assassin's experience, though she had to admit it worked.

Moving around the bar, she stared at the row of bottles lining a shelf behind the bartender. Most of the liquors here were of the cheapest sort, and not always safe to imbibe, but there were a few tolerable drinks familiar and some that had other uses besides getting drunk.

She lifted a brown earthenware bottle with no label yet a cork stopper in one end. "Anyone know what this stuff is?"

For the first time in some while, Curval rolled his head around to glance in Rgia's direction. "Nebrarian potato rum."

Rgia looked over the bottle. How could the man tell from the plain, flat muddy color and the typical shape and condition of the bottle? "You sure," she asked.

Curval nodded. "I can smell it from here."

The assassin glanced to her brother seated with Spider and Kilchus at a table, the three of them plopping down cards between themselves, a small pile of copper coins to one side the pot for the one who took the round.

Jarin could only shrug back at her. "I guess he's got a good nose."

Such a thought seemed more unbelievable than all Sadhe Teth's magic.

"I'll take your word for it," Rgia said to the knight. "But is it any good?"

"It'll get you drunk," Curval said.

He provided no other answer.

Rgia shrugged and slid the bottle into a worn leather haversack she had found in a back room. Not one to waste time, she had taken it upon herself to lift a few possibly useful items from the tavern while waiting for Teth to return. Slipping the sack's shoulder harness around her head, she found the weight not overly burdensome. Not one drawn to drink on a regular basis, Rgia could still respect liquor's benefits when it came to cleaning wounds and helping the suffering. Plus, such hard drink had a tendency to burn easily, which promised its own benefits.

A noise not unlike that of a weak explosion came to all their ears, causing the three card player's to put aside their game and stand at their table while Rgia turned to face the entrance of Chump's Squall. Only the slumbering bartender and Curval showed no signs of interest, the big man taking another slug from the bottle on his table.

When Sadhe Teth pushed through the swinging doors, his old man's face was bright with a smile.

"You did it, didn't you?" Spider asked, seemingly nervous.

"See for yourself," Teth said, stepping aside from the doors.

A soft thumping noise followed. Several soft thumping noises. Then a groan as the doors swung inward yet again.

Kilchus and Jarin's eyes went wide, and even Rgia almost took a step back.

The figure making its way into the tavern was a hulk, larger than two men, barely fitting through the doorway because of its commodious shoulders and girth. Scraggly, graying hairs hung down from atop a massive head, and eyes filled with rage looked out from a face flush with a meaty complexion. The thing was barely recognizable as human because of its size, and the only signs it was female were the pair of gargantuan breasts hanging beneath the thin, grungy tunic wrapping the body.

Adding to the inhuman aspects of the bulky, limping character was the replacement of one leg with what appeared to be a boot of steel plate, a single greave starting at the knee and riding down into a dulled shoe of metal.

"It's her," Spider managed to whisper.

Only Curval did not appear impressed as the large figure's baleful eyes roamed over him. The knight did not even seem to take notice of the monstrosity before him. He simply took another drink and continued to stare straight ahead.

"For those of you who not know her," Teth said, still grinning, "allow me to introduce to you Mama Kaf."

The woman-thing grunted and growled.

This time Spider managed to lift his voice. "It really is her."

"Of course," Teth said. "I promised to return with her."

Looking over those gathered, Mama Kaf's gaze finally came to rest on Spider. There was a glint of recognition in her eyes. She did not seem overly pleased to see him, but she made no remark as the small man with gray hair shuddered.

"Let us find you a seat," the wizard said, pulling a chair free of a table.

The big woman glanced down at the chair, then ignored it, tromping past Teth and the table.

"Of course," Teth said, shoving the chair out of the way. "Such flimsy seating would never hold her."

Rgia's eyes lit up as the massiveness of Mama Kaf stomped directly toward her. For a moment the assassin did not know what to do, but then she saw the other woman's gaze was not upon her but upon the row of bottles. At the last moment, Rgia slid to one side and out of the way.

Mama Kaf stamped to a halt directly in front of the bottles. She did not take a moment to peruse them, to make a choice, but grabbed up the closest at hand. Then she slammed the bottle's neck on the side of the bar, sending the cork flying as the neck shattered.

"By Ashal," Kilchus muttered.

Next the big woman lifted the remains of the bottle and tossed back her head. Without her lips touching the jagged, broken glass, she poured the liquor into her open mouth, the lips smacking every few seconds.

Soon the drink was gone.

She slammed the bottle onto the bar, where the last of the bottle crumbled into a thousand pieces.

Spinning around on her good leg, she faced the others, her eyes gazing over them yet again in a fashion most malevolent. Finally her look came to the wizard.

"You promised Darkbow," she said, her voice nearly guttural.

Teth came toward her, his hands out in front, almost supplicating. "And you shall have him, my dear. First we need to find you some proper clothes, and perhaps a weapon. Then, some planning is in order. After that, this Lieutenant Darkbow will be yours."

"Wait a second," Kilchus stormed from his table over to the wizard. "Darkbow is *mine*. I lay claim on him."

The massive woman's eyes glowered over the Sword, looking at him as if he was of no more significance than a gnat.

"I believe the good woman here has a prior claim," Teth tried to explain.

Kilchus huffed, his hands balled up at his side. "I don't give a damn. The man owes me, and you made a promise."

Before anyone could react, a giant fist lashed out, catching Kilchus beneath the jaw. The blow lifted the man off the ground, no small task as Kilchus had size to him, then dropped him to the floor. He lay there unmoving.

Teth snickered. "I believe that settles the debate."

***

Kron was first through the door into the back room of Randall's chambers. His boots skidded to a stop on the stone flooring as he faced the figure stretched out upon the cot. There was no denying the flesh of Randall's face held a pinkish glow, the skin natural looking, *alive* looking. It was more difficult to tell the slender chest beneath the white wrappings lifted and fell, but there could be no doubt the healer was alive.

"Kron?" Nodana came up behind her man, placing a hand against his back. She, too, stared down at the sleeping figure of Randall Tendbones.

Then Gris came into the room, took one glance at Randall, then sidestepped the first comers. He rushed to kneel next to the healer, then leaned over and placed an ear against Randall's chest. He stayed in that awkward position for nearly half a minute, then jerked back from the supine figure.

"Impossible," the captain said, the single word little more than a whisper.

"Apparently not." Kron's eyes blurred with tears as he wrapped an arm around the crying Nodana, pulling her into him as she engulfed his side with her own limbs.

Gris stood, rubbed tears from his eyes, then looked over at Kron. "How?"

"I do not know," the man in black said, his words not completely untrue. "Randall ... I know he is a powerful mage. I saw things in Kobalos that ..." His words ended on nothing.

Gris stared for a moment longer, then his attention was diverted as the healers from the hall began to trail into the room.

Suddenly Althurna appeared again, her hair brushed back from her face, her features filled with ecstatic joy as she pressed forward, dropped to her knees next to the cot, and placed her arms across Randall, her head against the sleeping healer's chest as she closed her eyes.

"It's a miracle," she said, her tears dripping down onto the white cloth encircling the young man so recently believed dead.

24

As before, news of Randall Tendbones flowed through the city like the rush of waters from a bursting dam. More than a few prayers of thankfulness were offered to Ashal, and more than a few bottles of wine or harder drink were tossed back in the name of the healer. At the main barracks where hundreds had gathered to begin the clearing away of debris, the city guards and workers alike paused in their tasks to send up shouts of cheer before sharing drink from bottles and flagons. Even the recently-arrived army camped outside the city walls shared in the jubilation, none too few of the soldiers dropping to their knees and bowing their heads while facing the city walls. Everyone seemed to know Randall, to be affected by the healer and his miraculous survival.

Not all believed it was a true miracle. Word of such events could not be trusted, as most were aware, so the general consensus was that Tendbones had never actually been dead but had only seemed that way before recovering. Even those closest to the healer had to question.

"I've never seen anything like this," Captain Gris said with a shake of his head as he and Kron exited the healing tower, giving room to the many healers clustered in the halls around Randall's rooms.

"Healer Wesler will determine if it was the work of Ashal," Nodana said, she and Montolio right behind the two men.

The captain and his lieutenant paused and glanced back at the woman. It had been an unusual remark for Nodana, the wizard not being known for religious sentimentality.

But she did not seem to care, her face lit with a wide smile. "It might be divine intervention," she said. "Wesler has even asked for a body of priests to help in the determination."

Gris did not appear believing. "I'm not sure what difference it makes, miracle or not."

Nodana shrugged. "Perhaps it makes no difference, or perhaps it does. I'm willing to wait and see what Randall has to say."

"If he wakes," Montolio said next to her.

The others looked at him, none overly pleased at his words.

"My apologies," Montolio said, "but the fact of the matter is Randall has not woken, and he might not come to his senses for some time, if ever."

"We can only pray," Nodana said.

"I think we can do more than that," Gris said. "I for one will be calling on the mayor to send the city's best hospitalers and apothecaries to see Randall."

A trio of figures appeared from the healing tower, pushing their way through the smiling and joking healers at the entrance.

"I believe I can be of help as well," Lalo the Finder said as he approached, Eel at his side and a grinning Stilp not far behind.

"What do you mean?" Gris asked.

"If I may," Lalo said, "I would like to offer my house as a proper place of rest and recovery for our healer. It offers much more quiet and solitude than can be found here." He motioned toward the caucus of healers growing louder at the door.

"You would have to ask Wesler," Kron said.

"I already have," Lalo answered back. "He approves."

"And you would need to speak with Althurna," Kron said. "I'm not sure she would be pleased with the arrangement."

"I've done that as well," Lalo said, nodding to Kron. "She said the decision will be yours."

"Mine?" Kron asked.

"Yes," Lalo said.

"Why me?" Kron said. "I was under the impression the woman did not care for me."

"I cannot account for her personal opinion," Lalo said, "but it does seem she holds a level of trust in you, and she recognizes you as Randall's closest friend."

Kron's face turned scarlet.

"What of Althurna herself?" Nodana asked. "She won't want to be far from Randall."

"We have plenty of room at the mansion," Lalo said, nodding toward Eel and Stilp. "With only the three of us residing within, there will be no difficulty in finding room for Lady Althurna. As well, I can provide chambers for any number of healers, as I expect Randall will need constant watching for some time."

"It sounds as if you already have all this worked out," Gris said.

The Finder beamed. "Thank you, I have."

"Why?" Kron asked. "You and Randall were never particularly close."

Here Lalo's face looked almost sorrowful, his eyes dipping for a moment. "True enough, but on more than one occasion the healer has served my household and served it well, and I am not unaware of what he means to the people of this city."

"What about moving Randall?" Montolio asked. "Won't that be a danger to him?"

Lalo nodded. "There is a certain level of risk, but Healer Wesler seemed to believe that risk could be alleviated through the use of magic."

"I'm willing to help," Nodana said.

"As am I," from Montolio.

"I can't see any reason not to go along with it," Gris said, looking to the man in black. "Kron?"

For a few moments Darkbow did not speak. He stared at the cold cobblestones beneath his boots, the man obviously deep in thought. "It is a generous offer."

"I realize you are familiar with my house," Lalo said, "but if you have any concerns, you are more than welcome to drop in tonight or any other time convenient to you and take a look. In fact, I would appreciate your opinion upon which room Randall should be placed."

Again Kron said nothing for some time, then he looked up, facing the Finder. "Lalo, we have not always seen eye to eye --"

Stilp let out a chuckle.

"-- and I admit you surprise me," Kron went on, "but I agree to your terms."

The Finder smiled. "Would you like to come by tonight? We could discuss the arrangements, then perhaps have Randall moved in the morning?"

"That would be fine," Kron said. "Six bells?"

"Perfect." Lalo beamed again. "I'll see you then."

The Finder smiled one last time, then turned away with his retinue and proceeded to their carriage parked not far away.

"What now?" Montolio asked of those remaining.

Captain Gris gave a low shrug. "What else? We do the best we can for Randall, and we get on with life, at least until he shows signs of improvement. I need to get back to the barracks and coordinate that mess so we can begin the rebuilding as soon as possible."

"Do you mind if I trail along with you?" Nodana asked. "I have a few spells which could ease the heavy lifting."

"It would be much appreciated," the captain said.

Kron looked to Montolio. "I suppose you and I should make our way to the Asylum. With everything that has been happening the last few days, I fear our squad will be behind on their training."

"And the need for them has been proven more than ever," Gris added.

Darkbow nodded at the words, then looked to Nodana. "Dinner tonight? Perhaps after I have met with Lalo?"

She reached forward and grabbed one of his hands. "I'll be looking forward to it. Why don't I stop by the Asylum after I'm finished at the barracks? Montolio and I need to talk over the magics we'll use for moving Randall."

"Until then, I will miss you," Kron said, squeezing her hand and leaning forward to kiss her on a cheek.

***

Jarin pulled back his hood as he entered the tavern, pausing inside the swinging doors for a moment to shake off the outer cold. "I looked all over, but this was the best I could find," he said, holding up a rod of ash as long as his leg and as thick as a man's wrist, at its top sitting a block of black iron shaped like the head of a hammer. "Found it over at the Docks, sitting there all lonesome."

Mama Kaf slurped down the last of her drink near the bar, tossed the bottle over her head where it smashed on the floor, then grunted and trudged forward. She grabbed the sledgehammer out of the assassin's hand, then held it up before her face, her sunken eyes looking out from within prodigious lumps of flesh to stare up and down the length of the stolen tool.

The room waited in silence, Rgia and Teth and Spider now seated upon stools fronting the bar, a swollen-jawed Kilchus sitting across from Curval, who still did not bother to look up.

Finally Mama Kaf grunted again, lowered her new weapon and rounded toward the bar again, one pudgy hand already seeking another bottle.

Jarin let out a sigh, then crossed to his sister. "I don't suppose you found any proper clothing to fit her?"

Rgia nodded toward a booth near the back of the room where a pile of rough cloth sat upon the table. "There was a stack of old sail cloth in the back. I'm thinking it's the best we can hope for. I'm no seamstress, but I can probably fashion together a simple tunic and maybe a shawl or cloak."

With a dark gaze for Mama Kaf's back, Kilchus stood and marched over to the mage and the assassins. "So what's the plan? When are we doing this?"

"Tonight," Teth said. "We need the hours to fashion Mama Kaf decent garb, and to rest some more. After dark the temperature should drop again, meaning there will be fewer eyes on the streets, and possibly bleary-eyed soldiers at the Asylum."

"You think their guard will be down?" Kilchus asked, a smirk of unbelieving on his lips.

"Oh, they've been alerted," Teth said. "They couldn't help but be after recent events. My setting fire to their barracks alone will keep their heads up for some while, but the dark and the cold will give us some little benefit. Until then, I suggest we eat, drink and rest."

Kilchus threw another nasty glance toward the monstrous woman breaking the top off another bottle at the bar. He lowered his voice when he spoke. "What about Darkbow? Who gets him?"

Teth sighed, showing clear frustration. "The person who gets to him first, Kilchus. A silly contest will benefit us nothing."

"Yeah, but can we trust her?" the Sword asked, thumbing toward Mama Kaf. "What's in all this for her?"

"Vengeance," Teth answered. "Relatively straight forward as far as I'm concerned."

"What about *after* Darkbow?" Kilchus said. "You really think she'll hang around?"

The ancient wizard stared at the big woman's back for a moment, then nodded. "I believe she will. What else does she have? She is like the rest of us, without family or prospects. Besides, I'm not sure this Lieutenant Darkbow's death will sate her sense of retribution, and there are the other targets you seek, the Finder and the captain."

Kilchus did not appear pleased. "I thought you said we could get all of them at once."

"I hope so," Teth said, "but we must be prepared for any eventuality. Will the captain be at the Asylum? Possibly, but he also has duties of import elsewhere, especially at the moment with his barracks. As for the Finder, it is less likely though not impossible he will be at the Asylum."

Teeth ground together in the Sword's jaws. "You promised me."

"Yes, I did," the wizard said, "and I mean to keep that promise. Whichever of your enemies we do not eliminate at the Asylum tonight, they will be dealt with. I will personally seek them out and finish them, if that is what you wish, but only after the bones are in my hands."

"That wasn't our agreement," Kilchus said.

"It is the best I can offer at the moment," Teth said. "If you think you can find your revenge on your own, you know the location of the door. There are seven of us now, Kilchus, which should be more than enough to allow us to manage the Asylum, at least with my magic keeping any possible onlookers at bay."

"What of the ghosts?" Kilchus asked, here smirking. "Think you can handle them?"

Teth's eyes grew narrow for a moment, then he turned to Spider. "You have some experience with the Asylum, correct?"

The thief nodded, then looked to Mama Kaf. "But she was one of the ones who actually went inside."

"Yes, I'm aware," the wizard said, twisting around on his seat to glance at the big woman. "It was souls from the Asylum which caused her condition."

"Her coma?" Rgia asked.

Teth nodded. "I cleansed her of their influence, and can do the same again if I have to."

Spider shuddered visibly, such notions obviously giving him anxiety.

"But it should not come to that," Teth went on. "Before we arrive at the front door, I will cover each of you with protective wards which should keep the spirits from being able to harm you."

"I thought ghosts were immune to magic," Kilchus said.

"They are, more or less," Teth said, "but only magic directed toward them. Think of what I will provide as a shield blocking your minds from their influence. Most likely you won't even need me there."

"But you *will* be there, right?" Kilchus asked.

The wizard turned toward the Sword. "Do you want me there, Kilchus? You keep grousing about the promises I made to you, yet you seem unbending in your desire for revenge."

"What's *that* supposed to mean?"

"It means I could conceivably keep the arrangement between us if, while the lot of you are tackling the Asylum, I distanced myself and took care of any stragglers on your list of those needing executed."

Rgia shook her head. "I don't like it. We can deal with any others later, Teth, especially if what you say about the bones making you more powerful is true. There is no need for us to take such a chance."

"Wise words." The wizard nodded.

But Kilchus suddenly looked excited. "No, no. It makes perfect sense. We take out the Asylum guards and get the bones, maybe take out Darkbow along the way, and Teth, you go off to finish Lalo and Gris."

Rgia glared at him. "It is a stupid notion, parting our forces at the very moment of our attack. I wish Teth hadn't even brought it up."

"What say you?" Kilchus asked, turning to Jarin.

But the assassin did not have time to answer. The massive form of Mama Kaf smashed another bottle against the bar's top, then she spun around and marched toward those huddled together further down the length of faded pine. She stomped her way up to Kilchus, then glared down upon him, a sight not common to the swordsman as it was rare anyone was large enough to tower over him.

"We kill them all," she said, her voice like that of a bear. "All at the same time."

Then she brushed past the Sword and made her way toward the pile of sail cloth in the back.

"I suppose that settles that," Jarin said.

25

As it had for millions of years across the northern portion of the continent dubbed Ursia by the tongues of men, winter brought the dark sky early. Torches and lamps and candles were set alight throughout the city of Bond, and commoners, dignitaries, and nobles alike settled before the warmth of their hearths or camp fires. The city slowed, becoming but a shadow of itself compared to the daylight hours and the warmer months.

Around the blackened skeleton that made up the remains of Bond's main barracks for the city guard, work came to a standstill. This night far fewer of the guards remained on the scene, nearly all of them having found temporary placement within the army encampment beyond the city's walls, the handful remaining behind acting on orders as protectors for the scene, though what they were protecting no one could quite say.

At the healing tower in the Swamps, the usual comings and goings of the injured and sick had returned as the temperature had dropped and the awe surrounding the living Randall Tendbones had somewhat diminished with the hours. Still, a stream of healers and priests came and went from Randall's rooms, all of them interested in the young man's survival. Not once did Althurna leave Randall's side, the woman commonly sitting on the floor next to his bed, her arms stretched across him in a protective manner, her glances daring anyone to refuse her her station of guardian.

In taverns throughout the city, drinks were tossed back, meals eaten, stories shared, quite a few of them about Randall himself. That night Midge Highwater set a new personal record for himself, landing more coin than he had in all his years of sharing tales, his spot for the night a table just inside the doors of the Rusty Scabbard.

Along the Docks, silence roamed as no boats or ships docked or set out into the busy waters of the three rivers. The university area in Uptown was also quiet, the classes finished for the day, the students withdrawing to the dorms and the professors to their private abodes. In Southtown, shops closed up for the day, along with the many other types of businesses to be found in the district, and the separate healing tower found there locked its doors for the night, as it rarely was open during the hours of darkness, unlike its cousin tower to the north in the Swamps.

The mansion that had once belonged to Belgad the Liar and was now home to Lalo the Finder was lit well from within, with only a pair of torches burning outside at the iron gate allowing access to the grounds around the building.

The Asylum also remained quiet, only showing a few lights burning inside, the two guards at the gated entrance keeping warm with a small fire built to one side.

All in all, the streets were practically empty. The cold weather and the cloudy sky above nearly guaranteed few would be rambling forth on this night.

It had taken nearly a year, but it was finally dawning on Spider that he had made a mistake in walking out on the household of Lalo the Finder. It had been little more than a spur-of-the-moment decision at the time, based upon Spider's hopes of joining the winning side in an upcoming scuffle. Since then he had allied himself with one madman after another, and now here he was serving Sadhe Teth and the circus of maniacs surrounding the wizard who claimed to be thousands of years old. Kilchus, Jarin, Rgia, Curval, and now Mama Kaf, all were killers, as likely was Teth. None of this boded well for Spider's own future, the master of thieves decided.

Leaning against the frame of the Squall's front doors, he stared through a window into the dark streets beyond, some few lights coming to his limited view of the Docks and the river vessels bobbing there.

Thoughts had been swirling around in his head all afternoon, and he had finally decided on a course of action, though he feared it could get him killed, especially if Teth or the others suspected anything. Time was slipping away from him, however. Soon there would be no hours left to him, not even minutes, in which to step aside onto a different path.

Shoving away from the door, he turned to find Teth seated near the bar, the wizard leaning upon the bar's top, his head in his hands as if slumbering. Curval and Kilchus sat at a table not far from Spider, the two swordsmen paying no attention to one another, merely staring ahead and occasionally drinking their drinks. The women had disappeared into the back sometime earlier to work on Mama Kaf's new clothing. Jarin had gone upstairs for a few hours of sleep in one of several empty beds available there. There was no sign of the bartender, the man either having fled or been disposed of by one of the crew.

Spider slowly made his way over to the wizard, not wanting to draw attention from the swordsmen if he could help it. There was little concern for immediate danger, but no need to take chances by bringing Kilchus or Curval into the conversation.

"Teth," he said with a low voice as the neared the mage.

The wizard lowered his hands and sat up straight, showing he had not been asleep after all. He turned in his chair to face the thief.

"What is it, Spider?" he asked.

The thief hesitated. Once he voiced the next several words, there would be no turning back.

"Yes?" Teth asked, annoyance riding his words.

"I've been thinking," Spider said. "I know you think the seven of us are enough for tonight's task, but with you going off to deal with the Finder and Captain Gris, that means our numbers will be down to six at the Asylum."

"And?"

"Well, they're likely to have a wizard of their own there," Spider pointed out. "Montolio."

Teth snickered. "My understanding from you is the man has no real skill. I believe the lot of you can handle him, especially as you, Spider, have some magical training of your own."

Spider's head bobbed up and down. "You're probably right, but I would feel better if we had at least one or two more men with us."

Now the wizard sighed heavily, showing frustration. "I'm not going to put off our plans for another night simply because of your fears."

"It wouldn't take all that long," the thief said, hoping he sounded hopeful and helpful. "We're just across the street from the Docks. I could check out a few of the other taverns, see who I could round up. People know me, after all, and I shouldn't have too much trouble getting a few toughs to join in with us."

Teth still did not appear convinced. "How long would this take?"

"An hour, maybe two," Spider said. "I could catch up with the rest of you on the way to the Asylum, and bring anyone I pick up along with me."

Waiting. Waiting. Would the wizard bite? Spider's nerves edged close to breaking as the mage turned from him, staring at the wall behind the bar.

Finally, Teth glanced back at the thief. "Make sure you find us before the main group reaches the Asylum. I will have to leave them then, and yours will be an important role."

Spider could barely hold in his glee. "Right, sure, I'll be there."

"Go, then."

Spider didn't have to be told again. Spinning around, he nearly ran out of the tavern, the swinging doors flapping back and forth behind him, the wizard staring after his trail.

"Want me to follow him?" Kilchus offered, glancing to the mage.

"No." Sadhe Teth shook his head. "Whatever he's up to, let it be on his head. If he's thinking of betraying us, he will soon wish he had not. If he doesn't show for the Asylum, then the rest of you will have to find the bones without him."

"Yeah, he's probably our weakest link," Kilchus said.

"I've been thinking the same thing." Teth turned away, closing his eyes once more and placing his chin in a hand, giving his old body the rest it needed despite his own anxiousness at having the bones in his hands.

***

Kron stepped from the warmth of the Asylum's front hall into the growing chill of early night. As he closed the door behind him and turned to walk down the hill to the gate and the road, he forced down a yawn that had been trying to escape him for some while. He had not slept at all the night before, laying there with Nodana in his arms, and the events of the last few days had drained him, physically as well as emotionally.

The fight on the roof. Randall's murder. Now the healer's apparent return from the dead. The escape of Kilchus. The chaos of the barracks. It was all weighing upon the dark-garbed figure of Kron Darkbow, not even thirty yet and feeling as if the world bore down upon him.

Reaching the gate, he gave off a quick salute as one of the guards pulled open the clanky door for him, allowing access to the street. Smiling at the small fire the two guards had put together, Kron nodded to them and went about his way, taking to Beggars Row, the street fronting the Asylum.

As he made his way along a crossing road that would take him to Cabbage Street, Kron caught sight of the lights of the Royal Bear tavern several blocks to the east of him. His steps closed as he thought of the place. The Bear had been where he and Nodana had shared their first night, meeting for a meal, a glass of wine, then traipsing upstairs together; at the time the Asylum had still been under construction and offered no respite for two lovers, and in the haste of their excitement Nodana's apartment and Kron's room at the Rusty Scabbard had seemed too far away.

A night at the Royal Bear it had been, then. A night to remember.

The thought brought a smile to Kron's lips, especially as the Bear wasn't exactly the kind of place one would want to take a woman for wooing.

He laughed at his own thinking, then continued on his way to Lalo's, taking his time as there was little need to hurry. The Finder was not going anywhere. Randall was alive again and in good hands. Kron would meet with Nodana later tonight for dinner, then would return to her place for a much-needed rest. Perhaps they would discuss moving Randall in the morning, or maybe even future plans once the paperwork was completed concerning the estate of Kron's parents. Maybe they would even make love yet again.

Such notions kept him warm as he marched along to the mansion.

Soon reaching Cabbage Street, he turned down an alley.

Which was how he missed Nodana coming from the barracks as she made her way up the road toward the Asylum, the two missing one another by mere seconds.

***

The horse screamed as Spider yanked on its reins, bringing the animal and himself to a halt in front of the gate in the wall surrounding Lalo the Finder's mansion. Dropping to the ground, Spider slapped the animal on its rear, sending it on its way into the night. He cursed the beast as it fled from him, the damned horse having been nearly more trouble than it had been worth. Then again, what could he expect from an animal unfamiliar with him, an animal he had stolen less than a half hour earlier.

But no time for a silly horse.

Spider opened the gate and rushed through, not pausing to close it behind him as he rushed up the driveway of gravel to the large house. He was glad to see plenty of light within, meaning Lalo and the others had not sought early sleep. It might just save their lives, Spider supposed.

At the front door he wasted no time and knocked, then knocked again, and again. Time was of import here and now. Teth's band would be on its way soon to the Asylum, and Teth himself could very well appear soon right here. Spider had no way of knowing if Teth would single out Lalo first or Captain Gris, but Spider still held some loyalty to the Finder and to Stilp, even to Eel to some extent. Besides, Gris could take care of himself and was often surrounded by a small army. Lalo only had Stilp and Eel, which were no match for anyone.

Except maybe me, the thief thought.

Before he could think further, the door in front of him was tugged open. Standing there was Stilp.

"What do you want?" Stilp nearly shouted. Then noticing who was outside the door, his attitude changed, a sly grin growing on his lips. "Well, well, the prodigal returns. What are you here for, Spider?"

"I've got to see Lalo."

Stilp laughed. "Have you lost your wits? You don't exactly have a good history here."

"I know, I know. I can apologize later for all that." Spider glanced over his shoulder as if someone would spring up behind him at any moment. "But I don't have much time. I've got to speak with Lalo."

602

"I don't think that's going to happen. You might as well turn back the way you came --"

Spider stepped up to the door as if to push his way inside, but Stilp moved in front of him to block the way.

"Hey! None of that!" Stilp shouted.

Holding up his hands in supplication, Spider's words nearly rambled. "Look, Stilp, I've got to warn the lot of you about Teth ... I mean Falk. Yes, Falk."

"Lord Falk? You know where he is?"

"Yes!" Spider spat out. "But he'll be coming here soon, and he's got it in for your master."

"Okay, but who is this Teth person?"

Frustrated, Spider stamped the ground. "There's no time to explain! You've got to let me see Lalo!"

The youthful bodyguard Eel Sidewinder suddenly appeared at Stilp's back. "What's going on here?"

Stilp pointed at Spider. "Says he's here to see Lalo. Has some warning about Falk coming here to cause trouble."

Eel's eyes narrowed as he glared at Spider. "Is this true?"

"Close enough," Spider said, his words rushed. "Look, I can't be seen here or they'll kill me. You two have got to get Lalo and clear out before Teth gets here!"

"Who is this Teth?" Eel asked.

"That's what I wanted to know," Stilp said, rolling his eyes.

"It's Falk, okay?" Spider said. "Falk and Teth, they're the same person, though not exactly."

"What does that mean?" Stilp asked.

"I don't know!" the thief shouted. "It's complicated, but he's a powerful wizard and he could be here any minute now, and he's planning on killing Lalo."

"I'll get the boss and see what he has to say," Eel said, slapping Stilp on the back before rushing off.

"Spider, old friend, have you maybe been hitting the bottle tonight?" Stilp asked.

The thief stamped again and turned his back on the door, looking out to the street to see if there was any sign of Teth or anyone else. "I'm not drunk, and I've not lost my mind. Kilchus wants --"

"Kilchus? Is he with Teth or Falk or whatever?"

The thief spun back around, nearly frantic. "Yes! Yes! Yes! And if the lot of you don't get out of the house soon, there's no telling what will happen! You know what happened at the barracks?"

His face full of confusion, Stilp gave a slow nod.

"Well that was Teth," Spider snapped out. "He's a wizard, the most powerful I've ever seen. And he's coming here to spill blood. If you don't get a move on soon, there'll be --"

"What is all this about?" came a new voice from the room beyond.

Spider recognized the speaker as the Finder, and decided he had had enough. He pressed forward, shoving Stilp back. For a moment the two men teetered on the doorway's brink, pushing against one another, their arms locked together, then their feet slid out from underneath and they crashed to the ground together, Spider on top, knocking the breath from Stilp's lungs.

Rolling aside, Spider lunged to his feet, but brought himself up short when the tip of a short sword presented itself beneath his chin.

At the other end of the sword was Eel. "I would not suggest moving right now," Eel said.

Out of the corner of his eye, Spider could see the lanky figure of Lalo the Finder. "I'm sorry about Stilp, honestly --"

"No problem," Stilp grunted from the floor.

"-- but there's a powerful wizard on his way here and he plans on killing you."

"What makes you say this?" Lalo asked.

"They recruited me into their crew," Spider said, trying to speak as fast as possible. "Actually it was Kilchus who recruited me, but there are others, a pair of assassins, brother and sister, a big knight in partial plate, and ... oh, hell, I almost forgot. They've got Mama Kaf."

"Mama Kaf?" Stilp questioned as he pulled himself to his feet.

"Impossible," Lalo said.

"No, no," from Spider. "Teth ... you know him as Falk ... he was able to bring her out of her sleep. She's up stomping around and angrier than ever. Wants Darkbow's blood, that's for sure."

"Sounds like Mama Kaf," Stilp had to admit.

"We've still only got his word for all this," Eel pointed out, the end of his sword never wavering.

"Perhaps." Lalo stepped forward next to his bodyguard to put himself in the thief's sight. "However, Spider isn't prone to being the most courageous of individuals, and I'd have to question why he would come here telling such a tale if there wasn't some truth to it."

"Boss, no offense," Eel said, "but true or not, I'm wondering why he came here at all."

"Out of loyalty!" Spider pressed forward, only the steel against his neck stopping him from moving further. "I admit I was wrong to leave last year, and I admit I've made a lot of mistakes, but this time things are going too far. This Teth, he's powerful, and dangerous. All of you, you've got to get out of here, and then we've got to find some way to stop him. I don't know what he's trying to do other than to steal some bones from the Asylum, but I know he's up to no good, whatever it is. The others only stick with him out of desperation, but I couldn't live with myself if I let something happen tonight."

"Bones?" Lalo asked.

"Yes, bones," Spider said. "I don't know what they do, but they're supposed to have some magic to them or something."

"I've heard Captain Gris and Lieutenant Darkbow discuss these bones," Lalo said, nodding. "The subject came up more than once while we were at the healing tower."

"See?" Spider said.

"He's the boss of thieves," Eel pointed out, "so how do we know he's not trying to get us out of the house just so he can rob us?"

"What thieves?" Spider blurted. "There are no other thieves! Anybody else I'd had working with me has run off because I'm so lousy at my job. I've got to be the worst master of a thieves guild of all time!"

Lalo nodded again. "I tend to trust his word, gentlemen, at least so far. Anyway, it's not as if we have that much here worth stealing."

"There's the tapestries and maybe some of the books," Stilp said.

"And wherever could I sell them without you bunch finding out?" Spider asked.

The Finder held up a hand. "No, I think it best we do as he says and leave, at least for the time being. We can report all this to Captain Gris, then perhaps sup at the Scabbard."

"Thank Ashal," Spider said, his shoulders drooping.

"But we'll take you with us, just in case," Lalo said with a grin.

"No," Spider said.

The end of Eel's sword taped the bottom of the thief's chin. "And why not?" the youth asked.

"I have to get back," Spider said. "They're planning on hitting the Asylum, and if I'm not there, they'll come looking for me. Believe me, none of us wants that to happen."

"And what if they have questions about where you've been?" Lalo asked.

Spider gulped, visibly not happy with the question and the notions it arose. "I'll lie as best I can. It's all I know to do. When things go down at the Asylum, I'll try to slip away if possible. But Teth, he's crazy, spouts off about being thousands of years old. If something's not done about him, there could be a lot more trouble."

"So they're going to attack here and at the Asylum?" Lalo asked.

Now Spider sighed. "Yes, yes, but can you hurry. It's not safe for any of us to be here."

Lalo looked to Stilp. "Lieutenant Darkbow is to arrive at any time."

"Kron can take care of himself," Spider said. "He's fought demons and everything else."

"I have to agree, boss," Stilp said.

Eel continued to stare into Spider's eyes for a moment, his look harsh, then in one swift movement he stepped back and returned his sword to his sheath. "I'll remain behind, give Kron a warning if he shows."

"I'm not sure that's prudent," Lalo said.

"No, I'll stay," Stilp said with a huff. "Eel, no offense, but you've got to watch the boss. If anybody stays back, it should be me."

Spider threw up his arms. "By all that is holy! You people are going to get us all killed by standing around here yacking!"

"Quite right." Lalo touched Eel on a shoulder. "Bring around the carriage."

With a last stern look at the thief, the bodyguard rushed off.

Then the master of the house turned to Stilp. "Go upstairs and fetch my satchel from the library. It'll have everything of immediate importance, the rest can wait."

Stilp strode off in a hurry.

Now Lalo turned upon the thief. "I thank you for the warning, but I must tell you, Spider, if this is some kind of trick, I will make sure you pay heavily for it."

"No trick, Finder," Spider said. "I've been an ass, I know, but that doesn't mean I want you or good ole Stilp dead."

Sounds of Stilp working above drew the Finder's attention to the stairs leading to the second floor. "Perhaps we will be in luck and Master Darkbow will arrive before we leave."

When there was no response, Lalo looked back to the open door. Spider was gone, vanished into the night.

A rapping at the front door caught Montolio's attention. He set aside the scrolls he had been looking over, various writings concerning the teaching of alchemy, and pushed away from the desk in his small office. Walking down the hall to the Asylum's entrance room, he could hear movement ahead of him and then words being spoken, though he could not make out what was being said.

Upon entering the front chamber he found Sergeant Nickel at the open front door, Frex Nodana standing just inside.

The sergeant turned to the second lieutenant. "Sir, Lady Nodana is here to see Lieutenant Darkbow."

"Thank you, sergeant," Montolio said as he came up to the two women. "You may return to your studies."

"Yes, sir," Nickel said with a salute before striding away into the depths of the Asylum.

Nodana chuckled as she closed the door and removed her cloak from around her shoulders. "What do you have them studying now?"

Montolio took the garment and hung it upon a wall peg. "Nothing too strenuous, though you wouldn't think so to hear them grumble. Just basic defenses against ensorcelement."

The master of the mages guild laughed again. "Mostly simple mind defenses."

"That's what I keep telling them," Montolio said with a grin, "but they act as if I'm teaching them the most convoluted secrets of the universe."

"Well, I hope I'm not interrupting."

"Not at all," Montolio said. "I'm finished with them for the day. Just having them put in some extra study time to make up for my absences the last couple of days. Is there anything I can do for you?"

"I'm waiting for Kron. We're supposed to have dinner together." She wrapped her arms around her shoulders, shivering from her recent jaunt outdoors. "But I wouldn't say no to a cup of warm tea or cider."

"Of course." Montolio led her along a hall to a small kitchen where he used a pitcher to pour water into a kettle, which he promptly placed atop an iron stove. Bending over to stoke the nearly dead fire beneath, he said over a shoulder, "How were things at the barracks?"

Nodana took a seat upon a stool. "Slow. The weather doesn't cooperate much."

"Were you able to help?"

"Oh, yes. A few hovering spells made the moving of debris much easier than it would have been otherwise."

The stove's fire coming back to life, Montolio closed the small iron door there and moved to a counter where he opened an earthenware jar and used a wooden spoon to scoop tea leaves into a waiting mug.

"Are you thinking the same magics could be used to move Randall?" he asked, still working.

"That's my thinking," Nodana said. "I've been wondering if Kron and I shouldn't stop by the tower tonight and mention the idea to the head healer, to see if he has any apprehensions about such."

Montolio waved her off as he moved around the kitchen. "Don't worry yourself. You and Kron enjoy the night. I'll stop by the tower after the two of you are gone."

"Are you sure?"

"Absolutely," Montolio said. "Kron shouldn't be at Lalo's for more than an hour at most, so it won't be too late by the time he arrives. I'll be more than glad to speak with Wesler, and to look in on Randall and Althurna."

Nodana smiled. "My thanks to you. I know Kron's mind won't stop going over this Lord Falk and whomever else might be out there posing a threat to the city, but he could use an evening free of complications. Besides, I have something that might take his mind off things."

"Really?" Montolio said.

Nodana couldn't help but smile again. "Yes. I've a surprise for him."

***

The early winter night was already cold, keeping Beggars Row empty of casual pedestrians and the normal foot traffic. Not even a horse or buggy or wagon could be found in motion along the length of the east-to-west road that traveled from the Docks to the Asylum and slightly beyond.

Sadhe Teth and his crew had the street to themselves, with only occasional glimpses from behind windows or doors which soon closed. Cold or not, the citizens of the Swamps recognized trouble when it was brewing, and none of them wanted any part of it. Calling upon the city guard was a useless task as there was no crime being committed, at least not yet, and even though Teth's gang was filled with wanted individuals, few could discern their faces from a distance and even fewer could have placed names with those faces.

As slow as she was with her perpetual limp, Mama Kaf led the way, making use of her new sledgehammer as a cane, her steel leg apparently heavy and not allowing for swift movement. Behind her walked the twins, Jarin strutting off to the right, Rgia sliding along from shadow to shadow on the left, the woman assassin sidestepping the occasional glow provided by hanging oil lamps. In the center was Sadhe Teth himself, the mage walking with his head back, his nostrils flaring, breathing in the chill of the night, his eyes haughty, his pale hair combed straight back atop his balding head. Next nearest to him was Curval, the big knight's sword strapped to his back, his demeanor sullen and silent, his shoulders hanging low as if a mountain rode upon his back. Bringing up the rear came Kilchus the Sword, the man looking none too pleased and ready to spill blood to soothe the anger swirling within him, one hand gripping the hilt of the sword at his belt.

The band strolled straight up the middle of the road. With the exception of Teth, who seemed not to care, and Mama Kaf, so bent upon vengeance, all eyes watched for the slightest movement from within any shadows. Every so often hands would go to weapons, then retreat a moment later. Their walk was not brisk, but cautious, though not overly slow. It helped that the mere sight of Mama Kaf's monstrous bulk frightened away any with a sense of curiosity.

As a black iron fence surrounding a cemetery came into view, Teth held up a hand. "We stop here for a moment."

Everyone halted in their tracks except for Mama Kaf who continued on several more yards before finally slowing to a pause and looking over a shoulder with one malevolent eye.

"I need to make a few preparations," the wizard said as answer to the big woman's stare, then he went to work muttering a handful of ancient, mysterious words, his hands raised in front of his face as his fingers traced unseen images in the air.

Teth's eyes closed and his head leaned back, his dry lips parting to exhale a mist that grew and grew, building into a whirling column not unlike that of smoke. For a moment this gaseous funnel continued to twirl, then a fissure sprang within its center, splintering the mist into two columns. Again it split apart, and again, multiple miniature whirlwinds darting about the wizard's head.

Then Teth gasped and his chin snapped down to his chest.

The gaseous streams shot away from him, one darting toward each of his comrades. Only Rgia was fast enough to avoid an oncoming trail of fog, but even she could not derail its purpose for more than a handful of seconds. The mist sprang upon them and poured itself into the mouths and nostrils of its targets, causing the men and women to jerk and cough. After a moment the mist was gone, seemingly swallowed by those in the streets.

Kilchus slammed a fist into his own chest. "Teth! What the hell have you done to us?"

"Protection, my boy," the wizard said. "I promised to shield all of you from the spirits at the Asylum, and I have now done so."

"Maybe tell us beforehand next time," Kilchus said, appearing as unhappy as ever.

It was at this moment Spider appeared from an alley and ran up to the group, stopping next to Jarin while placing his hands on his knees and breathing heavily.

"Looks as if you've been in a hurry," Kilchus said.

"Yes, Spider," Teth said. "Where have you been?"

For another moment the thief could not answer, then finally his gulping of air slowed and he stood straight. "I told you. Been down at the Docks trying to get some others to join us."

"It seems you have been unsuccessful," Teth said.

Spider shrugged. "Sorry. All I could do was try."

The wizard stared at the thief for a moment, Teth's eyes seeming to dig into Spider's soul, then he shrugged as well. "That is too bad, but I believe we have enough. Come, we are near the Asylum, and soon I must be leaving you for our other objectives."

Spider moved in behind the group, taking a place near Curval as they continued on their way.

Closing in on the graveyard, Kilchus moved up to Teth, keeping his voice low. "You realize he came from the opposite direction of the Docks, right?"

"I am aware," the mage said, his words also spoken under his breath. "If he has betrayed us, all will be revealed, and he will pay a most dear price. But keep an eye on him."

***

Stepping out from the shadows of a side street, Kron Darkbow spotted the back end of a carriage as it trundled away from the front gate of Lalo the Finder's mansion. Soon enough the vehicle disappeared into the darkness, leaving Kron with questions. Who had been at the Finder's place? Or if it had been Lalo himself within the carriage, why had the man left knowing Kron was to arrive?

There was no way to answer, so Kron moved toward the gate itself, starring through the bars and up the hill to the large house. Some few lights burned within, but of most interest was the front door standing open.

Pushing his way through the gate, Kron sped up the hill, his instincts telling him something was amiss.

On the front porch he paused, staring inside the well-lit front room. Nothing appeared out of place. No untoward sounds came to his ears. There were no unusual scents. He could see straight through the room to the second set of open doors into the main hall beyond.

Odd.

Putting a hand on the dagger at his belt, Kron eased to one side of the open doorway before him and slid up to the aperture.

It was then the patting sounds of footsteps came from inside the house. A moment later Stilp made an appearance, the man's head down as he focused upon buckling a thick leather sword belt around his waist over top of his tunic. From one side of the belt hung a short sword, the blade Kron recognized as one of Eel's sparring weapons from their days training together.

The man in black couldn't help but grin. Stilp wearing a sword was a sight to see.

Just as the buckle snapped closed, Kron stepped into the front room, allowing his steps to be heard.

Stilp's head shot up, a frantic hand snapping onto the handle of his sword.

Kron let out a chuckle. "What are you doing wearing a sword?"

The brown-headed man took a step back. "You're not going to hit me, are you?"

Kron tilted his head to one side, giving Stilp a look of curiosity, of questioning, of weighing a decision. The two had not always been on friendly terms, and more than once Kron had allowed himself to use poor Stilp as a punching tool.

But not this night. "No," Kron said, "but seeing the house empty but for yourself, and seeing the sword on your belt, I have to assume something is wrong."

Stilp looked over Kron's shoulder to the night outside, then, "Shut the door. I don't know how long we've got, but it's probably best if we go out the back way."

Ever prudent, Kron moved further into the room and closed and locked the front door behind him. "What is this about, Stilp?" he asked as he turned back to Lalo's employee.

"Spider was here," Stilp said, his speech fast as he tried to explain in as little time as possible. "I don't understand it all, but apparently Falk is on his way here to kill Lalo, I guess out of vengeance for turning them in to the city guard."

"Who is this 'them?' The others working with Falk?"

"I don't know who they all are," Stilp said, "but Kilchus is one of them for sure. And you won't believe it, but they've got Mama Kaf?"

"Mama Kaf?" Stilp was right. Kron didn't believe it. The woman had been left an invalid in a permanent slumber after attempting to slay Kron at the Asylum. The Asylum's ghosts had been the cause of her undoing, as well as that of those who had worked with the woman. "It can't be her."

Stilp shrugged. "Spider says it was."

"And you believe Spider?"

"Doesn't matter what I believe," Stilp said. "The boss believed, and that's all that's important. Now, come on, let's go." He motioned toward the back of the house.

Kron crossed the room to the much smaller man. "So where are Lalo and Eel now?"

Turning toward the long hall that made up the next chamber, Stilp looked over a shoulder to Kron. "They've gone to Gris to let him know. After that --"

The front door exploded.

<u>26</u>

The two guards lay crumpled in sleep near the gate of the Asylum's outer walls, Sadhe Teth's last gift to his followers before taking off to deal with other enemies. A steel foot kicked its way through the guards' small fire, stirring up sparks as Mama Kaf shoved open the gate and led the way onto the Asylum grounds.

The others followed the big woman, cautious glances along the street revealing there were no witnesses, either because of Teth's magic or the cold and dark of the early night.

As a group they tromped up the hill, Rgia scanning from shadow to shadow for any signs of an enemy while the rest watched the few lights burning behind the Asylum's windows. Halfway up the hill, Kilchus called for a halt.

Mama Kaf continued on ahead another dozen steps, but finally she turned around and glared at the others, her new rough garb hanging from her shoulders like a tent.

"For all Teth's talk, he never came up with a proper plan," Kilchus told the others. "How should we got about this?"

"A little late to discuss strategy and tactics," Rgia said.

The Sword glared at the assassin. "I was thinking we would just kick our way in the front door, but now that we're here, I'm not sure that's the best idea, especially without Teth."

Rgia snickered.

Kilchus ignored her and turned to Spider. "What do you think? You and Mama Kaf were in on that assault here before."

"Yeah, one that failed," Jarin said with an evil grin.

A growl sounded from deep within Mama Kaf's throat.

"What of you, Kilchus?" Rgia asked. "You were a guard here for a few days. Surely you know the ins and outs of the place."

"Not as much as you might think," the Sword said. "Most of our training was out of doors when I was here, so I didn't get much of a chance to get a feel for the place. I remember there was some talk about a back exit, but apparently its hidden."

"What of the roof?" Jarin asked. "Any access up there?"

Kilchus shrugged. "I don't know. Probably."

Mama Kaf growled louder this time. "You fools do realize while you're standing around blabbering, whoever is inside the Asylum is probably watching your every move?"

Rgia laughed again. "Oh, I realized that as soon as we came through the gate, but wanted to see how all this would play out."

Quiet until then, it was Curval who strode forward, making straight for the Asylum's front door. He said not a word to the others but marched onward, reaching up to unsling his mighty sword.

"I guess the decision has been made for us," Jarin said.

"I suppose so," Spider added.

And the others followed.

***

"*They come.*"

Montolio nearly spilled the mug of tea in his hands.

Concern appeared on Nodana's face and she sat forward, reaching across the table of the Asylum's kitchen. "Are you all right?"

"You didn't hear that?"

The other mage shook her head. "What was it?"

"The ghosts," Montolio said. "They ... spoke to me. They've done it before."

"What did they say?"

"I think it was a warning. The last time it was a warning."

As if to prove his words, "*Prepare for battle.*"

Montolio sat up straight and placed his wooden mug upon the table. "That was *definitely* a warning."

Before Nodana could ask further questions, he sprang from the table, "Wait here," then he darted from the room.

Rushing down the hall to the lengthy front room, Montolio found his six recruits coming up the stairwell from the basement.

"Lieutenant, what was that?" one them asked, the man's face gray with trepidation.

"You heard it?" Montolio said, stopping in front of his students. "All of you?"

Six heads nodded in the affirmative.

Montolio rushed to a window, looking through the glass and between bars into the night. There was little to see, the torches inside the room sheening off the glass to block much of his view.

"Damn it," he muttered.

"Lieutenant, what do you want us to do?" Sergeant Nickel asked.

For a moment Montolio hesitated, still trying to see anything outside. He thought he caught movement nearing the Asylum's front door, but he couldn't be sure.

Pushing away from the window, he rounded on the six guards, noting the looks of fear in their faces. All had received the basic training of city guards, all wore studded leathers and carried short swords and daggers, all were young or relatively so and in good health, but they were yet unprepared for the threats that had seemed prominent of late. There was no telling what lay beyond the Asylum's front door, but Montolio could guess it was something more deadly than what his group was familiar tackling.

"Okay," he said, giving himself another moment to think. He wasn't much trained for this himself, and wished Kron was on the scene. Still, he would not surrender. They could have escaped out the back exit, or he and Nodana could magic the lot of them away, but there were the bones to consider, the obvious reason for this new assault. There was no telling what could happen if those bones landed in the hands of Falk or whomever.

"Okay," he repeated, looking to the six before him. "Nickel, round up four crossbows, then place yourself and three others as archers on the second-floor landing." Here he pointed to the lowest level of the walkways across the front of

612

former inmate cells. "Take up defensive positions there, and don't be afraid to target whatever comes through the front door ... or any other threat for that matter."

"Yes, sir," Nickel said.

Montolio pointed to two of the largest men. "Sorry, fellows, but I'm going to need you near the entrance."

Fear remained steady in all eyes, but the two burly fellows nodded back.

"Swords out, but give the crossbowmen their shot," Montolio said to the two before looking to the group as a whole. "All right, let's get to it."

The city guards broke up, rushing off to their appointed tasks and places. The lieutenant watched them for a few seconds, glad to see everyone was doing what they were told and proud of them.

Then he rushed back down the hall to the kitchen.

He found Nodana standing by the room's exit.

"I heard," she said, concern there.

"Good," Montolio said as he came to a halt, "because I think we're going to need your help."

***

Mama Kaf raised her sledgehammer to a shoulder, ready to pound upon the Asylum's heavy front door.

"Hold on a moment there," Spider said, approaching. "Why don't we try something a little more subtle in case we haven't been noticed yet?'

The big woman glared at him once more, but she stepped aside giving him room.

Spider stepped in front of the door, staring at it, his eyes following the beams of thick wood and the iron bands, finally settling upon the lock itself.

"Magic will not work," Curval said, his voice surprising everyone. "Sadhe Teth already made the attempt."

"I know." Spider brushed aside the knight's words, then moved closer to the door while kneeling to study the lock at a better angle. After a few moments, one of his hands dipped into a pouch strapped to his belt, then withdrew holding several small utensils. "But there's more than one way to get through a door."

He went to work like an expert, each hand twisting and turning the miniature tools.

Until there was an audible *clicking* sound.

Spider grinned, pocketed his tools and stood away from the door. He had no desire to enter the Asylum first, or at all, but a sense of accomplishment rolled through him.

"Now you may enter," he said, motioning from Mama Kaf to the door.

The big woman didn't hesitate. Her sledgehammer on one shoulder, she grabbed hold of the a handle and yanked the door open.

Four arrows hurtled toward her.

The first smashed into her new steel shin, the arrow shattering upon impact. The second sailed over a shoulder, barely missing Spider before vanishing into darkness. The third sank into her left thigh, the fourth slamming into her massive right breast.

She grunted, swayed on her feet, then bound forward as if nothing had happened.

A burly fellow in orange on her right slashed out with a short sword, but despite all her size, Mama Kaf was faster. The end of her sledgehammer sprang forward, catching the man across the face. His knees buckled and he collapsed to the floor.

Another guard came from her left, his sword stabbing in. This time Mama Kaf was not fast enough, but it did not matter. Kilchus was suddenly there right behind her, his sword lashing across the guard's attacking arm, taking the limb off at the elbow. The guard screamed as blood sprang from his wound in a spray, only to be removed from his pain by a punch from one of Mama Kaf's gigantic fists. The enemy dropped to the ground unconscious and Sadhe Teth's minions poured into the Asylum.

A man dressed in blacks and whites appeared from a hall at the far end of the room.

"Montolio!" Kilchus shouted, taking off at a run for the mage.

But the distance was too great.

"Ice!" Montolio shouted, pointing a finger.

Kilchus the Sword's arms and legs locked in place. He could no longer move. All he could do was stand frozen in place, his blinking eyes the only outward sign he still lived.

A guard pounced from over the second-floor balcony, a dagger in one hand as he landed atop Mama Kaf. It was like hitting a mountain. Kaf did not move, not so much as a budge, but the man atop her grunted out the air from his lungs as he tried to find purchase on top of the large woman while also bringing up his weapon for a stab.

Mama Kaf reached up with a meaty hand and wrapped fingers like giant sausages around her attacker's throat. Squeezing, she kept him from drawing in more air, and before he could bring down his steel for a blow, she slammed him onto the ground at her feet. A cracking sound followed, either the floor or the man's neck, but he no longer presented any danger.

The other three guards behind the second floor railing worked frantically to load arrows into their crossbows again. Their comrades were falling and falling fast, and none wished to join the fray with that monster woman at the head.

Nodana gasped at the carnage as she came out from the shadows behind Montolio.

"Help me!" Montolio cried to her before turning back to face their foes.

Coming out of her surprise with a look of resolve, Frex Nodana nodded and stepped up next to the other mage. Her hands outstretched, her fingers working in the air, she muttered words of magic under her breath.

A hazy blue smoke burst up from the cracks in the floor, roiling around the legs of the attackers clustered in front of the Asylum's entrance, climbing up those legs.

"No!" Rgia Oltos shouted, her brother right behind her. She slid past Mama Kaf and to one side of the frozen Kilchus. Her hands flashed again and again, sending forth a hail of daggers pulled from hidden folds and pockets of her leather garb.

Seeing the oncoming danger, Montolio jumped in front of Nodana, the point of a flying dagger catching him in his right shoulder. Before he could react, another length of steel buried itself to the hilt in the meat of his right leg. He cried out and dropped, leaving the other mage open to the barrage of incoming missiles.

Still Rgia kept throwing her daggers, more and more of them appearing in her hands an instance before leaving her touch to careen across the distance to the target.

Three crossbows launched arrows.

Curval came up next to Mama Kaf, his giant sword whirling in front of the pair of them to knock aside two of the crossbow bolts. The third arrow tagged the knight's metal-plated chest and would have torn on through to flesh if he had not spun to one side, the arrow skidding across steel to bury itself in the Asylum's front door.

It was then a dagger struck Nodana. The blade barely touched her, grazing across her left cheek, but it was enough to divert her attention. The blue smoke dissipated as quickly as it had appeared, drifting away into nothingness. Then another dagger buried itself in the folds of her robes, causing no harm but frightening nonetheless. And then a third dagger found a home in her side, not far from the liver.

She screamed in pain and dropped to her knees.

The daggers stopped flying

Seeing the wizards as the most dire threat, Mama Kaf hefted her sledgehammer and trudged across the room toward them.

Sergeant Nickel jumped down from the steps leading to the landing where the other two guards worked at their crossbows again. Yanking her sword free of its leather sheath, she charged the giant figure approaching the pair of downed mages.

Jarin caught her in the side with a shoulder, knocking her off her feet into a wall. Shaking off her pain and her helmet, she tried to stand only to be met with a flurry of punches to the face. Sergeant Nickel slumped down.

As the last two guards cranked back their crossbows, Mama Kaf stood over the two mages. Montolio cringed in anguish, his eyes closed and his hands grasping at his wounded leg. Frex Nodana lay panting, one hand grasping the hilt of the weapon in her side, her wide eyes of defiance glaring up at the monster before her.

Mama Kaf chuckled.

Then the hammer came down.

And again.

Neither mage sat up. Neither mage moved.

Kilchus abruptly found himself able to move once more.

Crossbows twanged.

Fear and nerves showed themselves as both arrows missed their marks, slamming into the wall beyond the infiltrators and cracking apart.

"Get them!" Jarin yelled, pointing to the two remaining guards.

Kilchus joined the young assassin in a charge up the steps of the landing. The two guards dropped their crossbows in a panic and reached for their sheathed swords, their hands fumbling. Kilchus stabbed with his long blade, ending a life, while Jarin pushed past him to bring down a dagger from upon high, the steel burying itself in a shoulder and dropping the last of the protectors of the Asylum.

It had all taken a matter of seconds, and not a single one of Sadhe Teth's followers had fallen.

Stomping down the stairs, Kilchus pointed at Spider hovering near the Asylum's exit. "You! Your our wizard, so find those bones so we can get the hell out of here."

Spider nodded and closed his eyes, folding his hands together in front of his stomach.

Rgia moved to close the outside door, finally blocking the cold air from floating in through the opening. When she turned around, she grinned at the Sword while walking over to retrieve her thrown weapons. "Jumpy, Kilchus? Afraid a horde of city guards are about to descend upon us."

The man frowned at her. "No, but all the same, I'd feel better if Teth was here."

"It was you who wanted him to take out the Finder and Captain Gris," Jarin pointed out as he came down the steps behind the Sword.

"Yes, it was," Rgia said as she bent next to the unmoving, bloody figures of Montolio and Nodana. "But Teth agreed to it awful quick. Doesn't make sense, splitting our forces like this. Makes me wonder."

"Wonder at what?" Kilchus asked, slinging the blood from the end of his sword and sheathing the blade on his belt.

Rgia didn't answer, a shadow looming over the two downed mages blocking her view from finding all her daggers.

She looked up to see Mama Kaf still standing in place, the big woman's chest heaving as she stared down at the two mages, the sledgehammer gripped in both hands.

"Darkbow is not here," the massive figure said.

"Get used to it," Kilchus said with a chuckle. "Teth isn't exactly one to keep his word."

Rgia pulled several of her daggers to her, wiping them clean on the fallen Nodana's robes. "That's another thing that worries me."

"Found it!" Spider blurted out, his eyes snapping open.

"Well?" Kilchus asked, looking to the little man.

"It's in the basement," the thief-mage said, "locked away in a strong box. And there's nobody else here but us, so I don't think we'll have any problem retrieving it."

"What about the spooks?" Jarin said, showing some little fear as he looked around the room as if expecting an undead spirit to lunge at him from any corner.

Another dagger cleaned and put away, Rgia said, "Brother, if they could interfere, they would have by now."

***

A rain of steel and brass shrapnel and wood shards slammed across the entrance room of the mansion, followed by the front door knocked off its hinges. No time for Kron to react, the door smacked the side of his head, sending him to the floor, the door landing partially on top of him. Stilp screamed and crouched, bringing up his arms to shield his face, though some few splinters still managed to impale him, bringing up red spots along the arms of his tunic.

Then silence ruled as dust settled.

The only sound Stilp could make out was the beating of his own heart.

Until the gentle tapping of footsteps from outside.

Stilp looked up just as an old man in dingy robes and a cloak appeared in the shattered doorway. "Falk."

The old man grinned, stepping into the relative warmth of the room. "I take it the Finder is no longer present."

Before Stilp could answer, he caught a glimpse of the downed Kron Darkbow. He crawled over to the motionless figure in black beneath the remains of the heavy door. Reaching out, his fingers hesitated. There was a gash of red across Kron's forehead, and there was no sign of the man breathing.

"By Ashal, you've killed him," Stilp stated, looking up at Teth, fear filling the little man's eyes.

"So much the better," Teth said, still smiling. "I presume this fellow in black is the famed Kron Darkbow? If so, one less complication."

Stilp slumped back to sit upon the floor. "I suppose now you kill me, too."

"Not necessary," the wizard said, a hand brushing aside the idea. "I am mainly here to kill time, to allow Kilchus to believe I am serving his interests while in fact he serves my own. I don't really need the Finder dead, nor you, though coming here I believed I could perhaps tie up a loose end or two, which I've accomplished with Darkbow's demise. Besides, you will be dead soon enough. *Everyone* will be dead soon enough."

A flash of darkness came over the old man's eyes, then he turned, his cloak flapping about him and he walked back into the night.

Part 3:
Ashes

<u>27</u>

Pain. It encompassed him, encircled him. It was all that was. Only pain. There was nothing else to his existence, nothing else to the outside world. All he knew was pain.

And the darkness. There was that. Or was there? Even the dark seemed filled with terrible, ripping anguish that ate away at his very soul, at his very being.

A flutter of light. What *was* that? Something other than darkness and pain? Could it be? He mustered up his remaining strength, trying to reach for the light, but he felt as if on fire, the flames eating away at him, tearing at him, leaving him a shriveled nothing of a person.

The light faded.

It did not help that his thoughts swam amongst themselves and against themselves. He could not remember anything other than the pain. Had there ever been a past in which the torment had not existed for him? There were no memories of such a time.

Yet, there were faces. Yes. Faces. He could recall them. His mother, his father, his brother, that beautiful girl in a far off land. What had been her name? And how could he recall that the land was far off?

The memories came rushing back to him.

Lycinia. Yes, that had been the name of the country, his place of birth. He had been an artist, a painter, a sculptor, a student, all wiped away by foolishness, by the sizable gambling debts his brother had brought upon the family. Montolio had fled those debts, unable to pay and feeling little remorse for the drunk who had created them.

Montolio. That was his name. Even through the pain, he could now remember as much.

Other faces and names flashed before his mind, helping to assuage some of the burning. Dark hair, dark clothing, dark sword ... Kron. Yes, Kron. A woman, only a few years older than Montolio, dark hair, short hair, robes, a wizard like himself but more powerful, more skilled and experienced in the ways of magic.

Nodana.

Frex Nodana.

"Nodana!" The word ripped from his throat in a scream, waking Montolio to the world.

He could do nothing for long minutes but lay there blinking in the weak light of the Asylum's entrance room, a cold wind flowing over him, shivering his already pained body. One of his legs, it scorched his inner self, but the worst pain was to his head. His skull felt as if crushed beneath the weight of a mountain, his sight blurry and shaking. His shoulder also burned, but that was nothing as compared to his leg and his head.

Blinking, he found he lay in a small pool of blood. Was it his own? Probably, but likely not all.

Those daggers, the flying daggers, they had never seemed to end. The woman who had thrown them must have been a master mage herself, otherwise she was the fastest human Montolio had ever witnessed, and armed to the teeth with all those small blades.

But he could not think about her now. There was Nodana to think of, and Captain Nickel and the others. What had happened to all of them?

Montolio tried to move, but his limbs quaked and it was as if he was buried in mud. One hand rose a few inches from the Asylum's floor, then plopped back down into scarlet gore, splattering red across his face. He lay there, ushering in new levels of strength he feared were beyond his capacity.

Think! he told himself. You are a wizard, trained by the finest sorcerers of all Lycinia. You might not be a healer, Montolio, but you've been taught more than a few curative and invigorating spells.

He closed his eyes again, giving himself a moment of rest. He lay there in the blood, unable to ignore the wounds and the pains shooting through his body.

Gritting his teeth, he spat and opened his eyes once more. Whispered words of power tumbled from between his lips. Immediately he felt himself a little stronger. It was not much, but it girded him for more to come. He spoke further words, a little louder than before, and the pain eased from his body. The wounds would still be there, the blood would still flow, but at least the pain had lessened by far, allowing him to shake off the worst of the delirium.

He braced himself with his hands and pushed off the floor, nearly slipping in the blood. Once his arms were straight, he leaned back and sat upon the wet floor.

Laying before him was Frex Nodana, her face twisted away from him, her body laying at an unusual angle, her arms above her head, her legs bent as if she had been running.

"Frex," he managed to say.

There was no response.

Slowly, gradually, Montolio stretched forth a hand and placed it on her side. The body was warm, moving slightly with the rise and fall of her chest.

Montolio closed his eyes and sighed. "Oh, thank Ashal she's alive."

When he opened his eyes once more, he took in the blood pooling around her side where a dagger had been stuck, now a narrow wound empty of its weapon, and another, smaller circle of blood on the floor beneath her head.

"Nodana?" Leaning over her, Montolio reached around to touch her chin. Again, there was no reaction to his word or his touch.

He gently tugged on the chin, turning the face around so he could better see it.

And he almost dropped her head back upon the floor.

Her forehead had been shattered. The skull was obviously indented, bashed in at a spot above her eyes, cracked pieces of the bone protruding through red gore and gray mush. Her eyes stared directly ahead, flat, unmoving, no sign of life behind them, yet she lived somehow, her lungs taking in air.

Montolio had to fight back bile building in the back of this throat. As gentle as possible, he lay her head back against the floor.

Then he cried.

***

Stilp sat in shock upon the floor, his eyes unfocused, staring off into a corner. In the past there had almost always been someone around to tell him what to do, Lalo or Belgad or even Kron in some circumstances, but now there was a large empty house with only a body in front of him. The few times Stilp had taken charge of a situation, it had always been at the behest of another, but now without a boss he was at loss. Lalo and Eel had gone to the main city barracks in Southtown, or whatever was left of the place, leaving Stilp alone. Now Darkbow was dead, laying there on his side beneath that big door, so what to do? Who to report to?

Pushing himself up on his knees, he finally blinked, focusing his sight. There was a smaller guard barracks there in the Swamps, the place little more than a station house with an office and a bunk room for a handful of soldiers. He would have to go there first, he supposed, to report what had happened. Then what? Find the Finder? And after that? Where would they go? Surely Lalo wouldn't suggest they come back to the mansion.

A soft moan stirred Stilp from his thoughts. For a few moments he believed the sound came from himself, a supple call to the seeming futility of life, then he heard the sound again, louder.

"Kron!" Stilp grabbed the heavy, battered door that lay across the man in black and pulled it away. At first the door would not come easy, but he used muscles he did not know he had and soon enough the wood scrapped against the marble floor to one side.

Looking down, he could now see Darkbow was breathing, a sign of life that had been hidden by the door. Also, Darkbow's eyes fluttered beneath a red scrape across the front of his head.

"Holy Ashal, you're alive!" Stilp shouted.

"What?" Kron managed to mumble.

Stilp shot to his feet. "You stay right there, okay? Stilp will go and ... uh, I'll get you some water ... no, no, I'll get you a bandage. Does that sound right?" He gave a crooked smile.

"Stilp?" Kron rolled over onto his back. He groaned louder as his eyes snapped open to stare at the ceiling. "What in hell happened?"

"It was Falk," the other man said, dancing slightly on his feet, he was so happy to see Darkbow alive.

"He was here?"

"Yes, he was. Now don't you move. I'll be right back."

Kron held up a hand. "Hold a moment. What did Falk hit me with?"

"A door."

Kron's eyes opened wider. "A door?"

"Blew it off the hinges, actually," Stilp said. "Never seen anything like it."

Easing a hand up to his side, Kron pressed upon the floor and lifted himself to a sitting position. Doing so caused great pain to his head, bringing him to wince again. When he opened his eyes once more he could plainly see the damaged door next to him and the shattered opening to the outside, splinters and bits of metal spread across the front room.

"Magic?" Kron asked.

"Looked that way to me," Stilp said, "though I never heard of Falk being a mage."

"Why didn't he kill me?"

"Don't know for sure," Stilp said, "but he did say some weird things, stuff about fooling Kilchus, or something like that. And that we're all doomed ... no, no ... that we're all going to be dead soon."

"Dead?" Shaking his head to clear his vision, Kron grimaced as more pain racked his head. Then his eyes grew wide once more. "The bones. He has something in mind for the bones."

"Bones?" Stilp said. "I don't know about that."

"Did he say anything else?"

"Not really. He blew up the door, gloated a little, then turned and left."

"But he mentioned Kilchus? By name?"

"Yes, sir."

Kron sat there for a few moments in hopes of his pain lessening, but it did little good. His vision went from normal to cloudy and back again, occasional lights at the corners of his sight. His head felt as if it had been squeezed in a vice with a steel pick shoved into his forehead for good measure. He was leery of getting to his feet, afraid he would stumble, or possibly even disgorge his last meal considering the roiling in his stomach. But he had to act. The attack on the mansion made little sense, not even as a diversion. Something else was going on, and Kron believed it probably had to do with the bones. Was Falk trying to steal them this very night? That would mean an assault on the Asylum, but why wasn't Falk there himself? Apparently the lord had said something to Stilp about misleading Kilchus, so did that mean Kilchus was trying to retrieve the bones?

There was no way to answer any of those questions while sitting on a cold marble floor.

"Stilp, I need a healer, now."

"I'll go get one."

"Before you do, make sure --"

A knocking came from the front entrance.

Stilp and Kron looked around to find the carriage driver Scratch standing in the opening, one hand raised as he had just knocked on the wooden frame where the door had once stood.

"I was told to come here," the old man said.

***

"Lieutenant?"

The word had been slurred, and had come from behind. Montolio tried to twist around to see who had spoken, but a stabbing ache bolted through his head, causing him to wince and cry out.

Sitting there bleeding, Montolio slowly reached up to touch his forehead. There was a gash there, long and still wet, though there were signs of crust growing around the edges. It had been the giant with the hammer who had caused the blow. The only thing that had saved Montolio from a shattered skull had been him twisting away at the last possible moment. By all rights he should not be living.

"Lieutenant, is that you?" someone said, once more the words slurred.

Steeling himself, Montolio planted his hands on the floor at his side and turned to one side.

What he saw made him gasp. Sergeant Nickel lay sitting up against a wall, her legs outstretched, her face marbleized black and blue and brown. Her eyes puffy and swollen shut, one edge of her lip torn, a trickle of blood working its way down to her tabard.

"Sergeant?" Montolio asked.

Nickel coughed, spitting up blood, then groaned. "Is that you?" she repeated.

Montolio pulled himself over to the woman, now closer and better able to examine her. Several of her teeth were missing, but her jaw did not appear shattered. Her face was swollen to the point of being barely recognizable, but she breathed well.

"Nickel, it's me," he said. "Hold on for me, okay? I'm going to get help for all of us."

"Sure," the woman managed to say with a weak chuckle that spilled more blood from her mouth. "Not going anywhere."

Closing his eyes once more, Montolio drew upon his own soul to power further magic. The very act would weaken him, but he needed to heal his body as much as possible. Someone had to get aid. He spoke a few more magic words and managed a wave or two of a hand, then felt flushed as more of his pain drained from his body. The wounds were still present, but at least he could think and act more clearly without the trouble of dealing with the pain. The magic would not last long, perhaps a quarter of an hour, but he hoped that would be enough.

Wobbling, he rolled over on to his feet, paused to catch his breath, then pushed to standing while avoiding looking further at Frex Nodana. There was little he could do for the damaged mage until he could find assistance, preferably a skilled healer.

Once he stood, the scene unfolded before him.

Carnage lay everywhere. There were bodies strewn near the front door, which hung open to bring in the night's cold air, and across the landing on the second floor. How many were dead and how many were alive, the wizard could not know without further investigation, but from what he could see, there would be more dead than living.

Montolio groaned as a bit of the pain ached back into his leg. Looking down, he grasped the hilt of the dagger protruding there, forgotten by its thrower, and tugged. It was not the smartest thing to do, blood splurting from the wound as more pain hit him hard enough to cause him to double over.

After a few moments the magic kicked in and he found the strength to stand once more, the dagger falling from his fingers to clatter on the floor.

Then he remembered. *The bones.*

"Oh, no."

Montolio spun around and limped into the darkness of the hallway, making directly for the stone steps that took him into the dreary basement. Below he grabbed a torch from a wall and nearly stumbled ahead. He already knew what he would find, other torches along the hall revealing an open door at the end.

Leaning against the door jamb, Montolio stared into the room, holding his light before him. The heavy chest where the bones had been kept was shattered into kindling, most likely the work of that sledgehammer. Forcing himself to shuffle forward, he held the torch high, hoping beyond hope that perhaps the bones were still present, had been dropped or forgotten.

But fortune did not favor him. The bones and their leather wrappings were gone.

As the carriage trundled away from the smaller guard barracks in the Swamps, Kron rested his head on the back seat, his eyes closed.

From the front, Scratch slapped the reins, speeding his horses along.

"Scratch?" Kron said.

"Yes, Sir Darkbow."

"No need for the 'sir.' I'm no noble."

"Yes, sir."

"I've been meaning to ask you," Kron went on, "who was it sent you to the mansion?"

"It was Master Storyteller Highwater, sir," Scratch said, keeping his eyes on the road before them, dodging the occasional pedestrian.

"Midge?" That didn't make any sense.

"Yes, sir. It was him."

"Did he say anything else?"

"Just that I was to take you to the Swamps healing tower," Scratch answered.

"Did he say why?"

There was no answer from the front as the driver pulled the carriage around a corner, then a shrug. "I presumed he thought you'd need a healer, sir, which if you don't mind my saying, looks to be the truth."

Kron couldn't argue with him about that, believing himself to possibly suffer a concussion. His vision continued to swim and the pain in his skull was absolute. Without Stilp and Scratch's help, he doubted he would have been able to climb into the carriage on his own. Now that Stilp was with the city guards, Kron only hoped Scratch would be enough to help him down from the wagon, though there would probably be other hands available at the tower.

The tower? No, not the tower. Not yet.

"Scratch, forget about the tower for now," Kron said.

"My apologies, sir, but I was told that under no circumstances was I not to go to the tower first."

"By Midge?"

"Yes, sir. He's the one who paid me."

"But I wish to go to the Asylum first."

"He said you would say that, sir, and for me to tell you that you could do no good there until you was healed up."

"No good there?" That meant something *had* happened at the Asylum, which was what Kron had been fearing ever since waking up on Lalo's marble floors.

Kron tried to sit up, thinking he would jump from the carriage if necessary, but his wound forced him back in the seat. He could barely stand, let alone dive from a moving vehicle and run on foot to the Asylum.

He cursed from the back seat.

"Again, my apologies, sir," Scratch said.

Kron did not have much longer to grumble from the back, for soon enough the driver pulled the carriage to a stop in front of the healing tower's front door.

The door was open, a number of healers in white robes apparently waiting for them, their exact numbers difficult for Kron to ascertain in his condition.

A middle-aged, gray-haired man in the familiar whites stepped ahead of the others and approached the carriage. "Scratch, is it?"

"Yes, sir, Master Wesler," the driver said with a nod to the back seat. "This is Lord Darkbow. I was told you'd be here for us."

"That we are," Wesler said, climbing onto the side of the wagon, his eyes busy looking over Kron.

"Can you tell me what's happened to you?" he asked the man in black.

"Head struck," Kron said. "I think it might be a concussion. My vision is blurred, and I can barely keep to my feet."

The chief healer nodded and jumped down from the wagon. "Very well. We'll have you up on your feet as soon as possible." Here he offered a smile. "We might be lacking Randall's skills at the moment, but we can still perform a few miracles from time to time."

"How is Randall?" Kron asked.

The smile died on the healer's lips. "The same, unfortunately."

Wesler turned away then, waving for others to come forward. Three large fellows in white rushed up to the carriage and began to lift Kron from the back seat.

"Wesler!" Kron called out while being hefted to the tower's door.

The chief healer appeared at his side. "Yes?"

"Who told you to be ready for me?" Kron asked.

"It was Master Highwater," Wesler explained. "He said time was of the essence, that you would need immediate healing."

At that Kron allowed his head to lag back against a pair of stout arms. How had Midge known? And what was happening at the Asylum?

***

As Montolio came up the stairs from the basement, he found Sergeant Nickel sitting forward, a hand to her head. A groan from somewhere else in the room told the mage at least one more of them alive.

Stumbling at the top step, Montolio forced himself to drop to a knee. The magic was already fading from his body, and his strength waned. Even his wounds tingled, the sensation of pain on the verge of slamming into him once more. He could not allow himself to be overcome. Huffing in air that did not come easy, he realized he might well be the only hope for the room's survivors, especially Frex Nodana.

Then a new voice came onto the scene. "What ... what happened here?"

Montolio looked up. At the front door stood one of the two guards who had been stationed at the outside gate, the man's eyes agog, one hand lifted to the side of his head as if he was trying to recall something.

"Here!" Montolio shouted out to him, trying to stand once more but falling forward, his hand landing in blood and sending him sliding onto his stomach.

The guard from the door rushed forward. "By Ashal, lieutenant!" Then the man stopped, sight of the blood, of a severed arm, of the battered sergeant, and of Frex Nodana's head wound, bringing him up short.

Sloshing around in a pool of blood, Montolio landed on his back. "We need healers here."

The guard's face remained discombobulated, full of shock. "Sir?"

"Go, now!" Montolio shouted. "Healers!"

The loud voice seemed to wake the guard. "Yes, sir!" he said, then turned and trotted from the room as fast as his legs would carry him.

28

Sadhe Teth floated in space high above the city. Not in his physical form, no, as that would be impractical during such a cold time of year, but in his spiritual form. His body rested in a bedroom above Chump's Squall, where he had left it and his current companions, those fools.

Flitting about, staring from one end of the city to the other, even his spectral form could not help but grin. The bones were his once more, tucked away within the folds of his robes, and now there was no one with the might to stand against him. Tendbones was dead, and from Teth's survey of the city, there were no others with the power to stop him.

He laughed, thinking of Kilchus and those other idiots doing his bidding. It had been so easy to manipulate them. He would not need them much longer, and only kept them around now as added protection in case something should go awry with his plans, which he could hardly fathom at this point.

The bones in hand, it was time for death, for *everyone's* death. At least everyone within the city. Teth had performed similar magics long in the past, and they had made him the most powerful mortal wizard of any mage. But now the cities were so much larger, the human race had spread itself so much further upon the lands, and there were so many more souls worth sacrificing to his own goals of power.

His estimate was there were at least three hundred thousand people living in or directly around Bond. The number was nearly staggering to him. Thousands of years earlier, the largest city had been but ten thousand souls, souls which had fed him for millennium. He could scarcely imagine his magical power after three hundred thousand had fallen to his means. That combined with the bones would make him as strong as any god who had ever existed, and this brought a heated sense of exhilaration to Sadhe Teth's stolen heart.

Now he had to decide upon a plan of action. How should he go about the task? He had considered flooding, but the time of year was wrong. Still, a winter flood would not be impossible, not for one of his power, but it would be impractical, straining his reserves with little reason. Fire from above, spewing flames from the heavens, appealed to Teth's sense of fear mongering and his destructive inclinations, but that too was impractical. There had to be another way, something simple, something that would allow him to accomplish his task with a minimum of effort upon his part.

He also had to decide upon a place. Such powerful magic would take time, perhaps hours, and he wanted little chance of interruption while also having a fine view of the fruits of his labors.

High above the city, he spun slowly, his unseen eyes flickering from one place to another. He pondered the tallest structure in the city, a steeple in the northern neighborhoods, but decided against it as the single room at the top would likely be quite small, possibly even stifling, though he had to admit it would make an excellent viewing spot. He wanted some place with open air, a rooftop providing a view of the city in all directions. Any number of warehouses could have served, but most were packed near the rushing waters and only offered limited views. The university in the northwest also posed a number of larger structures, but Teth sought someplace more centralized.

Finally his gaze came upon the middle of the Swamps, the closest to an actual center of the city. A wide variety of tenement buildings of size were options, but one edifice stood out among the hundreds of others. Large and round with a flat roof, it would offer a complete perspective of the city.

The Swamps healing tower.

Teth couldn't help but laugh.

Then something danced across his vision. He blinked in surprise. Something else fluttered by him, and his spectral head jerked away. Spinning around, he found hundreds upon hundreds of white flakes tumbling down from the sky above.

Snow.

He laughed again.

Another question answered.

***

By the time Scratch's carriage pulled up in front of the Asylum's gates, four wagons had already been brought onto the grounds and placed atop the hill at the building's entrance. Six burly fellows in orange now guarded the gate, flurries of snow lingering on the edges of their shoulders and helmets as a dozen of their comrades came and went from inside the building to the wagons and back.

Kron stepped down from the carriage, his legs wobbly as his boots touched ground.

From the back of the carriage, Chief Healer Wesler looked out over the man in black's shoulders. "I've already assigned three healers here, and more will be on their way."

"My thanks," Kron said without looking back.

The healer jumped down on the other side of the carriage and worked his way around the horses to Kron. "How are you doing? Still lightheaded?"

"No," Kron said, which was only partially a lie. Most of the dizziness had faded, but every bump of the carriage ride had made his vision swim. On firm ground once more, he did not seem to be suffering the ill effects, but he could not guess how long that would last. The healers, magical and otherwise, had done everything for him they could. His head wound was nearly gone, only a red blemish was all that was left, but he still did not feel up to his full self. Time and rest were needed, but those were luxuries at the moment.

"Scratch," Kron said, looking over a shoulder to the driver, "I don't believe I will be needing your services further this night, but thank you for being there when necessary. This will be remembered."

"And thanks to you for your service to the city," the old man said. He opened his lips as if to say something further, but then seemed to think better of it and snapped his horses' reins, the animals pulling the carriage way into the night.

With Wesler following, Kron made his way through the gates, nodding at the stoic faces of the guards on duty. Following the path up the hill, the light from the Asylum's open door and windows allowed them to make out the comings and goings of more city guards, as well as the occasional healer.

"What are they doing?" Wesler asked with a squint as they tromped across a growing layer of thin snow.

"They're carrying out wounded," Kron said.

As they neared, it became apparent Kron's words were true. Two wagons were being utilized for the living, the other two wagons for the dead. So far all those in the back of the wagons wore orange tabards, including the groaning figure of Sergeant Nickel.

Kron paused a moment next to the sergeant's wagon. "Nickel."

"Lieutenant?" the woman said with eyes swollen closed.

"It's me," Kron said. "How bad is it?"

A tearful cry erupted from the sergeant's throat as she sat up in the bed of the wagon. "They worked through us like we weren't even there, lieutenant. They had a ... a giant! We hit it twice with the crossbows, but it didn't even slow the thing down. It kept swinging that giant hammer from side to side."

"A hammer?" Kron asked.

"Yes, sir," Nickel said, "and there was a woman, the fastest I've ever seen. She must have thrown a hundred daggers in the blink of an eye."

Seeing the woman upset, Kron placed a hand on her left shoulder, easing her back into a reclining position. "Find your rest, Nickel. You've earned it. I'll handle things from here."

"Yes, sir."

"Sounds like magic," Wesler commented as he and Kron moved away.

"Possibly," Kron said, "but I've seen some who could manage such tricks without sorcery."

"This sounds familiar to you, then?" Wesler asked.

Kron nodded. "Perhaps. I recently witnessed a woman who could be as fast as the sergeant here says, though I don't know about a hundred daggers."

"What about the giant?" Wesler said.

"It reminds me of someone I've encountered in the past," the man in black said, "but it couldn't be her."

Nearing another wagon, Kron glanced in the back to find a corpse missing most of an arm. Darkbow's face went white, then he ground his teeth together and looked in another wagon to find another body, that of Corporal Noktl.

He grabbed a nearby guard. "Where is the second lieutenant?"

"Lieutenant Montolio is inside, sir," the man said, pointing to the open door to the Asylum.

"Montolio!" Kron called out as he rushed to the entrance, Wesler right behind.

The scene before them was one of horror. A guard near the door used a push broom to sluice a stream of blood toward a drain in the floor. Several more guards and healers huddled together around a figure near the opening to a hallway. More guards worked atop the second-floor landing, the men and women there carrying an unmoving, bloodied person toward the stairs leading down. Montolio sat in a chair in a corner, blood splattering his clothing, one leg outstretched and covered with fresh white wrappings, a healer leaning over him and draping a bandage over his head.

"Right here, lieutenant," Montolio said, his voice weary, his eyes straining to open as if fatigued.

Kron and Wesler made directly to the second lieutenant.

"Was it Falk?" Kron asked.

"I didn't see the man," Montolio said, wincing as the healer finished with his head wrapping, "but Kilchus was with them. And Spider."

"Spider?" Kron said.

"Yes," Montolio said. "I didn't know any of the others. There were a pair, man and woman, who looked like one another enough to be twins, the woman as fast with throwing daggers as anyone I've ever seen. There was some fellow with a two-handed sword, his chest covered in plate with markings of a Caballeran knight. And then there was this ... woman? I guess she was a woman. Massive. Wielded a sledgehammer as if it were nothing."

"Lieutenant Darkbow," Wesler interjected, motioning toward Montolio. "My apologies, but this man needs seeing to before serious questioning."

Kron nodded, then stepped out of the way.

"Excuse me," Wesler said, moving past the man in black and shuffling aside the other healer. Then he said to Montolio, "Sir, would you mind sitting still for me for a few moments?"

The mage nodded, wincing again as he did so.

Wesler closed his eyes, said a few words under his breath, and his hands gave off a faint yellow glow. He reached forward and pressed his fingers against Montolio's chest. Almost immediately the second lieutenant sat up a little straighter and his eyes brightened.

The chief healer opened his lids and stood back. "That should keep you going for some time, but you still need several days in bed."

"Thank you, master healer," Montolio said.

"I'll be seeing to the others," Wesler said, moving on to the gathering near the hallway.

"Oh, damn," Montolio suddenly said, shaking his head as if a bad memory had returned.

"What is it?" Kron asked.

The second lieutenant looked over to the group Wesler had joined. Montolio's eyes filled with pain and sorrow.

"What?" Kron looked to the circle of healers and guards, several of them leaning or kneeling over a downed figure. "Who is it?"

"You might not want to look," Montolio said.

The words were like a challenge. Kron strode over to the group, pushing past a pair of guards and leaning over a stooping healer. Almost immediately he wished he had taken Montolio's advice.

Nodana lay sprawled upon the floor, dried blood having pooled around her head. Worst of all was the smashed forehead, splinters of bone sticking out among curdled flesh and pulpous gore. Her face was unblemished, showing no signs of anguish, her short, dark hair laying back above the massive wound.

Montolio pushed himself up from his chair and limped over to the lieutenant. "Kron."

For a long minute the man in black stared, his face impassive. He did not flinch nor blink. There were no signs of change in his face. He did not even breathe.

Then, "Is she alive?"

"Barely," Wesler said to one side. "They've not moved her yet because they've been afraid to. Now that I'm here, I'll use magic as best I can to lighten her and make her more rigid for moving. We'll have her in the tower within a quarter an hour."

"Can you do anything for her?" Kron asked.

"To be honest, I don't know," Wesler said. "Damage like this, I've never seen anyone recover, at least not fully. If only Randall Tendbones would wake."

"Yes, if only," Kron said, looking up to the chief healer. "Do everything you can for her, please. And price is no deterrent, if you should need to call in outside help."

"I'll do everything I can, and then some," Wesler said.

Kron turned away to the second lieutenant. "What about the bones?"

Montolio was taken back by Kron's sudden shift in topic, the seeming lack of remorse. But the wizard knew better. It was not that Kron did not care. The man in black was simply operating on a war footing, keeping himself busy while not allowing himself time to dwell on Frex Nodana. There would be time enough later for mourning. For now, there was work needing done.

Montolio blinked. "The bones are gone. I checked already."

"Are you able to move much?" Kron asked.

Montolio nodded. "I can now, after Wesler's help."

"Then show me," Kron said.

***

With her eyes closed, Mama Kaf sat on the floor in the middle of the room, her back against the bar of Chump's Squall. Her breathing came labored, ragged and throaty. The one arrow still extended from her breast while the other lay next to her wounded leg, a sizable, bleeding tear showing where the second arrow had been recently removed.

Kneeling next to Kaf, Rgia used the hem of the big woman's clothing to wipe blood from a small dagger, then slid the blade into its hiding spot beneath her left arm. Standing, she turned to face the rest of those in the tavern.

"I've never seen anything like it," she said. "She took those arrows as if they were nothing."

"We all saw it," Kilchus said, tossing back a drink from the front end of the bar near the exit.

"Is there anything you can do for her?" Spider asked, sitting at a table across from the unmovable Curval, the knight staring into a mug of warm ale.

Rgia shrugged. "I dare not take out the other arrow. The head is wedged between ribs and into her lungs. I'm surprised she made the hike all the way back here before succumbing."

Jarin appeared from a back room, a bundle of torn rags wadded up in his hands. "Will these do?"

"They'll have to." Rgia took the tatters and took a knee once more to wrap Kaf's bleeding leg.

Kilchus slammed his glass onto the bar. "Where the hell is Teth? Shouldn't we be doing something besides sitting here waiting for the guards to show up?"

"He's upstairs," Spider said. "Said he had to do some scrying."

Kilchus spun around on his stool, glaring at the small man. "What the hell is scrying?"

"He's taking a look around the city using his magic," Rgia explained, tightening the makeshift bandage.

"And what good will that do?" the Sword asked.

"It will do plenty," Teth's voice answered.

632

With the exception of Mama Kaf and Curval, all in the group looked to the back of the room where Sadhe Teth appeared from a hallway.

The ancient wizard walked forward, pausing next to the downed Kaf. "Is she going to make it?"

Rgia shook her head. "I think not. At the very least, she shouldn't be moved."

"Pshaw!" Teth spoke a few words under his breath, then leaned down, one hand grasping the arrow protruding from the large woman's chest. His hand flared as if aflame for a moment, then he tugged on the arrow.

It was as if he withdrew a knife from wet clay. There was no blood, and the flesh closed itself and sealed over.

Teth stared at the arrow in his hand, then tossed it aside. "She should do well. Give her a few minutes."

As a sign he was correct, the big woman's breathing already sounded better, stronger.

The wizard looked up to Kilchus, then marched directly to the man, almost on top of him, forcing the Sword to step away from his stool and stand.

"Darkbow is dead," Teth said.

Kilchus said nothing for a moment, gauging the hard stare he received. Then, "I thought the Finder was your target."

"He was, initially," Teth said, "but he was not present at the mansion. Unfortunately for Darkbow's sake, he *was* present. But no longer."

"What about Gris?"

One edge of the wizard's lips rose almost in a snarl, then he turned away to stare at the others. "The captain and the Finder will be my next targets." It was a lie, but there was no need for him to tell the others of this. They would learn the truth in due time.

Teth glanced over a shoulder at the Sword. "But there are some preparations that need taking care of first."

Kilchus rolled his eyes. "What now? First you wanted these bones, which you've got, and then you give further delays?"

The mage turned again, glaring, leaning into the Sword. "I will take out the captain and Lalo in one stroke, without even being present in their vicinity, and without anyone else knowing what has occurred. But to do this I must perform a ritual that will take some little time, and I will have need of a place which will allow me to see as much of the city as possible."

Spider frowned. He was no expert, not by any means, but he did know something of magic. He had never heard of anything similar to what Teth proposed. "Why do you need all that? Can't you just --"

Teth spun on him, the mage's nostrils flaring. "I think I've had about enough questioning for one night."

"Where are we going?" Jarin asked.

"The Swamps tower," Teth said.

Rgia stood. "The healing tower? The place will be bustling after the Asylum. It'll be crawling with city guards."

"Not on the roof," Teth remarked, "and there is no need for concern. I will ensure we will not be interrupted."

Kilchus held up his hands facing the wizard. "Oh, no. You're not magicking me up onto a roof in the middle of the night. The last time you carried me around like that, I lost my lunch. And in the dark, hell, I might fall off the side of the roof."

"What about her?" Jarin said, pointing to Mama Kaf.

The big woman sat up straighter, opening her eyes. "I will be fine."

Teth smiled. "See?"

"I'm not going," Kilchus said, wrapping his arms together before his chest.

Mama Kaf rolled to one side, shaking the floor, then gripped the edge of the bar and pulled herself to standing, the wood of the bar groaning beneath the effort. Her eyes locked on those of the Sword and she stomped directly over to him, her size and shadow imposing.

"Darkbow is dead, but still I fight on," she said. "You will do the same, or you will answer to me."

Kilchus said nothing. For a moment there was heat in his return gaze, but then his eyes shifted to the floor.

"It is settled," Teth said. "Everyone retrieve your weaponry, and whatever else you wish to take with you. We will be leaving shortly."

***

There was no doubt about the missing bones once Kron saw the destruction of the huge lock box in the basement.

"He has what he wants," Darkbow said.

"But what does it mean?" Montolio asked, holding up a torch behind the man in black.

Kron spun around. "Whatever it is, it can't mean anything good. The bones have been his goal all along."

"And Randall?"

"He considered Randall a threat," Kron said. "Apparently the only *real* threat to him, to Falk."

"Are you sure it's Falk?"

"I didn't see the man, but according to Stilp, Falk was at the mansion."

"What about Randall? Why would he be a threat?"

Kron hesitated a moment, weighing his words before he spoke. "Montolio, Randall is much more than a simple healer. Allow me to leave it at that."

The mage nodded. "Very well, but with Randall out of the scene and the bones in Falk's hands, what do we do?"

Again Kron said nothing for a few seconds. He stared past the wizard and the flames of the torch into the basement hallway beyond, light and sound from stairs at the far end revealing the guards and healers still worked above to move Frex Nodana.

"He will be overconfident," Kron finally said.

"What do you mean?" Montolio asked.

"He thinks Randall immobilized, possibly even dead. He has these bones, for whatever purpose. He will think himself untouchable."

"Are you positive?"

Kron nodded. "I can't know for sure, but it seems we are dealing with someone who has an ego, who is overly confident in their own powers."

"Yet he's been so cautious," Montolio said. "He didn't face Randall on his own, and he sent his crew to do his dirty work for him here at the Asylum."

"Because he didn't have the bones. Remember the barracks? Randall had been neutralized, and there were no spirits there to pose a problem. Now with the bones in his hands, he likely will think himself even more powerful."

"But we don't even know why he wanted the bones."

"True enough, but at the very least it seems he can draw power from them, which alone could be a threat, especially if it's true the bones belonged to some ancient god."

"Fine, but what do we do about it? Can we even guess where we should look for him?"

"He will have no reason to hide," Kron said, "not with Randall out of commission."

A spark lit in Montolio's eyes. "Which means if he's as powerful as Randall thought he was, any mage should be able to find him with ease."

"Exactly," Kron said. He moved to one side and marched past the wizard and down the hall. "Come with me."

Montolio did as he had been told, following the man in black to another door, this one heavy and dark and apparently locked as Kron whisked out a key from within his cloak and proceeded to open the door.

"I don't think I've ever been in here," Montolio said. "It was only a closet on the architectural drawings."

"A rather *large* closet," Kron said as he borrowed the torch and held it inside to rush away shadows as he lit another flame on the wall inside the room.

From the darkness appeared a chamber barely large enough for the two men because of a sizable table in front of the entrance and a weapons rack built into the wall beyond. The rack ran the length of the wall and held numerous weapons of various sorts, spears, swords of different sizes, a halberd, crossbows, long bows, short bows, recurve bows, pikes, more pole weapons with names Montolio did not know. Laying across the table was a lengthy white sheet, which Kron pulled away and dropped onto the floor. More weapons were revealed, but of smaller sorts. Daggers, throwing darts, flat but rounded projectiles with points, arrows of various lengths and makes, smaller bows and crossbows, smaller swords, a mace. There were even a pair of small grappling hooks, each tied to a string of thin, silken cord. The weapons were laid out with room between them so no two touched other than the smallest, some of the throwing darts and the daggers.

In the middle of the table were several earthen canisters with wide mouths, large corks stuffed into them. It was to these Kron reached first, prying open a cork to look within. Montolio leaned around the lieutenant to stare into the jar.

"I'd wondered what you'd done with all those," the mage said.

The jar was filled with a half dozen clay balls about the size of large berries.

"The others you made are there," Kron said, gesturing to the rest of the jars.

"Smoke and fire?" Montolio asked.

Kron nodded. "Even some of those experimental ones containing holy water."

"What do you intend?"

"I intend to do something about Lord Falk," Kron said, "at least once you find him for me."

"Are you sure you're up to this?" Montolio asked.

It was a prudent question, but one needing asked. Kron had to admit to himself he was not in top form. His head still ached somewhat and his steps did not come as fast as he would have liked. Still, he had surprise on his side. Falk and the others most likely believed him dead.

"Someone has to be up to it," Kron finally said.

"Okay." Montolio took the jar from Kron's hands and placed it on the table. Retrieving a small leather sack from one side, he began stuffing it with the grenados. "But tell me, how many of these do you want to take with you?"

"All of them," Kron said.

29

An unseen wall of invulnerability seemed to resonate around the seven as they casually made their way along the streets of the Swamps, flakes of white crystals drifting down in their wake. No one came near. No one accosted them. The few pedestrians out on the streets disappeared down alleys or through doorways. No city guards patrolled. Not even windows were opened by the curious. The bloom of lights behind doors and windows darkened as they passed. No one watched.

Sadhe Teth's magic worked well, Rgia had to surmise as she trudged along behind the massive figure of Mama Kaf, Jarin and Spider coming up behind the woman assassin, Curval with Teth and Kilchus in the rear.

It was an eerie feeling knowing one could not be stopped, could not even be watched at the whim of a single person, even if that person was supposedly a powerful wizard of unknown years. The night itself was quiet, providing no sound whatsoever other than the gentle patting of the group's own shoes or boots. It was as if they had the world to themselves. Combined with the growing cold of the night, the sensation brought shivers to Rgia's spine. She hoped such would not hamper her abilities with her daggers, if the blades should be called upon.

After some while the seven neared the square in front of the healing tower, though it was still out of sight around the corner of a three-story tenement building. From ahead there came the sounds of people working, the huffings and puffings of heavy lifting, the scattered words of orders being given, of feet moving frantically, of carts creaking, of animals.

Then all at once, the noises stopped.

***

It could always be worse. That's what Sergeant Nickel told herself the whole ride from the Asylum, every bump in the back of the wagon like a needle being driven into her skull. But for each stab of pain, she offered a thanks to the Almighty Ashal. She could have lost an arm. She could have had her head busted in. She could be dead. But she wasn't. A few bruises to the face, eyes barely open, she had been through just as bad before. Her body would heal, and now she had memories to provide her with more experience, to make her a better guard, a better sergeant. Live and learn, she told herself in the back of the wagon, because otherwise there was only death.

When the wagon finally creaked to a stop, someone said, "We're here," and Nickel knew the speaker, likely the driver, meant the healing tower in the Swamps. That's where they were headed, after all.

Barely able to see anything through her puffy eyes, Nickel reached out with a hand and felt the hard wooden slat that made up the side of the wagon. Putting her weight on the board, she lifted herself to sitting.

"Hold on a second there, sergeant," another voice said. "We'll have you out in a moment."

Nickel sat and waited with patience. Around her she could hear the heavy breathing of men and women at work lifting the other wounded from the wagon. This went on for a few minutes, Nickel counting her blessings all the while.

Then someone said, "All right, sergeant. Your turn."

A hand grasped her about a shoulder, though a gentle hand, and Nickel could just make out a shadow moving in front of her blocking off the dancing light of a flame somewhere, perhaps a torch.

Then the hand slipped away, followed by a thumping sound in the back of the wagon.

"What the hell?" someone said.

Nickel wanted to ask what had happened, but suddenly her head was swimming. The sensation was different than the pain that had been racking her head since the Asylum. She felt loopy, out of control, her chin dropping despite her best efforts to keep it up.

Around her she could hear other thumping sounds. It came to her that these were people dropping to the ground. But what caused it? There had been no sounds of a fight, no attack.

Mumbled words came to her from one side and she tried to look in that direction. Fighting to open her eyes, Nickel thought she saw the image of a white-robed healer leaning against the wagon's wall right next to her, but then the face cloaked by a white hood slipped down, dropping. Another thudding sound followed.

"What in the ..." But Nickel couldn't complete whatever it had been she was going to say. Her senses dulled and she dropped back flat onto the wagon's bed.

Soon gentle snores rose from around the healing tower.

***

The snow continued to fall. Not in great big gulps, but in a thin sheen that lay upon the ground and the surface of everything it touched. The sight would have been quite beautiful if killers had not walked the streets.

Now leading the way, Mama Kaf tromped into the open square fronting the healing tower's entrance. Still some ways distant, the group could see a pair of open wagons had been hauled up with their backs to the doorway standing open. Silence roamed the area. Even the footsteps of the seven were now muffled by the snow. Stranger still, there was no movement from or around the tower.

As Sadhe Teth's party grew closer, shapes began to form on the ground and around the open door. People lay on their sides and their backs, some few even on their faces, most of them city guards and healers, a few apparently citizens there for healing. All appeared alive, though barely. Mists of fog exuded from between their lips, and their breasts rose and fell. In the back of the wagons were found a few other city guards, all of them looking battered or worse, and Jarin could not help but grin at the familiar faces, nor could he hold back a chuckle at the sleeping horses tethered to the wagons, the animals dormant upon their hooves.

"It seems you've taken care of the guards," Kilchus said as the group came to a halt before the open entrance to the tower.

Sadhe Teth smiled and nodded. "That I have, and this is only the beginning."

"I'm still not going to let you magic me up to the roof," Kilchus said with a snarl.

"Fine," the mage said. "I prefer someone stay down here on the ground, in case of unwanted intrusions."

"Intrusions?" Spider said, glancing around at those slumbering. "What kind of intrusions?"

"My sleep magics only extend so far," Teth explained. "I could have enveloped the whole city, but do not wish to exert myself, at least not yet."

"So you're saying someone could come along?" Rgia asked.

Teth nodded. "It's not impossible."

"Great," Kilchus said, spitting off to one side. "If word of the Asylum hasn't spread yet, it will once people start noticing everyone is asleep here at the tower. The city guard will arrive in no time."

"An hour, that is all I need," Teth said, hoping he was correct. "Then we will have no more worries, none."

"Meaning Captain Gris will be taken care of?" Kilchus said with a squinting eye. "And the Finder?"

"*All* our opponents will be vanquished," Teth said.

"Then let's get to it," Kilchus said. "The sooner we are finished, the sooner we can get out of here."

Again, Teth nodded, then turned to Mama Kaf. "Lady, if you would be so kind, I prefer your presence here on the ground with our friend Kilchus here."

The big woman glared at the Sword, but then she grunted an acceptance.

"Good," Teth said, walking through the snow toward the tower's door. "The rest of you, come with me."

"Where are you going?" Kilchus asked the mage's back.

"Up to the roof," Teth said, pausing in the opening to glance back over a shoulder. "Did you expect I was going to use magic when there are perfectly good stairs available?"

The wizard chuckled at this and disappeared inside, the assassins and Spider giving off grins at the Sword's expense, Curval remaining stoic as he followed the others indoors.

"Son of a bitch," Kilchus muttered before looking around for a place to avoid as much of the snow as possible.

***

The blood had been swept away, yet a blemish of crimson lingered upon the floor. Bodies had been removed, the wounded taken away, the wagons withdrawn to another locale. The city guards had left, occupied with the dead and the living alike. The building was nearly empty but for two figures, one entirely in black, the other wearing a mixture of black and white.

Kron stood in the middle of the Asylum's front room, his black boots resting upon the scarlet stain of men who had served under him. His hands worked over his body, counting, counting, counting. A sword on his hip. A dagger on his belt. Another, smaller dagger sheathed within a boot. Three darts tucked into the back of his left glove. A small grapnel with attached cord hanging from the back of his belt. On his back a soft leather quiver filled with arrows. A bag of grenados hanging near the hilt of his sword. Other grenados, four in all, tucked away within hidden pockets of his cloak.

"I am ready," he said.

Montolio approached and handed him a small bow. "Are you sure you don't want me to go with you?"

Kron took the weapon and tugged gently upon the string, testing its strength. "No. Someone needs to get to Gris and let him know everything that has happened. And you're in no condition for fighting."

The wizard placed a hand on Kron's shoulder, drawing the man in black's dark gaze. "Kron, these aren't street thugs. You can't go this alone."

Letting out a sigh, Kron strapped the bow to his back next to the quiver. "Montolio, I appreciate your concern, but I've dealt with killers most of my life, trained killers. And I'm not exactly unskilled when facing magic. You tell me Falk is in the vicinity of the healing tower, so that is where I must go. There is no telling what he will do there, and Randall might be in danger once more. I need you to raise the alarm, because if Gris doesn't come charging in with a small army, my chances are little to none. Besides, I will not be alone. There are guards at the tower now."

It was clear Montolio wanted to say more, but the words did not come. He could tell it was futile to try to sway Kron further, so all he did was give a single nod.

Then Kron strode forth from the Asylum.

***

The trap door snapped open and back, blowing up a spate of white powder. The handle of his sword extending above and behind his head, Curval looked up from the ladder. Stretching all around him was the flat, round roof of the Swamps healing tower, the distant edges protected by a crenelated parapet. Above was the dark sky, the main light source half a moon, its glow lingering upon millions of falling white flakes. The snow lay in a short layer across everything.

"Well?" Jarin said from below.

Curval grunted, then climbed onto the roof, turning slowly to look in all directions. Still spotting no threat, he waved up the others.

"About time," Jarin said, ascending the ladder to land next to the knight.

Spider followed, tugging his cloak tighter as he entered the cold, snowy night yet again.

Then came Rgia and Sadhe Teth, the old wizard taking the offering of a hand from Curval to make it to the top.

"This will do fine," Teth said, staring over the roof's top to the lights of the city beyond.

"You couldn't have picked someplace inside, someplace warmer?" Jarin asked.

Rgia looked to her brother. "Have you taken Kilchus's place as the group nag?"

The wizard let out a chuckle. "I understand young Jarin's concerns, but to perform this ritual properly, I prefer to see as much of Bond as possible."

"And once you're done, we won't have any more enemies, right?" Jarin asked.

"Sounding like Kilchus more all the time, little brother," Rgia said.

Teth chuckled more. "Yes, when I am finished, our enemies will be vanquished."

"Where do you want us?" Rgia asked, turning to the face of Lord Falk.

"Here," Teth said, gesturing at the still open trap door. "There is little to fear with my sleep magic permeating the area, but I think it best to guard the roof's main access point."

Jarin dipped a toe under one edge of the trap door and slammed it closed. "This sleep magic of yours, will it affect anyone?"

"Anyone not under my protection who enters its territory," Teth said. "I suppose it's not impossible a mage with a hint of power might be able to circumvent my magic temporarily, but even if that were the case, who would be looking for us? And up here? Tendbones is vanquished, as is Darkbow. The others are of little concern, and will soon be dealt with."

"Quit being such a worrier," Rgia said to her brother, but it was mostly a show. Inside, she too was filled with concern. She had never trusted Sadhe Teth and did not now. Whatever the mage was up to, she doubted it only pertained to him eliminating their enemies, specifically Lalo the Finder and Captain Gris. She only spoke now in the wizard's favor in order to make Teth believe in her full cooperation, and of course because she derived more than a little glee in disparaging her boresome brother.

Jarin stuck his tongue out at her, making her laugh.

Teth frowned. "If these childish antics are done, I will retreat some distance to give myself room to begin the ritual."

No one said a word in response.

"Very well," Teth said. "Curval, come with me."

With that the wizard advanced into a wall of flurries, the heavy figure with the big sword on his back following right behind.

"What about me?" Spider asked.

Rgia pointed to the trap door, which was quickly being covered once more with snow. "You stay here with us."

***

"Damn the winter," Captain Gris spat as he fought the reins of his riding beast. Beneath the white powder a thin layer of ice had already formed upon the surface of Coin Bridge, making the trek across worrisome and potentially dangerous. The hooves of the horses, two dozen of the beasts in all, kept slipping when they didn't crack though the ice.

Gris glanced over a shoulder to the other riders following him. None of his people were faring any better than himself. The snow had grown thicker in the last few minutes, forming a wall of pale fluff in every direction. It was becoming difficult to see beyond a few feet.

As his horse skidded a few inches, the captain brought his eyes back to front and he cursed again. After working at the barracks most of the day and helping Frex Nodana, he had been visiting with the general at the army camp outside the city, trying to organize plans for construction at the barracks. General Hagen had promised aid, especially with labor, and Gris was more than willing to accept the cooperation.

But too much had happened in such little time, only hours. First had come a report from the barracks that Lalo the Finder had been looking for him, then had come word of something happening at the Finder's mansion, followed soon by news from Montolio of an attack upon the Asylum involving slayings. As if that had not been enough, a rider from the Swamps barracks had brought Gris a note from a sergeant informing the captain there was something odd happening at the healing tower there, people falling asleep whenever they approached the building. The written message from Montolio also mentioned the healing tower and that Kron was headed there.

It all stank of magic, as far as Gris was concerned, and it all stank of Kilchus and Falk and whatever other bastards had joined their little band. If the damned weather would only settle down for a few minutes, the captain would take his riders down Dock Street to meet up with others who were supposed to be approaching from the main barracks in Southtown.

His horse slipped again, this time nearly spilling the captain from his saddle. "Damn the winter!"

***

Sadhe Teth stopped near the back of the roof. A curtain of white encircled him, making it almost impossible for him to see the alleyway beyond the short wall running the edges of the building. Glancing back, he could no longer see his companions other than Curval only a handful of steps behind.

"You may wait here," the wizard said.

With nary a word or a look, the knight clanked around and faced back the way they had come, one hand reaching around to unstrap his big sword and bring it around for a solid, two-handed grip. There the man stood, staring into the snow.

For the first time Teth felt a pang of guilt for what was to come. Curval had been the best of companions, doing as he was told without questioning, almost always silent but providing protection when needed. It was too bad he would be dead within an hour or two.

Shrugging, the ancient mage turned back to face the wall of snow that now completely shrouded his view of the alley. He could not allow any sense of loyalty to sway him. He had come too far over too many centuries to fail now. He had failed once, long ago, and had paid the price for it. Unbeknown to the old gods, he had planned for the eventuality. Now he was here, thousands of years later, ready to strike once more, to protect humanity once more. It was only too bad thousands had to die in order for him to protect the species as a whole.

Breathing in the cold of night, he felt the sting of the chill upon his lungs. Closing his eyes, he fought back against a cough. This old body, it would have to be exchanged for another soon enough, once he had completed the ritual. Being the youngest, Jarin was the most likely candidate, though Teth had to admit he had a certain curiosity about taking Rgia's form as he had never ensconced himself within the body of woman. But there would be time to make the final decision once he was finished here on the roof.

Opening his eyes, he waved a hand over the rooftop in front of him and a circle of snow whisked itself away to leave a dry, empty place for him. Groaning at the age of his stolen body, he sank to his knees and pulled his cloak closer about his chest. Within the folds of that cloak his hands went to work unfolding the leather sack that held the bones of a god best forgotten.

He could feel the power dormant within the bones, the power of two gods, one who had engulfed another. With this power Sadhe Teth would perform a magic he had conducted only once before, long ago, with dire results for thousands. He had gained power then, enough to ensure his survival over the centuries until being awoken by digging fools, but there was so much more power to be gained now with the deaths of so many. Only then would he be able to unearth the gods, wherever they might roam, and only then would he have the might to destroy them.

It began now.

He closed his eyes once more and placed the bones atop their leather wrappings on the rooftop in front of his knees. Clasping his hands together as if in prayer, he began to mumble words of strength, words from a language forgotten by all waking men but himself.

It was then the falling snow grew heavier, thicker, and the rooftop began to creak as a thin layer of ice formed beneath the kneeling figure. Within seconds that sheet of ice began to grow, spreading out gradually from the mage, crackling softly as it went, a hoary growth with purpose.

<u>30</u>

The world had become a tomb of white. Everywhere Kron looked there was a wall of snow blanketing his vision. Sound was practically dead, even his boots silent as they padded atop the silvery powder. The cold embraced him, embraced everything, seeming like a living thing trying to envelope all. His breaths came in misty plumes, and his heart raced within his chest.

Yet the cold was not unfamiliar to Kron Darkbow. Having spent much of his life in the Prisonlands further north with surrounding mountains, he found the harsher elements more tolerable than did most of his fellow Ursians. Still, he could not help but shiver as he trudged over the snow, his cloak open before him to allow for easy use of his bow and access to the other weapons he carried.

Leaving the Asylum behind him, he made his way through a maze of back alleys, believing it best not to approach the healing tower from the front. The going was slow and difficult, in no small respect because he could not see far beyond his immediate vicinity, but he knew his paths well and kept close to the walls to help guide him. He was aided in that there was little wind within the confines of the alleys. Going unseen within the maze was an easy task, much of the moon's light sheltered by the surrounding walls and the stream of falling crystals, and helped by Kron's chosen black garb, yet he realized he would stand out when in the open, all that dark clothing in a sea of white. Still, hiding was not his main goal while traversing the alleys because he did not care much if he was noticed. It was only when he neared the tower that he did not wish to be seen as he did not know what he would find there, nor where his potential opponents would be within the tower.

Up ahead a wide eaves several stories above provided a narrow respite from the worst of the snow. Easing into the space, Kron shook the white powder from his shoulders and the hood of his cloak, then placed his back against a wall.

The back of the Swamps healing tower lay a dozen yards away to his left, the alley continuing around in the same direction behind the building. To the right of the large building was another, more narrow alley which looped around to the open square in front of the tower.

It was while standing there trying to decide which path he should take when Kron noticed several things almost at the same time. The temperature near the healing tower had dropped considerably, causing his hands to quiver even within the warmth of his gloves. Stranger still, he noticed a thin frost growing down the side of the tower, tendrils of ice clawing their way toward the ground and leaving behind a silvery sheet. The growing ice and the growing cold seemed unnatural to Kron, perhaps a sign of eldritch powers afoot.

Less unnatural was the last thing Kron spotted, a trail of prints in the snow of the alley that led around to the front of the building. The prints barely appeared visible, the falling powder working to cover them, but it was obvious someone had been marching back and forth. Someone was on sentry duty.

Kron reached up over a shoulder and hoisted an arrow from his quiver, nocking the arrow against the string of his bow.

He waited with patience for several minutes to see if this unknown marcher would appear, but nothing happened. It was time for Kron to move ahead, the trail of prints making his decision of direction.

Before he could move, a wave of numbness rolled over him. This was not the cold. The sensation ate away at his mind like fingers massaging his thoughts, pressing down upon him. Kron suddenly wanted sleep. He wanted to lay down there in the snow and to snuggle within the relative warmth of his cloak. The feeling nearly overwhelmed him, and the only thing that kept him from following through with the suggestion of sleep was his recognition of magic being used against him. Either a spell had been focused upon him or a protective ward had been placed around the area. He was familiar with such magics, and fortunately trained in thwarting them.

He blinked, steeling his nerves, forcing back the tendrils of magic attempting to overpower his own will. Nearly anyone could fight such magics, but most had not the training or experience necessary. It was mostly a matter of one's willpower battling against the effects of ensorclement, and few had more willpower than Kron Darkbow.

He blinked again and felt the magic draining away. He shook off the last vestiges of the spell, ready to shuffle forward once more through the snow.

A shadow moved ahead of him in the alley leading to the front of the tower.

Kron remained in place, pulling back the string of his bow, aiming the arrow down the alleyway.

Further movement, then a figure took form within the falling snow and the hint of light from the sky above.

"You," the voice of Kilchus the Sword said.

"Yes, me," Kron answered in reply.

Kilchus stepped forward, revealing himself fully as he hefted his sword. "You're supposed to be dead."

"You would not be the first to make that mistake."

The Sword smirked and chuckled, shaking his sword. "So, what now? We fight man to man?"

Kron said nothing this time.

Kilchus lifted his sword higher. "Put down your bow, lieutenant. Put down your bow and face me like a man. Back at the Asylum you sucker punched me, and I never got the chance to show you --"

The arrow caught him above the eyes, sinking deep within his skull. For a moment Kilchus stood on wobbly legs, his eyes crossing as they stared up the length of the wooden shaft protruding from his head. Then those eyes rolled back in upon themselves and he collapsed in the snow.

Kron Darkbow did not bother to look at the dead man as he stepped over his body.

***

The scene that unfolded before the front of the healing tower was one shrouded in a mystery of white. Snow lay upon everything, keeping hidden the truth of the various bulky shapes presented there. It took nearly a minute before

Kron's eyes recognized what appeared before him, revealed by the light of low-burning torches near the open entrance to the building, that opening shedding some light of its own. Slowly the outlines of several wagons became apparent to the man in black, as did the snow-draped horses lashed to the vehicles, though smaller shapes upon the ground remained a mystery until Kron stretched forward a boot to brush away some of the white powder.

A face going blue revealed itself to him. Kron recognized that face as belonging to one of the city guards who had been stationed in front of the Asylum.

Glancing around, Kron counted nearly a dozen similar shapes covered with snow, all of them slumbering individuals.

Slinging his bow over his head so the shaft of the weapon hung down his back, he went to work dusting the snow from the figures upon the ground. It took several minutes, but he soon had their faces clean, and a swift check proved everyone was still alive. They would not remain alive, however, unless he acted fast. The snow continued to fall and the temperature continued to drop, and those left to the elements would not last long.

Kron rushed to the tower's entrance and glanced inside, hoping beyond hope to find someone, anyone to aid him. He found nothing but sleeping guards and healers slumped to the floor in the outer hall.

Back outside he grabbed the closest snow-covered form by the ankles and dragged the person inside of the tower, torches hanging along the hallway providing light as well as some small warmth. Returning to the cold, he lifted another person and carried them indoors. Again and again he made the trip, his arms growing more tired by the moment, occasionally his footing slipping on the snow.

It took some time, but eventually everyone he could find on the ground or in a wagon had been brought inside and laid out next to the inner wall of the hallway.

After tugging closed the outer door, Kron planted his hands on his knees and allowed himself several seconds of rest. His head was hurting again from the blow earlier in the night and his breathing came heavy. At least no new enemies had presented themselves while he had been busy saving the others.

Looking up and down the hall to the many sleeping forms there, he wondered how long the magic would last and how long those in rest could survive. It was then he also noticed the faint outline of frost growing down the inner walls of the tower, just as he had seen outside. Though the hall was much warmer than the outdoors had been, he could already feel the temperature slowly falling. There was more magic involved here than a simple sleeping spell. Falk or whomever was up to something powerful.

Kron straightened. He had no more time to waste. He had to find Falk and his gang, and he had to put a stop to whatever they were doing.

But where to begin his search? He was fully convinced his enemies were here at the tower, but it was a large building with hundreds of rooms across multiple floors. Where could they be hiding, if they were even hiding?

Upon reflection, Kron decided his foes would be on one of the upper floors, most likely the top floor, possibly even the roof. No one else had attacked him, which told him he was relatively alone there near the main entrance, perhaps alone on the whole ground floor. But the floors above? And what of the roof? If Falk were performing some kind of winter or elemental magics, which the growing frost evidenced, then the roof might be a logical place to attempt such, giving the spell caster direct access to the elements and a wide view of the region.

Kron turned and marched down the hall. He could not take the time to look in upon every room, but he would have to go floor to floor for at least a cursory look for evidence of his enemies.

First, however, there was someone he wanted to visit.

Just in case.

***

There were more sleeping people staggered out around the entrance to Randall's rooms. More and more Kron realized he was dealing with powerful magics. In the past he had witnessed few others with such talents, Randall being one of them, and his concern grew. He had tackled powerful magic users before, but he had always had allies at his side. This time Kron was alone.

Yet that did not sway him from his course of action.

Pulling aside several of the slumbering figures, he opened the door to Randall's office and entered only to find a pair of healers slumping near the next door, the one to the inner chamber. Once more Kron moved aside the sleepers, wishing he could do more for them but knowing the best way to help them was by defeating whomever was responsible for the spell cast upon the tower.

Opening the inner door, he found a surprise, though not a pleasant one.

Randall lay on a cot as he had the last time Kron had seen him, the healer breathing gently beneath a sheet, but beyond him lay another unmoving figure upon a makeshift bed.

Nodana.

Kron did not enter the room for a moment, his lover's presence bringing him pause. Then he steeled his nerves and pressed forward, working his way around Randall to stare down at the woman whose bed he had shared on many occasions.

Her face was impassive, making her look like just another sleeper among hundreds. Covered by a sheet up to her chin, she had been cleansed of grime and dried blood, her head covered in layers of bandages, of which Kron was thankful. He did not know if he could stand to see the damage to her forehead again.

Another man might have cried. A lesser man might have raged at the universe, which Kron had been known to do. Yet he was not the first man, and no longer was he the second. What life gave him, what it brought to him, it just as often took away. He had learned as much and rarely expected otherwise. He would not shed a tear for himself because there was little need. His pain was selfish, foolish, unworthy of himself and of Nodana. It was only her pain that mattered, and as far as he knew, she was beyond pain. And he had made her a promise, not so long ago. Revenge was not his goal, would never be his goal again as long as he lived, at least not consciously. Revenge served little purpose, only bringing more pain to a world already filled with such. What he sought now was a reckoning, an account of balance, and someone within the healing tower would suffer his appraisal, his judgment, for otherwise Kron Darkbow could not live with himself. If he could not halt the ever present darkness of men, at least he could abate its growth and seek to keep it from affecting others, those who were innocent, those needing saving.

He turned from Nodana and faced Randall. Leaning forward, he stared down into the marble-like countenance of his friend. There were still no signs of awareness.

A sigh of resignation escaped Kron's lips. His hopes had been small, but at least they had existed. Now they fled from him. Randall was not awake, not able to lend a hand in these most dire of circumstances.

Kron would have to go forward alone.

Standing tall once more, he walked from the room into the front office.

And was brought up short by a massive figure filling the outer doorway to the hall.

Mama Kaf glared at him, her eyes poking out from her fleshy visage.

"So it *is* you," Kron said. Then he wasted no more time on words, unslinging his bow and quiver and placing them on Randall's desk as there was not enough distance to prepare the weapon before his foe could be upon him.

Pulling his sword free of its leather scabbard, he watched as the big woman grinned and hefted her sledgehammer. She took a step forward, her mass making the confines of the room appear all that much smaller. The floor seemed to shudder beneath her weight.

***

A third soldier in orange dropped to the ground.

"Ashal damn it all," Captain Gris said from his saddle.

A sergeant standing by looked up to the officer. "Sir, you want me to send in another?"

Gris stared over the scene before him, the blanket of white covering everything along the street leading to the Swamps healing tower. Three of his men were now asleep, though apparently no worse for their slumber. Behind the captain, two dozen others waited, men and women in leather armor and orange tabards, their heads helmeted, swords and spears in their hands. Each soldier shook with cold beneath the confines of his or her cloak. The snow itself was bad enough, as was the cold lingering upon the air, but the ground was now covered with a layer of ice stretching out for hundreds of yards beyond the tower and still continuing to grow.

"Any word from the other roads and alleys?" Gris asked the sergeant.

"Reports say its the same everywhere," the sergeant said. "As soon as anyone gets within a hundred yards of the place, they fall right off to sleep. Even the surrounding tenements are quiet."

The captain cursed again. "I don't suppose we've a mage yet?"

"Not yet, sir," the sergeant said. "I've sent riders to find Master Nodana and to the Asylum for Lieutenant Montolio."

Gris grumbled. As too often had been the case of late, there was too much going on of which he knew nothing, and it all seemed to have ties to magic. That new special squad couldn't be up and running fast enough, as far as he was concerned.

"Send a rider to the university," he said.

"Sir?"

"We need a wizard as soon as we can get one, sergeant," Gris said. "If Montolio is in no shape for this and Lady Nodana can't be found, then we have to make use of whomever we can."

"Yes, sir." The sergeant rushed off with his orders.

"Now, Kron," Gris said, staring into the sheet of tumbling snow before him, "where are you in all this nonsense?"

***

From experience, Kron had learned Mama Kaf was quite swift despite her bulk, even when she had had only one leg. Now that she had two legs once more, one of them seemingly of steel, she proved herself as fast as ever.

He barely had time to bring the end of his sword down into a guard position before she tromped straight for him. Her big hammer slammed down from her shoulder, and a quick slide to one side was all that saved him from a shattered skull. As it was, the hammer's head smacked into the floor, cracking stone.

For a moment the huge woman was off balance, her weapon lowered. Kron slashed across from right to left with his sword, the blade slicing through thick cloth and flesh to leave a line of red upon her right forearm.

She showed no sign of having suffered the wound. The hammer came up again, ready for another blow.

Kron jumped back, his boots avoiding the two sleeping healers behind him. He glanced down at the pair, realizing their lives were in jeopardy. Seeing Mama Kaf heading towards him once more, Kron dove to his left behind Randall's desk and away from the slumbering healers.

The head of the hammer crashed into the side of the furniture, sending splinters flying and shoving the heavy piece desk aside to reveal a hunkered Darkbow. Kron looked up into eyes filled with rage. His own gaze was nearly as harsh as he lunged straight for the woman, his sword leading the way.

Faster than he expected, the sledgehammer swung back between them, the metal head sparking against his own weapon and blunting it aside.

Man and woman nearly chest to chest, they could have been lovers they were so close.

Having no room to swing his sword, Kron twisted the weapon in his hand so the blade pointed to the ground. He brought up the thick pommel, punching toward Mama Kaf's face.

The move apparently surprised her. Her eyes went wide just before the blow struck, catching her square on the nose. Cartilage crunched and blood splashed. The big woman swayed back on her feet, her mighty weapon dropping from her hands. She teetered, her eyes rolling back in her head.

Kron took a step back, bringing up his sword for another strike.

Then the woman blinked and her eyes focused once more upon her hated enemy.

Kron screamed and stabbed.

To no end.

A hand the size of a large gourd wrapped itself around the lengthy blade plunging for the woman's heart. Kron tugged on his weapon, cutting into the flesh of the hand and spilling more blood, but he could not budge his sword free from those fingers. Mama Kaf yanked down, pulling the sword from Kron's grasp. With a laugh, she tossed the blade over her shoulder.

Kron shifted his feet, one ahead of the other, then snapped up and forward a kick, the heel of a boot cracking into his enemy's sternum. Again the big woman swayed, thrusting her arms out and back to hold her balance, but again she did not go down.

The kick had the man in black unsteady for a moment. By the time he straightened his stance and brought back a fist for a straight punch, his opponent was already in motion.

Mama Kaf howled in delight and pounced, her arms out wide before swinging around to engulf her foe. Kron found himself locked within her grasp, pulled into her chest so he could barely breathe. She squeezed, pulling him tighter. A cracking sound followed, causing him to cry out in pain. He tried to bring back his head for a butt to her face, but there was not enough room, and his arms were trapped within her arms, giving him no chance of throwing a punch or using his hands.

She leered down upon him with a ghastly smile, chuckling from her throat as she reared back, lifting him off his feet. Another cracking noise sounded and Kron cried out again, his hands flailing uselessly beneath her tightening arms.

Were his hands useless?

Instead of pushing up in an attempt to break her grasp, he forced one of his shoulders down, forcing his hand down to fumble at his belt, searching for a dagger, for anything he could use as a weapon.

His gloved fingers drummed against something hard, then grabbed for it, wrapping around it. Yes, a dagger.

He flipped the small weapon around until its pommel was in the palm of his hand, then he jammed the blade forward with all his might. Steel sank deep into flesh and a wet warmth flowed down between the interlocked man and woman.

Mama Kaf growled and reared back further, taking Kron with her. Blood spilling down her legs ran onto the floor, bringing with it a slippery surface. Her footing skated as if upon ice. For a moment she held herself up, then her steel foot skidded out from underneath her.

She dropped like a mountain, crashing onto her back, shaking the floor. Kron landed atop her and found the arms around his back loosened for a moment. He grabbed his dagger, pulling it free of flesh and spilling more crimson. His blade flashed toward her throat, but she thrust up an arm like a tree trunk and the steel only managed to slice across an open hand.

Grunting, Kron climbed the woman, pushing himself up her massive frame until he sat atop her chest. He raised the dagger high overhead, gripping its handle in both fists as her meaty fingers scrambled to grab at him.

Just as his knife came barreling down, one of her hands wrapped itself within his cloak and tugged, yanking him backward. His blade missed its mark, only sliding into the meat of a shoulder as he found himself forced off the big woman and onto the floor.

Leaving the dagger sticking in his opponent's flesh, Kron pushed himself away from her, sliding through her blood as he crawled to where his sword had been thrown.

His back to Mama Kaf, he never saw her roll over and find her footing once more, but he could hear her grunting and groaning, her thudding steps. He knew she would be coming for him.

Just as he laid a hand upon the hilt of his sword, he felt himself pulled back again. The woman had him by the cloak once more, using his own garb as a line to reel him in.

Unfortunately for her, his fingers tightened upon his sword's grip just as she yanked him to his feet. He spun, lashing out blindly with the blade.

Hardened iron and carbon sank through flesh and muscle and bone, the sharpened steel finally coming to rest several inches within the big woman's side.

Mama Kaf screamed, throwing up her arms again as she stumbled back, taking her foe's sword with her.

Kron did not contest losing his weapon, but watched as Mama Kaf fell against the remains of the desk, the wood splintering from the heavy weight of the woman, cracking and giving way beneath her. She crashed to the floor with the shattered furniture under her, a dagger protruding from a shoulder, a large sword ensconced within her side just beneath ribs. She lay on her back for a moment, then tried to sit up, but a stream of blood escaped her lips and she collapsed, spitting up more of the crimson.

Then she lay all but still, her eyes fluttering, her chest slowly rising and falling.

Kron continued to watch, not trusting her and giving himself precious moments of rest.

Minutes passed. He still watched.

Then she gasped. A red bubble escaped her lips, then burst. Her body shuddered and seemed to sink back further, almost as if the floor would envelop her. A last sigh pressed its way out of her lungs, then her head drooped and her eyes went flat.

She breathed no more.

31

The weather continued its slow growth of cold, and the snow stopped falling. Common knowledge was that snow would cease dropping when the cold grew too intense, but Sadhe Teth knew this to be misguided folklore. There was no such things as too cold for snow. More accurately, the temperature lowered to a degree in which there was too little moisture in the air for the snow to form properly, but such a situation was rare and imperfect, thwarted by warm updrafts or even mountains.

In this instance, the snow had stopped falling because Sadhe Teth had wished it so. The ground and the rooftops were covered for miles by at least six inches of the cold, white powder, in some places drifting up to heights of several feet. That was enough to do the job, Teth believed, and there was little need for more snow to fall as it obscured his sight. He wanted to see as much of the city as possible. He *needed* to. Not for his magic to work, but because he wanted to witness the death of an entire city as it occurred around him. He wanted to hear the panic and the screams. He wanted to see the chaos.

His ritual not yet complete, it was only a matter of time, perhaps half an hour. Then the deaths would begin. They would not all occur at once, not even within a short span. Perhaps days, maybe a week. But slowly all those within the city of Bond would be frozen and dead, and Sadhe Teth would reap their souls for his own magic, making him the strongest caster of spells in the world, likely within all of time. Not even the gods themselves would be able to stand against him.

The first to die would be his allies, those at the center of his growing web of magic. The loss would be unfortunate in the case of Curval, who had proven himself so loyal, but Teth would not miss the others. Rgia was the most intelligent and the most skilled, but she was also the most untrustworthy in many ways, especially as she herself did not trust Teth in return.

The thought nearly caused the mage to laugh, almost breaking his concentration. Of course Rgia had reason not trust him, and she would learn the truth of this soon enough.

But then it would be too late for anyone to stop him.

Even now, his foolish comrades guarded his back. He had no reason to look around, for he could still feel the knight's presence not so far from him, and occasionally he could hear the others rustling about or murmuring to one another at a distance. Teth could hear little of their words, but every so often he could make out one of them complaining about the snow and the cold, almost making the wizard laugh again.

If they only knew.

Through the thin cloth of his leggings, Teth could feel the cold seeping out and away from him, the frost growing and spreading, eventually to cover all of the city. His ritual would be complete long before the growth finished its expansion, but the ice would continue to spread until it overran the walls of the city. The rivers would freeze solid. Men and women and children alike would perish from frostbite or worse. All life would become extinct.

Then Sadhe Teth would be all powerful, unstoppable. Then he could scour the world for the gods, those he was sure still out there in hiding. They would pay for all they did to him thousands of years ago. Teth would blight them from the world. He would erase all vestiges of them that remained, the few there were in ancient tomes and carved upon stone. Most importantly, he would slay them, all of them. Only then would mankind be safe. Only then would mankind be able to find its own destiny without the interference of deities or Zarroc alike.

With Sadhe Teth as overseer of all, of course.

***

Something ground together like broken glass in Kron's back as he moved. He could not help but wince at the pain as he pulled his sword and dagger free of the dead woman's massive body. For a moment he registered the look of surprise and anguish on her face, then turned away. There was nothing he could do for her in death, and in life she had wanted nothing from him other than his own murder. Using a piece of her clothing, he wiped his weapons clean and returned them to their scabbards. Then he moved over to the shattered desk and found his bow and quiver, most of the arrows now broken and useless.

Slinging the quiver over one shoulder and gripping the bow in hand, he slowly turned and scanned the room. There was nothing for him here. No enemies, no friends, only the dead and those sleeping.

Moving toward the door, he bit back a cry of anguish. He was sure at least two of his ribs had been cracked, perhaps broken, but fortunately his fight with Mama Kaf had left him with little other damage, at least none that could hamper him seriously.

Entering the outer hall once more, he walked slowly, his bow up, a hand ready to grab an arrow from his back. Cautiously he made his way around the floor, glancing in at open doors and ignoring rooms closed off to him.

He managed to discover a handful of herbs which he recognized as able to deal with much of his pain. Dunking them in warm water for a few minutes provided a weak tea and relief for his bones. But he could not tarry more than a handful of minutes.

Finding no one awake on the ground, he made his way up the stairs to the second floor, each climbing step feeling as if a knife of ice had been shoved into his spine.

He was less familiar with the second floor of the tower, but found the layout much the same as the lower floor, a hall running the length of the outside, rooms of various sizes with various purposes within the central portion of the building.

And still no one awake. No enemies, no allies.

The third floor soon presented itself, and again, nothing, no one.

Still positive his remaining enemies were near, only the roof was left for him to check.

Standing at the bottom of the stairs leading up to the roof's trap door, he paused, waiting, thinking. The ceiling above him was thick, as was the door, and he could hear nothing. Not that it mattered. They were there. He was sure of it. But to go charging up through the trap door would only lead to a fool's death. There had to be another way.

Grunting at his pain, he hung his bow over a shoulder and proceeded back down to the ground floor. Soon enough he was outside in the cold again, though the snow no longer flew down from above.

He moved around to the alley where he had left Kilchus, again ignoring the dead man, and glanced up the frozen outer wall to the ledge of the roof three stories above. His gloved hands already finding the grappling hook within his cloak and working at unwinding the attached silken cord, he was thankful for the herbs he had found to dull most of his pain. Still, in normal conditions and with good health, the climb would have been a simple one for him, but with a cracked back and a layer of ice upon the wall, he was not so sure the climb would be a safe one. At the least, it would not be a swift ascension.

Still, better to take his time and surprise his foes than walk into their midst.

He twirled the grapnel over his head.

***

His elbows in his hands, his boots hidden in snow above the ankles, his shoulders quaking, Jarin Oltos the assassin was not a happy man. He shooshed one boot from side to side in front of him, clearing away the snow resting there to reveal the trap door once more.

"This is stupid," he said, staring off into the pale expanse that was now the city of Bond.

"At least it's stopped snowing," Spider said.

With a sour expression, Jarin turned and stared at the smaller man standing behind him near the short wall that made up the roof's edge. "At least you've got a cloak."

Spider grinned. "I guess that leather armor isn't all that warm."

"Shut up, you two," came another voice.

Jarin turned around again, facing his sister's back, the woman several yards away from him, her attention focused on the alley to the north. "What is it now, Rgia?" he asked.

"I heard something," she said.

Her brother chuckled. "You're always hearing something. It's because you worry too much. No one is coming, because no one knows we're here. And even if someone should show up, Teth's magic knocks them right out."

She waved a hand for his silence.

Instead of complying, he only laughed again.

Rgia twisted around, glaring at him, daggers suddenly in each of her fists.

"What?" Jarin asked with a grin, holding up his hands in mock defense.

"Don't test me, little brother."

Spider snorted from behind Jarin. "You two, if there *is* anybody out there, they sure as hell will hear us with all your jabbering."

The woman squinted past her brother to the little thief, glared a moment further, then turned back to watching to the north. "At least Teth could have given us some light so we could see."

Jarin glanced to the sky. "The moon is a bit narrow tonight, isn't it, what with the cloud cover and all the sn--"

An arrow appeared in his stomach.

Grunting, he stumbled back, both hands going to the shaft protruding from his flesh.

"Darkbow!" Spider shouted, hunching down near the crenelated wall.

Rgia crouched, her knees touching the snow, her eyes darting in all directions but seeing nothing but black night, her daggers out at her sides. "It can't be him. He's dead."

Waving a hand wildly to keep his balance, Jarin groaned, his legs nearly buckling and taking him back to Spider. Nearing the thief, he glared at him with eyes filled with pain and rage. "You knew! You knew it was him!"

"The arrow." Spider pointed at the assassin's bleeding gut. "It's all black."

Jarin glanced down, grimacing at the blood-slicked projectile causing him so much anguish. When he looked up again, there was no faith behind his eyes. "You lie."

Twaaang!

Rgia rolled to one side just as a second arrow smacked into the snow where she had been huddled but a moment earlier.

"There!" she yelled, pointing with a knife into the darkness.

Her brother seemed not to hear her words. Instead, he focused all his hate upon Spider. The assassin's free hand drew forth a dagger while his other hand grabbed tighter at the arrow in his belly. "Traitor!"

"No!" Spider shouted, pushing away until his back was against the wall.

"You fools, he's right on top of us," Rgia said to her brother and the thief.

Again, Jarin did not hear. He loosened his other hand and lunged with the dagger, the blade slashing into Spider's ribs as the assassin's free hand grabbed at the thief's throat. Spider tried to fight back, but he was smaller and less experienced, having avoided fighting whenever possible. The master of thieves cried out as the dagger carved through into his side, then he tried pushing his opponent away, all to no avail.

"Damn it!" Rgia nearly panicked. She glanced to her battling companions, then looked toward Curval and Sadhe Teth. The wizard still knelt as he had for some while. The knight stood his ground, showing no sign of attending to his comrades, his back to the wizard's, the big sword out, gripped in both hands, the end of the blade planted in the snow.

Another twanging sound, and the third arrow caught Jarin between the shoulders as he grappled with Spider and lifted the smaller man off the roof's floor. Rgia's brother howled with pain, dropping the thief to his boots in the snow. Still, the men did not stop fighting. Spider was too panicked, and had not noticed the most recent arrow. He fought as well as he could, having no weapon at hand, his fingers clawing for Jarin's throat, grasping the neck, the two men entwined like wrestlers.

It was then Rgia saw what was to happen. Her brother loomed over Spider, whose back was bent against the short wall around the roof. They scrambled against one another, neither doing much damage, both in pain, neither paying attention. Jarin had Spider off his feet again as they locked arms and necks, the assassin pressing forward, not aware of his footing, of his location.

"No!" Rgia screamed.

But it was too late.

With an upthrust arm and a shout, Spider went over backwards, his other hand enmeshed within Jarin's collar. Jarin could not help but follow. For a moment it seemed his weight and better balance would keep him on the edge, but then a tug from Spider pulled him over as well.

The two disappeared in silence into the darkness of the alley below. The only noise that came up from that black well was the thudding of their bodies upon snow and stone.

For the first time in her life, Rgia Oltos went into shock. She stood, slowly, her arms lowering to hang at her sides. A wind whipped at her hair, brushing strands across unblinking eyes. Her brother was gone. She hated him, had always hated him, but he had always been there. He had been more trouble than he was worth, was never as good at anything as he believed himself to be, but still, he was her brother. No one had the right to kill him except for her, the only other living family member, as was the code of Provenzano assassins.

She stared for long seconds to where her brother had fallen to his death along with a man barely worth being spit upon.

Then the fury erupted from inside.

She whirled around, her daggers out once more. "Damn you, Teth! Damn you, Curval!"

The wizard remained in place, and the knight betrayed no sign of having noted the conflict.

Rgia growled and twisted around to face the night, to face the darkness from where the arrows had come. "Show yourself, demon!"

And he did.

Kron Darkbow slid from the shadows like an apparition, tossing his bow and empty quiver to one side. His black garb concealed nearly all of him but his face, but a weak glow from the snow showed the outline of his figure and the cloak flapping behind him.

Roaring her rage, Rgia charged at the man, her daggers coming from both directions. With her soft boots wading through snow six inches in depth,. Kron had all the time in world.

With a snap of a hand, three black darts shot across the expanse between the two combatants. One went wide of its mark, helped along the way by a stray wind. The other two darts found a home in the woman's chest. The wounds were small and not deep, but they were enough to startle her, to bring her up several feet short of her foe.

Kron had made a mistake when fighting this woman before on another, similar rooftop. He had tried to match her speed with his own, and to match her ferocity. He should have known better, though in fairness to himself he had not been familiar with the woman nor her style of combat. His younger self might have been able to match her zeal, but he had never seen a mortal who could match her for speed. Yet no one could move overly fast in heavy snow. He smirked as he brought forth the dagger from his belt and the other short blade from his boot, one weapon brandished in each hand.

One of her daggers came up and brushed away the darts sticking into her. Then she howled and charged again, her eyes flashing hate.

Her steel came from both sides. Kron met her blade for blade, metal scraping metal, sparks flashing in the night. Then she attacked from above and below at the same time. Again, his weapons met her own, blocking them, knocking aside the assaults.

She kicked at him, but he twisted, her boot glancing off his side as he whirled, his cloak whipping around and smacking her in the face, blinding her for but a moment.

But a moment was all it took.

Rgia blinked, then the next thing she saw was a fist flying straight for her face. The blow caught her direct, jerking her head back and sending her falling. A black glove dropped a dagger and caught her by the throat before she hit the snow. In pain, her eyes filled with tears. Nearly off her footing, she panicked, flailing with her daggers, hoping for a lucky stab or a slash that would bring freedom.

No freedom came.

One of her blades lost itself within the folds of his cloak. The other he shunted aside with steel of his own. Then he pulled her into himself, dropping his other weapon and wrapping an arm around her free elbow, locking his other arm around her neck. His cloak fell about them, shielding them from the outside world as she allowed herself to come to him. She saw an opportunity, thinking it foolish of him to pull a knife fighter into close environs. But Kron Darkbow was no fool. Groaning at the pain in his back, he lifted her off the ground, causing her neck to crack from the pressure and weight.

Rgia tried to free her other hand, to pull it out of his cloak, but the dagger was stuck there. Letting the weapon go, she pulled back the hand and thrust it up in an attempt to jam a palm into his chin. His head turned away at the last moment, then slammed forward, his forehead cracking into her face. Blood splashed from her nose as more pain lanced her soul, causing her to scream.

Still, she fought on.

Seeing no other way, she brought her legs up, trying to wrap them around the much larger figure. Kron saw it coming and released her neck, nearly dropping her into the snow.

Landing on her feet, she grabbed him by the hood of his cloak, the cloth hanging to one side. She tried to pull it over his head to blind him, but then he let go of her other arm and tackled her, his limbs wrapping around her waist.

His weight alone would have been enough to take her down, but Rgia Oltos was skilled with balance and footwork. She managed to keep herself on her feet, her head and arms above his back. Her one hand still holding a dagger, she saw a prime opportunity to stab him in the back.

But Kron had skill and footwork of his own. He squeezed and lifted her again, forcing the air from her lungs in a hefty grunt. He forced her backwards, their legs nearly entangling as he kept pushing and she fought to halt their momentum.

Only at the last moment did she see where he was taking her. She brought her dagger up for a stab to his back. He continued to propel her forward. Her dagger flashed. He shoved, releasing her.

The razor's edge of steel sliced across his left shoulder as she went over the crenelated wall, falling with a scream.

Kron stood there bleeding from his shoulder, his eyes locked on the darkness of the alley below, his breathing heavy, his body tired.

Then he turned away to retrieve his daggers and darts.

32

The ascent up the rope and the ice-slick wall had been as strenuous and nearly as perilous as the melee on the rooftop. That combined with the fight had done Kron's back no favors, and now that his adrenaline was flooding from his body along with any aid from the healing herbs, he once more felt the aches and pains climbing up his spine. The dagger wound to his shoulder did not help, though a quick staunching with a piece of cloak ripped from the hem kept his life's fluid from much draining. His head still felt woozy from earlier in the night, and exhaustion nearly devoured him. All in all, he was not in top condition, but he had been in worse shape and faced worse odds.

While loosing his arrows he had kept a watch on the heavy figure with the big sword and the crouching person behind him, all the while expecting the man with the plated chest to wade into the combat. When that hadn't happened, Kron had been caught by surprise. It also concerned him the kneeling figure did not stir, making Kron think this must be the wizard, whether Falk or not, and that the mage was busy with some kind of spell or ritual. Considering the extent of recent events, Kron could not imagine the magic being of anything good.

Makeshift bandages wrapping around his shoulder and across his chest, his daggers returned to their sheaths, Kron once more returned his attention to the pair near the back of the building. He sauntered forward with caution, breaking out his sword as he went.

It was only when he neared within a few dozen feet that the big man with the plated chest stepped forward, raising his heavy blade into a high guard position, the end of the sword aimed at Kron, the weapon's handle near the armored figures bare head. This was not some mercenary or simple soldier. Kron Darkbow knew a trained, experienced swordsman when he saw one.

The man in black slowed, keeping his own sword in a low guard slightly to his right, ready to swipe the blade up for a block if necessary.

As the two silent warriors neared one another, the wizard behind them remained unmoving on his knees, as outlined by the moon which fought its way between a haze of clouds.

The image of a horse upon his enemy's chest plate brought Kron to a halt. His foe was a knight of Caballerus.

The knight also stopped, the two staring at one another across a short distance. Their gazes heavy, the two men recognized in one another a familiarity with death and disaster, and perhaps a familiarity with a sense of honor.

Kron allowed the tip of his sword to dip further, almost touching the snow in a sign of seeking respectful discourse. For a moment the other man did not move, then he nodded and brought his heavy weapon down into a standard guard at his side. The two still faced one another with opening positions, but there had been notes of accommodation.

"We do not have to fight," Kron stated flatly.

"You waste your time," Curval said.

His sword lowering even further, Kron nodded behind himself in memory of the combat moments earlier. "I see you did not help your friends against a lone combatant, which makes me believe you a man of honor."

The knight's teeth ground together before he spoke. "They were not my friends."

"Then who were they?"

"Murderers and thieves. Comrades only for necessity."

Kron raised his left hand and pointed at the kneeling wizard. "And him?"

"My ward," Curval said.

"Ward?"

"He is my charge, the one I protect."

A thousand thoughts chased themselves through Kron's mind. His body weary, he much wanted to avoid combat with this man, but he needed to get to the wizard to thwart whatever evil was being played out. It was then Kron recalled recent history. He gambled with his next words.

"Much like your king?" he said.

Curval's eyebrows rose, and for a moment the end of his sword quivered. "You dare speak of Lord Alexandre?"

"I would dare much when those I cherish have been harmed," Kron said.

An edge of the knight's lips rose in a snarl. "What would you know, being a man without a king?"

"A man without a king? Like yourself, you mean?"

The knight's face flared red with rage. "My land's king was slain by scoundrels of the lowest sort."

"Much like those who now attempt to bring harm to *my* land," Kron said.

"This land is a mockery of all that is right," Curval said, his every word dripping with disdain. "It is ruled by those only skilled in deception."

"It is ruled by those freely elected into office."

"There is little difference."

Kron stared at the ground for a moment, allowing his sword to stoop further into the white. It was apparent to him his opponent might not be a man with whom to be reasoned. Yet there was one more verbal and emotional tactic he could employ, for Kron wished to avoid this fight not only because his physical condition had deteriorated, but because he sensed a hint of dignity still buried deep within his foe.

"The people of West Ursia might be fools to trust in their lawmakers," Kron said, "but men of honor, men such as yourself, they can guide the people along better paths."

The words seemed to bring the knight up short for a moment. He stood stunned, but finally he found his own words, his eyes growing wet. "I served not only a king, but one of the most noble creatures who ever lived, and he was slain on my watch. You cannot imagine the shame I feel."

"You are wrong. I know such shame. I have failed many in my time, but I find others for whom to live, others to help, to serve, to honor."

Curval paused again, but then slowly stood to one side, freeing a hand from his sword to point back at the kneeling wizard. "Here is my master now. It is in him I find my honor. He gives me a reason to be. He gives me something in which to believe."

"And what is that?" Kron asked. "Do you know? Look back over the past week. What good has been wrought? Look at your master now as he prepares his magic, as he schemes. Do you sense any good coming from this?"

Again the knight appeared stunned. He glanced from the mage back to the figure in black several times, then he gave a short shrug. "He has given me life after my fall, and now I know nothing else." His empty hand returned to the handle of his sword where he tightened his grip and took a defensive stance once more. "Let us be done with this."

Kron's gaze fell along with his spirits. There was to be no avoidance of combat here. He let out a sigh and squared his shoulders, lifting his sword for battle.

The two men came at one another at the same moment. Curval's heavier blade swept in overhead from his right, Kron's upraised weapon knocking aside the steel with a stout thrust.

For a moment the pair were almost chest to chest. Kron twisted his sword around, bringing up the hilt for a punch at his opponent's face, but the knight was fast despite his size and armored chest, the man jumping back in time to avoid the blow.

Kron pressed his momentary advantage, flashing his sword around in a wide arc he knew to be foolish and dangerous to himself, but also potentially threatening to his foe. Curval showed no fear; he waited for the long sword to swish past him, then he slashed forward and down. The stroke would have cut the man in black from head to groin if he had not been more swift than his enemy. Seeing his doom approaching, Kron followed the trajectory of his own weapon and twirled himself away from the center of the fight, his boots sending up a flurry of snow before he came around and faced the knight yet again.

The two halted for a moment, catching their breath in the frigid night air, staring at one another across a short distance, their swords raised again to their sides.

"You are reckless," Curval said.

Kron bound forward, going for an over cut aimed for his opponent's head. As expected, Curval brought up his own blade, the two swords clashing together in their centers. Proving the knight's opinion of him correct, Kron let go of his sword's handle with his left hand, the glove darting forward to grab both blades where they met in an attempt at disarming. Using his leverage, Kron jerked on the weapons, trying to pull both to him, but the knight was stronger and familiar with the move. Curval twisted his sword, the edge cutting through leather and stinging Kron's hand with a line of red as the bigger man pulled away.

Ignoring the new pain, Kron lashed out wild with his sword, sweeping his opponent back another step.

The pair stopped for a third time, glaring at one another as their breathing came heavy, their swords at the ready.

The moment gave Kron time to think further.

"I don't know much about your King Alexandre," he said, "but I had always heard he was a goodly man who served his people well. Like he would do, I am trying to save my own people."

Curval snarled. "Shut up."

"Would you allow harm to those lesser than you?" Kron asked. "Is that a knightly virtue?"

The questions seemed to infuriate the knight. He charged, his sword held high for a moment before swinging around from one side. Kron barely had time to defend with his own blade, but he only halted his foe's momentum for a moment. Curval was heavier and stronger as was his sword. The bigger man shoved with his blade's edge, thrusting Kron back several steps.

Then nearly faster than Kron could see, the knight's sword spun back and around overhead for a downward jab. It was a move fueled by anger and, though a swift assault, it left the attacker open. Kron shifted to one side, his footing perfect despite the snow, as the knightly sword stabbed through the air where he had stood a moment earlier. Then Darkbow pressed forward with the tip of his own weapon, aiming for his opponent's heart.

Only to be brought up short by that chest of steel plate.

The two men almost touching once more, Curval grunted a laugh and rounded an elbow into Kron's face. The blow struck direct, snapping Kron's head back and sending him reeling with his arms out wide.

Somehow the man in black managed to keep one hand upon his sword, but it did him little good as the knight tromped forward and with both hands brought his own steel down with all his strength. The strike would have killed if Curval had meant it to, but he had not been aiming for Darkbow himself. Instead, the larger sword battered into the smaller one, steel striking steel as Kron's weapon was struck from his hand.

Yet even without a sword, Kron was not defenseless. Blood now covering his bottom lip, he recovered from being hit, one hand diving to his belt for a dagger, the other trying to retrieve throwing darts.

As skilled as he was, however, he faced an opponent similarly formidable.

Before Kron could draw any of his weapons, Curval stepped in close and swung high with his sword. The move caused Kron to duck low, keeping him from bringing forth further tools of conflict. Unfortunately for the man in black, it also brought his chin within striking distance of Curval's knees. The knight kicked up, a padded patella smacking Kron directly beneath the chin.

The blow sent Kron rolling away, his sight filled with bright lights, his jaw numb. An unseen kick to his back sent him into the snow where he landed on his back.

When he managed to blink away his most recent pain, Kron rolled over and looked up to find the knight standing above him, towering over him, legs on either side, the large two-handed sword gripped above Curval's head with the long blade pointed at Kron's chest.

Laying there dazed, his mind not fully working, Kron could think of nothing he could do to save his own life. Words escaped his lips without his knowing what he was saying and whether or not the words were true. "Would you dishonor your king's memory by this?"

The end of the sword plummeted down, then stopped mere inches from Kron's chest. At the other end of the lengthy weapon a pair of red-soaked eyes stared with anger and hate.

The world came to a standstill.

Then Curval lifted back his head and roared to the heavens, his sword shaking in his hands, his raging throat shaking all of eternity. Raising the sword once more, he swung it up high over a shoulder as if to slash down upon his foe.

Instead, he flung the heavy weapon far to one side. The length of steel and its wrapped handle disappeared into an ocean of white, sinking down beneath the surface.

Before Kron could react, the knight stepped over him, turned and walked several feet away, then came to a halt. The big man's head sank between his shoulders, and as he wrapped his face in his broad hands, those shoulders wrestled with themselves, trembling up and down. The knight cried out his pain, his torment. He wept for a king he had not been able to save, for an ideal which had seen its day.

Spying an opportunity, Kron inched back in the snow, then rolled over and scrambled for his fallen sword. Finding the weapon, he seized it and spun on his rear and sprang to his feet.

He found himself facing Curval once more, the burly figure with the plated chest having turned around without moving closer.

The knight glared once more at his foe, the eyes crimson and filled with anguish. Tears rolled down his quivering face.

Kron stood his ground, his sword ready for action.

But no further action was needed between the two.

"Do as you will," Curval finally said.

Then he turned away for a last time and padded through the snow.

Remaining wary, Kron watched each step of the armored figure. The knight made his way to where the trap door lay hidden once more beneath several inches of snow. The toe of a thick boot pushed aside the snow, then the big man leaned down and tugged open the door, slamming it back upon its hinges.

Only when the knight had vanished below, pulling the trap door closed yet again, did Kron allow himself an exhale of relief.

Then he turned to the wizard.

Who had still not moved.

<u>33</u>

Kicking up snow as he waded forward, his sword out at one side and prepared to strike, Kron came at the mage from one side, curving around until he could make out the man's profile beneath the light of the moon. The fellow appeared well into his old age, his head nearly bald with only a few wisps of white hair fluttering in the gentle breeze. The lines of the wizard's face sank deep within the flesh, giving him an appearance of being carved from ancient, dark wood. The cloak about his shoulders and the robes beneath seemed as thin as webbing, the paleness of the garb almost giving him the countenance of a healer. His eyes remained closed, though his lips moved slightly despite the fact no words could be heard coming forth.

More unusual to the man in black was the circular clearing of snow around the old figure. Instead of the white powder, a ring of thin ice concealed the floor of the tower's roof beneath the mage. Right away Kron recognized the ice as the same filaments of frost he had witnessed growing upon the building in the lower quarters.

Standing there for several moments, Kron awaited a reaction. All the wizard's protectors had fled or been removed, so now the mage was alone. Surely he would rise to defend himself.

Or not.

Because he made no move other than the silent mumbling of his lips.

"Lord Falk?" Kron asked.

There was no response.

Kron took a step forward, lifting his sword as if to strike.

Still no response.

"Defend yourself, sir."

Nothing.

Kron let out another sigh, this one filled with irritation. "I will arrest you, sir," he said, "by whatever means necessary."

The old man continued kneeling and muttering, perhaps in prayer.

The sword dipped. A sense of fairness kept Kron from wanting to harm the mage, especially as the man appeared defenseless. Yet Kron also knew the appearance could be a deception, thus he kept himself wary.

Leaning in close, the man in black reached out with his free hand and grasped the wizard by a shoulder.

Eyes snapped open. "Remove your hand from me. Now."

Pulling back his torn glove and leaving a mark of red upon the shoulder, Kron could not help but stare as the old man's face craned around almost as if no neck connected the head with the body. It was at that moment, delving into those glaring eyes, that Kron realized he dealt not with a mortal enemy, but with a power most ancient. That glare, it was filled with not only animosity but with evil knowledge beyond timeworn, an evil from an era when man was young.

"You think you have halted me," the old man said, finally standing, his body fully turning to face the man in black, "but you reckon not with some hedge wizard, my fool. My ritual is not disrupted, but is all but complete. It would take but a matter of moments for me to finish with it. Your disturbance delays the inevitable but by minutes at best. You may have fought your way through my allies, even those most trustworthy, but my power even now swirls around us unseen by the likes of you, only awaiting my patience to continue, to complete the binding and to finish what I have begun."

"You are not Lord Falk." The words slipped from Kron's lips without him meaning to say them.

The bald head snapped back and laughed to the heavens. "As I said, a fool! Of course I am not Lord Falk. No mere mortal could fathom the depths of my power, or to the powers for which I reach."

Kron took several steps back, his sword wavering, but then a coldness caused not by the night or the snow overwhelmed him, clawing up from deep within himself. He squared his shoulders and gritted his teeth. There was no one else here to stop this madness, no one but Kron Darkbow, and too many had already given their lives along this monster's journey. And while Kron stood alone, he recognized his foe did as well.

The man in black raised his sword in both hands. "Whatever your name, wizard or demon, let us end this."

The mage known as Sadhe Teth chuckled. "You think you can harm me with your flimsy steel?"

Kron glanced to the sword in his hands, then he shrugged and sheathed the weapon. "I suppose not. I am familiar with magics that can protect a wizard. No arrow can pierce your flesh, no sword can cut your skin. Fine with me. I'll simply beat you to death."

And he raised his fists to do that very thing.

The mage pointed at him. "I will bring your worst nightmares to life!"

Kron chuckled. "I have already lived my worst nightmares. I doubt you can show me anything I have not already witnessed, that you can show me any level of hell I have not already conquered."

The old man grinned, waving a hand around his head. "But what of your favored city? Are you prepared for its very death?"

Death? Of a whole city?

Teth laughed once more as the realization grew in Darkbow's eyes. "Yes, I mean to claim every soul in this retched metropolis. This city is mine!"

It was then the truth became apparent to Kron. The cold weather, the growing frost upon the ground, it all made a dark sense. This madman before him utilized the lowest of magics, those powered by the souls of others. The more who died at this monster's hands, the more powerful he became. Kron had personally witnessed such dark magics on more than one occasion, though rare they were. But here and now, this insane creature dared to take such magics to an extreme, by annihilating an entire city, which would make the madman as powerful as ... what? A god?

This could not happen. Thousands would not die for the whim of one power-hungry bedlamite.

"No," Kron said, stepping forward, his fists raised higher.

"You claim yourself this city's protector?" the mage asked.

"I do."

The wizard's eyes sparkled with their madness, their evil, as he raised his own hands, but not into fists. "Very well, then. Let us see you protect against *this*."

His hands waved and his fingers snapped and words as old as time escaped the wizard's lips.

And he exploded outwards in a giant mound of bosky flesh.

***

Several stories below, a healer's eyes flickered open.

***

Kron found himself engulfed within a mass of folding, gelatinous muscle and sinew and plasm, all the color of a dead man's eyes. One moment he had been facing the wizard, ready to strike with his fists, then his opponent's skin had bubbled out black and erupted in a matter of seconds into this monstrous thing surrounding the man in black.

Kron had no footing, but found himself lifted from the ground and tossed around as if he were a babe. He flailed with all his might, but there was nothing to hit which he could see other than an all-encompassing wall of flesh. There was no central target, not a face nor an eye.

The stench was the worst, like a wet dead thing pulled from a swampy grave, the smell overpowering and nauseating to the stomach. Fighting back spasms within his throat, Kron also had to combat the oily touch of this thing that surrounded him, pressed in upon him. From all sides, every inch of his body was forced up against a sweaty slickness that reminded him of the skin of hooked fish pulled to shore, but instead of the fish it was Kron who was floundering with no air to breathe.

The pressure was nearly too much, and the lack of air did not help. The man in black pushed back with all his might, making some little headway here and there, just enough to give him a little room to flex his lungs, to breathe in miraculous air, though air that smelled of the grave. Still, it seemed not enough. As soon as he gained an inch of room, the overpowering presence would roll around him further, tightening, digging in at him, pushing against him.

Soon giving up on freeing himself, Kron saw few other options than to fight back directly. His sword being useless as there was no room to draw the large weapon, he forced a hand down to his belt and grasped a dagger by its hilt, tugging the blade free of its scabbard. There was barely room to make use of the short steel, but he managed to twist a wrist around to stab and slash.

All to no avail. Trying to cut into the living wall of flesh was like trying to slice through thick, oiled leather with a dull wooden spoon.

Abandoning his dagger, Kron tried grasping with his fingers, pressing them into the mounds of rolling putrescence. For a moment he believed he had some luck, as his digits seemed to press back and into the skin sweeping over him. But just as soon as he felt a grip, the surrounding barrier of meat would reel away and undulate within his touch before springing forward again.

His vision was gone, filled with nothing but darkness, and his breathing grew more and more coarse. From the damage he had already taken that night, pain was growing in his back, his head, his wounded shoulder and his sliced hand. The enveloping beast had that effect as it pushed in open him and rolled him end over end, forcing itself upon his wounds and bruises, bringing fresh anguish.

Growing desperate, Kron once more sought a centralized target for his wrath. There had to be something within all this chaos and turmoil, something which he could focus upon. Yet there seemed nothing, not a sign of the old wizard, no sight of anything resembling a mortal man, only darkness with the occasional glimpse of dark, raw flesh like meat gone bad.

Infuriated, Kron pushed himself back with his arms and kicked forward with his legs. He gained some few inches, allowing him to breathe in again, though the stench sent his head into a swirl. For a moment he believed he had heard a grunting sound. Had he scored a hit against his foe?

He did not know, and would not be given the chance to find out.

Tendrils as thick as ropes shot forth from deep within the muscular thing that had been Sadhe Teth and wrapped themselves around the limbs of Kron Darkbow, pulling the swordsman in all directions. For a brief second Kron thought he caught sight of rows upon rows of round objects of various size, not unlike the suckers of an octopus, but such seemed impossible.

Then those tentacles grabbed hold of the man in black and ripped at his clothing, the small suckers not unlike hundreds of small mouths proving their existence by chewing and tearing away at him.

Kron jerked and writhed, fighting as best he could against the terrible mouths working their way down to his flesh. It would be moments before he was chewed apart unless he could do something.

His bow dropped and useless without arrows, his steel blades no good against this unholy foe, his punches and kicks fruitless, there were but two choices left to him, his throwing darts, also likely useless, and the favorite of all his weapons.

Grenados.

Fire.

His dagger hand still near his belt, he squirmed in desperation, his fingers stretching, searching, clawing for the small leather sack that possibly contained his salvation. Once more the engulfing monster squeezed in upon him, cutting his air down to nothing as the hundreds of small, hungry mouths tore at his garb, pulling away much of his cloak while tearing into his leather gloves and boots.

Yet he would not surrender. Not to death, not to the inevitable, not to this eldritch beast. His fingers worked, running along the belt at his waist, probing what felt like leather cords tied together, moving past as he realized he touched his climbing rope and grapnel, also impractical in this situation.

A pair of the tiny mouths bit into his lower right jaw, cutting into his flesh with a dozen miniature teeth, drawing forth blood and sucking. Kron would have screamed, but he had no air, the tentacles wrapping themselves tighter and tighter.

His vision went white with spots, the onset of unconsciousness, as more blood leaked from his wounds, and his back and head ached as if a giant hammered away at him.

Then his leather-clad fingers brushed against something soft, something with give. It was the sack of grenados.

Frantic, he plunged the hand down, tearing at the small bag's bindings, two of his fingers fumbling with a small, round object. A grenado. He had it. Then dropped it. But his hand was still in the bag. His fingers twisted around, found another of the clay balls, gripped and pulled, palming the small incendiary weapon.

With all the strength left in him, Kron Darkbow tugged his arm up and away from himself as if reaching for the sky. Within the palm of that cut, bleeding hand was the lone grenado he had managed to free.

It was all or nothing now.

He ducked his head, flipping the remains of his cloak's hood over his face, then brought the grenado down with all his might upon the living flesh of his terrible captor.

The clay cracked and hell was born.

Light and flame roared forth to bring sight of the entwining, unworldly terror to Kron's eyes along with fresh levels of pain as fire engulfed his left hand and rolled up his arm to lick at his chest and covered face. He shouted out from the burning and flinched away as far as he could, but there was nowhere to go as the fire streamed over his body. Then the massive bulk holding him screeched and shuddered and Kron found himself tossed into the air, his burning limbs whirling as he sought purchase upon anything.

Something cold and wet and gelatinous slapped him across the face, and Kron's head snapped to one side as if punched by a god's mallet. He plummeted through cold air for the longest of times, then landed hard in a puffing of freezing white powder.

Laying there, every inch of his body feeling as if one fire, Kron allowed himself to breathe in the chilled and much needed night's air. Smelling his own cooked flesh, he shook his head to clear away his dulled vision, then blinked and found himself huddled in the snow on the rooftop of the Swamps healing tower. His hands gripping one another in front of his face, he stared down at the blackened, raw meat covering his fingers, the leather of his gloves no longer evident, having been chewed or burned away. Swirls of black smoke circled themselves up and away from what remained of his skin, and he sat back to stare down his chest and legs to find much of his clothing gone or ruined, his weapons mostly missing. The pain was like a thousand insects crawling over his body, each tiny creature nipping away at the remains of his flesh with pincers covered in acid. It was all he could do not to scream and surrender to madness.

At least he was alive, and despite the beatings and the burning he had suffered, he was free once more, though his condition was atrocious. Grenado fire generally acted like a glue, adhering itself to its target and burning until there was nothing left to burn. Fortunately for Kron, his opponent had taken the brunt of the explosion, the giant mound of tentacled flesh having covered most of Kron when the grenado cracked, and falling into snow several inches in depth had helped.

Reminded of his foe, Kron gritted back pain as blood dripped from between his teeth and he craned his head around looking for the monster that had nearly slain him.

No longer the tentacled beast but in his original form of Lord Falk, the wizard was a dozen feet away on his hands and knees, his cloak and robes aflame as his body shuddered. Half his face was blackened and charred, the other half still appearing normal but filled with obvious anguish, the eyes shuttered, the mouth open in a soundless scream as the fire cascaded along his frame. His eyes snapped open, the lashes burnt away, and for a moment those wide orbs stared at the cause of all the pain, then the throat gave itself voice and the wail became real, loud, echoing across rooftops.

Sadhe Teth rolled over and over in a desperate attempt to vanquish the flames eating away at him, but it did little good, even the snow powerless to assuage his pain. Within a matter of seconds his clothing was gone, burned to strips of ash that danced away upon the wind. Still the wizard rolled, the grenado fire now down to the flesh and tearing away at him.

The sight was almost enough to bring remorse to Kron Darkbow's heart, but he thought of Randall and Nodana and all the others slain or wounded by this monster's doing. It was then all pity fled the man in black's heart.

Rolling, screaming, fire. It continued. The mage shuffling through the snow one way, then another. Slowly the flames began to die, and when finally extinguished left behind was a darkened crisp of a man, more than half the skin burnt down to black leather, madness wheeling around within the mage's eyes.

With a last sorrowful moan and a sigh, Sadhe Teth dropped onto his back in the snow. He lay there with eyes closed, his chest slowly rising and falling, his blistered lips working as if trying to say something.

Looking around for a weapon of any sort, Kron became surprised his sword remained strapped to his hip. Wincing at the pain of gripping the weapon's handle, he drew the sword forth and forced himself to crawl closer to the nearly dead mage because nearly dead was not good enough. Dragging his sword behind, the man in black left a trail that looked as if a snake followed him.

Next to the fallen figure, Kron gritted once more and forced himself to stand, lifting his sword for a killing stroke.

Eyes snapped open within the charred mess that was Sadhe Teth's face. "That is twice now you should be dead."

"I waited for you to lead the way," Kron said, stabbing down with his heavy blade.

But the sword's edge skidded off the burnt flesh as if striking stone.

Teth croaked out a chuckle and somehow managed to roll onto one side, looking more like a melted, disfigured puppet than a human being. "Still a fool. You forget my wards of protection."

No, Kron had not forgotten. He had simply believed the magic would have been nullified after the damage his foe had taken. This wizard was more powerful than Kron could have imagined, even after witnessing the horror the other man had turned himself into for a period of time.

Stepping back, Kron tossed his useless sword to one side. Then he raised his fists again, more pain rushing through him as his blackened digits curled together.

Rising to his feet, the mage turned to Darkbow. Teth's lips had been burned away, leaving him with a permanent grin like that of a death's head. Wavering on his bony feet, he motioned for his opponent to approach. "That's it. Fight me, young man. Punish me."

Recognizing a ruse when he saw one, Kron hesitated. But what choice did he have? He had no more weapons, and even if he had, they would have been useless. He moved forward, snapping a fist at his enemy.

Just before the hand landed, Sadhe Teth's face lit up, his vicious smile growing even wider in triumph.

Flesh touched flesh, a hand upon a shoulder, and Kron Darkbow immediately realized his mistake, that all of his fights throughout the night would be nothing as to the one confronting him now.

The man in black was no longer within his own body, or at least he could not feel his own burnt, battered, bruised flesh. He found himself floating nude, within a domain of undulating gray, reminding him somewhat of being trapped within the wizard's tentacled form except here Kron remained unfettered, able to move, able to breathe.

"Welcome to your own mind," a voice said.

Spinning around, nearly tumbling, Kron saw Teth a goodly distance away, the wizard appearing hale and hearty once more, again donned in robes and cloaks of white.

"Though you are not in the best of conditions, I am in need of a younger man's body," Teth said. "Prepare to lose yourself, forever."

The mage stretched forth his hands as if reaching for Darkbow.

A pain stabbed Kron in his eyes, blinding him and knocking him back into the nothingness of where he floated. He felt fresh tentacles, now with claws, tearing away at his skull. There were hundreds of the scrambling tendrils, each working to break into his mind, to burrow deep within himself, to strip away his thoughts and his memories, to steal them, to remove him from himself.

Forever. As the mage had said.

Yet there were few men with more strength of will than Kron Darkbow. After a moment of estrangement, he fought back, his mind throwing up shielded walls, his fists swinging at his enemy now unseen, not striking but delaying any approach. Kron kicked with his legs, then realized he was not truly in his body and that his appendages did little good here. He had to fight back in a different manner, in a way unfamiliar to him. But fight he would.

There was a shout of surprise from somewhere, followed by a snarl of anger and then a cackle of delight. A booming sound thudded throughout Kron's thoughts, the wizard's powers striking as hammers against Kron's defenses.

"I give you that your are strong," the mage said, his voice cunning, "but it is only a matter of time. Surrender and end your pain!"

"No!" Kron cried out.

Another level of anguish hit Kron, a wave of desperation rolled over him, throwing him back again and again, forcing his mind into a whirlwind of darkness that bottomed out into a never-ending bit of nothingness.

For a moment, all seemed lost.

Then someone said, "Enough."

And it all ended.

Kron found himself on his back in the snow yet again. Blinking, he sat up, groaning as his body's torments returned to him. He discovered Teth only yards away, the ancient, burned wizard naked again and hunkered down, his hands grasped in front of his face to shield his shattered features. The mage cried tears that rushed down between fingers now more like claws.

Kron's attention could only remain upon the old man for a moment, however, for off to one side a bright amber luminescence lit up much of the rooftop, its radiance warm and gleaming off the man in black's skin and highlighting the flat snow as well as the cowering mage. Within the light stood a figure in white.

"Randall," Kron managed to say.

The healer stepped forward, the nearly-blinding glow fading as he did. He appeared hale. There were no signs of wounds upon him, and he was dressed in the fresh white garb of his station. Around his feet the snow began to recede, melting into rivulets and then slinking away toward the edges of the roof as he approached the two downed men.

Kron tried to stand, but his body refused him. The best he could do was lift himself up onto his elbows, and even that brought a grimace of pain.

Not looking to his friend, Randall held up a delaying hand. "Wait," the healer said.

Kron stirred no further, enraptured with the scene unfolding before him.

Randall crossed to the ancient mage, leaving a wet expanse in his wake. Sadhe Teth did not show his face, but kept his hands curled before his visage. The old man's body shook as if he were in tears, his head bobbing up and down.

The healer paused in front of the prostrate figure, lifting a flat hand above the bald, singed head of gray and black flesh. There the hand wavered.

"It ends here, now," Randall said, his words little more than a whisper. "Your goals must be denied, whatever the final outcome."

The ancient head craned back, wide, lidless eyes glaring up above two holes where a nose had once been and a lipless grin all of teeth. "You are not one of the old gods," Teth said, flecks flying from his mouth.

"No," Randall said, shaking his head.

"Then how have you the power to thwart me?" Teth asked. "*Why* thwart me?"

"I am He Who Walks Among Men," the healer answered, "the god who cares."

"*Ashal.*" The word barely slipped out of the ancient wizard's mouth.

Randall nodded. "My power is not my own, but for all."

Sadhe Teth snarled. "Yet you hide among these mortals."

"For now."

"Then you are not deserving."

"I will reveal myself when the moment is most opportune," Randall said. "Until then, men are not ready."

Teth tried to stand, but his frame betrayed him and he sank to his knees once more. "You fools, all of you. You *need* me. The old gods, they are still out there. I can *feel* them. One day they will rise again, and without me, all of you will fall."

"On that day we will meet them with swords in hand," Kron said.

"And with goodwill in our hearts," Randall added.

"On that day you will be burned to ashes!" Teth shouted.

"And you offer a better alternative?" Randall asked. "The deaths of thousands?"

"I do what is necessary."

"To your own benefit," the healer said.

"Power comes with responsibility," Teth yelled, bounding up and forward, somehow finding his feet. "Sometimes to save, one must destroy.

Randall made no response, standing in place, showing no fear.

"You, your powers are the strongest of all," Teth said, leaning forward, his claws raised as if to grab at the healer. "Thus I claim them for my own!"

With that the old man lunged, his hands falling on Randall's shoulders.

An explosion of light blossomed from the two, forcing Kron to raise a battered arm to cover his eyes. Between his fingers he could make out silhouettes of the men grappling, arms locked in place as they shoved against one another, neither seeming to win. All the while glowing rays broke forth from them, darting in all directions to light up the night as if the sun had risen.

"Your body will be mine!" Teth shouted from the maelstrom of fluorescence. "Your soul!"

"I think not," Randall said, his voice calm.

The old wizard craned forward, pushing with his blackened, stick-like arms. Randall held his own, not giving an inch nor pressing for one.

Then it all ended.

The light died.

The naked, skeletal figure of Sadhe Teth jerked away from the healer, cowered for a moment, standing transfigured as if frozen, then crumbled apart into a black dust. A wind swept in, lifting the ashes of the dead mage from the rooftop and whisking them off into the shadows of the night. All that remained of Sadhe Teth were a few tatters of burnt clothing and an open leather sack with bones resting atop it on the ground.

"It is done," Randall said.

34

"Sir, someone got through."

Captain Gris jerked around in his saddle to face the sergeant reporting to him. "Thank Ashal. It's about damn time."

The sergeant looked up from the ground, her eyes shaded by the brim of her helmet. "It was Corporal Swish, sir. We're sending in a detail behind him to make sure he makes it to the tower unmolested."

"Good job, Sergeant Lidra," Gris said with the first smile of the night. "Let me know the minute you receive the next report. If everything is well, we'll move in behind them."

He crossed a leg over his saddle and dropped to the ground. Things were looking better than they had in hours. The night was warming, the snow was slowly melting, and that annoying and dangerous layer of frost had all but disappeared. Now the first of Gris's people had managed to make some headway toward the Swamps healing tower, the other half dozen volunteers all having fallen asleep upon nearing.

Surveying the road ahead of him, Gris had known for hours heavy magic was at work. It had consoled him little that a dozen other riders had been with him throughout the ordeal, and that he had been backed by more than a score of his own men and women as well as a smaller contingent borrowed from the army troops camped outside the city. It had been a long night with little headway, and not a mage had been found to lend a hand with the situation. Repeated messengers had been sent to the university and even to some of the private homes along Mages Way, but there had been no responses; Gris was sure the weather was to blame to some extent, but still, one would think at least one local wizard of some power would have had the guts to lend a hand. Then again, most of the university's mages and those of Uptown generally considered themselves above such tasks as helping out the local city guard. Gris made a mental note to speak with the mayor about this, of trying to reach out more to the local magic community; the new special squad might help some in those regards, but more would need to be done.

Turning to the sergeant once more, Gris opened his mouth to give orders, but a dark carriage approaching from the south caught his eye as it pushed through slush.

"Lalo," the captain said with a nod as the vehicle pulled to a stop and a side door opened to reveal the Finder climbing down.

"There are many rumors this night," Lalo said as he came up to Gris. "I hope the worst of them are not true."

Glancing back over a shoulder up the road to the tower, the captain frowned. "I hope you are right. We should find out soon enough."

Finished. Kron sank onto his back in the remaining snow and wet, his body so numb he barely felt the water sopping his tattered clothes. Whatever the mad mage had hoped to accomplish, it had been ended. Where Kron himself had ultimately failed, Randall had saved them all, or so it seemed. Regardless, the city was safe. Kron could rest now, even if it was the eternal rest of the dead.

He closed his eyes, allowing the numbness to roll over him.

"Not so fast."

A gentle hand landed upon Kron's chest, and the man in black's mind turned inside out. For the briefest of moments it felt as if lightning scoured his body from one end to the other, then he spasmed and his teeth clenched and a wave not unlike a cool breeze spread across him.

Kron's eyes snapped open. He found himself staring into Randall's smiling face, the healer kneeling next to him.

Giving himself a moment to recall where he was and what had happened, Kron found himself no longer in pain. His skin did not feel as if branded, his head no longer ached, and his back felt as good as ever.

"Thank you," the man in the torn black clothes said, sitting up and finding himself still on the roof of the Swamps tower.

Randall leaned back but remained on a knee next to his friend.

Glancing around, Kron saw there were no signs of his enemies. Either they had gone over the ledge of the building, fled or been disrupted completely. It was an unnerving sensation to know those one had vanquished were no longer in evidence, yet it was more unnerving to know those one loved remained in pain.

"What happens now?" he asked.

Randall finally stood, moving back to give Kron room to collect himself. "Now? The city carries on as it has before. The threat is past. He was planning to kill everyone within Bond, to freeze them, then claim their souls for himself. I have to admit, it would have made him quite powerful, but only someone diabolic or insane would contemplate such, let alone attempt to go through with it."

The sounds of a city awakening came to their ears, rumblings from below and words being passed on the streets, and Kron hesitated to take in the return of life before finally climbing to his feet.

"That is not what I meant," he said, brushing at himself as if his remaining garb was worth the trouble. "What about Frex?"

The healer's eyes dipped and a frown of sorrow crossed his lips. "I saw her below before coming up here. I'm sorry, Kron."

"There is nothing you can do?"

"Her spirit has already fled," Randall explained, "but even if it had not, there is little I could do. The body I can heal with ease, but the mind is another matter."

"Yet her body lives."

"It does," Randall said, "though she is not within. Her mind has been shattered beyond repair."

"What will happen to her?" Kron asked.

"As long as we are able to feed her and provide her with drink, she should survive for some time. How long? I could not tell you. Days, weeks, perhaps months or even years. The spark of life within her body will fade when the

Creator deems it best."

Kron looked to his friend. "Can you ... " His words trailed away.

But Randall knew the question. "Again, I am sorry. There is nothing I can do for her wherever she has gone. A true god could possibly provide you a better answer, but I only claim godhood because men once foisted it upon me."

"The Creator?" Kron asked.

Randall nodded. "Alas, men are rarely aware of him, let alone worship him in any fashion. If he would but speak to us."

"Yes, if." Kron turned away, his eyes going to the leather wrappings and the stolen bones left behind by Sadhe Teth.

Bending over, Kron secreted the bones within the leathers and tucked them under his arm, standing. "What should be done with these?"

"Give them to me," Randall said, holding out a hand. "I'll make sure to --"

"I don't want to know," Kron said, the package traded between the two. "The less anyone knows about them, the better."

"Yes, they do seem to be tempting," Randall said, hiding the bones within the folds of his cloak.

Kron slowly turned and looked out over the city, now growing darker as the snow melted and the moon winked its way between fewer and fewer clouds.

"Kron?" Randall asked.

"Yes?"

"If there was anything I could have done for her, for anyone, I would have."

The man in black looked back over a shoulder, a thin smile lacking mirth upon his lips. "You didn't know, Randall, so no use blaming yourself. This is the life we are given, and we must make the best of it we can."

"Yes," the healer said with another nod. After a moment, he added, "I suppose we should go downstairs and greet those who are waking."

"You go on. I'll be down soon enough."

"Are you sure?" the healer asked. "Even without that madman's magic, it's still winter and pretty cold up here."

"I'll be fine," Kron said.

"At least allow me to bring you a cloak."

The man in tattered blacks looked to his friend again. "Do as you see fit." Then he turned back to stare out across the city.

"I'll do that." With one last sorrowful look, Randall exited toward the roof's trap door.

***

The healing tower was caught in a sea of turmoil. Fortunately, no one had been killed, but more than a few injuries had taken place as a number of those who had fallen asleep had done so on their feet, leaving them with head wounds and the like upon waking. The healers quickly went to work and managed to take care of their patients, both new and old, in due order, along with some help from the city guards on hand and those freshly arriving.

Even with the damage minimal, confusion reigned. None knew what had happened, the cause of it all. There was speculation from those who had been to the Asylum earlier in the night, but no one could say for sure what had happened or if it could happen again.

Randall's appearance brought more than a few shouts of joy from healers, patients and guards alike, and he promised he would explain more of what had happened after he met with Captain Gris, who himself was soon on the scene.

Meeting in a private room, words passed between the healer and the captain of the Bond guards. There were still many questions, which both men guessed would never be answered. Foremost on their minds was the identity of the wizard from the rooftop. It did not seem to be Lord Falk, though the man had worn the Ursian knight's body. Then there had been the recent discovery of several bodies around the tower, including the infamous Kilchus the Sword and Mama Kaf and Spider, and some not known to the local constabulary. Randall could tell Gris nothing more than perhaps that Kron held some answers. At least the danger seemed to be over, the bones now in Randall's position, the healer promising he could do away with them permanently.

Upon learning of the fate of those at the Asylum, including Frex Nodana, the captain's face became grim.

"How is Kron taking it?" he asked.

"Mostly in silence," Randall answered, "but maybe you can pull words from him."

"Where is he?"

"Still on the roof," Randall answered.

"By Ashal's rope, what is he doing up there?"

"You would have to ask him," the healer replied. "I suggest taking him some clothing, at least a cloak."

"That bad?" the captain asked.

A look was the answer. Both were familiar with Kron's experiences in combat, and this would not be the first time the man in black walked away from a fight in little more than rags.

Soon enough Gris found a sturdy cloak and procured some robes from a healer. After that he made his way up to the roof of the healing tower where he was pleased to find the snow all but gone, only puddles left behind as a reminder, and a night that was gradually warming to tolerable temperatures.

But he was not pleased to find his friend near the back wall of the large building, Kron's hands placed upon the wall between two crenels as if he were sitting down to eat or pray. The look on Kron's face was blank, his eyes motionless as he stared straight ahead.

With hesitation, Captain Gris moved toward his friend's back, the cloak and robes extended. "I brought you these."

For a moment there was no response, then Kron turned, his movements gradual, almost mechanical. He did not raise his eyes to the captain's face, but glanced at the garb.

"My thanks," he said, taking only the cloak and pulling it around his shoulders.

Then he turned back to the wall and stared further as if Gris was not there.

"You won't find any answers out there," the captain said.

"I know."

"Hell, Kron, I'm not sure there are any answers anywhere. These things ... they happen."

Kron bristled, the cloak at his shoulders scrunching near his neck as he bared his teeth. "There are answers aplenty. The greed of men, their lust for power, their inability to see others as themselves."

"Surely there is more to it than that."

Craning his head around, Kron glared at his friend. "Gris, the only difference between the common thief and the most depraved of men is that one steals your money, the other your soul."

The captain stared back for a moment, choosing his words before speaking. Then, "I'm not sure I follow what -- "

Kron cut him off. "The Asylum's lease with the city, it is for six months, is it not?"

The change in subject caught Gris by surprise. Flustered, his words were stammered. "Yes, I believe so."

"Good," Kron said, turning back to look out from the tower. "Then let this be my six-month notice of leave from the city guard. I'll be your lieutenant and train your men for those months, but then I'm out."

Another surprise of the night as confusion became clear on the captain's face. "But ... we need you."

A wave of a hand as if to brush aside the topic. "In six months I'll have some of your sergeants ready to train the underlings, and perhaps you can find others."

"Don't do this," Gris said. "Kron, I know it's not enough to offer my condolences, though it's all I can do, but you shouldn't allow Nodana's fate to change who you are. Randall even suggested there might be some little hope for her. I can't imagine --"

A raised hand chopped his words short.

"Gris, do you know the city guard is?" Kron asked.

After a moment of hesitation, the captain said, "We are the protectors of the city. We watch not only the boundaries of Bond, but work with the citizenry in policing the interior."

Kron snickered. "That's a politician's answer."

"It is the best I can offer at the moment."

The man in black twisted around and looked to the captain again, this time his eyes less hard. "We are not protectors, Gris. We are refuse men. We clean up the messes, when we can, but little more. Rarely if ever do we prevent a travesty from happening."

Gris let out a sigh. "We're not wizards. We can't know what men will do before they do it."

"That's not good enough!" Kron's head snapped back to stare across the city.

A wall of silence grew between the two men, the wind flapping at Kron's cloak and torn clothes, Captain Gris standing there with a robe folded beneath one arm. The noises of the city came to them, now sounding more natural than earlier, the snow nearly all but gone and no longer keeping the night's carousers indoors.

Seeing no alternative, Gris turned to leave, but then brought himself up short. "I realize this is not the time, but I'll need to speak with you about what happened tonight."

"In the morning," Kron said.

The captain waited for a few moments, but no more words were traded. He looked to his friend with concern, then nodded and left the rooftop.

With the departure of the captain, several minutes passed of silence, cold and darkness.

Then, "He is gone," Kron said. "You can come out now."

A figure stirred from within a pocket of shadows, stepping out into the moon's glow near the wall a dozen yards to Kron's right.

"How did you know I was here?" Midge Highwater asked.

Kron glanced to the master storyteller. "I didn't know it was you, but there was someone."

"I should have hidden myself better."

"How?" Kron asked. "Magic?"

There was no immediate response. The storyteller only stared back at the man in black for a moment, then he turned to face the night and the city, looking out upon the expanse as had Darkbow, in silence.

"You're more than a storyteller," Kron said, his eyes still upon the other man. "A wizard, maybe. Or a god."

"Ashal is the only god," Midge said.

"The only god worshiped *now*," Kron said, "but not the only god ever known to men."

Midge looked to him again. "So you think I'm a god?"

"You're something. How else did you know to send Scratch to Lalo's mansion for me? And you've been here all along, watching. You could have stepped in at any time during the fighting, but you did not."

"When did you notice my presence?" Midge asked.

"As soon as I climbed over the outer wall," Kron answered. "I was preparing my bow when I caught an impression of your shadow out of the corner of my eye. I almost sent an arrow your way."

"You seemed to have things well under control without my aid."

"Except it was Randall who saved me," Kron said.

"You think so?" Midge said. "You think Sadhe Teth was not already defeated?"

"What was that name?"

"Sadhe Teth. The wizard you burned."

"You knew him."

A moment of reluctance, then, "I knew *of* the man."

"Again, you are more than you appear, Midge Highwater."

"Storytellers learn a lot over the years," Midge said, "especially one as old as myself."

"Which is how many years exactly?"

Midge grinned. "Let's just say it's been a long time."

"As you would like, but tell me," Kron said, "why were you here? You did not interfere, so why watch?"

"Curiosity," Midge said, "and for once to have an eyewitness view to one of my stories."

"I think it was more than that. You were not affected by this Sadhe Teth's sleep magic, which tells me you had a purpose beyond being a mere witness."

"*You* were not affected," the storyteller added.

"And I was not here to be a watcher," Kron said. "Besides, I had to fight against the magic."

"How do you know I did not do the same?"

"Maybe you did, but it doesn't feel right."

Midge chuckled. "Allow an old man his secrets."

"I will," Kron said, "but curiosity has ahold of me. If you were not here only as a witness, then I can only surmise you had another purpose for being here."

"Such as?"

"As a protector."

"*You* are the protector of this city," Midge said. "Teth so much as pulled it out of you."

"Merely words before a fight, nothing more."

"You think so?" Midge asked. "Others have tried to supplant the famous Belgad the Liar as overlord of the city's underbelly, yet none have prevailed. Time and time again it has been you who has fought back and kept the equilibrium within Bond. I have seen your potential, Kron Darkbow, and as more than a swordsman. I've seen you best the guild masters of this city, and I've known you to face some of the worst terrors this world has to offer. If anyone could lay claim to protector of this city, it would be you."

"But I do not," Kron said.

"Hmm. Not yet. Perhaps some day."

"Perhaps." Kron stared for a moment longer at the old man before him, then he turned away again to look across the city. "I am sorry, Midge, but it would seem you are not to give me direct answers this night. Maybe that is as it should be. If you please, however, I would be alone."

The storyteller turned partially away, then halted, glancing to the man in black. "Just remember one thing, Kron Darkbow. Whatever you might suspect of me, whenever you need a friend, I can be there for you. But only if you wish it."

A nod was the only reply. Kron's eyes never left the horizon.

A last look filled with pain came from the storyteller, then he vanished into the night.

It was only then, when totally alone, that Kron allowed the tears to well in his eyes and to fall to the ground.

35

Days later and more than a thousand miles from Bond, Randall Tendbones stood atop a mountain range in his homeland. It had been nearly two years since he had visited Kobalos, yet he felt no remorse nor any love for the place. Kobalos was a hard land with a hard people, and Randall's father had been the hardest.

He stared out at the Northern Sea stretching before him to the grays of the horizon, the water the color of steel with flecks of white here and there. Off that expanse blew a cold wind, and as high as Randall stood, where even the mountain goats did not traverse, he would have been dead if not for a magical aura surrounding him. The temperature alone would have frozen him near solid, but there was also a lack of air, not even enough to keep a man alive.

Turning to face the south, the healer who was a god spotted for what he had come. A red line glowed a mile or so away within a crevice between two crags that reached for the sky like the upturned talons of dead dragons. The place was known as The Forge. In truth, it was a small rent in the world's surface, a preview of what lay far beneath rock and soil. Melted stone bubbled up within the narrow defile, consistently turning over and over, laying a level of warmth for some distance around.

Randall had been here once before when he was a boy. His father had made use of The Forge in creating a handful of magical rings, one for each member of the royal family. Randall's own ring lie hidden within his new desk back at the Swamps healing tower in Bond. He had not worn the device sense returning with Kron from Kobalos, and he saw no reason to wear it now. The rings had been signs of the house of Verkain, and Randall no longer made a claim to royalty. A different king ruled here now, and Randall had given up his right to the throne.

He sighed. He had seen enough of his homeland, the black mountains, the dreary shoreline, the dead waters. It was time to perform his task.

Raising his arms, he spoke words of magic and lifted himself from the top of the mountain. He flew lower, following the mountainside and heading in the direction of the molten rocks that was The Ford.

As he grew closer, the temperature rose and rose until it was near unbearable. Again, magic protected him.

Staring down at the churning red and orange and yellow and black earth, the god reached within his white cloak and pulled forth the bundle that held the bones of another deity. Randall looked to the cracked leather package within his hands for a moment, then he flung out an arm, sending the bones and their casing sailing across the distance.

There was a flash of flame, then the package vanished, dipping below the surface of the lava. A dark bubble rose up, burst, then it too vanished.

Sighing again, Randall lifted his arms once more. He rose higher into the sky.

Then came a popping sound.

And he was gone.